Margo Mysteries

Volume 1
Books 1 - 7

Margo Mysteries

Volume 1
Books 1 - 7

by

Jerry B. Jenkins

MOODY PRESS
CHICAGO

© 1985 by
JERRY B. JENKINS

Library of Congress Cataloging in Publication Data

Jenkins, Jerry B.
    Margo mysteries.

        Contents: v. 1. Margo. Karlyn. Hilary. Paige. Allyson.
Erin. Shannon.
        1. Detective and mystery stories, American. I. Title.
PS3560.E485M28 1985 813'.54 85-5661
ISBN 0-8024-4329-x (v.1)

1 2 3 4 5 Printing/RR/Year 89 88 87 86 85

Printed in the United States of America

CONTENTS

To each reader
of the Margo Mysteries
who has kindly taken the time
to write and let me know
of his or her enjoyment.
Your letters have meant more to me
than I can express.
Thank you.

MARGO

ONE

THEY SAY MORE WOMEN THAN MEN ATTEMPT SUICIDE, but that more men are successful. I guess women are just attention-seekers. That's why I couldn't figure out this girl. Hers was an attempt without observers.

I had just finished a fairly successful job interview and had reason to believe I might be working in the Atlanta Tower as a commercial artist within a couple of weeks. Maybe not, though. Someone would be bound to recognize me as the jerk who couldn't even find his way back to the elevator.

For sure no one would recognize me as Philip Spence, the hero who kept a girl from committing suicide. No one knew. It was one weird suicide attempt.

In looking for the elevator I found myself in a little hallway, one of those meaningless crannies you find when you're lost in a skyscraper. It leads to a window — that's all. Maybe it was the architect's joke.

I spun around to head back to the main corridor, and there she was. I almost ran into her. "This is a great place for meditating," I joked.

She said nothing, but she looked as if I had offended her. That irritated me. I mean, the place wasn't private or anything. I let the million dollar question spew forth: "What are you doing here?"

She ignored the question. "Do you have to be here now?" she asked. I was surprised at how feminine she sounded, despite her disposition.

"I guess not, if you're busy," I said. I wanted to see her smile, or at least loosen up. "Is there much to do here?"

She just sighed. No smile. Trembling, she drew her clenched fists slowly to her face. Suddenly I didn't feel so funny.

"Hey, listen, what's wrong?" I asked. "Are you hiding from someone?"

"No," she said, annoyed. "I'm trying to get up enough courage to jump out that window." I knew the window was there, but for some reason I turned to look.

No crowd, no public drama. *She's serious,* I thought.

"If there was one place I didn't expect to see anyone, it was here," she said, crying.

I decided to challenge her, to make her see that she didn't really want to go through with it. "The window isn't even open," I taunted. "What are you gonna do, run through the glass?" I let that image dance on my brain for a few seconds. She'd have made a real mess in the alley thirty floors below.

My strategy didn't work. She was becoming even more determined, staring at the window. "Do you want me to open it?" I asked.

"Would you?" she said softly, as if it would be the kindest thing I could do and she'd be ever so grateful.

"Hey, come on now," I said. "What's the problem?"

She grew cold again. "If I'd wanted to tell my story, I'd have left a note," she snapped. "Open the window."

Well, she had no idea how to open the huge thing, and there was no way she was going to go through safety glass. She pushed at the window angrily.

So I opened it. Not because I wanted her to jump, of course, but because something told me that this girl was going to have to choose to live by turning down a bona fide opportunity to die.

The dirty Atlanta air blew in. I turned to her and motioned like an usher toward the window. She didn't move except to shiver. When she took a half step toward the window I decided not to block her path. She stopped.

"Leave," she said.

I couldn't. I could do all the rest. I could tell her to go ahead, and I could challenge her, and I could try my amateur psychology on her, but I would never have been able to live with myself if I had left her to jump.

"You know I could keep you from jumping," I lied. "All I would have to do is grab you and take you away from the window." I'm not a big guy, but I think I convinced her.

"But you won't stop me, will you?" she pleaded.

"What will I tell the reporters? That I didn't even try to talk you out of it?"

"I have no reason to live!" She was shouting now.

"Do you have a reason to die?"

"Having no reason to live is reason enough to die," she said. It was ominous. A truism. I had no answer.

There was silence for more than a minute. Then I started talking, saying things I hadn't thought about saying.

"What if you knew somebody loved you?" I began.

"No one does," she said.

I could hardly hear her.

"Not my family. No one here at work. No one anywhere."

"Someone cares," I said. "God cares." I hadn't said anything like that since high school when I had come back from a youth retreat all fired up.

But now it wasn't an obligation. I wanted more than anything to convince this girl that God loved her.

I hadn't cried in front of anyone since I was twelve years old, but I didn't care. She was looking at me now, straight into my eyes. "Listen," I pleaded.

She walked past me toward the window and stood staring at the floor, chin tucked tightly to her chest. Putting both hands on the edge of the window, she tried to slide it shut. No way. She looked at me with a helpless smile. I helped her close it.

"I'd have never guessed you for a *Margo*," I said. We were in the second-floor coffee shop where she worked. "Ready to talk yet?" She shook her head. "At least tell me this," I said."Why did you wait until you were off work to head for the window?"

She shrugged. She wouldn't even look at me.

"You're not going to tell me about it, are you?" I said, resigning myself to it. I felt a little guilty about being so curious, but it's not every day I encounter a suicidal waitress.

"I don't know yet," she said.

Two of her waitress friends stopped by to ask if she was all right. She nodded to each. They looked at me warily.

"See?" I said. "People care. Your friends care."

She looked as if she wished I hadn't talked her out of jumping. "They don't care at all," she said quickly in a whisper. "What else could they say to someone who's sitting here crying in her coffee? Anyway, they'd just love to have something to talk about."

"You're really a case, you know that?" I said, shaking my head the way a mother might over a kid who has sloshed home through every puddle. Margo didn't take it that way.

"Thanks a lot," she said. "You know, for a while I thought you really cared."

Now I was offended. I wanted to blast her for messing up my day. I had been elated to find that God could use me to share His love with someone, and I had been glad to help. I hadn't even minded that this girl thought of no one but herself, never asking whether I really had the time to baby her.

"What do you want?" I asked. "Really, what do you want?" I tried to sound as sincere as possible. I figured I was at least entitled to hear her tale of woe, and I for sure wouldn't get to if she thought I resented her taking my time. I really wanted to explain to her what God could mean to her, but she was hardly in the mood for that yet.

"Do you really want to help?" she asked. "Right now, I mean."

I nodded tentatively. I'd have bet my life she was going to ask me to leave her alone. Wrong.

"I would like to talk about anything but today," she said deliberately, as if she had thought it out for a long time. She even stopped crying and became surprisingly articulate. "I'm not ready for your sermon," she said, raising her eyebrows as if to assure me that she hadn't intended that to be a low blow, "but I would like you to just tell me about yourself. If you don't want to talk to me, I'll understand."

More self pity, I thought.

She read my mind. "No," she said. "Really. It's not fair of me to be so mysterious, and I appreciate what you did for me up there today. I'm not ready to talk about it. Can you just talk to me and not be offended if I happen to look bored or don't seem to listen?"

"I could," I said, "but I might not enjoy it." Her jewelry, simple and expensive, told me she wasn't just another coffee shop waitress looking for some bucks before moving on.

"You're not really a waitress at heart, are you?" I asked.

She was staring out the window. "I said I wanted *you* to talk," she said. "Could we please just save my story?"

"I will get to hear about you then?"

"Yes. I don't know — "

"Margo, listen. I've known you for what, a half hour? I don't know anything about you except that you really wanted to kill yourself a little while ago. Needless to say, I'm not experienced in this, but I have to believe you want to be alone right now."

"No. You're right that I really don't feel like talking *or* listening, but I don't want to be alone."

Obviously, I couldn't stay with her indefinitely. "Why don't you go home and try to relax?" I said. "Here's the phone number at my apartment. My name's Philip Spence, and if you need something, you can call me any time of the day or night."

She didn't like it, but I think she realized there were no other options. "Are you going to be all right?" I asked as I slid out of the booth. She pressed her lips tight and nodded. She was crying by the time I left the coffee shop.

All the way to my apartment I pondered why I had made myself available to her. Was it because I cared? Or because God was caring through me? Or because there was simply no other choice? Who would leave someone helpless? Maybe I had just been courteous. I had done the only right thing, hadn't I? I just didn't know.

My apartment, which doubled for an office from which I worked on and sold my free-lance illustrations, was as homey as it could be without a family. I had been getting by free-lancing, but that was because the apartment was my only major expense. With the economy as it was, I had been scouting for a full-time commercial art job, one that would leave me time to free-lance in the evenings if I wished, yet pay enough so I wouldn't have to if I didn't want to.

I had gone the three-piece-suit route for my interview that day, guessing at the conservatism of my potential employer in this Southern city. I wound up looking more conservative than Mr. Willoughby did. Owners of art studios and advertising agencies can afford to wear corduroy jackets and turtlenecks, I guess.

He seemed impressed with my work, even if my vest had thrown him a bit. He would be calling me within a few days about a staff job as an illustrator. My parents would love it. They had always been suspicious of my free-lancing, though I had made a lot of money in each of the last two years. "Why don't you get a job?" my mother often asked. "And why don't you find one here closer to Dayton?"

They were good people. I had written to Mom about looking for a full-time job. My free-lance accounts, good as they were, could end in a week if budgets needed tightening. The loss of one good account could mean a third of my income. I needed money now and for the future. Somehow I knew in the back of my mind that "just the right girl would come along," the way Mom always said. I didn't enjoy living alone, and while my only serious romance had ended in disappointment in college, I looked forward to what I hoped was inevitable.

The phone took me from my half-eaten steak. *It might be Margo.* I let it ring again to collect my thoughts. *What if she's just slashed her wrists? I'll wish I'd stayed with her.*

It was long distance from Dayton. "How'd it go?" Mom asked. "Did you get a job?"

"Not yet," I said. "But maybe."

"Oh, I hope not," she said. "Try here in Dayton. You've made a name for yourself. People here know you're good. You know Carl Ferguson could use a good artist." We'd been through it before.

"I know, Mom. I appreciate it. Maybe if nothing turns up here."

"Have you been going to church?" she asked suddenly, characteristically changing the subject.

"Oh, not as much as I should," I admitted. Not for months, was the truth. I had no excuse. I just slept in on Sundays.

"No better place to meet a girl than in church," Mom said.

"That's a fact," I agreed. "You wouldn't believe where I met a girl today."

Mom didn't know whether to be excited or skeptical. She wanted me to meet girls, but until she knew where I'd met one, she wasn't about to sound enthusiastic.

I told her all about Margo. She was thrilled that I had told Margo about Christ. She even had Dad listen in on the extension phone. I must say I was glad to be able to tell them about it, as a sort of absolution for having been so lax in my church and general spiritual life, and for insinuating to Mom that I had been to church even off and on lately.

When I finally hung up, my steak was cold and my Coke was warm. I threw the steak back on the broiler as the phone rang again.

"I've been trying to reach you for an hour," Margo said.

I suppose I should have felt guilty for not having kept my phone open for Margo's call. I didn't. What did she expect — an apology? How was I supposed to know she'd call right away?

"I had a long distance call from home," I explained.

"I need to see you," she said.

"From my parents," I said.

"Can you get away soon?" she asked.

"In Dayton, Ohio," I said.

"You're not listening," she whined.

"Oh, really? OK, where do you want to meet? At the coffee shop?"

"That's all I need," she said. "To be seen with you there again. The rumors would never quit."

We settled on an all-night restaurant about halfway between our apartments. It was a twenty-minute drive, giving me time to guess whether Margo would be in the mood for talking or for listening.

She could have listened by phone, I decided. Maybe she was ready to tell me, in person, what had caused her near suicide.

TWO

"You'll never understand, Philip," Margo said at the restaurant, "but as soon as I quit crying and went home, I stuffed myself."

"You're right, I don't understand. I would've been too upset to eat."

"That's what I mean about not understanding. I eat when I'm upset."

"And now you want to eat again?"

"Yes."

"I'm not your father. Go ahead and order."

"Eat something with me?"

"No, I had a steak — at — oh, no. I've got half a steak burning in the oven! I've got to go."

"No, you don't. How high is your oven turned?"

"About three hundred," I said.

"It won't be any more burned by the time you get home than it is already. And it won't start a fire."

She ordered, and the waitress pretended not to mind that I wasn't having anything. She even said it was OK if we sat and talked awhile. She didn't know how long "awhile" was going to be. Neither did I.

It didn't do much for Margo's ego, but I yawned through much of her story. Not that the story was boring, but it was late, and I'd had a full day.

"You don't want to hear this," she'd say every few sentences.

"No, really, I do," I'd say, through a yawn.

I'd been right about her not being just another waitress looking for quick cash. She was from a well-to-do Chicago family, and she was the daughter of a judge. I really wasn't ready for the next bit of news; her *mother* was the judge.

The way she ate made me hungry. Margo went on trying to tell me her life story while I looked around for the waitress.

Her story was depressing and totally humorless. She'd been popular through grade school and the first couple of months of high school. Then she suspected her mother was seeing another man. Her parents' marriage had been only cordial for about three years, and Margo had sensed something was wrong, though she didn't understand what it was.

"The change was so gradual it sneaked up on me," she said. "I'm not sure just when I realized that they didn't seem to love each other anymore. They were compassionate to me all right, but they showed more affection to me than to each other. They couldn't have known how it hurt me.

"I found myself dreaming of the good old days. I'd see Mr. and Mrs. Virginia Franklin, sleeping in separate rooms and treating each other more like neighbors than spouses, and I'd cry myself to sleep. All I could think of was my childhood. Trips to the zoo with Mommy and Daddy. Being carried when I was too tired to walk. Seeing them look into each other's eyes and smile."

Margo talked of the autumn of 1963 with particular pain, and I felt as if I were intruding on her history.

"I remember the coming out party my parents threw for me," she said. "It was everything my suburban Winnetka friends expected, according to the *Chicago Tribune* social page. I was a freshman in high school then, but the football games, homecoming, and being a debutante left me flat. I wanted our family happy again."

She had been a reader of novels and classic romances and began to dream of a guy who would sweep her off her feet and somehow replace the security she was losing as her family fell apart.

"By November I was no longer smiling, and everyone noticed, especially the guys. Mike Grantham broke the news to me about President Kennedy's assassination. He was so sensitive, so caring. I hoped he would invite me to the Christmas Ball, but by then I had become depressed and irritable. My status as the daughter of a hundred-thousand-dollar-a-year garment executive and a judge suddenly meant little to the 'in' crowd."

I looked around again for the waitress and finally caught her eye. "We can save the rest of the story, I guess," Margo said.

"No way," I said. "I've invested this much time, I want it all." While I ate, Margo kept talking.

"At first, I had little to go on in suspecting my mother had a lover, but it was enough. I basically knew when she had trials scheduled, and everyone knew when the big social events would demand her appearance. But Mom was gone too much at other times — like during the early evening — and she was always coming home late. I asked Dad about it and told him it could only mean she was seeing another man. That hurt him and I was almost sorry I had mentioned it. He confronted her, and she denied it. He believed her. I didn't.

"Still, the marriage was over. Mom and Dad were seldom seen together socially, and by the end of my sophomore year, Dad had moved out. I was crushed."

"Whatever happened with Mike what's-his-name?"

"Nothing. We chatted between classes now and then, but a mealy-mouthed, shy math major took me to the prom, and I had the feeling we were doing each other a favor — his asking and my accepting, I mean. When I closed my eyes, I was dancing with Mike."

"Who was Mike dancing with?"

"Whoever he wanted. Bouncy, skinny cheerleaders."

"Did your parents ever get divorced?"

"Yes, and I was more disgraced than my mother. She talked to me only to hassle me about my appearance, and I talked to her only to accuse her of cheating on Dad. It was a cold war."

"Did you know for sure she was seeing someone else?"

"Oh, sure. She argued on the phone often with a man she called Richard."

"Did she know you knew?"

"No, I really don't think she did, and I've always thought she was incredibly naive about that, especially for a judge."

"Did you ever find out who this Richard was?"

"You're getting ahead of me."

"Sorry." I was just trying to hurry the thing along. It was interesting, like I say, but I couldn't really see the link between a divorce ten years ago and a suicide attempt today.

"My dad visited me now and then, and he chose to respect, admire, and believe Mom. He decided the love was simply gone and was quite content to believe there was no other man. I resented that I got only a half hour chat with him every few weeks, so when I was a senior I staged a suicide attempt."

It was Margo's first and last attention-getting effort. To me it was one of the more transparent cries for help I had ever heard of. Even Margo had to fight a smile as she told it. "Daddy had called and asked if he could visit me while Mother was working one day. I said yes, hung up, and downed thirty aspirins. Then I sprawled on the living room floor with the empty bottle in my hand, and was conveniently (and violently) ill when he arrived forty-five minutes later."

"He obviously saw it for what it was," I commented.

"Not at first. He couldn't put it together, and I still regret that. All he could do was assume that his visit had somehow pushed me to attempt suicide."

"But you got his attention?"

"Oh, yes. And I've fantasized a thousand times since, remembering Daddy carrying me to his car and racing me to the hospital. Even as sick as I was, I wouldn't have traded the experience for anything. I was Daddy's for several hours."

"Did you talk?"

"Yes, but I couldn't bring myself to talk about Richard. Mother had been arguing with him on the phone nearly every day. I was sure they were fighting and that they might break up. That gave me hope Mother and Daddy would get back together. From what Daddy said, though, I knew he still chose to believe there was no other man."

"How did your mother react to the aspirin bit?"

"Oh, that really did it between us. She became openly hostile. Once she told me she wished she had a daughter to show off at social events. That really hurt, as you can imagine.

"She begged me not to tell anyone about the aspirins. I would have loved to have told everyone, just to disgrace her, but I was embarrassed about it, too. I finished high school with no more dates — not even with the math major — and grades that qualified me only for a local junior college."

"Did you go?"

"No. No one from Winnetka, and certainly not the daughter of Virginia Franklin, went anywhere less prestigious than Northwestern University, so I went nowhere. I worked at the public library, read, slept, ate, fought with Mother, and prayed that Mike Grantham was still single."

"Did you really think you had a chance with him?"

"Don't forget my reading, Philip. I read stories where the girl always got her man. I was enchanted with the South, and I planned to run off one day to Atlanta, develop some charm, and return to look up Mike. Somehow, in my daydream, I always thought of him as Michael. My biggest dread was that I would run into him before I got my head straight."

"Did that ever happen?"

"I'm getting to that."

"Sorry," I yawned.

"One day late in nineteen seventy I answered the phone while Mother was outside for a few minutes. It was Richard, only he thought he was talking to Mother. 'Virginia,' he said, 'this is Richard. Can you come to Inverness right away?' "

"Did he realize he was talking to you and not your mother?"

"No. I just said, ' Sure,' and he hung up. Then mother came in."

"Wait. Now, did his talking about Inverness give you any clue to who he was?"

"Yes, I guessed almost immediately from reading the papers everyday. It was only a hunch, but the assistant state's attorney, Richard Wanmacher, was from Inverness, a smaller town but every bit as exclusive as Winnetka. I had never put it together with Mother's Richard."

"Were you sure now?"

"Not until Mother came in. As matter-of-factly as possible, I told her that a Richard from Inverness had called and wanted her to come there right away. I don't know how long it had been since I had seen her blow her cool. She flushed and bristled and said, 'Nonsense, I don't know anyone from Inverness.' I said, 'Maybe it was that guy from the state's attorney's office who lives out there.' And she said, 'Oh, well, yes, perhaps.' "

"Wow."

"You haven't heard anything yet, Philip," Margo said. "Mom made a quick call from the kitchen phone when she thought I was in my room. I wasn't. I was on the stairs listening. Mother was hissing into the phone like a snake. 'I'll kill you, Richard. Don't think I won't,' she was saying. It was something about his even thinking of staying with his wife after all of his promises to Mother.

"That night I knew I hated her. From then on it was hard to think of her in a good light, even in childhood memories. I began to dream exclusively of Michael and me and our future — "

"Well?" I said after a minute of silence.

"I'm tired," Margo said.

"You ought to be. It's one A.M. But I want to hear what happened."

She looked at me coldly. I knew her well by now, what she dreamed about, what hurt her, what she wanted in life. At least, I thought I knew.

"I'm talked out," she said flatly, staring past me.

"Are you sure?" I said, "Or have you just come to the part that's hardest to talk about?"

"You guessed it," she said, making a stab at sounding light.

"Do you want me to talk you into it?"

She laughed a pitiful laugh. "That was a good question. You're as sensitive as I always dreamed Michael would be."

I shot her a double take.

"Oh, don't read anything into that," she said.

"Really, as much as I admire you for listening to me and for caring, I'm smart enough not to go falling for you."

I feigned offense. "And what is *that* supposed to mean?"

"You know," she said, smiling. Then she was serious. "For one thing, I know how to protect myself from pain, in spite of my somewhat fanciful dreams."

I debated badgering her to tell me the painful part of the story, but I somehow sensed there were two parts to it. First there was whatever was so painful at home nine years ago. Then there was whatever had pushed her past the brink and forced her to that window on the thirtieth floor today — well, yesterday now.

Margo saved me the begging. "I want to finish this tonight," she said.

"This morning," I corrected. "And don't forget the former steak in my oven." She didn't smile.

"Mother killed Richard Wanmacher," she said.

I was speechless. "How in the world do you know that?" I finally managed.

"Mother slammed the phone down after talking with him that night, ran upstairs, rustled through some drawers, ran back down, and sped off."

"To Inverness?"

"Where else? When I woke up the next morning, she was on her way out the door to head for court in Chicago. I'll never forget the headline in the paper — "

Margo's voice trailed off. She paled. I waited, but I didn't ask.

" 'Assistant State's Attorney Slain; Wife Charged,' " she said slowly.

"Wanmacher's wife was charged?"

"Isn't that ironic? The only motive ever suggested was that she suspected he was seeing another woman. Mrs. Wanmacher admitted that was true, but she never said who the woman might be, and the press had no idea either."

"Your mother's name never got into it?"

"Never. Mrs. Wanmacher maintained her innocence and fought the charge for three years."

"Was she innocent?"

"Of course! I told you, Mother did it."

"How can you be so sure?" I asked.

"For one thing, the gun. Richard was shot through the eye from a foot away with a twenty-two caliber pistol. It was the pistol in Daddy's dresser that I was never supposed to touch as a child."

"How do you know it was that gun?"

"Because as soon as I read the story in the paper, I looked for the gun. It was gone."

"You know that doesn't prove a thing."

"Maybe it doesn't prove anything legally, but I'll bet if that gun were found, it could be proved."

"You don't know your mother went to see Wanmacher. You can't even be sure you talked to Wanmacher. It could have been coincidental that a Richard from Inverness called your mother."

"But you agree the odds are that it was the same Richard she had been arguing with by phone for weeks?"

"OK, I'll buy that."

"Then it was probably her lover," Margo said.

"Probably."

"I'm saying her lover was Wanmacher."

"Why?"

"Because after his death, the phone calls stopped. She was left with no one. Not Daddy. Not me. Not Richard. She even tried to get close to me. That proves she was desperate."

I sat staring.

She continued, "When Mother reached out to me, I found myself hating her more. I told her once that I knew about Richard. She covered well. Then I asked her where Daddy's gun was. She said she thought he had taken it with him and that she hadn't seen it for ages."

"Is that possible?"

"I asked Daddy, without telling him why I was asking, 'What ever happened to that gun you used to keep in the bedroom?' "

" 'It's probably still there,' he said."

"You didn't tell your father?" I said.

"Are you kidding? He chose to believe there was no other man, and I'm supposed to tell him that there not only was, but that Mother murdered him?"

"Who did you tell?"

Margo said nothing. She shoved her plates aside and went to the washroom. When she returned I asked her again.

"Who did you tell?"

"Only you, Philip," she said.

I shook my head violently. "You're putting me on," I said. "You hate your mother, and you have reason to believe she killed a man, and yet you tell no one?"

"You forget that I love Daddy. This would destroy him."

"And it would eliminate the possibilities of your dream-world Michael too, wouldn't it? Who would want the daughter of a murderer?"

"I thought of that, too."

"Incredible."

The waitress came to clear the table. "My shift is over," she said. "You can stay, but can I give you your check now?"

"Sure," I said. Margo took it as her cue to head for her car. I paid the check and caught up.

"I still don't know how you got to Atlanta, or what happened today — nine years after the murder — to make you flip out."

"Flip out?" she said, walking quickly.

"Wrong term," I admitted, "but remember where we met."

Margo stopped and thrust her hands deep into her coat pockets. Rain began to fall gently, and right there on Peachtree Drive in Atlanta, more of the story spilled out.

"I kept badgering Mother about Richard and the gun, never actually using the name Wanmacher and never actually accusing. She knew I had no evidence, so she continued to brush it off. But she did begin encouraging me to get out on my own. She even decided to finance my venture to Atlanta. She paid for my flight here and sent me the money to buy a car and get set in an apartment.

"I took the money that time, but I told her that I couldn't take any more. I started sending her checks back, but she wrote and told me she was putting them in my account for whenever I needed the money. When I got my job, I started paying her back for the trip and car, but she's never cashed the checks."

I shivered. We leaned against a building. "Go on," I said.

"You're tired," she said. "And so am I. Should we pick this up somewhere tomorrow?"

"No. If you don't want to talk about it, I understand. But if you're only thinking of my fatigue, forget it. I'm already functioning on automatic, and my apartment must smell like a charcoal grill. Why don't you ride with me there so I can turn the oven off? We can talk on the way, and then I'll bring you back here to your car."

"You aren't going to try to take liberties, are you?" she said as we walked to the car. We both laughed for the first time since we'd met.

In the car her sense of humor vanished. "I haven't talked to Mother for over a year, and except to send me bank deposit receipts, she hasn't written to me either. I have corresponded with Daddy every few months, but its been on the surface. I figured if Mother could stay on the bench with murder on her conscience, I could pretend I never knew her."

"How about your dreams of Michael?"

With that she broke down and sobbed. I drove to my apartment and ran up to turn off the oven. The place was pretty smoky. I opened the windows and went back to the car. It was raining hard now.

The car windows fogged us into our own world. Margo cried as she talked, and I worried that all this honesty had backfired. Instead of releasing her from the haunting thoughts that led to our first encounter, my compassionate listening had brought her right back to where she'd been. "You don't have to tell me tonight," I said.

"I want to now."

"OK."

She spoke slowly and deliberately. "Since I left home I've dreamed about Michael during the day and the murder at night. I can see Mother pulling into Richard Wanmacher's driveway, and him coming to meet her as she gets out of her car. He gets right up to her when she shoves the twenty-two in his face and fires — "

"You sound as if you were there."

"After hearing Mrs. Wanmacher tell of her husband walking out of the house to his death, I can picture it perfectly."

"She saw the murder?"

"Yes, but not the murderer. Mother met him between her car door and the headlights, and the lights blocked Mrs. Wanmacher's view of her."

"You're still talking about nine years ago, Margo. What happened today?"

"This happens to me every day! Don't you understand?"

I nodded. "What ever happened in the case?"

"After several years of continuances, mistrials, and changes of venue, Mrs. Wanmacher was acquitted for lack of evidence. Today I learned that a man in Chicago was arraigned for the murder — an old foe of Wanmacher."

"That made the Atlanta papers?"

"No," Margo said, and she was sobbing again. I waited. She cried and cried.

"I waited on Michael at the coffee shop today," she said softly. "I know I'd never have had a chance with him anyway, but — he said, 'I never would have dreamed you'd wind up a waitress!' "

"That hurt."

"Not as much as the fact that he was sitting there with his wife and baby."

That would have been enough to send any dreamer to the window, but that wasn't all. Margo continued:

"Michael said he assumed I had heard about Mother's latest bit of notoriety. I almost fainted. 'No.' I said. 'What's that?' "

" 'She's been assigned the Wanmacher murder case,' he told me. 'They've charged a Chicago mobster, and your mother will be trying the case.' "

THREE

Bill Jacobs, a psychology major at the University of Georgia, lived just down the hall from me. He could hardly believe my story.

"It's not my story," I reminded him. "It's Margo's, and I believe it."

"You do?"

"Shouldn't I?"

"You want the opinion of a friend or a budding psychologist?"

"Whatever."

"As a friend, I'm dubious, but I assume you have no reason not to believe her. I'll bet she's good at spinning a yarn."

"You don't think the suicide attempt was serious?"

"Sure I do, Phil," Bill said, "if she was really doing it in private until you happened along. I don't doubt she's suicidal. I doubt that this bizarre twist — her mother's trying a man for a murder that she herself committed — would be enough to push Margo to the brink."

"Maybe you're right," I said, "but just seeing Michael again wouldn't be quite that devastating either."

"Agreed."

"Then what really set her off?" I asked.

"You don't see it yet, do you?"

"You're the psych major. Let's hear it."

"OK," Bill said. "A man comes between a happily married, or seemingly happily married, man and his wife. The daughter retreats into unreality as her secure world begins to crumble. When she discovers who the other man is, she can see only that he is to blame for her parents' deteriorating marriage. She doesn't suspect her father of also running around on his wife. She doesn't suspect her mother of having become a tramp. She simply feels compelled to rectify the situation, to put things back the way they were. So she shoots the 'other man.' Her mother knows it and uses her knowledge to force Margo out of town, unable to do much else and keep her own secret. So there's a stand-off for a few years. But now the case winds up in Mommy's court. Margo figures she can't keep her guilt hidden much longer, so she heads for the window."

"I sure hope you're wrong."

"I s'pose you do, Philip. But you'd better decide before you get in any deeper with her."

"You mean I should be afraid of her?"

"I wouldn't think so," Bill said. "Unless your discovery that she's the murderer would force her to react violently again. Until then, she has no reason to harm you."

"This is crazy," I said. "We're talking about a fragile human being. I'm not buying that she could have committed the murder."

"Then why the guilt? Why a suicide?"

"Is it possible," I asked, "that everything hit her at once and it was simply too much for her? I mean seeing Michael would be traumatic enough, even if he weren't married. Add to that the continuing neglect of her father, her idol. And then the memory of the murder is forced upon her again. She feels unloved, without even the hope of winning her Michael anymore. Like she told me, she had no reason to live, and that was reason enough to die."

"Maybe," Bill said. "Maybe you should be the psychologist."

"No, thanks. Your types are too suspicious."

"Well, I maintain that she's the guilty one, and something else, too."

"Which is?"

"You don't want to hear it."

"Of course I do."

"No, really. I'm sorry I got into it."

"I'll bet I know."

"What?" Bill said.

"You don't want to hear it," I said, laughing.

"OK," he said. "You win. I say the religious line you fed her is just going to give her another cover for her guilt. And if she's a murderer, you're gonna wish you'd never used it just to get her away from the window."

"That isn't the only reason I 'fed it to her,' " I objected. "And what if she's telling the truth?"

"Then she's gonna be mighty disappointed when she finds out there's no real value for her in religion."

"If I thought there was no value in it for her, I'd never have brought it up."

"You didn't just hit her with it to keep her from jumping?"

"No," I said, without enough conviction.

"You're not sure, are you?"

"Why don't you drop psychology and go into law?" I said.

"Why don't you drop religion and get into reality? If you really believe this stuff, and I'm beginning to fear that you just might, what are you going to tell her next?"

"First of all, I haven't said anything about religion. I'm talking to her about a person."

"I know, I know. Campus Crusade for Christ has made the rounds, and I've heard the whole pitch. It's still religion, and pie in the sky is not going to help this Margo. Murderer or not, she's suicidal, and you'd better have something practical to offer."

I couldn't get Bill's challenge off my mind. Margo had told me that she wasn't ready for my "sermon." I took it to mean she might be soon. She at least had postponed her own death because I promised to tell her of Jesus' love for her. Or had it been just because I seemed to care? I decided I wouldn't mention "religion" to Margo again until she brought it up.

Margo called me late that evening. "I went to work today," she said.

"You're kidding."

"No, I needed something to do, and I didn't want the people at work to think I've quit."

"Why not?"

"Because I haven't. And anyway, I haven't heard your sermon yet."

"I wish you'd quit calling it a sermon."

She ignored me. "If it's as good as you made it sound, maybe I'll be around awhile."

"You weren't ready for it yesterday," I said.

"That was yesterday. I'll be ready tomorrow. I'm going to bed now, but I just wanted to thank you."

I could hardly believe she had gotten up for work after having gone to bed so late. I sure hadn't. I had slept until noon before talking with Bill, and wound up doing a few pencil roughs until Margo called.

It was mid-morning the next day when the phone rang and a woman's voice asked for Mr. Philip Spence. It was a secretary at the art studio where I had applied for a job. I was to meet with Mr. Willoughby for lunch. That sounded good. It wasn't likely he wanted to have lunch with me just to say no to my job application.

"We like your stuff," Mr. Willoughby said over salad. "I wish we could hire you full-time."

I winced. "You wish?"

"I know we interviewed you for the full-time spot, but we're really looking for a beginner — somebody we could pay ten thousand a year or so to do cleanup work, keyline, paste up, that sort of thing."

I admitted I didn't relish a full-time job cutting and pasting, and that I wouldn't be able to work for that little at this stage in my career.

"We've got something else you might be interested in," he said. He described an account he had recently landed that called for illustrating a series of textbooks. The client wanted cohesiveness and hundreds of small illustrations in a particular style. "I showed him some of the samples you left with me yesterday, and he likes your technique."

"That's good to hear."

"The catch is that he would like to print these books within the year."

"Meaning he needs the illustrations when?"

"He needs a hundred illustrations a month for the next six months. All pen and ink, all basically the same size and format."

"Sounds boring," I said.

"Does fifteen dollars apiece sound boring? That would be nine thousand in six months, or less than six months if you choose to work faster."

"Make it an even ten thousand and I'll start tomorrow." It was a crazy thing to say. I'd never had such an easy and lucrative assignment offer, and here I was risking it for another $1,000.

"OK, the manuscripts are in my car," he said.

I was thrilled with the job, boring though it might be. I could complete four drawings in three hours each evening and spend my days trying to solicit more business. It was a free-lance artist's dream.

That evening Margo showed up at my apartment. "I'm sorry I didn't call," she said. "I can't go to work anymore; I'm going to quit. I can't handle it." She waved a newspaper as she talked. She hadn't even taken off her coat. She worried me. This was the Margo I had first met, but at 78 rpm.

"If you've got something to tell me about God, you'd better get on with it," she plunged on, "because I'm not gonna be around here long."

I hadn't said a word. I felt like the center of a merry-go-round, turning as she circled the room. Finally I sat down. Margo didn't. When she paused for a split second I said, as nonchalantly as possible, "I got a great assignment last night."

"Don't you even care, Philip?" she pleaded. "Haven't you been listening?"

"Margo, I've been listening, but you haven't said anything. Yesterday you worked and seemed to have your head on half straight for the first time since I met you. Now you come here unexpectedly and rattle on about doing away with yourself. And I don't even know — "

She cut me off. "I didn't mean suicide. I meant I might be going to Chicago. I can't sit by here and pretend nothing is happening while Mother is in Chicago trying someone else for her own crime. I could never live with myself. I have to go there."

"You mean your mother is actually going through with trying the case?"

Margo unrolled the Atlanta newspaper. A three-inch story announced the trial date a month away in Virginia Franklin's court. "Margo, do you honestly believe your mother could have murdered Richard Wanmacher and still have the guts to try someone else for it?"

"You think because she's going through with it, that proves her innocence?" she said, incredulous.

"I've heard of scoundrels," I said. "But this would beat everything. How could she sleep?"

"I've wondered that for years," Margo said.

"If you went, would you expose her?"

"No."

"Then why go?"

She had no answer.

"What would you do?" I persisted.

"I'd go to the trial and make Mother uncomfortable. Maybe she would confess."

"A woman who would have the audacity to try a man for a murder she committed would be so intimidated by your presence that she'd confess? Let's be realistic. Are you sure you don't want to go so *you* can confess?"

It hit her between the eyes. She slumped to the couch. "Is that what you think?" she said, beginning to sob. "Tell me it's not!"

"Margo, all I know is that you're not making any sense. You've got a month before the trial. At least keep your job until then. If and when you feel the need to go to Chicago, it had better be to tell the truth. Otherwise don't go."

Margo sulked through the next three days at work and called me every evening to remind me how hurt she was that I would suspect her. We both watched the newspaper for more information about the upcoming trial.

I had a good start on my illustrating project and hit the sidewalks every morning to drum up more business. I wasn't having much luck, and as it turned out, that would be for the best. The opportunity to talk with Margo about Christ hadn't clearly presented itself, but I knew it would, and that drove me to start praying and digging into my Bible as I hadn't done since high school.

I wasn't getting a lot from my study and prayer that would specifically help Margo, but I felt closer to God than ever, and I prayed almost continually that He would give me something to say just to her. A verse, a word of encouragement, anything. Meanwhile, I gave her every book and article I could find. I was recommending apologists I hadn't even read through yet.

I started going to church again too, but Margo would have nothing to do with it. "Not a chance," was all she'd say. "I'll get my sermon from you when I want it. Anyway, when am I supposed to read all your propaganda?"

One day the morning paper carried the story that the defense attorney had filed a motion for a change of venue, charging that the judge had been a personal friend of the deceased. They had worked in the same district and had been involved in many trials together.

"Mother can't argue with that," Margo said, when I showed her the article. "There's no way she can deny they were colleagues, at least friends professionally."

"Even if this works out the way you think it will, Margo, you've still got problems. The same ones you've had all along. Maybe your mother will be forced to turn the trial over to another judge. It's likely she'll be happy to. But what will change?"

Margo didn't answer and it hit me then that Bill Jacobs might have been right. If Margo herself were guilty, the idea of her mother handling the trial would likely scare her half to death. "Your reaction makes me wonder again if you might be involved in this thing yourself," I said finally.

"You've thought so all along," she said quietly.

"No, frankly, I haven't," I said. "I just don't see how the truth will hurt you, if what you're telling me is the truth."

"Don't you see?" she said. "It won't hurt me; it will hurt Daddy. And that will hurt me. I couldn't do it to him."

"You simply can't keep this to yourself," I said.

"Watch me," she said.

The next day's paper reported that the change of venue motion had been denied when Judge Franklin stated unequivocally that she had never known the deceased outside a courtroom situation.

About three days later Margo received a letter from Frederick T. Wahl, attorney for the defense of Antonio Salerno. It stated that she was to come forth with any information about her mother's social or personal relationship with Richard Wanmacher and/or any information regarding the whereabouts of one Olga Yakovich.

"I had almost forgotten about Olga," Margo told me. "She was our housekeeper for about six months before the murder. They could have learned of her only from Daddy. If I knew where she was, I wouldn't even have to worry about whether or not to tell what I know."

"You think your housekeeper knew, and would testify if she were found?"

"Maybe. If I heard all the phone calls, surely Olga did too, and she never did get along with Mother."

"Margo, what if they can't trace Olga? What will you do?"

She wouldn't answer.

"Hasn't the time come to quit running? If your mother murdered Wanmacher, it's going to come out."

"Then let it. I don't have to be the one to make it happen."

"I think you do, and I think you know you'll never have peace until you do."

"If that's peace, I'll stick with turmoil, thank you."

FOUR

Margo's next message from Defense Attorney Wahl was a simple telegram:

MISS FRANKLIN: HAVE YOU INFORMATION CONCERNING 1) ANYTHING OTHER THAN A PROFESSIONAL RELATIONSHIP BETWEEN MR. RICHARD WANMACHER AND JUDGE VIRGINIA FRANKLIN, OR 2) THE WHEREABOUTS OF MRS. OLGA YAKOVICH? RESPOND SOONEST PLEASE.

"They're serious, Margo," I said. "You can't ignore them."

"Then I'll lie," she said.

"No, you won't."

"And why won't I?"

"Because if you do, I'll assume you've lied to me. Have you?"

"No!"

"Not about anything?"

"No!"

It was obvious that Margo wanted to tell me something, but I kept badgering her. "I haven't lied to you, either," I continued. "I told you I know Someone who loves you, and I do."

"Don't you think I know that?" Margo asked. "All my life I've known there was a God and that He wanted me to do what was right."

A weak, "You have?" was all I could say.

"Of course. That's why I haven't slept well for years. I've known all along it was wrong not to tell. For a while it got worse every day. Then it got so six to eight hours would pass sometimes without my even thinking of the murder, but I dreamed of it every night. And anyone who reminded me of Daddy or Mother, or anyone named Richard or Michael would set me off and I'd be good for nothing for days.

"Before Michael showed up at the coffee shop with his wife I had had a feeling of dread for about a week. It was as if God were telling me that something was about to break and I'd have to come forward. Something, I think God, was impressing upon me that I would soon be through running."

"Wasn't that sort of a relief?" I asked.

"I can see why you'd think so. But I considered the options and decided that there was no way I could tell what I knew. It would be too painful for me and for Daddy."

"And it would snap whatever shred of hope you were still clinging to that the three of you would be a happy family again."

Margo turned slowly to face me, as if repeating my words in her mind. Her face contorted into a tear-fighting grimace. Her lips quivered and she blinked furiously. "I guess you're right," she managed, the tears gushing now. She made no attempt to hide her face. It was as if she wanted me to know that I had struck home, and that now I would have to share her grief. I felt strangely privileged as she sat, now wide-eyed, virtually crying to me. I could think of nothing to say.

"You look like you're losing weight," I said finally, feeling absurd.

She didn't react.

"I mean, I thought you said you ate when you were upset."

She wiped her face and shook her head in an act of toleration. "I ate my troubles away up to this point, but now that things are really starting to get hot, I have no appetite."

"Maybe that's good, huh?"

"I don't see how it makes much difference. I'm on a dead-end street anyway. You've got me talked or scared out of killing myself, but I can guarantee I'm not enjoying living either."

"You could if you'd let me tell you about the love God has for you."

"In spite of the mess I'm in I'm s'posed to take consolation in the fact that God loves me?"

"Frankly, I can't identify with a problem as serious as yours," I admitted. "Mine all seem pretty trivial. But I can tell you, He's never failed me. And I've failed Him often."

"You know," Margo said, "I'd been thinking that God was reaching out to me, but I was running. I thought He was after me because of my secret. When you told me He loved me, it just about blew me away. I'd heard the phrase *God is love,* but I never once thought He could or would love me."

"He does."

"You know, Philip, I don't think anything else you could have said that day would have worked." (I couldn't wait to tell Bill Jacobs.)

"You would have jumped right there in front of me?"

"Absolutely. When you refused to leave, you have no idea how close I came to jumping anyway."

I shuddered. "But you didn't because you liked the idea that God loved you?"

"Not really." Now I was puzzled.

"I think that possibility, along with the fact that you really seemed to care, made the difference."

"Did you really think no one would have missed you?"

"I knew it."

"And what do you think now?"

She smiled faintly, then changed the subject. "What am I going to do about the telegram, Phil?"

"You know what I think you should do."

"If I answer truthfully, will they make me go to Chicago?"

"Likely."

"Since you're badgering me into this, will you go with me if I have to go?"

"Oh, boy."

"That's what I was afraid of. I don't think I can do it on my own."

"I'll tell you what," I said, "you make your own decision about how you're going to answer that telegram. No blaming it on me. Then we'll decide about my going to Chicago with you, if you have to go — but it won't be because I talked you into anything."

"I have to know that you'll go with me before I answer the telegram."

"We don't know how long you'd be there. What would I do about my work?"

"I didn't know free-lance artists worked," she said with a smirk. "And what about that hotshot job you've been bragging about? The one that takes you only a few hours a day to keep up with? Why don't you get ahead and then you can take some time off?"

"I'll think about it," I said. "But we've got to make a deal. I won't even consider it unless you tell all you know in this thing. I'm not going up there with you if you're gonna tell some but not all."

"That one *I'll* have to think about."

I knew I was only a few days away from some serious spiritual talk with Margo, and I searched every Christian book and magazine I had for just the right words. On Sunday the pastor talked about not putting God in a box and expecting Him to do everything the way we think it should be done. I filed it away for future reference. One of the things Margo would surely ask would be how a loving God could allow such a tragedy in her life.

As I was working on textbook illustrations the next night, I tried to imagine myself in Margo's position. She had quite a decision to make, a lot more important than my decision whether or not to go with her to Chicago. I didn't want her to take it for granted, but of course I would go. It would mean working twelve hours a day or more on the illustrations first, but it would be worth it. Very little about Margo irritated me anymore, and I found myself wanting to help her, not just feeling obligated. Besides, I had to meet Virginia Franklin. She just had to be one of a kind.

I made one tactical error with Margo. When she came to me with her decision I nearly blew the whole case. "I want to tell the truth," Margo said. "If you'll stick with me on this, I want to get it done. What's the next step?" I told her to respond to the telegram with a simple yes to the first question, that there was more than a professional relationship between Richard Wanmacher and Virginia Franklin, and a simple no to the question concerning Olga's whereabouts.

"That's not the whole truth, though," she said.

"I know. Don't worry — they'll be back to you for the whole truth."

I was way off. A few days later we read that the lawyers for Salerno had not won just a change of venue, but had gotten the case thrown out of court for lack of evidence. The prosecution lawyer was astounded at the timing of the decision and admitted that the murder case would probably never be solved. "There are no other suspects," he told newsmen.

Margo and I puzzled over the story and the fact that there had been no follow-up on her telegram. "Maybe there's more on it in the Chicago papers," I said. We drove to the library and dug out the last several issues. What we read made us agree with the prosecutor. The timing was weird. The defense had asked for a few days to bring more evidence on their change of venue petition, but before any of what they found was brought up in court, the case was dismissed.

Slowly it began to make sense to me. "I shouldn't have had you respond only to the defense attorney," I said. "He doesn't care about the relationship between your mother and Wanmacher past its use in getting his client off the hook. A hoodlum's lawyers are going to be hoodlums, right?"

"I'm not following you."

"Figure this. Wahl gets your telegram, goes straight to your mother, shows it to her and scares the life out of her. Her daughter is about to spill the beans. She makes a fast deal. She'll throw the case out on a technicality if he'll destroy the telegram and tell no one."

"Makes sense."

"Of course it does," I said, clapping and drawing angry stares from two librarians. I felt like Sherlock Holmes.

"But what now?" Margo asked.

"You still willing to tell the truth?"

"If it'll do any good."

"It will if you tell the right people. Don't let me talk you into it, but if you really want to get this off your chest, tell the U.S. attorney for Northern Illinois."

"Why him?"

"He'll hassle Wahl and his associates for not pursuing your telegram. He is the one who must file murder charges against your mother. I never should have expected mob lawyers to be friends of the court."

Margo was stony.

"What's the matter?" I asked.

"File charges against Mother?" she repeated. "Philip, I can't do it. An innocent man has been cleared. Isn't that enough?"

FIVE

I was so certain Margo would call during the night that I slept fitfully, imagining the phone ringing every hour or so. She didn't call. I debated calling her the next day, but I decided to wait.

Some quick figuring told me that I would need 450 hours to complete my 600 sketches. To finish in thirty days would mean an investment of fifteen hours a day. I didn't think I could maintain a pace of four sketches every three hours for a whole day, but maybe I could work faster in the morning and average my twenty a day.

I dug out the manuscripts and began logging a basic idea for each drawing along with alternative options for several. Late in the evening I found myself half finished and realized that Margo had not called. I called her.

"I put out a fleece," she told me.

"Sounds awfully biblical for a non-religious type," I said.

"I'm not totally ignorant of the Bible, you know."

"OK, OK, what was your fleece? More important, what did you decide?"

"I'm going to do whatever I have to do. I can't live with this anymore."

"You're doing the right thing, Margo," I said. "What was your fleece?"

"I decided that I'd believe God wanted me to do it if you called me before I called you."

"That's ridiculous," I said. "You knew I'd call you if you didn't call me."

"I didn't know for sure that you'd call, and don't make fun of my fleece. It was sheer torture, wondering if you would get tired of all this and forget me. Anyway, my fleece included a time limit."

"Really? And I called at the very last second, right?"

Margo was silent, hurt. Finally she spoke, "Actually, you had until midnight, if you must know."

"You're convinced now that you should tell all? You're not doing it just for me?"

"No, Philip, but I can't do it without you."

"You know it's going to mean a trip to Chicago."

"Will you go with me?" she asked. "I won't go unless you go with me."

She sounded so desperate. I toyed with needling her about putting conditions on God's will, but she seemed so fragile. "You'll be interested to know that I'm halfway through the planning on my big job, and I've figured a way that I can do the whole thing in thirty days."

"Then you'll do it? You'll go with me if I have to go?"

"Yes, but you'd better know now that there'll be no ifs about it. You inform the right people of what you know, and they'll want you in Chicago — that's all there is to it."

"I'd better do it quickly before I change my mind."

"I thought you were convinced this is what God wants you to do."

"Doesn't God ever change His mind?" Margo asked, seriously.

"Not out of fear, and never about what's right or wrong. Listen, Margo, if I'm going to help you with this, you're going to have to help me get my work done. Let's get some supper and we can talk about it."

I picked up Margo at her apartment, but we didn't go out right away. "I thought we were just going out for a sandwich," she said, reacting to my turtleneck and sportcoat.

"Come on," I said, "don't you know an invitation for a date when you hear one? I distinctly said, 'Let's get some supper and we can talk about it.' That's about as debonair as I'm going to get."

"Well, I'm not going anywhere in a sweater and jeans when you're dressed up," she said.

Margo changed into a pants suit. It was the first time I had seen her in anything but her uniform or grubbies. She looked great, but that was all I wanted to say. She was just too impressionable.

"I know we're only pretending," she said, as if reading my mind. "But I'm going to enjoy my first 'date' in years."

She did seem to enjoy it, too. I exaggerated a lot of chivalrous moves, taking her arm, opening doors, ordering for her, and accusing her of offending all feminists. She laughed each time, and I bowed often. During dinner I raised the subject we had met to discuss.

"Can this wait?" she whined. "You're going to spoil the atmosphere."

I stuck out my lower lip and cocked my head. "Up to you," I said. "But we've got to talk soon."

"I'm off tomorrow," she said. "Let's talk then, and we can keep this evening for just our date."

I eyed her warily and she laughed quickly, assuring me that she was taking it as lightly as I was. "OK," I said.

I got to know Margo a bit better that night. More at ease than I had ever seen her, she seemed to come into her own in a world of even mock formality. She knew where to stand and sit and what to say and how to move. She was playing it for all it was worth. Anyone who cared to notice (and few, if any, did) would have thought she was being dated, and she loved it. I didn't mind. I felt benevolent.

She forced lightness into the conversation at every point. The heaviest we got was when she admitted that her favorite pastime was no longer reading. "It's television," she said flatly. "When I'm not working or sleeping, I'm watching. I know it's garbage, but I am literally hooked. I hate to miss anything. Sometimes I fall asleep watching and the test pattern is humming when I get up for work.

"There are lots of books and magazines I'd love to read, but I buy them and bring them home and they sit unopened, or quickly scanned, while I watch TV. It's a drag."

"That *does* sound like a drag," I said. "Let's talk about it tomorrow. Can you pass up some television to come over and help me finish my preliminary stuff? This isn't going to be easy, working all day every day — "

"But you'll do it for me, right?" she interrupted.

I didn't smile. It was true, I would do it for her, and I didn't want her to take it lightly. It was going to be an unbelievable job, and I was going to ask her to help me a lot. I wasn't going to feel guilty about it, either.

"I don't give up my favorite programs for even a good book, and you want me to give them up for you?" Her eyes were dancing.

"You'll be giving them up often if you help me as much as I need you to during the next month," I said.

She was still smiling, but I wasn't. "Oh, Philip," she said. "You know I will."

Realizing how stern I looked, I exaggerated my frown and growled, "Good, see that you do." Margo laughed, and I took her home.

At her door I flipped on a British accent. "Such a lovely evening, m'dear," I said. "We must do it again soon." Kissing her hand was as much pretending as I wanted to do. I turned on my heel and headed for the stairs.

"When?" she called after me.

"Give me until about three to finish my planning."

"OK," she said, "I'll see you then."

I got home at about 11:00, but I wasn't tired. I had a lot of work to do in the morning, but I didn't feel like going to bed. I didn't feel like doing anything. I sat staring for about an hour and fell asleep on the couch. In the morning, as I finished listing sketch ideas from the manuscripts, my mind kept drifting to the night before and how unproductive it had been. I worried that Margo might have made too much of it, and what I would do if she had. I decided to be a bit cool to her for a while so she wouldn't get any ideas. *Don't flatter yourself*, my conscience chastised.

I finished my preliminaries and had been napping for an hour when Margo arrived. "How did you know I hadn't eaten?" I asked.

"Just guessed," she said, opening a dish of homecooked chicken.

"I want to be serious for a minute, Philip," she said as we ate. "I've been goofing around, but I really do want to know what it's going to take to free you to go to Chicago with me and what I can do to help."

"I'm glad you want to be serious," I said, "because it's not going to be easy.

"First we have to give you a reason to go to Chicago. I've dug out the name of the U.S. attorney for the Northern Illinois district. He's James A. Hanlon."

"What do I tell him? And how?"

I advised Margo to tell Hanlon in a simple, handwritten note that her information, probably incriminating her own mother, Judge Virginia Franklin, had apparently been used to clear Antonio Salerno, but had not been pursued beyond that. "While it makes sense that my mother would not favor pursuing it," Margo wrote, "doesn't it seem that Attorney Frederick Wahl, as a friend of the court, would have checked into it further? I am ready to tell what I know. Are you interested?"

Margo and I went to the post office together and sent the letter with every precaution possible. It was air mail, special delivery, marked *personal, important,* and *confidential,* was insured, and a return receipt was requested. Once the letter was on its way, Margo seemed distant. "If he doesn't do any more with it than Wahl did, I'm going to forget it," she said. "I don't know if I can talk myself into this again."

On the way back to my apartment, I told Margo how many hours a day I figured it would take to do all my work in thirty days.

"Wow," she whispered.

"And I'll need help. But I can do it," I said. "How much money do you have?"

"Why?"

"You're going to have to trust me, Margo. Even if I get this work done, I likely won't be paid for about six weeks. The client has to like it and pay the studio, and the studio has to pay me. That takes time. I have only a few hundred dollars, and I'm going to have to leave that here for rent. Who knows how long we'll be in Chicago?"

"I've got about six hundred dollars."

"Oh, that'll be more than enough. We'll use that to get to Chicago and to exist on until my money comes. Then I'll pay you back and still have enough to live on for several months, if necessary."

"I hope it's not necessary," Margo said.

"So do I."

"But my providing money isn't going to keep me from my TV. What else do you want me to do?"

"I want lots of little things done," I said. "I hate to ask, but it's the only way we're going to pull this thing off."

"Just name it, Philip."

"OK, if I'm going to be sketching for fifteen hours a day, I'm going to have little time for anything else. Can you bring me food after work?"

"Didn't I prove it?"

"Yeah, and it was good."

"What else?"

"I may need errands run. Mail, supplies, sketches delivered."

"Sorry, my social calendar is full this month."

I blinked.

"Seriously, Philip, this will be fun. What else do I have to do? I leave that stinking restaurant every evening and sit home eating and watching TV. This will be the best time I've had in months — years."

"Don't get carried away. I thought you'd feel like a slave."

"No way, especially not when I think of why I'm doing it."

"Just to help your best friend, Phil, right?"

"No, because my best friend, Phil, is helping me."

"I have two other conditions, Margo."

"Oh?"

"First is that we do not discuss what's going to happen in Chicago until we're on our way there. There's no way I can concentrate on my work if we try to hammer out strategy during the day."

"OK."

"The other condition is that I get to talk to you about God during our trip to Chicago."

Margo was fidgeting. "Why is this making me nervous?" she asked.

"Is it a deal?"

"I guess. But can't we talk about Mother and what I'm going to do in Chicago before we talk about God?"

"If we start talking about that, there'll be no time to talk about anything else. Anyway, what we both get out of our discussion about God may help determine what you'll do in Chicago."

"What are you hoping, Philip?"

"That's a loaded question."

"Really, what are you hoping will happen?"

"You really want to know?"

"Yes."

"I'm hoping that you'll realize how much God loves you, and that it will make you want to receive His love gift. After that I just hope you'll see how righteous God is and how He will honor you for doing what's right."

"Which means what?"

"Exposing the entire truth in Chicago."

"For you that sounds neat and complete and the only thing to do, doesn't it?"

"Yup."

"How do you think it sounds to me?"

She caught me off guard. It had been easy to say what I would do. But what if it really were me? "Uh — "

"It sounds like a nightmare," she said.

"Which is what you've been living for years, right?" Margo nodded.

"Are you still game?" I asked.

"Do I have a choice?"

I began sketching at eight o'clock the next morning and was still going strong when Margo arrived ten hours later. "I'm already ahead of schedule," I told her.

"And what have you eaten?"

"I've been gnawing on pretzel sticks and sipping Coke all day," I said. "What've you got?"

"Something you can eat while you're working," she said.

"Good, what?"

"Pretzel sticks and Coke."

"Oh, no — "

"No, really I brought something from the restaurant. It has to be heated."

I kept sketching while Margo talked. It slowed me down a bit, but I was getting tired anyway, and it sure was a change of pace from ten hours in a quiet apartment.

"When I stopped home to change, my TV stared at me forlornly," she said.

"Forlornly?" I mocked. She set the hot meal before me, and I continued to work as I ate. She looked at the sketches and I looked at her. Her features were soft, her eyes dramatic. I didn't say anything.

"I like them," she said. "I s'pose I'd like them more if I knew their significance."

I showed her the manuscripts for the books and my notations for the required sketches. She was fascinated.

"You know, I never saw any of your work before," she said.

"I guess that's right, come to think of it," I said. "Sorry."

"So am I. I'm not a professional, but in my opinion you're exceptionally good."

"That makes you a professional," I teased.

"How come you don't hang any of your work around the apartment?"

"Never thought of it, I guess. Anyway, I sell most everything I do."

"There's something sad about that," Margo said.

"What?"

"I don't know," she said.

Margo ran the first several sketches over to the art studio and mailed some letters for me. She returned just in time to answer the phone. I winced. "What if it's my mother?" I said as she picked up the receiver. It wasn't.

"It's the art studio."

"Yes, sir." I answered.

"Was that your wife?" Mr. Willoughby asked.

"No, just a friend," I said, knowing how it sounded.

"Uh-huh," he said. "Listen, Phil, I just wanted to tell you what I thought of the first sketches."

"You've seen them already?"

"Yeah. I just got back from supper. I can't speak for the client, but I think we're smack on the right track and I wanted to encourage you."

"That's good to hear. I'll be anxious to know what the client thinks."

"Me too. I'll let you know as soon as I can. Probably in a few days."

Six

Earl Haymeyer looked too young, short, and thin to be a detective, but his credentials said he was a special investigator for the office of United States Attorney James A. Hanlon. Haymeyer wore a three piece suit and carried an attaché, but he also carried a snub-nosed .38 and spoke quickly.

"My boss was a personal friend of Richard Wanmacher and is a bitter enemy of both Wahl and Salerno. He has always suspected some sort of an affair between Judge Franklin and Mr. Wanmacher, but he never knew anything for sure. He spent years trying to nail someone for the murder, and was very suspicious of Judge Franklin when the case against Salerno was tossed out. Then he got the letter from your girl friend."

"She's not my girl friend," I said. "Just a friend."

"We're not amateurs, Mr. Spence. When my boss couldn't reach your girl friend by phone, we sent a telegram."

He pulled a copy from his brief case. "MISS FRANKLIN: HAVE BEEN UNABLE TO REACH YOU BY PHONE. CALL IMMEDIATELY. JAMES A. HANLON."

"When she still didn't call, I was assigned to locate her. I traced her phone number to her apartment complex and left a message at the office there. They told me where she worked."

"You could have reached her at her place late at night," I said.

"Or here at your place any other time, right?"

"Well, yeah. Y'see, I — "

"I know, Mr. Spence. I was just getting worried about her."

"You were worried? Why?"

"Because I've also been keeping a tail on Mr. Salerno."

All I could think of was that he would be no match for the notorious hit man, who had been charged with murder nine times but never convicted. Haymeyer saw it in my eyes.

"We're not amateurs, Mr. Spence," he repeated. "Mr. Hanlon and I wondered why Judge Franklin would make a deal with a hit man and his lawyer until your girl friend's letter arrived. Then it made sense, especially when my sources showed Salerno arranging a trip to Atlanta under a phony name. You see why we wanted to get ahold of Margo quickly?"

"Tell me."

Haymeyer was impatient. "Margo's letter tells us that her info, implicating her mother, was ignored by Wahl. But Salerno is cleared and heads for Atlanta. Adding up?"

It was, but I continued to look puzzled. I wanted to hear it all.

"I think old lady Franklin contracted to have her daughter taken out of the picture."

"You're kidding," I said, knowing immediately how it sounded. Haymeyer pursed his lips at me, but left the we're-not-amateurs line unrepeated.

"How did you find me?" I asked.

"We found Margo first," he said. "When Salerno actually started heading south by car,

I flew down here and met Margo at the restaurant. She's in a motel room now, but she told me all about you, and that she won't go to Chicago or say any more unless you're with her."

"Did she say I was her boyfriend?" I asked.

"She said the same thing you've been saying," Haymeyer said. "But you're *not* her lawyer, and we're — "

"Not amateurs," I cut him off. We both smiled.

"I'll take you to her," he said.

"How do I know you're really working for Hanlon?" I asked.

"I thought you'd never ask." He produced the original of the letter Margo had sent Hanlon. "You don't suppose I found this in the garbage, do you?"

I talked Haymeyer into letting me drop off the rest of my completed sketches at the art studio, and in the process I got more encouragement from Mr. Willoughby. He said the client was thrilled, but was concerned about how fast I was working.

"What does he care, as long as the stuff is good?"

"He hasn't complained about the artwork, Philip. He just wants you to know that you're a couple of months ahead and that you can slow up if you wish."

"I might just do that. Could he pay you so you can pay me for what's done so far?"

"No problem."

On the way to the motel, Haymeyer showed me several photographs of Salerno. "We figure it won't take Salerno long to track down Margo once he gets here, which should be sometime late tonight."

"Won't he have to learn her schedule or something before he tries anything?"

"Very good, kid. You've been watching TV, haven't you? Tomorrow's Sunday. Does Margo work on Sunday?"

"Usually, but not tomorrow."

"Salerno will have to figure that out. He'll probably show up at the restaurant and go to her apartment when he realizes that she's off work. If she's not there he may wait, or he might start asking questions that lead him to your place."

"Meanwhile we're jetting off to Chicago, right?"

"Not quite."

"Oh?"

"What you don't realize, kid, is that we have several objectives."

"We?"

"The U.S. attorney's office. First is the safety of Miss Franklin, not to mention you."

"Please mention me."

"Second is to solve the Wanmacher murder case, which my boss, not to mention the public, wants very much to see."

"Is there a third?"

"Yeah, and that's why we're not jetting off to Chicago while Salerno is looking to blow Margo's head off."

"I guess I'm ready for door number three, Monty."

"You do watch television, don't you, kid?"

"Why do you call me kid? You can't be much older than I am."

"So it makes me feel older; am I forgiven?"

"What's your third objective?"

"To nail Salerno. In the act."

"In the act?"

"Of murdering Margo."

It hadn't dawned on me until that instant that I was in over my head. Talking Margo out of killing herself had been the most traumatic experience in my life. Everything since then had seemed slow motion, even a visit from a government detective who told me Margo was being stalked by a mob hit man. But Margo as live bait?

"You can't really let her stay in Atlanta while he looks for her, can you?"

"We can and we will. I have some associates on the way right now. Our plan is to let Salerno have a good look at Margo and her schedule. We'll be watching her and him all the time, and I hope we'll set him up."

"You hope?"

"Frankly, despite his eluding conviction in nine previous arrests, and despite the fact that we believe he's guilty of twice as many successful hits, I think we've got a real chance here."

"Why?"

"He's limited by his *modus operandi.*"

"Which is?"

"Clean and messy at the same time. Sawed-off shotgun."

I was speechless. Was this real?

Haymeyer continued. "Salerno is good, maybe the best, with a sawed-off. But this is not the kind of hit that can be pulled off in public. And it's not Salerno's style to come in shooting. If it was, he'd have been locked up years ago.

"No, he's very cool and crafty. He lies low, is seldom noticed, even when asking someone's whereabouts."

"Why is that?"

"He uses simple disguises. He's very ordinary anyway. He doesn't have the sinister look that people expect after seeing too many cops and robbers on TV. His average build and appearance lend itself to disguise and anonymity."

"When and how does he make his, uh, hits?"

"He takes his time. He makes a lot of money, and he makes sure. My guess is that he'll watch Margo for four or five days until he is sure of the one place he can nail her without the chance of anyone interfering."

"I think I'd rather see her hustled off to Chicago."

"Then what would we have? A hit man on the loose, still looking for her — and for you, for that matter. If he follows her, it's going to lead to you, you know."

All I could think of was that neither Bill Jacobs nor my parents would ever believe this.

"There's something else," Haymeyer said. "If we don't get Salerno, who's going to give us what we need to put away old lady Franklin?"

"Margo."

"I've heard Margo's story. It's heavy, but it'll never stand up without Salerno admitting that he was paid by the judge to kill Margo."

"Did Margo tell you about Olga?"

"We've been looking for Olga ever since Wahl and his boys stumbled onto her name during the Salerno pretrial."

"How did they get onto her?"

"Through Mr. Franklin is all we can figure."

"That doesn't sound like something he'd say, based on what Margo told me," I said.

"We figure it was an innocent comment he made in response to questions about anyone who had contact with Mrs. Franklin at the time of the murder. Wahl was really pushing Judge Franklin at this point, and he wanted to discover and use any and every name that might fluster her into throwing out the case."

"Margo's name was the one that did it, though, right?"

"It appears that way. We've talked to Mr. Franklin, and he's convinced not only that Mrs. Franklin can in no way be suspected, but also that she never was unfaithful to him. I think the judge figures he's not worth worrying about, or she'd have sent Salerno after *him.*"

"She must not be worried about Olga either, then?"

"I'm not so sure," Haymeyer said. "Like I said, we haven't been able to locate her. I'd hate to think she's already been eliminated."

"What a nice way to say it," I said.

Margo looked like a scared puppy. Haymeyer looked nonplussed that we didn't embrace.

"Where could Olga be, Margo?" I said.

"I have no idea," she said. "I never really knew her, and I didn't hear from her after she quit."

"She quit?" Haymeyer said, taking off his top coat and shoes and stretching out on one of the beds.

"Yes, just after the murder. I always figured she knew about Mother and Richard."

Haymeyer rolled over quickly and grabbed the telephone. He placed a person to person call to Hanlon in Chicago. "Jim, Earl. I've got Margo and her boyfriend here, and we're going to try to flush out Salerno. . . . Yes, I've already requested Barnes and Warren, if that's OK. . . . Good. Listen, Jim, is there someone there who can work full time in tracking down this Olga what's-her-name?"

"Yakovich," Margo offered.

Haymeyer wheeled around. "Right, Yakovich. I think she might be key in this, Jim. If anything goes wrong with Salerno — " Haymeyer paused, and I saw the fear in Margo's eyes. "Oh, no, I don't mean that," Haymeyer was saying. "I mean if he won't talk once we get him. We'll get him."

He sounded so certain.

That evening detectives Jim Barnes and Bob Warren arrived at the Atlanta airport and called Haymeyer at his motel room. They were each instructed to rent a car and to meet us at the Omni, Atlanta's professional sports complex. "The Hawks don't generally draw as many fans now that they are playing without Maravich," Haymeyer told his two men. "But with the Seventy-sixers and Doctor J. visiting tonight, we'll be unnoticed in the crowd."

"It's just like a date," Haymeyer told Margo and me. "You go to the game in Philip's car. It's unlikely Salerno will have the faintest idea where to find you yet, but we'll not appear to be together anyway. We three will sit behind you. When we sit down, you two lean back as if bored with the game. We will sit forward and talk with each other so you can hear. You'll get the whole picture, but don't look at us, and don't say anything to us. My guess is that Salerno is in Atlanta by now, and he'll be following every lead to get at Margo. He's no amateur either."

Haymeyer dropped us off at my apartment, where we got in my car and headed for the Omni. We arrived early and were fascinated by the crowd and the game, but we found it hard to talk. "Where's God now?" Margo asked.

"Only you could make that sound original," I said.

I tried not to look around but found myself constantly watching for Haymeyer. When he arrived I almost didn't recognize him. He was wearing a Hawks hat and was carrying a box of popcorn. We leaned back, still looking straight ahead, and he leaned forward. "Look all around the stadium," he said quietly, "and you'll see Bob Warren in the green pullover, heading this way."

Margo looked one way and I looked the other, and we both eventually spotted Warren. He too had popcorn and a Hawks hat, but he looked out of place — older, gruffer, and tackier than Haymeyer.

"Jim Barnes is coming from the other way," Haymeyer said. We caught ourselves looking too quickly. Tall, thin, and blond, Barnes looked like a country gentleman out for a night of fun with his buddies. He was Warren's age.

The three detectives were boisterous about the game and the bets and the beer, but during the time-outs and between quarters they all leaned forward, elbows on knees, and chatted seriously in low tones, just loud enough for Margo and me to hear. Occasionally, though they were talking seriously, one would smack the other on the back or lean back and laugh uproariously, spilling something.

"Margo," Haymeyer said. "I'm going to talk about your schedule for the next few days. If you don't understand something, just turn and say something about the game to Phil and I'll repeat it. If you miss something altogether, we can talk about it later. If you understand, just shake your head as if to rearrange your hair." Margo shook her head and I turned to look. Her hair was beautiful. She was scared. So was I. I took her hand.

"That looks good, Philip. Just like a date. Now after the game you just take her to her place and then go home." I almost turned around. With Salerno in town I was to leave her alone in her apartment?

Haymeyer leaned back in his seat and called for a vendor. After buying an ice-cream bar he leaned forward to unwrap it. "Will you leave her safety to us?" he hissed. "Bob has already rented an apartment on her floor and will be there before you are. She will be under constant watch. It's unlikely that Salerno will show up there tonight anyway. Jim has rented a place in your building, Philip, though not on your floor. He'll be close whenever Margo is there, but there's no need for him to be on your floor otherwise. Salerno won't want you without Margo.

"Jim, I want each of us to visit the restaurant once in the next three days. None of us will be there more than once, in case Salerno is watching and notices a pattern. Margo, if you have a message for us, write it out and give it to us with our bill. The key is for you to maintain your usual routine. Any time, remember, *any time* you find yourself alone, walk very quickly and do not linger. Keep moving. The key is to make Salerno think that the only place he has a chance to get you is in your apartment, either while you're asleep or watching television."

Margo turned to look at me. "You don't understand something?" Haymeyer asked. I wrote a question on my program and dropped it beneath the seat. Barnes picked it up and read the question while passing it back to me. "Thanks," I said.

Barnes said to Haymeyer, "He'd rather the trap be laid at his apartment so Margo won't be alone."

I could tell from the sound of Barnes' voice that he was as annoyed as Haymeyer, who leaned almost to my ear and said sternly, "Philip, we know what we are doing. Leave it to us. There is no way we'll let Salerno get into Margo's apartment while she is there. If he tries, we'll nail him before he gets through the door. What we want is for him to get into the apartment when we have a dummy there. If he puts a load of buckshot through a dummy, we have a strong case. If he tries to get in before we think he will, and Margo is there instead of a dummy, we'll take him immediately." I settled back, nodding.

"There's something none of us should forget," Warren said. "We don't know Salerno is even aware of Margo. We don't know that's why he's here, or even that Mrs. Franklin let him off because of Margo's message to Wahl. We're going to approach the case as if he's here to get her, but we're only guessing. Let's not forget that."

Everyone nodded and Warren clapped Haymeyer on the back. "Gotta get goin'!" he said, and reached across to shake Barnes' hand.

"See ya," Barnes said.

Twenty minutes later the 76ers were sure of victory and many fans were leaving. "Stay until you see us leave," Haymeyer said. "Give us about a ten minute lead. I'm staying at the motel, and Barnes will be at your place by the time you get there, Philip. He'll nod to you in the hall when you get to your apartment. If he doesn't, call me immediately."

I was tingling with excitement and fear on the way to Margo's apartment.

"It's ironic," she said with a shiver, "not two weeks ago I wanted to kill myself. Now someone is going to try to do it for me."

"He won't succeed, though," I said, trying to sound brave. "These guys, Haymeyer and his boys, are too good." Margo said nothing. "Have you read those articles I gave you?" I asked.

"Yes, but I'm not thinking about them right now," Margo said. "If you had a Bible, I might read that." I leaned across her and popped open the glove compartment. I gave her a *Living New Testament*. "It's easy to read," I said.

"And that's what I need, right?" she said.

I blushed. "I mean it's easier to understand. At least for me."

"You're not as well read as I am, remember," she said, sounding chippy.

"What's wrong, Margo?"

"Oh, nothing," she said. "It's just that I'm about to have my head blown off, and my only friend in the world thinks he's got an edge on brains because he's a man."

"Now I'm a chauvinist?" I said. "I do think I have an edge on reality, though; I haven't thought about suicide."

"Oh, that helped," she said.

"I'm sorry. I didn't mean it to come out like that."

"It's OK, Philip, I deserved it. It's just that Haymeyer never asked if I wanted to cooperate in this scheme. I haven't even had time to think about it."

"There isn't time," I said.

"Time isn't the point, Philip."

"What is the point?"

"That I feel nothing toward the man who is hunting me down. I don't even feel anything toward the woman who's paying him to do it."

"You don't?"

"No, and that's the problem. I should hate her, but all I can do is wonder why my own mother would want me killed."

"You know why."

"Sure I know the pragmatic reasons, but how did it come to this? Is she so afraid for her own neck that she would kill her daughter? She threw away her marriage and family for what? A man? What was so special about Richard Wanmacher that she would sacrifice her family for him, and then hate him to the point that she would kill him?"

"She did the same for you. She loved you and now she hates you."

"Oh, it hurts to hear those words from anyone but me."

"I know, and I'm sorry."

"You may be sorry, but no, Philip, you don't know. How could you know?"

Margo was right. It choked me up to think of my own mother. Overprotective, possessive, eccentric perhaps. Old-fashioned. Devout. I would never belittle her again, not even to myself. What I would give for my mother! And what I would give if Margo could have a mother like mine.

"Philip, I am about to risk my life so a murderer my mother hired can be trapped into implicating her. Yet I feel no anger. I just feel alone, abandoned."

"You have God."

"I do, but not in the way you think."

"I don't follow."

"No, you don't, Philip. I don't say this to put you down, please believe that, but I think you're too naive to see how I have God when I have no one else. In all that you've shown me and told me and given to me to read about God, I've learned more about Him than I think you know."

I was shocked. What could she have learned about God that I hadn't known?

"You've been trying to reach me with intellectual arguments," she continued. "You thought I would need every barrier and doubt eradicated. You've given me evidence and reason and verses and everything else. It has all been reassuring, but that's not why I asked Jesus to be my Christ."

"You did? When?"

"When is irrelevant now, Philip."

"But why didn't you tell me? Didn't you think I'd want to know?"

I knew you'd want to know, but I wasn't sure why. Was it because you wanted to tell your Sunday school class or pastor or your friends or your parents? Was I a trophy?"

"You don't really think that, do you, Margo?"

"I don't know. I know I was more than a trophy for you at first, when you approached me with God as an alternative to death. That is beautiful, because that's what I have discovered Him to be. The antithesis of death."

Margo sounded so cool and calculated. Perhaps I had been out of my league intellectually, in spite of my subconscious chauvinism. It seemed that she was begrudging, almost attacking the fact that she had found Christ and careful not to credit me in any way.

"It's not that I'm ungrateful, Philip. And if it weren't for what I'm going through, I'm sure I wouldn't be picking you apart. It's just that you have communicated something to me that you didn't mean to communicate, and that very thing was what led me to Christ."

I was almost irritated. "What in the world was it?"

"It's so simple," Margo said. "In all the things you said and gave me to read, it wasn't the arguments that made the difference. It wasn't anything but the fact that I had God in you."

"Careful."

"No, I won't be careful. I'm not trying to flatter you, don't you see? Good grief, God uses you in spite of yourself. Your faith and your Christianity — and even your God is so small to you that you limit Him."

She was rambling on nervously, watching each street sign as we neared her place, probably hoping that we wouldn't arrive too soon. Haymeyer had cautioned me not to sit in the car and talk, and not to drive around the block in front of her place. He wanted Salerno, if he was watching, to think everything was normal.

"You see, Philip, God used you in the most simple and profound way possible. He loved me and cared about me through you. When I was immature and half insane with fear and guilt, He somehow allowed you to cope even though you really couldn't care and probably couldn't have coped."

I was hurt, and it showed.

"Don't misunderstand, Philip. You *are* misunderstanding. I can tell. That's my whole point. You thought you were God's mouthpiece. You weren't. If I had listened to your arguments and had taken seriously all of what your fundamentalist theologians call — what is it, apologetics? — I could have debated this thing for years. I likely would not have made the decision that I did."

"I had nothing to do with it, then?"

"Your nervousness is limiting your logic now too, Philip. You had everything to do with it, because in all of this, the only place I saw God was in you. Hearing you, knowing you, reading your literature only proved to me what an unlikely candidate you were to be used of God. When you first mentioned to me that God loved me it nearly blew me away — "

"Bad choice of words."

She ignored my grim humor. "But what you said was a shred of hope. I wanted evidence that God loved me, as you said He did."

"I tried to give you evidence."

"And all I needed was to see that you cared. Didn't you ever ask yourself why you were involved?"

"As a matter of fact, yes."

"Then you should be able to see it. There was no reason for you to care. Sure, you're a nice guy and all, but your arguments and attempts at convincing me were just evidence that the real you was just trying to do the right thing. It was Christ in you that convinced me."

"I don't know how to feel, Margo. Are you chastising me?"

"No. In fact, I don't think I would tell you to change in any way, except maybe to realize what's important and what isn't. In a way, you had to be the way you were for the chemistry to be just right. Had I not seen your humanity in all your efforts to convince me of God's love, I'd have never seen the contrast in the way God used you in spite of yourself. It had to be the way it was."

"If my arguments were all so futile, why didn't you say so?"

"I guess because there was something strange going on. You were loving me, almost, without knowing it. Not the romantic kind of love, but with God's love. I looked to you for unconditional love, the kind you talked about, and the kind I read about. God loved me unconditionally through you, and you hardly knew it."

I had nothing to say. For sure, I had underestimated Margo's mind. "You have unusual insight," I said finally. "I've always heard that when you're trying to win someone to Christ you should just let God use you and trust his Spirit to do the work."

"That's what happened, Philip. Every time I tried to pray, it seemed as if God were telling me not to listen to you so much as to watch you love me. It was as if He were saying, 'This is how I love you. Through Philip.' "

"That's almost scary, and sort of embarrassing and humbling, too."

"Philip, I love you in Jesus. I can say that because I know you love me in Him. I love you because you loved me first. That's why we love Christ, according to one of those articles you gave me."

"Then you did get something from them?"

"You're missing my point, Philip," she said, patiently. "I got a lot from them. Mostly I learned what to look for in you. I saw it, in spite of you."

"I don't know whether to feel thrilled or insulted."

"Feel used. God used you. I don't understand why you haven't seen this in your Bible reading. Isn't that what the Bible is all about?"

"Yes, but I guess when it becomes old to a person, he misses the real point — the living part of it."

"You didn't miss it, Philip. You just hit it without knowing it."

"One of my problems is the problem of every Christian I know: the discipline of daily Bible reading."

"Why do you have a problem if you believe it's God's Word?"

"If I knew the answer to that one, I could save a lot of people a lot of grief."

"No, really, Philip. Do you realize how that sounds? You tell me you believe this book is the Word of God. I couldn't hope for anything better than to have the Word of God in a book. Then you tell me that the people who believe this are the ones who have the trouble reading it every day. Why?"

"I don't know, Margo. I do know that every time I force myself to read and study, I am thrilled. God gives me something special. If it's not a specific answer to a need of the day, it might just be some encouragement in the way a psalm is worded or in the way a writer has praised God. Still, it's a struggle to read it faithfully."

"I don't know whether I'll ever understand why a person has to force himself to read something he loves," Margo said. "All I want to do is read the Bible. Will I lose that desire?"

"You might. You're going through what many people call the 'first love of Christ.' I think it's even called that in the New Testament."

"It's all so clinical. I hope I don't fit into some prescribed pattern. I'm going to read the Bible tonight. If Antonio Salerno wants to blow me away tonight, I'll die reading the Bible."

"You've become an amazingly mature Christian overnight," I said, only half joking.

"I'm not saying I'm not scared. I'm still puzzled about a lot of things, too. Somehow, I am convinced of the unconditional love and the ultimate wisdom of God. If a person who goes through what I've been through can say that, you know only God has convinced me of it."

"That's for sure, Margo. That's what I figured would be my biggest hurdle: convincing you that God was in this whole mess."

"There you go. Your biggest hurdle? You were going to convince me of it? Never. Only God could do it, and not with words."

We both spotted Bob Warren in the lobby, sitting in a stuffed chair and smoking idly. Our eyes met briefly. Margo left me at her door and went in with the *Living New Testament* tucked under her arm. When I returned to my apartment, I saw no trace of Jim Barnes — not in the parking lot, not in the lobby, not on the elevator, not in the hall. I walked slowly, trying to be totally alert. I spent a long time unlocking my door and began to panic when I still didn't see him.

"Call me immediately," had been Haymeyer's instruction.

"Room three thirty-three please," I said. His phone rang six times.

"There seems to be no answer, sir."

"Ring again, please, I know he's there."

She rang the room again, eight times. "I'm sorry, sir."

SEVEN

I imagined the worst and kept calling Haymeyer's number. The desk clerk finally offered to leave the message light on in his room and was obviously relieved to have me off her back. Margo's line was busy, so with nothing to do but worry, I took a walk in the building, hoping to see Barnes.

I passed two medium-sized men about five minutes apart, certain each time that I had discovered the hit man Salerno. I hadn't, of course, but I would have suspected a poodle at that point.

The phone was ringing when I got back to my apartment, but I didn't get to it in time. I called Haymeyer.

"No, sir. Now, please, I said I'd have him call!" the operator snapped.

I called Margo. Still busy. I slammed the receiver down. The phone rang.

"What have you been doing?" Haymeyer demanded. "For a half hour your line is busy, and then I get no answer until now."

"I've been trying to reach you, Earl," I said. "Barnes is not here and Margo's line is busy and — "

"I know all that. I'm calling from Margo's. Meet me at the drugstore on your corner in half an hour, and I'll fill you in. Let's not talk by phone."

"What's up? Is Margo all right?"

"Let's not talk by phone," Haymeyer said sternly, and he hung up.

"Yes, Margo is fine," Haymeyer said at the drugstore as we scanned magazines. "It's just that her mother called, and Margo thought we should know. She called Warren and he called Barnes when I couldn't be reached."

"Why couldn't you be reached?"

"I had a message to call Chicago and didn't want to call from my room. I was out making the call when they were trying to reach me. When I got back and didn't get an answer at Barnes's room, I headed for Margo's."

"Why couldn't you call Chicago from your room?"

"Salerno may not be alone here. It's possible our phones are tapped."

"Even mine?"

"Most likely yours. I'm still hopeful Salerno is not aware that we're here in Atlanta, but you can bet he's aware of you. If he finds out we're here, it may scare him off."

"That would be nice."

"No, it wouldn't. I think the phone call from Judge Franklin tonight may play right into our hands."

"What was it all about? Margo says Mrs. Franklin rarely calls, and never just for chitchat."

"It wasn't chitchat, Philip. It was a setup. First of all, she wasn't calling from home. Margo heard street noises. That's smart."

"Why?"

"Because if she is working with Salerno and wants Margo snuffed, it would look bad to have a call to Atlanta on her bill the day before. She underestimated Margo, though. It was stupid to call from a pay phone and expect Margo to think she was calling from home.

"Mrs. Franklin said she was passing along a message from Margo's father, whom she claimed to have seen recently. He wanted her to be sure to be at home tomorrow evening at nine so he could find her there when he calls, she said."

"You sure it's a setup?" I asked.

"Yup. We made sure Margo's phone was not bugged and had her call her father. Luckily she caught him at his apartment, and he seemed pleased to hear from her. She made no mention of the message from Mrs. Franklin, and neither did he."

"Earl," I said, "what are the odds that Mr. Franklin wouldn't mention the coincidence of Margo calling the night before he planned to? Or that he wouldn't ask if she'd gotten a message from her mother?"

"The odds are he would, Philip. You're catching on."

"What do you suppose is happening?"

"It's pretty transparent. Judge Franklin is so intent on Salerno completing the job that she's helping out. Do you suppose Salerno has any idea where Margo might be tomorrow night?"

"By the phone in her apartment."

"Right."

"What are you going to do?"

"Watch Salerno, and use a dummy."

"You've spotted Salerno?"

"Warren thinks he has."

"He *thinks?*"

"That's enough for me, Philip. We don't take chances when it comes to safeguarding a witness."

"That's good to hear. What about a witness's friend?"

Haymeyer loved the idea that Margo and I were going to church the next morning. He said he and Barnes would meet us there while Warren stayed at Margo's building to keep an eye on Salerno. "What do people wear to church in this town?" he wanted to know.

"Same as everywhere," I said. "Dress up, and carry a Bible or you will stand out as a stranger."

"I want to look like anything but a stranger," he said. "I'll pass along any more info when I greet you after mass."

"It's a *service* in this church," I said.

"OK, when I greet you after the service. They do greet each other after the service, right?"

I picked up Margo the next morning and saw her in pastel for the first time.

"It's a step," she said. "I'm not sure I'm really ready for light colors, but I feel like I am."

"I think you are," I said, staring too long.

Margo admitted that she had hardly slept, but had read until about 4:00 A.M. "I did feel a little more secure knowing that Mr. Warren was in the building, but every noise froze me to the bed. I prayed a lot."

Barnes and Haymeyer were a sight, each carrying Gideon Bibles from Earl's motel. They shook hands with us like old friends and smiled as they talked. Jim told us that the Atlanta Metropolitan Bureau of Investigation had determined that Salerno was in Atlanta alone and had stuck close to Margo's building. They were betting that no phones were tapped.

He also said that a check with the phone company revealed that Salerno had called a Chicago pay phone at 1:00 A.M. "There's no way of knowing," Barnes said, "but we think he called Judge Franklin."

Haymeyer advised us to maintain a normal routine for the day, so Margo and I planned to go out for dinner, then go to my apartment so I could do some more sketch-es before the evening service. I was to have her back at her apartment in time for the bogus phone call at nine o'clock. Haymeyer said he would get more instructions to us during the afternoon.

"I have a new appreciation for hunted animals," Margo said at dinner. "Honestly, Philip, I feel so vulnerable, and I have the strangest feeling for Mr. Salerno."

"*Mr.* Salerno?"

"I suppose that sounds a bit too respectful, doesn't it? I have no respect for him, of course, but have you ever wondered what kind of background a man like that must have had? Was he ever loved? Ever cared about? Ever disciplined? I mean, he's not the troub-lemaker type, not just an attention seeker. He's the opposite. He's smart and quiet and motivated — by what?"

"Money."

"But is that all? Isn't something missing? Could just money be worth giving up conscience? He has prestige only among a tiny group of people. Does he have a wife, a family?"

"I don't know," I said, as if I didn't care. I realized that I didn't, at least not as much as Margo seemed to. "Why do you care, Margo?"

"I don't know. I really don't. A week ago, a month ago for sure, I wouldn't have cared at all. I might even have been capable of killing a man who wanted to kill me. I know I was capable of killing myself. I almost did. I would have if God hadn't sent you there.

"That must be it, Philip. I was capable of killing because I hated myself. Antonio Salerno must have a terrible self-image. He must hate himself to be capable of hating another person enough to murder him."

"You were brutally honest with me last night, Margo, and I think I learned a lot about myself from it. So, let me be honest. I can't seem to muster any concern over *Mr.* Salerno as you call him. He's sin personified, and he needs to be dealt with."

"How does God deal with sin?"

"He judges it. His wrath comes down upon it. He is righteous and will not tolerate it."

"Wrong."

Margo sounded smug. Here was a day-old Christian telling me I was wrong about the judgment of God. "I'm not wrong, Margo. You are."

"Did God judge you or me, Philip? Weren't you trying to convince me for days that God is a God of love? Does God love Tony Salerno, or does He love only you and me?"

"We're talking about a two-bit free-lance artist and a manic-depressive, possibly sui-cidal daughter of a socialite as opposed to a professional killer! I'm not saying God can't love Salerno. I'm just saying God hates his sin and Salerno's probably past the point of no return." I knew when I said it that I was wrong. If God loved everyone and offered a free gift to all who would receive it, then that would have to include a mob hit man as well. Margo was going to be one intriguing Christian, taking God at His word right down the line.

"I don't know about you, Philip, but I'm going to try to show Salerno that God loves him. Not just tell him, but show him."

"How?"

"I'll visit him in prison. I'll do things for him. I'll be so nice to him he won't know what hit him."

"Good grief, Margo. This is morbid. Have you considered the possibility that he may be scared off this time and track you for months?"

"I don't even want to think about it."

"Neither do I."

"Philip, you sound like you're arguing against Christianity."

"I just want to be realistic. After last night, maybe arguing against instead of for would be more appreciated."

"Oh, poor baby," Margo mocked. "Is the baby hurt because his efforts went unappreciated?"

I said nothing, letting her taunt linger in the air so she could hear how cruel it sounded.

"OK, I probably do owe you an apology for being so confusing last night. I think you got the point, but let's don't talk about being realistic. Had I been realistic, I'd have jumped out the window. There's nothing less realistic than asking God to forgive your sin and Christ to be your Lord."

"Until you've done it," I said. "Then it makes sense."

"Exactly," Margo said. "We agree."

I wasn't so sure.

We continued our discussion at my apartment, and I got no sketching done. "Is there a chance that we're arguing and playing games with semantics because we're both scared to death?" I asked.

"I'm sure that's true," Margo said. "I'm sorry." She sounded beat.

"You're tired," I said.

"Yes, I sure am," she said, staring out the window and talking in a monotone. "Can we go for a ride?"

I said I guessed it would be considered routine for us to take a Sunday afternoon drive. I assumed she wanted to nap, but not in my apartment — and certainly not in hers. Barnes and Warren were waiting there for Salerno to leave her building just for a few minutes, for a paper or something, anything, so they could get in and plant a dummy. We were to stay away.

Margo leaned her head against the car door window and was asleep before we'd gone a mile. She felt secure with me, in a car, and moving. I didn't, I felt followed — and I was.

At first I thought I was being overly sensitive. Sure, the same gray sedan had been behind me for a long time, but that could be coincidence. The guy was probably just going my way. After about ten miles on the freeway, I decided to take a familiar exit so I could determine for sure that it was only my imagination. I didn't want to get into a section of town that would pen me in if I did need to keep some distance between me and whoever was tailing me.

I exited about one hundred yards ahead of the gray car and waited at a light to turn right. Just as the light changed I caught a glimpse of him in my rearview mirror. It was a Plymouth, and he was exiting too. I turned right and kept my eye on the mirror to see if he'd follow. I let my breath out slowly when he went straight through the intersection. My heart pounded. False alarm.

I took another right to head back to the freeway. He had taken two quick rights and was behind me again, closer now. His sun visor was down so I couldn't see him very well. He was a block behind and maintained the distance as we both turned right again onto the freeway.

I accelerated but he matched my speed. Margo stirred. "Where are we?" she asked.

"Nowhere special," I said, shakily. "Just driving." She looked at me hard and long. I tried to smile and determined not to look in the rearview mirror while she was watching me. She put her head back down and closed her eyes. I shot a glance at the mirror. The gray car was almost in my blind spot to my left rear. What would he do on a busy expressway? I alternated between the two middle lanes every half mile or so, pretending not to see him. I didn't want to give him the chance of running me off the road. There was no way he'd dare try taking a shot while driving. Besides endangering himself, he'd have bad odds of a direct hit.

I signaled and moved into the left center lane. For the first time he moved behind me and up on the right. Margo's side of the car. I couldn't let him get even with her. I shot into his lane, sending him into a long screeching slide and rolling Margo nearly into my lap.

"What's happening?" she screamed.

"Stay down! I think it's Salerno!" I put the pedal to the floor and moved into the far right lane ahead of a semi, whose driver blasted me with his air horn. An exit appeared on my right and I began a long swerve to make it while riding the brakes to pull back from about eighty miles an hour. The mirror showed the gray Plymouth passing the semi on the shoulder and exiting a couple of hundred feet behind me.

I hit the accelerator again, only to jump on the brakes, and skid up to the pump at a gas station. "Stay down!" I told Margo as curious heads turned from inside and outside the station. The Plymouth went past the station and came in from a far entrance, pulling up on the other side of the same pump from the opposite direction. The door of the Plymouth flew open and the driver lunged out. I slammed my car in drive and was about to speed off when I saw his face.

It was Haymeyer, and he was furious.

"Follow me back to my hotel!" he said, teeth clenched. He drove away in the Plymouth as I sat with my arms at my sides, forehead resting on the steering wheel, and Margo staring at me, saying nothing.

"Fill'er up, sir?" a young boy said, knocking on my window.

I shook my head slowly and drove out of the station. Just as I pulled onto the street the car coughed and died. I was out of gas.

"Rub it in," I told Margo on the way to Haymeyer's. "Enjoy yourself. Tell me how stupid it was to assume it was Salerno."

"I thought it was him, too," she said. "And I don't get any enjoyment from your stupidity — I didn't mean that. I mean, I don't think you're stupid. I think you're wonderful."

"You're tired," I said.

"Yes, but I won't apologize for saying that. You are wonderful."

"You're humoring me. Don't."

"I give up."

"Don't do that either."

"Well, Philip, it's just that you can dish it out but you can't take it. You tell me for weeks that I'm somebody, that I'm worth caring about. God uses you to teach me that, I tell you that you almost got in the way of His message, and you figure I don't appreciate you. You're wrong. I appreciate you. I treasure you. Can't you just let me tell you that without saying I'm patronizing you?"

"OK," I said. "I'm wonderful." We laughed.

"I'm scared," Margo said.

"So am I."

"What took you so long?" Haymeyer asked as he opened his motel room door.

"I figured I'd get gas as long as I was there," I said. Margo stifled a giggle.

"Why were you following us?"

"Didn't you realize we were keeping you under constant watch?" Haymeyer said. "Honestly, Philip, sometimes I think you know what's going on and that you might even be an asset, and then you pull something like this. Had I wanted to follow you without your knowing it, I would have. I stayed in plain sight so you'd know. Didn't you recognize the car? You rode in it the first day I was here."

"That was at night," I said.

Haymeyer shook his head. "Is there somewhere you can go until this thing is over?" he asked.

I shook my head. "Not unless you want me to go to Dayton."

"Maybe we should all go back to Chicago to try to track down Olga, and we could leave Salerno down here alone. You'd like that, wouldn't you?"

Haymeyer was still furious, and I didn't know whether to take him seriously or not. "I'd like what — going to Chicago or leaving Salerno alone?"

Haymeyer turned his palms up and rolled his eyes toward heaven. "What did I do to deserve this?"

Margo was smiling.

"Margo would like to see Salerno left alone," I said. She fired a double take at me.

Her smile was gone. "If you think *that,* you missed my whole point," she said.

"All right, all right," Haymeyer said. "Let's stay cool. Margo's going through a normal reaction of concern for her stalker. You're both jumpy. Philip, I was kidding about your leaving town, especially to go to Chicago. Salerno would be onto us for sure.

"Right now he's holed up in his apartment at Margo's building. He did go out early this afternoon for about a half hour, and the dummy has been planted.

"Now both of you listen very carefully. After church tonight, Philip, take Margo home as usual. Walk her to her door. See her inside and then leave. Do not linger or look back. Go to your car and head straight for my motel. Ask the desk clerk for a message, and a key will be in the envelope I have left for you there. Go to my room and wait. Keep the door locked, but be ready to open it immediately should you hear Barnes's voice.

"Margo, when you get inside your apartment, don't be startled by the dummy in your chair. Turn on a few lights and the TV and leave immediately. Take the east stairs down four floors and go down the hall to the west stairs, which will take you down three more flights to the basement garage. When you get to the garage, Barnes will pull up in a dark green Ford four-door. When you're sure it's him, get in the back door and lie down on the seat until he tells you to sit up. He'll take you to my motel room and will stay there with you and Philip."

Haymeyer repeated the instructions word for word, then added: "Maybe you two can teach Barnes how to pray and the three of you can pray for Warren and me. We want to catch Salerno *in* the apartment. If it works any other way, we won't have him on anything serious enough to make him talk."

We didn't hear much of the sermon that night. We had our own concerns in mind during the prayer, too.

"How are they going to be sure Salerno doesn't see me leave?" Margo asked as we drove to her place.

"Haymeyer figures Salerno will watch us come in from somewhere in the lobby downstairs. He'll sit tight there until he sees me leave. Then he'll head for your apartment. Since you're leaving right after I do, you'll be gone by the time he gets there."

"How do they know he won't take the stairs?"

"They're hoping he'll think it would look too suspicious."

"I don't know what I think about all this figuring and hoping," Margo said.

"They're not amateurs, Margo," I said.

As we walked through the lobby of her building to the elevators, I saw Salerno. He wore a brown denim sportsuit and low-cut boots. His hair was combed straight back and was darker than his blond mustache. He wore tinted eyeglasses and held an unlit cigarette. We walked within six feet of him. He was slouched in an overstuffed chair and never moved or even looked at us, at least until we had our backs to him.

"That was him," I said on the elevator.

"Who?"

"The guy slouched in the chair. That was Salerno."

"I didn't even see him."

"You're kidding."

Margo didn't answer. I wished I hadn't said anything. Maybe she had held out a hope that he wouldn't show tonight. At least this way she knew he was in the lobby and not lurking down the hall.

I squeezed Margo's hand and whispered that I would be praying for her. "You know what to do, right?" I asked.

She nodded and unlocked her door. I turned and headed toward the elevator. When I got on, Bob Warren got off, nodded to me ever so slightly, and walked down the hall the opposite way from Margo's apartment. I felt better — until I got to the lobby. Salerno was gone. I hoped he had taken another elevator and not the stairs.

I waited at Haymeyer's hotel room for exactly six minutes before I heard Barnes's voice outside the door. "Philip, open up," he said loudly. Once inside, Margo sat on the bed, her face in her hands. Barnes bolted the door.

"Now what?" I said, relieved to see Margo.

"We wait," Barnes said. "And I'm as anxious as you are. We weren't followed. I'm tempted to go back and help, but it'd be over by the time I got there."

"You think so?" I asked.

"Sure. We had Salerno spotted in the lobby when you two walked in. By the time I picked up Margo and drove outside the garage, he was gone."

"I noticed that too," I said.

Barnes nodded. "It won't be long," he said. "Salerno won't spend much time in the apartment." He flipped on the television. "As soon as he fires two shots, he's out of ammunition. All Bob and Earl have to do is wait until he 'murders' the dummy, then they move in and take him."

"You don't think he smelled the stakeout and took off?"

"Nope. Somehow, I don't think he knows we're around."

"Will all those other charges he's been tried for help convict him?"

"No," Barnes said. "He was acquitted. That means, believe it or not, that Antonio Salerno has a record as clean as yours or mine. Wanmacher thought he had Salerno cold at least a half dozen times but never saw a judge put him away. In fact, Wanmacher had Salerno in court so often, Jim Hanlon figures Tony had a motive to kill him."

"That's how Salerno got involved in the Wanmacher case?"

"Yeah, but I think Hanlon knew he didn't do it and just charged him to irritate him and Wahl. Don't tell Earl I said that, even though I think he agrees."

"Hanlon never thought Salerno killed Wanmacher?"

"I don't think so. Sure, Salerno had threatened Wanmacher, and he had a motive of sorts. But a twenty-two between the eyes is not Salerno's style."

From the ten o'clock news on television we heard, "Shots have been fired at the Kenilworth Arms apartment building on Atlanta's south side. More details as they become available." Margo lay on the bed, staring at the wall.

Barnes stood quickly and began pacing. "They said shots, plural. If it was only two, they probably got him. If it was more, they may have killed him. We don't want that."

"Could Salerno have shot Earl or Bob?" I asked.

"I doubt it," Barnes said. "They're not amateurs."

"Neither is Salerno," I said.

Barnes pursed his lips and shook his head.

"Does Salerno always empty both barrels?" I asked.

"Always. The first one does the job. The second is his trademark. It's his way of saying, 'I don't shoot and run. I linger and make sure.' "

I glanced at Margo. She appeared catatonic.

Barnes switched channels with every commercial for the next twenty-five minutes, hoping for more news about the shoot-out. Nothing. It was another hour before Haymeyer and Warren returned. Margo was still, I was watching television, and Barnes was reading. We all stood when we heard the key in the door.

"We had Salerno underrated," Warren grumbled as he sat on the floor.

"You mean *I* had him underrated," Haymeyer said. "I never should have expected him to fall for a dummy."

"Start from the beginning," I said. "Did you get him? I want to hear it all."

Warren answered, "Yes, we got him, thanks to Earl. It was close."

"I *had* to salvage it after I realized he was on to the decoy," Haymeyer said.

"C'mon," Barnes said, impatient. "Let's hear it from the top."

"OK," Earl said. "We had men from the Atlanta Bureau stationed on each floor and in the lobby for backup. Another waited just outside the stairwell door near Margo's apartment. Warren was at the other end of the hall, just around the corner. I used the same elevator to the seventh floor that Salerno had used. I was behind him by about a minute and a half.

"When the elevator opened I could see from there that Salerno was in Margo's place and had left the door open about two inches. I expected him to shoot immediately, but after several seconds I turned off the elevator to keep the door open, kicked off my shoes, and tiptoed down the hall. Through the door I saw Salerno sneak up behind the dummy. The TV was loud, and he probably figured Margo hadn't heard him come in. He waited just behind the dummy, and I think it was then that he realized 'Margo' hadn't moved all the time he was in there.

"As he shook the dummy I realized how foolish I had been to try to catch a pro with an old trick, and I knew if he didn't fire, we'd have nothing solid enough on him to make him talk in exchange for a lighter sentence."

"This is where it gets good," Warren said, eyes gleaming.

"Well, we were lucky it worked," Earl said. "I knelt and pulled Margo's door shut, hoping to spook him — "

"And it worked," Warren said, clapping.

Haymeyer continued, "Salerno whirled and fired, blowing the door knob over my head. I dashed for the elevator and dove in just as Salerno burst through Margo's door and sprayed his second shot down the hall."

"Who shot Salerno?" I asked.

"No one," they said, almost in unison. "When Salerno fired his second shot, he was out of ammunition."

I turned to Haymeyer. "Did he try to run?"

"No way," Earl said. "When we heard that second shot, we all converged on him. He was through. He just dropped his weapon.

"Philip, remember our three objectives?"

"Yeah."

"I think two have been accomplished. We kept you and Margo safe, and we've got something good on Salerno. Now we have to hope he'll sing for his supper."

"Exactly what have you got on Salerno?" I asked. "Since he didn't shoot the dummy, I mean."

"First, we've got him on breaking and entering," Warren said. "You should have seen him. I swear he got in that room quicker and more smoothly than if he'd had a key."

"That's a felony," Earl said. "And possession of a sawed-off shotgun is illegal in any state."

"But the biggie," Warren said, "was when he fired at Earl. The first time he was just shooting through the door, and it might have been hard to prove that he intended anyone bodily harm."

"But when he fired again as I dove into the elevator," Haymeyer chimed in, "that was attempted murder. We'll let him think about that one for awhile. Then we'll see if he'd like to talk about one Virginia Franklin."

With that, Margo broke down. Haymeyer put his arm around her. "You've been tight for a few days, girl. Let it out."

"You don't understand," Margo managed. "None of you do. Don't you see? My mother tried to have me killed. I didn't really believe it until you described him stalking my dummy. He was going to kill me on orders from my own mother!"

EIGHT

When Margo calmed down, Haymeyer arranged for a room for her at the motel. She went to bed and the rest of us went out for a midnight steak. "This was going to be a celebration," Haymeyer said, "but I can sure see Margo's point. What a bummer. Her own mother. Have you met her, Philip?"

"No. I just met Margo a few weeks ago."

"You want to go to Chicago with us? Margo will have to come anyway."

"She won't go without me," I said.

"We're hoping we can talk Atlanta into delaying arraignment on Salerno until after he can be extradited to Chicago to face charges of conspiracy to commit murder. It might be difficult because attempted murder is really the more serious offense. If we can implicate a judge, we've got two people involved in a very serious crime, though, and the conspiracy happened before the attempted murder."

"What happens in Chicago?"

"Well, we're going to make things very uncomfortable for Mrs. Franklin."

"How?"

"Hanlon hasn't decided yet. If Salerno talks, it will be easy. If he doesn't, Jim may try to get Mrs. Franklin to think Salerno's talked anyway. She's pretty cool though, and she knows the law. She was a great lawyer and judge in her prime."

"Really?"

"Absolutely. She was for sure the most respected woman trial judge in Illinois."

"Was?"

"Until her marriage went on the rocks and she started bad-mouthing her own daughter in public."

"You're kidding. I don't think Margo is even aware of that!"

"Oh, it was sickening. I guess she was ashamed of her because of her weight. You can't tell it now, Philip, but Margo was somewhat overweight when she was younger. Hanlon used to grouse about it after a social function. He'd come back to the office complaining that Mrs. Franklin was poking fun at her own daughter again."

"What would she say about her?"

"Oh, I don't know. I guess she said she would have brought her daughter to the function if she could find a tent to fit her — stuff like that."

"That's disgusting."

"Yeah, and Philip, being overweight or an embarrassment to a mother is hardly grounds for murder. I believe every word Margo says. The old lady is as guilty as she can be, and I want to help the boss prove it."

"So do I."

"You might be able to help," Haymeyer said. "I never told you what my phone call from Chicago was about the other night, did I?"

"No, but I figured it must have been important, since you didn't want to return it from your room."

"It was about Olga. The Chicago boys traced her through IRS to her son at Northwestern University in Evanston. According to him she's financing his education with money she won from the Illinois State Lottery and is living on Lake Shore Drive under a phony name so her friends won't come asking for money. You don't know Chicago, but Lake Shore Drive is ultra."

"Boy, that was some piece of luck for Olga."

"Yeah, too much luck. She never reported any winnings on her subsequent income tax returns, and according to state records she never won a dime from the lottery."

"Then where's she getting the money to live on Lake Shore and put a son through college?"

"You tell me."

Barnes and Warren left for Chicago the next day. Haymeyer stayed with Margo and took several written depositions, "just so we'll have everything straight when we get to Chicago and have to go through all this again."

Haymeyer told me he was sure Margo was out of danger but advised me to keep her at the motel until I could drive her to Chicago. He left on Tuesday with instructions that we should be in Chicago within a week. "Better have her quit her job and get out of her lease," he advised. "I doubt she'll be back here for a long time."

The day Haymeyer left I got a check for $4,000 for my textbook sketches. It was the most money I had ever received at one shot, but I could hardly get excited.

Margo spent most of her time at the motel unless she was out eating with me or watching me sketch. She wanted to rest before making the trip, and that was fine with me. What wasn't fine was her insistence on visiting Tony Salerno at the county jail. I refused to even hear of it. I was to know where she was every second, but on Friday, when I couldn't find her at the motel or the restaurant or anywhere, I felt down deep that she had gone to see Salerno.

When I got to the House of Corrections I toured the parking lot for about twenty minutes before spotting her car. I raced inside and asked if Margo Franklin had been admitted to visit a prisoner.

"Yes, sir, about a half hour ago. She's still there."

"I want to see the same man," I said. "I'm a friend of Margo's." I was searched, authorized, stamped, badged, and read a list of regulations. Four heavy doors later I saw Margo, sitting, waiting.

"I'm sorry, Philip, I had to come."

"Have you seen him yet?"

"No, he's talking with his lawyer."

"Wahl is here, huh? I'll bet they're trying to get him out on bond, or at least push for his extradition to Chicago. That's home to these guys, and I'll bet they think they've got a better chance beating the conspiracy charge. There's no way they'll beat the attempted murder charge here. The longer they can put that off, the better they'll like it."

Margo seemed relieved that I was off the subject of her being at the jail, but I came back to it. "What do you think you're going to accomplish?" I asked.

"I've told you before. I feel for Salerno. I want to tell him that he is loved, even that I love him."

"Good grief, Margo, this isn't a game. All he has to do is tell Wahl that you visited, and your mother will be the next to know. Haymeyer doesn't want your mother to know that you were involved in helping nail Salerno."

"You don't think she knows already?"

"I would have thought so, but Haymeyer thinks she'll assume that he trailed Salerno here at Hanlon's request and that Salerno was careless."

"Oh, Philip, if she's following developments at all she knows my apartment got shot up. How could I have not known what was going on?"

"She still won't know that you know she's involved."

"How will my visiting Salerno prove that I know she's involved?"

"I don't know," I admitted. "OK, I still think it's a bad idea for you to talk to Salerno, but if you're determined to go through with it, at least keep quiet about your mother."

Margo seemed to relax, realizing that I was not going to try to keep her from seeing Salerno. It would have done no good. She had a mind of her own and knew what she wanted. Who was I to tell her what to do? "At least let me be with you when you talk to him," I said.

We saw Salerno through safety glass and talked to him through telephones. Wahl was with him, a bit too pleased to see us. He talked first. "I suppose you're wondering about what happened in your apartment the other night, young lady." Margo stared at him. "Simply a case of mistaken identity. Had nothing to do with you. My client doesn't even know you. You don't know him, do you?"

Margo and I looked at each other. Wahl beamed. Salerno never took his eyes from Margo's. How could Wahl expect us to be so naive? How did he think a dummy had been planted without Margo having known she was being stalked?

"Hope that clears it up for you kids," Wahl concluded. It was ludicrous.

"I want to talk to him," Margo said, pointing at Salerno. Wahl handed him the phone. "I want you to know that God loves you and that I love you, Mr. Salerno. No matter what you go through during the next several weeks, I want you to always know that someone loves you." Salerno never moved. He just stared. He said nothing. The scene reminded me of when I had first met Margo. For some reason I had loved the unlovable. Now she was doing the same, only to an infinitely greater degree.

Wahl was still smiling and Salerno staring as we left. Margo was boiling. "I wanted so badly to demand to know if my mother had told him to do it," she said, her eyes afire. "And that Wahl! There's one I haven't been given any love for yet. Pray for me."

"Pray for *me*," I said. "I still haven't seen anything in Salerno but a creep."

When we got back to my apartment I called Haymeyer in Chicago. "You shouldn't have let that happen," he said when I told him of our visit to Salerno. "I was counting on you. Can you get Margo to Chicago, or should I send someone for her?" He was being sarcastic, and it smarted.

"We're leaving tomorrow," I said.

"You can bet old lady Franklin knows all about your visit already. No doubt Wahl keeps in close contact."

Haymeyer told us to come directly to United States Attorney Hanlon's office when we arrived in Chicago. "If for some crazy reason Wahl and Mrs. Franklin think Margo really isn't aware of the plot, let's keep them thinking it. We'll have Margo keep a low profile here for a while."

Margo and I took turns driving my car and got to Chicago late Saturday night. "It sounds crazy," she said sleepily, "but I have this desire to see Mother, being so close and all."

"You mean you really would like to confront her?"

"No, just see her. I remember her as she was, not as she is. I don't know the woman she has become. Even during my teen years when I felt rejected by her, there was a lot of Mommy left in her, in spite of herself. After Richard was murdered, she became an animal, never the same. I can't dwell on it, Philip. I may never be able to. To think that she would have me killed! Do you realize that it was only the chance timing of our letter to Hanlon that saved my life?"

"I guess you're right," I said.

"That was God, Philip."

"Right again."

It was nearly midnight, and we were tired, but Margo insisted on showing me a reminder of her childhood. We drove north on Lake Shore Drive toward Evanston.

"So this is where Olga lives, huh?" I said. "In one of these big, dark buildings. I hope she's enjoying it. They don't look like they're worth that much money."

"It's not the building or the furnishings," Margo said. "It's the location. Lake Shore Drive is the place to be if you want to flaunt it."

Farther north, Evanston was beautiful. "It always is at night," Margo said. There was a quaintness about it, street lights on ancient poles, eight-bedroom mansions guarding acre lots.

"This looks more like the place to flaunt it," I said. Margo didn't respond.

A few miles north Lake Shore Drive became Sheridan Road. It was darker and more winding. "It's just around the next curve," she said.

"What is?" I said, just as it broke into view. The Baha'i temple gleamed majestically against the blackness of the night sky. It was like a three-dimensional picture card I'd looked at through a special lens box as a child — literally breathtaking.

"What faith is it, Margo?"

"I never checked into it much," she said. "It was just here. It was God to me. People came to look, and I guess they even held church services, but I never went. It was so beautiful that I was afraid of it. I guess it was like the Wizard of Oz to Dorothy. So powerful, so awesome that it was frightening. I longed to know the God of this place, but I resented the fear it instilled in me when I walked around it at night.

"When no one else was near, it seemed as if I were being watched as I walked. Can we walk?"

"It's late, Margo. Are you sure you want to?"

She was sure. I parked and we walked around the temple. It was after one o'clock in the morning, but we were not alone. There were a few couples and a family or two, just walking, looking. No one spoke. It was eerie. I felt for Margo and her childhood fears. Nothing made the temple look real. Not from any angle. It could have vanished with my next blink. But it didn't. It loomed bright and yet shadowy, its dome lighting the sky, its pillars posing questions for young debutantes who gazed at it while walking alone at night. Their families were worshipers of things, goods, money, prestige, power, position. The young girls knew already that those were symbols of the shallowness of life.

If there was something in the temple, they wanted it. If there was nothing, they would resign themselves to the battle for position and forget their childish wonderment at the glistening monolith.

"How does it look in the daytime?" I asked.

"Like it's waiting for the night."

Margo drove on the way back to Chicago. She took a left off the main drag. "Where you headed?"

"Home," she said.

"Margo."

Don't worry, Philip. I just want to see the place, and I want you to see it. It's only a few blocks from here." She took me through a heavily wooded area and into a section where the huge homes weren't so far apart. "That's it, there, through the trees."

"Wow. Your mother still lives there alone?"

"Yeah, isn't that weird? I imagine she entertains, and no doubt she has live-in help. But otherwise, she's alone."

"How many bedrooms?"

"Just seven."

"*Just* seven? Margo, that's the Winnetka in you. There's a light on."

"Yes, in my old bedroom!"

"Who would be in there at this time of night?"

"Who else?" Margo said. "Is it too much to hope that Mother is sitting on my bed, crying over how near she came to having me killed and thankful now that Salerno failed?"

It was too much to ask, and I barely heard her last few words as she swallowed her sobs. I was tired; we both were. She pulled off the road and fell into my arms. We held each other and cried for several minutes. I felt so sorry for her that I would have given anything for it all to have been a nightmare. "We've got to get going, Margo."

I got out and went around to the driver's side while Margo slid over. Elbows on knees, she held her face in her hands and cried softly all the way back to Chicago. I rented us each a room at a downtown Holiday Inn and handed over her key without a word.

"How's she holding up?" Haymeyer asked in the morning after pulling me aside at the United States attorney's office.

"I'm not sure," I said. "She took me to Winnetka last night, and it was hard on her."

"She didn't want to drop in on the old lady, did she?"

"No, but we went by there well after midnight and a light was on in Margo's old room."

"Wow."

Haymeyer introduced us to James A. Hanlon, the United States attorney for Northern Illinois, and it took me a while to get used to his plush office. He was a stocky six-footer with a reputation for incorruptibility.

"Earl has told me a lot about you, Philip Spence," Hanlon said, carefully enunciating both names. "You can't do anything officially, of course, but the rest of this investigation will be quite tame compared to the Atlanta activity. I see no reason why you can't tag along, *if you agree to be under the supervision and direction of this office whenever you are with one of my agents.*" He had a way of talking in italics.

"I understand," I said, tingling. "Fine." I could hardly wait to get started. "Where will Margo be during the investigation?"

"Sometimes with you, sometimes not," Hanlon said. "Your rooms at the Inn are fine with us. Just stay accessible. She is technically in our custody, and this case could go to court anytime."

"Have charges been filed?"

"No, we're waiting until we've got it all but locked up."

"What will that take?"

"Something good from Salerno, or from this Yakovich woman, or from the judge herself."

"Which looks most promising?"

"None. Salerno and his lawyer are claiming he was pulling a petty theft — with a sawed-off yet — and was unaware of any connection between the occupant of the apartment and the judge who had recently thrown his case out of court. The judge has not been contacted by this office, though I imagine she's expecting us. She doesn't know Margo's in town, though, and we want to keep it that way."

"And Olga?"

"She would be our best chance because she's not a professional from either side of the law, but we still haven't found her. Her son might be the key. He's sworn to secrecy about her address, and you know, I think he believes her story about the lottery. If we surprise him by telling him what's at stake, he may just be shocked into putting us onto his mother."

"It might scare him into tipping her off, though," I said.

"It'll depend on how we do it, Philip. You wanna go along?"

"Sure."

Jon Yakovich was earnest, a bit irritated, and very concerned. "I already told my story," he objected.

"I know," said Haymeyer, "but I was out of town and didn't get to hear it. Hit us with it again."

Jon said his mother had won money in the state lottery and was financing his education with it, saving some, and living in anonymity on Lake Shore Drive with the rest.

"Can't you tell us where, Jon? There are thousands of people on the Drive. We'll go door to door if we have to, but it could take months."

"Why should I? She wants to remain hidden. If her friends find out where she is, they'll beg for money. The worst part is, she'd probably give it to them. She's a generous person."

"Then why doesn't she let them know?"

"I don't know. It surprises me, too," Jon said. "She once said that if she ever came into a lot of money, she'd give most of it away. Maybe she's changed her mind because she feels she needs it. Once she told me she felt she deserved it after all she'd been through. Coming from the old country; Dad dying twenty years ago."

"Could there be another reason she doesn't want her friends to know, Jon?"

"What are you suggesting?"

"That she didn't get the money from the lottery, and that if her friends found out about it, they might also find out where she got it."

"What are you saying?"

"I'm saying that most people who win the lottery are happy to share the news, and that a person like your mother would be happy to even share some of her winnings."

"Maybe that's true, but what does it prove? Where else could she have gotten the money?"

"Didn't she work for rich people on the north shore?"

"Yes, but she hated them. She always resented their money and how little it seemed to mean to them. They wouldn't have given her anything. When she first got a job up there in Winnetka she thought it would be the chance of a lifetime. But they were so tight they paid her less than people in Chicago. Can you imagine?"

"Did that upset her?"

"Yes, it did. She was extremely angry in her own way. She brooded."

"Would it have made her mad enough to steal some money?"

Jon stared at Haymeyer. "No," he said finally.

"You say that with conviction."

"Well, I know because she used to look for money. She hoped they'd leave cash around that she could lift unnoticed."

"Then she wouldn't be above taking money?"

"No, so what? She had a hard life. She always wanted me to have an education. Her daughters both died at birth. She is a tired, bitter, hard-working old woman. The lottery was a gift from God."

"Oh, come on, Jon. You don't believe she won the lottery, do you?"

"Why don't I?"

"Did you ever know her to buy a lottery ticket?"

Jon didn't answer. "What do you want her for?" he asked. "Stealing lottery tickets?"

"It's not funny, Jon. Your mother could be in very big trouble."

"What kind of trouble?"

"Big and serious. If she is involved in something bad, we have reason to believe she could help us and do herself some good."

"Tell me what it is and I'll tell you where to find her."

"Let's do it the other way around, Jon. You tell us where, and we'll tell you what."

"No deal."

"It's up to you. We'll find her on our own, but the longer we wait, the harder it will be for her to get a break."

"At least she'll know I didn't send you to her."

"And we'll tell her you could have made things a lot easier for her."

"She'll understand," Jon said.

"She'll have a long time to think about it," Haymeyer said. He left his business card.

"We'll have a message from Jon waiting for us when we get back to the office," Haymeyer predicted in the car. He was right.

"You make sure Mother knows why I sent you to her, for her own good, but don't tell me what it's about. She wouldn't want me to know. If she wants to tell me, she can." He gave us an address.

No one answered our knock. We waited at the end of the hall for six hours before a short woman with black-dyed hair and a plain beige coat trudged from the elevator to her apartment door carrying a twine-handled shopping bag in each hand. She set them down to fish for her keys, and Haymeyer moved in.

He flashed his badge and identified himself as a special agent for the United States attorney's office. "Olga Yakovich?"

"No," she said huskily. "Don't know no Yakovich."

"Do you know Jon Yakovich?" Haymeyer needled.

"What's the matter with my Jon?" she demanded. "Come in. Talk to me. What is problem with Jon?"

"No problem, Olga," Haymeyer said. "We just wanted to be sure it was you."

Olga put her groceries away, looking totally out of place in the beautifully furnished apartment. Her clothes were plain and off the rack. She wore no jewelry. She sat heavily on the sofa.

"Jon send you to me?" she asked with a whine.

"For your own good, Mrs. Yakovich. He didn't want you in trouble. He doesn't know why we want to see you."

"Olga don't know either," she said, glaring.

"Yes, you do."

"No."

"We want to know where a housekeeper gets the money to live here and send her son to Northwestern University."

"Lottery. I win three-hundred thousand dollars. Get some every month. You check bank account."

"We have, Olga. We have also checked your income tax reports. You haven't paid taxes on your winnings."

"I am ignorant old woman. I know nothing of taxes."

"You are not ignorant, but letting your income show in your bank account without paying income tax was stupid."

"So what's wrong?"

"You didn't win the lottery, and stop insisting you did. We have access to those records."

"I didn't have name listed because I wanted friends not to know."

"Get off the case, Olga. We have access to the actual records. You did not win, and no money has come to you from the state of Illinois. Where are you getting your money?"

"Why should I tell you?"

"If you tell us and help us get who we're really after, we might be able to help you get a better deal from the law."

"And if I don't tell you?"

"We'll find out soon enough, and there will be no mercy for you."

"I think about it."

"Don't think too long, Olga. We're working on this around the clock. You help us, and we'll help you."

"Why didn't Judge Franklin send Salerno after Olga?" I asked Haymeyer on the way back to the office.

"She's probably got a system that would bring information to light if she is harmed.

It's not hard to do. It could be through her bank, a lawyer, or even her son. If she is killed a document is publicized, probably implicating Mrs. Franklin."

"How much is she hitting Mrs. Franklin for?"

"About three thousand a month."

I whistled through my teeth. "What's next?"

"We'll have to put a little pressure on Olga, I think," Haymeyer said. "She's tough and smarter than she appears. She knows we have little without her, and she's not likely to come to us. We're going to have to scare her, trick her, or convince her."

"I like option number three."

"That's the idealist in you, Philip. This is where our job gets tedious, but there are no shortcuts. The tough ones never get handed to us on a platter. We've got to go after them."

"I think I'll stick to art."

Hanlon wanted to know how Haymeyer planned to pressure Olga.

"What do you suggest?" Haymeyer replied.

"It sounds to me like Jon could help, if he knew the whole story, straight, with no games, no guessing. You come right out and tell him, blow his mind. Let him see it right there on the table so he doesn't have to guess at the consequences."

Haymeyer studied his boss. I nodded and Hanlon caught it from the corner of his eye. "You agree, Philip?"

"I'm closer to his age," I said. "I think I'd buckle and help put pressure on my mother in the same situation."

"Why don't you talk to Jon alone, Philip?" Hanlon asked.

Haymeyer straightened up. I looked at him, eyebrows raised. "I'm not against it," Earl said. "It just took me by surprise."

Hanlon smiled. "It's up to you, Earl, of course. This is your investigation."

"You're the boss, Jim," Haymeyer said. "If you think this will work, I'm for it."

"The important thing is whether you think it will work," Hanlon said.

"I'm just wishing I'd thought of it, that's all," Haymeyer said.

We all laughed.

That night I took Margo out for dinner and told her all about my day. "It was really exciting. I felt like a detective."

"Did you ask Olga any questions?"

"Not one. They didn't let me get involved at all. But tomorrow I have an appointment with Jon Yakovich again. It should be interesting. I'll keep you posted."

"Could I go too?"

"Hm. I doubt it. I'll check with Haymeyer. What would be the advantage? Did you know Jon?"

"No," Margo said.

"What would you think about dropping in on Olga eventually?"

"I'd have to think about that one. It would sure have impact, wouldn't it?"

"The only problem is that at this point, Olga thinks Haymeyer is fishing. She doesn't realize that he already knows the answers and is simply looking for her to confirm them. She thinks he is simply aware that she is getting her money from somewhere other than the lottery. Your showing up would tell her immediately that she has been found out."

"But without actually saying so to her, Philip. It might be a great move. I think I could do it."

"I'll talk to Haymeyer and Hanlon."

"Well, what do *you* think?"

"I think it might be valuable if it becomes necessary, Margo."

"What is the alternative?"

"Just my seeing Jon for now."

"I'd like to be involved," Margo said.

"Why?"

"Not for revenge, if that's what you think. I just want this mess over with."

"I believe *that*. How are you doing?"

Margo shifted in her chair. "I'm OK, I guess. I'm praying a lot. Reading my Bible. Losing weight."

"I noticed."

"You did not."

"No, really, I did."

"You didn't say anything."

"We had too much else to talk about."

"I need to hear it."

"OK, you look like you've lost weight."

Margo laughed. "I think about you all day," she said.

"That's the kind of stuff *I* need to hear."

"I pray for you, too. Are you praying for me?"

"Yes, I think of you often and pray that God will comfort you and give you something out of this. I don't see what good can come of it, but I am willing to trust Him for it."

"Maybe He'll give me you out of this," she said carefully.

"That was rather bold."

"Do I care?"

"Obviously not. But you've already got me, Margo, and you know it."

NINE

"Do not, I repeat, do *not* tell Margo where Olga lives," United States Attorney Hanlon said the next morning.

"I didn't," I said.

"See that you don't," Haymeyer horned in.

"I said I won't already!" I said, rolling my eyes.

"Good grief, Earl, is this kid gonna screw us up on this?" Hanlon said, "Because if he is, maybe we'd be better off — "

"He won't, Jim. He didn't really tell her anything important." Haymeyer turned to me. "But don't tell her much of anything from here on out, OK?"

I nodded.

"If she goes to see Olga, it could cost us the whole case. Can you see Jon Yakovich without telling Margo about it?"

"Sure. I already told her I was going to see him, but I won't — " Hanlon and Haymeyer swore in unison.

"He's not catching on, Earl," Hanlon said. "Tell him he simply can't say anything to anyone. This is a highly confidential federal investigation of very serious charges."

Hanlon was telling Haymeyer what to tell me as if he didn't want anything to do with me.

"Do we have to tell you every little tidbit that's confidential, Philip?" Haymeyer asked.

"No."

"I'd be glad to, but I thought you'd know."

"Well, Earl, you told Margo lots of stuff in Atlanta. I figured it was OK to tell her because she's involved."

"You have no idea how much I didn't tell her. Or you either, for that matter."

"Me? What don't I know about this?"

Hanlon and Haymeyer glanced at each other. Haymeyer raised his eyebrows. Hanlon nodded. "This is confidential now," Haymeyer said, as if I didn't know. "It seems that Wahl and Salerno are pushing for extradition to Chicago."

"That's not really a surprise, is it?" I asked. "I mean they've got a better chance up here than down there, don't they?"

"Yes, but that's not the reason they want to come here. They know they'll be coming here anyway. The key is, they want to come immediately."

"So?"

"So, why would they want to come immediately? It seems they'd want to stretch this thing out as long as possible, right?"

"I guess," I said.

"The problem," Haymeyer explained, "is that Salerno's life was threatened last night."

"In the Atlanta jail?"

"Yup. There's no faster grapevine than behind bars. Someone found out why he was there and threatened to do him in tonight after dark."

"For shooting at a cop?" I asked. "Wouldn't they be proud of him?"

"Not for that," Haymeyer said patiently. "For attempting to kill a woman."

"You mean there's some sort of code?"

"Absolutely. No women or children."

Hanlon tipped his chair back. "We can't have him moved up here in one day, but we can't risk someone nailing him. either. We're asking Atlanta to put him in solitary confinement until the day after tomorrow. By the time he gets here, he'll already have a roommate."

"A roommate?"

"A cellmate. One of our guys. Larry Shipman is a sort of free-lance police reporter for a couple of the papers and radio stations here, and he does some undercover work for us now and then, too. Very little of what he gets for us can be used in court, because he gets it any way he can, but it sure helps us know where we stand."

"I don't follow."

"For instance," Haymeyer said, "He might just come right out and ask Salerno for a lot of information. Even if he got it on tape, Salerno could say he had just been bragging. We'll send Shipman in anyway and see if he can get anything out of Salerno."

Hanlon and Haymeyer had agreed that I should visit Jon Yakovich alone. I found him in his room on the third floor of the dorm and asked if he wanted to take a walk with me. "Not if you're going to tell me about Mama," he said.

"I just want to ask you some questions."

"We can do that here."

I said OK, but before I could sit, he grabbed his jacket and I followed him out. We walked diagonally across the campus. It was dark, yet majestic, and clouds were moving quickly overhead.

"Storm's coming," Jon said finally, his feathery blond hair flying.

"Your mother is in deep trouble," I said. "And if she doesn't tell the U.S. attorney's office what she knows, they may find out anyway and she could go to jail for blackmail."

Jon stopped short and whirled around. "Blackmail?" he repeated, incredulous. He smiled faintly. Either it was impossible to believe, or he was half a hair proud of his mother for pulling it off. "You don't mean blackmail," he said.

"That's exactly what I mean," I said, and I told him the whole story quickly. Jon sat on a bench and tucked both feet under him. "It sounds to me like this Judge Franklin is in bigger trouble than Mama," he said.

"For sure. That's why if your mother helps us nail Mrs. Franklin, she could do herself a lot of good."

"She's pretty well off now, wouldn't you say?"

I shook my head. "No, I sure wouldn't."

"And you want me to talk to her, convince her to tell what she knows?"

I nodded.

"How much good will she do herself?" he asked.

"No promises," I said.

"None?"

"Only that if she doesn't talk, she'll suffer eventually."

"That means I will too," Jon said as thunder rolled in the distance. "She's been a good mother. Maybe I can help her."

Jon had promised he'd talk to his mother that evening, but as Hanlon, Haymeyer, the newly introduced Shipman, and I waited for his call, prospects appeared dim. Shipman was more articulate than he appeared. He was scruffy, knowledgeable about police matters, and very much in love with newspaper work. "I'm taking Larry down to have him booked at the county jail," Hanlon said. "You can reach me by radio if I'm not back when Yakovich calls."

By the time Hanlon returned, Larry Shipman was alone in a cell built for two, waiting for Salerno.

"Yakovich called just after you left, Jim," Haymeyer said. "He told his old lady he knew everything and that she should cooperate. She told him he was no son of hers if he believed such things and ordered him out of her apartment. He's pretty shook up."

"What do you think?" Hanlon asked.

"I think she'll be calling us," Haymeyer said.

Margo was angry that I had been advised not to tell her what had gone on. "I'm going crazy here," she said. "I pray, I read my Bible, I think about you. Now I can't know what's going on?"

"I'm sorry," I said.

"I know it's not your fault, Philip. But can't you tell me something if I promise not to do anything or tell anyone else?"

"Who would you tell?"

"Good question. Can't you tell me then?"

"No."

"Oh, Philip! I'm not kidding, this is driving me nuts."

I called Haymeyer at home. "Sorry to bother you," I said, "but can't we do something for Margo's sake? It's too much for her to be in the dark about everything."

"What does she want to do, talk to her mother?" Haymeyer suggested sarcastically.

"Hey," I said, "how about if she talked to her father?" I tried to say it quietly, but Margo spun around, nodding her head so vigorously that her hair fell down beside her face.

Haymeyer was silent for several seconds. I waited. "Let me check with Hanlon on this," he said finally.

Margo was ecstatic. "Oh, thank you, Philip! I haven't talked with Daddy since Atlanta — "

"Haymeyer's just checking, Margo. You know the odds are against it."

"I know they'll let me see him," she said, ignoring me. "I just know it." She turned on the television.

"I think I'll wait in my room," I said. "It won't look good, our being in the same room."

"To whom?" Margo asked mischievously.

"To your father," I said. She threw a cushion at me as I left.

I was exhausted and fell asleep within minutes after stretching out on my bed. I slept fitfully, images playing in my mind. Margo, Jim Barnes, Bob Warren, Earl Haymeyer, James Hanlon, Larry Shipman, Jon Yakovich, Olga, Frederick Wahl, Tony Salerno, my parents. *My parents!* I rolled over and sat up quickly.

What if they had tried calling Atlanta? I flipped the light switch and squinted against the blinding whiteness, groping for the phone.

"I didn't mean to wake you."

I jumped. Someone was in the room! I shielded my eyes and peeked between my fingers. It was Wahl. "I followed you from Hanlon's office," he said, sitting and crossing his legs. He was immaculately dressed, as he had been in Atlanta. My heart cracked so loudly against my chest I could hardly breathe.

"Then you know where Margo is," I said.

"I have no beef with Margo. We made our point to her mother when Salerno got into her apartment in Atlanta."

"You made your point?"

"Yes, I think Mrs. Franklin is convinced that we are capable."

I was totally confused. "But Salerno blew it in Atlanta."

"For himself, maybe," Wahl said, smiling. "But he wasn't there to hurt the girl anyway. Salerno wouldn't take a job like that. Judge Franklin wanted some proof of our capabilities, that's all. We had to locate her daughter, and then demonstrate that we could kill her, but without hurting her. We did that."

"Salerno wouldn't have killed Margo, even if she *had* been there?"

"No way."

"Why are you telling me this?"

"Proving capabilities again. I could have killed you while you slept."

"You?"

"I *could* have. You understand, I don't do that sort of work myself. I simply see that it gets done."

"I'm not afraid of Salerno, as long as he's in jail."

"Come now, Mr. Spence. You think Tony Salerno is the only man I represent?"

I shrugged. Was I still dreaming? The phone was ringing.

"Don't answer it," Wahl said.

"They'll come for me," I said, feeling like an actor in a B movie.

"I'll be gone by then," Wahl said. He talked fast while the phone rang and rang.

"Our point is this. Mrs. Franklin does not want to be responsible for any more deaths."

"Any *more?*"

"Oh, come on. You know she killed Wanmacher. The point is she doesn't intend to be convicted of that. Without Margo or Olga, they've got nothing on her. That means she has to keep both of them quiet, and, like I said, she doesn't want any more deaths. The money is keeping Olga quiet." He paused meaningfully.

"And what's she gonna do about Margo?"

"We think we've solved that little problem. One of my associates is with her right now. He's telling her that you've been murdered in your room and that she should keep her mouth shut if she doesn't want the same to happen to her father."

"You're going to kill me?"

"Certainly not. I already told you no. I don't do that work. But when I leave, don't be too sure that you're alone."

With that Wahl left, slamming the door.

I froze. Still half prone on the bed, I tried to move without making any noise. If I could just bolt through the door before anyone came out of the bathroom or closet. But what if he was under the bed? Or waiting outside the door? And where would I go if I did get out?

I leaned over as far as I could without putting my hand on the floor. The blood rushed to my head as I looked under the bed. I heard a noise. Was it in the closet? The bathroom? Outside? I put one foot on the floor. My chest heaved as I fought to breathe without gasping. Should I turn off the light and take my chances? No, he might have a flashlight and then he could see me without my seeing him. I stood on one foot and edged toward the closet. Maybe I could duck into the closet and he would think I had left. But what if *he* was in the closet?

Should I wait until Haymeyer arrived? But what if it hadn't been Haymeyer on the phone? What if it had been Margo? Would she come up? I couldn't let her. I toyed with just waiting until he made his move, but it seemed hopeless and endless. I prayed silently. *Lord, if it's going to happen, let it happen quickly. Take care of Margo.* Bible verses rang in my head, but they made no sense. They weren't verses of comfort, but rather old standards like Genesis 1:1 and John 3:16.

"Should not perish..." hit me as ironic, and I pulled open the closet door. No one. Now I knew he was in the bathroom. Could I do what Haymeyer had done to Salerno? I leaned around the corner. The bathroom door was ajar about three inches. Could I reach it without being seen? Didn't the gunman hear Wahl leave? Why hadn't he come out blasting?

I took three quick steps toward the bathroom door, and though my arm was nearly paralyzed with fear, I grabbed the knob and yanked the door shut. I turned to dive away from the door but slipped on the rug and fell as I heard a banging from the bathroom.

I rolled over and hid my head with my arms, finally realizing that the noise was the soap on a string I had hung on the hook behind the bathroom door. It tapped slower and more softly and then stopped. There was no other noise. I ran to the front door and fastened the chain lock. I went back to the bathroom and listened. Nothing. I opened the door and reached in to turn on the light, causing the soap to bang again and my heart to resound, but no one was there. I collapsed on the tile floor, my back against the bathroom door.

I gasped for air and every muscle ached. I felt as if I couldn't move, but a loud knock at the front door made me scramble to my feet. I shut and locked the bathroom door, turned off the light, and lay in the bathtub, pulling the shower curtain shut.

The porcelain was cold against my face and hands. I could hear my heart. I prayed that the soap string would quit tapping. Someone was kicking the front door. The lock broke and the chain snapped. I quit breathing.

"Philip!" The voice sounded familiar. I couldn't respond. The soap still swung on the bathroom door. I reached up to pull back the shower curtain just as Haymeyer kicked open the door and stood crouching in the darkness, both hands on his gun.

"I'm OK," I managed, as he turned on the light.

He swore. "Someone visited Margo," he said. "She thought you'd been murdered."

"So did I," I said. He helped me out of the tub. I could hardly walk. I flopped onto the bed and Earl called Margo.

"He's OK, Margo. I'll bring him down in a while."

Haymeyer told me he had come to talk Margo out of seeing her father, arriving just after Wahl's man had delivered his threat. Margo had tried to call me, and when she got no answer she ran out of her room and into Haymeyer's arms. She was hysterical. He told her to stay in her room with the door locked, and he bounded up two flights of stairs down the hall to my room. "I thought you'd had it," he said.

A half hour later Margo and I sat unashamedly with our arms around each other. I stared into her eyes and she cried softly. "They got the desired response," I said.

"What do you mean?" Earl asked.

"I'm through," I said. "I'm willing to leave it alone, take Margo away, and forget it."

"Give it twenty-four hours," Haymeyer said.

"Give it nothing. It's not worth it. Who needs it?"

"You're afraid," Earl said.

"For Margo, yes. Nuts, for me too. Sure I'm afraid. I'm scared to death."

"I could kick myself for not being as careful here as we were in Atlanta," Haymeyer said. "But it won't happen again. From now on it's round-the-clock protection for both of you."

I was so wiped out I didn't even bother to argue. We'd get some rest while Haymeyer's men stood guard, and then we'd be long gone.

After Margo and I were moved to adjoining rooms at the Jackson Hotel near the Loop, Jim Barnes, Bob Warren, and another pair of special agents traded off standing guard over us. For the next few days we rested, played word games with our bodyguards, and watched television. We also spent time praying and studying together.

"You're in this as deep as any of us now, Philip," Haymeyer told me one night. "You've been threatened by the real mouthpiece for the organization in this town. If and when the time comes, I hope you'll testify against him before the grand jury."

"Forget it," I said.

"You're kidding."

"No, I'm not. I already told you, it's not worth it. I'm not going to get shot up or see Margo hurt, just to help you bag these creeps."

"Is that what your Bible tells you?" Haymeyer said, looking at me with disgust.

Margo turned to me as if she expected an answer. I shrugged and turned away.

"I'm tempted to withdraw your protection, Philip," Haymeyer said.

"You're not serious."

"I sure am. Why should I protect you? What are you to me?"

"It's your job to protect a citizen who has been threatened."

"But you haven't been threatened, have you? You're not willing to say you've been threatened, so as far as I am concerned, you haven't been threatened. How long are we supposed to protect you? Forever? We haven't got the men or the money. Someday, unless you help put these guys away, they're going to get you and Margo and anyone else who gets in their way."

I pretended not to hear him, but every word echoed in my brain. I had badgered Margo to come to Chicago at any cost to do what was right. Now, here I was backing out of the most important responsibility I had ever faced. My parents would never believe this. *My parents!*

"How much can I tell my parents?" I asked Haymeyer. "I'd better call them. They've probably been trying to reach me in Atlanta for days."

"Don't tell them anything," Haymeyer said. "Just let them know where you are and that you're here on business."

"Does this mean you're looking for a job?" my mother wanted to know. "You should check with Mr. Ferguson here in Dayton, Philip."

"I know, Mother. Maybe I will, and I promise I'll come by there before heading south again."

"How's the girl you met?"

"She's fine, Mother," I said.

Just talking to Mother made me realize I would have to do the right thing. I could live in fear all my life, or I could come forward and do what I had been encouraging Margo to do all along. It gave me a new perspective on her problem, except that I didn't have a murdering mother to worry about.

It was late on Friday night, and Bob Warren was standing guard outside my door. Jim Barnes and Margo and I were watching television when Haymeyer called. "Philip, Hanlon has decided the time has come to fill in Mr. Franklin for his own protection. We've been watching him since you and Margo were threatened, but Hanlon wants him to know what's going on. See how Margo feels about it, and if she gives the green light, we'll talk with him tonight."

Margo was anxious for her father to know, and she wanted to see him. "It won't hurt him so much if he knows that Mother didn't really want me killed."

"It's time you were told a few things, too, Margo," Barnes said. "Larry Shipman has gotten next to Salerno since he was extradited to Chicago."

"What did he find out?" Margo asked.

"It took a few days," Barnes said, "but Salerno finally bragged about the fact that he almost killed you. He said that the organization and your mother had been negotiating for a long time on favors the judge could come up with in exchange for the mob's scaring you, and Olga if necessary. He told Shipman your mother had instructed that you be scared but not killed, and that she thought it had been a success."

"She thought?"

"Right. Salerno says he went in there with every intention of killing you."

"What about that women and children code?" I asked.

"It exists," Barnes said. "And very few hit men have ever violated it for less than double their normal asking price. Salerno said the organization was going to pay him fifty thousand dollars for this one. He thought it was too good to be true, and was a bit careless. He didn't do a final preliminary check of Margo's apartment and found himself facing the dummy."

"Why did he shoot his way out?" I asked. "Wouldn't it have been better for him not to shoot at all?"

"Oh, yeah, and that's the funny part, if any of this can be funny. The same thing happened to Salerno once before. Not a dummy. Just that he smelled a stakeout. There was no target, no dummy, no nothin'. He just dropped his weapon and threw up his hands and all they could get him for was possession of the sawed-off."

"So why did he come out shooting in Atlanta?"

"If he'd known it was a police stakeout, he wouldn't have," Barnes explained. "He thought he'd been set up by the mob."

"Why?"

"He didn't know. There's a lot of jealousy between hit men. Prices and contracts and all that — the news gets around. Every hit man in the East knew Salerno had a big contract and was about to violate the code. When he spotted the dummy and heard the door shut, he figured it was kill-or-be-killed, so he blasted away."

"So they were actually going to go through with killing me."

"Yes, Margo, but your mother doesn't know it. Right now she is pleased with the organization."

"Why did they tell Margo they'd murdered me?" I asked. "And why did Wahl tell me that Salerno never intended to kill Margo, and that I wasn't alone in my room?"

"Why not, Philip?" Barnes said. "If those guys ever told the truth, they'd confuse each other. Whatever works, whatever furthers their cause, whatever terrifies you, they'll say it."

"I still take some consolation in the fact that Mother did not intend to have me killed," Margo said.

I pressed my lips tight and shook my head. She noticed.

"I have to agree with Philip," Barnes said. "I suppose it can make you feel better in a way, but remember, she misread them. Why didn't she realize that they might kill you anyway, just to show her who's boss? And now who will they kill to show her their strength? Your father?"

"I want to see him," Margo said.

By midnight, Mr. Franklin had been told the entire story and was brought to my room. I was surprised at his height. He was thin, which made him seem even taller than he was, and graying. He and Margo held each other tight and long. He was ashen. "You never wanted to believe that Mother was seeing Richard Wanmacher," Margo said.

"I knew all along she was seeing someone, of course, Margo," he said just above a whisper. "I didn't want to admit it to you because I thought you were only guessing. I thought if I denied it all, you might decide you were wrong."

"But I knew, Daddy. I wasn't wrong."

"I know. You were a young woman I treated as a child, and I'm sorry." Mr. Franklin looked helpless, vulnerable. He seemed self-conscious about talking so personally in front of strangers, but he continued.

"You know, Margo, I never dreamed the man was Wanmacher. I detested him, and I thought your mother did too. He was so smug at parties. I made twice as much money as he did, but he treated me the opposite. I couldn't stand that condescending attitude."

"Daddy," Margo said gently, "I've finally gotten over the shock that Mother killed Wanmacher. Do you find it as hard to believe as I did?"

"I don't know," Mr. Franklin said, his shoulders sagging. He still had his coat on. "If he ever treated her the way he treated me, she could have killed him. Richard Wanmacher was one killable person."

"I heard her threaten him, Daddy."

"That's what they tell me. You know, I can just hear him telling her that he couldn't see her anymore. Not that he's sorry, just that she'll get over it eventually. Wouldn't that infuriate you?"

"How do you know what he said?"

"I'm only guessing, honey," he said. "I just know what kind of man Wanmacher was. Arrogant, a smartaleck. Syrupy. I despised him."

"Mr. Franklin," Haymeyer interrupted, "did you ever tell your wife how you felt about Mr. Wanmacher?"

"Dozens of times. I always got the impression she agreed. That's why I never suspected they were seeing each other. I still find it hard to believe. Like I say, I knew there was someone else. There had to be. But not him. He was the cockiest, most arrogant — "

"I think that's what attracted Mother to him," Margo interrupted.

"If it was, she found in him something she never would have found in me."

"What's that?" I asked. Mr. Franklin looked at me. It seemed to bother him that I would ask a question without having been introduced.

He shrugged. "Cockiness," he said. "She always wanted me to act more self-assured, richer than I was. 'Virginia,' I'd say, 'you're always going to be a more impressive woman than I am a man. So you show off and I'll watch.' " He shook his head slowly. "I did always love her, though. Oh, I loved her."

"You still do, don't you, Daddy?"

"No, I don't think I do. I'm not capable of loving a woman who could risk her own daughter's life just to scare her. What if you'd been killed?"

Mr. Franklin broke down and Margo comforted him.

"I'd have never forgiven her," he said. "Never."

TEN

The phone rang early the next morning. It was Haymeyer. "We just got a call from Olga Yakovich" he said. "She wants to talk, and Hanlon wants you in on this. I'll be right over to pick you up."

"What we need," Hanlon said back at his office, "is the murder weapon. The proverbial smoking pistol."

"Olga has to have it, doesn't she?" I asked.

"Of course," Hanlon said. "It's her bread and butter."

"Maybe it's what she wants to talk about," I suggested.

"Maybe," Hanlon agreed. "But remember, she can use that gun against us the same way she's using it against Mrs. Franklin."

"How's that?"

"She knows we have nothing solid without it. She can tell us she's got it, but she can demand all kinds of promises from us before she produces it."

"Then you can get her for withholding evidence, right?" I said.

"Very good, Philip," Haymeyer said sarcastically. "Then we've got an old washwoman for withholding evidence when we want a judge for murder. No, sir, that's not for me. I want that gun with as few promises from us as possible. Once we've got the gun, we've got Franklin."

"I'm not excited about nailing this Yako-what's-her-name on blackmail, Earl," Hanlon said. "I mean, I want her, but I'd make a lot of concessions, even to the point of seeing her stay out of jail, if she'd come up with the gun."

"She might want more than that, Jim," Haymeyer said.

"What more could she want? She's guilty and should get several years!"

"She might want her name left out of the whole thing. Protection for her son. Lots of stuff."

"Boy, I hope not," Hanlon said. "That's all we need."

"Maybe we should go before the grand jury now with what we've got," Earl said.

"Let's see if they'll come back with a true bill so we can arrest old lady Franklin."

"Go before the grand jury with what we've got now?" Hanlon echoed. "On what charge?"

"Conspiracy to murder Margo Franklin. Conspiracy to obstruct justice. The murder of Richard Wanmacher."

"Earl, you're dreaming! We have no hard evidence that she conspired to murder Margo. Even Salerno says she thought he intended only to scare Margo. She did conspire to obstruct justice, a serious charge, especially for a judge, though nothing like conspiracy to commit murder. But even the obstruction charge hinges on a mobster's testimony. She could just argue it is an attempt by the mob to get her because she's an honest judge."

"You're right, of course," Haymeyer said, seeming disgusted with himself. "Maybe we should forget the conspiracy charge for now and go after her on the murder."

"All we've got on that one is Margo's word," Hanlon said. "And right now something else is sticking in my craw, Earl. Mr. Franklin seems to have had more of a motive to kill Richard Wanmacher than his wife did. We may need to rethink this whole case."

My mind whirled. Everything had pointed so clearly to Mrs. Franklin, but when I stopped to think about it, how did I really know it wasn't her husband? How could Margo know? Maybe he was in this with Wahl, to get revenge on his wife and to eliminate a judge who was troublesome to the mob.

Hanlon was continuing to outline strategy. "The first thing we have to do is talk with Olga," he said. "If she's ready to talk, there's no telling what we may learn."

Hanlon and Haymeyer agreed to let Larry Shipman and me go along to see Olga. "Yeah, let's really scramble her brain," Hanlon said. "I may regret it, but I'd like to let her see that we mean business and that the best she can do is to tell all, produce the gun, and hope for the best." We stopped by the jail to pick up Shipman and headed for Olga's.

"If you're ready to talk, I'm ready to listen," Hanlon said when she opened the door. "You will either confirm what we already know, or I will begin litigation against you."

"Litigation?" Olga repeated, frowning. Her eyes studied each of us. Larry Shipman could barely keep a straight face. With less a stake in this than any of us, he was simply enjoying the tension, the drama. He seemed to be writing his story in his head.

"I want not to talk to so many," Olga said, "I will talk to you and you." She had pointed to Hanlon and me. "You nice to my Jon," she told me.

Olga took us to one of her bedrooms. "I take money every month," she said, when she had shut the door.

"Yes, yes, go on," Hanlon said.

"I take money every month because I have gun used to kill lawyer," said Olga.

Hanlon shot me a now-we're-getting-somewhere look and pressed Olga for more information. "Where is the gun? You'll have to turn it over to us, you know. It's a serious offense to withhold evidence in a murder case."

Olga stared at Hanlon, her jaw set.

"Olga, we can't do anything for you without the gun."

"What I get if I give you the gun?"

"We'll do everything we can for you."

"Want guarantee."

"We've got enough on you now to put you away for years," Hanlon said, his coldness catching me off guard.

"I not say anything more unless I get guarantee. I want no jail, no name in papers, no harm to son, no nothing."

"You don't think you should have to pay for your crime? You have withheld evidence in a murder case. You have blackmailed Mr. Franklin. You have virtually stolen the money you've spent on this place and on your son's education."

"Nothing," Olga said, not batting an eye at the mention of Mr. Franklin. "I want guarantee nothing happen to me."

"I can guarantee a lot will happen to you if you don't tell us, Olga. I will charge you with what you have already admitted voluntarily. I have not forced you to say this. You have not been under arrest, but I will put you under arrest if you don't tell us."

"Olga watch TV," she said. "Nothing I say so far can hurt me. Olga have rights."

"You're right," Hanlon said. "You also have my phone number."

Hanlon, Haymeyer, Shipman, and I went back to Hanlon's office. "Where would Olga stash the gun?" I asked.

"Anywhere," Haymeyer said. "If she were smart she'd put it in a safe deposit box."

"If she were really smart," Hanlon said, "she'd have kept it in that apartment all these years, or maybe even in her purse. No one would suspect."

"You know, that gun is not only her meal ticket but her life insurance," Haymeyer said. "The murderer has to want her silenced, but can't do a thing as long as that gun remains hidden."

"If Olga were really stupid — " Shipman began.

"Which she is — " Haymeyer said.

" — if she were really stupid," Shipman continued, "she'd move the gun from wherever she's got it now that the heat is on."

"If she were going to do that, she'd have done it already," Hanlon said.

"Let me finish," Shipman said, sitting on the edge of his chair. "This old broad is shrewd and dumb at the same time. She'd be better off leaving the gun where no one has seen it all these years, but my guess is that she's moved it."

"To where?"

Shipman waved both arms. "I'm getting to it, just listen. What would be the most desperately stupid thing for her to do right now?"

"I thought *you* were going to tell *us*," Haymeyer said.

"I may have to if you don't guess. On the other hand, if you don't guess, it probably isn't worth speculating about. I know it's a long shot. Just a hunch."

Haymeyer and Hanlon looked at each other. I hadn't said anything from the time we'd left Olga's apartment, but something was gnawing at me too. I'd been so quiet that Shipman and Haymeyer and Hanlon had all but forgotten I was there. It almost startled them when I spoke. "Jon," I said. "Jon might talk her into letting him hold the gun."

"Yes!" Shipman shouted, clapping. "Wouldn't that be the most desperately stupid thing for them to do at this point? Maybe Jon lied to us about her kicking him out!"

Haymeyer and Hanlon were already on their feet, grabbing their coats. I sat with my chin in my palm. "She wouldn't," I said quietly. "Wahl's cohorts would have been watching Olga — she's got to know that."

The three men were on their way out. I followed. "What does Olga know about Wahl or anyone else?" Hanlon asked. "She'd be just dumb enough to do this."

Haymeyer hadn't driven so fast with four people in the car before. Several times we narrowly missed jumping the curb on tight corners, as he sped north to the Evanston campus.

"It's just a hunch, a long shot," Shipman kept shouting.

"We have to check it out," Hanlon said. "Philip, you'd better pray that we're onto this before Wahl is."

Haymeyer slid onto the sidewalk in front of the dorm, and we ran up the steps to the third floor. A crowd had already gathered outside Jon Yakovich's room. Students milled about, some turned away holding their mouths. My heart sank.

"Oh, no," Haymeyer said. Hanlon swore. Shipman bullied his way past the crowd.

"Police! Clear the way!" Shipman shouted. "Move out!"

The blood covering the floor was already dry. "It's a Fred Medima hit," Haymeyer told Hanlon as he pushed his way through. "Ear to ear with a straight razor while he slept. The kid had only enough time to arch his back in reflex. It threw him onto the floor where he bled to death in a minute."

I kept pressing forward, though I knew I didn't really want to see. I had known this kid — slim, soft spoken, a slight accent. Loyal to his mother. Defiant when talking about her. Now, in an attempt to give him a good life, she had gotten him murdered.

Jon Yakovich's eyes were open. His teeth were bared. His fingers clutched a sheet and a blanket near his neck, where a gaping wound had let his life's blood gush forth. Only landing on his back had kept him from losing more blood. The heart had long since stopped beating, and blood had coagulated on his neck.

"That's how we know who did it," Haymeyer said, pointing to the straight razor. It had been wiped perfectly clean and had been closed and laid beside the victim's head. Plastic overshoes, which had left perfect impressions in the blood, had also been removed and left behind with a pair of surgical gloves.

"It's the arrogant announcement Medima always makes," Haymeyer said. "It's like Salerno's second shotgun blast."

"How can you stand this?" I asked.

"I can't, Philip," Haymeyer said evenly. "That's why I'm here."

"If the gun was ever here, and we all know it was, it's gone now," Hanlon said.

Olga opened her door carefully. "I hoped it was you," she said, studying our faces. "I think something happen to Jon. What happen to Jon?"

"Why?" Hanlon asked.

"I get call, say no more money come. I can say what I want and it not hurt because I not have gun now."

"What did you do with the gun, Mrs. Yakovich?"

"I give it to Jon," she said. She looked at us, her eyes questioning, pleading. I looked away, and she knew. She cried. "All I wanted was guarantee," she sobbed.

"You've got it," Hanlon said.

"Don't want it now," she said. "Don't want nothin' now."

Eleven

The color drained from Margo's face when she heard the news. She sat on the bed in her hotel room and trembled.

"I know it's terrible," Haymeyer said.

Margo shook her head. "That was the name," she said, her throat tight.

"What name?" Haymeyer asked.

"That was the name the man used who was here the other night. The one who told me Philip had been murdered."

"He told you his name?"

Margo nodded, tears welling up. She folded her arms and rocked back and forth.

"What name?" Haymeyer persisted.

"Medima," she said.

Hanlon jumped up and began to pace. "I can't believe they sent Medima for a scare job," he said. "Of all the arrogant — "

"They sent Salerno to Atlanta to scare her," Haymeyer reminded him.

"Salerno meant business. Can you imagine Medima stooping to verbal threats?"

Warren and Barnes shook their heads. "Incredible."

"This Yakovich murder was definitely the work of this Medima?" Mr. Franklin asked.

"Definitely," Haymeyer said. "He's so thorough, so precise, and so consistent, no one could imitate it."

"And he was in my room!" Margo sobbed.

"That's it," I said. "This is too much. How much more can Margo take? Let's confront her mother and get this stopped."

Margo rolled onto her side and hid her face in the blankets. "You may have a point there, Philip," Hanlon said. "Margo, listen." She sat up, staring at him through her matted hair. "Would your mother be capable of ordering a murder like the one you just heard about?"

"How should I know? She let them scare me. She killed Richard Wanmacher. What wouldn't she do? Who knows?"

"Come on, Margo," I said. "I know it doesn't make much sense right now, but there *is* a difference between killing someone in a fit of passion and ordering the mutilation of an innocent college kid."

"I don't know," Margo said. "I just don't know what to expect from her anymore."

"Well, Jim," Haymeyer said, turning to Hanlon, "where does this leave us? Looks like Judge Franklin has the gun, and we have witnesses to protect."

"Let's move them one more time," Hanlon said slowly, his brow wrinkled. "Get them in a suite, all together, with Barnes and Warren taking turns on watch. Salerno thinks Shipman was just moved to a different building in the House of Corrections, so maybe we'll put him back with Salerno and see what we can get."

At midnight we were moved to a small hotel on the Near North Side. It was a dive compared to where we'd been, but the top floor had a suite with three bedrooms and a reading room and was situated perfectly for protection. After we were settled, Mr. Franklin, Margo, Bob Warren, and I just sat. Barnes posted himself in the hall. No one said much, but we were too tight to sleep. We jumped when the phone rang. It was Haymeyer.

"Hanlon just promised Olga complete exoneration if she'll tell her story to a grand jury. She says it's Judge Franklin who's been paying blackmail. She'll tell the grand jury everything this once and the transcript may be used later, but then she's out of it. She never has to talk again."

"Will it work?" I asked.

"Can't hurt," Haymeyer said. "Hanlon had toyed with the idea of just confronting Judge Franklin, but the decision at this point is to get the charges filed. We're going after her for the murder of Richard Wanmacher and conspiracy to obstruct justice."

The next day, though I was exhausted from lack of sleep, Haymeyer agreed to let me go with him to Virginia Franklin's court. His purpose was simply to rattle her a little if he could.

Margo had described her mother, but I could hardly wait to see her. I imagined her hard, tough, weatherbeaten, sophisticated. I was wrong on almost all counts.

We sat near the back and waited for her entrance. Haymeyer explained the case to me quickly. It was a stock scandal; a broker was charged with fraud.

"All rise!" My heart jumped. We stood and I stared as she walked in. Her robe made her look even tinier than her five feet, two inches. She didn't look nearly Mr. Franklin's age, but could have passed for forty. Her black hair was up, expensively done. Her complexion was perfect. She looked soft, loving, motherly. She smiled slightly as she sat down.

I couldn't take my eyes off her. She was a picture of professionalism, class, sophistication. She spoke gently, but steadily. "I believe you were calling a witness when we recessed yesterday, Mr. Trine." I wouldn't have been more surprised if she had shouted obscenities.

Haymeyer said something to me, but I ignored him. I was captivated. Virginia Franklin had to show some evidence of the character Margo had described, but she didn't.

"Want to meet her?" Haymeyer asked.

I answered without looking at him. "Would Hanlon approve?" I asked. "Is she supposed to know I'm in town?"

"Would I suggest it if Hanlon disapproved? I'll tell her you're a friend of mine. She already knows Philip Spence is in town, but she won't know you're Philip Spence."

Judge Franklin was listening carefully to the lawyers and the witnesses, her eyes following the conversation. She took notes occasionally, but never looked away from the speakers. She sat with her back perfectly straight.

"Court will break for lunch soon," Haymeyer said. "Let's go back to her chambers and see if we can greet her."

"What will she think about your being here, knowing you're on her case?"

"It will blow her mind, I hope."

We waited near the door of her chamber with the deputy bailiff, a friend of Haymeyer. "She's going to stop this trial this afternoon," the bailiff said. "Told me so herself. She says she's gonna hafta insist that the prosecutor come better prepared to her courtroom."

"She'll just stop the trial?" I asked. "Doesn't she have to wait until the defense moves for a dismissal?"

"You'd think so now, wouldn't ya?" the bailiff said. "But I seen her stop a trial herself more'n once. Did it here not too long ago in the Tony Salerno hearings."

From inside the chamber we heard a door open and close as the judge entered from the courtroom. "Your honor, Mr. Haymeyer is here to see you, ma'am," the bailiff said, knocking.

"One moment, please," she said, lyrically. In just seconds she opened the door. Her robe had already been put away and she wore a skirt, blouse, and blazer. "It's so good to see you again, Earl," she said, taking Haymeyer's hand and looking him squarely in the eyes. "And who is this young man?" If she'd had an accent I'd have sworn she was a Texas socialite, the perfect hostess. Not a trace of hardness, suspicion, or bitterness. She was one charming and attractive woman.

"This is Bobby Boyd, Virginia," Haymeyer lied. "He's a law student from Ohio State and is visiting to get some exposure to the courtroom."

"How nice," Mrs. Franklin said, taking my hand. She was so soft. She seemed sincerely interested in me.

"It's a wonderful school," she said, catching me off guard. "Is Clarence Hill still there?"

"Clarence Hill?"

"Yes, in the law school. He's been there for years."

"He might be. I'm in pre-law, so I'm really not fully aware of the law school faculty."

"Greet him for me if you should meet him, won't you?"

"Sure will."

"Will you and Bobby have lunch with me, Earl? I'm about to send out for a sandwich, and I'd so like to visit with you."

I could hardly believe she would ask him, but Haymeyer accepted. Our lunches were delivered from within the building.

"I was sorry I had to throw the Salerno case out," Mrs. Franklin said. "I know how hard you worked on it, Earl. And I wanted to see Wahl lose one for Jim's sake."

"Hanlon was hungry for that one, Virginia," Haymeyer said.

"But you know there wasn't enough evidence there," she said. "It irritated me." She looked directly into his eyes and spoke daintily. "I want as much as anyone to have Wahl and his syndicate connections out of Chicago for good. And I'd like to be responsible for their sentencing. But I cannot allow improper charges to violate justice in my court."

I was stunned. This woman was guilty of murder, yet there she sat, acting virtuous and nearly convincing me, though surely not Haymeyer. She insisted she had done the right thing in spite of her "firm belief that Wahl and Salerno and the likes of such men should be imprisoned." She was "forced to rule in their favor when the evidence simply wasn't there."

My mind reeled. This woman was nothing like I expected. Could Margo be wrong? Could she have misjudged her own mother? *Mr.* Franklin seemed a more likely candidate for a murderer than this woman.

"We're all after the same goal, aren't we, Earl?" she asked, begging the only logical answer.

"Yes, we are," Haymeyer said lifelessly. "You never cease to amaze me, Virginia."

She bit into her sandwich and raised her eyebrows as if to say, "Oh? Why?"

"You're always on top of things. Don't you ever get rattled?"

She waited until she had swallowed. "Oh, my, yes," she said, winking at me. "You know very well" — and here she slowed her speech dramatically — "that I get rattled whenever I encounter shoddy investigative work, lazy research, or insufficient evidence. But I must say, Earl, with you that is a rare occurrence." She entwined her fingers on the desk before her and smiled at both of us. I smiled back.

"She's some kinda woman, huh?" Haymeyer said, as we headed for Hanlon's office.

I didn't respond.

"You were charmed, weren't you, kid?"

"Yes, I guess I was."

"You were supposed to be. You know what I was supposed to be?"

"What?"

"Scared."

"Did she scare you?"

"Yup. She made it clear that she will not be threatened. She will not be rattled. She will not be intimidated. And we are going to have to build a tight case against her or we won't have a chance. She might even have figured you out with that innocent question of hers about the law prof. She was a trial lawyer once, you know, with a reputation of going for the jugular.

"I'll bet if you looked into it you'd find there is not now, nor has there ever been, a law prof named Clarence Hill at Ohio State or anywhere else. The biggest problem is what I've got to tell Hanlon."

"Which is?"

"That she appears ready to stonewall it."

"How can you tell, Earl?"

"It was obvious. She's well rested. Energetic. She doesn't know her daughter was almost killed. She thinks she was just scared and that everything is going according to plan. She's looking forward to this fight. She's challenging me to come up with hard evidence, because otherwise she'll fight till the end and beat it."

"Could she?"

"You'd better believe she could. We'd better be right on the money, no shortcuts, no assumptions. Just hard evidence."

At Hanlon's office Haymeyer relayed the conversation to his boss. "She was in prime form, huh?" Hanlon said. "I don't know if I like that or not."

"I know I don't like it," Haymeyer said. "Why can't it be easy? Wouldn't you think we could shake her up? We've got everything but the gun. We've got Margo, Olga, and even what Salerno's been telling Shipman."

"It's not enough, Earl, and you know it," Hanlon said. "There's not a judge in this town who would convict a peer of murder without a piece of hardware on the evidence table, and from what you say, there's no chance Virginia Franklin is going to give us a break."

"Not even if she were confronted by Margo?" I asked.

Haymeyer and Hanlon looked at each other. "I really don't think so," Hanlon said.
Haymeyer nodded in agreement. "This woman is like a bullet in a sponge. Soft on the
outside and — "

"I can't believe she could sit there knowing that Earl and her daughter were nearly
killed in Atlanta and pretend that she knew nothing about it," I said. "She didn't even
mention it. She had to know that Jon Yakovich has been murdered. She reads the papers, doesn't she?"

Hanlon and Haymeyer nodded. "She knows her stuff," Haymeyer said. "She's not
going to give us a thing."

"Not on her own," Hanlon said. "Shipman got a message to me this morning. He
says Salerno has been talking with Wahl, and they're about to blow Virginia's case for
her."

"How?" Haymeyer asked. "And why didn't you tell me?"

"How could I? You and Philip have been singing her praises so I can't get a word in."

"So what was Wahl supposed to have told Salerno?"

"Shipman says the syndicate is upset with Virginia for calling Olga and for having the
gall to read them out about the Yakovich murder. Sure enough, they found the gun in
Jon's room, but they're holding it, threatening to call in an anonymous tip and let us
find it so we can add it to Olga's testimony and put Virginia away."

"What are they holding out for?"

"She's throwing out a stock fraud case this afternoon for one of their guys."

"We know," Haymeyer said. "She's bragging that one up herself." He mimicked her
sweet voice. "Got to have enough evidence, Earl."

"Won't she try to keep Olga from testifying too?" I asked.

"I doubt it," Hanlon said. "But we've got Olga in safekeeping anyway. Once she gets
her testimony on the record, she can leave town. The irony now is that Virginia Franklin is no longer being milked for three thousand dollars a month by a pathetic old
housekeeper. She's being blackmailed for the freedom of syndicate goons. Where will it
end?"

"I'm more encouraged than when I came in here," Haymeyer said.

"Why?" I asked.

Hanlon smiled.

Haymeyer answered. "In a very real sense, my boy, we've got a talented bunch of
terrorists on our side. It's Jimmy Hanlon's office and the Chicago organization against
her honor, Virginia Franklin."

"I might bet on Mrs. Franklin," I said. "Anyone who can be that low and come off
that sweet has got to be somethin' else."

"That she is, Philip," Hanlon said. "That she is."

Olga's testimony before a secret grand jury that afternoon came tearfully and halting-
ly. It took more than four hours. "It rang clear as a bell," Hanlon said grimly. "We'll
know the jury's decision soon, but there's not a doubt in my mind. We'll get a true bill
calling for Virginia Franklin's arrest so we can file charges."

"What then?" I asked.

"Then she finds herself a lawyer and fights our motion for a change of venue."

"Why would you move for a change of venue?"

"We'll maintain that every judge in Chicago will be sympathetic and should disqualify himself. She'll fight it, and we'll be thrilled when she wins. While it's true that most of these judges would protect her, they'll turn on her like scorned lovers if hard evidence comes into the picture. Then we'll be in the driver's seat."

"Won't she figure that out in advance?" I asked.

"Ouch," Hanlon said. "You just heard an ingenious plan from a brilliant U.S. attorney. Give me some credit, kid. This Franklin is shrewd, but she's never tangled with me before." Hanlon thumped his chest with his thumb and grinned. He was only half kidding. He looked forward to the fight as much as Judge Franklin did.

"Will you give the syndicate anything in exchange for helping?" I asked.

"Not a chance," Haymeyer said. "You give breaks to the first timers, like Olga. We'll give the syndicate nothing. Hang it. They'll lead us to Virginia, and she'll lead us to them."

TWELVE

"I have this incredible feeling," Margo told me the next morning. "I've been praying and reading and thinking, and I feel a deep sense of security."

"I wish I did," I said. "I'm finding it easier to pray now that I'm in danger, but as for security — "

"*You're* the veteran Christian," she chided gently. "You should be telling *me* where security comes from. My family's been devastated for years, so it's not like I just lost it. I have new security in God, and in you, I hope."

I cupped her face in my palms. She looked tired. "You're gonna be a good Christian," I said. She smiled.

"I want to grow," she said. "If I didn't have all this on my mind, I think I could really get into it."

"I can't concentrate on anything, either. Especially after meeting your mother."

"She's something, huh?"

"She's something."

Barnes had been chatting with Mr. Franklin in the hall so we could be alone for about ten minutes. He knocked and entered. "Haymeyer was just here," he said. "The grand jury is not happy."

"You're kidding."

"No. They don't like the fact that Olga will not testify in an actual trial, and especially that there is no weapon. Hanlon was really hassled for coming in with so little. Margo may have to testify."

"So *little?*" Margo said. "Didn't Olga tell them everything?"

"Sure, but why should they believe her? There's no proof the money she's been getting all these years came from your mother. Without the weapon, the grand jury doesn't want to ask for charges to be filed against a judge, especially one of the stature and reputation of Virginia Franklin."

"I can't testify against Mother. I could have when I thought she wanted me killed, but not now," Margo said. "I don't want to. I want to keep out of this. And don't think it's just because she's my mother. I'm scared. For Daddy, for Philip, even for Olga. It seems they'll stop at nothing."

"The grand jury said that without the testimony of Salerno or Wahl or you, Margo, they didn't want to open a can of worms."

"What does Hanlon plan to do?" I asked.

"I think he wants to talk Margo into testifying."

"Is there any way I can avoid it?" Margo asked when Hanlon and Haymeyer arrived late in the afternoon to persuade her to testify.

"There's one possibility," Hanlon said. Haymeyer and Barnes edged closer. Warren was standing guard outside. Mr. Franklin sat on the floor, his back resting on the side of a bed. "We could tip off Mrs. Franklin. It may backfire, but I think it's a chance we have to take. If she thinks the case is about to become public knowledge, it may force her into some sort of a defense, regardless of her cool facade."

The phone rang. I answered and handed it to Hanlon. "Are you certain?" he said. "Wait until Earl Haymeyer and I can join you. Don't touch anything. No, we have Mr. Franklin right where we want him. He's in our custody on another matter." Hanlon hung up, a grin on his face.

"We've got our break!" he said, clapping. "Barnes, get to Shipman and find out what Salerno is saying. Earl, come with me. That was Ewald from the office. Someone called in an anonymous tip. They say we'll find the Wanmacher murder weapon in George Franklin's car."

Mr. Franklin stood quickly. "What?"

"It means they've played into our hands, if it's true," Haymeyer said. "It sounds as if your wife talked them into using the gun to implicate you so the heat would be off her. They want the attention off her too, because if her reputation suffers, so will all their favors in court."

"But won't the gun implicate me, if it's found in my car?"

"We'll worry about that later. Right now we just want to prove that the gun is the one that killed Wanmacher. That'll be the biggest break we've had in this case in years. Then our suspects, instead of being person or persons unknown, will be you and Mrs. Franklin and Olga and Margo, or someone who might have stolen that gun from your home in Winnetka."

"Now *I'm* a suspect?" Margo said.

"Technically," Hanlon said. "Now all we have to do is establish alibis for anyone with a motive."

"First," Haymeyer said, "we have to make sure we've got bona fide evidence."

Hanlon stood and put on his coat. "Right." As he opened the door he casually turned back to Mr. Franklin, now sitting on the bed. "By the way, sir, we need your permission to search your car."

Mr. Franklin waved at him. "Get out of here," he said. "You've got it."

"Can I go?" I said.

"If you hurry, loverboy," Haymeyer said. I winked at an unsmiling Margo. She mouthed a soundless goodbye. I could sense Hanlon and Haymeyer's excitement as we drove to Mr. Franklin's apartment house about ten blocks north.

"I've got to hand it to Wahl," Hanlon said. "Pretty crafty of him to have his boys plant the gun while we've got Mr. Franklin. We gave them the perfect opportunity, and we didn't even plan it."

"Don't say that, Mr. Hanlon," Haymeyer said in his weak British imitation. "I was about to take credit for it."

Ewald and Davis, two young agents from Hanlon's office, were already in the underground garage at the apartment building. They stood by Mr. Franklin's car. Hanlon tossed a huge key ring to Davis who began trying the various keys. "We're too nervous," Hanlon said.

Haymeyer shot him a doubletake. "Why?"

"We should have just asked George Franklin for his keys."

"Of course," Haymeyer said, sticking his tongue between his teeth and stifling a laugh. "Here we stand, breaking into the car of a man we have in custody." Ewald and Davis laughed too, but I felt spooked. I shivered and wished we could get on with it. Then the lock popped.

"We'll even let you guys do the looking," Hanlon said, "but when you find the gun just let it lie. I've got a nice *Baggie* from the crime lab, and I'll sack it myself."

Davis opened the hood and Ewald the trunk while Haymeyer edged toward the front passenger door and peered through the window to the glove compartment. "Come on, Earl," Hanlon said. "Let them find it. Haven't you had enough fun in your career?" Hanlon was enjoying himself. "Save the glove box till last," he said. "That's where it's going to be. Give me a complete search of the car, but save that glove box till last."

The agents removed the spare tire and pulled up the matting in the trunk. Inside the car they looked under the floor carpets and yanked out the backseat bench. Ewald slipped a glove on his right hand and felt under the dashboard. "Nothing," he said to Hanlon. "You want to check the glove compartment yourself?"

Hanlon shook his head, but Haymeyer stepped forward. "I will."

"Now, Earl," Hanlon said. "Let these guys do their jobs. Unlock the glove compartment, boys."

Haymeyer looked embarrassed. Hanlon wanted to see the gun as much as he did, but the United States attorney wanted to savor it. Both stared in when Davis shined his flashlight into the compartment. There was no gun. Hanlon swore. He pushed Haymeyer out of the way and grabbed Davis's flashlight. "Let me in there," he snapped.

He reached into the glove compartment and swept maps, pencils, note pads, a screwdriver, and a change purse out onto the seat with one motion. The compartment was clean. He slammed it shut and lay on his stomach on the front seat, reaching underneath and groping in the darkness. He yanked at the carpeting.

Backing out of the front seat, he hit his head on the roof. He flung the front door shut and climbed in the back, ripping out the bench seat again and looking in vain for the .22. Haymeyer thrust his coat back and jammed his fists on his hips. He walked to the front of the car, and slowly raised his right hand and crashed it down on the hood. He swore.

Hanlon was out of the car. "They're loving every minute of this," he said, lips pursed. "They're probably watching. Keep your eyes open."

"And we thought we were so close," Haymeyer said. He turned to Agent Ewald. "Call this number and get permission from George Franklin to search his apartment. We'll wait for you at his door. It's seventeen D."

"Let's not be stupid," Hanlon said, already cool. "This could be a setup. Let's not just barge in."

Haymeyer suggested that Hanlon take the elevator to the seventeenth floor while he and I and Davis took the stairs to guard against any surprise. We stopped to rest at the eighth and fifteenth floors, and when we came down the hall on seventeen, Hanlon was waiting just off the elevator. "Stay here," Haymeyer told me. I was puffing and scared. I backed up against the wall and watched from three doors away.

Hanlon got an affirmative nod from Ewald on the permission from Mr. Franklin. Haymeyer stationed the two agents on either side of the elevator. "Better stay away from the door," Haymeyer whispered to Hanlon, who never carried a gun.

Hanlon backed away and Haymeyer drew his revolver. He stood to the right of the door, reached out with his left hand, and knocked loudly three times. He pulled his arm back quickly and we all waited. I heard nothing — not even a breath. Earl waited about a full minute and knocked again, leaning his ear near the door, but keeping back far enough to avoid any firing from inside.

Ewald slipped behind Haymeyer and handed him a thin strip of metal. Haymeyer deftly jimmied the lock, turned the knob, and pushed the door open, again stepping back behind the wall. With his pistol out front, he edged into the doorway and flipped on the light. Ewald and Davis followed him and opened the bedroom, bathroom, and closet doors. "It's empty," Haymeyer called out. Hanlon and I joined them.

It took over an hour to go through the pockets of all of Mr. Franklin's clothes. Hanlon was angry. Haymeyer was determined. I moved a pair of old shoes so I could look deeper into a closet and noticed that one shoe felt heavier than the other. I put them next to each other on the bed and called for Earl. Everyone hurried into the room.

"One of those shoes has something in it," I said, backing away as if the shoes were contaminated.

"It's probably a sock," Hanlon said.

Haymeyer picked up one shoe. He hit it on the toe end. Nothing. He tossed it back into the closet. Taking the other shoe carefully in his hands, he sat on the bed. "Uh-huh," he said, looking at Hanlon. "We've got something here."

Something was stuck deep in the toe end of the shoe. Haymeyer tapped it twice but it didn't move. He held the shoe up to the light and peeked in the end. "It feels hard." He shook the shoe and tapped it two more times. When he squeezed the sole from both sides and held the shoe vertically, heel down, the obstruction was freed and slid into view. A *Smith & Wesson .22*.

"Bingo," Hanlon said quietly as Haymeyer looked up and into each face. "Pretty as you please."

The Chicago crime lab called Hanlon four hours after the gun had been delivered. The weapon was completely clean of fingerprints, had not been fired for years, had one empty shell, and a test bullet had markings that matched perfectly the markings on the bullet found in Richard Wanmacher's skull. The gun was registered to George Franklin.

"We've got our murder weapon, but the grand jury won't like where we found it," Hanlon said.

Meanwhile, Larry Shipman had been playing up to Salerno, flattering, idolizing, baiting; Salerno had eaten it up. He was keeping Larry up-to-date every day. "Salerno says the plant was the old lady's idea," Barnes reported.

"Maybe she's not so smart as we thought," Hanlon said.

"I don't know," Haymeyer countered. "If I were her, I'd want someone other than the organization to have that gun, and I'd want them to find it just where we found it."

"Salerno told Shipman that the old lady insisted on the plant in exchange for future favors," Barnes said. "Whatever that means."

"It could mean a lot of things," Haymeyer said. "Who knows what they've got on the docket? Maybe a raft of syndicate trials are in the works."

"That's not all," Barnes said. "Salerno told Shipman that the bartender at Mr. Franklin's favorite watering hole is going to swear that on the night of the murder he heard Franklin vow to kill Wanmacher."

"Where were you that night?" Haymeyer asked Mr. Franklin. "When was it again?"

"November eleventh, nineteen seventy."

"I couldn't tell you, but I've been in *The Place* bar almost every evening for the last ten years, so that's a good bet. I know the bartender well, and I can't believe he's going to testify I talked about Wanmacher."

"I wouldn't be too sure," said Barnes. "According to Salerno, the place belongs to the syndicate."

"If he does say that, he's lying. I never bad-mouthed Wanmacher to anyone but Virginia, and even then I had no idea she was seeing him. I might have been capable of killing him, had I known, but I didn't."

"Of course you didn't, Daddy." Margo was crying. "How is this thing going to end?"

No one knew, so we said nothing. Margo's question rang in our ears and haunted us for the next three days. Mr. Franklin listened courteously as Margo told him that God loved him and would carry him through this. "Your mother always said my job was my god, honey," he'd say, at least once a day. "I guess she was right."

"Do the people who work for you know where you are now?" Barnes asked one day, just making conversation.

"Only Bernie. He's my right-hand man. He always knows where I am. I'm nothing without Bernie. He won't tell anyone. Watches out for me like a mother hen. Everyone else thinks I'm on vacation."

"Would Bernie know where you were the night Wanmacher was murdered?" Barnes asked, his mind working double-time.

"It wouldn't surprise me. He's got a memory for things like that. I'll bet he'd know where he was when he first heard about it. That's the kind of a guy he is."

Barnes grabbed the phone. "It'd be something if I helped break this case, wouldn't it?" He smiled and looked at each of us. It wasn't just the recognition he wanted. Margo and I had decided that Jim Barnes cared a lot about us. "How do I get ahold of Bernie?"

Mr. Franklin dug out his own business card. "Just ask for him at this number."

"Bernie? This is Jim Barnes, special agent in the office of U.S. Attorney James A. Hanlon. Listen carefully, please. I am with your boss, Mr. Franklin. He tells me you have a sharp memory for detail. Before answering, I want you to listen to my question two ways. Whichever jogs your memory, answer it. This is very important to Mr. Franklin and could help us a great deal.

"I want to know if you have any idea where Mr. Franklin was on the night of November eleven, nineteen seventy. Now, don't answer yet. I know your memory isn't quite that good. Let me ask it this way. Now, think. Are you familiar with the Richard Wanmacher murder? . . . Good. I want to know if you can remember where you were when you first read or heard about it." Barnes kept his ear to the phone for a moment, then wheeled around and frowned at Mr. Franklin. "He wants to talk to you. He remembers, but he doesn't want to tell me."

George Franklin took the phone. "What is it, Bernie? . . . Oh, that's right! You were with me . . . No, it's all right. Listen, tell Mr. Barnes here. It's OK, Bernie. It's great. Tell him."

Barnes was ecstatic. "You'll swear to this in court if necessary? . . . Super! Now don't tell anyone anything, not about this call, not about anything."

"Well, where were you?" Margo asked when neither Barnes nor her father offered any information. Mr. Franklin cocked his head. Barnes shook his.

"I'm sitting on this one," he said. "I'm gonna hold it as our ace."

"Even from us?" I demanded. "Come on, Jim, this is stupid. You can tell us. Why can't you tell us?" I was livid. So was Margo.

"*You're* going to tell us, aren't you, Daddy?"

"Not unless Jim here gives the OK."

"Come on, Jim," Margo and I said in unison. He just grinned.

It was his, all his, and he wanted to tell Haymeyer and Hanlon. His chance came when they arrived early that evening. He hustled them into the empty room and all we could hear was Hanlon smacking his hands together and Haymeyer asking if he'd checked it out. "No," Barnes said. "I just believed him."

They came back into our room. "It's not a matter of doubting his story, Jim," Haymeyer was saying, irritated. "It's just a matter of being sure. And there's only one way of being sure. Check it out."

Barnes took the phone behind the door and did whatever checking he hadn't done with whatever source he'd been reminded of.

"Why can't we know?" I asked Hanlon.

"The fewer who know, the better," he said.

"Who would I tell?"

"Maybe Mrs. Franklin."

"I'm going to see her again?"

"Tomorrow."

"Why?"

"Because we're going over there to mess her mind a little."

"Haymeyer and I already tried that once, remember? It didn't seem to bother her in the least."

"Well, it'll bother her tomorrow," Hanlon said. "We're going to ask her to appear before a grand jury to tell why her former husband might have had a motive to kill Richard Wanmacher."

"Can't I know before we go what you found out about Mr. Franklin?"

"No."

We visited Mrs. Franklin at her home the next afternoon.

She greeted each with a smile and a nod and a mention of his name. "Earl. *Philip.*" So the masquerade was over and we were into the heavy stuff. She knew me, as she had all along.

Mrs. Franklin asked us to sit down, and she pulled her long lounging gown up under her and sat on the couch. She was totally collected.

"I think you know why we're here," Hanlon began.

"You're going to have to tell me," she said, smiling, and I knew she wanted to add, "just like you'll have to work for every other tidbit in this case."

"We're here to ask you to testify for us. I want you to tell the grand jury why your former husband might have had a motive for killing Richard Wanmacher."

Virginia Franklin never flinched. "I had heard, of course, that George was somehow implicated in the murder. How did you come to suspect him?"

"An anonymous tip led us to his place, where the murder weapon was found. Everything matched."

"Well, I'm afraid I won't be of much help to you, Jim," Mrs. Franklin said. "I can think of no reason why George would have wanted to murder Mr. Wanmacher. They were only casual acquaintances, and George never had anything but good things to say about him as I recall."

Hanlon sat dumbfounded, trying desperately to take it all in stride. He had expected Mrs. Franklin to appear shocked that George had been accused, but to admit quickly that she had always wondered.

"He didn't suspect that you were seeing Wanmacher?" Hanlon tried, putting into Judge Franklin's mouth the words he had so badly wanted to hear.

"Seeing Mr. Wanmacher?" Virginia repeated. "Did George say that? I never saw him, as you put it, and if George thought I did, he was wrong. Our marriage had ended long before Mr. Wanmacher was murdered, as I recall. Anyway, Mr. Wanmacher was a married man."

She said it as if she were just slightly insulted that Jim Hanlon would dare to accuse her of seeing him. By calling me by name, she had as much as admitted that she knew what was going on, but she was giving Hanlon nothing. Framing Mr. Franklin was her idea, but now she refused to help put him away.

"Well, there's no reason to call you as a witness for the prosecution then, is there?" Hanlon said.

"You could call me, Jim, but I'm afraid I wouldn't help your case."

On the way back, Hanlon was stony. "Why doesn't she jump at the chance to put him away? It would take the heat off her and she'd be home free. Until we spring George's alibi."

"Maybe it looked like a trap to her, Jim," Haymeyer said. "It was coming too easy, right to her doorstep. Sure, it was her idea, but maybe she didn't expect us to run to it so eagerly. She knows we suspect her. She figured we'd only reluctantly switch to suspecting her husband. When it happened so fast, she smelled a rat."

"You're probably right," Hanlon said, banging his open palm on the steering wheel.

"Does she think we'll go ahead and prosecute George?"

"I doubt it," Haymeyer said. "We've got enough on him, especially if that bartender is ready to come forward and testify against him. But she knows we know George didn't do it. The only thing we'd gain by trying him would be to taint her reputation. It would have to come out that she was seeing Wanmacher, and that would hurt her."

"She's got us over a barrel," Hanlon said. "The grand jury is going to insist we file against George, and we'll have to pull his alibi out of the hat now."

"That's it!" Haymeyer said. "She knows nothing about the alibi, so she thinks George will be charged. She can protect her reputation while George is being set up by the bartender. She looks lily white, and we've got the murder weapon, found in his apartment. She can even come to his defense somewhat with that no-motive line of hers, knowing full well that we've got enough to nail him."

"There might be a way to get her," Hanlon said. "Let's have Philip tell her about Mr. Franklin's alibi. How would she react to that?"

Haymeyer was puzzled. "I don't get it, Jim."

"We'll have Philip tell her he got permission from us to see her. He can appear to be foolishly telling her our plans, acting as if she should just turn herself in because we've got her figured out."

"So what will come of that?" Haymeyer persisted.

"I can only hope, Earl. What have we got now? It's only a matter of hours before the press and the public start asking for my head or Mr. Franklin's conviction. Our backs are to the wall. We've got to try to rattle her."

"You should know by now that she doesn't rattle."

"But something *has* to get to her."

At Hanlon's office I was briefed for two hours and then taken back to the hotel. Margo was anxious to hear what had happened, but I was too tired to talk. Haymeyer filled her in, and I went to bed. The next morning I was to call Mrs. Franklin and tell her that I had been given permission to talk with her about the whole matter. My head was crammed with alternate responses to every possible reaction she might have during our conversation.

I didn't sleep well and often caught myself wide-eyed in the darkness, trying to imagine meeting with her alone. More than once I dozed off, dreaming that I had already called her and that I was now in her living room. I had told her that I knew everything and had asked her if she could tell me how much of it was true. In my dream she sat prettily as usual and smiled at me but would not answer. She looked right through me. I wasn't there. She wasn't real. She didn't breathe or move or blink. She just sat, looking, smiling, silent. Then I would open my eyes and stare again into the darkness and try to pray. *Lord, let this end for Margo's sake.*

Once I woke near dawn and realized that it was Sunday. I wondered if Hanlon and Haymeyer would let me take Margo to church. That possibility made me forget about my meeting with Judge Franklin, but only temporarily.

By 7:00 A.M. I was more exhausted than when I had gone to bed. I showered and dressed and knocked on Mr. Franklin's door. He and Margo were already up.

"How is she?" I whispered.

"She didn't sleep well. You don't look so good either."

"I think I'll just sit around for a while," I said. "Tell Margo I'll see her in an hour or so."

I stuck my head out the door of the suite and said good morning to Bob Warren who was sitting guard in the hall. He gave me a thumbs-up sign. "Good luck today, Philip." I nodded and went back in to the couch in the sitting room between the bedrooms. I left the lights off.

With my hands folded in my lap I sat nearly dozing for about twenty minutes. It was a melancholy morning. Very quiet. Margo tiptoed out. I didn't look up. "How are you?" she said.

"Dead."

She sat next to me and took my hand in hers. "I've been reading my Bible," she said. Still staring at the floor, I smiled. "That's a good Christian. What were you reading?"

"Psalms."

"I need a psalm today. I'm going to see if I can take you to church."

"I'd like that."

Neither of us spoke for several minutes. I felt lifeless. I was so tired, so mentally drained. Yet I was glad I could try to do something for Margo. As tight as I'd been, and as scared and repulsed as I had been by the danger, I had been through nothing compared to her long ordeal.

I laid my head back on the couch and looked at the ceiling. My breathing was even and deep, as if I were asleep. I was sad for Margo. Poor, sweet Margo, whose nine-year nightmare was coming to life. Despite it all, she was somehow able to be sensitive to me.

Emotion welled up inside me. What a beautiful, beautiful person she had become in just the last few weeks. How could she grow with such pressure?

"I love you, Philip," she said quietly, not raising her head.

It was too much. How could she be thinking of me now? Tears poured from my eyes and rolled over my ears to the back of the couch. Her grip on my hand was steady, and she did not move.

I sat up and buried my head in my hands, sobbing. She put her arm around my shoulder and her tears fell on me.

"I'm not worthy of your love, Margo," I said.

THIRTEEN

By 9:00 A.M. our suite was crowded. United States Attorney James A. Hanlon brought Earl Haymeyer and Agents Ewald and Davis to join Jim Barnes and Bob Warren. Larry Shipman had been "released" from jail and came to report on the latest from Salerno, which wasn't much.

Salerno had been strangely quiet for the last two days, except for grumbling that his lawyer, Frederick Wahl, was trying to get him sent back to Atlanta to answer the attempted murder charges. "It's as if he wants me sent up," Salerno has groused to Shipman. "I'm guilty down there."

"Are you guilty up here?" Shipman had asked him.

"Sure. But with old lady Franklin stonewalling it, they've got nothing on me. If they get me up here, I'm taking Wahl with me. He was there when I got the assignment from Judge Franklin to scare her daughter. And he was the one who put the fifty-G price tag on Margo's head."

Margo winced.

"You sure you want to hear this?" Hanlon asked.

She nodded.

"Maybe we should admit that we're not going to file charges against Salerno right away," Haymeyer said. "To keep from getting shipped back to Atlanta, he might rat on the judge, and on Wahl."

"It's a thought," Hanlon said. "Let's see how hard Wahl pushes for his release. I'm sure the whole organization is nervous about having a restless big-mouth behind bars, especially one who sees little hope.

"Anyway, people," Hanlon continued, addressing the whole group and reminding me of a grade school teacher I'd had in Dayton, "today is a big day. If we can't get Mrs. Franklin to tip her hand, we're going to tip it for her. Earl is heading the strategic end of things, as usual, and he has instructions for everyone."

Hanlon stepped over Mr. Franklin and sat on the couch. Haymeyer began: "Philip will call Mrs. Franklin in about ten minutes and ask to see her at one o'clock at her home. He has already been briefed on how the conversation should go. Right now it all hinges on Mrs. Franklin's availability.

"Agents Ewald and Davis will stay with Mr. Franklin and Margo here. Mr. Hanlon and I will follow Philip in one car as far as the northern limits of Chicago, and then we'll circle back. Jim Barnes will pick up the tail there and will follow Philip to Winnetka. Then he'll circle back.

"Bob Warren will be under a blanket in the back of Philip's car and will remain there all the time Philip is with Mrs. Franklin. By following Philip in two separate cars and having Bob in his car, we'll be able to protect Philip from any interference, although we don't expect any.

"Bob will have a radio, so we can contact Philip if we think he's being followed."

I raised my hand. "Any chance I could take Margo to church this morning?"

Haymeyer looked at Hanlon who gave him an it's-your-case shrug. "Let me think about that," Haymeyer said. "If you choose a church in the suburbs it might be a good way for us to test our surveillance plan. I'll let you know.

"Anyway, Philip, when you're through talking with Mrs. Franklin, just head right for Mr. Hanlon's office. We are fairly certain you will be followed from Winnetka, even if you aren't followed on your way there. If these guys don't know where this hotel is by now, there's no sense leading them straight to it."

"They have to know where it is by now, don't they Earl?" Davis asked.

"We've always taken different cars and different routes," Haymeyer said. "But I wouldn't be surprised if they're watching. That's why you and Ewald will stay here. I don't care if they know where we are, as long as they know they can't get to our people.

"It's time for Philip to call Mrs. Franklin. Let's have total silence while he's on the phone."

My hand shook as I dialed. As Mrs. Franklin's phone rang for the fourth time I looked up at Haymeyer. "She's got to be there," he said. "Where would she go this early on a Sunday?"

"Certainly not to church," Margo said.

"Franklin residence."

I was surprised it wasn't Mrs. Franklin. "Uh, yes, uh, Mrs. Virginia Franklin, please."

"I'm afraid she's sleeping right now, sir. May I take your name and number?"

"Just a minute," I said, covering the mouthpiece. "It's some woman, the cleaning lady, I suppose. Mrs. Franklin's asleep. Should I leave this number?"

Hanlon shook his head vigorously and barked rapidfire instructions: "Tell her it's very important to wake Mrs. Franklin. She'll talk to you."

"It's very important that I talk to her," I said. "Could you wake her and tell her it's Philip Spence?"

"I hate to, sir. I have strict orders."

"Tell her that I insisted. I'll take the blame."

"One moment, sir."

My heart pounded. "Be cool," Haymeyer whispered.

"Easier said than — hello? Mrs. Franklin? I'm sorry to bother you so early."

"That's all right, Philip," she said huskily. "I'm embarrassed to be sleeping so late. What can I do for you?"

"I'd like to see you today, if I could."

She hesitated. "Alone? I mean, I'm not sure I understand."

"I have gotten permission to come and talk with you," She didn't respond, and I didn't know what else to say. I glanced at Haymeyer. He clenched his fist to encourage me. "Your daughter is of mutual interest to us," I said finally. Haymeyer nodded.

"That is true, Philip," she said, immediately cool again. "I don't know what you want to talk about, but I could see you sometime perhaps this evening."

"No, I mean like around one o'clock," I said, wincing.

"Oh, you have a schedule?"

"No, I'm sorry. I guess any time you're free would be OK."

"No problem, Philip. I can see you at one. Where shall we meet?"

"At your house," I said.

"My goodness, you do have it all planned, don't you?"

"I'm sorry," I said. "I — "

"No, no, that's fine, Philip. I'll look forward to seeing you then."

"I almost blew it, huh?" I said after hanging up the phone.

"No." Haymeyer said. "She knows what's happening. The fact is that she's not afraid of you. She'll see you any time anywhere. I don't think she believes this was your idea, which it wasn't. But I'll bet she'll give you an earful today. With no one else listening, she might even talk freely about what's been going on."

"You really think so?"

"Why not? She'll be coy with me or with Hanlon, but she'll probably tell you anything just to scare you or amuse herself. Who's going to believe you? She'll just deny it later, if necessary."

"Then what's the point?"

"The point is that if you can get her to admit she's behind this whole mess, maybe you can start talking about things that will get to her."

"Like what? I haven't seen anyone ruffle her yet."

"Like me," Margo said.

"Right," Haymeyer said. "Like Margo. We can't be sure. Maybe this woman is so cold and calculating that she can't be shaken. And maybe even her own daughter means nothing to her anymore — I'm sorry, Margo, it may be true — but at least it's a chance."

"How about church?" I asked.

"Where?" Haymeyer asked.

We checked the phone book and found a Bible church in Evanston. "How's that?" I asked Haymeyer.

"OK with me. Maybe even perfect. What time would you get out of there?"

"Around twelve thirty or so, I guess."

"Great. Even if she has tipped off anyone that you're coming, they'll never expect you to leave this early. We'll follow you there, and Barnes can follow you from the church to her house.

"What about me?" Barnes asked.

"Good question, Jim," Earl said. "Can you stay in the car all that time?"

"During church? How long is it?"

"Over an hour," I said.

"What if you and Hanlon dropped me off somewhere en route to the Franklin house and Philip could pick me up on his way from the church?"

"OK," Haymeyer said. "Sounds like we're all set."

Margo stepped close to Earl. "No, we're not all set," she whispered. "I want to go with Philip."

"You are going with him, girl. Then, we'll pick you up in the church parking lot when he heads for your mother's house."

"That's what I mean," she said. "I want to go with him to see Mother."

Haymeyer stared at her. "Margo, please let me handle the strategy, will you?"

"I really want to go, Earl. Why can't I?"

Hanlon caught Haymeyer's eye from over Margo's shoulder. He spread his palms as if to ask, "Why not?" Haymeyer glared at his boss. "It's your operation, Earl," Hanlon insisted.

"OK, Margo, listen. We have to talk this over, the boys and I. I'm going to come to a decision while you're in church. If I'm in the parking lot, you come with me, understand?" Margo didn't respond. "If I'm not there, you go with Philip."

Margo's look told Haymeyer she was determined to go with me. "Margo," he said, "I don't want trouble from you. You weren't in on the briefings, you don't know what is supposed to be said or not said. You might just blow the whole thing."

"If my name is supposed to rattle Mother, won't my presence rattle her even more?"

"Is that why you want to go?"

Margo sat down wearily. It was hard for her to talk, and the other agents looked away. "I want to go because I miss my mother, all right?" she said. "Is that a good enough reason? I want to see her again."

"I can sympathize with that," Haymeyer said. "But that feeling is going to make you take her side. You're not going to want to see her break down and admit her part in this, are you?"

"Is that what you think she'll do? You've got her underestimated."

Haymeyer was confused. "Are you proud of your mother's deceit?"

"Do you really think Mother will crack?"

"She just might," he said. "I think Philip is ready for her, and I think if anyone can get to her soft spot, he can."

"Why?"

"Because he loves you."

"How do you know?"

"He told us."

Margo looked quickly at me. She couldn't respond. The news had come to her in the form of a begrudging argument.

Haymeyer continued. "If your mother loves you, she'll feel something toward Philip. She'll understand him a little. She'll sense what he feels for you."

"And if she doesn't still love me?"

"Then maybe he can at least make her feel remorse over what she almost did to you."

"I still want to go."

"Why!? Don't you understand?"

"I understand perfectly. You're the one who doesn't understand, Earl. I want to see my mother one more time before I know for sure that she's the person I've hated all these years. When she admits it, when it's all out in the open, I'm not going to know her. She'll spend the first few minutes with Philip just feeling out where he is. She'll be her old charming self. I want to see her at her best one last time. She so seldom cracks. When she does she's going to be devastated, never to charm anyone again, not even in deceit."

"And what about when Philip nails her to the wall? What about when your presence, and his love for you, and his knowledge of the facts, and the news that she almost got you killed, hits her with full force? Are you going to want to be there then?"

"Yes."

"I can't believe it," Haymeyer said, wheeling around. "How can you say that?"

"Because I don't hate her anymore. You can't understand it, but God has forgiven me for hating her. He's helped me understand her a little. I'm still hurt, and bitter about a lot of things, but Mother suffered too. Her life wasn't what she thought it would be. She tried to take things into her own hands and she hurt herself, she hurt me, she hurt Daddy, she killed Richard, and ruined his wife.

"She's been suffering all along, but she hasn't been able to tell anyone, like I have, and she'll suffer more. I think most of my suffering is past. When Mother's defenses crumble, what will she have? A virtual stranger in her house, zeroing in on her weak spots, haunting her with what she's done to me."

"So what are you going to do, Margo?"

"I'm going to forgive her." The agents traded glances. They thought Margo had flipped, and they appeared anxious to get to Haymeyer so they could advise that she be tranquilized, or at least kept away from Winnetka. "She'll have to answer for everything she's done. I can't and won't try to stand in the way of that, and I'm not saying any of it was justified. But I have no right to avenge what she's done to me. I want her to know that someone still cares about her."

Haymeyer was speechless. When he finally said something, it was to change the subject. "Just in case I decide you can go, Margo, you'll have to be briefed."

While he filled her in, I tried to talk with Mr. Franklin. He looked sick, sitting on the floor with his chin tucked to his chest.

"Philip, how can she love like that? I never loved anyone that much, certainly not Virginia. I hate her. I hated her when she just bugged me to be more image conscious. I hated her more when we got divorced. But when I learned she'd been seeing Wanmacher, and might have killed him, and then scared Margo and almost got her killed, too — "

I put my hand on his shoulder. His words came slowly. "I'll never forgive her for what she's done, and I don't understand how Margo can."

"She can't," I said. "Any more than you can or I can. By ourselves, we aren't capable of that kind of love and forgiveness."

"I know I'm not," he said.

"Only God can love like that," I said. He looked away and nodded, signaling the end of our conversation.

At 10:30 Haymeyer finished with Margo and she went to change clothes. "That's some girl you've got there, Philip. I don't like this, but I'm willing to go along with it. If Mrs. Franklin doesn't come around, don't belabor it. I don't think you should be there for more than an hour."

Haymeyer and Hanlon took Bob Warren in their car and gave me the keys to another. Mr. Franklin stayed with Shipman and Ewald and Davis. Barnes was already on his way to the church, where he would wait to follow us to Winnetka.

Margo sat close to me in the car on the way to Evanston. "So you love me, huh?" she said.

"Not really, but it sounded like the right thing to say at the time."

She smiled. "This still hurts," she said, suddenly serious.

"I believe that," I said.

While we waited for the service to begin, Margo said it had been a long time since we'd been to church together.

"It just seems like a long time. Do you remember what the sermon was about?"

"Hardly. That was the night I was almost killed. All I remember is praying through the whole evening. I'll be praying all morning this time."

"Me too," I said.

"About what?"

"About confronting your mother, of course."

"Not me, I've already got that one settled."

"Then what'll you be praying for?"

"That Haymeyer will see the wisdom of letting me go."

"Why don't you channel your energy into praying for me, then? Haymeyer already told me you could go."

Margo stiffened as we left the church. Haymeyer was in the parking lot. She looked at him defiantly. "I'm going, aren't I?"

"No, Margo, and don't you dare make a scene." He was so forceful that Margo backed down. Haymeyer pulled me away. "We've spotted a tail," he said. "I can't risk Margo's going along. You don't have to go either, you know."

"I'll go."

"Good, but be careful. Don't do anything foolish. Talk straight with Mrs. Franklin; don't take any garbage. You each know exactly what the other is up to, so make sure she understands that. We've already got Warren in your car, so just head up there."

I caught Margo's eye as she walked with Hanlon toward Haymeyer's car. There was no time to say anything. It didn't seem right to leave her that way. I felt incomplete as I pulled out of the lot.

"How you feeling, kid?" I jumped. It was Warren.

"I almost forgot you were back there," I said.

"You better know I'm back here, partner. From what they tell me, you may need me this afternoon."

"Thanks a lot."

"You're just getting straight stuff, Philip. You'll always get straight stuff from me."

"So what's happening, Bob?"

"Well, you were followed to the church. When the car went around the block to find a spot to wait for you to come out, I jumped in here."

Static came from Warren's radio. "Ten-four," he said. "That was Barnes, Philip. We've got ourselves a tail again. Can you see anyone?"

I checked the rearview mirror, as I had all along. "No, is Barnes sure?"

"Of course, he's sure. And you may never see your tail. That's how good they are. Anyway, they know where you're going. They just want to be sure you're alone."

"Would they have spotted Barnes?"

"It's possible, but remember, he's pulling out of the picture as soon as you're in the driveway. They'll quit worrying about him. I'm their problem, and they don't know about me, I hope."

I was sure I'd be blown away when I left the car to go to the house, and told Warren so. He tried to put me at ease. "They don't want you, kid. Anyway, if they *were* going to hit you, they'd do it inside the house."

"*That* helped," I said.

In spite of his reassurances, I never felt so vulnerable as when I was walking toward the front door. I hardly breathed, my heart pounded, my legs wobbled. I rang the bell. The housekeeper, in her coat, opened the door and greeted me. Then she left.

The overdone hospitality of Virginia Franklin was gone. "Hello, Philip," she said, rather formally. "I find it interesting that they sent you in to do battle with me."

"Maybe it's because I love your daughter. Do you?"

"It's irrelevant. What is relevant is how you're going to try to break me. How are you?"

"I just tried. I guess I'm through. If your daughter means anything to you, what can I say?"

"Not much. But as long as you're here, why don't you tell me how Hanlon's case against me is going?"

"Oh, I imagine you know."

"Yes, I suppose I do. Any new developments?"

"What do you know already, Mrs. Franklin?"

"Well, I know Hanlon's aware of my dealings with Wahl and Salerno. That was rather transparent, but hard to prove." Her eyes danced. "How're they going to prove that one, Philip?" I shrugged. She settled back comfortably on her couch.

"They've got Olga's word on the blackmail money. Again, hard to prove, right?"

I shrugged again. I was appalled. What a contrast she was to the charming woman I had met earlier.

"They've got Margo's word on my affair with Richard. Impossible to prove, in spite of Olga's corroboration. You see, my husband was always totally ignorant of that relationship. He hasn't got the guts to lie, so he could never testify against me. Who would believe him anyway? If he said it, he would seal his own doom. You know what they've got on him already."

I nodded.

"Well, Philip. Where am I weak? I've got a former husband who still finds it hard to believe that I killed a man. As much as he can't stand me, he's going to pay for my crime. Isn't that nice of him? And I've got a tacky so-called daughter who thinks her testimony about my midnight ride is going to put me in my place. What do they have on me, Philip? What's going to do me in?"

"Three things," I said, surprising myself with my calm.

"I can't wait to hear them," she said, edging forward. She was loving it.

"First will be the syndicate."

"Oh, come now. Who's going to believe I would deal with such low-down characters?" She was smiling.

"Let me finish." She nodded. "It's not someone finding out about your dealing with them. It's them. They don't like to owe favors."

"They can't help it. They need me."

"You're not letting me finish. I've got three points, and I'm not through with the first one yet."

"Oh, that's naughty of me, isn't it, and me a judge at that. I'm so sorry, Mr. Spence. Please continue."

"The syndicate doesn't need anyone they can't scare. What would you say if I told you that what happened in Atlanta was a mistake?"

"I'd say you were wrong. It worked perfectly according to plan, except that Earl Haymeyer sniffed it out. No harm done. It was a scare job, anyway. Salerno might do some time, but my mission was accomplished."

"Yours was, but Wahl's wasn't."

"Is this point number two?"

"No, we're still on number one. Wahl promised Salerno fifty thousand dollars if he killed Margo."

"Nonsense. Salerno never got fifty for a job in his life. Anyway, he'd never hit a woman. And why would Wahl want Margo hit?"

"To show you where you stood. You see, Wahl had you misjudged almost as drastically as you had him misjudged. He thought your daughter was dear to you and that was the only reason you wanted her scared instead of murdered."

Mrs. Franklin threw her head back and looked at the ceiling. The position of her neck made her sound laryngitic. "You don't know what you're talking about," she said.

"Don't I? Let me ask you something. If your daughter means nothing to you, why didn't you just have her killed? It would have looked like revenge from the mob for past sentences you've handed down. Margo would have been silenced for good. You wouldn't have cared, would you? She's a tacky, so-called daughter, right?"

"Philip, how do you know they were going to cross me and kill Margo?"

"Let's get to point number two, shall we?" I said. She was so seldom frustrated that I wanted to milk it, but she wouldn't let go.

"Tell me how you know this."

She had put me in the driver's seat. "All right," I said. "Through Salerno. He's a big-mouth. One of Hanlon's men got next to him in jail, and Salerno's been singing ever since. He doesn't much like the idea of going back to Atlanta to face attempted murder charges either. He's going to tell about conspiring with you to scare Margo, and he'll implicate Wahl in the process."

"Nonsense. Wahl will call him a liar and so will I. Who would ever believe I conspired with a mobster to scare my own daughter?"

"Maybe you're right," I said. "Margo finds it hard to believe."

"En garde, eh?"

"You're more naive than I thought, Mrs. Franklin. If you think Wahl is with you, why did he promise Salerno a bundle to kill Margo?"

"I still don't believe that one."

"You could take my word for it. But then, what do I know? I'm the one who thought you still had a shred of love left for Margo. Don't you even care to know how she is?"

"Sure. Why not? As long as you're here, how is Margo?"

"You're trying too hard, Mrs. Franklin. You're dying for some word from Margo."

She stood. "I'm not! She abandoned me when I needed her. I tried to get close to her, but she kept taunting and accusing."

Something had broken loose in Judge Franklin. She was defending her feelings toward Margo.

"Why do you hate her?" I asked.

"Because she wouldn't respond. I had no one. I tried to make up to her. I bought her things, I paid her way to Atlanta, I started a savings account for her. She left me alone."

"She's sorry," I said. "That's point number two."

"Don't give me that," Mrs. Franklin spit out, turning quickly and facing me. "She can't throw an apology in my face. Who does she think she is?"

"Didn't you just say she abandoned you? She wants your forgiveness."

Mrs. Franklin snorted and threw her head back. She began to speak but just let out a loud sigh. She set her jaw and returned to the couch. As she sat down, she hid her face and fought tears. "If I forgive her, she'll have to forgive me." She paused. "And how could she?"

Mrs. Franklin thrust her hands beneath her and sat staring at the floor. I began to tell her of the Margo she never knew. "I met her in the Atlanta Tower," I said. The judge nodded in recognition. "Not in the second-floor restaurant," I said. "On the thirtieth floor. She was about to jump out the window." Mrs. Franklin's shoulders tightened, but still she wouldn't look at me. "I talked her out of it by telling her that Someone loved her, that Someone cared. It was hard for her to believe, but it worked because she wanted so desperately for it to be true.

"I told her that God loved her. Do you want to know what she told me?"

Mrs. Franklin made no response.

"She told me that she started gaining weight when she lost her security at home. She dreamed of the good old days. She'd see you and Mr. Franklin sleeping in separate rooms, treating each other like neighbors, and she'd cry herself to sleep. All she could think of was her childhood. Trips to the zoo with Mommy and Daddy."

"Don't," Mrs. Franklin whispered, but I continued.

"Being carried when she was too tired to walk. Seeing you and your husband look into each other's eyes."

Mrs. Franklin hid her eyes with one hand and waved at me with the other. She'd had enough. I leaned forward. We were sitting directly across from each other, almost knee to knee.

"Well," she said finally, "it was a gallant effort, and I commend you. But I have come too far. I'll not be giving it up this easily." She forced a smile.

"What do I tell Margo? That you refused to forgive her?"

"Just tell her she's not going to con me into asking her forgiveness by pretending that she wants mine."

"You don't have to ask for her forgiveness, Mrs. Franklin. She asked me to tell you that it's yours already, no strings attached. Whether you ask for it or not."

Her lips trembled and she turned her head away. Then her mouth curled into a smirk. "That's just too touching," she said, dripping sarcasm. "I've come this far — I'll keep going."

I stood and began moving toward the door. Mrs. Franklin didn't move. "Don't think you've got me on the ropes, Philip. I'm fully aware that you haven't gotten around to point number three. The first two didn't do me in, as you promised. I want to hear number three."

"I'm embarrassed," I said. "Frankly, I never thought we'd get to three."

"Had me underestimated, did you?"

"For sure," I said. "Anyway, Mr. Hanlon told me that he would have to deliver point number three personally. And he also advises that you have a lawyer present."

"It must be a winner," she said, never missing a beat, though her face still betrayed her cocky tone. "His place or mine?"

FOURTEEN

Amos Chakaris, a former Illinois secretary of state and semiretired lawyer, arrived at Hanlon's office with Mrs. Franklin early in the evening. He was a tall, fat, white-haired man, obviously an old friend of both Mrs. Franklin and James Hanlon. The United States attorney seemed surprised and genuinely pleased to see Chakaris.

Mrs. Franklin showed little surprise at seeing Margo, except to comment on her weight loss. Margo looked as if she wanted to run to her mother and began to cry softly when the judge treated her as if she were a casual acquaintance.

"Now what's this all about?" Mrs. Franklin asked sweetly, as soon as we had all been seated. "And where's everyone else?"

"You know where they are, Virginia," Hanlon said. "And you also know what this is all about."

"You'd better let me speak for you, Virginia," Chakaris said. "Jim, is my client about to be arrested and charged?"

"Yes, unless she chooses to cooperate."

Chakaris appeared slightly amused. He was genuinely convinced that Virginia Franklin could not be guilty of anything serious enough to involve the United States attorney. "Virginia has told me nothing, Jim," he said. "What is this, some sort of conflict of interest or complicity?"

Mrs. Franklin smirked at Hanlon behind her lawyer's back. "So you're even going to make it hard on Amos, huh, judge?" Hanlon said.

"Why am I here?" she said, brows raised.

Chakaris leaned close to whisper to Hanlon. "Jimmy, we've known each other a long time. Can't we clear this up without these kids here?"

"They aren't kids. This is the judge's daughter and her boyfriend. They're as involved as anyone. Amos, we're filing charges against Mrs. Franklin for the murder of Richard Wanmacher and conspiracy to —"

Chakaris leaped from his chair and began stomping back and forth, rubbing his hand over his mouth. "Why didn't you tell me, Ginny?" he complained. "I can't come in here prepared to represent you unless I hear your side."

"My side of what?" she asked. "What's it all about, Amos?"

Chakaris pulled Hanlon off to the side and demanded to know why Mrs. Franklin hadn't been informed. "She knows," Hanlon insisted. "Can't you see this is a game? We've got her dead to rights. I've got a secret grand jury testimony, a deposition from Margo, and evidence of syndicate involvement."

Chakaris looked at Margo and me over his shoulder and pulled Hanlon into the hall. Mrs. Franklin edged forward and patted Margo on the knee. "So how've you been?" she said. Margo pulled away.

"I don't know you," she said.

"You never have," Virginia said. Margo hung her head.

"You are too much," Haymeyer said.

"Hello, Earl," Mrs. Franklin replied kindly.

I couldn't believe it. She casually lit a cigarette, crossed her legs, and let her shoe dangle from her toe.

Chakaris and Hanlon returned after several minutes. "I want to talk to my client," the old lawyer said.

"I have nothing to tell you," Mrs. Franklin told him. "I'm totally in the dark on this, and I simply want to go home as soon as you clear it up."

"Then maybe I should tell *you* what it's all about," Chakaris said.

"I'd rather hear it from Mr. Hanlon," she said, smiling.

Chakaris spread his hands, palms up, and shrugged. "Do your thing, Jim."

Hanlon turned to Haymeyer. Earl stood and faced Mrs. Franklin who remained seated.

"Mrs. Virginia Franklin?" Earl began. She cocked her head in affirmation. "You are under arrest for the murder of Richard Wanmacher and for conspiring to obstruct justice by contracting with Frederick Wahl and Antonio Salerno to keep Margo Franklin from coming forward with evidence in a murder case. You have the right to remain silent."

"I am quite aware of my rights, Earl, thank you very much. My legal counsel is here, and I waive the right to silence."

"Not so fast, Virginia," Chakaris said.

Mrs. Franklin turned icy. "I'm not guilty, Amos, and I will not go to trial. I want countercharges filed. I am being charged without evidence, and I want to see Mr. Hanlon suffer for this. I happen to know that my former husband murdered Richard, and that Jim here has the evidence to prove it."

"Yes, Mrs. Franklin, I do have some evidence here against your former husband," Hanlon said. "Would you care to see it?"

The judge eyed him warily, then shifted her eyes to Chakaris who sat down and turned away from her.

"What is it?" she asked.

"Do you know Bernie?" Hanlon said, toying with her.

"Bernie who? You mean George's Bernie? Of course. He'll do anything for George. Run for his paper, run for his slippers, just like a puppy dog."

"Well, Bernie remembers where he heard about the Wanmacher murder."

"Good for Bernie," Mrs. Franklin said, attempting to regain her composure. "All George ever talked about was Bernie's memory." She dragged on her cigarette, but kept her squinting eyes on him.

"He got the word about the murder before the newspapers did, Virginia," Hanlon said gently. "He got the word from a desk sergeant at the sixteenth precinct station. Know why he was there?"

Mrs. Franklin waved him on.

"He was bailing George out of the drunk tank. George had been there from two hours before the murder until nearly dawn. I have here a copy of the log sheet, verifying that he was behind bars while Richard Wanmacher was being murdered."

Hanlon held the log sheet before Mrs. Franklin's eyes. She looked past it to his face, her lips tight. She whirled to face Margo. "All right!" she said. "I can't protect you any longer!" Margo's mouth dropped open. "She did it," Mrs. Franklin said. "She thought Richard had broken up our family and — "

"It won't wash, Virginia," Haymeyer broke in. "We have Olga's testimony that Margo never left the house that night. And we have both Olga's and Margo's word that you left in plenty of time and were gone long enough to have shot Wanmacher."

Chakaris stood and thrust his mammoth hands into his pockets. He sat down again immediately when Margo stood and faced Mrs. Franklin.

"Mother, you are killing me." Margo said, on the verge of tears. "You wanted me scared into silence and almost got me killed, and now I wish you had. I thought the last nine years were a nightmare, but this is unbelievable. What will you come up with next?

"Doesn't it matter to you that you're pulling this on your own daughter? I knew you when you were warm and good. What are you now? When I realized what you had done and how far you had gone to cover up, I remembered the good times and took some solace in them. Now what am I to do? You're erasing my good memories. All I see is this woman I don't know. Do you know my mother?"

Mrs. Franklin looked at her quizzically.

"I used to call her Mommy," Margo continued. "She loved me and she loved my daddy and she was warm and kind and good. I haven't seen her for years. Do you know her?"

Mrs. Franklin bit her lip. She trembled.

"Mother, no one believes you. What you need is support and forgiveness. And you have it."

"I do? From where?" Mrs. Franklin's eyes were ablaze.

"From me."

"Have I *hurt* you?"

"What do *you* think?"

Mrs. Franklin put out the cigarette she'd been ignoring. She spoke slowly, "I don't think, Margo. I haven't thought for years. When I think, I hurt. When I think of what your life must be like, I hurt."

"Well, I've hurt too, Mother. And I'm hurting now. I thought I was hurting before, but I didn't know the meaning of the word. Seeing you like this hurts me more than anything."

"Stop! Why are you doing this to me, Margo? Don't you think I know what I've been doing? How much do you think I can take? Sure you've been hurt, but look what I've been through. What do I have left? I know I'm grabbing at thin air, but air is all I've got. Now you stand here and tell me I'm not what I used to be. That I'm killing you by being this way. Well, I ask you, what am I supposed to be like? What is the dignified thing to do now?"

Margo stared at her mother. "I want you to accept my forgiveness."

Virginia's face was contorted. She shook her head. "You can't forgive me," she said. "You simply cannot. I won't let you. It's impossible."

"You don't want my forgiveness?"

"What will it do for me? Your forgiveness would belittle me — crush me. I would be humiliated even more, if that's possible."

"But I offer love."

"Margo, you're loving my memory. You can't love me now."

"I can and I do."

"You can't love me!"

"God is loving you through me." Margo's tears were flowing freely now. "I hate the things you do, and I pity you. But God lets me love you in spite of myself."

Mrs. Franklin broke down. I thought I'd never see her cry. "Margo, Margo," she said. "What should I do?"

Margo embraced her. "Give it up, Mother. Just give it up."

"I'll suffer. I'll pay. You know I'll be sentenced. And I'll be alone."

Margo held her closer.

"You'll never be alone. God loves you, Mother. I love you. You'll always have me."

And Margo would always have me.

KARLYN

If Margo meant what she said about the fact that her mother would always have her, what would it mean to Philip and Margo's future? If her mother was indeed sentenced to prison, as the woman herself had predicted, Margo's life would continue in chaos.

Who is leaving threatening messages in Karlyn's apartment, and why? And what can Margo or Philip do about it?

ONE

VIRGINIA FRANKLIN WOULD BE SENTENCED TODAY. As painful as that would be for her, not to mention her daughter, Margo, a major chapter in my life would echo shut with her cell door — and I couldn't deny that I was glad.

Margo was quiet, almost icy, as we drove to the Lake County, Illinois, circuit court with James Hanlon and Earl Haymeyer not far behind. The arraignment and brief trial had been as rough on Margo as everything that had led to her mother's confession. But the sentencing, which promised no surprises unless the judge had been stricken with some overwhelming compassion or — to read the newspaper accounts — some incredible stupidity the night before, would prove even rougher.

Amos Chakaris, the former Illinois secretary of state and semiretired lawyer representing Mrs. Franklin, had won several concessions in the case, in spite of heavy civic and media pressure to see the full brunt of the law fall on Judge Franklin.

Chakaris had so far kept her out of jail. The usual bond in such a case is about a quarter of a million dollars, of which the defendant must come up with ten percent. Probably because the defendant in this case was a Cook County circuit court judge, the Lake County judge quadrupled the figure.

Mrs. Franklin's former husband, George, on whom she had tried to blame the murder at one point, offered to post the $100,000. She refused his offer, so he set up a legal defense fund for her. When he received virtually no contributions, he announced that an anonymous donor had come up with the money.

Her temporary freedom allowed Virginia no false optimism. During the more than four months since her original confession, she seemed to worry most about the conditions she would face at the women's facility in the Pontiac State Penitentiary.

She had not been a circuit judge in the criminal courts for sixteen years without knowing that she would be sentenced, pure and simple. A plea bargain to lessen the charge from first to second degree murder was successful, provided that Chakaris not seek any more concessions. He agreed, and the next day inadvertently broke his promise.

"Your Honor," he had said at the obligatory evidence trial, "there is the matter of protective custody when my client is incarcerated."

"Mr. Chakaris, I made it very clear yesterday that there would be precious few luxuries allowed in this hearing. On the other hand the court is grateful for the cooperation the defense has exhibited to this point in not dragging this out more than necessary."

"If Your Honor please," Chakaris continued, "I believe this is a matter of utmost urgency and see it as much more than a luxury. The very life of my client may depend on it."

"On protective custody?"

"Absolutely. Judge Franklin will encounter women in that facility whom she has sent there. And even the ones she hasn't sent there will know who she is and will be more than happy to strike back at authority by humiliating her and possibly even attacking her. I would request that Your Honor consider stipulating that she be segregated from the general prison population."

The judge agreed to consider it, but there was little more to hope for other than the reduction of the charge. That probably would make the difference between a life sentence and one of ten to twenty years (with parole consideration allowed after three years, but highly unlikely).

The newspapers and the public had reacted as you would expect to a pious judge who not only murders her lover — who happens to be an assistant state's attorney — but then also tries another man for that very crime, scares her daughter by nearly having her killed, works with the syndicate to implicate her own husband, and avoids suspicion for nearly nine years.

Now her quick confession and eagerness to take her punishment rang hollow in everyone's ears. They wanted to see her all but strung up, and no Lake County judge was about to risk his reputation by slapping her wrist.

The judge had at first resisted Chakaris's plea for a reduced charge in exchange for her cooperation, but the prosecution encouraged him to concede it if she would implicate syndicate leaders as well. What it boiled down to was that all her collusion and related crimes were ignored, the charge was reduced, and the judge would consider having her segregated at Pontiac. That was as far as he would go. The sentencing itself would tell how tough and/or dramatic he wanted to be with a courtroom full of reporters.

Margo stared out the window on her side of the car. I reached across the back of the seat to touch her shoulder. I felt her relax until I said, "Well, what do you think will happen today?"

She turned sharply toward me and stared until I was forced to take my eyes from the road and return her gaze. When I looked back to watch the road, she said, "You make it sound like a basketball game. Who's gonna win?"

"I didn't mean to make it sound that way, Margo. I just know you're as curious as I am about the possibilities."

"Curious? That's what you think I've been? Curious?"

"Margo, please," I said. "Don't accuse me of being insensitive. You know that even if it didn't come out right, I didn't mean anything by it."

She looked away again, and I felt as if a heat lamp had been turned off. "So what do you think will happen?" she asked. "Be honest. I want to know what you really think."

"I'm not optimistic," I admitted.

"I'm not either," she said. "What do Earl and Jim think?"

"The same."

"Wonderful," she said sadly.

The parking lot was crowded and the press was coming. By now they knew "Margo's guy" had been heavily involved in the investigation. The first parking place I found was too close to the surge of reporters. I backed out quickly and wheeled around to the back of the building.

It was no use; we weren't going to get inside without having to answer questions. "I really don't need this today," Margo said, as if she might need it some other time.

I would have thought we had been asked everything in the book and that the media would grow tired of us, but we got the same questions every time. "Is it true you're secretly married?"

"No."

"Are you living together?"

"No!"

"Are you going to be married?"

"I haven't been asked yet," Margo said.

"Are you going to ask her?"

"No comment."

"If he asks you, will you accept?"

"No comment."

"You mean you might not?"

"I mean I don't know. I'll think about it if it happens. Excuse us, please."

"Where will you live? What will you do? Do you think your mother will be sentenced for life?"

"Please!" I said. "Leave her alone. Let us through." But there was nowhere to walk.

"Do you think she'll get a life sentence?"

Now I was angry. "She can't get a life sentence on a second degree charge," I said. "You know that."

"Have you studied law? Are you really just an artist?"

I ignored the question, kept a firm grip on Margo's arm, and began walking through the crowd. Microphones were literally poked into our faces, and I heard one tap Margo's teeth. She recoiled and I drove a straight-arm into the reporter just as a muscular arm grabbed my own and led both of us through the crowd and into the building.

It was Earl Haymeyer and his boss, Jim Hanlon. The United States attorney towered over the wiry Haymeyer, and as soon as we were inside, the attention of the press turned to him. "Mr. Hanlon, is it true you'll be running for governor?"

"If I say yes, will you leave these kids alone?"

"Sure! Is it true?" By now we were safely inside the courtroom and Earl had returned to Hanlon's side. That night on the news, Chicagoans heard Hanlon's reply:

"No, I just wanted you to leave them alone. We already have a governor, and I have a big enough job for now." (It wasn't true. He had told us the night before at the hotel that he was going to enter the race.)

Margo had a rolled up *Daily Herald* in her purse, along with a dog-eared paperback copy of *Psalms and Proverbs*. She handed me the paperback and unrolled her paper, but somehow I wasn't in the mood for Scripture right then — any more than she was.

It wasn't that we didn't know where our strength came from. In the last several weeks we had read and studied and discussed more of the Bible than I, for one, had ever done in my life.

And Margo. She was the brand new Christian, yet she wanted so badly to offer some spiritual help to her mother and father that she ran circles around me in searching for answers. She read everything either of us could get our hands on, listened to tapes, and went to church every Sunday and sometimes during the week.

It had become more and more difficult to sneak away with Haymeyer or one of his men and get somewhere without being noticed, but that was part of the fun. It had even taken our minds off the ordeal we had been through and the fact that we would soon witness Margo's mother's sentencing.

And now here we were. At the crisis hour, we wanted to read the paper. Maybe we had already found our answers and our strength. We didn't need to cram at the last minute. I set the Book between us on the bench and read the paper over her shoulder.

FRANKLIN SENTENCE EXPECTED TODAY, the headline read. The article recapped the whole bizarre story and wondered at the turn of events that prompted a daughter who "turned" on her mother to sit directly behind her in court and provide moral support.

Margo looked up from the paper when her mother came into court with Amos Chakaris, stood, and embraced her. No one would ever understand it; certainly not the press. Reporters were puzzled over my role in the whole affair until Margo one day had just blurted it out: "Philip is the one who encouraged me to do the right thing."

Once they had pounced on the fact that I had been involved from the beginning, they dragged out details of my having been allowed to hang around the investigation. Haymeyer even allowed once that I had been of some help and had showed "an instinct for our kind of work." I had been a minor celebrity for a few days, which was not at all like I had dreamed notoriety would ever be.

I was hounded more than ever, switched hotel rooms and phone numbers every few days, and could hardly go anywhere without a strategic plan.

Margo and I had read the rehash of the story so many times that we instinctively knew how far into the articles to look for any new material. While Mrs. Franklin was deep into a quiet discussion with Chakaris, Margo and I locked our eyes onto the newspaper account of various experts' speculation about the length of the sentence.

Hanlon and Haymeyer slid into place beside Margo. "How you holding up, girl?" Earl asked. Margo had never liked his calling her that, but he seemed so fond of her that she decided not to say anything about it.

"I'm OK," she said, forcing a smile.

"And you, Picasso?" he said, leaning past her. I just nodded.

The judge entered, and we stood.

Two

"Hear ye, hear ye," the bailiff sang out, "the circuit court of Lake County, Illinois, is now in session, the honorable Judge Stephen Gregory presiding. You may be seated. The State of Illinois versus Virginia Franklin."

The prosecutors remained standing, as did Mrs. Franklin and Amos Chakaris. He was obviously worried, though this should have been a cut-and-dried case of admitted murder and a normal plea bargain to second degree. His hope was that by throwing his client upon the mercy of the court, he could get her the minimum sentence for that charge.

He had seen a lot of days in the courtroom, even more than his fifty-nine-year-old client. Chakaris, a swarthy, heavy man, was red-faced and sweating, in stark contrast to the defendant who was stylishly dressed as usual, hair done right, makeup just so, formally stern, standing rigidly.

At a meeting of all of us, except Mrs. Franklin, at the hotel the night before, Chakaris had told Haymeyer and Hanlon that he just didn't understand "why Gregory wants to be so stubborn on the sentencing.

"Jim, Earl, you know it's customary in cases like this, where there's an early confession and plea and the usual amount of bargaining and concessions, for the judge to discuss the sentencing with both sides before the formal hearing. Why wouldn't he do that? Is he grandstanding? If he is, I'll appeal this crazy thing to the state supreme court and let the boys in Springfield decide if the guy is fit to sit on the bench."

"You'd appeal a case where your client has pleaded guilty?" Hanlon asked.

"I'd appeal the sentence, Jimmy. If the judge is so all-fired concerned about surprising everyone — us officers of the court included — with his sentence pronouncement, maybe the guy has a problem."

"Amos," Haymeyer broke in, "you know Gregory has an impeccable record. They wouldn't assign someone to a case like this who had a spot or blemish. The man is sound and fair."

"I know that, Earl," Chakaris said. "That's why I'm worried about the sentence. Virginia and I agreed a long time ago that by going this route we'd stand the best chance of getting the thing over as quickly as possible and get the best deal we can. If he's gonna pull some stiffer-than-appropriate sentence out of his hat tomorrow, I may be forced to drag the case even further."

"I hope not," Margo interrupted.

"Well, I hope not too, honey," Chakaris said. "But you wouldn't want your mother to take a worse sentence than she should just because of all the publicity this case has received, would you?"

"I have no idea what an appropriate sentence is for the crime and everything that went along with it," Margo said, defeated.

"She's right, Amos," Hanlon said. "You've gotta admit that a judge who hid her guilt for nine years — "

"I know already, Jim. I know. OK?" Chakaris said, a meaty hand in front of him. "I just don't like going into the courtroom unprepared and dreading a surprise. This poker face has served me well over the years, but I'm going to be uncomfortable tomorrow."

And he was. "Will the parties approach the bench?" Judge Gregory intoned now. Chakaris stepped aside to let Virginia Franklin move toward the bench first. His eyes darted, his lips were pursed. A nice minimum sentence with parole consideration after three years would be a victory, he had often said.

The assistant prosecutor had spoken little during the proceedings, but the brief closing statement had fallen to him. His boss would ride the political wings of putting away Judge Franklin, and he would cut his own teeth on this scrap. "The people of Illinois are grateful to the defense for its cooperation in these proceedings. We feel it has contributed to the efficiency and economy of the hearings."

"Mr. Chakaris?"

"Thank you, Your Honor, and thank you, counselor. I do wish to speak, yes." The big man grasped Mrs. Franklin's elbow. "My client is guilty. She is remorseful. She is repentant — "

"If I may interrupt, Mr. Chakaris," the judge said. "You are aware, of course, that the verdict was handed down at the last hearing and that the sentence I am about to pronounce has already been decided upon. I would ask that your closing remarks not in any way resemble a further attempt to petition the bench on behalf of your client."

"Forgive me, Your Honor, but it is most unusual that neither side has been informed in advance of the sentence, and I fear that any objections I may have after the fact will be futile until I would take the case to Springfield."

"Mr. Chakaris, I find it regrettable that you are now marring what have been most expedient hearings with open threats to appeal a decision you have not even yet heard."

Chakaris sighed loudly and gestured with his free hand. "I admit that I sound desperate and pessimistic, but this is most unusual. We have no inkling whatever of the possible sentence. I feel at a loss to not be able to challenge it."

"May I remind counsel that you submitted that any and all other charges be dropped in lieu of the murder charge if Mrs. Franklin would turn state's evidence on those matters?"

"Which she did, sir."

"And mightn't anyone in her predicament, Mr. Chakaris? You also asked at the eleventh hour that I consider having her segregated from the general prison population."

"And I hope you have, Your Honor."

"Of course I have, and I am pleased to be able to say that it will be so stipulated, but that is precisely what has delayed my decision on the exact sentence until shortly before this hearing."

"If Your Honor would grant, could we recess to chambers so that we might react to the sentence before it is read in open court?"

"Mr. Chakaris, you are acting like a child before his birthday party. You can't stand the suspense."

"The analogy hardly fits," Chakaris replied. "I'm certainly not looking forward to this surprise, and I pray you aren't looking forward to springing it on us."

"That was entirely out of order, counselor."

"I'm sorry, Your Honor. I withdraw the statement and ask that it be stricken from the record."

"I'm going to have it stricken from the record," the judge said, nodding to the court reporter, "but let me take you back to law school first. You have been a respected barrister and public official for more years than I have been on the bench, and you should know that it is I, not you, who asks that remarks be stricken from the record. And it is I, not you, who suggests recesses to my chambers. Is that understood?"

"Yes, sir," Chakaris said without emotion. "May my client speak?"

"Of course. Mrs. Franklin?"

Virginia Franklin had not spoken in the courtroom during any of the hearings. Even the guilty plea was entered by Chakaris. "I am throwing myself on the mercy of this court," she said. The judge nodded impatiently, looking helplessly to Chakaris. Suddenly the old fire came back to Mrs. Franklin. "Is there a problem with my statement already?" she challenged.

"No, ma'am," the judge said. "Except that this entire hearing is becoming redundant. We know the crime, we know the plea, we know the evidence, we know the verdict. We even know, and have been reminded of it every time your counsel has spoken, that you are repentant and remorseful and are throwing yourself on the mercy of this court. Do you have anything new to add to the record? Because if not, I would like to pronounce sentence, and I wish not to have you or your attorney respond. Is there anything else?"

Chakaris and Mrs. Franklin looked at each other. Chakaris raised his eyebrows and shrugged. To him any further discussion was pointless. "If your honor would indulge me," Mrs. Franklin said, "and not make it any more difficult by looking condescendingly upon me, I would like to enter one more statement into the record."

The judge looked down at his papers and made some notes. Without looking up, he said, "You may proceed with a *brief* statement."

"I just want to express my gratitude and love to my daughter — for her courage and for doing what she knew was right in spite of everything." Mrs. Franklin's voice quavered and Margo's eyes filled. "She helped me put an end to a nine-year nightmare, and I find myself strangely thankful."

The judge looked up, suddenly formal and silent. "Thank you very much," he said finally, his eyes scanning the principals before him. "Is there anything else at all?" No one responded. The courtroom was silent except for the swishing of the artists' sketch pads and the scribbling of reporters' pens.

"Mrs. Virginia Franklin, you have confessed to and been found guilty by the people of the state of Illinois of second degree murder in the November 11, 1970, murder of Richard Wanmacher. I have taken into consideration your cooperation and plea in this matter and wish to remind you again of the extraordinary generosity of the prosecution in reducing the charge.

"However, due to the nature of your station in life, which for many years had been as a circuit judge in the criminal courts of Cook County, Illinois, I find the crime and your subsequent actions equally reprehensible. You need no lecture on why the leaders of society ought also to be its moral models.

"To try a man for a murder that you yourself committed, to then attempt to implicate others of even your own immediate family, and to force investigators to the hilt before finally coming forward to acknowledge that you were without further recourse, constitutes an arrogant thumbing of your nose at the laws of this state, the laws you were sworn to uphold.

"It is, therefore, my ruling that you shall be immediately turned over to the custody of the Illinois Department of Corrections to be imprisoned in the women's facility at the Illinois State Penitentiary at Pontiac for a period of not less than twenty-five years."

THREE

Amos Chakaris caught a stumbling Virginia Franklin in one tree trunk of an arm, but his objection and the judge's refusal to act upon it could not be heard over the commotion. Reporters sprinted for the phones, observers for their cars. Judge Gregory, who would be the darling of the six o'clock news, left in a flourish.

Margo tried to get to her mother but was pushed away by Chakaris himself who didn't realize who it was and was merely trying to protect Mrs. Franklin. "We'll appeal the sentence, we'll appeal it," he kept whispering to her.

"Mother, I'll see you tomorrow," Margo shouted as a corrections officer guided Mrs. Franklin away from Chakaris and the crowd.

Haymeyer and Hanlon's unmarked sedan awaited us as we stepped out a side door. "Get in," Earl said. "Jim says we should take you back to the hotel and bring you back here later for your car." A quick glance at the horde of media people surrounding my car convinced me of the wisdom of that idea. We climbed into the backseat, and Haymeyer pulled around to another exit where the enraged Chakaris stormed out and jumped in without a second thought.

We were several blocks from the courthouse before he asked, "What am I doing with you guys?"

"You really want to go back there and get your car now, Amos?" Hanlon asked. The big man shifted to look out the back window, nearly knocking me into Margo's lap. "Sure don't," he said. "Sure enough don't."

"Well, it'll all be over by tomorrow morning," Haymeyer said. "Philip, I want you and Margo to feel free to stay the night in your rooms." It was just details, but when he was through with business, there was nothing to talk about except the hearing. And no one wanted to do that.

Margo finally broke the ice. "Are you going to appeal, Amos?"

"Well, frankly, there's no hurry," he said. "Even if it were reduced to the minimum she wouldn't be eligible for even parole consideration until three years. That gives us that long to make noise."

"Three years," Margo repeated. "When can I visit her?"

"You can see her briefly before she goes tomorrow," Chakaris said "And then you won't be able to see her again for three weeks. Then you can see her a half hour a week after that." Margo stared at him. "I'm as upset about this as you are, Margo," he said.

"I doubt it."

"I suppose you're right," he admitted. "She isn't my mother. But I hope you know I did everything I could. I believe we have a real shot at getting the sentence reduced. There didn't seem to be many grounds for his invoking the maximum."

Margo raised both arms and let them drop. "I know you did everything you could, Amos, and I'm grateful. It's all in your hands now. I'll be moving to Pontiac to be as close to her as possible. She'll need me. This will be too much for her. I don't know how she'll be able to stand it. I'd like to go to my room for a while."

Hanlon, Haymeyer, Chakaris, and I glanced nervously at each other. "Let her go," Hanlon whispered to me. Haymeyer spoke to her.

"You going to call your father?"

"I suppose. I know now why he didn't want to be in court for any of this." She dug in her pockets for her room key, coming up with it in her left hand and a folded piece of paper in her right. "What's this?" she asked, looking at us as if we had planted it there.

She opened it and read silently. "Earl, look at this."

"Where'd you get it?" he asked.

"I don't know. It wasn't there when I left this morning."

"What is it?" I asked, miffed that I had not been the first one she showed it to. Hanlon followed me to Haymeyer's side and we read it together:

"Margo:

"I desperately need you and your boyfriend's help. I beg you not to turn me down. If you will listen, call me tonight at 9 at 555-7733. Karlyn M."

"What do you make of it, Earl?" Hanlon asked.

"Someone must have given it to her in the crowd today," Earl said. "Either when the press was surrounding you two or right at the end of the hearing. You don't know who it was or what you might be setting yourself up for if you reply to it, so I wouldn't advise doing anything with it until you know who this Karlyn M. is."

"How am I supposed to determine that?"

"I don't know," Haymeyer admitted. "But let me check out a few things while Jim takes Amos and Philip back to their cars. You go ahead to your room and call your father and get some rest. We'll talk later, OK?"

We hardly spoke on the way back to the courtroom parking lot. Amos was one whipped lawyer. He just sat shaking his head. We'd been through it so many times that we were sick of it. My original intuition had been right. Mrs. Franklin would be transported to Pontiac the next day, and I would be done with it for a while.

The only thing that bothered me was that Margo had said she was going to move to Pontiac. Surely I could talk her out of that. There was little reason to move that far away when you could see a prisoner only a half hour a week anyway.

"What do you make of the note?" I asked Hanlon.

"Got me," he said. "Could be a prank. I don't even want to think about it. It isn't that I don't care for you and Margo as much as ever, Philip, but this one is not likely to fall under the jurisdiction of my office, and frankly I'm glad not to have to worry about it."

It made me feel good to know I wasn't alone in my relief over the end of the Virginia Franklin case. "But why is Earl getting involved then?" I asked.

"Oh, I wouldn't say he's getting involved. He'll probably just call Larry Shipman, his journalist friend, and see if he knows anyone who was shooting videotape when you two walked into court today. Maybe he'll see someone on the tape who could have slipped Margo the note. If it happened in the courtroom at the end, though, there'll be no record of it."

"How can Earl stay out of it?" I asked. "He's a born detective, isn't he?"

"I hope not," Hanlon said.

"Why?"

"Because I want to talk him into hanging up the gumshoes and being in charge of security for my campaign. If I win, Earl can have any law enforcement job he wants in Springfield. I'll probably even endorse ol' Amos here for secretary of state again."

Chakaris, who had been dozing, opened one eye and grunted. "I'm through with politics," he said. "Seventy-one is too old for the courtroom too. I was like a senile old fool today."

"Nonsense," Hanlon scolded. "You did what any self-respecting lawyer would have done, and you'll look good on the record too. It'll probably help you get the sentence reduced."

"Do you really think so, Jimmy?" Chakaris asked, gratefully. "You always were a good law student."

I had the idea when I shook hands with Chakaris in the parking lot that I might never see him again. He would quit practicing law except to appeal Mrs. Franklin's sentence. As for me, I didn't know what I would do.

I followed Hanlon back to the hotel I'd stayed in for the four-and-a-half months of arraignments and hearings. Hanlon and Haymeyer had moved us all out of hiding downtown once the Mafia leaders began to be picked up on Mrs. Franklin's information. That way, too, we were close to the court. When Mrs. Franklin was safely on her way to Pontiac the next day, our security would be pulled off and we'd be on our own.

That would be fine with me. I was tired of being trailed or accompanied everywhere. Hanlon checked out of the suite where the bunch of us had met — along with our security agents — almost every night for the last several weeks. Now only Margo and I and our 'round-the-clock guards were left in the hotel from the original group.

Haymeyer was still on the phone when I entered my room. "Philip's here now," he said. "We'll be leaving shortly. Thanks, Larry. We'll see ya."

I dropped onto the bed. "Earl, please tell me we're not going anywhere," I said.

"You don't have to if you don't want to," he said. "But Shipman has a friend who shot a lot of tape while you and Margo were going into court today. He'll put it on a machine anytime we want to see it."

"What time is it?" I asked.

"Just after three."

"Can I take a nap first?"

"And what am I gonna do, lover boy? Sit here and watch? I don't have a room in this joint anymore, you know. And this case is unofficial anyway. This is on my own time. I'm just as curious about this note as you are."

"Maybe more so. I wish it would go away. I'm intrigued, sure, but who needs more excitement than I've had in the last several months? I just want to relax a while, get back to my drawing, decide what I'm going to do about Margo."

"Well, it's up to you, Philip," Earl said. "Though somehow I can't see you letting this one rest until you find out what it's all about."

"Me? Why?"

"Because that's just the way you are. You're like me. The real motive behind my work is curiosity. Sure, it's helpful to society. I try to keep the streets safe and all that. But the fun of the job is in finding the answers. The search. I'll tell you what — if that isn't what you like, how about if I go see the tape and let you know if I find anything, hm?"

Haymeyer stood and pulled on his coat.

"Not on your life," I said. I called Margo to tell her we'd be back by early evening.

"Daddy took the news well," she said. "I think he's going to be all right. I'll try to start seeing more of him now."

"You going to go to bed early and sleep through?" I asked.

"I don't think so. I'll probably be ready for a little company by the time you two get back."

"Tell her to stay up and we'll take her out for a nice dinner," Haymeyer said. She liked the idea.

As Earl and I got into the car, it hit me that Margo sounded as confused about the future as I was. How was she going to see more of her father in Winnetka and her mother in Pontiac? And where did she think I'd be all that time, or did she care? We'd been thrown together so dramatically and unrealistically that we had never had time to sort out our relationship.

We had grown dependent upon each other, and there was no doubt in anyone's mind that we cared about each other. Although we had never talked about it, everyone who knew us considered it a foregone conclusion that we would wind up married when this was all over.

I wasn't sure how either of us felt about that. Maybe we both realized that we needed time to recuperate and perhaps even to be apart for a while. I hoped that everything I felt for Margo had not been artificial because of the situation. I didn't know what she was feeling for me anymore.

I had learned enough about Chicago to know that when Haymeyer exited east off the Edens Expressway onto Tower Road and took it to Glencoe Road, we were taking the long way to Larry Shipman and the television station. "Where are we going, Earl?" I asked.

"Larry isn't expecting us for another few minutes. There's something I want to show you, anyway."

FOUR

Haymeyer pulled onto a side street and parked in front of a quaint two-story building about a half block long that housed a drugstore on one end and a women's boutique on the other. Various shops occupied the middle properties on the first floor while the second story housed an optometrist, two dentists, a podiatrist, and some attorney's offices.

"There are also six flats upstairs," Haymeyer said. "Pretty nice too. Only one occupied right now. The others were just redecorated and should be filled soon."

"How do you know all this?"

"I own the building."

"You own this building? I thought you lived downtown and worked sixteen hours a day."

"I do. Or at least I did. I've made pretty good money the last few years, and I've hardly had any expenses except eating and sleeping. I don't even own a car, or at least I didn't until a few days ago when I ordered one. I've always driven 'company' cars."

"You know, Earl, it embarrasses me how little I know about you. After all the time we've spent together, I realize we have been so wrapped up in Margo and her mother that we never really talked about you. Are you married?"

"Widower."

"I'm sorry."

"It's all right. I was an idealist who worshiped her and haven't been able to even think of anyone replacing her. I have friends, but no one special."

"How long has it been?"

"Six years. And we were married six years too."

"No children?"

"One. Institutionalized. I see him now and then. He doesn't know me. Junior."

"Sounds like a lonely life."

"I don't let it get lonely, Philip. I work all the time, and I love my work. Always have."

"Then what's all this?" I asked, waving at the building.

"Just a little security and a place to live. I had money stashed away that inflation was eating up, so now I've got something that will provide rent income and will allow me to fail in my own business."

"Your own business? C'mon, are you going to make me drag this out of you sentence by sentence?"

Haymeyer laughed. "I guess not. Look at this," he said, pulling a letter from his pocket. The envelope was addressed to Mr. James A. Hanlon, U.S. Attorney for Northern Illinois, State of Illinois Bldg., Chicago, IL. "You can read it," he said.

"Dear Jim:

"It's been rewarding and unforgettable. I'm flattered by your hints that I would always have a place with you wherever you go and whatever you do, but you know as well as I do that I'm a detective first and foremost and always.

"I wish you the best in your run for the governorship, will help you in any way I can, and would bet against all odds that you'll win and be a great one. Maybe when you become president I'll consider the leadership of the FBI!

"Meanwhile, wish me luck on what I've always wanted to do. I've got an income-producing property in a great location and I'm going into private practice. 'EH Detective Agency / Private Investigations' has a ring to it, don't you think?

"You'll know who to come to when you need it done right. And I promise not to take any penny ante cases like trailing unfaithful spouses.

"Thanks for understanding, Jim. I'd like this effective April 1.

"As always, Earl Haymeyer."

"That's less than a month away," I said. "How's he going to react?"

"You can never tell with Jim Hanlon," Earl said. "He may pout a little, but he won't try to talk me out of it. We've always been real close on the job and not so close off the job. He's not a meddler. He'll want me to stay, which will make me feel good, but he won't make me feel guilty for leaving."

"You can't ask for more than that."

"You sure can't," Earl said, pulling away. "I'll show you the building sometime soon. You're going to need an apartment anyway, aren't you?"

"I don't know, Earl. I appreciate the offer, but I don't even have a source of income right now. If I'm going to stay near Margo, I'll have to get back to Atlanta and move my stuff. I don't know where she's going to be, and I don't think she does either. If she's bound and determined to move to Pontiac, I may settle up here after all. I can't see living there. I would have very little work outside a metropolitan area."

"We're going to have to talk about your career," Earl said. "Maybe tonight after dinner."

It was chilly by the time we rolled into the Channel 8 parking lot in the Loop. Larry Shipman let us in by a side entrance. I had met him early in the Virginia Franklin investigation when Hanlon had used him as a plant in the jail to bring back information. Shipman was a sort of free-lance everything. He hung around newspapers and TV stations until they gave him work to do, and he also worked with Earl and Jim when they needed him.

"I looked at the tapes," Shipman said. "Tell me what you're looking for and I can probably punch right to it."

"Well," Haymeyer began, "Margo found something in her pocket when she got back from the hearing."

"Got it," Shipman said, beaming.

"You're unbelievable," Haymeyer said, shaking his head. "Are you serious?"

"Of course! You know I don't kid around."

They both laughed. "You know," Larry continued as he fast-forwarded the videotape machine, "I could work for you and Jim for nothing, just for those appreciative exclamations you come out with now and then."

"I'll remember that," Earl said.

"Please don't," Shipman said, stopping the machine and restarting it at regular speed. It was weird to watch myself opening the door for Margo and then trying to move into the building before the press closed in.

"You see, Earl," Shipman said, "there are several people in this crowd who are not press. Many with no recorders or cameras or microphones or even notepads. They are just bystanders who see the commotion and want to be in on it. Now watch. As they realize that they can't hear anything anyway, they begin to fall away. Then all you've got is the core of reporters and maybe just one or two outsiders."

Larry cut the sound and punched the slow motion button. "Now watch carefully," he said. Incredulous, I saw the press crowd in close enough to jam the microphones in our faces and saw myself build to a boil in slow motion. Larry cut the speed one more time until it was coming an image at a time.

A microphone tapped Margo's tooth, she jerked back, and my arm shot out toward the reporter. Just as I made contact, Margo and I were scooped up by Haymeyer and

Hanlon and steered through the crowd. "Did you see it?" Shipman asked.

"Yeah," I said. "I nearly flattened that reporter."

"You missed it," Shipman said, giggling. "Did you see it, Earl?"

"Yes, but I wouldn't be too hard on Philip. He's still a kid in this business, but he has potential. Run it back again, Lar. And, Philip, this time don't watch your own performance. Look for what we're looking for. The note *w*asn't placed in Margo's mouth or in your hand, was it?"

"No," I said sheepishly.

Shipman backed up the tape a few seconds and ran it again. The microphone hit Margo's mouth and I made my move, but this time I forced my eyes from the action and watched Margo's coat. "Right there," we said in unison. A short blonde woman, about twenty-five, slipped the note into Margo's pocket just as Margo's head snapped back. The woman was nearly bowled over by Hanlon as he and Haymeyer pushed through behind us.

Shipman stopped the tape just as the woman crossed in front of the camera. In spite of the emotional strain obvious on her face, she was striking. She wore a light trench coat of dark blue and a thin scarf. She was made up like a model, and her yellow hair was cropped close and hung just short of her shoulders.

"Not bad, huh?" Shipman asked, but I didn't know if he meant the girl or his work.

"Not bad, Larry," Earl said. "Now can we jump ahead and see if the cameraman got a shot of everyone leaving the courtroom?"

"He did."

"Then let's see if she was in the group."

"She wasn't."

"Boy," Haymeyer said, "you don't miss a trick, do you?"

"Nope, and thanks for the compliment."

"That was no compliment. That was next week's pay. Anyway, if she wasn't in the courtroom, she probably had no interest in the trial."

"Does she look like a Karlyn?" I asked.

"I dunno," Shipman said. "What does a Karlyn look like?"

I shrugged. "I just wonder if she is the writer of the note, or just the messenger."

"Good question, Philip," Haymeyer said. "If you went to work with me, would you settle for compliments instead of paychecks?"

Shipman laughed. "Anything else I can do for you gents?" he asked.

"Nope, we gotta go," Haymeyer said. "You'll hear from me soon."

"Why? Is this on Hanlon's budget?"

"Even if it's not, this one deserves more than compliments, wouldn't you say?"

"I won't argue with that. What was in the note, by the way?"

"Can't tell you yet. Trust me."

"Always," Shipman said.

We called Margo before we left Chicago, allowing her enough time to be ready when we arrived. "Tell her to dress up," Earl said. "I'll take you guys to a place we haven't had time for until now."

She looked only a little less tense than she had at the trial, but she said she felt a lot better. "I just don't know what I'm going to do now," she said.

"Neither do I," I said. "Why don't we postpone thinking about it until after dinner. Let's try to put our brains in neutral until we're ready to make some plans."

"I was hoping you'd take charge," she said, leaning her head on my shoulder. "Even if taking charge means postponing action, that's fine with me. There are just a few things I have to do. I have to get out of my hotel room, get back to Atlanta, pack my stuff, move it to Pontiac, and find a job and a place to live."

"I hate to put a wet blanket on all those wonderful plans," Haymeyer said, "but you seem to be ignoring a little responsibility that rolls around at nine tonight, just a couple of hours from now."

"Do you really think I should call this girl, Earl? I'm not ready for any more escapades for a few years."

"Read me the second sentence in that note again," Earl said.

Margo dug for the note, then read aloud: "I beg you not to turn me down."

"Can you ignore that?" Haymeyer asked.

Margo looked at me and sighed with resignation. "I was desperate once too. I'm glad you didn't ignore me."

FIVE

Earl took us to an exclusive French restaurant in one of the luxurious hotels near O'Hare International Airport. It didn't take long for us to break our promise not to talk about the future until after dinner.

"Your plans don't seem to include me," I said.

"Sure they do. You dragged me up here from Atlanta in your own car, and I assume I have a round trip ticket." She poked me in the ribs to assure me she was kidding. "Seriously, Philip, there are so many things to think about now that I don't know what to do about us. Don't you agree that we need time to just think it through?"

"No doubt," I said. "It'll probably cost me, though."

"Cost you what?"

"Cost me you."

"Why do you say that?"

"Oh, you'll start thinking about the whole situation and realize that our relationship was forced from the start. Out of sight, out of mind, end of Philip."

"Oh, poor baby," she said.

"Shed me a tear," Earl said.

"Keep out of this," I said. "How can a guy have a pity party with you two around?"

"Want us to leave?"

"Cute."

It was eight o'clock and we were eating. We had avoided much talk of Karlyn, other than a description of her for Margo. "What should I say to her?"

"I think you ought to try to shock her," Haymeyer said. "Unless she tells you what she wants right away and gives you her full name, treat her as a nuisance and tell her what you liked about what she wore today."

"Really?"

"Sure, it'll scramble her mind a little. Force her out into the open. Why didn't she come to you openly?"

By eight forty-five we were racing down the Kennedy Expressway toward the Loop. "What if I don't call her in time?" Margo asked.

"All the better," Earl said. "Let her wonder a little. We don't want to be too late, but I do want to do it from Jim's office where we can tape it and also listen in."

"Jim won't mind?" I asked. "Since it's not federal business?"

"I'll pay for it," Haymeyer said.

"And who'll pay you?" Margo asked. "Moneybags and I here are in no condition to be engaging a private detective."

"Consider it a free introductory offer," Earl said. He winked at me and Margo cocked her head.

"You'll have to let Earl tell you," I said.

"Later," he said.

Margo shook her head. "I can't keep up with you two."

Hanlon was there when we arrived, surprising Earl. Haymeyer filled him in and asked if he could use the phone equipment. "You know you don't have to ask," Jim said. "Especially considering what I'm going to ask you tomorrow."

"You're going to ask me tomorrow?" Earl said.

"Yup."

"Then I'd better give you this tonight."

"Should I read it now?"

"Not if it's going to change your decision about the phones."

"It won't, but I have the feeling this is one I should save until I get home."

"Suit yourself."

"I'm leaving now, Earl. Let me know how this thing turns out. And do lock up. I'm sorry. I know I don't have to tell you that, of all people."

"You're right, boss. You know me by now." The two shook hands, almost as if Hanlon had already read the letter. He might as well have. He knew what it contained.

"If I know Jim," Earl said a few minutes later, "he won't be able to wait until he gets home." He moved toward the window and looked down on Hanlon waiting. For his car to be delivered from the underground garage. Margo and I peeked over his shoulder.

Hanlon opened the envelope and read the letter under a streetlight. He looked up from it and just stared across the street at nothing. He let both arms drop, the envelope in one hand and the letter in the other. His shoulders sagged wearily as he stood motionless in the cool spring air.

He crumpled the envelope and dejectedly tossed it into a trash can, then carefully refolded the letter and slipped it into his breast pocket. "Get on the phone, Margo," Earl said. "We've got work to do."

Margo dialed the number and Earl started the machinery. He and I listened in on extensions in the same room. The number rang and rang, six times, then seven. "If she answers now, hang up immediately," Haymeyer said.

Margo shot him a puzzled look.

"Just do it," he said. "You don't want to be made the fool of. We don't know who this is or what she wants. We need to take the upper hand right away." The phone rang for the tenth time. And then she answered.

"This is Karlyn," she said in a whisper. "Who is this?"

Haymeyer motioned for Margo to hang up, which she did, reluctantly.

"That's good," Earl said. "No problem. We know she's there and we can call her back. We'll train her to answer immediately or she'll get no cooperation. This time I want you to talk to her only if she answers within the first three rings."

We waited a few minutes, then Margo dialed again. Karlyn answered on the fifth ring; Margo hung up before she could say anything.

"See how this puts us in the driver's seat?" Earl asked. "She had us over a barrel, and now we've got her wondering if she's going to hear from us at all."

"Us?" Margo said. "She doesn't even know about you."

"All the better. Call again."

Margo dialed. Karlyn answered immediately but said nothing.

Haymeyer put his finger to his lips. "Don't hang up," he mouthed. "But do make her talk first."

Margo waited.

"This is Karlyn. Who's this?"

"Who did you expect?" Margo said, surprisingly calm.

Haymeyer closed his eyes and gave her the "perfect" sign with his finger and thumb. He was amazed. She was doing well even without his coaching.

"Is this Margo?"

"This is Margo."

Margo was melting. It was against her nature to make someone squirm, and she was obviously about to make herself available to Karlyn. But before she could, Haymeyer repeated his silence signal.

"Are you the Margo whose mother is a — I mean your mother was sent to — was in court today?"

"Yes, my mother is the judge who murdered a man, and you know who I am because you saw me today. You were wearing a blue coat. Karlyn, what can I do for you?"

"I'm in trouble and I need help," she said quickly. "When you were in trouble, someone helped you. Will you help me?"

"I don't know. What kind of help do you need?"

"I can't tell you by phone. Will you meet me?"

"Where?"

Suddenly Karlyn was suspicious. "Is anyone listening in on this?" she asked.

Haymeyer shook his head, but Margo said, "Yes." Haymeyer winced.

"At least you're honest," Karlyn said. "Who's listening in?"

"Philip."

Haymeyer motioned for me not to say anything.

". . . and a friend named Earl," Margo said. Haymeyer gazed up as if in prayer. Karlyn hung up.

Margo immediately began to redial, but Haymeyer cut her off. "Let's not press her," he said. "She needs us a lot more than we need her. She's made contact, and if we let her sweat it out, she'll be back."

"But she doesn't even know our number," Margo said. "Why do you insist on tormenting her this way?"

"I'm not trying to torment her, Margo. But this woman may wrap her tentacles around your life and bleed you to death emotionally before she'll tell you what it's all about. You must show her that you want to help, but that you won't be taken advantage of. Actually, this is none of my business. You showed me the note, but you didn't ask my help. I'll understand if you want me to stay out of it."

Margo appealed to me with a look. "It's up to you," I said. "This is more hassle than you need right now. Earl can only help."

"Of course I want your help, Earl," Margo said. "I just want to feel free to question you, even to challenge you sometimes. Is that asking too much?"

"Not at all. Let's call Karlyn back and tell her that she can either tell you what her problem is now, over the phone, or she'll have to wait at least a week to meet you because you have personal matters to attend to."

"Which is true," I added.

"It certainly is," Margo said.

When Margo called again, Karlyn sounded fearful. "Do you want to help me or not?"

"I'm perfectly willing to help you," Margo said, "because someone helped me when I needed it. But I'm afraid I'm going to have to be just as firm with you as my helper was with me. I will not meet you alone because I don't know who you are or what your intentions are. And I need to know your full name."

"I'm Karlyn May."

"At least one person will be with me when I meet you, and it will have to be a place of my choosing. It will not be before a week from today, so if you need help more quickly than I can give it, you should look for it somewhere else."

Karlyn was silent for a long time. "I'll wait," she said finally. "Call me a week from today at eleven A.M. at this number, and I'll meet you and whoever else you trust anywhere you say." She suddenly sounded fragile. "And thank you very much."

Haymeyer was happy. "You did well, girl. Very, very well. I'm as mystified as you are. but at least we've got Karlyn May playing on our turf now, not hers."

"The trick now is to keep this off my mind for the next week," Margo said. "I'm going to have to count on you to help me with that, Philip."

I said I'd do what I could, but that I thought the best thing to do now was for Earl to get us back to our hotel where we'd switch to the custody of our security agents for the last time.

"It's still early," Earl said. "At least let me show Margo my building first."

Six

Margo readily agreed because she figured she would get the scoop on what Earl and I had been hinting at before. She was right. Only she got more than she bargained for. And so did I.

A fancy set of keys released the burglar alarm so Earl, the new landlord, could show us around. It was impressive. He told Margo he planned to live in the building while letting a real estate firm handle the business of collecting rents, hiring out repair work and complaint answering, and generally running the place.

"And this is where my office will be," he said, flipping on a bank of second floor lights to illuminate a huge room, bare except for a set of furniture that had not even been uncrated yet. "What do you need an office for, if you're not going to run the building?" Margo asked.

"You'll see," Earl said. "This kind of thing excites me. I love new equipment and setting things up. Since I've never had my own office or business before, this is better yet. The sign painter comes tomorrow."

"The sign painter?" Margo said.

"To put my name on the door. In old-fashioned block lettering it'll say, 'EH Detective Agency/Private Investigations.' "

"Why old-fashioned?" Margo wondered. "You're a modern-type detective, aren't you?"

"Oh, sure, I use modern equipment and techniques, but I never let them get in the way of good, old-fashioned hard work and horse sense. This business is nothing like you see on television where the guy squeals around in a hot car shooting at everybody in sight. The majority of cases are solved by persistence and know-how."

Earl tore the cartons away from his furniture and revealed equipment that would fit the lettering on the door. It was new, obviously expensive stuff designed like the furniture of the thirties. He had a rolltop desk, Bank of England chairs, a ceiling fan, even quaint desk lamps.

"Well, Earl Haymeyer," I said, "if you aren't just an eccentric old cop after all."

"You didn't know that?" he said with a grin. "The three-piece suit and the briefcase threw you off, did they? Well, I'm more eccentric than this. Want to see where I sleep?"

"I'm not so sure."

Earl led us to a tiny apartment next to his office. The furnishings were sparse — though tastefully arranged — consisting of a single bed lodged next to an open window and covered with sheets, one electric blanket, and a pillow; a dresser and mirror; a table and wood chair; and a huge easy chair.

On one side of the room was a gigantic walk-in closet ("where I store everything I own and my meager wardrobe"), and a full bath. The place was carpeted, painted, papered, and cozy.

"I love it," Margo said. "But why the open window?"

"Just another of my eccentricities," Earl explained. "I always sleep next to an open window and crank the blanket up as high as I need to."

"By 'always,' I assume you mean during reasonable weather?" Margo said.

"I mean always. In the summertime the window is wide open and I don't need the blanket. In the winter, when the windchill factor is way below zero, the window may be open only an eighth of an inch and I bury myself under the blanket with just my nose sticking out for air. Ah, you don't want to hear it. Suffice it to say, I like fresh air, keeping cool, and sleeping comfortably."

"What are your days like, living alone?" I asked.

"Pretty structured. I read the paper in my easy chair, first thing every morning. I skip breakfast and have my other two meals either out or delivered from a greasy spoon down the street. When the office is opened in a few days, I'll eat them there instead of here."

"It's neat, Earl," Margo said. "It really is. Right now I wouldn't mind a little structure in *my* life."

Margo and I waited in the car while Earl locked up and left a note for his new secretary in case she arrived at the office before he did in the morning.

"I need to tell you, Margo," I said, "that I can't see my moving to Pontiac, even though I don't look forward to being apart from you."

"I know, Philip," she said, taking my hand. "I want to be with you, too, but Mother needs me. I know it's not fair to you. You need to be near a big city so you'll have enough work. Maybe this will be good for us. You stay in Atlanta and I'll stay near Mother. If we're meant to be together, it will happen."

It wasn't that I disagreed with her — in fact, she made sense. "But Atlanta is an awfully long way from Pontiac," I said. "It would mean expensive phone bills and long trips to see you."

"Maybe you'll decide you don't want to see me."

"Or maybe you'll decide you don't want me to," I said. We stared at each other while we tried to put words into each other's mouths that we really didn't want to hear.

"That's not really what we want, is it?" I said. Margo looked down and shook her head.

Earl returned and started the car.

"I want to be near you and I want to be near Mother," Margo continued. "I really have no choice."

"But *you* do, Philip," Haymeyer interrupted.

"Sure. I can move to Pontiac if I want to, but how will I survive?"

"No, but you don't have to stay in Atlanta either," Earl said. "Chicago would be a ten times better market for you. Why do you think I brought you two whipped puppies tonight? To show you my soon-to-be office and my eccentricities?"

Margo and I looked at each other. "So what are you driving at, Earl?" she said.

"I need Philip," he said. "I've got clerical help coming from an agency, but I can't afford any more personnel. I don't know how the business will go and, frankly, I need a partner I don't have to pay much."

"Earl," I said, "I love the kind of work you do and I suppose if I had to choose and could start my life over again, I wouldn't care if I didn't have art ability and could just study crime detection. But I do. I'm an artist, born and trained. I know nothing about your work."

"But you just said you love it, and that's oozed from you since we first met. You've been a stumbler and a bumbler just like all of us at first, but you caught on fast. You know people. You understand them. Best of all, you're curious. I know you couldn't just give up your art, any more than I could give up sleeping next to an open window in the winter. That's why I have a proposal."

"You've had this all planned out — what you were going to say and everything?" Margo asked, admiration in her voice.

"I've thought about it a lot, yes."

"So, let's hear it," I said.

Earl accelerated onto the expressway. "I've held open one apartment, almost identical to mine. It's just down the hall from my office, maybe twenty steps. I could rent it tomorrow with no trouble, but I'll let you have it for as long as you work for me. I'll teach you the business, and I can give you a thousand dollars a month."

"I can't live on that in Atlanta, Earl, let alone Chicago — especially on the North Shore. I've heard about the cost of living up here, and I've gotten a little taste of it during the last several weeks."

"I know that, but where else can you get a free apartment? And if we eat on the job, I'll pick that up too. I'll pay your car expenses, everything. And I'm not asking you to give up your free-lancing. What you do with your own time is your business. What do you say?"

I looked at Margo.

"Oh, no, you don't," she said. "Don't expect advice from me on this one. Sure, I'd love to have you a little closer to Pontiac, but it's still more than a hundred miles away. I'm doing what I have to do, and while it hurt me to do it, I decided without hearing from you. You're going to have to do the same."

"Can't you just tell me what you think?"

"Philip, only you know if what Earl is saying is true about your love for his kind of work. Could you supplement your income with illustrating? Would you enjoy working for him? Do you trust him? It's a big decision only you can make."

She was dead right as usual, but I wasn't about to decide right then. "How long can I have?" I asked.

"I'd like to know as soon as possible, but I won't push," Earl said. "I'll say this: I don't want there to be any mistake about it; we won't be business partners, and we won't really be partners on the job either. We'll work a lot together, but I'll be in charge. You're no kid anymore, even though you're a novice at this. You'll be allowed all the usual mistakes, but only once. If you can't learn to avoid repeating errors, it won't work.

"I'm confident you can do it, but some day my life may depend on you, so I want it clear before you decide: you would be the subordinate, I would be the boss. You would be the student, I would be the teacher. You can speak your mind, but when I make a decision, it's a directive.

"Just like in the military, somebody's got to make the decisions because somebody is better, smarter, older, more knowledgeable, more worthy of leadership."

"And that's you," I said.

"You'd better believe it," he said. "And I don't want you thinking this would in any way be some cushy, fun job. You'd enjoy it, but you'll also learn what a grind it can be."

SEVEN

Mrs. Franklin didn't look like a woman who had spent her first night in jail. Petite and pretty, she looked ten years younger than she was. Margo and I were allowed to see her for fifteen minutes before her trip to Pontiac. All the former judge could talk about, it seemed, were the differences in life-style she would face.

"I will wear a denim jumper. Can you imagine? I haven't worn a jumper in nearly fifty years, and I don't ever remember wearing denim."

"You'll find it comfortable," Margo said lamely. Her mother nearly spit.

"You know, Margo, as a judge I toured Pontiac once. It was overcrowded *then*, and that was years ago. It had been spruced up for our visit, no doubt, but they couldn't disinfect everything. The stench still came through over the ammonia. I saw the dead eyes, heard the screams and catcalls. I got a view of prison life from that. Enough to know that I'm not capable of handling it."

Margo was startled. "What do you mean by that?"

"I will have no identity. No dignity. I will be stripped and showered and photographed and processed and quarantined. I will be segregated physically, of course, but unless I'm in solitary confinement — which would kill me — I'll still be able to see and hear the other women. It isn't that I don't know I deserve this. I've sentenced a lot of men and women to Pontiac, and even after visiting there I was convinced it was appropriate punishment. But I don't consider myself a hardened criminal. I won't be able to survive."

"Mother, you keep saying that. Can't you devise some plan of action, a way of keeping busy? Won't you have access to a library and study classes? And won't there be work to do?"

"Sure. I'll be working with the women I'm not allowed to live in the same cell with. Manual labor will certainly take my mind off my troubles, won't it? The first time a guard turns her back, I'll probably be killed.

"Reading and studying? What can they teach *me?* I could teach them. I've got a library at home to rival that of most law schools. What do you suppose will tempt me at the Pontiac prison library?"

Margo didn't respond. Her mother was rambling. And she was right. It would be horrible, especially at first. The contrast in life-styles could push her to the edge of suicide. She wanted comfort, but there was little Margo could say. You don't argue with a former lawyer and judge.

"I'll probably never see you again," Virginia said, lips trembling. "You whom I have never loved the way I should and from whom I never accepted love, even though you tried hard. Do you love me, Margo?"

Her daughter nodded, unable to speak. "I will be alone," Mrs. Franklin said. "I won't survive."

"Nonsense, Mother," Margo managed. "You can have a visitor in three weeks. I'll be waiting by the door. And then I'll see you every week for as long as you want me to."

"You can't come that often."

"I can if I'm living in Pontiac."

"What?"

"I'm moving to Pontiac as soon as Philip can get me back to Atlanta. I told you that you would always have me, Mother, and you will. I'll get a job and a place, and I'll be there when you need me."

Mrs. Franklin stared at the floor. She shook her head slowly. "I don't understand you," she said. "You would do that for me? I can't ask you to do that. I can't let you."

Margo put her hand over her mother's. "You can't talk me out of it."

"Margo, you deserve a life of your own, don't you see? I've done enough damage. Don't make me live with the guilt of tying you down to a prison town in the middle of nowhere. I could be there a long time — if I live." Margo started to argue, but Mrs. Franklin cut her off. "You should be with Philip. You're right for each other. Please don't move to Pontiac, Margo. Please don't."

"Mother, frankly, it's good to hear you worrying about someone else for a change, and I don't mean that to be unkind. But I *will* be moving to Pontiac, and I *will* be visiting you every time they'll let me. If you channel some of that caring attitude you just showed me, maybe you can help some of the women down there.

"Maybe you can teach a class on criminal law. Maybe you can even get better books into the library. Maybe you can work with the chaplain in helping counsel people."

"Wait, wait, wait," Mrs. Franklin said. "I've been impressed with you and your young man and what your religious interest seems to have done in your life — "

"Mother, I've asked you not to call my faith in Christ 'religion.' It's not religion; it's a relationship with God."

"You lose me every time with that relationship business, as well as that 'it's not a practice, it's a person' doubletalk. Anyway, it's working for you and you've certainly been kinder to me than seems humanly possible under the circumstances, but don't expect me to hook up with any chaplain or goody-two-shoes group in the hope that I'll get religion, or God, or whatever. Be encouraged that your old mom is impressed by you and Philip. And promise me that if you do settle in Pontiac, you won't think it entitles you to preach to me every week. If that's your motive, maybe you aren't so noble after all."

"Don't suspect my motives, Mother. I'm going to be there because I want to be, and because you need me. You're in no position to be requiring promises from me. No, I won't preach to you, but I'm not saying I won't pray for you. And I'll give you things to read. If that library is as limited as you say, maybe some of the stuff Philip gave me to read will look appealing to you after a while."

"Will you write to me, too?" Mrs. Franklin asked, switching emotional postures so fast I could hardly keep up.

"Of course I will, Mother. And I want you to stop berating yourself. You are paying for what you did, and whatever debt to me you feel is outstanding has been forgiven. You're paid up. You owe me nothing, and I will not be put off by you. You've got me whether you want me or not."

"I want you, Margo," Mrs. Franklin whispered, standing to embrace her daughter across the table. A department of corrections officer tapped on the door.

"One minute," he said.

"At least I don't have to ride all the way down there in a jail wagon," Mrs. Franklin said. "I get to ride in luxury in a Dodge station wagon." Margo tried to smile at her mother's attempt at levity, but she suddenly began to cry.

"You're going to get me crying too, Margo," her mother said. "It'll be all right."

"I'm supposed to be telling you that," Margo whined.

"Oh, don't buy this whole little-girl-lost bit of mine, honey. I'll survive because I'm a tough old bird and always have been."

Margo looked at me and we shook our heads. Was the woman crazy, or was this just her defense mechanism? A deputy entered and reached for Mrs. Franklin's arm.

"You don't need to touch me," she told him. "I'm perfectly capable of walking to the car." A matron put her hand on Mrs. Franklin's arm as she moved out the door. "Do you have to touch me?" Mrs. Franklin demanded, nearly shouting.

"No," the matron said meekly. And Mrs. Franklin walked in front of her, looking as much like a socialite out shopping as a murderer on her way to a twenty-five year's sentence in the state penitentiary.

Margo didn't speak for the first hour and a half of our drive to Atlanta. She faced the passenger-side door and laid her head on the seat back. She didn't move, but I knew she wasn't sleeping. She was crying.

"Anything I can say or do?" I asked. She shook her head.

I reached over and rested my hand on her side, just above the waist. She covered it with her own and we rode in silence for miles. When her hand fell limp, I knew she had fallen asleep.

She didn't have much to say when we stopped to eat. I asked her if she wanted to drive. She didn't. I decided to drive straight through, hoping to reach Atlanta by midnight. "I'm going to need you to talk to me sometime this evening," I said.

"About what?"

"About anything, just to keep me awake."

She turned toward me and tucked her legs up under her. "I'm going to miss you, Philip," she said. "You don't think my decision to move to Pontiac was an easy one, do you?"

"I don't know," I admitted. "You never seemed to waver on it."

"I'm not saying I have any second thoughts about it. I just want to be sure you don't feel left out or hurt."

"I don't know what I feel."

"Understanding, I hope."

"I care about you," I said. "You know that."

"So does Earl Haymeyer," she said, "but he doesn't care where I live."

"He doesn't care for you the way I do."

"How do you care for me?" she teased.

"You know."

"You've never told me."

"I've never told you? You can't tell? Do you think all this has been the result of pity for you? If that's all it was, you've cost me several months of my life."

She grinned. "How much do I owe you?"

I pretended not to be amused.

"Philip, I'm only teasing you, don't you see? I just need to know where we stand. I'm confused and I don't want to presume anything."

"I am too."

"I hoped you wouldn't say that. One of us has to know what's going on here, or we're headed for a dead end."

"I hope not."

"So do I, but Philip, if neither of us knows his own mind, how are we going to know what to do?"

"Maybe this separation will be good for us."

"That sounds familiar. Are you going to take the job with Earl?"

"Of course. I've never wanted anything so badly in my life. Except you."

"You want me?"

"You know I do."

"You've got me. When you can't stand being without me anymore, just write and tell my mother that you're coming to get me and that she'll be on her own after that."

"Be serious."

"OK, I'll be serious," she said. "If you wanted to work for Earl so badly, why didn't you tell him when he first suggested it?"

"You really want to know why? Because I was afraid you'd think I was being too hasty, frivolous, impulsive."

"Aren't you?"

"Probably."

"That's all right. I'm more impressed with the fact that you're worried about what I think of you."

"I have been for a long time."

"And I've never thought anything but the world of you for all that time," she said.

"But just out of gratefulness for my help, right?"

"No, I don't think so."

"Well, if we're so stuck on each other, how come we're both convinced that being apart is the right thing?"

"For one thing, we have little choice. I see no way around it unless I abandon my mother or you forget making a decent living."

"But is it fair that we can't be together, especially when we know we're right for each other?"

"Who said life was fair? God's ways haven't seemed entirely fair to me since I've become a Christian. He just does what He knows is right for me, and eventually I see that He was right from the beginning."

"And you put this in that category?" I asked. "God's will for us?"

"Since we have no choice, yes."

"What if we had a choice?"

"I hope we'd choose His way. This time He has made His way simple to find. We simply have no options. That gives me a certain sense of peace, even though I wish it could be different somehow."

"Margo, just what are we going to do if your mother's situation doesn't change for several years?"

"You'll become either a famous artist or a famous private detective who's independently wealthy and can make it anywhere."

"Even in Pontiac, Illinois?"

"Even in Pontiac."

EIGHT

We picked up Margo's car in Atlanta and moved out of our apartments. Three days later our two-car caravan pulled into Pontiac. I was towing a rented trailer with all our earthly belongings.

Finding a room for Margo was not difficult. The first ad we pursued was for the upstairs in the home of an old woman about a mile and a half from the prison. It included a bedroom, a bath, and a sitting room, plus some storage. Once we got her moved in, I called Earl.

"How soon can I move to Glencoe?"

"How soon can you get here?" he said. "You're going to accept my offer then?"

"No, I was just curious," I deadpanned.

"Not funny," he said. "You can move in anytime you want. When'll it be?"

"Pretty soon," I said. "Margo's not even going to look for a job down here until she gets back from talking with Karlyn up there. We'll be heading that way soon."

A few hours later I got Margo checked into a North Shore hotel and then started moving my stuff into my new apartment. There was plenty of room for everything, including my drawing board. Earl then put Margo and me to work supervising the interior decorators who arranged the furniture and put the finishing touches on his offices while Earl himself was tying up loose ends with Jim Hanlon. And he had been right: the sign on the door looked just right.

"So how did Hanlon take your resignation?" I asked later.

"Just like I thought he would. He wanted to know if it was final or if anything could change my mind. I told him a hundred thousand dollars a year might turn my head. He told me to leave my head right where it was. In fact, he said if I just checked in with him each day until April 1, he'd tell me whether or not he needed me. I guess things have really slowed down since your mother-in-law's trial."

"My mother-in-law? Not so fast, Earl."

"Tell me you didn't wish she was."

Margo pretended not to hear the conversation. She was more worried about Karlyn. "Can I call her early, as long as we're here?"

"I wouldn't," Earl said. "For one thing, the EH Agency isn't geared up for any cases yet. Give us a few days. By a week from when you last called her, we'll be ready to really check this thing out. It'll be a good one for Philip to cut his teeth on. That reminds me. What do you two think of these?"

Earl fished around in a box of supplies for a brown paper bag from which he produced two square boxes. I slid the top off one to find business cards inscribed with the EH Detective Agency name and phone number, and also "Philip Spence/Special Investigator."

"I ordered them the day after I talked to you, Philip. Just got 'em today. I'm glad you didn't turn me down after that kind of a cash investment in your future."

"What made you so sure?" I asked.

Haymeyer answered by asking Margo, "Did you have any doubt?"

"Nope."

"It was obvious in your eyes, Philip," Earl said. "And I'm glad to have you."

The phone rang. "Hello, yourself, Governor Hanlon," Haymeyer joked.

Margo and I wandered out and down the hall.

"I love you, Margo," I said suddenly. It just slipped out and brought her staring eyes right to mine. "I do," I said. She swallowed and said nothing.

When we returned, Earl was off the phone. "Do you suppose I could take Margo out to dinner tonight?" I asked him.

"Without me, you mean?" he shouted. "Girl, do you trust this man without a chaperone?" Margo laughed. "Of course, Philip," Earl continued. "Jim and I are meeting tonight anyway. In fact, why don't I just not see you two for a few days until we call Karlyn. My hunch is that Hanlon will officially let me go tonight. He's got a young guy he wants me to chat with, my heir apparent no doubt. Meanwhile, I'll see if anyone anywhere has anything on Karlyn May. There can't be too many people around with that name."

"Where will you look?" I asked.

"Everywhere. You'll find, Philip, that in our line of work we make a lot of friends, do a lot of favors, and owe a few too. A bushel of buddies from the local PDs owe me a quick check of their microfilm files. I want to know anything at all about Karlyn May, a short, blue-eyed blonde, about twenty-five. That's all some of them will need to go on. If she had a parking ticket, a jaywalk warning, anything, I'll know about it by the time I see you again. I'll find out where she is taking her calls too. Have a good time."

As Earl headed for the door, Margo said, "PDs?"

"Tell her, Philip," he said. "She's gonna need a lot of teaching."

"Right," I said, as if I knew what he had meant by the initials. He left.

I looked at Margo sheepishly.

"So what did he mean?" she said.

"Uh, let's see. He said buddies at local PDs owe him stuff. And these people have some kinds of files — "

Haymeyer, who had obviously been listening at the door, popped his head back in. "Police departments," he said. "PDs. Don't forget to lock up, kid."

At dinner Margo teased me. "That was the first time you told me you loved me all by yourself."

"By myself?"

"Don't you remember? In the heat of the investigation of my mother you must have said something to Hanlon and Haymeyer about it because Earl said he thought you could get to mother because you loved me."

"Oh, yeah. And I've never told you myself until now?"

"Right."

"I'm sorry."

"That you love me?"

"You know what I mean."

"I told you first, remember?"

"I sure do."

"Do you really, Philip? Are you that romantic that you remember when I told you?"

"It's hard to forget. It was the only time."

"I still don't believe you remember."

"All right. It was a Sunday morning, before church, the day I would see your mother for the last time before her confession to the murder. We were in the suite between our hotel rooms."

"You're right as rain, inspector. I'm impressed."

"Must you always mock?"

"I'm not mocking, Philip. I'm impressed, I really am. And I'm sorry I haven't told you again since then, but I had a reason."

"And what was that?"

"I wasn't going to tell you twice before you told me once."

"That was a little childish, wasn't it?"

"Maybe, but why force myself upon you? I didn't know how you felt, except for that secondhand information once. I just didn't want to put any undue pressure on you."

"Loving me would put pressure on me?"

"If you didn't love me it would have, don't you think?"

"I suppose."

"You know, Philip, when I was a kid I loved romantic stories. I always have. But as I got into my last years of high school and beyond, I decided that love meant nothing. Family love had fallen apart. I didn't feel love for my mother, and sometimes I thought I pitied my father more than loving him. And as for true love and all that, to me it was an illusion, a selfish feeling, a syrupy, self-serving fantasy. How could anyone know what love really was?"

"And now?"

"I still don't know *what* it is. I just know that it is, and it's real. And there are different levels of it. There was the unconditional love you felt for me when I was in trouble and wanting to kill myself. That was God-love. I know God is the author of all love. But this exciting, heart-pounding type of love that makes me want to look right into your eyes and tell you without embarrassment, that's the elusive love I never thought I would fall into."

"Aren't you afraid of analyzing it to the point where it becomes academic?"

"No. Do you want me to stop talking about it?"

"No, I don't," I said. "I get a kick out of your being so straightforward and sure about it. It's not the way they talk about it in the movies, but it leaves me breathless just the same."

"You know what the best, the really best, part of it is, Philip? I mean, do you know how it is that I know this is the real thing and can be sure of it?"

"No, but I get the distinct impression that you're going to tell me."

"It's because as thrilled as I am to know that you love me — and I've known it at least as long as you have — I consider loving you even more of a privilege."

"I'm embarrassed."

"Don't flatter yourself, Philip. It's not because you're Prince Charming — though to me you are. It's just the way you let me love you. You don't drag it from me, beg me for it, play games with my emotions. You just let me show you, allow me to enjoy you, and you don't turn me away."

"Why would anyone ever want to do that?"

"You've seen it before, haven't you, Philip? I've had friends who dare each other to love them. They make it a psychological tug of war. We've been close to that when we've skirted the issue. I'm so glad it's out in the open now so I can just tell you. It excites me to just sit here and tell you to your face that your loving me is just icing on the cake. The cake is the privilege of loving you."

"I wish I'd said that."

"You have, many times. I waited to hear you say it out loud, but I haven't really doubted your love for a long, long time."

"I don't even know when it happened," I said. "Do you?"

"Not really. For me it might have been when I was holed up in Chicago in protective custody and you were out with Haymeyer and Hanlon trying to put the whole case together against Mother. You were so considerate of me and seemed anxious to see me when you got back. I was miserable, yet I looked forward to being with you. All of a sudden I needed you, and not just for conversation. In fact, it scared me that I began to depend on you so much. That's when I started really evaluating my feelings. I didn't want a phony feeling of love just because you were all I had and because you had helped me through a crisis."

I didn't know what to say. I was flattered, thrilled, humbled. She was so sure of herself. "I always wanted to be an articulate suitor," I said. "I'll never be able to match you. Just know that I love you, and that I hear you."

"I can't ask for more than that," she said.

NINE

One of the things I appreciated about Margo was that she rarely spoke seriously unless she had thought it all out first. And once it had been thought out, there was no stopping her. She'd give it to you with both barrels.

Margo had already figured out many mysteries of the Christian life that had eluded me as a "lifer" (a Christian since childhood) and explained them to me like a female seminary student. And now she had explained her love for me and even mine for her. I had never met anyone like her, and I wasn't about to let her go now.

"I've come to a decision," she said.

"There's more?" I said.

"This separation is going to be rough on us, especially now that our feelings are completely out in the open. And you are the cause for that."

I shot her a double take.

"Well, Philip, if you hadn't said what you said, I wouldn't have said what I said tonight."

"You wouldn't?"

"Did you think I was just waiting for a chance to be alone with you before springing it on you? I could have told you all the way to Atlanta, couldn't I?"

"True enough. So what have you decided?"

"I've decided that if my feelings for you are real, then true love means that I want the best for you, even if that means that I am not what's best for you. It would hurt, and I wouldn't understand it, but I would live with it."

"What in the world are you talking about?"

"I'm talking about being far apart, starting new lives. We'll meet new people. Our love might be diverted."

"I doubt it."

"I do too, and it's wonderful to hear you say that, but get my point: I will despair being without you, Philip. I will hate it. I will probably be tempted to forget staying close to Mother and just run to Chicago. But I won't do it. I won't worry that just because you're not in my grasp, or even in my sight, that I'm losing you."

"Well, you've got another one on me. That's exactly what I'll be worrying about."

"But here's the way I figure it — do you want to hear this?"

"Absolutely," I said.

"OK, if because of the distance and all the other factors I somehow lose you, even to someone else, I will rest in the fact that God wants only the best for you. If someone else is better for you than I am, then if I really love you and consider loving you a greater privilege than being loved by you, I will be able to accept it. I need to love you enough to be willing to let you go. And I do. I think."

I laughed. With that last "I think" she went from being the self-assured, articulate woman to the little girl who hoped she was right. "I'm glad you added that," I said. "I was beginning to feel like a commodity you were willing to sell or trade if it was best for the business."

"You weren't really, were you, Philip?"

"No. In fact, your thoughts are noble and beautiful. I love you, everything about you. Being loved by you is overwhelming. I guess I'm more selfish because I don't want to lose you. I wouldn't accept it. I wouldn't agree with God or anyone else that someone else would be better for you. Call it what you want, I'm not as Calvinistic as you are."

"Calvinistic? I knew I should have read everything you gave me."

"You read enough. A Calvinist is basically one who believes that what happens is what was supposed to happen. Let me tell you something in my own crude, nonromantic, slightly blue-collar, Dayton versus Winnetka way: No chance I'm going to lose you. I may not be as mature in my love for you as you are in yours for me, but then my expression of love was the one that slipped out suddenly. Yours had obviously been pondered for weeks."

"Months," she corrected.

"Church tomorrow?"

"I'd love it."

Earl Haymeyer had been right about Hanlon's wishes. He asked Earl to give a pep talk to the new man and then to feel free to get started on his own agency. On Monday morning, after he showed me where I'd land in the office, he told me to call Margo at her hotel and have her come in. "I want to brief you both on Karlyn May."

It was obvious that Earl was thrilled to have his own place. He strolled around the office in shirt sleeves, pinning notes to himself on corkboards all over the room. He had every piece of equipment and paraphernalia any police department detective squad room could have. Hardly anyone knew he was in business yet, and he had no idea if Karlyn May could pay for what he was willing to do for her, but he was ready. It was a case, and he was working.

"The girl has no family," he told us. "She was orphaned at three and raised in a children's home in southern Michigan. She became a bit of an incorrigible and was transferred to a home for older girls in the Chicago area when she started high school in 1968.

"She went through a series of troublesome times, skipping school, shoplifting, generally raising cain with lots of boyfriends. Somewhere along the line she found religion."

"Do you mean religion, Earl?" Margo asked. "Did she get involved in some cult or Eastern group, or did she become a Christian?"

"Well, girl, you see a difference there that I've never seen. In my mind, religion is religion. You've got yours and she's got hers. I couldn't tell you if hers is different or not, but I can tell you what group she got involved with."

It was a campus group Margo had never heard of, but I had. I smiled. "She's one of us," I told her. Earl looked puzzled, and I knew I hadn't done myself any good in planning future discussions with him on the subject.

"Whatever," he said. "She got involved with this group and became quite outspoken, had some sort of a conversion experience, and even went so far as joining in Christian outreach types of activities. My sources tell me she really changed. She had been a fringe student in a bad crowd and all of a sudden she threw that over for a nice appearance and a pleasant personality.

"Her grades improved, she was named to the homecoming court her senior year at Arlington High School in 1972, and she even spent a couple of years at a junior college in Palatine. She's held the same job for the last six years as public relations coordinator for a Des Plaines electronics firm. As best I can tell, she has told no one there or anywhere what's troubling her. Besides you, Margo. Still want to get involved?"

"We can't abandon her before we start," Margo said. "Anyway, if she's a Christian, we have a lot of common ground."

"Religion is all we need with her background to make her a real basket case," Earl said.

"If she's a Christian," Margo said forcefully, "she's got more than religion and it's the best thing for her."

Haymeyer raised both arms in surrender. "Whatever you say. I'm just thrilled that my first case might be a religious weirdo. I just wish I could start with a nice, clear-cut missing person or something."

"I hope you're not prejudiced against Karlyn already," Margo said.

"Let's try not to jump to conclusions, OK?" Haymeyer said.

"I won't if you won't," she said, smiling.

"Remember, at eleven we call her. She's taking the calls at a pay phone about three blocks from her apartment."

"How do you know all this stuff, Earl?" I asked.

"You'll learn, Philip, that with a name and a description, you can discover almost anything you want about anyone. Would you like to see the readouts on you and Margo?"

"You're kidding."

"Not at all. Here."

By giving our names and all the other information Haymeyer knew about us to his friends with access to the computers in the capitals of our respective states, he had come up with our social security numbers, educational records, employment, traffic and criminal records, and current crime-related activity. At the bottom of both was the notation: "Principal in the Virginia Franklin/Richard Wanmacher murder trial, Lake County, Illinois, March, 1980."

"I'd say we're up to date," I said.

"I'd say we're in a police state," Margo said.

TEN

Margo scared Karlyn May when she asked her on the phone if her boss at the Des Plaines electronics firm knew she was missing work because she was waiting in a phone booth for a call.

"How do you know where I am?" Karlyn asked.

"I know a lot more than that, Karlyn. I even know that you're a Christian."

Silence.

"Is it true, Karlyn? Are you?"

"Well, yes, but — "

"Did you know that Philip and I are too?"

Silence.

"Karlyn?"

"Are you?" Karlyn said. "Are you really? Tell me you are." She had begun to cry.

"We really are. Philip's an old pro. I'm a newcomer. But yes, we are."

"How does it feel to be an answer to prayer? I couldn't have hoped that the people I reached out to would be Christians. It was too much to ask. At first I wanted help from Christian acquaintances, but I'm so scared and confused, I didn't know who to trust."

"You can trust me, Karlyn," Margo said, "and I'm going to ask you to trust me even further. I want you to meet me at Philip's apartment in Glencoe, and I want you to let me also bring our friend Earl. OK?"

"Who is this Earl?"

"I'll tell you when you come. You must trust us. Earl can probably help you more than Philip or I can, so I want him in on this from the beginning."

Karlyn hesitated. "I guess I have no choice."

"You have a choice, but I want you to choose to trust us."

Margo told Karlyn how to get to my place and encouraged her to put in a half day's work before coming. "Meet us after dinner tonight, say at seven."

By late afternoon, Earl was high from his first day at his own business. The secretary had gone home, we sat around trying to guess what Karlyn's problem was, and Earl ordered sandwiches from his favorite haunt. A delivery boy brought them at about six-thirty.

For as neat and trim as Earl is, he's the kind of a guy who can take a huge bite from a greasy burger with everything, stuff it into one side of his mouth, talk while he chews, and not really gross you out. He's as articulate and quick while eating as when not.

"I'm guessing boyfriend problems," he said "But it could be anything."

At about ten to seven a car pulled up outside. Earl stepped to the window and peered down. "I can't see who it is," he said, "but the driver isn't taking any chances. If it's Karlyn, she worried she's been followed. She's just sitting there with the motor running, leaving herself lots of room to take off if someone pulls up."

"What do we do now?" Margo asked.

"You told her how to get in and up to Philip's apartment. Let's go and wait for her." Haymeyer swept the sandwich trash into the wastebasket, cut the lights in his office, and led the way down the hall. My apartment was on the same side of the building, so Haymeyer was able to watch Karlyn from there too. She stepped from her car while it was still running, looked in every direction, then reached back in to shut it off.

"It's her," Haymeyer said. "And she is a beauty, just like the tape showed."

She took the only entrance that led from the outside to the apartments and we heard her moving cautiously down the hall. Margo answered her knock. She seemed relieved to see Margo and greeted us all warmly, sounding a lot softer than she had on the phone.

"How can we help you?" Margo asked.

"First tell me about Earl, if you don't mind."

"There's no way around it," Margo said. "Right from the top you need to know he's a private investigator."

Karlyn stiffened and looked as if she felt betrayed. "You can trust him, Karlyn," I said, "if you can trust us. We value him as a friend and a professional. We trust him."

"I can't afford to pay anyone to help me," she said.

"I'm here unsolicited," Earl said. "If you ask more than I can give, I'll tell you."

"Thank you," Karlyn said. "I didn't expect this. I don't know what I expected. The only thing I do expect is that when I return to my apartment in Des Plaines tonight, no matter what time, someone will have been there."

"How do you mean?" Earl asked.

"I mean someone will have been there, just as someone has been in my apartment while I was at work or out anywhere for the last three weeks. Exactly twenty-one days."

"They wait for you?"

"No. They're never there when I arrive. They have simply been there."

"They make it obvious?"

"Not at first. About a month ago I first noticed that the light in my hall closet was on when I hung up my coat at the end of the day. I couldn't remember having turned it on for anything. I complained to the management of the apartment complex that someone had been in spraying for bugs or cleaning the carpet or something and had left my light on. They assured me no one had been admitted to any of the apartments for months. I apologized, assuming I had been mistaken.

"A few days later, my living room curtains were open. I always leave them shut during the day so people can't tell from the outside that no one's home. It makes for a depressing homecoming, but the first thing I do every afternoon is open them wide to the sun. That day, I came into an apartment already warm and bright."

"And you figured you had forgotten again."

"No. That's one thing I don't forget because I pull the drapes shut every night before bed. I wouldn't be able to sleep if I thought someone could see through my living room window. There was no way I had opened those drapes before going to work. It's simply something I don't do."

"Did you complain to management again?"

"No, they had told me that they would inform me before they let in anyone for any reason. And if the maintenance staff had to get in, they were to leave a card, so I'd know they'd been there."

"Is that all it's been?" Haymeyer asked "Just something that could be attributed to a poor memory if someone wanted to be picky?"

"No, like I say, after those two episodes another few days went by, then I noticed a strange one. I have a certain way I hang my clothes. It's with the open side of the hanger hook pointing out. That means I put the clothes away by reaching in past the bar and hooking the hanger back toward me. I've done it since chidhood. That afternoon I returned from work and noticed that two of my jackets were turned the wrong way in the front closet."

"Did you begin looking for little things like that all of a sudden?" I asked. "Is it possible that you had never really been that careful but that now these things jumped out at you because you expected them?"

"I know what you're driving at, but I don't think so. I'm weird that way. I do things a certain way and always have."

"So that was the third time something like that happened. How long was it before the next time you noticed anything?"

"The next day. The hangers were the first of three straight weeks of little messages. It's about to drive me nuts. I've had the locks changed. I've heard no noises, and no one has tried to get in at night. I've had friends stay over, without telling them why, and no one has seen or heard anything they've told me about.

"When I'm alone I sleep with pots and pans near the windows so any intruder would make a lot of noise if he came in. I push furniture in front of the door to make it harder to get in. I even stayed in a motel one night so I could get a full night's rest. The next day a bottle of milk in my refrigerator was empty. I would never leave an empty bottle in the refrigerator. Anyway, I had just bought it.

"I began to leave notes for the intruder I asked why he didn't just tell me what he wanted or leave me alone. The first note was ignored, I think, though my wall phone cord was looped up over the phone rather than hanging free the way I leave it. The second time, the note was folded in half and left right where I had written it."

Karlyn said she could hardly remember all the little things that had been changed in her apartment each day. "It's never more than one thing," she said. "Am I crazy? I know I'm not imagining it."

"I'm not so sure," Haymeyer said. "I want you to know that. The phone cord, for instance. Couldn't a friend have used the phone and looped the cord without thinking? Was there some reason that made you start worrying about an intruder three weeks ago? Could your mind be playing tricks on you because you did something or said something that made someone upset with you?"

"Not that I know of. Believe me, there have been too many things like this for it to have been my imagination. There are things I haven't told you."

"Such as?"

"A poster turned around to face the wall. Why would I do a thing like that?"

"Do you think you did it?"

"Not while I was awake."

"Are you a sleepwalker?"

"No."

"One night my barbecue grill — which I haven't used since last summer — was full of charcoal, brand new coals from my previously unopened bag. The bag was stashed against the patio railings as usual, but it had been opened and used."

"And your apartment is on the second floor, right?"

"How did you know that?"

"From the number," Haymeyer said. "It starts with a two. I just figured."

"What else do you know about me?"

"That you were under the care of a counseling psychologist for four years. Can you tell me what your basic problem was?"

"Well, it wasn't hallucinating, I'll tell you that. I wasn't insane or anything. I was a lonely, frustrated girl who never knew who her parents were, never felt loved, never felt accepted. My social worker said I had outgrown her when I received Christ and my life changed."

"I'd like to hear about that some time, Karlyn," Earl said. "But for now, did you happen to bring a change of clothes?"

"As a matter of fact, I did. What are you, a mindreader?"

"No, in fact I didn't figure that until I heard your story. No girl afraid of what she might find in her apartment during the light of day wants to go back alone to it in the middle of the night. Am I right?"

"You're right."

"Margo, can she stay with you at the hotel?"

"Well, she's certainly not staying here."

ELEVEN

"I hope we can get this solved before I leave for Pontiac again next week," Margo said the next morning. "I really like Karlyn and would hate to leave when this is only half done."

"Don't kid yourself," Earl said. "This could be a tough line. Luckily, right now it's all we've got to worry about. So let's worry about it. Did she say anything more last night?"

"She was pretty tired and the only things we talked about at the hotel were personal. Nothing of significance to the case, I would think."

"You don't know that, Margo. Everything in her life could be significant here. I need to know everything. Anything at all about her past or her work situation, anything."

"Well, she doesn't date much and has no real close friends. She's been involved in the same church for several years, but she likes the bigness of it and is not active other than attending regularly. People know who she is, of course, but she accepts few social invitations and while she has favorites among the people, there are none she would call personal friends."

"Strange," I said. "How could someone go to the same church for a long time without developing some friendships?"

"It may not be so strange to an orphan," Haymeyer said. "Remember she was probably deeply hurt as a child. A person should have at least a few vague memories of early childhood, unless they are too painful to deal with. She probably felt abandoned and has always resisted close ties with people who might dump her later.

"Let's remember to ask her about childhood friends. What time did she get away this morning?"

"Fairly early. We stayed up late to talk, but she slept well and said she felt good. She's even prettier when she's rested, gentlemen."

"Then why didn't you bring her around to say good-bye?" I said.

"For that very reason. She did ask if we would meet her at her apartment after work today. I told her I'd call and let her know. Is it OK, Earl?"

"Sure, but I don't want it to be obvious that we're with her. If anyone is really getting into her apartment only when she's gone, then her place is being watched. We want to be careful not to let the whole world know she has help all of a sudden."

"Earl," I said, "what do you mean 'if someone is really getting into her apartment'? Do you doubt her story?"

"No, not at all. It's just that the mind can play funny tricks. Think back on all the things she said were clues that someone had been in her apartment. Any one of them could have been the result of a memory lapse, something else on her mind, whatever. All but the turned around poster, anyway."

"How do we find out if someone's been getting in?"

"That I'll show you tonight."

Margo spent her day writing a long letter to her mother and going to the library. Haymeyer taught me how to dust for fingerprints and put together a composite sketch of a suspect with various facial parts already drawn on overlapping sheets of acetate.

"I could draw them faster than this," I said.

"Then maybe you'll be even more valuable to me."

He also taught me how to handle a gun — not to shoot, but how to load and unload and clean it. "There's no such thing as an unloaded gun," he said.

"One more time?" I said.

"How many times have you read about kids, or even parents, who have shot someone — or even themselves — and were then quoted, 'I didn't know it was loaded'? If you treat the gun as if it's always loaded, you'll never fire it at anyone unless you intend to."

I was amazed to learn that he had never fired his gun in the line of duty in all his years as a detective. "To watch television, you'd think you guys are always shooting it out with someone."

"Nope, in fact I've pointed it at someone only a dozen times or so. The rule is, don't draw your gun unless you're prepared to use it, and don't fire unless you're shooting to kill. The only time you should ever draw it is to protect a life."

"I don't care to carry a gun," I said.

"That's probably just as well, Philip. Eventually you'll probably find it necessary, but for now you've got the right attitude. I don't get any thrill out of carrying one, but it sure evens the odds sometimes."

Haymeyer had a Polaroid camera with him when we left for Des Plaines in his new nondescript Ford station wagon. "I didn't want it to look like an unmarked squad car, but it couldn't be flashy either," he explained.

We waited in the parking lot of Karlyn's apartment building until she returned from work. She acknowledged us with a tiny wave as she pulled in, but we did not respond. She had been instructed to leave the door ajar so we could just walk right in a few minutes later from another entrance.

Karlyn was in the living room looking for clues of the intruder when we walked in. Her deadbolt lock looked forbidding enough. "How could anyone get in here?" Margo asked.

"It wouldn't be easy," Haymeyer said. "The door could be popped with a simple tool in less time than it takes to open it with a key, but that deadbolt should be a deterrent to anyone but a pro, and even he would need time."

Karlyn led us to the bedroom, which was neat as a pin. She opened the closet. "Everything looks OK," she said. "Here and in the living room and the kitchen. That's eerie. That means whoever has been leaving messages for me the last three weeks knows I went for help."

"Don't assume too much," Haymeyer cautioned. "Have we seen everything?"

"All but the bathroom."

Karlyn walked past us from her bedroom and into the bathroom, but as we followed she turned and nearly bowled us over, terror in her eyes. "The shower curtain," she whispered. "Mr. Haymeyer, someone could be in the shower!"

Earl pushed us back into the hallway and asked Karlyn where the bathroom light switch was located.

"On your right," she said, barely able to speak.

Earl took off his suit coat and laid it over a chair, drew his snub-nosed .38 with his right hand, and inched toward the bathroom.

Reaching across his body with his left hand, he switched on the light and lunged toward the shower curtain, whipping it aside and dropping into a crouch, both hands on his revolver. "There's no one here," he said.

Karlyn was trembling. "You can say it's my memory or anything you want," she said, "but what girl living alone would close her shower curtain when she's not in the shower? I even check the closets before I go to bed to make sure no one's inside. If I left the shower curtain closed, I'd have to check behind it every time I walked by."

Margo nodded.

"How would you like to get out of here for a while, Karlyn?" Earl said.

"I would."

"Let's take a ride back up north so Margo can check out of her hotel. I'd like you to come back and stay with Karlyn until you have to leave for Pontiac, OK?"

"Are you kidding? I'm not so sure," Margo said.

"I'm not either," I said.

"You've never seen or heard this intruder. Right, Karlyn?" Haymeyer asked.

"Right."

"He comes only when you're gone and never at night?"

"So far — as far as I know."

"Then you two should be safe. Use your usual precautions, furniture against the door and all. For now, let's go back and get some dinner. Just let me shoot a few pictures first."

Haymeyer took two or three pictures in each room in an attempt to record things exactly as we left them. Then we were off, Margo and Karlyn in her car, Earl and I in his.

Dinner was nice, Karlyn was nervous, and Margo wasn't much better. She was anxious to help Karlyn, but she felt a little like a guinea pig, "or a sacrificial lamb," she said. The women weren't anxious to head back to Des Plaines, so we chatted for a few hours until Haymeyer told them they'd better quit putting it off.

"Philip and I will wait in my office until we hear from you that you're in and safe and locked up."

"And alone," Margo said wryly.

"Yes," Earl said. "And alone."

Earl was showing me his photographic equipment that allowed him to make internegatives of Polaroid prints and enlarge them when the call came that would force him to do just that.

"I don't know what to make of it," Margo said, "but Karlyn insists that the thermostat has been tampered with."

"Oh, brother," Haymeyer said, "we're reaching a bit, aren't we? I'm getting just a bit dubious. Let me talk to her.

"Hello, Karlyn? Listen, what is different about the thermostat? You know how those things can always be off a degree or two . . . Oh, it is? I see. Well, maybe there's a way I can check it. Meanwhile, get yourselves secured and try to get some sleep. You know where we are if you need us."

"What's up?"

"Karlyn says she never touches the thermostat. Two or three months ago she set it on automatic at sixty-eight degrees and never moved it. A little while after they got there, she noticed that the blower seemed to be running constantly, although the temperature seemed normal. She checked the thermostat and it was set at sixty-seven and manual."

"How do we determine if she adjusted it by accident or without thinking?"

"Come here. I'll show you. We can know for sure if anyone was in that apartment after we were."

TWELVE

It took Earl about an hour to make a huge enlargement of the tiny shot he had taken of the wall where Karlyn's thermostat was located. With a magnifying glass on a high contrast print, he could see that Karlyn had been right.

"When we left that apartment," he said, "the thermostat was set on sixty-eight and automatic."

"What now?"

"Sleep and then a stakeout. We'll find out just how sharp this bird is and if he knows when a place is being watched or not. We'll get there before Karlyn leaves for work and watch the place all day long. You're going to get a good idea of the occasional drudgery of this work. When we're not staring at parking lots and entrances and comings and goings, we'll be running for coffee, covering each other for catnaps, and interviewing people in the building about whether they've seen anything at all."

"Sounds like a drag," I said.

But it wasn't. I rather enjoyed showing people my new business card and asking if I could speak with them a moment. Few wanted to talk at first, assuming that I was trying to sell something. There was not a person on Karlyn's floor who didn't know who she was, though most had never spoken to her. Almost all referred to her in some variation of "that beautiful, quiet, little blonde."

No one had seen anyone coming or going from the apartment when Karlyn wasn't home, though most had noticed two men and a woman who entered after she did the afternoon before.

"I'm completely baffled," I admitted to Earl. "I suppose you've got it all figured out."

"No, but I'm not ready to throw in the towel yet. I can't admit I'm stumped, even if it's true. It might make a bad impression on you. But what did I tell you about perseverance? Somebody knows something, and we're gonna find out who it is."

With Margo in the apartment virtually all day everyday, there was enough activity to scare off any intruder. But that made it obvious that the place was being watched. As long as someone was there, no attempt was made to leave "messages." We learned nothing by interviewing more people in the building. A week passed and Margo began making plans to leave for Pontiac.

"I hate to do this to you, Karlyn," she said. "But I have no choice."

"I understand. But I'm sure going to miss you and all the time we spent talking and praying and reading."

"Yeah," Margo said, "and watching TV, and cooking, and eating. It's been fun, in spite of the circumstances."

"I guess Philip will just have to take over where Margo left off," Haymeyer said.

"Fat chance," Margo said, throwing a pillow at him.

"Seriously, I am about to turn this case over to Philip," Earl said. "I'm getting more and more business as my old contacts discover that I'm available. We need some hard legwork done before we get a real lead, and that's what you're here for, Philip."

I couldn't deny I was excited, but I told Earl I would need his counsel.

"I'll be around," he said. "Nothing I have lined up will take me out of town. You can talk to me anytime you want, but as of tomorrow morning, this one is yours."

"How do you feel about that, Karlyn?" I asked. "You sought out Margo, got Earl instead, and now I'm subbing for him."

"I'd feel guilty if I didn't tell you I'd rather have Earl on it, but if he feels you can handle it, who am I to say you can't? I can't pay either of you, so I appreciate any help I can get from anyone. Don't get me wrong. You're the one who helped Margo when she needed it, so you've got that experience."

"The cases are hardly similar," I said.

"And let's not let the consequences be similar either," Margo said, smiling.

Margo was more talkative than usual as we loaded her car the next morning. She was concerned about everything from the fact that she hadn't heard from her mother by phone or letter to what she should wear the first time she visited. "What does one wear to a prison?" she asked.

She double-checked that she had everything and slid behind the wheel. I got in the other side just to sit with her for a minute. She finally ran out of nervous energy and turned in the seat to face me.

"So — " she said.

"So," I said.

"So now you're a private eye."

I winced. She didn't want to be serious. "Yeah," I said, "and someday I'm gonna track you down." She leaned over and laid her head against my chest. I smoothed back her hair.

"This is not going to be easy," she said softly.

"Hm?"

"Leaving you."

"I know."

"I mean I knew it was coming, but I thought I'd be ready. I'm not ready, Philip."

"Neither am I."

"But we're not kids; we have no choices, do we?"

"No, Margo, we don't."

"I mean, if we were high school kids, I could just forget this trip. You could skip school. We could spend the day in a park somewhere and get yelled at when we got home. And maybe grounded."

"Those were the good old days," I agreed. "Only in Dayton there wasn't anything worth skipping school for."

"There was in Winnetka, only I was never invited."

"Skip school with me, love. Forget Pontiac and I'll forget my responsibilities to Earl and Karlyn. What do you say?"

"I say you're as crazy as I am."

"Just crazy about you, Margo."

"My, what a quick wit and tongue! How do you come up with 'em so fast? You should be in the movies!"

"You really know how to hurt a guy. You set me up for that dumb retort, you know."

"But I had no idea you'd just jump right in there with 'crazy about you'!"

"Oh, be quiet. I don't know if I'll ever survive your mockery."

"Here's hoping you get plenty of time to find out."

"You'd better get going," I said, looking at my watch. Margo looked up at me. I leaned down and kissed her.

"Oh, to be a kid again," she said. "I swear I'd forget this trip."

"You are a kid. Now get goin." I jumped out and ran around to her window.

"There are so many things I want to say," she said. I put my finger to her lips.

"Call me when you get there," I said. "Write me often. Let me know when you can come up, and make it soon." I took my hand away.

"Parting is such sweet sorrow," she said. "More sorrow than sweet." And she pulled away.

I'm not one who waves to cars as they fade from sight, so I just headed for Des Plaines. I tried to think about whether it would be right to get Karlyn's permission to tell her employer, or the police, or the apartment complex management what was going on. I decided I'd better check with Haymeyer first, but it was hard to keep my mind on the case.

All I could think of was how little time I had spent alone with Margo since returning from Atlanta. I missed her already and didn't need that while trying to make heads or tails of my first investigation. I called Earl.

"No. Philip. No police yet. Let me deliver the intruder to them when the time comes, unless we need them. And let's not say anything to the apartment managers because I haven't ruled out the possibility that they could be involved somehow. How else is someone getting into that place without force and without being noticed? As for her employer, that's entirely up to her."

Karlyn agreed to meet me for lunch, where I gingerly broached the subject of telling her employer what was going on. "It can only help you," I said. "Earl discovered that the personnel department is already worried about you."

"But what if it's someone there?" she said. "The word will get out and whoever is doing it will change tactics."

"Do you have any reason to believe it might be someone from work?"

"I don't have any reason to believe anything anymore," she said. "I've racked my brain to think of anything I've said or done to anyone that would prompt them to torment me like this. I scribbled a list of everything I could think of in the last year. I don't know what good it will do you, but you can see it if you want."

"Sure," I said, and read it as I ate. Karlyn just picked at her food. She had listed a minor traffic accident she had caused the previous winter.

"I didn't know how to report it or even if I had to," she said. "I thought the police report would go to my insurance company or something. I didn't mean to be so dumb. After about six months, I got a letter from the guy I hit, asking me to please inform my insurance company so he could get his car fixed. I did that, but a few months ago I heard from him again. My insurance company had contacted him, but no settlement had been made yet. He wasn't too happy, but he seemed like a nice enough guy. Worth checking out?"

"Of course," I said.

THIRTEEN

"Don't waste too much time on this insurance claim thing," Haymeyer warned me. "I ran across the same incident when I was checking her out. The guy is from out of state. All you need to do is verify that he's not been in Illinois during the last month and you can rule him out. It's pretty thin soup anyway, thinking that a victim of a fender bender would try to scare a girl to death."

"Makes sense, I guess," I said. "How many of the leads that sound good to me are going to become dead ends?"

"All but the last one."

"Very funny."

"Just hang in there, Philip, and don't expect it to be easy. Very, very often the tip that leads you to the answer will seem like coincidence or a stroke of luck."

"But it isn't?"

"Of course it isn't. It would be luck only if you had it drop in your lap when you weren't doing your homework. If you're working hard, you make your breaks. It's just like in sports. Doesn't it always seem like the team that gets the breaks wins?"

"Yeah."

"Think about it. It's really the other way around. The winner, the champion, the hustler is in a position to get the breaks. He makes the breaks. You may be looking in one direction and have something pop up in another, but you wouldn't know it if it slapped you in the face unless you were looking just the same."

"I'm not sure I follow, but I'm stubborn enough to stay on this."

"That's all it takes."

"I hope you're right. Is there anything else you ran across that I should know about so we don't duplicate efforts?"

"I'm sorry I didn't give you Karlyn's readout. I'll have it for you tonight."

"Say, Earl, this may sound weird, but do you ever just stop and think about a case? I feel I need to do that, but I feel guilty if I'm not driving around, talking to Karlyn, or trying to track something down. I need noodling time, or at least I feel I do."

"Exactly right, Philip. Remember when you and Jim Hanlon and I used to sit around with the other agents and maybe Larry Shipman and just brainstorm? Sometimes it lasted an hour or two, and we would just try to get inside someone's head and decide what we would do if we were him?"

"Yeah."

"Well, if you really hit a dead end, just drive to the beach and think the thing through."

"I'd probably wind up thinking about Margo."

"Then track down Larry Shipman. It'll be good experience for you because that's a job for any detective. No one ever knows where he is. Find him and see if he'll spend some time discussing the case. He knows nothing of it yet, so tell him and swear him to secrecy. In telling him, maybe something will break loose in your own mind. You may find him a step ahead of you, though. He's a thinker."

Shipman's phone-answering device told me that Larry was either sleeping or gone and that if I called again right away and he was sleeping, he'd wake up and answer, but that if I was a burglar and that didn't work, not to assume he was really gone or I'd risk getting my head blown off when I broke into his apartment. A really different kind of a guy.

I called back right away and got the same message, so I went to his place in downtown Chicago and banged long and hard on his door.

A neighbor told me he had seen Larry leave about an hour before, but the neighbor had no idea where he was headed. "You can bet it's either to the paper, the radio station, the TV station, or — "

"Or what?"

"Or the police department. You never know."

I called all those places. He had been to each, except for his favorite radio station, so I figured he was making the rounds of his haunts. They didn't expect him, but then they never expected him. I drove over and asked for him. "He hasn't been here," the girl said. Intuition told me to wait in the parking lot.

Intuition was right. I was encouraged. Maybe I could be a detective after all.

"Philip, my man, how ya doin'?" Larry said as he breezed into the studio. "You and Happy Haymeyer get that blonde caper settled yet?"

"No, and that's why I'm here. I'd like to bounce some ideas off you if you have the time."

"What'll it take?"

"Maybe an hour."

"Sure. Is this a freebie?"

"Fraid so."

"That's OK, Philip. I made a few skins off your future mother-in-law's case. I can give you an hour as soon as I'm through here. C'mon with me."

I followed him to the news director's office and listened as he played a few cassette recordings he had made just that morning. One was an interview with a fireman at the scene of a fatal fire. The other was with the mother of a hit-and-run victim.

"This is dynamite stuff, Larry," the news director said. "I don't know how you do it."

"It's all because of the praise and glory and money, and because of my little scanner radio that tells me where the cops are at all times."

"We've got the same radios, Larry, but even when we beat you to the scene, we don't get the interviews you get. That's what makes you our best stringer."

"That's music to my ears, but I bet you tell that to all the brilliant people you meet. Just wait till you find out that I use actors and make these things up."

"You'll be hearing from me soon," the newsman said.

"Hey, I haven't heard from you yet on last week's stuff."

"Are you serious?"

"Yeah."

"Larry, I'm sorry. You know we're usually pretty tidy on these things, especially with you. I'll call accounting right now and get it in the mail to you tomorrow."

"A likely story." Shipman laughed, tossing the man the untouched half of a roast beef sandwich. "We'll be talkin' to ya."

Larry is a constant mover, always on the go. He swept past me and was down the hall and out the door to the parking lot before I had hardly begun to move. He held the door open for me and then clapped, rubbed his hands together, and said, "Philip, let's talk blondes."

He directed me to a deserted Lake Michigan beach where frigid waves lapped not far from the car. "I want to hear it all, and you've got an hour of my prime time." He was dead serious and stared straight into my eyes for the twenty minutes or so it took me to tell Karlyn's story.

Shipman looked dubious about all the clues, especially after I said she had changed the lock. I concluded, "So Earl determined that someone for sure had been there by blowing up the picture of the thermostat and showing the different setting."

Shipman lowered his eyes and sat gazing at the dashboard. "Let's walk," he said and was quickly out of the car and down the beach. I ran to catch up. He said nothing for a long time, but just ran his hands through his hair and kept moving. Finally he stopped and looked around, as if the answer had just whizzed by and he had nearly missed it. "I want to see her place," he said abruptly.

"It's nearly time for her to be off work, and my hour with you is almost up," I said.

"Hey," he said, "did I ask for anything? No self-respecting journalist can ignore a real mystery. Just let me see her place. It's in Des Plaines, you say?"

We got there just a few minutes before Karlyn was due home from work. "I don't want to be here when she gets here," he said. "Let me just check it out quickly."

We went to her apartment and rang the bell, not expecting any answer, of course. But while I stood there, shielding anyone's view of Larry, he popped the door lock and nearly jimmied the deadbolt. "I could have been in in another minute or so," he said. "But then I know what I'm doing. No way anyone could have gotten in there fast enough to not be noticed. Not every day for three straight weeks anyway."

We went down and out and around to the back where Larry leaped from behind some bushes on a dirt incline and caught hold of the railing on Karlyn's patio. He pulled himself onto the ledge and climbed over the rail.

"Notice anything?" he called out.

"No, I can't even see you."

"Move over to where I jumped up from."

"I still can't see you."

"Move to your left about three feet and crouch. Now can you see me through the bushes and the railing?"

"Just barely."

"Then you noticed what I wanted you to notice."

"No, I didn't. I can hardly see you."

"That's what I wanted you to notice. Now if you can get up here, I'll show you what else you can't see."

It wasn't difficult, even though I am not as athletic as Larry. "Now look," he said. "Can you see anyone else's patio?"

"No, that's neat how they designed these for privacy, isn't it?"

"Ducky," he said. "Don't you see, Philip? If you can get around behind the building with no one seeing you, you can get onto the second floor patios without trouble. And once you're on the patio, no one can see you. Do you have any idea how easy these patio sliding doors are to open?"

"No, but you're going to show me, aren't you?"

Shipman placed both hands, palms out, on one of the glass doors, leaned in, and lifted. The entire side was freed from the bottom track. He could have lifted it out, but we heard the lock being turned from the hallway door.

"Karlyn's home," I whispered. "Let's get out of here before we scare her to death!"

We nearly knocked each other down trying to get to the railing, but Shipman got there first, neatly planted one hand and catapulted himself over the side into the bushes. The door clicked from inside. Another second and Karlyn would have a clear view of my silhouette on the curtain. I tried to do what Shipman had done but chickened out of letting go in mid-air and found myself hanging from the other side of the railing. As the front door opened, I let my hands slide down the rail until I hung out of sight from the concrete patio floor.

I hung there with scraped wrists and aching fingers, but Shipman was no help. He was trying so hard not to laugh that he was nearly crying, hiding his eyes.

"Hang in there," he whispered, causing himself to laugh even more. "I'm comin' to get ya, Tarzan!" He grabbed my ankles just as I heard footsteps inside and let go of the ledge. With Shipman holding my ankles, I hit the dirt incline headfirst, and we both bounced into the bushes.

We were like a couple of drunken sailors staggering out of there, I rubbing everything that hurt, Shipman trying to control his laughter.

"You're lucky I'm free tonight," he said in the car. "Let's see if we can get some time with Earl. The only thing better than this is hearing me tell about it." I was only slightly amused.

Haymeyer could hardly contain himself. "Are you hurt, Sherlock?" he asked.

"No, but I wish I was. I'd have something to show for my heroics."

"Well, did you boys come up with any leads, or did you just spend the whole afternoon monkeying around?"

"Boo," Shipman said.

"I learned that whoever is doing this is doing it from the back," I said.

Haymeyer and Shipman broke into mock applause. "Very good, Philip," Earl said. "Have mercy, Larry. The kid's gonna make it yet!"

"I can't win," I said.

"Seriously, Earl," Shipman said. "I do think there is one part of Karlyn's history that deserves our attention."

FOURTEEN

Earl and I looked at each other, as if to ask if Larry was being serious. "We're ready," Haymeyer said.

"The orphanage," Shipman announced. "Philip, how big are you?"

"About five ten and a hundred seventy-five pounds."

Haymeyer and Shipman rolled their collective eyes. "Philip, you are talking to trained observers," Haymeyer scolded. "I don't suppose you'll get in trouble with your church for exaggerating a bit, but at least tell us the truth. There's no way you're taller than five nine, and it'll be years before you see a hundred seventy-five pounds."

"OK," I said, "I'm five eight-and-a-half and a hundred sixty-four."

"What does all this have to do with the orphanage?" Earl said.

"My theory is this, gentlemen: a woman could get onto that patio just as easily as we did today."

"I'll grant you the physical part of it," Haymeyer said, "but is it logical? Is there anything else that says our man is a woman."

"Cute," Shipman said. "And yes, there is, if Philip got the story straight. Think about it. There have been no threats. No notes, no breathy, wordless phone calls. No weapons. Just irritations. Little things done a different way. Little things that only a woman might know would bother another woman."

"But why would this female enemy have to come from the orphanage? Why not the girls' school? Or high school? Or from work?"

"It's just a guess. Hurts inflicted at childhood are the deepest and most painful, aren't they?"

"I don't know, Dr. Freud. I'm just a flatfoot."

We all sat thinking about it. Finally Earl spoke again. "The scariest messages for Karlyn were the shower curtain and the folded note, but that was only because the one hinted at an ambush and the other seemed to be a direct answer to a communication. You may be onto something, Larry."

"Should we get Karlyn in on this discussion?" I asked.

"No, I'd sooner get Margo's ideas. I don't want Karlyn trying to figure out which girl she knew in the orphanage might be visiting her apartment everyday, when we're only guessing ourselves. Ask Margo when she calls, will you, Philip?"

Margo's drive south had been uneventful. "Tomorrow I'll be beating the bushes for work," she said. "I miss you already."

"I missed you first," I said.

"Don't be too sure. Philip, I really need to ask you something serious, if you have a few minutes."

"I have something serious to ask you, too, if you have the rest of your life."

"Really, Philip. I need your help."

"OK, I'm sorry."

"It's about Mother. I got my first note from her. She says she feels vulnerable there. Isn't that weird? Why should she feel vulnerable when she's separated from the other inmates?"

"I don't know. Maybe it's paranoia. After so many years in a position of power, now she's a nobody and she doesn't like it. What do you make of it, Mar?"

"I think she might be ready for a real spiritual push. I'm tired of trying nudges."

"I hadn't thought of it that way, but maybe."

"What do you think about my explaining all about why I became a believer in Christ? In a letter I mean, so she won't interrupt me or act embarrassed as usual. And then I'll tell her we can discuss it when I see her, or when she's ready."

"With that analytical mind of hers, that may be the best. You might do better on paper too."

"You know I've tried several times in person. I guess I'm just too emotional. I've never been able to talk her into anything either, and I'm still intimidated after all these years. I'm anxious to get something down and off to her soon. I'll be seeing her in a week or so, you know. I do need some advice first though."

"Like what?"

"Like what I should write."

"Hit me with what you had in mind."

"She already knows what I feel Christ has done for me, but my needs are not her needs. What do I tell her, Philip? I want to start with the fact that the Bible says she's a sinner and lost, and that she needs Christ to assure herself of eternal life. I just don't know how she'd respond."

"I don't either. For sure she knows she's done wrong. She's lived with that for years. Maybe you should emphasize that Christ offers her abundant life. You'll find that in John ten, specifically verse ten. And convince her that she can be free, even in prison. John eight thirty-two says that she can know the truth and that the truth will set her free."

Margo was silent.

I continued. "She needs to know that Christ's death paid for her freedom and that if she would give Him a chance to change her life, she might eventually adopt John the Baptist's philosophy in John three thirty. That would be the full cycle for her, Margo. From being the god of her own life for more than fifty years to getting out of the way so Christ can take over."

"That would really be something, Philip. That really would. What you're telling me is that if I know the book of John, I can write the letter I need to. Maybe what I should do is to read the book through a couple of times first."

"As long as you're going to do that, try it in a couple of different versions."

"Great idea. Thanks, Philip."

"Now, let me pick *your* brain for a minute."

"Sure."

I asked her what one little girl could do to another that would make her hate the first so much that she would harass her like Karlyn was being harassed.

"I'd have to think about that one," she said. "I don't have any experience with orphanages, but I imagine they can be pretty rough. Can you find out if there were boys there? That can lead to some knock down, drag out fights sometimes. But I suppose Earl is looking for evidence of a quarrel that was never resolved by a fight."

"I suppose."

"I'm sorry, Philip. I'll keep thinking about it, but that's all I can come up with right now."

Haymeyer and Shipman agreed that Margo was probably right about the unresolved quarrel. "But we want to be sure we aren't going off the deep end on the wrong idea," Earl said. "It's easy to build a case on a theory and then find out the theory itself is wrong."

"How often have *my* theories been wrong?" Shipman asked. "Don't answer that."

"You were sure right about Olga Yakovich giving the Wanmacher murder weapon to her son," Earl said.

"Yeah, but I was a few hours too late with that brainstorm, wasn't I?"

We were silent for a few minutes, reliving in our minds the horror of finding the body of that slim, young college kid on the floor of his room, a gaping wound where his throat had been slit.

"I'm not sure I'm cut out for this kind of work after all, Earl," I said. "I dread being too late in finding out who's playing games with Karlyn. If we found her injured, or worse, I'd never forgive myself."

"You have to forgive yourself sometimes, Philip," Shipman said. "I could blame myself for Jon Yakovich's death if I thought it was my responsibility to think like a criminal before the criminals do. But there was nothing I could have done about it. We raced over there as soon as we thought of it, but he had been dead several hours. What could I have done?"

"I just don't want us to be sitting around trying to think of motives and suspects while Karlyn might be already hurt," I said.

"Nobody's disputing that, Philip, and maybe that's why you are cut out for this business. You've got to care. If you don't, you'd just wait for the murders and then enjoy figuring out whodunit. That's not for me."

"Me either," I said.

"Then let's go to work," Shipman said. "I'm still trying to figure out why you, the best gumshoe in the state, and I, upon whom the entire city of Chicago depends for its news, are spending all this time helping an apprentice investigator with his first case, and for no bucks."

"I do appreciate it, guys. You know that, don't you?"

"What have you done for me lately?" Shipman asked.

"I gave you a good laugh in the bushes, and don't you forget it."

"I couldn't if I tried, believe me."

"Let's call Karlyn," Earl said.

She was anxious to have us visit her, though she was a little nervous when Larry showed up with us. Again we had to convince her that he was more than just another person getting involved.

Today's clue had been the bed covers turned back, the way it's done in nice hotels. "Fits my theory," Larry said, piquing Karlyn's curiosity.

"Which is?" she said.

Shipman looked to Earl for permission.

Earl nodded. "But first let me explain our new tactics. From now on we don't try to pretend we don't know someone has been here. We don't try to hide that we're looking for the person. I think the suspect wants to be caught because otherwise he or she would have tried something more severe. There's something darkly symbolic about the bed covers being turned back, and I don't like it. Could mean we're heading toward a confrontation. It would be nice to know who we're dealing with before that happens."

Karlyn looked sick. "I'm not sure I like what I just heard," she said.

Haymeyer leaned forward and rested his elbows on his knees. "I'm not trying to be tough on you, Karlyn, but welcome to the adult world. This is happening to you, so I'm through talking in circles about it as if it concerns someone else. You're being hassled and threatened and it scares you, I know. But you can't avoid the truth just because you don't like how it sounds. Keep your wits about you and stay with us. Don't hide behind us. Lead us to your pursuer."

"I don't have any idea who he might be!"

"Go ahead, Larry. Hit her with your idea."

Karlyn was fascinated and tried to rack her brain for memories of childhood battles. "There were many," she said. "Which one would lead to something like this?"

"Something unresolved."

"That was the one good thing about the home in Kalamazoo," she said. "For as strict as the matrons were, they didn't allow fighting and arguing to go unfinished. There was a complete airing of the problem and someone was always punished — "

Karlyn stopped and appeared to be deep in thought. "There was a girl," she said, "whom I liked so much that I wished she were my mother. She was only a couple of years older than I was, but she was a true friend."

"We need someone who wasn't necessarily a friend," Shipman said.

"Well, something happened with us," Karlyn said. "And she quit being my friend."

"Tell us all you can about her and the situation," Earl said, "and Philip will take notes."

Karlyn folded her hands in her lap and looked down. "I was six," she said carefully. "LaDonna was eight. LaDonna Finch. I thought she was the most beautiful girl in the world. I couldn't believe that she liked me too. We played together every chance we got, but we also had to work too. From age four on up, everyone had specific duties and were punished if they didn't do them.

"LaDonna always talked about her parents coming back for her some day. No one believed her because most of us didn't have parents, and those who did were not often visited by them. But LaDonna, the girl with the beautiful name, did. Her mother came about every six months and promised it would be only a little while longer before she would take her home again and she would meet a new daddy.

"It was a promise most of us had heard her recount so many times that many had stopped believing it. But I didn't. I wanted it to be true for LaDonna, but I didn't want her to leave either. She never knew how much I needed her to be my friend and protector. She stuck up for me all the time. That's probably why she never understood why I didn't stand up for her."

"You let her down?"

"Not intentionally. I could have saved her from a paddling if I had been more forceful. We were supposed to clean up the television room before visiting hours, and we were not allowed to leave until it was done. She and I were nearly finished when she saw her mother's car pull up. 'Oh, please finish up for me, Karlyn,' she begged. I said, 'Sure, LaDonna. You run and see your mother.' "

Karlyn looked up at us.

"She got in trouble for that?" Shipman asked.

"Miss Kepkey came in just a few minutes later and demanded to know who was supposed to be helping me. I said, 'LaDonna, but — ' and I was going to tell her that I had said I would finish up.

" 'I'll teach her for leaving all this work to you,' she said, and before I could say anything more, she left. I got to meet Mrs. Finch that day. LaDonna's mother had the same jet black hair cut in a pageboy that LaDonna had. She seemed so nice, nothing like I thought a mother would be like who left her daughter in an orphanage.

"While we were talking, Miss Kepkey interrupted and told LaDonna that she wanted to see her in her room as soon as visiting hours were over. Mrs. Finch asked if anything was wrong, and Miss Kepkey just said, 'Nothing that can't be handled.' Then she looked at me and walked away. I had a stomachache for days, every time I thought of that look."

"So what happened?"

"When Mrs. Finch left, LaDonna went back to her room. I followed her but waited outside the door because I knew Miss Kepkey was in there waiting for her. 'Well, aren't we just something?' she said to LaDonna. 'A pretty, black-haired girl and her rich, black-haired mama all gussied up and wonderful? And you think that entitles you to leave little Karlyn to do all the work?'

"LaDonna started to protest but Miss Kepkey told her, 'Karlyn told me how you left her with the whole job! Now bend over!' LaDonna started crying and saying it wasn't true, that I had said it was OK, but Miss Kepkey kept yelling at her to bend over."

Karlyn buried her head in her hands and wept. "I'm sorry. I haven't thought about this in years."

"Take your time," Earl said. "I really think we might be onto something here."

"Well, Miss Kepkey smacked LaDonna's bare skin with the paddle so hard and so many times that LaDonna screamed and screamed. I wanted to run away but I was frozen. Suddenly LaDonna stopped screaming and I heard her tumble to the floor Miss Kepkey kept insisting that she get up, but LaDonna wasn't moving.

"I ran to the headmistress and said, 'She's hurt LaDonna bad, she's hurt her so bad!' and I pointed down the hall. Mrs. Miller ran into the room just as Miss Kepkey was coming out, the paddle still in her hand. Mrs. Miller screamed when she saw LaDonna."

FIFTEEN

"Just relax for now," Haymeyer said. "When you're ready, tell us whatever else you can about the incident."

"I'm all right," Karlyn said "I can tell you. That was the worst, but things were never the same between LaDonna and me. She was never mean — she never had been — in fact, I don't think she had a mean streak in her." Haymeyer and Shipman caught each other's eye as if to say, *I'll bet.*

"Did LaDonna try to get back at you?"

"She never said one word to me for the last year she stayed there. Nothing. Not one word. I could hardly stand it. I cried and begged her to say hi to me, to hit me, to kick me, to yell at me, to take my toys, anything. I wanted her to acknowledge that I existed. She would come into a room and merely look at me. I'd smile, say something, or hand her something, and she would ignore me as if I weren't there. She kept it up longer than I ever would have been able to.

"I tried to tell her what had happened, that I hadn't really told on her, but she walked away. I followed her around, asking if she understood and if it was OK now. She never said another word to me."

"Did she speak to other girls?"

"Yes, but she was not the same girl she had been. She had been the happiest, cheeriest girl in the place, but now she was subdued. She was in infirmary for two weeks and her seat was tender for another two.

"I've not had a real friend since. I blame myself for losing LaDonna, even though down deep I know it wasn't my fault. I tried to make it right with her, but she just wouldn't listen. I think she was hurt even more deeply than I was. It could be that she never got over it. But she wouldn't be doing this to me now. It wouldn't make sense."

"Well," Shipman said, flopping back in his chair, "think what you want. I'd say you've got a possibility here. This is the very way deep-seated hostilities come out after many years."

"But nineteen years?" I asked.

"Why not? It depends on how deeply LaDonna's mind may have been scarred."

"Bizarre."

"For sure," Haymeyer said. "And you'd better check it out."

"Where do I start?"

"At the Creekside Home for Girls, Kalamazoo, Michigan, I guess."

"They won't tell you anything," Karlyn said. "At least they never told me anything."

"You tried to look up LaDonna?"

"No, my parents."

"Well, that's different. In fact, they'd probably have to give you that information now too, with the new laws. It's worth checking out. Maybe Philip can ask about that when he's there."

"You know what?" Karlyn said. "If I find out it could be LaDonna, I don't even want to know. I just want to go where she can't find me. I was almost to the point where I was over that hurt. But now this. I still can't believe she's got it in her."

"Karlyn," Haymeyer said, "you read about Margo and Philip in the paper, right?"

"Right."

"Can you imagine what it must have been like for Margo to live with the knowledge that her mother was a murderer?"

"No, I can't."

"But what's worse, her mother at one point plotted with the Mafia to have it look like Margo was about to be killed herself. Margo had a pretty tough time believing that her mother would do that."

"Never having had a mother, I can't relate, but I'm sure you're right."

"But Margo was right," I corrected Haymeyer. "Her mother only intended to scare her, not to really have her shot."

"But that didn't make Margo feel a whole lot better, did it?" Shipman said.

Karlyn put her fingers to her temples.

"What is it?" Haymeyer asked.

She raised a hand to silence him, as if she were in deep thought. "I just remembered something I hadn't thought about in years. Not long after LaDonna got her paddling, little things began happening to my room and to my bed, even to my closet."

"Like what?" Shipman said. "Like what's been happening here lately?"

"Not exactly. One day my closet door was nailed shut. Once my bed was shortsheeted. Another time a tiny turtle was left in my shoe. I don't know if it relates or not. I hope not."

"Philip," Haymeyer said, standing, "let's bid Karlyn good night, thank Larry for his time, screw on the sliding door lock that will secure it against anyone, and head back to Glencoe."

Karlyn was shaky as she got our coats from the closet. Larry applied the lock, "just for precaution," and told her to call Earl if any messages turned up the next day.

"I don't really think any will," Shipman said. "Unless they appear on the patio. I believe we've secured the only logical point of entry."

"We'll see," Haymeyer said. "This intruder has been crafty. It may take more than being locked out to discourage him."

"Him?"

"Her?"

"It."

"Philip, I think you should go to Michigan first thing tomorrow."

"What'll I be looking for?"

"The whereabouts of the former LaDonna Finch. On the one hand, I hope you find she's migrated this way. On the other, for Karlyn's sake, I hope it's a dead end and we find it's just some neighborhood Peeping Tom we can scare off, or put away."

I didn't know what to think. I believed in women's intuition, but it seemed Karlyn was just refusing to believe that her sweet little girl friend of so many years ago could have grown up into a bad woman. My only hope was that I could find someone at Creekside who would give me a solid lead.

There certainly were no other suspects. Although Karlyn had no close friends, she seemed to have no enemies either. Not one. Not even the man she had hit the last winter. When I finally reached him, telling him I represented her, he told me to assure her that he had been taken care of by her insurance company and was happy.

The reason it had taken so long for him to get back to me was that he had been in Bermuda for two weeks. "Unless he commuted to her patio everyday, " Haymeyer said, "he's not our man."

So who *was* our man? At first I wanted to track him down because it was my first solo job. Then Shipman and Haymeyer had been so instrumental in leading me this far that I lost the thrill of its being my own. Now my whole motive was to help Karlyn out of her misery. I believed she was safe in her apartment with the intruder intent upon bothering her only when she was away.

When I called her the evening I arrived in Kalamazoo, however, I realized that time was not on our side.

"An envelope was in my mailbox when I got home," she said. "It had no stamp and no postmark, No letter either. Just a blank sheet of paper."

I called Haymeyer, who told me he would get out to Des Plaines to see if anyone had seen a stranger near the mailboxes that day, but that I should not hope for much. "At least that sliding door lock is forcing our target out into the open a little more," he said. "Let me know what you find up there."

I figured the bold approach would lead nowhere the next day, so I tried something different. "Does Mrs. Miller still work here?" I asked.

"No, but you may talk to Miss Bloom. She's headmistress now."

Before she would answer any questions, she wanted to know all about me, who I was, what I was doing in Michigan, and all the rest. I simply told her I was an artist who was in the area looking for a friend of a friend. I asked Miss Bloom if it ever happened that a girl who lived at Creekside came back to work there on the staff."

"Not very often, but there is a woman with us now who was here back in the sixties."

"Could I talk with her?"

"Certainly."

A few minutes later I rose to meet a slender, pleasant woman who introduced herself as Roberta Burns. "Did you know Karlyn May?" I asked her.

"I vaguely remember her," she said. "Are you a friend of hers?"

"Yes."

"Is she still a blonde?"

"Sure is. She has talked about a Mrs. Miller."

"Oh, yes."

"Whatever happened to her?"

"She retired. She lives only thirty miles or so from here."

"Would it be possible to get her address and phone number? I'd like to greet her for Karlyn."

"I think so."

When she returned with the information on a card, I thanked her and asked if she also remembered LaDonna Finch.

"Oh, who could forget?" she said.

"Unforgettable?" I said.

"That beautiful black hair," she said. "I never really knew her though. She was much younger than I. Caused a few problems around here before she left as I recall, though."

"Problems?"

"I wish I could remember. Seems to me she had been a cheery little thing and turned sullen. It happens to a lot of orphans you know, at certain ages. Same was true with Karlyn when she became a teenager, as you probably know. I don't recall much of that story either, but I know she was transferred to the Chicago area for high school. Mrs. Miller will remember. She remembers them all."

SIXTEEN

I found Mrs. Miller in the tiny, former railroad roundhouse town of Constantine, Michigan. A robust, rawboned woman of silver hair, she was full of laughter and memories of "my girls."

She remembered Karlyn. "Of course. She and LaDonna Finch were extremely close for a while. They were such a pair, a little blondie and a little black-haired sweeties, both with those unusual and beautiful names. They weren't the oldest or the smartest or even the most industrious girls in the home back then, but they were among the nicest, and they were the favorites among the matrons."

"They were?"

"Yes, especially LaDonna. She had a lot going for her. She was not an unhappy girl until the time she was punished. It seemed to me that most of our workers were especially fond of her."

"But wasn't she *severely* punished?"

"Oh, yes, and I don't think she ever forgave Karlyn for that, though I can't imagine that it was entirely Karlyn's fault. LaDonna was punished by the one tough, little matron who resented the happiest girls, probably because she was not happy herself. We continually tried to weed out such women. We couldn't allow her to stay after that. We had hired her at a risk because she came with less than a perfect record at her previous job, which was at a girls' reformatory. I could never seem to get through to her that our girls were not at Creekside because of behavior problems."

"Has anyone ever told LaDonna what you just told me?"

"I doubt it. Of course, when you dismiss a woman like that, the girls never know why she's suddenly gone. They are not told what has happened."

"What ever happened to LaDonna?"

"She moved back with her mother to Grand Rapids. I was glad to see it. You always are when they are reunited with parents. And I was convinced her mother was a basically good, loving woman. I never did hear if she was able to get LaDonna back to normal."

"Back to normal?"

"Well, like I say, she was terribly hurt, and while we never had any direct evidence, we all knew that it was she who was pulling the dirty tricks on Karlyn, leaving things in her bed and what not. Oh, she was a motivated little girl. I never will know how she managed to nail that closet door shut." Mrs. Miller chuckled with the memory. I tried to.

"Karlyn still refuses to believe that LaDonna was capable of being mean."

"That's not surprising, Mr. Spence. But Karlyn should look at her own history. When she was told that her parents had been killed when she was three and that relatives who wished to remain anonymous had brought her to us, she demanded to know who they were and sulked for weeks when we would not tell her.

"The sweetest children change personalities. With Karlyn we had to recommend that she be transferred to an all-girls home in Chicago when she became rebellious in her early teens. Of course, I got the word a few years ago that she had come around to be a mature young woman by the end of her high school years. You always love to hear that."

"And what did you hear of LaDonna?"

"You know, I never did hear much more about her and it always troubled me. She had more advantages than most of the other girls, especially more than Karlyn. Yet her pain was so deep, I don't suppose I could hope that she eventually became as well adjusted as many of the rebellious ones do. She did write to some of the girls at the home, though."

"Ever to Karlyn?"

"No, and that worried me. Once I even wrote to her mother, asking if she couldn't talk LaDonna into burying the hatchet with Karlyn. I never heard back from either mother or daughter, and as far as I know, Karlyn never heard from LaDonna again either."

I hoped that was true, but I feared it wasn't. I needed to know where LaDonna was now, but I knew Mrs. Miller couldn't be very specific. I probed carefully.

"So LaDonna's mother remarried and took her daughter home?"

"No, I believe she took LaDonna home when she realized that she wasn't going to find another husband who wanted a daughter. I'm convinced she left LaDonna at the orphanage to keep her out of her way while she searched for another husband, but she finally gave up. Whether she ever married after that, I wouldn't have any idea. I completely lost contact with that family once LaDonna's letters stopped coming. I only hope she found some happiness in this world. I couldn't tell you where she landed. Of course, I couldn't tell you if I knew, knowing of her problem with Karlyn."

I was brought up short. "Her problem with Karlyn?" Not concentrating, I thought Mrs. Miller knew something I hadn't told her.

The old woman looked at me as if I were missing a strategic part. "Yes, the problem. Her silent treatment and the pranks — much too mild a word actually — before LaDonna moved home."

"Of course."

Mrs. Miller asked me to greet Karlyn for her and thanked me for the conversation. "I always enjoy reminiscing about my girls," she said, "though I have lost contact with so many of them. Many still write me, you know. Tell Karlyn she should do that."

"I will," I promised, but right then I was anxious to get to Grand Rapids. I had to find that girl.

As soon as I got inside the Grand Rapids city limits, I stopped in a phone booth and wrestled the phone book around so I could look up the Finches. I didn't know what the odds were that LaDonna had not married, or if there was a Finch anywhere who would know what became of her or her mother, and the phone book didn't help much either. The first half of it had been torn apart. As long as I was there, I checked in with Earl. It was good that I did.

"Time is a problem, Philip," he said. "Karlyn received another message last night. It was a letter, not hand delivered this time but mailed from Park Ridge. It said, 'How would you like to have *your* seat paddled until it bleeds?' "

"And I had begun wondering what I was doing in Michigan while Karlyn was in trouble in Illinois."

"Still wondering?"

"Hardly."

"Don't let me keep you from finding a phone book," Earl said.

"I want to call Karlyn and Margo real quick," I said. "And then I'll be back on the trail."

"Good luck."

I then telephoned Karlyn at her office.

"I'm not doing too well," she admitted. "But Earl said there was no way he'd leave me alone once he decides that something is about to happen."

"Of course we wouldn't leave you alone, Karlyn. In fact I hope to be back in time to help."

"I hope you are too," she said.

"I'll be praying for you, Karlyn, and I know Margo will be too."

"I appreciate that, Philip."

I called Margo. She was having no luck finding a job in Pontiac. "If I don't find something soon," she said, "I don't know if I can stay here. I'm not going to take just any old job. There are waitress jobs galore, but I've been that route before."

"If that means you might come back to Chicago and find work that would pay you enough so you could make weekly trips to Pontiac, I couldn't be happier," I said.

"That would be quite a job, Philip. If you find one like that for me, let me know."

When I told her what was happening in my search, she scolded me for letting her ramble about "my petty problems. You'd better find yourself a phone book and get to work."

I finally found a phone book intact, but there were no LaDonna Finches. Remembering Margo's telling me that single women often have themselves listed under an initial only so no one can tell that it's a woman, I checked under the Ls for LaDonna and the Ds for just Donna. There were several Ds. Finches under the Ds, along with the Finch Day Care Center, Finch Dog Hotel, and Finch Dress Boutique, but I decided to start with the half dozen L. Finches and hope for the best.

After getting four embarrassing responses to my asking for LaDonna — and wondering if I wouldn't have done better to study mechanical drawing by mail than to be in "our kind of work" as Haymeyer always called it — my break came.

"LaDonna won't be back for three more days," a man's voice said.

"Who am I talking to, please?" I said.

"You're talking to Frank. I'm just looking after the place while LaDonna's away. It's the first time nobody's been in this house for years."

"Frank, could I talk to you for a little while? I have just a few questions for you. I'm a friend of an old friend of LaDonna's."

"I haven't talked to anyone for so long, I might enjoy that."

Following his directions, I pulled into a long driveway that led to a modest two-story frame house set far back from the road. Frank was in the yard, clipping hedges.

"You said it's been a long time since nobody's been in the house," I began. "What did you mean by that?"

"Ever since old man Finch died years and years ago, Mrs. Finch been livin' here. Her daughter LaDonna's been with her now nearly twenty more, takin' care of her mama since she took sick here a few years ago. All that in spite of LaDonna workin' downtown. Now that she's gone, who knows what LaDonna'll do? She never did marry, ya know."

"You say her mother's gone now?"

"Yep. Died 'bout four, five weeks ago. Right after the funeral LaDonna hired me to house-sit and tend the yard. Told me she'd be back in exactly five weeks."

"And that's three days from now?"

"Yessir."

"Frank, where did she go?"

"Believe she went to Indiana, maybe Illinois."

"She didn't tell you where she could be reached?"

"Nope, just had me get her a map that showed Interstate Ninety-Four west. That'll take you just about anywhere you want to go, startin' here and goin' through Indiana and Illinois."

I thanked Frank and headed back to my car. "Who should I say come callin'?" he asked.

I stopped. "For ten bucks, would you not say anyone called?"

"Sure thing. Thanks."

I figured I'd be seeing LaDonna before he did anyway.

SEVENTEEN

I had just reentered Illinois when I stopped to call Earl and breathlessly told him everything I had discovered.

"Did you happen to find out what line of work LaDonna's in that allows her to take off that amount of time?"

"No, why?"

"Well, it would be good to know where she works so we could see if she has psychological problems now, if she's hard to work with or moody or whatever."

"Do you think we have time, Earl?"

"Probably not. I've sensed all along that the harassment has been building to something more ominous. That note about the paddling had to be a promise of action."

"What are we going to do?"

"I'll think about it. You get back here."

Shipman was in Haymeyer's office when I arrived. "I want help on this thing," Haymeyer explained.

"Great," I said "It's getting good, Larry."

Haymeyer said he would like to be with Karlyn when she got home from work, so we called her and then drove to Des Plaines to follow her home from her office. In her mail was a letter postmarked Park Ridge again. She opened it as we all stood in the hall. It read: "When I really want in, I can get in."

When Karlyn opened the door to her apartment, a cold gust of wind hit us. The glass on one of the two patio doors had been cut. It lay in huge pieces, obviously done with a glass cutter and suction cup that allowed the intruder to break it without a lot of noise and just lay the pieces down without shattering them. "Stay right here," Haymeyer said.

He and Shipman entered the apartment, Earl's gun drawn. I followed a few steps behind. No one was there, and nothing seemed to have been touched, except that the wind had blown open the pages of the magazine on the coffee table in the living room.

"Ship, get on the phone and get someone in here to board up that window."

"Why wouldn't anything have been taken or changed?" Karlyn asked, shaken.

"It was just a message," Haymeyer said. "By now she knows we could stake out the bushes. Maybe she subconsciously wants to get caught."

"I hope you'll oblige her," Karlyn said.

"Don't worry," Earl said. "I think we've got her right where we want her. The problem now is, we can't let you stay here alone anymore. She could make her move anytime. What I want to do is cut down her options. If she really has to be back to Michigan in a few days — and if we knew what her job was we would know for sure — let's give her only one chance at getting to you before then. For the next two nights I want you to stay in a hotel in Glencoe. You'll come back here every day after work to get your mail, and then you'll leave right away."

"Whatever you say, Earl. But then what?"

"The next day you can return with your clothes and everything, making it very obvious that you're back home to stay. My hope is that she'll think you feel confident to move back in and that'll give her just that night to do whatever she's going to do."

"And I'm the live bait?"

"You won't be alone. We'll come to your apartment during the day from various directions and even different floors. We'll stay out of sight of the windows, and when you come home, talk to us only in whispers and don't look at us. We want it to appear to anyone watching that you are alone as usual. Then when you go to bed, you will have one of us in the other room. Fair enough?"

"And when someone starts to break in?"

"We wait until she's committed herself, is fully inside, and obviously looking to do you bodily harm."

"How will you know that? When she's in my room with a knife at my throat?"

"We won't let her get that far."

"I don't know about this."

"It's the only way, Karlyn, unless you'd like us to use a stand-in for you."

"How about a dummy like you did for Margo in Atlanta?" I asked.

"This isn't set up for that, Philip," Earl said. "We don't know where this girl might be watching from or when. We have to assume she knows Karlyn's comings and goings. She's been right every day for weeks."

"But her time's running out," Shipman said. "Here's hoping your idea works, Earl. It would be nice to be able to catch her in the act so you can put her away for a while."

"Or get her some help," Karlyn said.

"You sound just like Margo," I said. "She always felt more for her pursuer than any of the rest of us. Personally I think what this girl has done to you already is nearly unforgivable."

"She probably feels the same about what she thinks I did to her years ago, but knowing God allows me to be able to somehow feel pity even for one who would torment me. Don't you pity her?"

Karlyn searched each of our eyes for the sympathy she hoped to find for LaDonna. Sad to say, she didn't find much. "Philip," she said, "you of all people should feel something for her."

I nodded lamely. Why was it that women like Margo and Karlyn seemed to have more depth of Christian character than I did? It bothered me for the next two days while Karlyn commuted from Glencoe to Des Plaines every day and often badgered me about having such feelings of animosity toward LaDonna.

She received no letter on either day, but when she stopped in at her apartment for a moment the second day after work, the telephone was ringing. "Don't cross me up now," a woman's voice said, and the line went dead. Karlyn ran down to her car and sped to Glencoe.

"I didn't know you were going to your apartment," Earl said. "It wasn't smart. You should have told us. It's obvious she knows when you're there and when you're not."

The next afternoon, the day before LaDonna was expected back in Michigan, Karlyn returned to her own apartment after work. "We're here," Haymeyer said from next to me in the closet when she came in.

"Hello," she whispered.

"And I'm in the corner of the kitchen," Larry said. "Don't be alarmed when you see me."

"I won't."

It was weird to be stationed in her apartment, out of sight of the windows and the door. "What should I do now?" Karlyn asked quietly without looking at anyone.

"Whatever you normally do," Haymeyer said, reclining next to me on the floor of the closet with a blanket and a pillow, reading a magazine.

During the course of the evening while Karlyn puttered around the apartment trying to look normal, she called Margo in Pontiac. She passed along Margo's love and reported that she was close to landing a job much like Karlyn's at a local printing plant. "She'll know tomorrow. And she can't see her mother for another several days. Mrs. Franklin has the flu or something."

"Oh, great," I said.

By about eleven o'clock, Earl and I were stiff and sore. Shipman was not where he could move much either. Our whispering had quit and Karlyn was getting ready for bed. "I'm getting a little nervous," she said.

"So are we," Earl said. "If you're not nervous now, you're not human."

"I must not be human," Shipman said quietly. "I'm excited."

"You're right," Earl said. "You've never been human. You're an animal."

"I usually shut the closet before I go to bed," Karlyn said.

"Come and shut it then," Earl replied.

"You're going to stay in there with the door shut?"

"Just shut it and go to bed. There's slats for air and we can hear. If she sees the closet door open, knowing how persnickety you are, she'll smell a rat."

"I won't be able to sleep," Karlyn said.

"No kidding," Larry said. "But unless you hear us leave, you can rest assured we'll be here. And we won't be sleeping either."

"Thanks, you guys," she said, sounding more like a little girl than I had ever heard her. "And be careful, OK?"

"To bed," Haymeyer said.

About an hour later, Karlyn's phone rang. She answered it on the extension in her room. The caller immediately hung up. She rose without turning on the light. "What do you suppose that was all about, Earl?" she whispered from the doorway.

"Probably just making sure you're here," he said. "Be patient and try to stay calm. We could have company soon."

Just before one o'clock, Earl and I heard footsteps in the hall that stopped just outside the door. "I didn't figure her for the front door tonight," Haymeyer whispered. From the kitchen came the faint sounds of Shipman jockeying for a better position to see and hear.

A note was slipped under the door and the footsteps retreated. I started to get up to get the note, but Haymeyer put a hand on my shoulder. "Let's give it a few minutes," he said.

"What's happening?" Karlyn asked. Shipman shushed her. We waited several minutes in silence. No one moved. Then we heard the patio railing squeak, so lightly that we wouldn't have heard it if we hadn't half expected it.

Haymeyer tried to get into position to see the patio through the slats in the closet door. "No good," he whispered. "But let's not move unless she comes in." We heard feet lightly touch the concrete.

"I can see her on the patio," Shipman whispered. "Small, wiry, lithe. It's her all right. She's leaning against the boarded-up side."

Something touched the glass and made scratching sounds. "What in the world is she doing?" I asked, barely audibly.

"She's probably cutting glass again." He was right. She tapped lightly until a piece came loose, held in a rubber suction cup. She now had a hole big enough to allow her to reach in and unscrew the sliding door lock Shipman had installed.

Haymeyer drew his gun and rolled up onto the balls of his feet, knees bent. "Keep me posted, Ship," he breathed. "I'm ready to move. Sit tight, Philip."

Gladly, I thought.

We heard nothing. Then Shipman was moving toward the closet, in direct view of the window. "What are you doing?" Haymeyer scolded.

"Earl, she's gone," he said. "She cut that glass and left it hanging on the suction cup, and then she just turned and jumped over the railing again. She's gone."

Haymeyer swore. "Leave the lights off. She may be back. This time we'll wait for her in the kitchen, all of us. If she comes in, I'll take her right then. Let's see that note."

I brought it to him, and he held it up to a thin shaft of light coming through the window. "It's just a matter of time," it read.

"She didn't expect Karlyn to get this until morning," Haymeyer said. "Is it possible that she's smarter than to try anything inside the apartment?"

"She's been pretty crafty so far," Shipman said. "Maybe this whole apartment assault has been a ruse."

"When is this going to end?" Karlyn asked. "You can't hold my hand the rest of my life."

"I hope it ends when we force it to," Earl said. "Not when she does. Meanwhile, let's get some sleep."

EIGHTEEN

Shipman taped the hole in the window and traded off standing watch with Haymeyer and me. Karlyn hardly slept.

While she got ready for work, I called Margo. "I want you to come up here between now and the time you have to start your job," I said. "I can't take it anymore."

"That's good to hear," she said. "I don't have any money, but I'll scrape some up somewhere. I'm bored to death here with nothing to do, and there's a lot I want to talk about. Living this far apart just isn't going to make it."

"My sentiments exactly. When will you be leaving for Glencoe?"

"Within the hour, love."

"If you get there before I do, just wait for me at Earl's office. I don't know when we'll be free today. Earl thinks it's going to break soon. I'll see you then."

As we waited I felt again for Margo and all that she had been through. It was unfair that so much of her life had been eaten up by the problems of her mother. And now those apron strings had reached right out of the prison walls and ensnared her again.

Tonight when I saw her again, I would take Margo to the same place we had been to a few days before she left. I would tell her all that I had been thinking about, and I would try to be as articulate as she had been the last time.

If I could somehow express to her all that she meant to me and how much I loved her and needed her, perhaps we could work out something more equitable than living more than a hundred miles apart. Especially if we were married. That is, if she would say yes.

By tonight I would know. She wouldn't be expecting the question, but like Earl had said so many times, "You're not kids anymore." I wanted to get this settled before she accepted any job offer in Pontiac. I couldn't wait to see her.

Earl's voice brought me back to the situation at hand. "We have to decide how we're going to keep an eye on Karlyn today. We shouldn't let her out of our sight Larry, why don't you start by bringing my car around."

Karlyn was pale and shaky. "I'm going to be good for nothing at work today." Dressed and ready to go, she sat at the kitchen table as if waiting for the coast to clear. "Are you going to follow me, or what?"

"At least," Haymeyer said. "I'm not sure what to do with you at work and at lunch and all."

Shipman tapped at the door. I let him in and he said, "Earl, let me see you for a minute." They went into Karlyn's bedroom and shut the door. Karlyn looked at me. I shrugged.

As the door opened again, Earl was saying, "Yeah, ask her."

"Do you ever leave your car unlocked or a window open just a fraction?"

"Never."

"Not even yesterday afternoon when you were thinking about finding us in your apartment when you arrived?"

"No way."

"Well," Shipman said with a sigh, "the window on the passenger's side is down about a quarter of an inch, and the windows are slightly fogged. Do you have that problem as a rule?"

"Only in the dead of winter. Never in the spring."

"Someone's in the car?" I said.

"Excellent, Philip," Shipman said, rolling his eyes.

Haymeyer looked at both of us as if to say, Shut up and let me think. "Feel brave this morning, Karlyn?" he said.

"How brave?"

"Brave enough to walk to your car as if everything is normal?"

"And where will you be?"

"We'll casually converge on your car, all at about the same time you get to it. Rather than opening the door, I want you to just drop to your knees by the left rear tire. Philip will be there at the same time. Just stay there until it's over."

"How do I get there?" I asked.

"Hold on. I'll get to you."

"And what if she just shoots me as I come near the car?" Karlyn asked.

"She wouldn't be that stupid. Try to get away in the car of the person you've just shot?"

"Anyway," Larry said, "there's no one in the front seat. I walked right by the car. She's in no position to hot wire the car and take off fast enough to try something like that."

"I'm putting my life in your hands," Karlyn said.

"It's totally up to you, kid," Haymeyer said. "We could just charge out there and storm the car, but I'd feel a whole lot better about it if her attention was on you rather than us when we make our move."

"That's just what I don't want — her attention on me."

"It's been on you for weeks," Haymeyer said. "That's why you won't actually get into the car. If you're kneeling where I told you, she would have to climb over the front seat and out the door to get to you. By that time, I've got her."

Karlyn sat thinking, fists clenched. "I'll do it," she said. "I'm tired of this and I want it over." She stood. Haymeyer said. "Are you ready?"

"Sure, boss. Where do you want me?"

"Just take the elevator up three floors, exit right and walk down the stairs to the exit at the end of the building. We'll watch from the window in the stairwell at this end. When you get outside, we'll send Karlyn from this exit. Try to time it so you reach the car from behind when she gets there from this end. Our friend in the car should never see you, Philip. When you both are about twenty steps from the car, Ship and I will get in my car and start a slow U-turn. We will appear to be pulling away, but as we get near Karlyn's car, Larry will pull in front of it and stop."

"Everybody got it?"

We all nodded.

"Ready?"

We nodded again and I moved out to the elevator. I stepped on and pushed the button for the fifth floor to the glare of the other passengers who knew before I did that the car was going down. "Takes the elevator for one flight down," a woman muttered. I had to step out and let them all off at the first floor, then reboard and ride up to five.

I hurried down the hall on the fifth floor and took the stairs down two at a time. Going down isn't supposed to be as exhausting as going up, but I realized when I hit the ground floor that I had held my breath most of the way. Now I was huffing and puffing as I burst out the door.

"Help me calm down, Lord," I prayed. "Slow me down, don't let me blow it." I tried to shorten my stride despite my crashing chest and shortness of breath, but my knees were rubbery. I must have looked like a toy, bouncing along the parking lot.

Karlyn came out of her exit, holding her purse and a small attaché case to her chest with both arms. She too was trying to look casual and not doing a good job of it.

Her car keys were lodged between her fingers. I slowed a bit so we would be about equidistant from her car. I tingled from the backs of my knees all the way up to my neck. She walked faster. I sped up. We were probably thirty steps from her car when Shipman and Haymeyer came out and got into Earl's car without even glancing our way.

I knew Ship was watching us in the rearview mirror. When we drew closer. Shipman shifted into drive and slowly pulled ahead. He looked over his shoulder and began a wide, slow U-turn. I glanced at Karlyn's car. I saw the slight fogging of the windows, but nothing else.

As Karlyn heard Shipman and Haymeyer coming, she hesitated and almost turned to look. I held my breath. She kept moving. Just as she pretended to reach toward the door with her key, I noticed movement in the car and dropped to my knees by the rear tire.

I grabbed the arm of Karlyn's coat and she tumbled on top of me, burying her face in my shoulder as the driver's side door opened.

Shipmen screeched to a stop in front of the car as Haymeyer skittered out and around to our side, sliding neatly to one knee with both hands on his gun. "Freeze!" he screamed. "Hold it right there!"

Karlyn pressed closer to me and over her shoulder I saw a woman's hand push the car door all the way open. She was prone across the back of the front seat and had been about to come out headfirst when Haymeyer confronted her. Now Shipman joined Earl and approached the car. All I could see was the woman's outstretched arms. In her right hand was an old wood paddle.

"This gal is more than two years older than you are, Karlyn," Haymeyer announced as he and Shipman pulled the hysterical woman into view, her feet trailing across the seat.

"I almost had you, you little brat!" she managed through her sobs.

Karlyn's head shot around.

"You're in trouble, young lady!" the woman shrieked as Earl and Larry wrestled her into Haymeyer's car. "You got me fired!"

"Miss Kepkey!" Karlyn gasped. "It's Miss Kepkey!"

"One of the things that really intrigues me," an exhausted Karlyn said a few hours later in Earl's office, "is where LaDonna was all this time."

"Me too," Haymeyer said, looking my way.

"Hey, did I do something wrong?" I asked. "What would you have done with the same information?"

"Probably the same, Philip. Don't feel bad. But I'm betting that a little *more* information would have changed the picture some. Call the Finch home and see if she's arrived."

A woman answered.

"Miss Finch?" I said.

"Who's calling, please?"

"My name is Philip Spence. I'm a friend of Karlyn May."

"Pardon me?"

"Karlyn May."

"That's what I thought you said. Let me sit down, Who did you say *you* were?"

"Philip Spence."

"And you know Karlyn?"

"Yes, ma'am."

"Do you know that I've been looking for Karlyn for years? She was my best friend when I was a kid, but something happened and we lost contact. How did you get my number? How did you know I knew Karlyn? I — "

"Do you want to talk to Karlyn yourself?"

"Why, yes!"

"Let me ask you something first, if I may. Where have you been the last five weeks?"

"Vacationing in Wisconsin. You see, my mother died recently and I just had to get away. I needed a long break from home and work, and my assistants are able to handle my day care center."

"Just a minute please, LaDonna. Karlyn, it's for you."

While she was on the phone, Margo arrived.

"Got any plans for lunch?" I said.

"Hardly. Is that an invitation?"

"Unlike any you've ever had," I said. "Keep your coat on."

HILARY

Margo quickly grows tired of living so far from Philip, but she is forced to leave Pontiac, Illinois, sooner than expected, and suddenly she is in need of a lawyer. Hilary, Margo's lawyer, discovers evidence Margo doesn't want to hear. It means danger to the people she loves.

ONE

IF I HADN'T LET MARGO SPEAK FIRST, we'd be engaged now.

Earl had told me about a charming little place for lunch just north of the Loop. Margo sat close in the car and lay her head on my shoulder. "I have so much to talk to you about," she said quietly.

"Me too," I said.

"But me first. How much time do we have?"

"Unless you've accepted a job you have to run back to Pontiac for, we have the rest of the day. Earl gave me the afternoon off."

"Any more cases coming up?"

"Oh, I'm sure. Earl got started on several while I was concentrating on Karlyn — on her case, I mean. We'll be starting in on something the first thing tomorrow morning."

At the restaurant I held her hands across the table. The moment was perfect for my big question, but I had promised to let her speak first. "I don't want to be away from you anymore," she said quickly.

So she was going to make it easy for me. "Me either," I said, my courage building. She put a finger to my mouth.

"I want to forget about Pontiac, move up here, get an apartment, and get a job that really excites me."

"What excites me is the thought of your being so close," I said. "Then we could — "

She quieted me again. "I can visit Mother once a week. It will be difficult and expensive, but I can see her only once a week anyway. I find myself coming up here to see you more often than that, and I can see you anytime."

"How would you like to see me every day for the rest of your life?"

She ignored me. "I suppose you're wondering how this all came about and what Mother might think of it."

"Uh, yeah, OK."

"Well, her last two letters — I can see her in three days, by the way — have been so insistent about my not staying in Pontiac but finding myself a career, that she has nearly convinced me. I still want to see her whenever I can, but every lonely night I spend down there confirms all the more that I need to move on, to grow. To grow *up.*"

"What do you want to do?" I asked.

"I want to do what you do."

I raised my eyebrows. Maybe the Karlyn May case had intrigued her, but there had been a lot of drudgery in it that she wouldn't have known about. What if she lost interest? And a woman in detective work? I was enough of a chauvinist to think twice about it. I smiled at her, not knowing what to say.

"I know what you're thinking, Sherlock," she said. "Afraid of the competition?"

I laughed. "What will it mean to our future?" I said. "I want to marry you."

The waitress brought our salads and we prayed silently. Margo looked at me, but I couldn't read her thoughts. "I've been thinking a lot about that too, Philip."

"And?"

"And I want time."

"Time for what? We've been together constantly for months, up until the last few weeks."

"I want to get to know you as a normal person, not as one who pitied me, or who led me to Christ, or who protected and helped me."

"I don't pity you — "

"Anymore."

"OK, anymore, but I do want to protect you and help you and whatever else goes along with loving you."

"But don't you see that there hasn't been a normal day in our relationship?"

"And you think there will be if you become a private investigator too?"

"The attention will be focused on someone else's problems, not mine. We've been so wrapped up in my problems that we haven't had a chance to breathe."

Margo had always been hard to argue with. "So what does it mean to our future?" I repeated.

"It means we'll get to know each other well. If you're still convinced in a few months that I am what you want, let's talk about it then."

"How come you make everything sound so cut and dried and businesslike? And how about you? Do you still have to be convinced that I'm what you want?"

"No."

"But if I asked you right now to marry me, you'd make me wait so *you* would be sure that I was sure?"

"You got it."

"Grief."

I was genuinely irritated, but I wasn't sure why. I couldn't blame her for wanting me to be sure, but I was insulted that she thought I didn't know my own mind. I pouted a while, but she ignored it. We ate in silence.

"You don't just *become* a private investigator," Earl Haymeyer said in his Glencoe office late that afternoon.

"Why not?" Margo challenged. "Philip did."

"No, Philip didn't. To get him his license, I had to verify that he had been personally involved in many of the investigations that led to your mother's arrest. I also had to pledge that he would be properly trained in the use of firearms before he is allowed to carry a gun, and that I would enroll him in an accredited six-week course on crime detection and prevention as soon as an opening arises. Your three-day qualifying screener begins tomorrow, Philip."

I was surprised.

"I just got the call a little while ago," Earl explained. He turned back to Margo. "If you think this business is fun, or you just want to try it as a lark, I don't encourage it."

"You know me better than that, Earl," Margo said. "I really want to do it. Maybe someday Philip and I will work as a team."

"That'll do wonders for your marriage," Earl said. "Anyway, where do you think you're going to work? There's not a detective agency I know of that would take a chance on a totally inexperienced young woman with no training, and, for all anyone knows, no aptitude for the work. Jobs are scarce and money is tight."

"You could teach me, Earl. Just like you're teaching Philip. In fact, Philip could teach me secondhand."

"There's no way," Earl said. "I've had a dozen cases dropped in my lap from old acquaintances. I won't even be able to train Philip the way I want to. That's why I'm glad this opening at training school came for Philip. It usually takes months to even get into a screening class."

"That just proves you need help, Earl," Margo persisted. "And that you'll have the money to hire more people."

"You're hopeless, Margo," Earl said. "I just can't encourage you, as much as I'd like to."

"How would you like it if I landed with some other agency? I will, you know."

"You probably would," Earl said. "I'll tell you what I'll do: I'll let you work in the office, and I'll put your name on the waiting list for a screening class."

"I don't want to be a secretary."

"You may be here for a while. I've just converted from a temporary to a full-time girl, and she could use some help. You could pick up a lot about the business by being in the office until we hear about your application."

"I suppose that would be all right. I really don't have a choice unless I want to take some other kind of a job in the meantime. And I am moving up here, job or not."

"I don't want you getting any false hopes, though," Earl said. "We were lucky to get Philip into a screening class as early as we did, and he had a lot going for him."

"Like what?"

I looked at Margo.

"I mean, what did he have going for him?" she said, trying to improve on her question.

"A little experience, a couple of well-placed references, things like that."

"Which I wouldn't have?"

"All you'd have on your resume is that you help out in our offices. The fact that you are a woman will not help you, as illegal as any discrimination might be. You should know that any law can be circumvented if every angle is studied enough. They could drub you out because of your sex and blame it on any number of other reasons."

"You're not very optimistic."

"I'm glad you're getting the point, Margo. The worst part is, you could get into a screening class and then fail to qualify for the six-week course, which follows a month or so later."

"The same could happen for Philip."

"Sure it could, but he doesn't have any natural barriers to overcome. And he does have some background now."

"Are you offering me a job in the meantime?"

"If you're willing to do clerical work, not grumble about it, keep your ears open, and accept an appropriate salary. I don't want you around here just biding your time, because your time may never come."

"Thank you, Dale Carnegie," Margo said.

That evening Margo showed me the letters she had received from her mother. They troubled me. They evidenced all the predictable bitterness of a woman who had been to the heights of power as a judge, now reduced to a denim-wearing number in a facility full of hard women. But there was more.

She complained of dizziness, lack of orientation, listlessness. She said she thought it was the "lousy chicken they seem to feed me every meal in my cell." Margo thought it was her mother's veiled request for the earliest possible visit allowed by law. I was left simply shaken by it.

For one thing, I wasn't aware that she was segregated from the other prisoners even for meals. And of all the things I expected from tough, old Virginia Franklin, physical problems were not among them.

One of the letters even told of an overnight stay in the infirmary. "That doesn't sound like your mother," I said.

"Oh, she's all right," Margo said. "She may be seeking a little sympathy. I'll find out when I see her."

"When is that again?"

"Three days from now. And I'd like you to go with me."

"We'll see. My qualifying class will be over, so maybe I can take a day."

Two

For the next three days I endured a battery of tests to determine if I had the psychological and physical aptitude to study crime detection and prevention. The tests were fascinating lessons in themselves. At the end of each day I drove back to suburban Glencoe for dinner with Margo, who had a ton of questions.

"You know there are a lot of things I can't tell you because we are sworn to secrecy," I said. "They remind us often that there are many people who plan to take the tests and would pay anything for an idea of what they contain."

"OK, what's your price?" she teased.

"I ought to report this attempted bribe."

Earl gave me permission to drive Margo back down to Pontiac and help her move north if I agreed to be back to work two days later. I was so keyed up over the tests that I would have been good for nothing to him anyway.

"How do you think you did?" Earl wanted to know.

"It's hard to say. Some of the questions seemed so ridiculously easy that I may have missed something. Others were Greek to me."

"That's the way it seemed to me years ago," Earl admitted. "And I was allowed into the class."

All the way to Pontiac, Margo tried to assure me that she knew what she was doing, and that if I thought about it carefully, I'd realize that her main motivation for moving to the Chicago area was to be near me. I believed her, but she couldn't hide the excitement in her voice when she talked of getting into detective work. That opportunity had a lot to do with her decision too.

When we arrived at her place, letters were waiting for her from both her mother and father. She opened the one from her father first. Shortly after her mother's trial, Mr. Franklin had moved to California to become a garment industry consultant. Now he told Margo of "a wonderful woman" he had met. "She's also a transplanted Chicagoan," he reported. "We've not dated long, but something tells me you might have a reason to visit me out here very soon."

"I can't believe it," Margo said. "He hardly ever saw any other women after Mother divorced him. Now he sounds ready to get married again after all this time."

"How does it make you feel?"

"Protective, I guess. I want to know who she is, what her intentions are, all that." Margo laughed at herself. "Listen to me," she said.

She opened the letter from her mother. "Perhaps by the time you read this I'll have already seen you. And that means I will have talked you into leaving Pontiac and following your head and heart to Philip and a career. That's what I want for you."

"She's in the infirmary again," Margo said flatly. "I don't guess I like that too much. Still complaining about the poultry not agreeing with her. I'm afraid she's just used to gourmet food."

I asked to see the letter. The rest had the usual complaints of a woman out of her element. No one listened to her or understood when they did listen. "It will be good to talk to you soon," she wrote, "just to have someone half intelligent to banter with. And yes, you may hit me once again with your Christian ideas, if you promise not to take more than half our time together with it."

"That should encourage you," I said.

"Sort of," Margo said.

I could tell the news of the infirmary was troubling her. Her mother wrote nothing of exactly why she was there.

"I'm going to call," Margo said.

I followed her to the hall phone. She dialed the prison. "I don't know who to ask for," Margo began. "I have a relative who's an inmate, and I know I can't talk to her . . . yes, in the women's facility. Thank you." She waited. "Hello, I don't know who to talk to, but I have a relative who's an inmate there . . . yes, a woman. . . . No, I don't know her number." Margo shuddered. "Virginia Frank — yes, that's right." Margo covered the mouthpiece and whispered, "I guess they all know who she is.

"Yes, I know she's in the infirmary and that I can't see her yet, but — oh, I can? Yes, if that's OK." She turned to me again. "They drop the visit and call restrictions when an inmate is in the infirmary. Hello? Mother? Oh, I'm sorry. I was told I could talk to her.

Well, could you tell me what's wrong with her? . . . How can I prove I'm her daughter without coming there? I'm due there tomorrow, but I'd come tonight if I could get some information. . . . I see. OK, thank you, nurse. . . . I'm sorry, doctor. I'll see you tomorrow."

Margo was upset. "She's sleeping now. I could have seen her a few days ago when she was put in the infirmary for the second time. She probably didn't even know that. They never told me. The doctor won't tell me anything by phone, and I can't get in there this late. I'll be anxious to see Mother tomorrow. And the doctor too."

I stayed at the local TraveLodge that night and met Margo at about nine the next morning. We could not visit her mother until ten, so we ate quickly and just drove around, trying to ease the tension. "I've got so much to tell her," Margo said. "She'll be glad to hear of my plans. At least I hope she'll be. Maybe down deep she really wants me to stay near her."

I let her ramble. In a strange way, I was anxious to see Mrs. Franklin again myself. We agreed that I would just greet her, talk a few minutes, and then leave while Margo looked for the right opportunity to talk to her again about God.

"One of these times we're going to get through to her," Margo predicted. "I just know it. The Bible says that God will give you the desires of your heart, and that's my desire. Can there by anything selfish about that desire, Philip?"

I thought for a moment. "Not that I can see."

"I know she was wrong," Margo said. "But she's long overdue for some peace and forgiveness."

"You already forgave her," I said.

"And God will too," she said, "but somehow she can't see that. I want to hook up with the chaplain here and start really working on Mother."

"Ganging up on her might not be the answer," I said. "Persistence is the key. The right time will come. It will all hit her at once, and she will be most moved by the fact that you cared enough to stay by her."

"I don't know if I ever prayed for anything so hard in my life."

"I know what you mean," I said.

"No, you don't. But thanks anyway."

The main receiving room looked less like a prison than the outside walls and gates did, yet that same cold formality permeated the place. Neither of us had been there before, of course, so we tentatively followed the signs to an information desk. Margo clutched my arm so tightly that I knew she wanted me to get us into the infirmary.

"We're here to see Virginia Franklin," I said.

"Your names, please."

"Philip Spence and Margo Fr — "

"There is someone here to see you, sir," the guard said.

"Pardon me?" I said. Margo stiffened. Then I saw Earl. And Amos Chakaris, the huge, aged lawyer who had represented Mrs. Franklin at the trial. My first impulse was to smile. "What are you guys doing here?" I asked, a little too loudly and much too cheerfully.

"Let's go in here," Haymeyer said, nodding toward an anteroom with heavy wood furnishings. I started to fall in behind the two men, but Margo hardly moved, holding me back. Her eyes were fiery. She wanted answers before she went anywhere.

"What *are* you two doing here, Earl?" she demanded, her voice echoing through the hall and turning the heads of other visitors.

Chakaris and Haymeyer looked at each other soberly for an instant and then at me. I was still puzzled. Margo wasn't. She knew they had news she didn't want to hear. "Please," Earl said, putting his hands on her shoulders and guiding her, stiff-legged, into the room.

"Please sit down, honey," Chakaris said, helping Haymeyer ease her into a straight-backed chair. Margo looked as if she wanted them to get to it. Her eyes were already filling. I sat dumbfounded.

Chakaris slid a tissue box across the table in front of Margo. She stared at Earl. "Your mother died early this morning, Margo," he said. She shook her head. "She was run down from a cold, and she wasn't adjusting. She didn't respond to medication and when she developed heart trouble, she had no reserves. She was gone quickly."

Margo closed her eyes and drew her fists up before her face. She trembled until her entire body shook. I moved to comfort her but was no help. She interlocked her fingers and pressed her lips against her hands. Still she shivered.

Amos started to say that it might have been for the best because she was so miserable in this place, but I signaled him to silence, knowing that Margo was probably preoccupied with the fact that her mother was much worse off now than she had been during her first few weeks in prison.

Haymeyer and Chakaris paced the room, not looking at Margo and occasionally staring out the window. "Do you want us to leave?" Earl asked. Margo shook her head.

"Do you want anything?" I asked.

She didn't respond.

"How long can we stay here?" I whispered to Earl. He shrugged. "Let's just give her some time then," I said. "And then we can take her home."

"Would you like to see her?" Chakaris asked softly. Margo nodded.

"I'll see what I can do," he said, and left.

"I don't understand," Margo said weakly. "Mother never wrote anything about having a cold."

Earl tried to explain again about how the combination of shocks to her mental and physical health had sneaked up on her, but Margo made a face and he fell silent.

Chakaris returned. Margo looked at him expectantly. He nodded. "When you feel you're ready."

"Can Philip go with me?"

"Of course."

Margo tried to stand, then sat again. "I guess I'm not ready," she said.

"There's no rush," Chakaris said. "The coroner is here because autopsies are mandatory in prison deaths before the bodies can be moved. I will see that she is transported back to Chicago for you, if you wish."

"Amos," Margo whined, "I don't know anything about this or what I should do — "

The old man raised both hands to silence her. "Shhh," he said. "You know I have always represented your mother. I have all her important documents and am executor of her will. She has stipulated where she is to be taken, what kind of service she wants, everything. I'll handle it. OK?"

Margo nodded gratefully and stood. As we moved slowly down the hall, Margo leaning heavily on me, Amos told Earl that the regular Pontiac coroner was not there. "This guy is from up north," he said. "I didn't even know he served the Department of Corrections."

THREE

Margo controlled herself during one last look at her mother's body, but as Mrs. Franklin was wheeled away, Margo broke down.

With Earl and Amos's help, we had Margo packed and ready to move to Chicago in less than an hour. She wanted to help, and we probably should have let her, but we insisted that she just sit and wait for us, as if grief and shock were exhausting. Later she admitted that they were.

During the drive north, Margo was mostly silent. And angry. "I don't want any of your platitudes," she said when I tried to console her. And I couldn't deny that trying to explain the good purpose of such a death was beyond me. In a way, her lashing out at me saved me some awkward moments; anything I might have thought to say seemed hollow when I even considered it.

"I'll be praying for you," I said weakly.

"Yes, I suppose you will," she said. "Why don't you just try holding me for now?"

I drove with one arm around her, traveling slower than usual, as if hitting a bump or swerving would injure her. After a long silence, she said, "I've got to call Daddy."

"Now?"

She shook her head. "When we get back."

"I wish I knew what to say to you," I admitted.

"Just ignore me for a few days, will you?"

"How can I, Margo? You don't really want me to, do you?"

"I mean ignore what I say. I'm not handling this well, and I don't know what I might say. I might even hurt you, Philip. And I probably already have." She was right. "But I need you to bear with me, to love me, to not give up on me."

"I would never give up on you, Margo."

"Not even if I said I thought God had made a mistake and that I might not forgive Him?"

"You don't know what you're saying."

"Of course I don't; that's what I just said!"

"It's not our pl — "

"Don't tell me it's not my place to forgive God or not forgive Him! I know all that! Please, Philip, don't preach at me now. Just let me be."

"Just let you be what? Angry at God?"

She didn't answer.

Earl opened an apartment for Margo in his building, not far from mine. "I'll want to get a place somewhere else as soon as possible, Earl," she said. "Philip and I don't need this kind of pressure. But I do appreciate it more than you know."

She called her father from Earl's office. "He's coming on the next plane," she reported.

"How'd he take it?"

"I couldn't tell. He sounded pretty stunned. He asked if he could bring his fiancée."

"And?"

"I've quit telling Daddy what to do. It's always been too easy, and it was what Mother did for so long. He needs to make his own decisions. I think it would be tacky to show up with a fiancée at his former wife's funeral, but it also makes sense to have her come along so I can meet her."

"So is he bringing her?"

"He didn't say."

Bonnie, Earl's new secretary, a matronly, fiftyish woman, silently took in our conversation, then stood and approached. She took Margo's hands in hers. "We've never met," she said. "But I feel I know you. I followed the story of your mother in the papers, and Earl has told me so much about you. I just want you to know how badly I feel about this and that I would do anything at all if there's any way I can help."

Margo looked at her incredulously, as if she could hardly believe that a stranger could be so kind. She couldn't speak. She fell into Bonnie's arms and cried loudly. The phone rang, but Bonnie didn't even make a move for it. She asked with her eyes if I would answer it.

"EH Detective Agency," I said.

"Yeah, uh, Mr. Haymeyer?"

"No, this is Philip Spence. Can I — "

"Oh, good, Philip, it's you. This is George Franklin, but please don't let on that it's me if Margo is there."

"Oh, OK, sir. How are you? It's been a long time."

"I'm OK, Philip. Listen, let me tell you something straight here. Gladys my fiancée, she's not real hot about my coming back there for this funeral. You understand?"

"I think so. Does that mean you're not, I mean, what does that mean?"

"Right, Philip. I'm not going to be able to make it, but I'd appreciate it if you'd tell Margo another reason, like maybe this threatened air traffic controllers' strike everyone's talking about. Tell her I'm afraid I'll get stranded in Chicago or something, and with the new business, you know I can't afford that."

"OK, is that all? Are you sure you don't want to talk to — "

"No, I'd appreciate it if you'd handle that for me, Philip."

I knew Mr. Franklin wanted to come. He had loved Mrs. Franklin for years after the divorce and was especially supportive of her during the trial, though she resisted all his help. Everyone knew he posted the exhorbitant bond so she was free until her sentencing, but she had never thanked him. Still, he would have come. It was now more of the same for George Franklin. A woman was trying to make a man out of him by making him do what she said.

I didn't care if I ever met Gladys.

"Daddy will be calling back with his flight number, Bonnie," Margo said. "Just let me know, and I'll pick him up at the airport. Philip, will you go with me?"

"Your father just called and told me to tell you that he's afraid of getting stranded in Chicago if this threatened air traffic controllers' strike comes off. He's not coming."

"Of course he is; let me call him again."

"Margo," I said, as gently as I could, "if he had wanted to talk to you, he could have." She glared at me. "What are you saying?"

"That he didn't want to disappoint you, but he is not coming, and your calling him is not going to change anything."

Margo sat at Bonnie's desk, refusing to cry again. I hung around, not knowing what to say or do. I wanted to criticize her father and tell her the real reason, but it would not have helped. "You don't have to stay with me all the time, you know, Philip," she said.

"It's no bother," I said.

"Yes," she said. "It is."

I got the point and left. Later Bonnie called me in my apartment. "When my husband died a few years ago," she said, "I didn't want my closest loved ones to hover. I wanted them there, or not too far away, but I didn't want them uncomfortable. You looked uncomfortable. Like you were pitying her."

"Well, I *am* pitying her."

"Of course, Philip. We all are. We just need to be whatever she needs us to be right now. For you that means to take charge. Don't wait for things to happen. Make them happen. Don't try to console her; just tell her what happens next and see that it happens. I'm going to talk Margo into staying at my place tonight. It's not far away, and I think she needs to just get away right now.

"But listen, Philip, when it's time for the funeral or meetings with the lawyers or whatever, just take charge. Tell her you're coming for her and then do it. I think she's reacting a little toward her dad, who doesn't sound like a strong man."

"If you only knew," I said. "Thanks for everything, Bonnie."

Amos Chakaris told me at dinner that night that Mrs. Franklin's will requested that only a few close friends attend an interfaith-style service and burial within twenty-four hours of her death. "Which is nearly impossible in this state because of the autopsy, but I think we can make it within thirty hours."

"And who suffers if you don't?" I said.

"Well, Philip," he said, "I understand what you're saying, but where I come from — or maybe I should say, at my age — we have real respect for the dead and for their predeath wishes. I'll feel much better if we do all we can to grant those wishes."

"What other wishes were there?"

"Most everything else simply involves disposing of the estate. I'm not really at liberty to discuss the details until it has been read to the principals, or in this case, the principal — Margo."

"Can I be there for that?"

"It's entirely up to her."

Chakaris and Virginia Franklin went back a long way. He spent much of the rest of the evening recounting the days when she had been the crackerjack prosecutor and he was one of her toughest rivals. "She was always the consummate professional with the highest standards. Nothing dirty, nothing underhanded, nothing personal. We respected and admired each other until the end."

"You admired her even after you found out she murdered Richard Wanmacher?"

"No. To me that *was* the end. I don't know how or why she happened to take that turn, but I do know it was a turn. When I knew her best, she was straight, unimpeachable, above reproach. Seeing her fall was one of the most painful things I have ever been through. In my mind, her death is the kindest thing that has happened to her since she decided to kill a man."

Chakaris said that the autopsy report bore out the infirmary doctor's evaluation of the cause of death and filled me in on the funeral details. He said he had been given the power to invite up to ten people — based on his knowledge of the deceased — whom he thought she would want there. He had decided upon former United States Attorney James A. Hanlon, Earl Haymeyer, myself, Margo, and Mr. Franklin. "Of course, Margo can bring whoever she wants, also."

I explained Mr. Franklin's plight — to Chakaris's puzzlement — and asked if Mrs. Franklin didn't have any other friends.

"Are you kidding? The woman abandoned most of her social, business, and civic contacts during the last several years. I hardly spoke to her for two years before she called me one night and asked me to represent her before Jim Hanlon.

"Any friends she might have had in the Cook County circuit courts have dropped her like a hot potato since the mob ties and the murder were revealed. Even people who pity her would not want to be seen at her funeral."

"So it will be a mighty small gathering," I said.

"For sure," Chakaris said wearily. "Tomorrow morning at ten at the interfaith chapel in Kenilworth."

I called Bonnie's place at about ten that night and asked if Margo was sleeping. "Not really," Bonnie said, "and she did want me to wake her if you called. Now remember what I said."

"Yes, ma'am," I said, with mock deference.

I told Margo I would pick her up at nine the next morning for the funeral and that Amos had said she could bring anyone she wanted. "Even Bonnie?" she asked.

"Sure, if she wants to come." She did. "How are you doing, love?"

"I'm OK, Philip. I owe you a lot of apologies, I know, but for now, I'm OK."

"You owe me nothing. I'll see you at nine."

"You're sweet. 'Bye."

FOUR

Even with me on one side of her and Bonnie on the other, Margo didn't do too well at the funeral. The service was predictably antiseptic, no mention made of any turmoil whatever in Mrs. Franklin's life, let alone that she had served time for murder. Nothing was said even of her contribution to society as a lawyer or judge. We could have been burying anyone, and indeed we were. We were listening to a canned funeral service that, but for the filling in of "her" for "him" and "Virginia Franklin" for "John Doe," was the same service held there nearly every day.

That didn't help Margo, and neither did the absence of her father. "I feel like an orphan," she said at one point. There was nothing I could say. I wanted to be her mother and father and lover and friend. When the "interfaith" clergyman said, "Virginia is now resting in the peace that is her reward," I feared Margo would be sick.

She was silent and shaky as we left the cemetery. Amos strode up and told her that he would read the will for her and for anyone else that she wanted present, "whenever you wish."

"The sooner the better," she said. "Can we do it this week?"

"If you're sure that's what you want," he said. "Would you rather wait?"

"No. I want to put all this behind me as soon as I can."

Amos agreed to call her later with a specific date and time. "Wait until you see *his* offices," Margo told me incongruously.

Several nights later I saw what she meant. Not far from Chicago's Loop, the three floors of a turn-of-the-century mansion had been refurbished to accommodate the prestigious law firm of Chakaris, Fenton, Henley, and Whitehead and its twenty-eight lawyers.

The will was to be read at 9:00 P.M., and I was amazed that so many of the staff were still at the office. Chakaris himself answered the mystery when he arrived. "Good question, Philip. Though our staff is among the best and most dedicated in this city, nine o'clock is a little late for this many to still be here. They're here because I'm here.

"You see, the bigger and older a firm becomes, the more legendary its partners become. We seldom rub shoulders with the staff much anymore, so if they get so much as a chance to greet one of us, they take it. And if they can impress us by simply being here late at night when they know we're in, so much the better."

"Does it work?"

"Oh, a little. I did the same thing when I was young, tried to look busy when the big boss came in. What they don't realize is that we are often in here late at night on unscheduled business they wouldn't know about. Fewer 'selfless' staffers are here then, I can tell you."

"How would all these people know you were going to be in tonight?"

"Oh, you'd be surprised how quickly word travels around here. Law offices are great for rumors and grapevines. Usually accurate, too. But I wouldn't kid myself that all these people are here on my account. The other partners have just as many impressionable staffers as I do. They're going to be here tonight too."

"Your three partners? The names I saw on the plate outside?"

"Right. At ten o'clock I'm giving up my semiretired role in the company. It will be the first change of names in the company in more than thirty years. I'm the original owner, and I took on Hollis Fenton more than forty years ago. A few years later we promoted Thomas Henley, then Clarence Whitehead. It's been Chakaris, Fenton, Henley, and Whitehead ever since."

"So this is a major move."

"You bet. Even though I semiretired a couple of years ago — with a party and the whole bit — I've remained active a couple of days a week. Now I'll be out, though I assume the boys will want to keep my name on the door and the stationery."

"So why is this such a big deal, making official what has been in the works for two years?"

"Philip, my boy, there will be fireworks tonight. Any time a partner leaves the firm, the other partners jockey for position."

"Isn't it automatic? I mean if they move your name from first to last in the lineup, don't the other three just move up in order?"

"Often yes, but that wouldn't cause the fireworks I predicted, would it?"

"No."

"Confidentially, one of the big boys is going to find himself out of the usual lineup, and possibly even voted out of a partnership."

"Can that be done?"

"It's complicated, but our firm is set up in such a way that the majority rules in a vote of the partners. That means no partner had better be alone on a vote, or he loses. If he can get one other vote, a tie forestalls any changes."

"Who's in trouble?"

"I can't tell you that. But I can tell you that my official resignation becomes effective before the vote on the order of the names, so I will not be a voting member."

"Is that significant?"

"Only because it allows me to sit back and watch. I would be concerned if the very minute I was out the boys voted someone in or out and changed the face of the business in a way I disapproved of. But that is their right."

"Is that what they'll be doing tonight, taking advantage of the fact that you have no vote?"

"No, Philip. If I was voting tonight, I would be voting with the majority."

A phone message came for Chakaris. Margo and I sat in silence. I was fascinated by the workings of this office and the power the partners seemed to have, but it was obvious that Margo could not concentrate on it. This would be an ordeal for her, and she simply wanted it over with.

"Don't take this wrong, Margo," I said, "but what do you think you will be left from your mother's estate?"

"I don't know. Some of the stuff from the house, I suppose. Daddy will get the house. I mean it's his anyway."

"How can that be? Didn't she win it in the divorce settlement years ago?"

"I guess. All I know is that he always made the payments on it. Still does, I think. I wouldn't know how much it's worth by now. They bought it more than twenty years ago, but for how much, I don't know."

A court reporter came in with his equipment in tow, informed the secretary of his presence, and sat next to us on a leather couch. "Big doings here tonight, huh?" he said. "This many people here to hear the Franklin will?"

Margo shrugged.

"Not really," I said. "Most are just staffers here."

"Oh," he said, taking in the dark wood trim and beautiful furnishings. "A meeting of the partners tonight, then?"

"How'd you know?"

"Either everyone on this staff has a trial tomorrow morning, or something's going on."

Chakaris's secretary motioned for the court reporter to come upstairs. "You may come along in about five minutes too," she told us. For some reason, I was nervous.

As we started up the stairs, a distinguished man in his mid-sixties came down as if each step was a surprise. "Good evening," he said with a slight bow. "You must be Philip and Margo. Charmed. I'm Hollis Fenton. So nice to meet you."

He was so smooth he nearly overwhelmed us. We were speechless. "Amos asked if I would introduce you to the lawyer who will be handling any of the detail work of the Franklin estate subsequent to the reading of the will."

"We'd be happy to meet him," I said.

"Her," Fenton corrected, a sliver of ice in his tone.

He led us upstairs to the door of the room in which the will would be read. From another wing came a young woman in her mid-twenties, tweed-clad, nearly six feet tall, with long, black hair, huge eyes, and an incredible face. I stared and Margo noticed, almost amused.

"This," said Fenton with a flourish, "is Miss Hilary Brice, attorney at law. She will be — "

"Thank you very much, Mr. Fenton," Hilary said, turning her back on him and motioning to us with a thin attache. "Will you follow me, please?"

Fenton was left broiling in the hall as Hilary closed the door. "Philip and Margo," she said, "I trust that the reading of the will would be the end of the legal association between you and our firm, but if not, I will be handling anything for Mr. Chakaris, who is retiring shortly."

She was crisp and to the point and, except for the quite obvious brush-off of Hollis Fenton, seemed pleasant and even a little shy. She certainly knew what to say and when to say it. I pictured Mr. Fenton in the hallway, plotting her demise. How could a young lawyer do a number like that on a man who had been a partner in the firm for forty years?

Amos sat at one end of a long wooden table, and the court reporter — already entering script — listened as Amos monotoned preliminary file numbers. "Are we all here?" he asked, looking up. I nodded as if I knew, then realized that I didn't.

"I believe so, yes," Hilary said.

"Off the record," Amos said, glancing at the reporter, "Margo, I am pleased to tell you before I read this aloud that you are about to become an extremely wealthy young woman."

Margo was nonplussed. She shot a double take at Chakaris and then at me. Hilary overruled a grin. "Get on with it, counselor," she said.

"Let the record show who is present," Chakaris began. "Amos Chakaris, senior partner in the firm of Chakaris, Fenton, Henley, and Whitehead, in his final official duty for the same — "

"Excuse me, sir," the court reporter interrupted, "but do you want all that on the record?"

"Do you mind?" Chakaris asked Margo. "This is, after all, really recorded for you."

"Oh, not at all," Margo said. "As long as you're not going to recount your entire legal history just for the books."

Everyone laughed. Chakaris continued: "Also Margo Franklin, daughter of the deceased — " That sobered Margo again. " — Philip Spence of Glencoe, Illinois, and the youngest and most beautiful junior partner this law firm has ever had, Hilary Brice."

The court reporter hesitated, Hilary pursed her lips and shook her head, and Chakaris resignedly said, "Strike that. There might have been one younger."

This time Margo was not amused, and Chakaris noticed. He quickly began the laborious reading into the record all the legal jargon:

"I, Virginia A. Franklin, of Winnetka, Illinois, being of sound and disposing mind and memory, do hereby make, publish, and declare this to be my last will and testament, revoking any and all previous wills and codicils by me made.

"The expense of my last illness, my funeral and the administration of my estate, wherever situated, shall be paid out of the principal of my residuary estate....

"I give all my personal and household effects not otherwise effectively disposed of to my daughter, Margo Franklin, if she survives me for thirty days, or if she does not so survive me, to my executor for disbursement as he determines...."

Finally, Chakaris got to the guts of the document. "I give all my residuary estate, being all real and personal property, wherever situated, in which I may have any interest at the time of my death, not otherwise effectively disposed of, to my daughter, Margo Franklin, if she survives me for thirty days...."

Chakaris read on and on, finally asking if there were any questions.

"Yes," Margo said, raising her hand as if in class. "Just what did my mother leave me? What did she own that is covered by that all-inclusive paragraph?"

Five

"I'm glad you asked," Chakaris said, grinning broadly and looking at his watch. I thought of his monumental meeting at ten. "Your mother and father purchased the lovely home you grew up in back in the late fifties for eighty thousand dollars. That was an extremely high price in those days, and the home has increased in value nearly ten times.

"As you know, your mother had great and expensive taste in furnishings, all of which are included in the home. The cars were disposed of at the time of her incarceration, but virtually everything on the property and in the house and garage now belong to you.

"To the best of our ability in the time we had before this reading, in conjunction with professional appraisers, our firm has determined that even after inheritance taxes — if you allow us to set up the legal shelters you are entitled to and we earnestly recommend — your personal net worth will increase by just less than one million dollars."

Margo was stunned. The import of it had not sunk in. I would have asked when and where and how the acquisition would take place, but Margo doesn't think that way.

Chakaris sat grinning at her. Hilary filled her attaché, preparing to leave. Suddenly Margo spoke. "Why has my dad been making the payments on the house all these years if it's my mother's house?"

Hilary froze. The smile died on Chakaris' face. The court reporter looked puzzled but entered the question.

"Strike that," Chakaris said quickly.

"I can't," the reorter said. "I mean, I shouldn't. You know that."

Chakaris started to insist, but Hilary cut him off. "He's right, Mr. Chakaris. Let's clear this up on the record. May I?"

Chakaris nodded. Hilary began, "Are you sure, Margo?"

"No doubt. I've known it for so long that there's no question in my mind. I can remember my mother talking about how much more money we had because Daddy was making the house payment, and sometimes she'd even make fun of him for it. Once she said, 'I may not be his any more, but he's sure mine.' "

Chakaris winced. Hilary pulled her papers out again.

"Mr. Chakaris," she said, "I have a copy here of the divorce decree. It was the last document on the case and shows clearly that Mrs. Franklin won the house and all equity on it to that point, and it stipulates also that she assumes the mortgage and all subsequent responsibilities for it, including payments on the loan and interest, taxes, insurance, and any and all major or minor repairs. What do you make of it?"

"I make of it that it's all we need," Chakaris said gruffly. But it was obvious he was troubled.

"Where do we go from here?" Hilary asked.

"Get Franklin on the phone. I want to know if he made the payments after she was awarded the house, and why. Meanwhile, this session is recessed until the principals are notified."

Chakaris thanked the court reporter and told him Miss Brice would be taking over the case. Then he turned to Margo. "Don't worry, honey," he said. "I'm sure it's just a minor detail. The house was your mother's free and clear. I don't know why a man would volunteer to continue to make house payments on a house he lost in court, but regardless, that gives him no rights to it, and now it is yours. If he's really a fool, maybe he'll still make the payments on it. There are a few years' worth to go."

"He's not a fool," Margo insisted.

"I'm sorry," Amos said. "I've met him and I know better than to say he's a fool. I do want to clear this up. You realize now that we are representing your mother's estate, and thus you in this matter?"

"Yes."

"Good. Stay close to Hilary. She's a good one." And with that, he was gone much more quickly and lightly than a man his size and age should have been. He slipped into another office down the hall at about a minute before ten, and Hollis Fenton followed him, trailed by two other nattily dressed gentlemen, no doubt Henley and Whitehead.

Just before we were about to leave the mansion, Hilary caught up with us.

"Is Mr. Chakaris in his meeting already?"

"Yes," I said.

"I have a message for him."

"I thought you were taking over the case."

"I am, but besides talking with Mr. Franklin's attorney, I learned that the air traffic controllers' strike is on. Mr. Chakaris won't be able to go to Florida tomorrow after all."

"What did you learn from Daddy's attorney?" Margo asked.

"Let's talk about that tomorrow," Hilary said.

"No, let's talk about it now."

"I really can't. I have to give this message to Mr. Chakaris and then be available if he needs anything. I'm sorry."

"Can we wait?" Margo asked, almost desperate. I scowled at her as if it wasn't such a good idea. She ignored me. Hilary hesitated. "We'll wait," Margo decided, and she sat down.

Hilary started upstairs but turned back. Margo looked expectantly at her. "It's all right with me if it's all right with you," Hilary said finally. I shrugged. Margo nodded. "This meeting could be a long one, and Mr. Chakaris thinks there will be, uh, that it will be, um, that there might be — "

"Fireworks," Margo said.

"Right." And Hilary trotted upstairs.

"Beautiful, isn't she?" Margo said.

"For sure," I said, a little too enthusiastically.

Margo and I talked quietly on a love seat at the bottom of the stairs while a half dozen young lawyers found reasons to jog up and down the stairs on real or imagined missions to second floor offices and files. They heard little more than we did for the first half hour or so. Things seemed to be progressing so smoothly that no voices were raised.

"I'm still mad at God," Margo allowed.

"Do you want to talk about it?"

"I'm not sure. It's hard to talk about without becoming emotional."

"Then maybe this is the place to talk about it. There are enough people around so you can't become too emotional."

"Philip, I just flat don't see how God could let Mother die before I had gotten a chance to really confront her with His claims on her life. How do you answer that? How do you fit that into the formula of everything working together for good to those who love God? I love God, and the desire of my heart was that my mother receive Christ. God disappointed me; He failed me. I feel horrible saying that. I know how it sounds. But what else can I think?"

"I don't know."

"Oh, great. That's beautiful. You know, Philip, I hinted at my feelings the other day hoping to give you time to get your answer together, to marshal your theological forces. I even told you that I didn't want your platitudes because I thought that would force you to really dig for an original answer for me. I need something now, and as honest as you're being — I really appreciate your admitting that you don't know — it doesn't help me. You're failing me too."

"You're not a very nice person sometimes, Margo. Did you know that?" She looked at me incredulously, as if wondering how I could say something so cruel at a time like this. Frankly, I wondered too, but I stayed with it. "No one can please you. You want your life wrapped up in tidy little packages, labeled and ready to be opened. Answers for every problem and question. Now that you're a Christian, God owes you a smooth ride, or at least the reason for any bumps in the road."

Margo was dumbstruck. She shook her head slowly. "You have no answers, so you attack me. Is that it?"

"To you, not having all the answers *is* an attack. An attack of realism. Who ever told you that life with God would be rosy? You want to be biblical? Look at Job. What did he do to deserve what he suffered? He was tormented *because* he was godly. Satan attacked him for that very reason. He was a pawn in a spiritual chess game. Is that fair?"

"You're evading my question. How does God explain promising me the desires of my heart and that everything works together for good to those who love Him, and then allowing Mother to die?"

"I don't know."

"What *do* you know, Philip?"

"I know that you'd rather be God than Margo; and wouldn't we all? You feel you could do a better job than He does. If you had His power and might and omnipotence, you'd made it all turn out all right. You'd decide what was good and what was evil."

"Haven't you ever felt that God treated you unjustly?"

"No, I haven't, but don't you dare accuse me of some false piety. My problem is self-image. I've been so convinced for so long that I'm unworthy of the love of God that I feel guilty when good things come my way and fortunate when bad things come that they weren't worse. My problem is that I feel I deserve so little from God that if He ever tried to balance the books with me, I'd lose everything."

"That *is* sick."

"Perhaps it is, Margo. At least I see it for what it is. And it at least keeps me from judging God or trying to tell Him what is right and what isn't. You know how He explained Himself to Job?"

"No, but I have a feeling you're about to tell me."

"He didn't. He merely challenged Job and asked him if he could do what God does. Could he have created all the wonders of nature? Job had to see his inadequacy. But think of Job's situation when God reminded him of all the wonders of nature. He had lost everything and was suffering."

"You're saying that God has a bigger plan and knows better than I do."

"In simple terms, yes."

"Does that mean I have to like it?"

"Would you, even if I said yes?"

"No."

"God demands only your trust and faith and confidence."

"He doesn't demand understanding?"

"He nearly forbids it. I know no one who claims to understand God. If you understand God, you are God and we don't need Him."

"The height of blasphemy."

"You got it. And have you ever wondered if that verse about God giving us the desires of our hearts should not be read a different way?"

"Like how?"

"I'm no theologian, and maybe I'm way off, but since it is hard to reconcile God promising us the desires of our hearts and then allowing loved ones to die when their salvation *is* the desire of our heart, try reading the verse another way. Instead of assuming it means that God will fulfill the desires we have in our hearts, could it mean that He will dictate to us what those desires should be? In other words, God will literally give us the desires of our hearts; He will instill them in us so they will be proper and in accordance with His will."

Margo was silent for several minutes. "Do you think I'm terrible?" she asked finally.

"Of course not."

"You said I wasn't very nice sometimes."

"You're not. You're a know-it-all who gets irritated when she doesn't know it all."

"So you *do* think I'm terrible."

"No. I think you're learning."

"Don't kid yourself. I've got a lot of reading, studying, and praying to do before I buy this package. Though I must admit I am drawn to your logic."

"You mean all my I-don't-knows sound logical?"

"I'm drawn to your *un*logic then. All of Christianity is illogical, isn't it? From the creation, to Job, to the virgin birth, the cross, the resurrection — "

"Perhaps I was fortunate to have been raised with it. I went through my periods of doubting, which forced me to study and claim Christ for myself, but sometimes I think there is value in being indoctrinated with truth."

"But think of the people who are indoctrinated with lies," Margo said.

"I have. It's scary."

Appearing suddenly at the bottom of the stairs were three or four of the law office staff. They craned their necks at raised voices from upstairs. Two men were speaking at once, and another — apparently the court reporter — was asking each to wait his turn so he could record it all.

When Hollis Fenton burst from the room, yanking on his knee-length overcoat, the personnel in front of us parted like the Red Sea. We stared full into Fenton's flushed face as he sped down the stairs.

Six

A few minutes later the meeting upstairs broke up. "You're still here?" Amos said.

"I want to know what Hilary found out from Daddy's attorney," Margo said.

"Yes, well, what *did* you find?" Chakaris asked Hilary as she approached from another room. "Here let's go into my office. I'm in no hurry to get home now with no reason to get up early tomorrow."

Chakaris' office was the most elaborate we had seen in the mansion. His bookshelves were empty, and stuffed boxes were piled near the door, but it was not difficult to imagine how impressive it looked lined with law books and paintings. "Henley will like this office," Chakaris told Hilary, chuckling.

Hilary looked pleasantly surprised. "Mr. Henley?" she said. "Not Mr. Fenton?"

"Let's talk about it later. What's the word on Mr. Franklin?"

"Not good. His lawyer says he's been making the payments on the house since the beginning. Says he had an agreement with Mrs. Franklin that this would give him the first option on the house if she should ever list it for sale."

"No problem."

"And — "

"And?"

"And that the house would revert to him if she preceded him in death."

Margo hid her head in her hands. Chakaris leaned his massive body back in his chair, scowling. Hilary sat with her brows raised. "I know what you're wondering," she said. "You're wondering if he has it in writing. He does. Or at least his lawyer says he does. He won't part with the original though. Says he'll send a photocopy."

Chakaris told the young lawyer that a photocopy would not be any good if she wanted to check it for authenticity.

"You want *me* to check this thing out?" Hilary asked.

"It's your case, kid. You know that. I've been officially off it since the reading of the will."

"Wait a minute," Margo said, as if they were missing some basic reason that the whole conversation was pointless. "Are you telling me that you're doubting my father's word? That I'm supposed to fight him for my mother's estate? I'd never do it. Forget it. If it's his, it's his. If he wants it, I don't want it."

"Girl, you're talking about a million dollars here," Chakaris said. "I appreciate your altruism, but let's get serious. Even a peach like your father can sour when the big money comes into the picture."

"Well, I won't let him sour; he won't have to. If she put in writing that the house is his upon her death, then the house is his. No way I'll fight him for it."

"Margo," I said. "Don't you think you'd better sleep on this?"

"No amount of sleep is going to make it all right to battle over my mother's will. This is like a bad movie, and I don't want any part in it. Daddy wouldn't try to take anything that was rightfully mine."

"You're probably right about that," Hilary said. "His lawyer seemed genuinely surprised that your mother had left you the house."

"I was surprised too," Margo said. "Perhaps she just forgot about the deal with Daddy."

"Your mother never forgot a detail in her life," Chakaris said. "Something really stinks here, and I'm going to find out what it is. I don't mind telling you that part of my reason is financial. If the house was included in the estate illegally, it considerably lessens the base value of the estate, from which we determine our percentage as executors."

"Amos, I'm disappointed," Margo said.

"Don't be. It's strictly business, and I'm trying to make you see that people will be hurt in this, whether you care about yourself or not. I'll no longer be with the firm anyway, so it won't affect me. Are you aware that I represented your mother gratis in her trial? Her funds were depleted quickly, and we're talking about tens of thousands of dollars' worth of legal fees."

"Why did you offer that?"

"I didn't. I tried to tell her not to worry about it for the time being, but she felt terrible about it. Your father tried to pay me, but I refused that, too. Your mother finally told me that she wanted our firm to try to sell her house if her appeal failed, and that we could take our fees from the profits, which would have been considerable after all these years of building equity."

"And she never told you Daddy was making the payments?"

"Never."

Margo was nearly in tears. "I don't understand any of this. Why would Daddy pay for the house unless he was going to get it someday? And why would Mother leave it to me if she knew it was illegal? She had to know it would never happen and would only cause me embarrassment."

Chakaris tried to be gentle. "Margo, it wasn't beyond your mother to do numbers on people. The last will was dated several years after your parents' divorce. She was willfully writing your father out of her will. That was the whole point of redoing it. We need to respect that."

"Was the will written after she had been arrested? I mean, if not, why hadn't she written me out when I was trying to expose her?"

Chakaris fidgeted. "She tried to. She wanted me to tear up her will and make you and your father fight over the estate. I told her your father would have no claim on it as a divorcée and that *you* would lose most of it to the state if she had no will. She still wanted to do that, but she never got around to it."

"This really brings back bad, bad feelings," Margo admitted. "I can't stand the thought of inheriting any part of that house or property now."

"Don't speak too soon," Chakaris said. "I'd never forgive myself if I let you sneeze at a million dollars. Anyway, you don't think your mother still felt that way at the end, do you?"

"I don't know."

"Yes, you do, Margo," I said. "You know she was very fond of you and showed it in her own feisty ways."

Margo nodded miserably. "This was supposed to be the end of my mother in my life," she said. "I knew it would be tough, but I thought it would be over after tonight. Pick up a few pieces of furniture and some keepsakes and be done with it. Now this."

"It's late," Hilary said. "Why don't you get some sleep, and we'll talk strategy tomorrow."

"There will be no strategy," Margo said. "But sleep does sound good." She looked at me. "Home, James," she said, still wry to the end.

Chakaris caught my arm on the way out. "Whatever you do," he said, "don't let her talk to her father. Anything she says to him or to his representative at this point could jeopardize her rights to the estate."

"Are you confident of her rights?"

"Until I see that document Mr. Franklin's lawyer claims to have. If it's legit and dated after the will I read tonight, we've got problems."

"What time is it in Los Angeles?" Margo asked in the car.

"About ten, I guess."

"I want to call Daddy from Earl's office before I go to my apartment."

"I can't let you do that."

"What are you talking about, Philip? You don't own me. You can't tell me what to do." I knew she didn't intend to sound so mean, but neither had I intended to sound so possessive.

"It's just not a good idea, Mar. You're dead tired. It's been a big, emotional day. Your father is gun-shy of you right now anyway because he knows he should have come to the funeral. Don't put him on the spot now."

"All I want to know is whether he wants the house, knowing that Mother left it to me in her will. If he does, then I won't fight him for it."

"That's just what Chakaris doesn't want you to say to your dad or to anyone representing him."

"Chakaris is representing me, not me him, you know."

"Correction. Hilary is representing you. And she's worth listening to."

"And worth looking at, judging by your reaction."

"Guilty."

"I can hardly believe my father has representation already. He doesn't need a lawyer to fight with me. I'm easy." Margo fell silent, thinking. "Do you really not want me to call Daddy tonight?" she asked suddenly. "Or are you just parroting Amos?"

"Both."

"I'll wait," she said.

The lights were on in Haymeyer's office when we pulled in. Earl and Bonnie were still at work. After we greeted them, I insisted that Margo go to bed, and I stayed to talk to Earl.

"Chakaris called about a half hour ago and told me the whole story," Earl said. "It's hard to figure. Mr. Franklin always hit me as such a Milquetoast. This isn't his style."

"What do you think Amos is going to do?"

"I know what Amos is going to do. He's hired the best detective agency in the Chicago area to investigate the thing and report back to one Heather Bruce or Hilary Brewster or — " Haymeyer dug through his notes.

"Hilary Brice," I said.

"Right. And the aforementioned detective agency is assigning its top — and only — junior staff member to the case."

"You're kidding. You don't think that's a conflict of interest?"

"Just because you're in love with one of the principals? Hardly. Anyway, I don't have time for a drive to California."

"Drive? You want me to drive?"

"You wouldn't want Hilary Bruce, or Brice, to drive out there all by herself any more than Amos does, would you?"

"Well, no, but drive?"

"That air traffic controllers' strike is indefinite, in case you hadn't heard. They're not even scheduled to talk for ten days. Nationwide commerce is going to be crippled."

"And the road full of trucks."

"You'll be driving one yourself."

"I can't drive a truck."

"Not a truck really. A four-wheel-drive job."

"Margo's going to want to go, you know."

Haymeyer frowned. "What do you think, Bonnie? Should I let Margo go?"

"You won't be able to keep her home," the secretary said.

SEVEN

"We've got the expense of two hotel rooms all along the way anyway," Haymeyer explained the next morning. "Margo, you can stay with Hilary."

Haymeyer said he would have Bonnie or the secretary in the Chakaris law firm arrange a meeting time with Mr. Franklin and his lawyer to officially examine the documents on both sides. Chakaris thought it would put the pressure on Mr. Franklin if Hilary went immediately and offered to let him see the will and all the attendant papers. "He can either put up or shut up," Chakaris summarized, according to Earl.

Bonnie helped map out our route, arranging for the rented four-wheel drive to be delivered, making hotel reservations, and checking the weather. "It should be clear sailing except maybe in the mountains," she said. "You seldom hear of much trouble in mid-April."

Margo and I busied ourselves packing as lightly as we could. She was anxious to see her father and wanted to call him and let him know she would be there, but Haymeyer and Hilary thought the surprise would be better. "Plus, anything you say now could threaten our part of the negotiations."

Margo insisted that she didn't care and vowed she would turn the house over to her father if he wanted it, whether he was legally entitled to it or not. "If he wants it that badly, I want him to have it. He must want it for some reason or he would never push it this far. He's never hurt a flea; he surely wouldn't hurt me on purpose."

Once, such talk spilled over in front of Haymeyer, and Margo started in again on the idea that God seemed distant and hard to understand. I was able to shut it off without being too obvious and tried to scold her later. "You don't want to throw a barrier in Earl's way, do you?" I said. "When the time comes to really challenge Earl to consider God in his life, we don't want to have posed unnecessary questions for him."

"You want me to be dishonest?" Margo said. "I do have questions about God and why He did this — I mean why He allowed this. I guess I agree that we have no right to challenge God's right to do what He wants, but what happens when we don't like what He does?"

"Then we tell Him He's wrong and that we could do better. We become proud and we become God and run the universe the way we want."

"If only I could," Margo said.

"You don't mean that."

"The point is that I can't. I have no power next to God. He does what He wants. People die and people hurt and people starve and things go wrong, and we are powerless to do anything about it. He lets it happen for His own reasons, and we just have to accept it."

"Can't argue with that," I said.

"But we don't have to like it."

"Of course not."

"You were close to convincing me with your Job argument, Philip, and while I confess I haven't read it yet, I assume I shouldn't argue with it if it's God's own example of answering my questions for someone else. It's His prerogative to ignore the question and change the subject to get His point across. But why is He piling one thing on top of the other, just when I'm about to get whatever point He has for me?"

"What do you mean?"

"This thing with Daddy. Has he had a personality change? Is he a Mr. Hyde? This is not the man I knew. I went through this with my mother. Do I have to face it with my father too? I don't know if I can take it. Why, Philip? Why?"

"I don't know."

"You know, your honesty used to thrill me, refresh me, uplift me. Now it irritates me."

"And how would you like a platitude instead? A sermon maybe? A trumped-up truism?"

"No, thanks. I get the point. But I still don't like it. Be patient with me, will you? And just ignore me."

"Yes and no. I will be patient, as long as you realize what a tough position you put me in sometimes. But no, I will not ignore you."

"I mean ignore me when I'm mean. I don't want to hurt you. I'm lashing out at God and things I can't control and I'm hitting you. I'm sorry. And what do you mean, the tough position this is putting *you* in? You mean other than that I'm shooting at you a little? That should be easier to take than what *I'm* going through right now."

"True enough. Let's compete for most-worthy-to-be-felt-sorry-for, OK? I know you'd win, but sometime just put yourself in my shoes. I am expected to defend the mind of God, which I don't understand any more than you do. I'm content to trust that He knows what He's doing, because I've believed that all my life. I admit this is easy to say when the toughest breaks are coming *your* way and not mine. I don't know how I'd feel if they were tearing up my world."

"My world isn't your world?"

"I can't win."

"Yes, you can. You've won my heart in spite of yourself."

"Marry me," I said.

"Give me a few days."

"Really?"

"Of course not. You don't want a bad Christian on your hands, do you? Just don't give up on me."

"We've already been through that."

"And you won't?"

"You know I won't."

"And it doesn't shock you, my bold talk against God?"

"I'm not saying I like it, Margo, but it sure beats being phony."

"Meanwhile you want me to be slightly phony in front of our godless friends, is that it?"

"Not really phony. Judicious maybe."

"Save my doubts and fears and challenges for the ears of someone who loves me and cares about me and who won't throw over his faith in the face of my tirades?"

"Are you being facetious?"

"Not until I got into that. Then it sounded pretty good."

I laughed. "Then you're right. That's what I want."

"Fair enough," she said.

Bonnie arranged an ambitious schedule. "With three drivers you should be able to make North Platte, Nebraska, in twelve or thirteen hours the first day," she said. "You're confirmed in two rooms at the Holiday Inn. It has a lot of features, but you'd better ignore them, eat well, and sleep long because I have you down for Cedar City, Utah, the next night. If you make that, you should be able to make L.A. the next evening, maybe even late afternoon."

"North Platte and Cedar City?" Margo said. "Sounds like the big time."

We were scheduled to leave the following Monday morning, and a meeting was set with Mr. Franklin for late Thursday morning. I had to coax Margo to go to church with me in Winnetka Sunday morning, hoping that the sermon would be on Job or the sovereignty of God or some other divinely coincidental topic that would illuminate her mind and prove that I had been right — not for my sake, but for hers.

But the sermon was on the love of God, the very attribute Margo was doubting. She listened intently and seemed to enthusiastically join in the singing and other aspects of the worship service, but I couldn't get her to talk about it later. "This is something I'm really going to need to work through, Philip," she said.

The next morning Hilary, Margo, and I pulled out of Glencoe and headed south to Interstate 80 and then to points west. I took the first driving shift of four or five hours, then Hilary would go four and Margo three. The girls brought books and magazines and snacks, but nothing was opened as the three of us got to know each other for a few hours.

After telling everything we knew about Amos and Earl, for the benefit of whoever among us knew the least, we told every joke we knew to avoid talking about ourselves. Then we could avoid it no longer.

Hilary was as curious about us as we were about her. She had followed the story of Virginia Franklin's murder trial in the papers and had been fascinated by the bits and pieces she had heard about Margo's and my relationship.

We filled in the blanks as best we could, and Margo even explained how she had come to believe in Christ as a result of my concern for her and the many things I had given her to read. She suggested that Hilary could have any of those to peruse if she wished, but Hilary politely refused.

"I hadn't realized how religious you two were," she said, matter-of-factly, "though Amos warned me — ah — told me a little about you. Earl said something too about the fact that you go to church a lot and all that. I hope you won't spend the whole trip trying to convert me," she added with a smile.

"From what?" Margo asked, as only she could.

EIGHT

"From nothing," Hilary said. "My father's parents had been pretty strict Baptists, I understand, and when he couldn't live up to their standards, there was a falling out that never fully healed. Religion is simply not discussed when his parents are around, and they never visited on Sundays because they couldn't stand to see him drinking beer in front of the TV when they thought he should be taking his family to church."

"So you didn't go to church at all?" I asked.

"Not really. My mother had been raised to go to church on holidays and sometimes sent us or let us go if other kids invited us. We went to summer Bible school and stuff like that, but I don't remember being in church just for a meeting since I was about ten."

Hilary was the third of four girls, had always been exceptionally tall and self-conscious about her looks, never dated much until college, and decided that she had been driven to succeed in school and a career by the desire to please her parents. "They weren't pushy or prestige-oriented," she said, "but take my father, for instance. All his goals are intrinsic. He has no qualitative or quantitative goals. All he wants is to be the best he can be at a given project. If it's working around the house, he doesn't have to build the best patio deck in the neighborhood or one that would fool a professional carpenter. He just wants to do the best he can do, and he doesn't worry about anything else."

"Not a bad philosophy," I said.

"My mother is the same way," Hilary continued. "She cared more about the fact that we were honest and displayed good sense than that we were popular or beautiful or anything else."

"Then how do you explain your sort of overachievement?" Margo asked. "You know what I mean."

"Sure. I guess it's just part of my dad's philosophy. I never had a goal of being a top student so I could qualify for law school. And I certainly never set out to be on the staff of the law review. I sent resumes everywhere, just like all the other graduates, but because I had done well in school and had written in the review, I guess the people at CFH and W were impressed, and I was asked to come for an interview."

"How many other students were invited?"

"Only a few. CFH and W interviews only about ten a year and hires just one."

"And you were it."

"Right. Two years ago."

"You've been there just two years and you're already a junior partner?!"

"I didn't strive for that, either."

"What did you strive for?"

"I just wanted to prove to myself that I was worthy of being hired. I spent a lot of time in the law library, and I did my homework. I worked a lot harder my first six months on the job than I did in my last year of law school."

"That's hard to believe," I said, "from what I've heard about law school."

"I'm not saying law school wasn't grueling. It was. Almost overwhelming. And I didn't exactly love it, though some students do — if you can believe them. I was intrigued by the law and wanted to do my best, and I felt my sex was a hurdle too. Right or wrong, I felt I had to be better than the men to be considered as good."

"It worked."

"I guess. Anyway, that first six months on the job in Chicago I worked as if I was afraid I would wake up and find that I had not landed a position with one of the most prestigious firms in Chicago."

"Then you did care about prestige."

"I'd lie if I said I didn't, but it wasn't most important. It was satisfying. It said to me, 'You're doing it. You're being the best you can be.' That didn't mean I had to become a junior partner within the first year and a half, and I'm serious when I say I have no bigger goals than that. I can't imagine remaining a junior partner until I'm fifty, but I would be satisfied if I did that job the best I could do it."

"Don't be silly," Margo said. "You'll be a partner before you're thirty, a judge by forty, and on the supreme court by fifty." We all laughed, but I wonder if any of us doubted that Hilary Brice could be such a pioneer if she really wanted it. The fact that she didn't live and die for it might be what would make it happen one day.

"I just want to keep doing my homework," Hilary said. "I treat every case as my top priority. I give it all I've got, give it the hours it needs, count on no one else to do my digging for me, listen to every bit of advice — from the partners I respect to the partners I don't respect, and from the colleagues I admire to the ones I don't. I don't apologize for it, and I don't talk about it much — which will be hard for you two to believe after I've gone on about it so."

"No," Margo and I said in unison. "It's fascinating," I said.

"Well, it wasn't fascinating to all my colleagues when I was named a junior partner," Hilary said. "And there was a partner who wasn't thrilled either."

"Mr. Fenton?" I ventured.

"I don't hide that well, do I?" Hilary said.

"No, it *was* rather chilly in the hallway the other night."

"I really shouldn't talk about it," she said, digging out her camera. We were quiet for more than an hour before she broached the subject again. "This isn't like me," she said, "but you two have told me so much about yourselves that I feel like I want to tell you about Hollis Fenton. You must swear to never mention it to anyone, especially Earl Haymeyer. He knows too many people that Amos knows."

We were all ears. Hilary wasn't really ready to tell us much yet, however. She wanted to apologize in advance some more first. "I live alone, you know, and there aren't many people I can tell when I have a personal problem. I shouldn't make this sound like it's still a problem, because I handled it, but I always wished I had had someone I could tell about Hollis. I mentioned it to Amos once and I think that really cooked things for Mr. Fenton. At first I was afraid Amos would defend his old friend, but there had been enough other bad reports that it was merely the straw that broke the camel's back."

"Are you going to tell us this story?" Margo asked with a twinkle.

"Probably not," Hilary said. "From this you wouldn't get the idea I'd be any good in court, would you?"

"No, but you probably are."

"Well, Mr. Fenton, who had been out of town when I was hired and who has always had a problem with women lawyers, refused to be impressed, even when good reports came back about my court appearances. He resisted the other partners' efforts to have me promoted to a junior partner."

"But he couldn't garner another vote, right?" I asked, remembering Chakaris' explanation of a few nights before.

"That's right. But I discovered later that my being voted in as a junior partner really took away Hollis' bait for me."

"His bait?"

"At one point during the earliest days of my tenure at CFH and W, Mr. Fenton called me at home and invited me out to dinner with him. It was strictly an invitation to a dinner date, no way around it. I laughed and asked if he was serious and if he knew I was just out of law school — the implication being that I was about forty years his junior. He said he was quite aware of it and that if it didn't bother me, it didn't bother him.

"I could hardly respond. I was in awe of this man who had such a reputation in the courtroom. I was nearly speechless in his presence, and now, on the phone, when I realized he was serious, I didn't know what to say. I told him I thought it did bother me, though I was flattered. The man has a son at a law firm in the suburbs, who is forty years old!"

"Fenton still married?"

"Divorced. Twice. And the kids from neither marriage can stand him. He is feuding with members of both families, though there is one son he tries to stay next to for some reason. Those were not exactly amicable splits. He's quite the ladies' man. He is often seen with women, usually younger than he, but not quite forty years younger."

"So what happened?"

"Well, he was dumbfounded. I got the impression he had never been turned down before, especially by a subordinate. He immediately tried to pretend he had been kidding and said, 'Seriously, Mr. Chakaris asked that I take you to dinner and counsel you about procedures at the firm.' I couldn't call him a liar, so I accepted.

"At dinner he was so complimentary it was embarrassing. He didn't try to take my arm or anything, but he treated me like a date and I kept having to get him back onto the subject of the law firm. He told me nothing that the secretary hadn't been telling me for days. I played it very icy the whole evening, and when he walked me to my apartment door I just thanked him and went in."

"Just like you did the other night, shutting the door on him?"

"I didn't do that."

"Yes, you did."

"I did? It's second nature to me anymore."

"Why? Aren't you afraid of him?"

"I was, but I decided that if I told Mr. Chakaris what happened and he told me that I should humor the man, I would simply quit. No job is worth that."

"Did you tell Amos?"

"Sure. And Fenton got in trouble, but not before he got into more trouble with me. After I told Mr. Chakaris — and it was obvious that Amos was upset with him — Hollis made a pass at me in the library at the law offices. Nothing gross, he just leaned over my shoulder at a table and whispered that being nice to him could mean good things in my future at the firm, especially since he was the heir apparent. I told him, without whispering, that the best thing for my future at the firm would he if he kindly left me alone."

"What did he do?" Margo asked.

"It stood him straight up. He flushed and said that I would regret that. I told him I doubted it."

"Would you have been so bold if you hadn't known of Chakaris' disapproval of his actions?"

"Are you serious? I don't know what I would have done if I hadn't had someone on my side. And someone who ran the firm, no less. I guess Hollis's courtroom theatrics had gradually gone from effective to ridiculous, and he was beginning to embarrass the firm occasionally. He was still a top lawyer, one of the best, but people were beginning to wonder about him, mostly people within the profession. Judges, too."

"So did he get into trouble with Chakaris?"

"You bet. He was taken off one important case, told to leave me alone — which he didn't — and was generally scolded by Chakaris, his lifelong friend and associate."

"He didn't leave you alone?"

"He told me that squealing 'like a schoolgirl' would keep me from progressing. When I became a junior partner, he was whipped. He has been civil to me only in front of strangers ever since, and then he is so sickeningly sweet that I can't take it."

"So what happened the other night in the big meeting of the partners?"

"I thought you'd never ask. Isn't it my turn to drive, by the way?"

I had driven for six hours without thinking of the time.

NINE

We were still short of Des Moines, Iowa, when we made our first pit stop with the gauge nearly on empty. Hilary took over at the wheel, and except for being a little tentative pulling out of the service station and onto the freeway, she handled the vehicle as if she had driven one all her life.

"Would you believe Hollis Fenton began actually trying to sabotage my cases?"

"No, I wouldn't," I said, "I can see all the rest, but isn't that a little childish for a man his age?"

"Isn't all the rest of it childish for a man his age?" Margo argued. "I believe it. What did he do?"

"I would get a message in court that 'someone from your office called and told you to call in before the hearing.' I would call and there would be no message. Then there might be a message to ignore some portion of my research because 'someone at the office said they had found further information on the subject and that it would have a bearing.'

"So I'd put off a crucial argument, hoping for some new insight someone had dug up for me, only to find out that no one at the office knew what I was talking about."

"Did it cost you any cases?"

"No, but very nearly. A couple of times I really had to scramble to salvage something for my clients."

"How did you know it was Fenton?"

"Legally speaking, I never did. It was just a gut feeling. Who else would it have been?"

"I don't know," I said. "Got any other enemies?"

"Not that I know of. I suppose there could be any number of jealous people of both sexes in my life, but I certainly have never done anything to cause it, at least willfully."

"I believe you," Margo said, "as much as I hate to be sympathetic to beautiful women. I do believe you."

I noticed a lot of snow piled on the shoulders of the interstate, though the road itself was dry and fast. We were making good time, but as the snow began to look fresher and more recently plowed, I began to hope that we weren't coming into something bad. When it was Margo's turn to drive, I told her to watch for wet roads ahead. "We'll probably have sunlight until we hit Grand Island or maybe even North Platte, but we could hit the tail end of whatever left these snow piles." I didn't think much more about it until we encountered rain, and then sleet, and were forced to slow to about thirty-five miles an hour.

I didn't like the looks of the huge snowflakes that were not exactly melting instantly on the interstate. The going was slow, but Margo refused to let me take over driving. And she was doing well. It was dark by the time we spotted the Holiday Inn at North Platte, and the snow caused deep slush puddles.

Bonnie had been right. The Inn was lovely, spacious, well-equipped. We had a leisurely dinner, and much too much to eat, and I told the women to be ready at six in the morning because we wanted to get to the end of this snowstorm. The truckers and other veteran cross-country travelers were already rumoring ten to twelve inches by morning. The eternal optimist, I believed it would stop and that our vehicle could get us through. When I peeked out in the morning, I wasn't so sure. I just wish I had had the sense to sit tight and keep our beautiful, comfortable rooms.

Margo was still getting ready when I went past their room, and Hilary slid their suitcases out into the hallway. I lugged them down to the car and wished I had brought more than a light jacket. The four-wheeler was buried in a drift, and I was forced to dig around for an old book to scrape the snow away. I hadn't dreamed of packing a scraper, let alone a pair of gloves. My hands were red and raw by the time I jumped in and started the engine. Still Margo and Hilary had not appeared. It wasn't like Margo to take long getting ready. In the rearview mirror I saw Hilary signaling me to come back in.

"What's up? Roads closed?"

"No, Margo just got a call from Earl. You want to talk to him?"

We skipped back up to their room, and I waited for Margo to finish. She looked troubled as she handed me the phone.

"There's an opening in a qualifying class for the detective school," Earl said. "Just wanted her to know about it. She'd have to start Wednesday morning. May not get another chance like this for ages."

"Oh, boy," I said with a sigh. "What do you think, Earl?"

"It's totally up to you guys. If she's serious about wanting to study this field, she'd better give it some thought."

"We don't have much time for thinking. We've got to get going to get out of this snowstorm, and if she's heading back, we can run her to the bus station right now."

"Let me know now," Earl said. "Bonnie can meet her at the station here."

"What's the word, Margo?" I said.

"I want to see Daddy," she said.

"She wants to go with us, Earl," I said, but Margo waved me off.

"It's going to be a painful meeting anyway," she said.

"Hold a minute, Earl."

"I'd better go back," she said. "I want to do this, and I don't want to know if Daddy is trying to do anything wrong. Tell Earl I'm coming back."

It felt strange without Margo with us. I found myself a little formal, more inhibited with Hilary than I had been the day before. "This is going to change our driving schedule," I said. "You want me to drive halfway and you take the rest?"

"Let's play it by ear," she said. "You may get tired driving that long. Maybe we should each drive until we need more gas, then switch."

"Whatever," I said.

"Yeah, whatever."

The interstate was already confined to one lane in each direction. Snow was whirling and blowing, and the gigantic flakes splattered against the windshield like cupfuls of rain. The four-wheeler handled the deep drifts all right, but after a half hour of slow going, we found ourselves last in a several-mile-long line of cars and trucks. When we hit a bend in the road, we could see how far the cars stretched out ahead of us. The radio already told the news of road closings heading east.

"That's encouraging," I said. "Maybe we're heading away from the trouble."

"Maybe."

I gripped the wheel too tightly and tired quickly.

Hilary tried to read, but the ride was too bumpy. She gave up. "You really love Margo, don't you?" she said.

"Yes, I really do."

"And you've worked through the idea that it might have been pity at first, because of her situation, I mean?"

"Yeah, we have. It *was* pity at first. But not now."

"That's nice. I don't think I've ever been in love."

"Well, I thought I was once before. I was engaged. There was no doubt in my mind that I was in love. It didn't work out and was painful for a while. But when I fell in love with Margo, it was so different, so incredible, that I knew I had never really loved before. Whatever it had been, it wasn't love. This, what I feel for her, is love."

"How do you know?"

"I just do. I love her so much that I would give her up if I was convinced that I was not what was best for her. I think that's a good definition of love."

"Is it yours?"

"I wish it was. Actually, it took me a long time to come to that way of thinking because I loved Margo so much that I was selfish and possessive about it. In fact, that philosophy is Margo's. She said it first, and I thought I could never duplicate it, though I knew I should."

"And now you really feel that way?"

"I do."

"Margo is a very special lady. I can tell. She's a deep thinker, in spite of her self-image problem."

"That was obvious to you?"

"A little. Of course, I know she's under great strain right now. That would take the self-confidence out of anyone."

"Where'd you get yours?"

"My what? My air of self-confidence?"

"Yeah."

"I don't know. I've always had it. People have always said that until they got to know me they thought I was arrogant. My profession hasn't helped. Neither has my height."

"But you're not cocky."

"I know that, but did *you* know it when you first met me?"

"No, I guess I thought you were pretty self-assured, especially the way you treated Hollis Fenton."

"Really that bad, huh?"

"I don't know. You made it appear as if he deserved it for some reason. And I guess he did."

"Anyway, I think most of my image is a result of shyness. I know I express myself well when I am forced to, and I enjoy speaking in meetings and in court, being in command of taking a deposition, or whatever. But unless it's all scoped out in advance and I'm prepared, I'd rather be in the background. Not easy for a woman of my height."

"Or beauty."

"Thank you."

"So you overcompensate?"

"I guess. I've never thought about it, but I know it doesn't do any good to try to act *un*arrogant or *un*conceited, if there are such words. You have to be yourself, and I just have to try to assure people that I don't think I'm anyone special, if I ever get the chance."

"I believe you, but you're wrong."

"I don't follow," she said.

"I believe that you don't think you're anyone special, just like I believe that you don't think you're beautiful. But you're wrong on both counts. Don't argue. The fact that you don't think you're anyone special is one reason you're so special. And not knowing how beautiful you are gives you a certain innocence that enhances even your beauty."

"Can we talk about something else?"

"I suppose we ought to."

But we didn't. We just didn't talk. The snow nearly belched from the sky in great waves. Visibility went to nil. More than once the great line of cars — now stretching farther than we could see in both directions — slipped and skidded to a stop, first for five minutes, then for twenty-five. A couple of times I jogged ahead to help push someone back onto the road. More and more it appeared that we might spend several hours stopped there. I was glad we had a full tank of gas. A six-pack of Cokes and a bag of pretzels didn't sound too appetizing to either of us, but it was all we had.

We were too far from anything to walk anywhere in this weather, and the sight of CB-equipped trucks in front and behind was comforting. At least they had news. Part of the news was that from North Platte east was open. Margo would get home. From where we were back to North Platte, however, just a few miles, was closed. We could see the result of it across the median. Miles upon miles of cars were going nowhere.

And the snow continued.

TEN

We drove at ten miles an hour or so for several minutes, watching cars slide off the road on both sides. There was nothing to say. Both of us were hoping something would break so we could either get out of the storm area or find a spot to settle in and wait it out. No one wanted to be stranded in a car all day and night on a snowy highway, even with fuel and a little food.

We were city people. I was not skilled in survival. I was willing to ration the food and use the engine sparingly, but the thought of just shutting the windows against the snow and being buried under drifts scared me.

When the line of cars stopped and two semis jackknifed on a bridge ahead, I started talking again, just to get my mind on something else. There was nothing else to do; they were too far ahead for me to run and help, and there appeared to be many people helping already. I wondered if we would move again at all that day.

"So, what happened to Hollis Fenton the other night?"

Hilary finished her paragraph, bent back the corner of the page, closed the book, and tucked it under the front seat. "One lousy book," she said. "You'd have to be stranded in the snow on a trip across country with no one interesting to talk to, to keep reading that thing."

"So what's the verdict? You gonna keep reading or have you found someone interesting to talk to?"

"I'm all ears."

"No, you're not. You missed the question."

"Don't kid yourself. I'm just not sure I want to talk about him anymore."

I was disappointed, but I knew it wouldn't be right to push. "Suit yourself," I said.

"OK, I'll talk about him," she said quickly, with a smile. "I just didn't want to appear too anxious."

College-aged kids in the car in front of us jumped out in shirt-sleeves to throw snowballs at cars and trucks across the median. The eastbound traffic wasn't moving, and probably wouldn't for hours until the state police could route them to open exits, so the little battle made the drivers' day. Many leaped out of their vehicles, laughing and retaliating. Our car was pummeled, but we weren't dressed for battle, so we just sat it out.

"He was, in effect, put on probation by the other partners, according to Amos. That means he is still a partner but will be listed second to last, just ahead of Amos, on the letterhead. The firm will be called Henley, Whitehead, Fenton, and Chakaris."

"How did Hollis take it?"

"You saw as well as I did. Amos said Hollis told the partners not to be too quick to print the new stationery. And then he rushed from the room. Amos thinks he was just blowing air. He's known Hollis a long time, through the good days and now the bad."

"Is the man incompetent?"

"I don't think so, and if anyone has a reason to think so, I do. I just think he's terribly proud and hates to have his feathers ruffled. He needs the job and the money and the prestige. Neither of his former wives have remarried, so his money is really chewed up by the time he sees much of it."

"How much would a guy like that make?"

"Oh, a few hundred thousand a year, I assume. The firm has been thriving for years, and he *is* a full partner. I don't think he has the guts to give that up. He still has the makings of a great lawyer. Sort of like an athlete who's past his prime but whose skills still put him ahead of most younger men."

"What *are* his skills?"

"Same as with any good lawyer. A good memory, a quick mind — especially on his feet or under pressure, though that's the skill that's eroding the fastest — persistent. That's the one he still has. He never gave up on me, first pursuing me and then trying to make things rough for me. He just never quits."

"Those could be wonderful characteristics in a nice guy."

"Absolutely. Also horrible in a dictator. Or a Hollis Fenton."

"So you don't think he'll quit the firm?"

"I don't, but who can tell what he might do? The demotion will be obvious and will humiliate him. I think what hurt him most was that he got no support from Amos, and they go back such a long way. Amos's official resignation became effective before the vote on the new lineup."

"Amos told us," I said. "Could it have happened the other way around?"

"Sure. It was totally Amos's decision. He could have hung in and voted before bailing out, but he would have had to vote against his old friend, so he did it this way."

"In effect he still voted, right?"

"Right. I just hope Hollis gets this thing settled in his mind, licks his wounds, and doesn't do something rash. He could join another firm, and there are plenty who would jump at the chance to get him, but he would likely try to do harm to our firm either by stealing clients or bad-mouthing us."

"It really puts you guys in the middle, doesn't it? Could you fire him, or vote him out?"

"The partners could. I don't think anyone wants that."

"Afraid of him?"

"Probably. Sad but true. Gone are the days when you fire the bad apple because it's the right thing to do. In earlier years, Amos might have done it. He'll leave it to Henley and Whitehead now. And they're super."

The trucks ahead had been straightened and were moving. It was several minutes before the movement affected us, and then the compact car in front of us slid sideways and couldn't move. Startling me, Hilary climbed down from the front seat and, with no more protection than a sweater over a blouse, bent at the knees and drove her shoulder into the left rear bumper, pushing the struggling car back into the deep ruts where it grabbed and began rolling. She hurried back to the accompaniment of appreciative honks from the cars behind us. I just looked at her and shook my head. "Trying to make me look like a lazy slob?" I said.

"You don't need my help," she said, ducking my playfully cocked backhand.

Still we barely crept along and by nearly noon we had covered less than fifty miles. Our schedule was shot. Even if the storm broke and the roads cleared within an hour, there was no way we'd make our next scheduled stop by that same night. Ominous weather reports on the radio made me want to keep pushing as long as even one lane was open. Hilary agreed. "I'm a pioneer all the way," she said. "Let's not quit moving until we have to."

We needed fuel and lunch so we took the exit at Ogallala, Nebraska. "Ever hear of this place?" I asked. She shook her head, neither of us realizing that it would be a place we would probably never forget. In trying to maneuver the overpass and pick my way through lines of trucks and cars already parked or stuck on both sides, I embedded us in a snowbank.

Hilary took the wheel and I rocked us from behind until the car was free, but not before the rear wheel covered me with slush. "I'm really sorry," Hilary said, laughing. "I don't know why it hits me funny. I really am sorry, even if I don't sound like it!"

Tentatively easing our way down a frontage road toward the huge truck stop that had drawn us like a mirage, I tried to blast past a stuck semi the way two pickups just had. They made it. We didn't. We were high centered in deep snow, and having nothing to dig with, we needed help this time. We couldn't even rock it, and neither of us could stand to be out in the weather for more than a few minutes at a time. For some reason, Hilary still thought it was hilarious. "I just figured out your name," I said.

I hung around outside the car, peering underneath and trying to look helpless, all the while keeping an eye out for a good Samaritan. A few people passed, but none stopped. Few cars were moving, though many were now lined up behind us. I shivered into the front seat.

"I hate to ask you to do this," I said.

"You want me to try to dig us out with something? I'll be happy to try — "

"No, you can't dig us out without a shovel, and if we had a shovel, I could do it. What I want you to do is what I just did."

"What'd you do? I didn't see you do anything but check out the situation."

"Trust me, Hilary. If you check out the situation, help will come. Don't make me explain it."

"And did you want me to stick a leg out into the road?"

"Don't be silly. If you don't want to do it, I'll understand."

"No, I'll do it." And it worked in no time. Hilary just got out, pulled her collar up against the wind, and surveyed our hopeless situation. A wrecker stopped behind us and a pickup in front. They nearly fought over the right to pull and push us out, finally agreeing to do both at the same time.

Soon we were again easing between closely parked trucks and trailers, ignoring the blocked entrance to the truck stop, and entering through the exit like everyone else. We waited in line for gas, then again for a meal, and decided to eat big in case we found ourselves stranded later. We didn't realize that for all practical purposes, we were already stranded.

After lunch Hilary waited in line to place a call back to Chicago while I picked through trinkets and junk in the attached "store" for some gloves.

"Only local calls, I guess," Hilary reported after ten minutes of trying to get a long distance operator. "You need an operator to dial outside this area, and both of them in this town must be busy."

"Be kind," I said, enjoying her. As I paid for the gloves and some more junk food to store in the car, I heard a woman at a switchboard reserving a room for a young trucker.

I asked her if she could arrange for two more rooms at the same place. "I'm pessimistic when I see all these truckers sitting around as if there's nowhere to go. They aren't willing to commit to a hotel room, but they aren't out on the road, either."

"The road west is closed after another twenty miles or so anyway," a trucker told me.

"That's all I needed to hear," I told Hilary. "Let's take those rooms if we can get 'em."

"He'll hold one room for an hour," the woman said, and she gave us directions to the Isle of Paradise.

"The Isle of Paradise," Hilary repeated. "I can't wait to see this."

"You'll have to park at the corner and walk about a quarter of a mile," the woman said. "His parking lot is closed, but the hotel is open."

Hilary stifled a laugh.

"You're a snob," I said.

ELEVEN

On the other side of the freeway, the bespectacled man behind the counter at the Isle of Paradise looked haggard. "This started yesterday, you know," he said. "A lot of the people who were stranded here last night want to keep their rooms in case they come back. They're out looking for open roads and if they're back by one, I've got to let them stay."

He looked as if he'd been there all night, and I soon learned that he had. "I can't plow the parking lot because the plow is in my garage at home. My wife can't even get from the house to the garage, so I'll be replacing the linens myself today. If everybody can just be patient, I'll get around to you."

Everyone in the lobby pledged their undying cooperation and sympathy for the owner's plight in exchange for one of the precious rooms, to be paid for in advance. And such rooms. It was obvious when we first got a look at ours that it would never work.

It was tiny, tacky, and dominated by one double bed. "It looks like I'm sleeping in the car," I said. Hilary just laughed. As a tribute to modern commercialism, the room was built around a beautiful color television that carried one local station and a cable hook-up that showed Atlanta Braves baseball games, of all things. Hilary sat on the edge of the still unmade bed. I stood awkwardly watching "I Love Lucy."

"I'll check back at the office," I said. "You want to try calling Chicago again?"

A few minutes later I was back with the good news that a young man next to us — who found himself in a suite of two private rooms with two beds — was willing to trade with us. But Hilary was still on the phone, and she did not look happy. I didn't make her tell me what it was all about until we had switched rooms.

"There's no phone in here," she noticed immediately. So it would be TV, messages taken at the office downstairs, awkward conversations, and isolated sleeping rooms until the weather cleared. Hilary had seemed amused by it all until she had placed that call.

"What's up?" I asked.

"I'm not supposed to tell you, Philip, but I'm not going to be able to keep it from you."

"What?"

"Margo sent a message to Earl. It said not to worry about her and that she would be back in a week or so."

"Where's she going?"

"Didn't say."

"No clue?"

"I guess not."

"Earl worried?"

"Not really. He thinks she can take care of herself, but he's not excited about the idea that she's missing this detective school opportunity."

"That bothers me too, but I'm more worried about the fact that she started whatever trip she's on in a snowstorm and that she didn't communicate with me."

"She told him to tell you, but he didn't want to. He doesn't want you to worry, and he feels it's important that we get to California."

"Where would she be going?"

"That's what I was going to ask you, Philip."

I was worried. She had not been in the best frame of mind lately, but whom could she go to? I wasn't aware of any friends she had between Nebraska and Chicago. What would be important enough for her to pass up this school opening she had been so excited about?

"Philip, there's something else."

"Hm?"

"There's something else. Something I haven't even told Earl yet. Mr. Henley's secretary told me they received a photocopy of Mr. Franklin's alleged agreement with Virginia Franklin about the house."

"Does it look legitimate?"

"Yes, and it could nullify the will Amos read for Margo. It calls for Mr. Franklin to keep making payments on the house for the extent of the mortgage and to pay Margo fifty thousand dollars on Mr. Franklin's acquisition of the property. It was dated later and would take precedence, and there is one other very interesting clause that ties the thing together, at least in my mind.

"The clause calls for an immediate cash payment to Virginia Franklin of one hundred thousand dollars for the ownership of the estate upon her death."

"So for a hundred thousand to Virginia, fifty thousand to Margo, and the mortgage payments he's been making, he gets a million dollar estate."

"Exactly, as long as Mrs. Franklin preceded him in death."

"And who would have predicted that?"

"Our firm, for one."

"I'm lost."

"The photocopied document sent to our offices, covering Mr. Franklin's interest in the estate, was under our own letterhead. It was prepared by us, and sure enough, Mr. Henley's secretary was able to locate our copy in the files."

"How could that happen without Mr. Chakaris's knowledge, when he was the executor of her will? Doesn't that sound incredible?"

"The document was typed by a secretary no longer with the firm and carries a clause that it was to be kept confidential even from other principals in the law offices. Which is against our policy, by the way."

"Why would Chakaris violate the policy of his own law firm? And why wouldn't he remember preparing the document for the Franklins?"

"Because he didn't prepare it, Philip. The initials at the bottom of the document are H.F./G.M."

"G.M. is the secretary who typed it, and H.F. is your favorite lawyer, right?"

"Right."

"Is it contestable?"

"Mr. Henley doubts it. He's going to send it on ahead to Los Angeles so I can have a chance to study it before meeting with Mr. Franklin and his lawyer."

"Hilary, what do you think is Hollis Fenton's interest in this?"

"I don't know, but I'm especially worried about it, now that he's been shafted at the firm. It's bizarre that he hid the document from Mr. Chakaris, thus leaving Mr. Franklin with the burden of coming forward with it. Mr. Franklin probably thought we knew all about it until we called him about why he was still paying on the house. There would be no reason for the document to still be confidential once his former wife had died."

"You would have thought he would come forward immediately if he thought his interests were being ignored," I said.

"I'm sure he assumed we would be getting to him shortly for the reading of the new will. He did have a lawyer ready to talk to me, though."

"Maybe his new love put him up to that."

With nothing to do, nowhere to go, no one to call, and nothing to say, I felt like putting my fist through a window. I paced the room. Hilary kept wishing aloud that there was something she could say or do. "Let's not worry until we have to," she suggested.

We watched television and read for several hours, finally venturing out into the blowing and drifting snow to the only two restaurants open in town, both on the same street as the motel. One was a pizza place and the other was The Hungry Eskimo, which we decided was too ironic a name to qualify for our first meal. We had a pizza, but somehow it didn't seem right to eat so somberly in such a festive place. I was miserable.

We trudged back to the motel, where a message waited from Margo. "I wrote it down," the man told me. "I couldn't make much sense of it, and she didn't leave a number."

It read: "Got your number from Earl. Sorry you're stranded. Don't worry about me. I'll see you soon."

"She ain't gonna see you soon if she's tryin' to get here from anywhere," the man said with a smile. I thanked him.

"What do you suppose she meant by 'See you soon,' Hilary?"

"Don't make too much of it. It may have just been used the way we always use it. It may mean nothing."

"But nothing else she said means anything either. I have to have something to go on. Do you think someone is holding her or has intercepted her or something? Someone who wants to make sure she doesn't survive her mother by thirty days?"

"Philip, you're really reaching now. She said not to worry. Sure, someone could have forced her to say that, but you're in no position to worry about it, let alone do anything about it. You'd better take it at face value and assume she's OK. It'll drive you nuts otherwise."

It was after dark now, and as I peered out the window of our suite I had to guess we'd be there another full day and night. The snowplows cleared one lane for both directions of traffic in the town, but no one was going more than a few blocks. The interstate was closed for fifty miles in both directions, and the police weren't even letting people try the overpass to the truck stop.

"So it's pizza or The Hungry Eskimo for as long as we're here" I said, trying to sound light.

It didn't work. Regardless of what I said on what subject, my fear and worry came through.

Twelve

By the next morning, Hilary was completely packed, her vote for total optimism, assuming we would be on the road again within a few hours. I was slouched in a chair, feet propped up on the at-least-ten-dollar "stylized" table, gloomily watching the national news out of Atlanta forevermore.

The weatherman didn't even know how to pronounce Ogallala, but he worked out a reasonable facsimile and reported that our adopted little snowbunny trap had been awarded the national Golden Shovel Award for the most snow in the shortest time — thirty inches in the past twenty-four hours.

Hilary even had her coat draped over a chair, as if ready to pop it on as soon as some all-clear signal were given. It was still snowing, albeit lightly now. I padded out to the balcony in my stocking feet and peered over the railing to the street. People were digging out cars and a few graders were clearing a little more of the main drag, but no one was really going anywhere.

"I'm going down to the office and see if anything's open," Hilary said. "Let me have the keys. I may drive to the overpass to see if we can get to the truckstop on the other side. Want anything in case I get over there?"

I said no. I had hung a six-pack of Cokes on the outside doorknob overnight, and an icy one with some cheesy tortilla chips made a sickening breakfast. It did, however, leave me less hungry. I searched the room for anything readable, but except for a local newspaper and its three-day-old prediction of spring weather, the only thing available was a Bible, "placed here by the Gideons."

I didn't even pick it up, but it prompted me to flip off the television and sit thinking and praying. My energy had been invested in worry and frustration, which even people without God would classify as a waste of time. People who claimed to live for God or who have Him living in them should have less reason than anyone for wasting time worrying. I prayed for Margo. I didn't feel much better, but I knew there was nothing else I could do.

I tried to go back in my mind to what I had been thinking before all the trouble started. It was about Earl and how afraid I was that something Margo or I would say or do would adversely affect our spiritual impression on him. I realized that it had really mattered to me because Earl really mattered to me.

Here was a guy who was more of a Christian in life-style and honesty and treatment of others than many professing Christians I had known. And yet he resisted any personal talk about Christ or the need for God in his life. I wanted to reach him, not for any selfish reason, but because he was Earl. He was the kind of a guy who would flourish in a relationship with Christ (and who wouldn't?), and about whom I cared very much.

I would never forgive myself if I spent a lot of time with Earl — especially while working for him — and never got to the point where I was able to articulate my faith to him. He knew where I stood, but he was convinced that "religion is all right for those who want it or need it."

And he didn't want it. Didn't see the need for it. Maybe his life-style was the very thing that kept him from what he really needed. And, being a lawyer, maybe Hilary could coach me on how to express myself better. While I was asking her how I could be more eloquent, maybe she would catch on to just what it was I wanted to communicate to Earl and appropriate it to herself.

I felt a little better. I had a project, something to think, talk, and pray about. It didn't lessen my worry over Margo, but at least it would assume some of the time burden in my troubled mind. I heard Hilary trotting up the stairs. It was nearly noon. The snow had stopped, but it was cold and the drifts were deep and foreboding.

"Let's get rolling, Sad Sack," she said as she knocked and entered in the same motion. I whirled around.

"You're kidding. The overpass is open?"

"I don't know about the overpass, but people are getting onto I-Eighty heading west. It's closed north where the north-south split comes at Big Springs, but we're going south through Denver at that point anyway, aren't we?"

"Yeah," I said, scrambling to throw my things together.

Soon we were part of the only traffic jam Ogallala, Nebraska, has probably ever had. There was still just one lane to be shared by cars going both directions on the main street. Local people were heading in, interstate travelers were heading out, and volunteers were holding one line of cars so the other could get through, then switching and stopping the movers so the waiters could go.

When we finally reached the stoplight three blocks from the motel, we headed left and got in line to convince the policeman on the overpass that we could make it. He wanted to know which direction we were heading. "Whichever is open," I said, wanting to get somewhere even if it meant backtracking.

"West is open for maybe twenty miles," he said. "Then you can go only south at the Big Springs split."

"Perfect. We're trying to go through Denver."

"I doubt you'll make Denver," he said. "But good luck."

It was eerie to see no cars on the other side of the median. The eastbound lanes had been closed for so long that other than a few stalled cars and trucks here and there, nothing was moving on that side. As for us westbounders, we were in a line that stretched as far as we could see, front and back, all going about twenty miles an hour and wondering why the fast-clearing sky didn't start melting the snow.

The pavement was wet but clear of snow in the one lane open to the west, but the drifts in the left lane were up to four feet deep. Though we were mobile and could have passed, there was nowhere to go. Every once in a while an eager beaver behind us would swing out into the left lane when it wasn't so deep for a stretch and try to pass a slew of cars before the big drifts rose up again. But when the driver looked for an opening to merge back in, those who had seen his folly determined to make him wait.

"You want me to drive?" Hilary said.

"No, thanks. I feel better doing something."

"So would I, but I suppose I have a little less on my mind than you do."

By mid-afternoon we had not progressed far. "If it clears soon and two lanes open, we ought to try to get as far as we can," I suggested.

"I think we ought to just hope to make Denver," Hilary said. "You're exhausted already, and this kind of driving — even for a fresh driver — is going to get old fast."

Occasionally the traffic stopped for five minutes, but the trouble — whatever it was — was so far ahead that we couldn't determine the cause. After one long stop, we passed the trouble about ten miles ahead. Two tractor-trailers had tried to open a closed exit. They got about a hundred feet into it and found themselves pushing a wall of snow that didn't want to be pushed.

At one point the whole line of westbound traffic was routed off the interstate, down an exit, through a small town and back on via a frontage road. As we exited we watched huge earthmovers attack the mountains of snow on the overpass. It was hard to believe when two lanes opened an hour and a half later and the braver souls — like ourselves — broke free and hit the speed limit. Soon we forked southwesterly toward Denver. The roads and the skies were clear and dry. The higher we got from sea level, however, the more our engine sucked air.

After one stop, where we switched places, I tried reading Hilary's book for a few minutes and gave up in disgust. "What is this, anyway?"

"Supposed to be a novel," she said. "But I think it's more of an experiment."

"Writing itself is an experiment for this writer," I said, stuffing the book beneath the seat. "Do you suppose we should have tried to contact our offices back there?"

"No. Let's call when we get to Denver. There can't be any news we can act upon unless it's 'Come home now,' and I want to see Denver anyway. I've never been there."

"Me either," I said, but I still wished we had tried to put a call through to Earl or to Hilary's office. "You gonna be hungry before this evening?"

"I don't think so," she said. "Let's just push on through. If it's this dry all the way, it shouldn't take long."

Suddenly I was exhausted. The driving had gotten to me, I guess. I also realized that I had not slept well the night before. Still worried, I was not as anxious now over Margo since directing my concern to praying for her. It had made me feel a little more positive, and I tried to take her message literally. She didn't want me to worry, and she said she would see me soon. I leaned my head against the icy window and tucked one leg underneath me. I was asleep in minutes.

When I awoke a few hours later, Hilary was picking through a snowy mountain pass, alternately accelerating and braking, watching the rearview mirror nervously as more impatient drivers — or locals who knew the roads and conditions — flew past. "Need some relief?" I said, startling her.

"No." She looked determined. "I want this experience. Unless you're afraid for your life."

"I trust you," I said. She smiled but never diverted her eyes from the road.

"I've been wanting to talk to you," I said. "We haven't really talked all day."

"There's nothing wrong with that," she said. "We don't *have* to talk all the time, do we?"

"No, but there's something specific I want to talk to you about."

"And you're going to bring it up now, when I need every reserve ounce of consciousness to keep us alive. It's getting dark, Philip."

"I thought you lawyers had minds like steel traps, or something like that."

"It's not our minds as much as our personalities, and mine is about to tell you to keep quiet."

"Oh, I'd like to hear *that.*"

"Keep quiet."

"Impressive."

It was all she could do to keep from laughing, but I knew she was right. This was no time for serious discussion, especially if we wanted to make Denver by the same night. We had no reservations, and we wouldn't be staying long because we wanted to start at about six the next morning and see if we could get as far as Las Vegas.

It was Wednesday evening. By now, Hilary's office had put on hold Mr. Franklin and his Thursday morning appointment. Without further trouble, we would make Las Vegas Thursday night and L.A. Friday afternoon. "You probably should have your office set the meeting with Mr. Franklin for either late Friday night or Saturday morning," I said.

Hilary seemed distracted. "What?"

"The meeting with Franklin," I repeated. "You're going to want time to wind down before seeing him, aren't you?"

"I can't even think about that now. Tell me later the time you think we're going to arrive, and we'll go from there, OK?"

"Sure."

"Was that the big subject you wanted to discuss?" she said.

"Hardly."

"The last time we talked at much length, you were trying to convince me how beautiful I was."

"And you're even more so when you're concentrating. You should see your profile."

"Seeing my own profile is something that will never happen, Philip. I don't even have to concentrate to know that."

A sign read: "Denver — 14 miles."

THIRTEEN

"Now I don't feel much like talking," I said an hour later after we had checked into our separate rooms and met for dinner at the hotel restaurant. "Can I save it until tomorrow on the road?"

"Please do. Did you reach Earl?"

"No, got Bonnie, though. No messages from Margo. I told Bonnie where we are and where we expect to be during the next few days. She's arranged our reservations in Las Vegas. I'll bet we'll be the only people there just to sleep before heading to Los Angeles. Did you reach your office?"

"Yes. I asked them to arrange my meeting with Mr. Franklin for Saturday morning. That will give me time to study the document before seeing him."

We had ordered and were waiting to be served. Hilary let her shoulders sag, the first time I had seen her relax her regal posture. She breathed a heavy sigh. "I'm tired," she said. "Really, really tired."

"Me too. I'm going straight to bed after dinner. You?"

"Yeah. Might call the office one more time, though. I think they should tell Earl about the document and the ramifications. He shouldn't have a man on this case and not know everything."

"They haven't told him yet?"

"They were probably assuming you would, Philip. I'll tell them."

"No! What would Earl think, getting that information from someone other than me? I had no idea he didn't know yet. I just assumed — "

"You can't assume anything. You know that."

"I've got to call him right now."

A few minutes later I returned to a waiting dinner. "I got the answering machine," I said. "I can't tell him that way. I'll call him from Vegas tomorrow night."

We ran into more mountain snow and slush in Utah the next day, slowing us more than we anticipated. But it did give us lots of time to talk. "I have a problem I think you can help me with," I began. "I have always had trouble expressing myself verbally. I can write things OK, but I'm not as good when speaking."

"You mean you're better on paper than orally, not verbally."

"What?"

"Verbally. You said you had trouble verbally. Not true if you can write. That's verbal, too."

"Picky, picky."

"Well, in a sense you merely illustrated your point. Perhaps word choice is a problem."

"Perhaps, professor. May I continue?"

"I'm sorry."

"Don't be. Anyway, Hilary, here goes: You know, I presume, that Margo and I are Christians."

"Christians? I thought you were Baptists or fundamentalists or born-againers or something. Most people are Christians, aren't they?"

"Well, no, not really."

"Well, Philip, certainly in America, if a person isn't an atheist or an agnostic, he would be either Jewish or Christian, wouldn't he? I mean if he has any normal church background at all it is going to be Lutheran or Methodist or Presbyterian or Baptist, right?"

"See my problem, Hilary? I need to tell you why you're wrong, but it's complicated. Let me try it this way: You know certain brand names have been diluted by imitation, like Band-Aids, Kleenex, and Jeep?"

"You mean where it originated as a brand name and then became so associated with the product that people call any bandage a Band-Aid and any tissue a Kleenex?"

"Exactly. That's what happened to the term 'Christian.' Originally it meant a Christ one or one like Christ. It was the term given to His early followers, who organized after His death and resurrection. They are the forerunners of the current Christian religion. But not everyone who calls himself a Christian is really a follower of Christ, wouldn't you agree?"

"Well, some may not be as devout as others, I suppose, or worry about it so much. But you're not saying that Lutherans or Presbyterians aren't really Christians just because they aren't as fundamental or old-fashioned as, say, Baptists or some others, are you?"

"What I'm saying is that not only are some Lutherans and Presbyterians not really Christians in the biblical sense of the word, but neither are some Baptists or some of any other denomination you want to name. The point is not in being religious or belonging to a denomination or even going to church every Sunday. We believe a true Christian is one who believes that Jesus Christ is the only way to God and who responds accordingly by trusting in Him for their salvation."

Hilary pursed her lips and raised her eyebrows. After breathing a vapor on her window and wiping it off, she said, "OK, I see your point. You think you and Margo and those like you are the true church, sort of the way the Jehovah's Witnesses and the Mormons and even the Moonies believe they are the true church."

"Oh, boy."

"That's not it?"

How was I supposed to explain it? I stalled, studying the dashboard before answering.

"Not really. It isn't a matter of being exclusive unto ourselves. It's just that Christ Himself said He was the way, the truth, and the life and that no man could come to God except through Him."

"Then there's nothing wrong with Christianity being exclusivist, if that's what the founder, or the namesake anyway, said."

"Right. But where we differ from those other groups you mentioned is that while they call themselves Christian too, they're just as wrong as the normal, everyday churchgoer if they add something or take away something from the gospel. I mean, some of those groups really have some strange beliefs."

"And you don't?"

"Not really. Fantastic things, yes, but nothing that's not in the Bible. We believe that Jesus was born of a virgin, lived a sinless life, died in our place for our sins, and was raised from the dead."

Hilary smiled. "You've got to admit that's pretty farfetched, but at least it's the commonly accepted belief about Christianity, from Catholicism to Protestantism. It's good to know you and Margo aren't weirdos, even if you do have some strange taboos."

"Like what?"

"Well, you don't drink or smoke or anything like that, do you?"

"No, but you don't either."

"But not because of any religious list of rules."

"Neither do we. There are Christians who are really outspoken against some things, but again, unless it's specifically in the Bible, it's simply a matter of personal conviction, not religious injunction."

"So why are you telling me all this, Philip? You in effect promised not to try to convert me on this trip."

"I don't remember that promise, but here's the reason. Margo and I believe in Christ so deeply and are so convinced that people who don't know Him are missing out on what life is really all about that we want to share Him with people. That's part of what Christianity is about. Christ told His early followers to tell the whole world about Him. We want to start with the people closest to us."

"Does that mean I should keep my distance or risk the strong-arm?"

"Forget that, will you? We don't want to tell people who know what we mean and still don't want to hear it. Anyway, if you believed something this deeply and felt it would make a life or death difference to your friends, I would be insulted if you didn't tell me."

Hilary thought for a moment. "You're right," she said. "I suppose I'd be a little hurt if you never told me about the most important thing in your life. I would also be insulted if you did tell me when I wasn't interested in listening. Which I don't think I am. Something about it bothers me. It's an intrusion, a condescension of some kind, I think. Do you mind?"

"I hadn't really intended to tell you anything about it yet," I said. "I was really looking for advice."

"That's the story of my life, Philip. It'll cost you a hundred dollars an hour, but fire away. How can I counsel you?"

"It's Earl. We want to communicate our faith in Christ to him. We're looking for the right opening because we don't want to put him off, insult him, hurt him."

Hilary shifted in her seat in what appeared to be a vain attempt at getting comfortable. "What makes you think he needs what you've got?"

"If I explained the whole setup to you, you'd understand that we believe that everyone needs Christ. That's the point. People who know Christ and trust Him with their lives are people who have life abundant. Those who don't will never truly be happy or fulfilled."

"And they'll go to hell when they die?"

"We believe that, yes."

"Well, let me tell you something, Philip: That's not good enough. Any first year marketing student can tell you that to reach somebody with a message, you have to know what his realized needs are. I'll bet that Earl Haymeyer isn't any more worried about hell than I am. If you want to reach him on that score, you have to convince him there is a hell, and that the God you believe in would send him there unless he became a Christian. Then show him how he can escape it. Want to take bets on the outcome of that?"

"That — or something close to it — used to work, believe it or not. Still does in some cases."

"And you could make a case for the fact that just because belief in hell went out with the Dark Ages doesn't mean that it doesn't exist. I don't think it does, but regardless, it's probably the wrong tack for Earl Haymeyer."

"We haven't said anything to Earl about hell. *You* brought that up." I shot a hard glance at her.

"So you think it may be a latent fear of mine?"

"I didn't say that."

"I know. *I* did. That was the one thing I remember from my brief religious — uh — Christian exposure as a child. Really a scary deal, choosing between heaven and hell."

"Agreed. But take Margo, for instance. She didn't come to Christ out of fear of hell. Her need was to have someone forgive her and love her and give her the abundant life I mentioned before. That's what the Bible calls it."

"It does, huh? That's nice. Abundant life. But anyway, even though you feel that it's your duty to tell everyone they need Christianity — "

"That's not what we tell them, for the reasons we talked about. The wrong evolvement of the meaning of the word."

"What *do* you tell them they need?"

"Christ. The person. Not the religion. Not the church. Not the denomination or any list of ethics. Our faith, true Christianity, is in the person of Jesus Christ. It's personal."

"OK, so you feel it's your duty, or you want to, or whatever, tell people about Christ. And you believe everyone needs it. Even if that's true, you know what's wrong with it? It's not as personal as you say it is."

"I don't follow."

"You tell me it's personal," she said. "And then you tell me that everyone needs it. If you make Earl Haymeyer feel like 'Everyman,' or like he should want and need this because everyone does, you can forget it."

"Keep going."

"If it's true that everyone needs Christ, and also that what they need is a person and not a religion or a church, then it *is* personal like you say. So you've got a dichotomy, and that's why it's so hard for you to speak coherently about it."

"You noticed?"

"Well, it's a tough one. Think of yourself as a marketing manager. You've got to sell widgets to everyone in the United States because your bosses have convinced you — and you believe them — that everyone not only could use a widget, but needs one. In fact, if they don't buy them, they'll regret it and you'll blame yourself for not selling them one."

"I'm with you so far."

"The only problem is, your market, that choice selection of buyers who all — and I mean one hundred percent, just like you've said — need widgets, don't know it."

"Don't know what?"

"That they need widgets."

"But you said I was convinced they needed them."

"Right, *you* are. *They* aren't. And what's worse, and what makes your job even tougher, is that you can't just advertise and convince everyone they need widgets. You know why? You've already hinted at it in your own example of the difference between Margo and the person who wants Christ in order to avoid hell."

"Tell me."

"They all need widgets for different reasons. You can't just barge in and say you need this because everyone needs it. That's what will make it an intrusion or condescending, like I said. It's your job to find out what need the widget will fill."

"But I still have to make the prospect aware of that need."

"Sure, but when you've taken the time to determine it, and you're right, he'll know you are right."

"And be more likely to respond to what I have to offer."

Hilary smiled and reached over to pat me on the head. "Even if it's true that everyone needs Christ to avoid hell, but you're going to reach them by showing them how He meets their *realized* needs."

FOURTEEN

Hilary and I had talked ourselves out. As we rolled on through Nevada, pushing for Las Vegas, we fell silent. Hilary did no more reading, and when I glanced at her during my turns to drive, she was either sleeping or gazing at the mountains that rimmed the horizon on all four sides.

I knew her arguments had left out the indispensable work of the Holy Spirit in a person's life. It takes more than marketing strategy, advertising, convincing, and all that. And yet, she had made sense. She had opened my eyes to the reaction of the unbeliever to the sharing of a Christian. And I hoped she had heard what I was really trying to say, all the while she was helping me say it. It was obvious she wasn't ready to be pushed.

The next morning we concurred that the Las Vegas nightlife and traffic could be heard from the windows of our respective hotel rooms until early in the morning. And when we went to check out, people were still playing the slots in the lobby at 5:30 A.M.

We were still very tired and regretted the decision to spend the night in Vegas, but it did perk us up to think that we were less than a day's drive from Los Angeles.

I took the first shift at the wheel and Hilary asked, "Can I get back to my lousy novel, or are we going to solve all the problems of mankind again today?"

I laughed. "You helped me a lot yesterday. Thanks."

"I won't know what to say if you and Margo ever get through to Earl. I'll feel partly responsible."

"We'll give you all the credit."

"Don't you dare."

Because we had time, we didn't feel rushed to get to Los Angeles. We stopped one time more than necessary for a snack and postponed our phone calls until we were in our rooms in L.A. We arrived just after noon and hung around the hotel lobby for a while, waiting for clean rooms.

I called Earl. "Why didn't you call last night?" he asked.

"It was late when we got to Vegas and even later in Chicago. What's up?"

"This whole thing stinks, Philip. It's gotten out of our hands, and I don't like it. Chakaris told me about this guy Fenton's involvement. What does Hilary know about him? Is he some kind of a jerk or something? Who does he think he is, pulling a separate deal with the Franklins and not letting anyone else even in his own firm know about it? Let me talk to her."

Hilary and Earl set up a conference call while I helped the bellboy get us moved into our rooms. Several minutes later, my phone rang. Chakaris, at his home, was on; Hilary, in her room, was on.

"Hi to everyone," Earl said. "Let's run this thing down now. If anyone has heard from Margo since Philip's message at Ogaloski or wherever that was in Nebraska, say so."

Silence.

"Anybody heard from Hollis Fenton?"

Silence.

"Anybody with any ideas? Let's start with you, Amos."

"I go back a long way with Hollis. It doesn't seem logical to me that he would be involved in some sort of collusion with one of my clients, but since that much of it is obviously true, I'm afraid I wouldn't put anything past him."

"Philip," Earl cut in, "you know Margo better than any of us. Where do you think she is?"

"I have no idea, Earl. I really don't."

"You have to guess, kid. I'm serious. We have to play some hunches here. Would she simply have gone somewhere other than with you or back to Chicago on her own?"

"I'd have to guess no. It doesn't sound like her. She was a loner before I met her, but not since."

"Things have changed since you met her, Philip," Hilary said.

"Yeah, but for all practical purposes her mother has been dead to her for years. I don't think it would change how she reacts to me."

"Earl," Amos said, "are you suggesting that Hollis might be with her for some reason, taking her somewhere?"

"I don't know, Amos. I don't know what else to think. I just don't like it. I think we ought to go under the assumption that Margo is in trouble, being threatened perhaps, held against her will. I know that's morbid and may have no basis, but we'd better cover the possibility just in case. Would that kind of a threat affect Hilary's negotiations with Mr. Franklin?"

"First of all, the question is academic, Earl," Amos said. "There's no way our firm will negotiate against itself. Hollis Fenton — whether he's still with us or not — was with us when he drew up the document that's causing all the trouble. It actually outdates a bona fide will that I drew up. If Hollis is representing Mr. Franklin, we'll insist that he find other counsel — or that Hollis leave our firm."

"Which he already may have," Hilary said. "So what's next, Earl? What do you want us to do?"

"Before you get into that, Earl," Amos said, "I need to tell Hilary that Margo's father is insisting that their meeting take place tonight at ten, not tomorrow morning."

"Why?"

"Didn't say. Just a scheduling problem. He was ready Thursday morning, and now he wants tonight rather than tomorrow. We'd better comply."

"Yes," Haymeyer said. "But demand first to know if they know where Margo is. You won't tolerate any games. Amos, can we say that the will is up in the air until we're satisfied that Margo is safe and responding on her own?"

"Sure."

"Then that's what we want to do. Hilary, do whatever else you were going to do, but insist that he tell you anything he knows about Margo. OK?"

Everyone agreed and we hung up. Hilary and I decided on an early dinner so she would have time to study the document from Mr. Henley that had been waiting at the desk. She couldn't keep from reading it at dinner. We agreed to meet at nine for the forty-five minute drive to Mr. Franklin's office. In the meantime I tried to sleep. And didn't succeed.

All we needed was more driving. I was dressed up and less comfortable than on the previous two thousand plus miles. Hilary was dressed for work, much the way she had been when Margo and I met her, but even more conservatively, if possible. She was striking, but mostly she looked professional. She would be taking nothing from Mr. Franklin or his lawyer, Hollis Fenton or not.

"I want to call his office from the lobby of his building before we go up to see if I can get a reading on what or whom we will encounter."

"Surely he'll have representation," I said.

"You'd think so."

Mr. Franklin's consulting service office was on the sixteenth floor of a thirty-story building that was virtually closed this late at night. A security guard pointed Hilary and me to the pay phones in the spacious lobby. Franklin answered his own phone.

"Mr. Franklin, this is Hilary Brice of the Chakaris firm. Philip Spence of the EH Detective Agency is with me. May we come up?"

Hilary hung up and said he had simply directed her to the proper elevator and didn't hint that anyone else was there. "We'll just have to be adaptable."

We didn't speak on the elevator. I stood with my hands thrust deep into my pockets with my suitcoat buttoned. Hilary stood straight with her leather attache tucked under her arm. If she was nervous, she didn't let on. We watched the floor lights blink to sixteen and the car floated to a stop. The door opened.

And there stood Margo.

She smiled almost smugly, and I couldn't even form the obvious question. She answered it anyway.

"I've been to Pontiac," she said.

"Why? How?"

"I took the bus straight into Chicago, rented a car, and drove down. Why? Because of the questions you asked me about my mother's letters, and because of something Amos said the day Mother died."

"Good grief," Hilary said. "We have a lot to talk about, but first, does your father know you're here?"

"Yes."

"Does he know you were in Pontiac?"

"No."

"Do me a favor and don't say anything, anything at all, until you're alone with us later." We heard footsteps at the end of the hall. "Promise me, Margo. Please."

"Promise."

"You must be Hilary Brice," Mr. Franklin said. "And hello, Philip. Good to see you again."

He led us to his office and to chairs around a small table. "I wanted you to meet my fiancée, but this is a little late for her. We'd like you to join us for an early dinner tomorrow at four-thirty."

"That would be fine," Hilary said, obviously anxious to get down to business. "Is your lawyer here?"

"I have a confession to make," Mr. Franklin said. "I don't really have a lawyer out here. Mr. Fenton of your firm represented me — us — on this, and when you called I pretended to be a lawyer representing me."

Margo was shocked at the mention of Fenton's name in association with the new document.

"Why did you feel the need to do that?" Hilary asked.

"I haven't been able to reach Mr. Fenton, and I've always felt a little vulnerable in such situations without representation. You understand."

"No, but if you say so," Hilary said.

"I suppose you want to see this," Mr. Franklin added, pulling the original document from the breast pocket of his coat. Hilary compared it with her photocopy.

"Do you have the cancelled check that shows you paid Mrs. Franklin one hundred thousand dollars for the option on the estate as spelled out in this contract?"

"Of course. My fiancée said you would ask for it. I also have a cashier's check here for fifty thousand dollars made out to Margo. Do you have title and deed to the property? I know Mr. Chakaris represented Virginia and filed virtually all her important papers."

"Daddy, why did mother leave me the house in one will and then leave it to you in another?"

"Margo, please," Hilary said.

"No, let me answer. At first it bothered me to know what she had done to you, honey," he said. "In fact, it still does. But then I realized that her request for fifty thousand to go to you before I acquire the estate was meant to heal the wound of her nullifying the previous will. I don't know why she chose not to destroy that will. I paid handsomely for my option on the estate through the years and then in the lump sum to your mother. She needed funds right then, and this was merely a business transaction. You have a nice inheritance and I have an investment that paid off, although in a not entirely happy way."

Margo burst into tears. "That must have been during the time that Mother was associated with the syndicate," she said. Mr. Franklin looked ashen.

"I don't want my client saying anything more right now," Hilary said. "I want you to know that you will not be nullifying a million dollar bequest with a payment of fifty-thousand dollars without a verdict in court."

Margo started to protest, but Hilary stared her down. "Please wait and talk to me later," she said firmly. "Mr. Franklin, we will be studying this carefully. I believe you intend your daughter no harm, but her counsel will not allow her to settle for five percent of what we feel she is entitled to. I recommend that you secure counsel or get hold of Mr. Fenton or do whatever you feel is necessary to represent your position."

Mr. Franklin was still shaken. He had never been the type to stand up to a strong personality in a woman. He merely nodded and stood. We left quickly.

"You didn't even kiss me when you saw me," Margo said in the elevator.

I held her close. "Well, I, uh, I didn't exactly expect to — "

"I know," she said. "Have I got news for you two."

FIFTEEN

"Let's save it for the hotel, Margo," Hilary said. "I want to be able to take notes and get it all. Anyway, we need to let your friends in Chicago know you're still in the land of the living."

On our way back, Hilary told Margo of Hollis Fenton's secret involvement. At the hotel Hilary registered Margo to share her room, then we all met in mine where Hilary reported on the meeting in a late call to Chicago. Mr. Henley was waiting up for it.

"OK, Margo," Hilary said when she hung up. "Shoot. What've you got?"

"First let me tell you why I wanted to go to Pontiac," Margo began. "I had been in shock the last time I was there and hardly remembered anything about it. I found it difficult to believe my mother had actually been locked up in that place. The only time I'd been inside the front gate was the day she died. I just wanted to go back.

"And I wanted every memory to return. I wanted to remember the phone conversation I had with the woman doctor the night before Mother died. And I wanted to reread her letters and scrutinize everything. I'm glad I did. I also wanted to investigate something Amos said just before I saw Mother's body."

"What was that?" I said. "He said a lot of things."

"He said he didn't know the coroner, that he wasn't the one from Pontiac who usually served the prison there. Remember that?"

"Barely. But so what?"

"I got the coroner's name from the death certificate and discovered he was from Park Ridge. The Pontiac coroner didn't even hear of the death until a week later. The guy from Park Ridge said he was called the night before and was asked to be there the next morning. Mother died at four-thirty A.M."

Hilary looked puzzled. "It does sound strange, Margo," she said. "But of course it doesn't prove anything. You're insinuating that someone in the prison had a premonition about your mother's death, or that someone was going to die?"

"Let me finish and then I'll tell you what I'm insinuating. The woman in charge of food service told me that only prisoners in solitary confinement are segregated from the others during meals. Prisoners normally segregated from social, recreational, and work functions have their meals in the cafeteria, separated from the other women by only about twenty feet of floor space."

"So?"

"So Mother talked about having meals in her cell. And having chicken for what seemed to her like every meal."

"Maybe she had been restricted to her cell for illness or disciplinary reasons," Hilary said.

"I checked all that. Don't you see? I demanded to see reports and log sheets. The people in charge didn't think I was looking for anything in particular."

"So what did you find?"

"I found that chicken was not served to any prisoner during the week Mother wrote about it. Not to the general population, nor to any prisoner in solitary or restricted confinement."

"Could your mother have been mistaken? You said she had been ill or out of sorts."

"No! She was not one to miss details, and she certainly knew when she was eating chicken! She wasn't dizzy or disoriented until she had eaten the chicken a few times. The chicken that it seems only she was served."

"What are you saying, Margo?" Hilary asked. "Exactly what are you implying?"

"That my mother was poisoned."

Hilary shook her head impatiently. "It would have shown up on the autopsy."

"Not if whoever poisoned her owns the coroner."

Hilary set her pen on her steno pad and entwined her long fingers. She stared at Margo, who seemed on the verge of crying again. "You don't want to know who is implicated first if there's anything to this," Hilary said.

"I know. Daddy. But of course he could not be guilty. We all know that."

"Yeah," I said.

"Well, not *all* of us know that," Hilary said. "He has a motive."

"For killing Mother? Never."

"His motive is the estate. The house. A little payment to keep you happy, and everything is his."

"That's not enough of a motive for Daddy. Why wouldn't he have killed her before? Anytime after the document had been signed?"

"It might have looked too obvious. This was convenient. How could a man in California get into an Illinois prison to do in his ex-wife? It was a perfect setup to make him look innocent."

"No way," I said. "I have to agree with Margo, Hilary, and I don't think I'm being naive. I believe that man loved his wife even to her death. He didn't need her million dollar estate. It doesn't add up, even though things look bad for him."

"The story is far-fetched anyway," Hilary said, paging through her notes. "It doesn't make sense that the prison officials were that free with their time and log sheets. Why would they show them to *you?*"

"Because I played the little-girl-lost bit to the hilt. And I was good. I didn't lie or cheat to get to see any of it. I just begged. I wanted to see some evidence of her last days. She never told me anything about a cold, yet her infirmary reports say she was heavily medicated against the symptoms."

"Maybe they showed you what they wanted you to see," Hilary said. "Another autopsy could prove what you're saying, one way or the other. Do you want us to petition to have the body exhumed?"

Margo grimaced. "Ooh," she said. "I don't know about that."

We sat in silence for a few moments before Hilary spoke. "Let me tell you something straight. I think this is all off the wall. Your mother simply didn't tell you about some of these details because she was upset or didn't think of them or didn't want to worry you. Your allegations are going to be hard to prove, and if they do pan out, the finger is going to point straight at the man with the motive, your father. Since he is just a few semester hours from canonization in both of your minds, you obviously don't want to see him face charges. So what have you got? You've got a situation you don't want."

"I'm telling you my mother was poisoned to death. I want to know who did it."

"If you are convinced your father is clean, you'd better come up with someone with a motive. Who would stand to gain by your mother's death? Someone with the influence to buy a doctor, a coroner, an autopsy, and a few bit part players."

"Think of the initials on that new document," I said, "and you've answered your own question."

"Fenton? Nah! Why would Fenton care? What would he have to gain? His percentage of the estate would hardly be worth the risk, unless he was getting a significant share of the gross."

"We've got to get hold of Earl," I said, dialing his office in Glencoe. I got the answering device. I rang Bonnie's apartment, forgetting how late it was in Chicago.

"I'm sorry to wake you, but I've got to get a message to Earl. Know where I can reach him?"

"Not really; he's on the move. Calls in every morning, though. Shall I tell him it's urgent?"

"It's more than urgent, Bon. He needs to call me from wherever he is as soon as he can. Tell him anything you have to, to get him to call me. I'll wait by the phone."

We ordered a snack from room service before the girls went to their room. Then I called Margo. "I haven't even told you how much I missed you and worried about you,"

I said. "Why didn't you tell me where you were?"

"I was afraid you'd want me to stay in Glencoe. I needed to do this, Philip."

"How in the world did you beat us out here?"

"Once I had my information, I took a bus. They don't stop for sleep, you know. They just change drivers."

"How are you feeling about all this?"

"As you'd imagine. I thought I was all through with it. All I know is that Daddy is innocent. How Hollis Fenton would get any of the money is beyond me. If Daddy thought Mr. Fenton had anything to do with Mother's death, he wouldn't have anything to do with him. And he surely wouldn't give him any money."

"Of course not," I agreed. But I fell asleep as puzzled as she.

The phone woke me at 5:00 A.M. I knew it had to be Earl.

"Where are you?" I asked groggily.

"Springfield, Illinois," he said. "A conference and some business. What's up? Bonnie said it was more than urgent."

I told him the whole story.

SIXTEEN

"One major problem," Earl said. " Unless Margo was lucky, she simply got her chain pulled in Pontiac. I just can't see anyone there giving her anything legit, especially if there *was* any collusion by insiders."

"Do you think it's possible there was, Earl?

"Anything is possible in that Franklin family. The poor woman couldn't even get to her grave in peace."

"Not many people do."

"I know. I know."

"What do you think? What can we do?"

"Well, for one thing, I want to get to Pontiac and see if I can corroborate anything Margo learned. I'll see if I can get Amos to meet me there, because he knows Hollis Fenton better than anyone. The thing I can't get to add up is Mr. Franklin's role. He just isn't the type of a guy who would have his former wife killed just to get her money. He doesn't need it, and he doesn't hold grudges. I've been in the business long enough that I shouldn't be fooled. I've seen apparent weaklings murder two or three people, but George Franklin isn't that type of bird."

"That's what Margo and I have been saying. Listen, do you really have time to go to Pontiac?"

"No, but I'll just forget this conference for now. Other business will have to wait. You and Margo are getting to be like family, and that makes you priorities."

"We appreciate that, Earl. But I feel badly about it. I should be doing the legwork on this."

"You are, Philip, but you can't be in two places at once. Good thing that air traffic controllers' strike was settled. Maybe I can get a small plane out of here this morning for some dirt road landing strip near Pontiac."

"I didn't even know the strike was over."

"That means you're doing your job. I'll call you as soon as I have something. What's your schedule today?"

"We're just meeting Mr. Franklin and his fiancée for an early dinner at four-thirty this afternoon. Between now and then, we don't know what to do."

"You'd better sit tight. I'll be getting back to you. Hilary will have a tough time holding off Mr. Franklin without a formal injunction against what appears to be his legal right to acquire the estate."

I rang Hilary's room. Margo answered.

"Sorry to wake you. Let me talk to Hilary."

"No, you don't. I'm the one who tracked down all the information. I want to be in on this. I'm not gonna sit by while everyone else decides my fate, like last time."

I told her Earl's plans. Meanwhile, Hilary stirred and tried to listen with Margo. "This is silly," she finally broke in. "Meet us for breakfast downstairs in a half hour."

"What if Earl calls?"

"He won't even be out of Springfield in a half hour," she said. "Anyway, we can be reached in the coffee shop here."

I'm sure I looked as bleary-eyed as the girls did, but breakfast woke me up. "Earl seems to think there's a missing link," I said. "He wants to find the connection between Hollis Fenton and your father."

"Somehow it's hard to imagine your father being totally unaware of anything underhanded in your mother's death, especially when he stands to gain so much," Hilary said.

"You don't know him," Margo said. "He didn't know she was seeing Richard Wanmacher either. I maintain that he is — just as you say — totally unaware. I wonder how he'd react if I played my hunch and told him I didn't want any money."

"I've been thinking about that too," Hilary said. "We need some kind of a lead on how Hollis Fenton thinks he's going to get his fingers into this pie. Unless he's getting a major share somehow, why would this all be worth it? Margo, why don't you see what you can find out? If you make noise like you're going to make it easy for them, maybe it'll flush them out."

Margo called her father from her room while Hilary and I remained in the restaurant. "What do you think she's going to find?" I asked.

"I don't know. I still think her father is just after the money, but you two are pretty convincing." Margo returned in about twenty minutes.

"Daddy says Hollis Fenton is flying out here today and will be at our dinner this afternoon."

Hilary's eyes lit up. "Amos wouldn't want me contesting another lawyer within our firm, but Amos isn't really my boss anymore. And Fenton may not be with our firm anymore either."

"I learned something else," Margo said. "His new woman has a lot of influence."

"I caught that last night," Hilary said. "When he said she told him I would want to see the cancelled check. How would she know that? She sounds pretty sharp. Unless she's a lawyer."

"I don't think she's a lawyer," Margo said, "but every time I asked Daddy a question about the document or the estate, he told me what she said and how she felt and what she advised. It's almost as if she wants this deal more than he does. They're both very anxious for me to just take the money, whether I want it or not."

"You think she's got him to commit part of his estate — which would include the inheritance if this is consummated — to her upon their marriage?" Hilary said.

"I've never heard of that," Margo said. "Would he be bound by it?"

"You bet he would, especially in this state. Then she just finds quick grounds for divorce and makes off with whatever percentage of his estate she's legally entitled to."

"And that's legal?"

"It happens every day, Margo," Hilary said.

"You're not saying that Mr. Franklin's fiancée had something to do with Mrs. Franklin's death, are you?" I said. "This is getting pretty wild."

"I don't know," Hilary said. "If she didn't have anything to do with it, she sure came along at a strategic moment in his life, didn't she?"

"I'd really like to meet this woman," Margo said.

"No, you wouldn't," I said. "I wasn't going to tell you, but she was the real reason your father didn't come back for the funeral."

"You said he said it was because of the air traffic strike."

"That's what he told me to say. But really, it was this Gertrude or Gilda — "

"Gladys," Margo corrected.

Hilary wrote it down. "Gladys what?" she said.

"Turner, I think. Do you remember, Philip?"

"No."

"When Earl calls again," Hilary said, "let me talk to him."

"You mean you don't think I'm an astute enough private investigator to pick up on the fact that he and Amos ought to try to check out this woman too?"

"You didn't remember her name, Philip," Hilary said.

"I do remember Margo saying Gladys was a transplanted Chicagoan."

"That's a big help. I'm sure any number of Chicagoans would know her, then, wouldn't they?"

"Why are you being sarcastic, Hilary?" I said. "I'm just trying to help."

"I'm just teasing, Philip. But saying she's from Chicago is like saying that your father was in World War Two and might have known my father."

"He was."

"Was what?"

"Was in World War Two. Was your father too, really?"

"Honestly, Philip. Yes, he was. Stationed in Iwo Jima."

"You're kidding! So was mine!" I said. "What year?"

"Starting in nineteen forty-two."

"I don't believe this! I'll give you my father's name, and you check it out with your dad, OK?"

"You can't be serious, Philip."

"Of course I'm not serious. We can both tease, can't we? My father was a camp clerk, stateside."

Hilary shook her head. "I must keep reminding myself that we're adults," she said.

"Mr. Spence?" the waitress said. "There's a phone call for you."

"May I take it in my room?"

"Surely. I'll have it transferred."

We paid quickly and ran for the elevators.

Earl told me he had reached Pontiac and was having more luck than he had hoped for because of the weekend staff on duty. "They're anxious to prove they know what's going on. Virtually everything Margo found is being substantiated. I talked to the Park Ridge pathologist. I think he's clean. He said he got a call the night before from a doctor down here, asking if he would perform an autopsy the next day because the Pontiac man was going to be off.

"I asked him if he thought it was a strange request, but he said he had been to Pontiac occasionally on other cases, so he didn't think too much about it."

"Earl," I interrupted, "what time of the night was he called?"

"Late. About eleven."

"Margo talked to a doctor in the prison not long before that. Why wasn't she told anything about her mother's condition if it was bad enough to alert a coroner? And didn't you and Amos tell us that Mrs. Franklin died early in the morning?"

"The report shows that she was discovered dead in her infirmary bed at four-thirty A.M.," Margo cued me. I told Earl.

"I reminded him of that," Earl said. "It was also on the death certificate. He said he had noticed that but assumed it was an insignificant clerical error and didn't mention it to anyone at the prison. His only other hangup with the case was that the doctor had told him of a cold, which he couldn't verify through the autopsy. The only problem he found was traces of a gastric condition that could have been brought on by something she ate. Not enough to hurt her, he said, but enough to get her into the infirmary. He feels a minor cold, hardly traceable, *could* have killed her because her heart did appear to have been in a weakened condition.

"When I was convinced that he might have been an unwitting accomplice, I asked him if there was any way Mrs. Franklin could have been murdered without his detecting it. He said there were many ways, but that since he went into the autopsy without any suspicions, it was routine. He based his search on the doctor's prognosis and found everything in order. At the time he had little reason to believe that she had not died, as the doctor said, as the result of low resistance to a heart attack, due to a minor cold. A more complete autopsy would have had to have been warranted in advance."

I asked Earl to wait a minute and tried to relay the conversation to Margo and Hilary. "I want the body exhumed," Hilary said flatly. I told Earl. Margo made a face.

"I'll mention it to Amos," Earl said. "He'll know how to get it done. He should be here any time."

SEVENTEEN

At about one o'clock Los Angeles time, Earl called again. "We have a court order to have the body exhumed, but it can't be done until Monday morning. Meanwhile, you want to guess how many Gladys Turners there have been in Chicago? Thousands, and many of them with records. You need to get a good look at this woman and get some more information out of her. Is it possible the reason she didn't meet you last night was because she wanted to find out who all was there before she showed her face?"

"Why would she do that?"

"I don't know. It just seems strange that she wouldn't meet her future step-daughter the first chance she got. And maybe there's someone she wants to avoid."

"We'll be seeing her this afternoon. Hollis Fenton will be there, too."

That was news to Earl, and he knew it would be to Amos too. He covered the phone and told him. When he came back on, I could hear the old man fuming in the background. "I don't think I'm going to be able to talk Amos out of coming out there," Earl said. "He's hot. He's heard nothing from Hollis since he stormed out several days ago. If I finish my investigation here, I may come out with him. A little surprise meeting between Amos and Hollis might not be a bad idea."

I asked Hilary where we were supposed to meet Mr. Franklin, Miss Turner, and Mr. Fenton. She took the phone. "At the Pub Club on Ventura Boulevard, Earl, but tell Amos I was kinda looking forward to confronting Fenton myself. It'll feel good to outlawyer him, no tricks . . . Oh, good. That'll be great."

She hung up and told us that Earl and Amos wanted us to delay the meeting until seven and they promised not to drop in on us until about eight. "Meanwhile," she said, "it's strategy time."

We spent the rest of the afternoon trading theories, wondering whether Gladys Turner was involved, whether Mr. Franklin was totally in the dark as usual, how he and Miss Turner had met, and just what we were supposed to get out of her that would help Earl put the pieces together. I would have liked to put them all together myself, but by now I was totally confused. I wondered if this business ever got easier.

Mr. Franklin had no problem with postponing the dinner a few hours, though he sounded a bit puzzled. The time dragged.

That evening Miss Turner was a surprise to all of us. She was of average height but was unusually thin and mousy looking. Her hair was made up in a ratted style from years ago, and she wore orange-tinted glasses. She was, however, dressed expensively.

"Hollis will be here shortly," Mr. Franklin said more than once, and he continually looked over our heads and behind us to watch for him.

Hilary tried to keep things social until Hollis arrived, and I knew she was hoping he would come before Amos and Earl showed up. The later it got, the more we wondered whether Earl had finished his work and if they were able to get a flight, knowing most would be fully booked after the lengthy strike.

Miss Turner, however, wanted to get on with business. "Exactly what do you have in mind, Miss Brice, that will stop this transaction?"

"I prefer to wait until Mr. Franklin's counsel arrives, if you don't mind."

"I do mind, but I don't suppose I'm going to change yours."

Hilary tried to kill the hard woman with kindness. "Let's talk about you, Miss Turner. Margo tells us you're a native Chicagoan."

"And how did you know that?" Gladys said, staring at Margo.

"Isn't that what you told me, Daddy?"

"Yes, but, you see, Gladys has less than happy memories from Chicago. She'd rather talk about Los Angeles."

Gladys's thin face broke into a reluctant smile, and she tucked her arm beneath Mr. Franklin's, though her body remained rigid.

"Here's Hollis now." Mr. Franklin beamed, rising as if to meet his salvation from an awkward situation.

Fenton was loaded for bear, smelling right, looking right, wearing the right clothes and jewelry, and even carrying the right portfolio. He was the epitome of the man in charge, and Mr. Franklin and I immediately deferred to his presence. Hilary, however, all but arched her back.

As he had been the first time we had seen him, Hollis Fenton was as smooth as silk. "George, it's good to see you again. Hello, Hilary, Margo, Philip, and this must be your intended. Why, Miss, uh, Turner, you're even more lovely than George said. The pleasure is all mine."

Miss Turner looked embarrassed and said nothing. I nearly gagged. Saying she was lovely was an insult to Hilary and all the other women he had ever made passes at, probably including the late Mrs. Franklin. "Are you ready to talk business, Mr. Fenton?" Hilary asked.

"Oh, my dear, let's eat first. I'm starved. This was originally scheduled for much earlier, and I haven't eaten." He signaled the waiter, ordered drinks all around, then grinned broadly as Hilary and Margo and I declined. "Then we'll have the best steaks in the house," he said, "and you may bring me the bill."

"I don't care for steak," Hilary told the waiter politely. "I suggest your taking our orders individually, and I will be paying for the three of us."

Mr. Franklin, Miss Turner, and Mr. Fenton ordered steaks. I wanted to as well, but I was getting into Hilary's nonviolent resistance, so I ordered roast beef. Hilary and Margo ordered fish.

Hilary smiled sweetly at Hollis. "Will both these bills be on Chakaris, Fenton, Henley, and Whitehead, or should I say Henley, Whitehead, Fenton, and Chakaris?"

"As a matter of fact, you shouldn't say either," Hollis said. "The firm of Fenton and Fenton will move into offices right here in Los Angeles in a few days."

"How nice for you. And for your son, I presume?"

"Yes, my youngest. He came with a real price tag, but he'll be worth it."

Hollis rambled on about his son and the new firm while we ate. Hilary was stony, but she appeared ready for battle. As dessert was served, she tore into Fenton. There was no buildup.

"Don't you think it looks a little strange that you and Mr. Franklin have a secret agreement, secret even from one of the principals — Margo here — and from the very firm you represented at the time you drew up the papers?"

"That was the wish of my client, dear. I cannot violate the wishes of my client."

"And who was your client? Mr. Franklin or Mrs. Franklin?"

"In this case, Mr. But she needed the money and he wanted a good investment."

"And what do *you* get out of this?"

"A percentage, you know that. We all know that. The deal is perfectly legal, and if you have no bona fide reasons we shouldn't complete the transaction immediately, I suggest you comply or face legal charges yourself."

"Don't be silly, counselor," Hilary said. "A lawyer who would violate the ethics of his own profession is a lawyer whose every move should be scrutinized, especially one who would stiff his own partners."

"In an archaic firm, at that," Fenton said. "And what will you gain by scrutinizing me? You know our document takes precedence on the basis of date alone, and there's nothing whatever illegal about it, despite the irregularities the client's confidence required."

"Excuse me, Hollis," Mr. Franklin broke in, "but are you saying that this contract was not known to others at your law firm?"

"George, let me handle this. Your former wife was embarrassed to be acquiring such a lump sum and simply asked that I — as an old friend and colleague — not tell Amos about it. It had to be filed separately because *he* had drawn up the last previous will."

Mr. Franklin still looked puzzled, but Hollis tried to ignore him.

"You said George was your client," Hilary pressed. "Why follow the wishes of Mrs. Franklin when you represented Mr. Franklin?"

"And wasn't Mrs. Franklin more than an old friend and colleague?" I asked.

"What are you talking about?" Fenton said, flushing. "And why are *you* talking anyway? This is none of your business."

"Hollis, let's get back to business," Hilary said.

"Yes, let's," he said, louder than before. "I have a right to know exactly how you're going to try to stop this transaction. We have a check cut for Margo, and I trust you have the title and deed to the property."

"No, we don't. And you can *keep* your check. Quite frankly, we have serious questions regarding Mrs. Franklin's death."

"You saw the body. You know she's dead. What more do you want?"

"We want to know how she died."

Mr. Franklin looked as if someone had punched him in the stomach.

Hollis Fenton spoke. "You know how she died if you talked with the attending physician and the coroner. It's all on record. I even have copies of everything with me. Don't you?"

"Of course I do. I just don't like it. I don't like the fact that Mr. Franklin's fiancée came into his life not long before he was to come into a million dollars."

Miss Turner bristled. Hilary charged on. "I'd be very interested to know if there isn't a prenuptial financial agreement between Miss Turner and Mr. Franklin that includes the very estate we're talking about."

Mr. Franklin looked at Hollis, who jumped in quickly. "That is totally irrelevant, and you know there would be no way for you to petition to see it. It would have no bearing, even if it existed."

"Which it does," Mr. Franklin said.

"George," Hollis said.

"But I'm proud of it. Gladys was jilted once and taken for all her savings another time. I am perfectly willing to assure her, legally, that the same thing will not happen again. She's protected should we divorce, but we will not be divorcing."

"Uh-huh," Hilary said, unconvinced.

"The details of any such document are irrelevant to this discussion. Even if we produced such an agreement, it would prove nothing. Miss Turner is practical and Mr. Franklin is generous. I, for one, think we need more of that in this country."

"Oh, shut up," Hilary said. "Honestly, Hollis, you sit here spouting like a Boy Scout after you've set this woman up for life at your client's expense — "

"Now wait a minute," George Franklin said. "If you're suggesting — "

"I'm suggesting, Mr. Franklin, that you've been had. Don't you think it a little unusual that you meet this woman, she takes an inordinate interest in you to the point of your falling in love with her, she tells you stories about her sad past that make you anxious to promise her anything, your promises are then legally contracted for by the lawyer who also encouraged you to take advantage of your former wife under the guise of helping her, and now you find that he never told anyone, not even his partners, about that contract? Does that not arouse any suspicion in your mind?"

"Ignore her, George," Hollis said. "She's just trying to get her client more than she's entitled to."

"Her client happens to be my daughter, Hollis," George said. "If Virginia intended to leave her the house, then perhaps she's entitled to it. I don't want to fight my own daughter for money or property or anything else. And Gladys, you *have* been pushing me to do just that. Both of you have. I trust you, but I'm going to need time to think."

"You'll have plenty of time," Hilary said. "We're going to do everything we can to slow the paperwork on your contract with Mrs. Franklin, and if I were you, I'd get the processing halted on your agreement with your fiancée too."

Gladys glared at him. "If you hold up that paperwork," she said, "it'll be the end of us."

"Gladys," Mr. Franklin whined. "This doesn't sound like you."

"After all I've been through," she said. "I could never trust another man."

Mr. Franklin put his arm around her. "All right," he said softly. "All right."

"While we're on the subject, Mr. Franklin, how would you feel if you knew your former wife was murdered?" Hilary said.

He could hardly comprehend her words.

Hollis squinted at her and shook his head. "What in the world are you trying to do?" he said.

Hilary ignored him and kept talking to George. "How long after Gladys came into your life did Mrs. Franklin die? How long after you promised her half your estate?"

"Enough of this," Hollis said. "You don't have to listen — either of you. It's ridiculous."

"Well, look who's here," Hilary said cheerfully as Amos and Earl approached. Fenton closed his eyes and opened them slowly. George Franklin tried to smile. Gladys Turner put her hand to her mouth and looked down.

EIGHTEEN

As two extra chairs were squeezed around the table, tense introductions were made and Hollis Fenton fought to maintain his composure. He asked through pursed lips to what he owed "the pleasure of this surprise?"

"My office — or my former office anyway — tells me that your resignation arrived in the mail this morning," Chakaris said. "Nice of you to have it come on a Saturday when only a few people were there."

"Well, I don't know if you've had a chance to see it or read it yet, boss, but it simply reiterates what I've felt all along: that working for you was a highlight, a challenge, and a privilege, and that I had to move on to get my name first on a firm's stationery."

"And we both know that's baloney, don't we, ol' friend? You've been on the ropes for the last several years, and you couldn't face me or the other partners with your final decision, which we would have eventually come to as well. You saved the partners a difficult task."

"So that's why you're here? To face me? To tell me good-bye? To tell me that I didn't give enough notice?"

"Well, the latter is true enough, isn't it? I mean, we're not the local factory with a line of welders waiting to get in and take over, are we? Your contract calls for ninety days notice and your assistance in screening junior partners to replace you."

"But that's not why you're here."

"Nope. We just want to listen in."

Hilary tried to recap the conversation, with Hollis interrupting with rebuttals and corrections every few sentences. But Amos was not looking at either of them. He may have been listening, but he was staring at Miss Turner. Occasionally she would peek up at him, only to lower her eyes again. Her hand still covered her mouth, though not as if she were startled, as when they had first arrived. She was simply sitting there with her left elbow on the table and her chin and mouth buried in her left palm.

Chakaris, whose voice can be as big as he is when he wants it to be, cut off Fenton's and Hilary's arguments by speaking over them to Gladys. "So, tell me about yourself," he said.

She cocked her head and looked at him, but kept her hand where it was. She pulled back a fraction so he could hear her past her cupped hand, and when she had spoken, she settled back into her former position. "Not much to tell," she said. "Sort of a nobody from nowhere."

"Oh nonsense," Chakaris said. "Everybody's somebody and everybody's from somewhere. Where've you lived, what've you done, who are you? C'mon, it takes an impressive woman to land a guy like George here. Surely he wouldn't be interested in a shy girl who won't even show her face."

Gladys smiled self-consciously and tucked her chin between her thumb and forefinger so he had a slightly better look at her. She answered his questions with monosyllables. "Is Mr. Fenton your lawyer too?" Amos asked.

"Not really," she said.

"As a matter of fact," Hollis cut in, "I worked up the papers between Mr. Franklin and Miss Turner without ever having met her. It was his idea. He knew of her bad experiences in the past and insisted upon protecting her legally. I had not met her until tonight myself. She's not the type of a woman who would procure a lawyer to challenge her own husband-to-be."

"No, I'm sure she's not," Chakaris said, smiling fatherly at her.

Chakaris had not taken his eyes off the woman for several minutes. Fenton kept asking if anything was going to be accomplished or resolved and if not, could he schedule a later meeting.

"No, sir," Chakaris said evenly, his eyes still locked in on Gladys. "I want to clear this up tonight. Do you know that a judge is sitting in my former office right now, sipping my coffee and maybe even sampling a little of Mr. Henley's hootch? You remember Mr. Henley, Hol, the guy who got the position you wanted so badly? The judge won't get himself drunk tonight, though. He never does. Especially when he's working weekends and has already given an order to have a body exhumed.

"He works on weekends only for old, old, friends. And even then he'll only do it when he can help those friends nail a rat."

"You're talking in circles, Amos," Fenton said. "And if you don't mind my saying so, you're being extremely rude to Miss Turner. I believe you're embarrassing the lady by staring at her so."

"Well, Hollis, I'm not talking in circles. I do have a judge waiting for my call. I told him that even if I didn't run into anything new out here, I would still call him and tell him of all the circumstantial evidence we had run into. I didn't expect you to make it this easy for me, Hol. But then you and Gladys didn't expect to see me here tonight either."

Amos waved to the maitre d' who brought a phone to our table. "And no, I don't mind your saying that I'm being rude to Miss Turner. Perhaps I am. But this lady, as you call her, is no Miss Turner. Unless she's been married since her first husband died, this woman has been Mrs. John Margolis for two decades."

Gladys pressed both hands to her cheeks and slid them up to cover her eyes as her glasses rattled to the table. She inhaled deeply and her knuckles turned white against her face.

"Well, old John died a lot of years ago, and I haven't seen Gladys since then. But she was one of those old, old friends I was talking about. And they're hard to fool, aren't they, honey?"

Gladys nodded, but her face was still hidden.

"Hollis, my pal, I'm going to call my judge in Chicago now. And I'm going to finish the story I started to tell him just before we flew out here.

"I don't know how you got enough bad chicken into Mrs. Franklin to make her sick enough to get her into the infirmary. And I don't know how you got the Park Ridge pathologist to help you without arousing his suspicion. I probably won't know until Monday just what it took to kill Mrs. Franklin, but I think the judge will agree with me that a warrant for your arrest, and that of Gladys Margolis, is appropriate.

"I believe he has the California contacts to have you detained for extradition to Illinois to face charges for conspiracy to commit murder."

We sat stunned, listening, wondering. Hollis Fenton's breath came in great rushes through his nose as he kept his mouth tightly closed. Chakaris let a pregnant silence hang in the air as he put his big hand on the phone. Mr. Franklin finally spoke.

"Please, someone, tell me what's going on." He looked pleadingly at me and at Earl Haymeyer.

"Even I don't know, Amos," Earl said. "You might as well give us all of it."

"Would you like to tell it yourself, Gladys?" Chakaris asked softly.

She shook her head.

"The woman Hollis says is Gladys Turner," he explained, "is Gladys Margolis. And she used to work in our offices. She was Hollis Fenton's secretary, and she typed up the agreement between the Franklins."

Chakaris looked pityingly at his former partner. "All I needed was a connection between you and Mr. Franklin, something that would justify your taking such an interest in his estate."

"I didn't want any part of this, Amos," Gladys said through tears. "He said it would be so easy, and that I wouldn't have to have anything to do with the murder. We were going to split the money after I got it from George. I've had a rough time since John died, Amos. I never got a break. Hollis said we could pull it off once you had retired and George moved to California."

"I wonder, Gladys," Amos said, "given the sad man Hollis is, how long you suppose he would have let you keep your half?"

"Gladys," George Franklin managed, just above a whisper. "I thought you loved me. I loved you."

"That was the sickest thing about this, and about you," she said with contempt. "Getting next to you was the easiest job I ever had."

Late that night, in Mr. Franklin's spacious apartment, Amos Chakaris sympathetically told George and Margo how he had hated to expose Gladys in front of everyone. "Giving Hollis his due didn't bother me a bit, but Gladys *has* had her share of rough breaks. Nothing that would justify what she's been party to, but rough nonetheless.

"I recognized something about her immediately, but I couldn't put my finger on it, and it *has* been a lot of years. I can't tell you how shocked I was when I realized who she was. When it became obvious that she was hiding from me, I just stared her down and racked my brain. When she spoke the second or third time, it all came back to me."

Amos asked to use the phone, and when he had left the room, Mr. Franklin said, "I feel like a fool. I've been made the fool so many times it's a wonder I can function as an adult. How can I be so gullible?"

"It's a hazard of your sweet nature," Margo said, but he didn't appear consoled. "Maybe you need me out here for a while to protect you and take care of you."

I rolled my eyes.

"I couldn't let you do that, Margo," he said. "One of these days you've got to start living your own life."

"So far 'my own life' has been horrible," she said. "Next I'll hear that someone is trying to kill you or Philip."

"There's a lesson in this for all of us," I said, immediately realizing how sermonic I sounded. It seemed everyone was looking at me with utmost toleration. "At least it was a lesson for me," I added weakly.

And it had been. There was no way Margo could argue with that. She had been concerned about her mother and now her father, and we had both hoped for opportunities to tell Haymeyer about Christ. Hilary knew where we were coming from spiritually, and our work with her was cut out for us. With the kind of business we were getting into and the undeniably strange family Margo had come from, no one knew what could happen to any one of us next.

I wanted to tell Margo that we needed to plan and work and pray about sharing our faith with our friends, but this wasn't the time. At least it didn't seem the time to me. But she surprised me.

"Philip's right," she said, coming to my defense, albeit not as quickly as I might have hoped. "I'm still in shock over Mother's death and what Daddy has gone through, but I don't feel like retreating and sleeping it off or running and hiding from it. I just feel like you never know how much time you have to tell the people close to you what's really important to you."

"Are we gonna get the whole pitch right here tonight, Margo?" Haymeyer asked.

"Only if you want it," she said.

"Not really."

"Your time is coming, Earl," she said with a smile.

"I know that. I was impressed with your work in Pontiac, and I'm anxious to have you working with me and getting back on the waiting list for detective school."

Amos returned from the phone to report that two arrests at the women's facility in Pontiac had already led to confessions and direct implications of Hollis Fenton. He pulled me aside. "Tell Margo if she wants to know and when you feel she's up to it: her mother was killed by an injection of air into the bloodstream. Almost impossible to detect through autopsy, but an orderly has confessed to it."

Hollis Fenton and Gladys Margolis would be found as guilty as the pair they paid to do the dirty work.

With the air strike over, we left the rented car and flew back together. All I could think of was that Margo had wanted to work with me so we could get to know each other better, predicting that all the problems we would face would belong to other people.

So far, she'd been wrong. Dead wrong. She could still call my love pity or sympathy. She could say our relationship was entrenched in trauma and crisis. And I couldn't argue.

All I could do was to stay close and hope she would realize that my love was constant, regardless of whether she was in trouble, in shock, or in mourning.

PAIGE

Earl Haymeyer meets Paige, someone to care for after having lost his wife years ago. She's everything he ever could have hoped for and more, but why are people telling lies about her? What secrets from the past still haunt her?

ONE

THE FOUR OF US WHO WORKED FOR HIM in his EH Detective Agency simply thought Earl Haymeyer was in love. It was unusual, sure — even out of character for him — but none of us fathomed how it would affect us.

Bonnie, our receptionist and secretary, had been with Earl just a few days less than I had — about a year. My fiancée, Margo Franklin, had been a special agent for about six months, following her training. And Larry Shipman, an old friend of Earl's since he had been with the United States attorney's office, had joined just a few months before.

Shipman is crazy. There's no other way to say it. He's an overgrown kid in his early thirties who never got tired of chasing police cars and fire trucks. He had helped Earl on some cases during my first few months on the job while he was a stringer for local newspapers and radio and television stations. He was also a part-time undercover man and jack-of-all-trades.

Margo and I have grown to love the Ship, especially his mock fear whenever Bonnie announces that Earl either wants him on the phone or is on his way to the office. "Now I'll be fired for sure," Larry screams, scurrying to look busy, as if he weren't the most valuable pro on the staff.

But the day Earl arrived unexpectedly at the office, and Bonnie tipped off the three of us on the intercom in the darkroom, Larry really did think he'd had it.

Earl had told us to wait for him before we tried developing the film he had shot the night before in total darkness. He explained that infrared light made it possible, and although Margo and I were skeptical, Shipman insisted he had "read something about that somewhere," as he always did when someone brought up something he knew nothing about.

Earl had left early in the morning to visit his thirteen-year-old son, Earl, Jr., who had been locked into autism since birth. Though the boy never knew Earl or his wife — who had died seven years before — Earl visited him at least once a month and generally stayed several hours to watch him play.

When Earl called Bonnie and told her he would be a little later than usual getting back, Shipman and I tried to convince each other that Earl would be just as anxious as we were to see the results of his infrared camera experiment. As usual, Margo argued for sanity. "He spent a lot of money on that camera, and he doesn't need you two rummies messing with the first roll of film he put through it."

"You don't have to be party to it if you don't want to," Shipman told her. "But I'm going to develop it and see what we've got. It's hard to believe there will be an image on the film. All he did was shoot his apartment without any light in the middle of the night."

Yup. I'm going to develop the film and blame it on Philip."

I laughed, and Margo and I followed him into the darkroom.

Larry was just hanging the negatives to dry when Bonnie announced Earl. "Boss's here!" she said cheerily, knowing exactly what we were up to.

Shipman jumped and swore.

"She's kidding," I said. "Next she'll use his familiar knock."

We heard three loud raps. Shipman's grimace relaxed into a smile as he finally realized it was just Bonnie scaring us. He swept to the door like an usher and opened it grandly while bowing at the waist.

"Oh, do come in, Grand Earl of Haymeyer," he exulted, stopping short when he discovered it was indeed Earl after all. "Hey, Earl, I'm sorry, man," he said. "I wanted to see how the film looked and — "

"That's all right," Earl said, shocking us all. "I took her out to dinner."

We looked at each other. Earl didn't sound like himself. Here was a man who had reached the heights as a special investigator for high government officials, had helped crack some of the most celebrated murder cases in Chicago history — including one committed by Margo's mother and another in which Mrs. Franklin had been the victim — and had been wildly successful in his own small firm in just more than a year of operation.

The man is usually all business. He is crisp, to the point, and impatient with ambiguities and people who speak in vague terms. And now he is guilty of it himself.

"You took *who* out to dinner?" Margo and I said in unison. Larry was puzzled too, but was in speechless relief that he had been pardoned.

"Paige," Earl said dreamily, his eyes not even focusing on us.

"Sit down, Earl," Shipman said. Earl just looked at him, then at each of us with a silly grin. Bonnie appeared in the doorway.

"Why don't you sit down and tell us all about it, Earl," she suggested.

He ignored her. "Paige Holiday," he said, as if we weren't there.

"I don't believe this," I said.

"Let me sit down," Earl said, passing up a chair right in front of him. He hoisted himself onto the darkroom counter and directly into a tray full of wash and three or four eight-by-tens Shipman had shot the day before. The wash cascaded out both sides of the tray and left Earl sitting heavily on the sticky prints, which were gluing themselves to his seat. He didn't notice a thing.

"I think," Bonnie said in great wisdom, "you'd better tell us about Paige Holiday."

"I'm in love," he said. "I'm going to marry her."

"Whoa!" Shipman whooped. "Does she know that?"

"Hm? Of course not. Unless she can tell how I feel about her."

"*We* sure can," I said. "So who is she? Where'd you meet her? How long have you known her?"

When Haymeyer looked at his watch, Shipman decided, "There goes the business. He has to look at his watch to see how long he's known her, but the greatest detective mind since Columbo is going to marry her, posthaste!"

"About seven hours, I guess," Earl said, grinning again.

"So you met her at the rehab center," Margo said.

"Uh-huh."

"Tell us about her," Bonnie repeated.

"I did. She can't wait to meet you all."

"No, tell *us* about *her.*"

"Uh-huh."

Bonnie looked at her watch. Her grown kids were coming for dinner, but she didn't want to miss this. Shipman fidgeted too, anxious to try to print from the dry negatives of the infrared experiment. Margo stared at Earl, as if hoping that a cautious silence would bring him out. I looked at Margo, remembering when I had been nearly incoherent about her.

"She's not real tall," Earl began. "She's not real skinny, nor is she overweight. She's sorta, I guess you'd call it, cuddly." We shot a collective doubletake.

"Well, I didn't cuddle her, of course. Yet."

"Earl!" Margo scolded.

"She has dark brown hair that hangs straight and is cut evenly at her shoulders. Her eyes are dark too, but they're deep and expressive, and it's as if she can look right past your face and into your brain. She's not any less pretty when she's not smiling, but when she smiles it's as if she's happy from the shoulders up. She just breaks into these wise and knowing and open grins that make you feel like you've made her day.

"She loves Little Earl, and all the kids. They hardly respond to her, or to anybody, but she just keeps giving and giving anyway."

We were enraptured. I hadn't heard Earl go on so since he talked about his first stake-out. He was a detective's detective, and until now I wouldn't have thought anything else in life could matter to him as much as his work. He'd had a good marriage and just the one child, and when his wife died, he threw himself into his career as never before. He had hardly dated in seven years.

"At first she was just the new girl on the staff to me," Earl said. "You know how I am with new people. She introduced herself and told me about how Little Earl has been getting along. It was just small talk after that, but not to her. Even when I just mentioned the weather, she stared deep into my eyes and listened. And if I said anything remotely funny, she seemed to really enjoy it."

"That's neat," Shipman said, as if he meant it. I think it even embarrassed him that he was so moved by Earl's infatuation. "Uh, how old is she, Earl?"

"Oh, maybe a year or two older than I am," he said. "Maybe forty."

"Available?"

"A widow. Loves kids. Has none of her own. Lost one at birth."

"Sad."

"Yeah, but she's not. She's dealt with it, I guess. She's really at peace with herself."

Margo and I locked eyes for an instant, wondering if she might be a Christian.

"I'd like to meet this woman," I said. "I really would."

"Me too," Margo said.

"Paige," Earl said.

"Hm?"

"Not 'this woman.' Paige Holiday. Someday Paige Haymeyer. I took her to dinner."

"You said that. How was it?"

"I don't remember what I ordered."

"I mean, how was the time with Paige?"

"Outstanding." He was grinning again, and we were all amused. And pleased. And just half a hair wary. She sounded like a wonderful person, one of those rare birds that is an instant hit with everyone. But could she really be available? With no attachments? And might Earl get hurt by falling so hard so fast, especially considering his background, temperament, and years of detachment?

"So you're going to see her again next month?" I ventured.

"Next month? Tomorrow noon."

"Earl," Shipman said, "you've got a business to run."

"I know that. And it'll survive. I'll be the better for this, I can tell you that. It'll make me a better detective, a better boss, a better businessman — "

"Sure," Shipman said, "and it'll improve your golf game, your racquetball, and your breath."

"Particularly my breath," Earl said, almost coming back to reality. "I'm bound to be more conscious of that."

"It's never been a problem," Bonnie said too quickly, almost motherly. She blushed when we demanded to know why she was an expert on Earl's breath.

"Well, anyway, I'm back," Earl said. "And what're you all still doing here this late at night? I wanted to develop my infrared film and surprise you skeptics with it in the morning."

"Well, the negs are dry," Shipman said. "You wanna print some?"

"Tell me you didn't already develop the film, Ship," Haymeyer said, almost whining.

"I already told you I did," Larry said, incredulous.

"Did what?"

"Developed your stupid infrared film!"

"Oh, OK. Let's see what we've got."

As Earl slid down from the counter, the tray flipped over toward him and splashed him anew. "What's this?" he said, reaching for the photographs stuck to his pants.

I just had to meet this Paige Holiday.

Two

We all peered intently at the negatives until we were convinced that Earl had been right, as usual. He had turned out the lights and shut all his curtains the night before, then shot a roll of film in the blackness while we stood mostly hooting at him.

"This could revolutionize our work," he had predicted. Margo and I bet he would have a roll of black ravens flying through an unlit coal mine. Shipman had been silent, not eager to be wrong either way. When we had told Bonnie about it the next morning, she advised against doubting Earl and his new gadgets.

"So we were wrong," I was saying now. It was obvious Earl and Shipman could pull decent photographs from the negatives. "Do we have to stay and watch you print them, or can we come back later and see the final product? We haven't eaten yet."

We dropped Bonnie off at her place — which was within walking distance, except on dark nights — then headed off to eat. When I brought Margo back to her car at Earl's office later, she was too tired to even come up. I lived in the building, so I was home. I kissed her good night, and she left for her apartment in Winnetka, a few minutes away.

I had brought Shipman a sandwich, which Earl ate, even though he had been out to dinner with Paige. "Just thinking about her makes me hungry," he said, shaking his head. He still smelled of freshly developed pictures, probably because he still had the remnants of a couple of them stuck to his pants. Normally he was a pretty dapper guy.

"Where's the Ship?"

"Went home. He's been putting in a lot of hours for me lately. I could never pay him enough. You either."

"But I'm learning so much, Earl. So is Margo. I know it sounds strange to disagree with your employer when he says he can't pay you enough, but we both feel good about being here, and we're both addicted to this business. We think it's because we've been learning it from you."

"And Shipman. Don't think you don't pick up things from him everyday. Sometimes I think he's more of a natural than I am at parts of detective work." Earl paused.

I almost nodded.

"Don't agree with that," he said. "Wanna see the infrared prints?"

They were impressive. Nothing like you get with a flash, of course, but there were some fairly contrasty prints of Earl's furniture. "I wish I'd put one of you in the picture," he said. "It looks as if a person would be identifiable, doesn't it?"

"It really does. Wanna shoot me now?"

It was eerie, "posing" in pitch darkness and hearing the shutter click. Earl said he was too tired to develop the new shots that night. "But let's look at 'em tomorrow when I get back from seeing Paige." And with that he was off into his fantasy again. "I just flat want to talk about her," he said.

"This is so unlike you. You know that, don't you Earl? I mean, it's all right for you to fall in love, but you're like a high school kid. I never thought much about what it would be like if you found yourself a new love, but I know I never expected this."

"I never did either, kid. I never expected to fall in love again. I knew if it ever happened, it would have to come out of the blue and hit me over the head, because not only have I not been looking for it, I've been running the other way. I've made myself unavailable, and when I see a TV show or a movie and find myself envious of someone in love, I push it from my mind. I almost wish I could do that now, but this woman has me."

"She has you?"

"Yeah. And she doesn't even know it."

"You don't think she knows how you feel?"

"I know people pretty well, Philip. Maybe not women as much as men, but my guess is that she not only feels nothing for me, but that she also has no idea of what impact she made on me."

"What makes you think so?"

"She just seems selfless. Her whole being reaches out. She's a friend, a listener, an others-first person."

"Wow. I wish someone somewhere was saying that about me."

"Yeah, those are some attributes, aren't they?"

"What would she think if you told her how you feel?"

"It would really mess her up, Philip. I hardly know the woman."

"I know you've got ten years or more on me, Earl, and it's none of my business, but if you hardly know the woman, what makes you think you're in love with her?"

"I don't know. But it's so real it has to be true."

"That doesn't sound like Haymeyer reasoning."

"Don't you think I know that? There's no reason in this. The woman knocked me off my feet, and I can't quit thinking about her. Maybe I'll find out she's got green toes or likes bullfights or something, and I'll lose it. Meanwhile, I keep dreaming of her in my future. If she's half the woman I think she is, she's twice what I ever hoped for since Janice."

"What would Janice think?"

"She'd be thrilled. They're two of a kind in many ways. Janice was selfless, though I don't think she was as at ease with strangers as Paige is. You really need to see her in action. She's something. Just alive, glowing, brightening her space."

I thought of a song, but said nothing.

"I could keep you up all night talking about her," Earl said. "You'd better get to bed so you can be to work on time tomorrow."

"What's the difference?" I said. "I hear the boss has a heavy date and won't be in anyway."

"A cuddly date, anyway," Earl said. "And don't kid yourself. I'll be in before I leave to see her, No tellin' when I'll get back, though. Philip, this woman — ah, go to bed."

Earl began tidying the office, as he did every night. It wasn't that Bonnie was not organized. She was. In fact, her desk and area were always pin neat. But Earl is fastidious and a compulsive straightener. When he's working, his office — and ours — can be total messes. But before he leaves for his apartment, just a few steps down the hall on the second floor of his building, he gets the office into the shape he wants to see it when he arrives the next morning — always early.

An hour later, as I finished my reading and sketching and was crawling into bed, I realized I had not heard Earl lock up and head toward his place, two doors down from mine. I threw on a floor-length terry cloth robe and padded to the office, where lights still burned. It was nearly midnight.

I figured Earl must have felt he was too excited to sleep and had decided to process the film he had shot of me. I crept in toward the darkroom, but noticed the light on in his own office.

I hadn't intended to surprise him, but my slippers made no noise on the carpet, and I found myself standing in his doorway, undetected. He sat on the edge of his chair, elbows on his desk, face in his hands.

"Excuse me, Earl," I said, startling him slightly. "I just thought you might be in the darkroom."

"Nope," he said, quickly rubbing his face with both hands. He had been crying. "Just leaving." He reached for his desk lamp and put us both in darkness.

"Don't try anything," he joked, his voice thick with emotion. "I have infrared eyes and can still see you." I didn't laugh, and he noticed. He put his arm around my shoulder and led me out to where the main office light was on. He wiped his face dry with his free hand.

"Philip, my man," he said, "you know that for all I think of you and Margo, I don't buy your religious thing. But right now" — and his voice began to break — "I feel so grateful to someone, that I just don't know who to thank."

"Grateful?"

"For Paige. Oh, I know it may never come to anything. But it's been so long since I've allowed myself to feel the stirrings, since I've been romantically interested in anyone. I had convinced myself that I would be better off shutting out that part of my life. Philip, if all I get out of this was today's thrill of adoring the woman Paige seems to be, it's enough to thank someone for."

I didn't know what to say. Should a person who doesn't really believe in God thank Him for a friendly, nice-looking woman who makes him feel good? She sounded like a Christian, but that didn't mean God was going to make a gift of her to Earl.

"I believe God is the author of all good things," I said, trying not to sound too pious or sermonic.

"Someone who knew what he was doing wrapped this package," Earl said. "I don't feel comfortable thanking God for it, but I am grateful. What a wonderful feeling, to have been awakened after so many years."

I had never seen Earl emotional. Never. It was strange. And nice. Perhaps in spite of the bizarre nature of his feelings, he was actually getting things in perspective after falling in love virtually at first sight. He was talking a lot more now about how nothing may come of it — and that this day may be his only good memory — rather than that he was going to marry her, no ifs, ands, or buts.

"I don't think I'm going to sleep well tonight," he said.

"I will," I said. He clapped me on the back and locked the office door.

"See you bright and early," he said, the way he had done nearly every night for a year.

"Bright and early," I repeated.

THREE

In truth, Earl enforced no regular hours on anyone except his secretary, Bonnie, who was to be in at eight and could leave anytime after four thirty unless there was an emergency. She usually stayed nearly as late as everyone else, sometimes into the early evening.

As for Larry and Margo and me, by midmorning Earl wanted us either in the office or out tracking down leads and sources for our individual assignments.

Larry and Earl had been working together on a suspected embezzlement ring at a big bank downtown, not far from where Larry lived. Shipman had gotten himself hired as a teller and made noises among his coworkers that he "could sure use some extra money," while Earl consulted with the executives and accountants to determine just how the siphoning off of funds was being done.

They felt they were close to something, and near the end of each working day, Bonnie, Margo, and I waited impatiently to hear of their progress.

Meanwhile, Margo was working on a welfare fraud case that came to Earl through his old friend and former United States attorney — now Illinois governor — James A. Hanlon. It was Margo's first case alone, and she was doing well. She wasn't playing undercover or anything, just asking a lot of questions in the welfare office and among check recipients.

I had been assigned to investigate the mysterious death of a teenage boy. He had been an athlete, a good student, a leader in school and in his church, yet he had been run over by a truck and killed in the alley behind an X-rated bar on the city's west side. His father had hired us, presumably to clear his son's name.

"What I can't understand was the trace of alcohol found in his blood," the tearful father told us one night. "I think I can take it if you find that Justin was not the boy we thought he was. But I just have to know."

Earl warned me later, "Mr. Keith is not going to like what you find, but he's paying a lot of money for the truth, so give it to him straight."

"What do you think I'm gonna find? You know this kid or something?"

"Nope, and don't jump to any conclusions just because I do after so many years in this business. Go into it with an open mind, hoping you can tell the man that his kid was kidnaped, force-fed booze, and was killed when he tripped in the alley, leaving the porn shop after trying to preach to the customers. But don't be surprised if you find that the kid played his parents' game Sundays and during the week, then turned into a junior Mr. Hyde on Saturday nights."

Larry Shipman cut in. "Why not just tell the old man what he wants to hear, regardless of what Philip finds? What would it hurt?"

"I couldn't do it," I said.

"And I wouldn't want him to, Ship, even though I know your motive is all right. Our whole business — the law itself — centers on truth. We can't let it erode, even around the edges, for whatever reason."

My investigation had led to Justin's best friend, a classmate people said had often been seen with the now dead boy. I would be interviewing him after school.

Strangely, after my midnight chat with Earl, I found myself awake at six o'clock the next morning. I usually need more sleep. I called Margo. She answered groggily on the fourth ring.

"Hey, you got to bed a lot earlier than I did last night," I said. "How come you're still asleep?"

"I'm not, hon, thanks to you. Anyway, I stayed up preparing for my interviews today. I think I'm onto something that could cost a few patronage workers their jobs. Anyway, what's up?"

"Wondered what you were doing for breakfast this morning."

Margo and I met at a place about midway between our apartments. Somehow she never looked like she had just got up. "How do you do it? I must look like I'm still in bed."

"I'm just full of natural sunshine," she teased, laughing.

"I'd love to wake up to your natural sunshine every morning for the rest of my life," I said.

"You're going to, Philip. I'm wearing this huge rock you're still paying for, aren't I?"

"Then why don't we settle on a date?"

"We did. We're having one now. One I shouldn't have agreed to. Imagine a suitor waking me up and giving me an hour's notice for a date. You'd really have to love a guy to let him get away with that."

"You sure have strange ways of telling me you love me."

"You want me to stand on the table and tell the whole place? I would, you know."

"I'm sure you would, Margo. No need."

We prayed and ate, and she told me about her case. "The mistake the crooks in the welfare office made was that they chose stupid accomplices. First, they chose friends who lived not far from where they do. Then when I started asking questions, they warned their friends not to tell me anything. So, instead of playing innocent or confused, the accomplices tell me straight out, 'My friend at the welfare office told me not to tell you anything.'

"I asked one woman why she got five checks for varying amounts in one month. She told me the welfare office explained it to her and that it was all right, but she couldn't remember the reason. She's been getting those checks consolidated into one now for the last three months. It's a whopper each time."

"You got enough for Earl to bring in the state authorities?"

"I think so. After today I should have the names of everybody inside the department who had anything to do with it. The names of those who received the checks were easy. Many of them were going to the same address under different names.

"One man was so sad. He said that the welfare office worker who was paying him triple his usual amount had promised him he wouldn't have to split the money with her this month if he promised not to tell me anything. So he didn't tell me anything."

We both laughed. It was hard to tell who were the bumblers — the unsuspecting accomplices, or the idiots who chose them.

"It's really strange," I said, "but it appears that all the active cases we're on right now are coming to a boil at the same time. You'll have enough after today, Ship and Earl feel they're really close at the bank, and I could wrap up this Justin Keith thing today."

"Really? Was Earl right? Is the father not going to want to hear what you're going to tell him?"

"I don't know. Right now it looks rather encouraging. I still haven't pieced together the last night of his life, but every single person I've talked with, from relatives to other friends, to teachers, to girl friends, all vouch for the kid's character. He really *was* a nonsmoker, nondrinker, not a rowdy, not ashamed to stand up for what he thought was right, respected and obeyed his parents, everything."

"What do you make of it?"

"I'm not sure, but somehow this Brian Dahlberg friend of his raises a lot of eyebrows when his name is mentioned. Justin's friends couldn't figure out that friendship. They couldn't imagine Brian having a lasting impact on Justin; they didn't seem a natural pair. Brian is a jock, like Justin, but he's a senior — a year older — and a rich kid. Has his own car, lots of stuff, lots of girls. He's known as a boozer and does drugs; nothing real hard, but definitely illegal. I'm anxious to talk to him."

"Let me know how it turns out."

I told Margo about my strange conversation with Earl the night before. She responded with silence. I let her think. Finally, she spoke. "Could it be that we've been right all along about Earl's tenderness? That's not the reaction of the tough, professional investigator, is it?"

"His head-over-heels bit wasn't, either," I said.

"No, but that's a little more understandable than that he would be moved to tears of gratitude for one idyllic day with a total stranger."

"He's going to see her for lunch today, you know."

"Yeah. What I wouldn't give to be a little mouse at that meal."

"Well, babe, no doubt we'll hear all we want to hear about it later," I said.

"And more."

"Right."

"Philip."

"Hm?"

"What do you think about the fact that all our cases are about to be wrapped up?"

"I think Earl will just pull all the stacked and waiting ones out of his drawer and start assigning them."

"I know that. And I'm hoping he'll trust me with an important one again. But what I'm getting at is sort of superstitious, I guess."

"You mean that all our cases coming to a head at the same time means something big might be on the horizon for the agency, just like when a bunch of male babies are born, people think we're going to have a war?"

"Yeah."

"We're kind of a small staff to have a war."

"Oh, Philip, you know what I mean. It's Earl's style to tell clients right up front that their case may be in our pending file for a month or two, in case they want to take it elsewhere. I'm just wondering what'll happen if he gets involved with Paige and doesn't want to take any cases himself."

"It'll just mean more work for us."

"But you know that's not good. We need his input and his energy. We need his presence."

"You make him sound like God."

"We need His presence, too, but let's face it. Earl *is* the EH Detective Agency — in more than just name."

"Somehow I don't think he'll give up any good cases for his new love."

"Don't be too sure, Philip."

Earl looked bleary-eyed at the office. He was scurrying around, making phone calls, barking orders to Bonnie, and generally trying to wrap everything up so he could get to the rehab center to pick up Paige at noon. The center was on his way downtown, and he had told Shipman that he would probably see him near the bank at the end of the working day.

"You look shot," I told him.

"Leave it to you for a cheery comment every morning," he said. "At least I look happy, don't I?" He turned toward Bonnie, who was eyeing him with wonder. "What do you think, Bon, should I tell Paige that I look this way because I had trouble sleeping last night?"

"She'll figure that," Bonnie said.

"But I'll tell her why," Earl said. "I'll tell her it's because of her."

"I wouldn't," Bonnie said. "Not if you don't want to scare her off."

"Your face will scare her off today," I said.

"Philip, you keep making cracks like that and you're gonna find out why I'm the only gumshoe in this office who has enough brains to carry a gun."

"Sorry, Earl. You really might want to splash some cold water in your face before you leave, though."

"What, and wake up? No way. As long as I'm dreaming, I might as well be asleep."

Bonnie shook her head. None of us had ever seen Earl like this. I mentioned to him that our cases all seemed to be nearing an end at the same time. "No kidding?" he said. "Maybe I should propose today, then put off starting the pending cases until we get back from our honeymoon."

He was laughing. Bonnie said, "I tell you not to even tell her why you couldn't sleep last night, and you want to propose today. Don't ask *me* for any more advice."

Earl packed his briefcase and gave the office one more glance. "You talked to this Dahlberg yet?"

"After school today. He gets out at one thirty."

"Has he seen you yet? Know who you are, I mean?"

"Nope."

"You know who he is?"

"By pictures and make of car."

"Why don't you see if you can watch him at lunchtime? Might give you an idea of what he's like, who he runs with, that kind of thing."

With that, Earl was gone. Bonnie and I shrugged. "He still thinks business occasionally," she said.

"And when he does, he's right on the money," I said. I called the school to find out when the lunch breaks were, then drove to Skokie South and cruised the parking lot until I found the black Pontiac Trans Am with Brian Dahlberg's father's license number.

I parked two rows away where I had a perfect view, and sat waiting.

FOUR

At about noon, just when Earl was probably opening his car door for Paige Holiday, when Margo was probably making the last of her notes from her morning interviews, and when Shipman was trying to get next to his fellow "employees" at the bank in Chicago, I saw a tall, loping, good-looking blond kid get into the Trans Am and start the engine.

He was alone, and I was surprised. He was supposed to be everyone's friend, a guy with a girl on each arm. He was supposed to be a less-than-model driver as well, though his father had paid off five of his last six violation citations. Today he was driving like a gentleman.

That made him easier to follow without being obvious. I hung back a half block and even let other cars get between him and me. He drove about two miles, away from the usual haunts of the Skokie South kids. He pulled into a crowded fast food place and stood in a long line. He stared at the floor.

I wheeled over next to his car, then stood in the same line. He placed a very small order for a big kid, went outside, and sat on a cement bench. I took my meal to a window seat and watched him from inside. It took him longer to finish a cheeseburger and a small Coke than it did me to finish twice as much.

He hardly moved, eating as if in a trance. It didn't appear drug-induced or anything. His eyes were clear and his body steady, but he looked tired, and sad. He was not at all what I had expected. A guy and two girls greeted him on their way out, eager to stop and chat, but he just pursed his lips and nodded at them, unsmiling, and they moved on.

When he stood and headed for his car I hurried to dump my trash and catch up with him. Just as he put the key in his door, I said, "Brian? Are you Brian Dahlberg?"

"Depends," he said slowly.

"I'm Philip Spence. I have an appointment with you at one thirty."

"Yeah, hi. It's not one thirty, is it?"

"No, but I just wondered if we could talk now. Will you get in trouble if you miss your last class?"

"Nah. I was going to cut it anyway so I'd be home in time to see you. Wanna follow me there?"

We had his parents' mansion to ourselves. "Housekeeper comes at two, but she won't bother us. C'mon up to my room."

The house was beautiful. His room was huge, easily accommodating a king-size bed, a console color television, a wall stereo unit, and even a pinball machine. "Play if you want," he said, flopping on the bed. I shook my head.

"You've even got a CB unit in your bedroom," I said, knowing I sounded like a hick.

"Haven't used it in months. It was sort of a status thing for my dad. One of my friends' dad told my dad he had bought his kid one for his room; next thing I knew, I had one. Dumb. I listened to it for a few nights and got tired of it. Never asked for it. Never asked for any of this junk."

"I want to talk about Justin," I said.

Brian rolled up onto one elbow and pointed to a chair. As I sat down he covered his mouth with one hand and breathed deeply through his nose. He said nothing.

"Justin Keith," I said.

He nodded. "Yeah, I know."

"How come you suppose no one knew where he was that night he died?"

Brian glanced up at me, deep into my eyes. He appeared almost puzzled.

"None of my other contacts had any idea where he was or who he was with that night, except his mother. She said he said he was going downtown with you, maybe to a movie or something."

"Why didn't you believe her?"

"I did. That's why I'm here. But she said you denied it the next day. She said you said you were home all evening doing your homework and that your father vouched for you."

"So that's it then, huh?"

"No, that's not it then. Your father didn't get back into town from a business trip until midnight that night. Your mother could have vouched for you, but she didn't. She doesn't remember where you were."

"But you figure I was with him."

"Yeah. Because he doesn't lie."

"No, you're right about that. He doesn't. Didn't. I can't get into any trouble unless I had something to do with his death, right?"

"Right."

"Well, I didn't have anything to do with it, except — "

"Except?"

"Except I got us into the place. I had the fake IDs. I talked us into there. I egged him on. I made the dare, and I even made him a deal."

"A deal?"

"I wanted to see how real the kid was. He was the only really straight-arrow type of a guy I had ever spent much time with. I liked him a lot. He kept wanting me to go with him to picnics with his family. Can you imagine? A picnic with *family?* And he wanted me to go to church with him. I couldn't believe it.

"He never hassled me about getting loaded or drinking or anything, but he never joined in. He even got me to see a couple of G-rated pictures. I hadn't seen one since I took my niece to *The Black Stallion.* He never wanted to see the kind of movies I wanted to see. Maybe he wanted to, but he felt he shouldn't. I played upon his naiveté. I finally talked him into it."

"Why are you telling me this?" I asked. "Only because you weren't directly involved in his death and know you can't get in trouble?"

"No, I would have told you anyway," he said, his breath short and his eyes darting. "I've lived with it for weeks, and I feel like a creep." He hung his head. "I *am* a creep. I ruined a perfectly good kid, just because I had nothing better to do. Do you know Justin excelled at things money could never buy? I can compete because my dad makes a lot of money. I can get by as a mediocre athlete and a crummy student. But why was Justin a good kid and a good student? Because he was, that's all. It was him. It came from inside, not from anybody's wallet."

Brian lay back and put his hands behind his head. "I don't care who knows. In fact, I *want* my parents to know. I want you to tell anyone you want." He swore.

"You wanna tell me about that night?"

"There's not much to it," he said. "I told Justin that if he was so concerned about my experiencing his kind of life, he ought to experience mine. We went to a straight movie, and then I took him to the X-rated place. I don't believe he ever drank before. I convinced him the bouncer would really be mad if he didn't drink and that we would either have to pay a lot of money or not be allowed to leave. The place really spooked him."

"Where was he going when he was hit by the truck in the alley?"

"To the bathroom. I pointed him down the hall, but he missed the door and staggered out into the alley. He was sick."

"The driver says he thought Justin saw him, but when he backed up, Justin stepped behind the truck."

"I know," Brian said. "I was so jealous of that kid."

"You mean of his life-style?"

"I suppose. But I never got close enough to figure out what made him tick. I'm more jealous of him now than ever."

"Now?"

"That's right. Now."

The boy rolled over onto his stomach and hid his face in a pillow. He wasn't crying. I guessed it had been a long time since Brian Dahlberg had cried about anything. I waited a few minutes.

"I want you to do something for me," I said. "When you're up to it."

"What's that?" he said from behind the pillow.

"I want you to tell Justin's parents what you told me."

He sat up and let his legs dangle off the side of the bed. "I don't know if I can do that," he said. "They'll hold me responsible. And they'll be disappointed in him, too."

"I don't think they will, Brian," I said. "Do you know what it looks like as it stands? Like he was a liar who went for some kicks and wound up getting himself killed."

"In other words, his father is worried about the family name?"

"No, his father doesn't care about his own reputation. He cares only about his son's, and about his own peace of mind. He thought he knew his son, and now he isn't so sure."

"He thought he knew his own son?"

"That sound strange to you?"

"Doesn't it to you?"

I didn't respond.

Brian sat seemingly on the verge of tears for several minutes. "So, you want me to make it clear to Justin's parents that he was all they hoped he would be, but that I was the creep they were afraid he might have become."

"I wouldn't put it that way."

"I would. And I will. They need to know."

"Should I get your parents' permission first?"

"Are you kidding? My dad would kill me. As it is, they'll want to leave town."

"I don't have any authority to ask you to do this, you know. I can simply tell the parents what I learned and ask them to keep it quiet. No one ever has to know."

"Then why do you want me to do it?"

"For the same reason you want to do it. The same reason that drove you to tell me when you didn't have to. You were looking for someone to confess to. You'd had enough of the sham. You live with *this* sham every day," I said, waving at the room. "I was easy. You knew I couldn't hurt you, and you had to tell someone. How about having some guts? Tell someone who isn't easy to tell. Tell someone who could tell others to protect his son's reputation. Tell someone who could ruin your — and your father's — reputation.

"But remember, you do it on your own. No laying it off on me. My job is finished. I found what I needed to find. I'll go back to my office and file a report with my boss. He'll trade it to Mr. Keith for more money than a little running around and asking questions is worth, and we can all go our merry ways."

We sat staring at each other.

I passed the housekeeper on my way out.

FIVE

By the time I got back to the office, Margo was there typing up her report for Earl. "Wrapped it, huh?" I said, but she was so into her work that she just stuck out her hand without looking up. I squeezed it as I walked by.

Bonnie was on the phone and mouthed, "Larry," to me, making me stop. She covered the mouthpiece. "He's really onto something big and wants me to get to Earl right away." She turned back to the conversation. "I'll do what I can, Larry." She never called him Ship or Shipman. Not even *Mr.* Shipman.

"What's up?" I asked when she hung up.

"Larry called on his break from a pay phone down the street. He says the accomplices at his level in the bank have let on that the real leader in the scam is high in the corporate structure." She was dialing.

"You mean maybe even someone Earl has been working with in trying to break the thing?"

"Hello, this is the EH Detective Agency calling for Mr. Earl Haymeyer; I believe he's with Mrs. Paige Holiday . . . Thank you." She covered the phone. "That's right, Philip. Luckily, no one but the chairman of the board even knows that Earl has a man working inside." I started to respond, but she quieted me with a finger. "Oh, they're not. Well, would you have him call his office immediately when they return? Thank you."

"Hope Earl doesn't get her in trouble with her superiors," Bonnie told me. "They expected her back at two.

"By the way, Earl asked me to give you these," Bonnie said, handing me a manila envelope.

I took it back to my desk, held it in my teeth while taking my coat off, then slid the contents out. "Ah, the pictures from last night. Have you seen 'em, Bonnie?"

She nodded, but now Margo was out of her trance. "*I* haven't! May I?" She gathered up her rough draft, made a few scratches on it, asked Bonnie to type the final version for her, and hustled back to my desk.

"I don't believe this," she said, staring at the grainy, high contrast black and white prints. "It's not even difficult to tell who it is. It's incredible. Where were these taken? That looks like my desk in the background."

"It is. I was standing right where you are, and there wasn't a light on in the place — not even out in the hall."

Margo leafed through the photos, letting out a faint whistle between her teeth, "Maybe this *will* revolutionize our work." The phone rang.

"If that's Earl, I want to talk to him," I said.

"Me too," Margo said.

"Who may I say is calling?..One moment please. Philip, it's a young man named Brian?"

"Thanks, Bonnie. I'll talk to you in a minute, Margo," I said, punching Brian onto my line. "Brian, how ya doin'?" I began, trying not to sound too eager.

"I'm not doin' too well, Mr. Spence," he said, "but I know what I have to do. What I want to know is, Will you set it up and go with me?"

"You want me to talk to the Keiths?"

"Yeah."

"I think I can do that. You ready to do it tonight? They'll probably be anxious."

"I guess I'd better do it now before I change my mind."

"Hey, Brian?"

"Yeah."

"You're doing the right thing, you know that?"

"I think I do."

"I'll call you back."

I rummaged around to find the Keith file and called their home. Mrs. Keith said she would call her husband at work and get back to me if there was any problem; otherwise she would plan on seeing us at seven. While I was dialing Brian to let him know, I heard Bonnie taking Earl's call. "Remember I want to talk to him," I hollered just as Brian answered.

"It's all set for tonight at seven, guy," I said.

"Could I ask one more favor, Mr. Spence?"

"Sure, and call me Philip."

"Yeah, Philip, would you mind driving too much?"

"Uh, no."

"I mean I just don't want to pull up — or drive away later — in my Trans; you know what I mean?"

"Yeah. I'll pick you up at six forty-five."

When I hung up, Bonnie was already off the phone. "I needed to talk to him," I reminded her.

"I know, but you'll get your chance. He's going by the bank around closing time to pick up Larry down the street. He wants you to meet him down there and to bring his tape recorder — "

"But I have to be back here in time to — "

"I know, Philip. I told him you seemed to be arranging something for this evening, and he said he was sure you could drop off his tape recorder if you hurried. I also told him that Margo had finished her assignment, and he said she should feel free to come along."

"Let me," Margo said. "I want to tell you about my day."

"Let you? Let's get going. Earl forgot about the traffic at this time of day, and I have to get right back."

Bonnie brought me Earl's metal tape recorder case. "Fresh tapes, batteries, and everything," she said, like a mother handing out lunch boxes at the beginning of the day. "Meet Earl and Larry at State and Randolph."

I didn't give Margo much of a chance to tell me about her day, though she did work in that she found more of the same information she had turned up before and felt she had solid cases against everyone she had determined was involved.

"It'll make Governor Hanlon look good, cleaning his own house, and it will make Earl look good to him again, as if he needed that," Margo said.

"As if *we* needed that," I corrected. "The gov will just try to steal him away for a state job again."

By the time I had brought Margo up to date on the Keith-Dahlberg deal, we were off the expressway and into the Loop. Earl and Larry were in Earl's car, parked at a meter. Margo tooled around the block while I dashed over with the tape recorder.

"I wanted the camera, Philip," Earl said. "Not the tape recorder."

I just about died. "You've got to be kidding," I said.

"I am," Earl said, and they both cracked up.

"You guys got nothing better to do than sit here thinking of ways to give me heart failure?"

"As a matter of fact, we do. We have an appointment with the bank officers for dinner tonight, from the chairman of the board through the president, the senior executive vice president, and all the rest. Including, I might add, the man behind this whole scheme."

"Why was he dumb enough to involve people at the teller level?" I asked.

"I wouldn't know," Earl said. "But I think the rest of the executive committee is clean. Maybe he knew he could never find help there and was afraid to try anyone else. There's Margo. You'd better go. I'll be anxious to hear about your talk with Dahlberg — "

"And with Dahlberg *and* the Keiths tonight," I said.

"No kidding? I'm anxious to read Margo's report, too. Now get going."

"How was Paige today?"

"Get outa here!" Shipman interrupted. "We don't have time for all that!"

Margo had passed but was waiting at a light. I jumped in just as it turned green, and she fought the traffic all the way back to Glencoe, arriving just in time to have sandwiches with Bonnie, ordered from the deli down the street. I kept glancing at my watch.

"What are you two going to do tonight?" I asked.

"I don't want to get too far from here with all the news you three will be bringing back," Bonnie said. "What time is Earl's meeting?"

"He didn't say, but it's for dinner. I don't know exactly what he's planning or why he wanted the tape recorder, so I can't tell you when they'll get back. If you two want to be close, you could stay in my apartment so you'll know when any of us get back."

Bonnie said she had some reading she wanted to get done, and Margo wanted to study for a night school course in criminology, so they took me up on my offer. "You'd better get going," Bonnie said.

Brian was waiting for me in front of his home. He wore a short jacket, and his hands were thrust into his jeans pockets, thumbs sticking out. He slid into the car and asked me not to leave yet. I put the car in park. "We've got a few minutes," I said. "If you want to talk."

He said nothing. He just sat. Once he glanced expectantly at me as if to ask if I had any last-minute advice. I didn't. He buried his face in his hands and breathed deeply, then wiped his mouth with one hand while turning to stare out the window at nothing. "OK, let's go," he said.

We arrived at the modest Keith home right at seven, and I had locked and shut my door before realizing that Brian was still in the car. I walked around to his side. The front porch light was on. I saw movement through the picture window. Brian stared straight ahead.

I leaned up against the car as if in no hurry, but after a minute I opened his door. "I'm not going to force you," I said. "But you're this far."

He looked up at me. "This sure isn't going to be easy."

I nodded. He stepped from the car and started up the walk ahead of me.

Six

Mrs. Keith opened the door before Brian could ring the bell. I looked past her and saw her husband waiting on the couch in the living room, still in his business suit.

"Brian, please come in," Mrs. Keith said warmly. "And you must be Mr. Spence."

She took our coats and led us to the living room where we exchanged greetings with Mr. Keith. He and his wife both had that hollow, dark-eyed look of the recently bereaved. They were pleasant enough, but guarded and curious. Brian asked about their two young daughters and the dog, and Mr. Keith appeared a bit agitated, anxious to get to the point.

After an embarrassing silence, I said, "Brian has come to talk to you tonight of his own accord. It won't be easy for him, but I think he realizes that his discomfort in no way matches your grief. I'll let him tell you in his own way whatever he wants."

Brian suddenly became concerned with straightening a strand in the shag carpet with his foot. "I, uh, I want to tell you of the impact your son had on me," he said finally.

"And then I want to tell you of the impact I had on him." He fidgeted, and Mr. Keith interrupted.

"Justin never thought he made any impact on you, as much as he tried." Mrs. Keith shushed him with a wave.

"I know, I know that," Brian said quickly. "That may have been true at first, but not totally."

It took him twenty minutes to tell the Keiths the story of a strange friendship between a middle-income, straitlaced kid, who broke into the "in" crowd because of good grades and athletic skills, and a dope-doing, not-caring, Cain-raising rich kid.

"I could never figure him," Brian said. "I kept thinking that if I could just get through to him, he'd see he was missing out on all the fun in life. When I finally realized he had everything and was everything that I had always wanted deep down, it was hard to admit, even to myself. I never told him; in fact, I got a little angry with him.

"He kept asking me to join his kinds of activities, family-type stuff, church, picnics, all that. I made a deal with him. I told him he would have to try my life-style first, then I would try his."

"That doesn't sound like the kind of a deal Justin would make," Mr. Keith broke in.

"You're right. I must have finally gotten to him on a night when his resistance was low. I didn't even tell him my plan. I just dragged him along. It was the first time he had ever let me take him anywhere he didn't really want to go."

"And the last time," Mr. Keith said coldly.

Brian stared at him and fell silent. When he spoke again, his voice was thick. "Anyway, he hardly had anything to drink. It made him woozy and sick. I pointed him to the bathroom, but he went right out the back door and into the alley. Maybe he was thinking of just getting out. The next thing I heard was that a kid had been run over, and I just split."

Brian put both hands on his head. "That bothers me more than anything, that I just left him there. I knew no one in a place like that would tell anyone who they had seen with him. In fact, they probably denied he'd even been in the place."

I nodded.

"Anyway," Brian said, struggling to speak, "I wanted you to know that he loved you. And — and that he was everything you thought he was. And that I feel horrible for having forced him to do something he didn't want to do. I know his death was an accident, but I don't think he would have been hit if he hadn't been sick from the booze." Brian clasped a hand over his mouth to keep from sobbing.

Mr. Keith pursed his lips tightly while his wife let tears roll silently down her cheeks. "It's not a nice story, Brian," the man said, his grief tinged with anger. "But it helps to know what you've told us."

"I feel responsible," Brian blurted.

Mr. Keith rose from the couch, a tall, angular, imposing man. He strode past Brian to a cold fireplace. "You *are* responsible," he said, a little too loudly.

Brian was stunned. "I'm sorry," he said, "and I want you to forgive me." The words sounded strange coming from the boy, as if they had never before passed his lips or even crossed his mind.

"I want to forgive you," Mr. Keith said. "With everything that's in me, I *need* to forgive you. Justin was wrong. I wish he could have resisted you. But he was younger. He idolized you."

Brian looked genuinely surprised. "I idolized *him*," he said, his eyes finally moistening.

"Well, you had everything you wanted, you were popular, you answered to no one. He thought you were worldly-wise, and you were."

Mrs. Keith cried openly now. Brian wiped his eyes and stood. He looked vulnerable and weak, despite his youth and size. "Will you forgive me?" he said.

"I don't know," Mr. Keith said. "Do you think we'll feel any better letting you walk out of here with a weight off your shoulders? Is the weight you drop going to fill the void in our guts? Our son is gone, boy. I need to forgive you for *our* sake, not yours."

"I understand," Brian said desperately. "I'd do anything to turn the clock back."

Mr. Keith looked to his wife, who looked as if she wanted to speak. "I have an idea," she managed, looking sympathetically at the boy and speaking carefully.

"It's not our place to forgive you. We can't exonerate you. And telling you everything is all right now will not bring our son back. Neither will it change you. Your memory of this will fade much more quickly than ours — "

Brian tried to protest, but she kept talking. "It simply will, that's all. It's only natural. You will go on not having to answer for anything. You may take more drugs and be irresponsible — "

"I've done no dope since Justin died."

"I suppose that's good. Anyway, Brian, you made a deal, and I'm going to insist that you keep your part of it."

Brian looked quizzically at me, and I raised my eyebrows. The woman continued. "You said Justin had to sample your life-style before you would sample his. He did, and it cost him his life. Now you should sample his. It may cost you parts of your life."

"What are you saying, Mrs. Keith?" Brian asked.

"I'm saying that the Keith family is ready to return to some semblance of normalcy. We will never forget our son, and right now I can't imagine ever even being able to stop grieving over him. But now that our minds have been put at ease about his own character, and we can piece together the events before his death — and yes, we can even put some of the blame on you — I think the best thing for me and my husband and our girls is to get back to the things that made us such a close-knit family when Justin was with us."

Mr. Keith was obviously puzzled. "What are you driving at, honey?" he said kindly.

"Family activities, church socials, outings, picnics, ball games. We've virtually forced the girls to do nothing the last several weeks while we sat around feeling sorry for ourselves."

"We haven't felt sorry for ourselves as much as we worried that Justin had been something we thought he wasn't," Mr. Keith said.

"I know, but we're at the point now where we must go on. We must live our lives in such a way that our daughters aren't crippled by this."

"Granted, but what does it have to do with Brian and his deal with Justin?"

"I'm going to invite him to go with us. I'm going to invite him so often that he'll have every chance he wants to fulfill his part of the bargain. And when he's had enough, he can just tell me or quit taking my calls. How about it, Brian?"

Before Brian could answer, Mr. Keith broke in. "Are you suggesting that the first time I try to loosen up in weeks, the first time I take my family out to the park where I taught my boy to catch a ball and throw a Frisbee, that I have to take along the boy responsible for his death?"

We all sat in silence. Mrs. Keith finally spoke to Brian, but it was for her husband's benefit. "Justin's dad will regret he said that in a little while. He'll realize how cruel it was and how much it took for you to come here tonight. He'll think about the fact that it will be just as painful for us to go on family outings with or without you now that Justin is gone. And he'll probably call you and invite you himself."

Brian shook his head slowly. "You know, Mr. Keith, I can forgive you for saying that, because it's the type of thing I would say if I were you. In fact, I would have said a lot worse, and I appreciate that you haven't done that. You know, when Justin first asked me to come with him to various family things, I couldn't think of anything I'd less rather do. I envied his relationship with you, but a softball game on a Saturday afternoon, when there were cars and girls and highs? Not for me. But right now I'd rather do that than anything I can think of. I can't guarantee it will change me or make me like Justin, and I'm not even sure that's what I want."

"But you do want to at least uphold your end of the deal, don't you?" Mrs. Keith said.

"You bet I do," Brian said, without emotion.

Something made me wish that the Keiths had evidenced more that would have given me the courage to ask them straight out if they were Christians. But they had not referred to God or Christ, and though I knew they were churchgoers, I didn't feel free to talk to them about it in front of Brian.

Mr. Keith leaned back on the couch and let his head fall back. As he stared at the ceiling, he began to cry softly. "Thank you for coming, Brian," he said, his voice strained because of the position of his neck. "We'll talk, huh?"

"Yeah," Brain said. "We'll talk."

Mrs. Keith saw us to the door. "I'd like to call on you again and chat sometime myself," I said. "Do you think that would be all right?"

"Surely, anytime."

Earl had warned me before about my penchant for wanting to "talk religion" to all my clients. My real target was Earl, because I figured if he could ever see his need for Christ, he might not scold me every time word got back that I had, as he always says, "mixed business with religion."

"It's not religion," I always tell him. "And it doesn't need to mix with anything. The people we deal with have needs."

"And we have intelligent, rational, scientific answers for them," he always says.

"Not for all of them, Earl. There are some needs that can't be met by the greatest detection techniques ever devised." But I never wanted to push it. Margo and I had prayed a lot and laid a lot of groundwork with Earl. Too much, in fact, to risk blowing it by being disrespectful or insubordinate. I had confined my "religion" to my own time, especially when I wanted to talk to one of our clients.

"Hey, Brian, I'm proud of you," I said, pulling up to his house.

"Yeah, well, I dunno," he said.

"Could we get together sometime for a Coke or something?"

"Sure, if you want. I'm no prize for a buddy, you know."

"I know," I said, punching him in the shoulder. "But listen, take the Keiths up on their offer."

"Her offer."

"Right. But do it."

"If I go on picnics with them and for Cokes with you, I'll have made more friends from this than I've lost."

"You just might be right."

I felt like telling him that I would be praying for him, but it just didn't seem right.

"I'll be thinking about you," I said.

"You will?"

"I will."

"Thanks. Me too."

Bonnie was napping when Margo answered my knock. I kissed her. "Heard from Earl and Larry yet?"

"No. How'd your meeting go?"

"Really something," I said.

We decided to leave Bonnie a note and talk in the car so we wouldn't bother her. Margo was strangely silent when I finished my story. She usually had a bundle of reactions.

"What are you thinking?" I asked.

"That you should have struck while the iron was hot."

"You mean talked to them about Christ?"

"At least to Brian. He sounds like he could really be open."

"Brian's problems aren't drugs," I said. "They aren't even money or attitude. Those are just symptoms. He needs an anchor, a right relationship with his universe."

"Exactly my point, Philip. Why don't you think he's ready?"

"It's just that some people need to be brought up to a place of higher receptivity," I said. "You can't just hit 'em cold. Even you needed to come up to receptivity from point zero, remember?"

"Philip, you're pontificating. You sure hinted enough about what you had to offer — if I would only give you a chance to tell me — that I at least wanted to hear it. What have you said to Brian to whet his appetite?"

"Nothing, really. But I *will* get back to him. Hey, here's Earl. Let's wake up Bonnie."

SEVEN

Margo ran upstairs to rouse Bonnie while I greeted Earl as he emerged from his car. "You look whipped," I said. "Where's Larry?"

"He lives so close to where we were that he just went home. Anyway, I got it all on tape, so you won't miss anything. Wait till you hear it tomorrow."

"Tomorrow! I'll save *my* story till tomorrow, but we've been waiting all evening. C'mon, we'll make you coffee or whatever you need, but you're gonna tell us tonight."

Earl smiled wearily and shook his head. "It wasn't that long ago I was just as crazy as you."

I helped him carry his stuff upstairs and suggested we meet in my apartment rather than the office so we'd be more comfortable. Margo sat on the edge of the bed where Bonnie still lounged under an afghan. Earl sat in my easy chair. I served him coffee and set a TV tray in front of him for the tape recorder. Then I flopped onto the floor with my back against the wall.

Earl checked his watch and said he was good for only about another hour. "I'm seeing Paige tomorrow morning." We all smiled and caught each other's glances.

"When are *we* going to meet her?" Bonnie asked.

"Tomorrow. She and I are having breakfast, and I'm giving my tired and successful troops the day off, on one condition."

"What's the condition?" Margo asked.

"That you meet Paige and me for a picnic in the afternoon."

We all liked the idea, but we were soon bugging Earl in unison to get on with the tape. He introduced it:

"Ship had finally gotten next to the tellers who were involved with the removal of the cash each day. They trusted him enough to offer him a cut in exchange for his help, but they said their top-level contact would not approve bringing anyone new into the picture, so they weren't going to tell him. Like the idiots they are, though, they told Larry who their man was: none other than J. Michael Lucas, vice-president in charge of customer relations. How ironic is that?"

"Unbelievable. So he was at this dinner tonight?"

"Sure was. And at first he didn't recognize Larry from the bank. When he did, he about dropped his teeth. You know Ship. Every time he caught the old man staring at him, he gave him a nod and a huge grin. Lucas just picked at his food, no doubt praying that if Larry was with me, he had not turned up anything that would implicate him in the embezzlement.

"I asked the chairman of the board if he minded if we taped the meeting. He said he didn't, so the first thing on the machine is the end of his permission. You'll catch a lot of miscellaneous pleasantries and table noises, but when the meeting gets going in earnest, you'll be able to make it out, I think."

Earl pushed the "play" button.

". . . no problem at all, though I assume it will become our property once your investigation is over."

"Certainly, sir. I record these just for my own information and will have no use for them once our dealings are finished."

The chairman of the board, in effect, brought the meeting to an order. "Gentlemen, please, I think we'd like to let Mr. Haymeyer tell us about the progress he and his staff have made in our behalf. He called this meeting, so we're hoping for good news and an end to our problem. Mr. Haymeyer."

"Yes, thank you. You men have not been aware that while I have been meeting with you over the past few weeks I had a member of my staff working in the bank. Your board chairman was the only one who knew this.

"Some of you may have realized when you were introduced to Mr. Shipman tonight that you had seen him at the teller windows recently. He is a member of my staff, and he's been working undercover in your behalf. I'm pleased to say that his findings have in many ways corroborated mine, and also that his findings have confirmed many of your own suspicions.

"Both Mr. Williams and Mr. Bennett, I believe, speculated that the problem revolved around the teller area and that cash seemed to be disappearing despite balanced books at the end of each day. When you men quizzed them, the tellers' stories were always the same; and they pledged their undying loyalty and interest in finding the culprits.

"Gentlemen, I believe Mr. Shipman has found the culprits. You'll be happy to know that while it involves four tellers, it involves no others at that level."

Earl turned the machine off. "I stole a look at Mr. Lucas here," he told us, "and he had begun to breathe again. I think he thought I was implying that we believed the problem began and ended with the four tellers, and of course that's what I wanted him to think." He turned the machine back on.

"Many of you gentlemen may be hard pressed to name all the tellers in the bank, but let me pass around this list of the names of the four, in case you might know any or all of them by name."

The chairman of the board spoke. "I want you men to know that Mr. Haymeyer and I have discussed at length what we would do if and when we tracked down those responsible for this, and I call it a travesty. As you know, I am very much concerned with the public trust. It's all a bank has to sell itself on, that and courteous service.

"It would not be in the best interests of our bank to prosecute these three men and this woman, because the police records are public domain. There would be no way to compute the potential damage to our business if word got out that we prosecuted four of our tellers for embezzlement. Our plan is to give these people the option of paying back the money in exchange for their being allowed to simply resign."

Earl spoke again. "Of course, we have plenty of evidence, and Mr. Shipman here is prepared to swear in court to what he has seen and heard, so should any of the four choose to put up a fight, the bank would win. I believe the guilty parties will see the light if we apply enough pressure, and I'm confident they will acquiesce."

Earl turned the tape off. "Right about at this point, the list of the four names got around to Lucas, and he studied them as if trying to put faces with the names. As he passed the note on he said something to the effect that he didn't really know any of them well, except maybe one. Then I began to lay the trap for him."

The tape came back in midsentence. Earl was speaking. ". . . if you have not already thought of it, you will. There is the real likelihood here that the news will get around the bank, among the other employees I mean, that four people are suddenly gone and the embezzling problem is over. They will begin to put two and two together, and you know the grapevine. Is there a way we can help? What will be your plan in dealing with this?"

The chairman of the board responded: "We may be forced to tell the whole story to our personnel and simply ask their assistance in keeping the lid on."

"Maybe," Earl said. "You may have no choice. But one of the things they'll be extremely interested in is the disposition of the guilty. If they learn that these people got away with paying back the money and going free, you may have an internal public relations problem. And those kinds of problems always seem to leak outside to the public. Then you've got a *real* PR problem."

Margo and Bonnie and I grinned and pointed at Earl, seeing what he was up to. The chairman of the board's voice came on the tape: "Mike, what do you think? What would you do in that situation?"

J. Michael Lucas cleared his throat and his voice cracked. "Well, I, well, I agree that this would be unfortunate, and something we would want to avoid at all costs." It was almost as if he realized that once he got rolling he sounded all right, so he began to pick up confidence and steam. "In fact, I think it would be appropriate to let it be known that we have warned these people not to try to remain in the banking business and that even if they should resign and cooperate with us in a payoff plan, this does not insure them against an unfavorable reference from us should they seek future employment."

"We might have a legal problem there, Mike," a voice said.

"That's the personnel director," Earl explained.

"Unless we had it in writing that it was part of the deal, we could be sued for casting aspersions on someone who has not been convicted of a crime."

"But we're being *kind* in not prosecuting them!" Lucas insisted. "They owe it to us to not try to use us as a reference. And that would virtually keep them out of the banking field."

"Which you feel is just," Haymeyer said.

"Absolutely," J. Michael said.

"And what would your reactions be, gentlemen, if someone at a higher level than teller had been involved in something like this?"

"That would be an entirely different story altogether," the personnel man said.

"Yes," the chairman said. "I believe I would be extremely interested in cleaning our own house, even to the point of prosecuting. There might be a temporary PR threat, but in the long run we'd be the better for it. We'd show that we are not above dealing with our own problems and demanding that men who have high positions of trust live up to their commitments. Wouldn't you agree, Mike? I mean, this is just as important an issue in customer relations, wouldn't you say?"

"Oh, even more so, sir. I agree wholeheartedly. We should spare no expense in that type of a situation. Tellers are gnats on a cow's back, but executives are, they are, uh — "

"We are the cows," the chairman said, obviously proud of himself and drawing laughter all around.

"Was Lucas laughing?" I asked.

"Not really," Earl said. "I was staring right at him." The laughter died, and the conversation continued. Earl was speaking. "Mr. Chairman," he said, "and members of the executive committee, I give to you the cow."

There was silence. "I gestured toward Mr. Lucas," Earl said. We heard gasps. "Lucas said nothing, he just blushed and glowered at me," Earl said. "Listen now. I'm talking to the chairman here."

There was not even a hint of any other noise. "Sir, I normally would consider it cruel to implicate a man in front of his colleagues, even if I were sure that he was in on such a crime — which I *am* sure of, by the way. But in this case, where Mr. Lucas has continually acted pompous and self-righteous, as he has evidenced even here tonight while his four young, sacrificial (albeit guilty) accomplices' careers come to an end, well, I just wanted to give him a chance to speak for himself. You helped me do that, sir, when I cued you to the PR questions. Past this point — after turning over to you all the evidence you'll need, and more, to prosecute this man — this is really none of my business. But may I add something?

"I believe when you receive your copy of this tape, it would be wise to turn it back a few minutes and listen to the man in charge of customer relations tell you the proper board reaction to a crime of this nature committed by a member of your own executive committee. And then, if you have ever respected that man's judgment, respect it now and act upon it."

"How'd they take it?" I asked.

"They were stunned, as you could tell. I'll take some heat for the way I did it, but not from the chairman. He shook my hand warmly before I left and said something about advising 'your Mr. Shipman' to try to keep a straight face, at least until he gets out of the restaurant. Shipper really was having a tough time not cracking up."

"Did you enjoy it, Earl?" Margo asked.

"At first I thought I might. And I still think it was the right thing to do. But, no. Not that he deserved anything better, but it's never pretty to see a man's life disintegrate."

"That's for sure what you were seeing," Bonnie said.

"You said it," Earl agreed.

We sat silent.

"I'm going down the hall to bed," Earl said finally.

I dropped Bonnie off at her apartment and followed Margo home to make sure she got in safely. "I can hardly believe we're finally going to meet Paige," she said as she left the car.

EIGHT

Margo and I had agreed to pick up Bonnie on our way to the picnic, but Bonnie called me late in the morning to change plans. "I can hardly believe it," she said, "but Larry just called and asked if he could escort me."

"Larry who?"

"Larry Shipman, of course. What other Larrys do we know?"

"You mean he wants to drive you? It's a little out of his way, isn't it? Why didn't you just tell him we were taking you?"

"I did, but he insisted. He's such a sweet boy. I'm more than old enough to be his mother. In fact, my married daughter is older than he is. But he said he and I would be the fifth and sixth wheels at the park unless we stuck together, so it looks like I have a date."

Margo thought it was neat. "Larry's just being Larry," she said. "Anyway, it'll give us a chance to be alone on the way."

I picked her up around noon, and we carted our picnic paraphernalia north to a forest preserve bordering Highland Park. We were the first ones there.

When Larry came tooling in he leaped from his car and ran around to Bonnie's side before she could get out. He swung the door open and helped her. She laughed and punched him. "Be nice!" he shouted, "or I'll treat you like the grandmother you are."

"You're already treating me like an old lady!"

"You want me to call you 'Mom' right here in public?"

Bonnie was loving it. We sat and chatted about whether we thought Paige could ever live up to her advanced billing. "Don't anyone get the idea that this is really going to be a nonworking day," Bonnie said, pulling her newspaper and several file folders from her huge handbag. "Earl called and asked me to stop by the office and pull the pending files. I imagine he'll be making some assignments today."

None of us really minded. Assignment day is the most fun day of each month for us. Earl talks about each file folder, shows us the photographs and documents and affidavits and leads — anything he's acquired during the initial interviewing stages — then asks for comments. It's like a classroom with the best possible teacher running the show. He asks questions, evaluates our answers, poses hypothetical situations, and challenges us to think. "What's the first thing you'll want to find out?" he'll say. Or, "What are you going to have to watch out for with this client? What if he says this, or what if she does that?"

It is always a stimulating time, and I often realize during my investigations that what Earl predicts is usually right. And when I ask the questions and look under the rocks he suggests, things start to come together.

"I don't suppose you'd let us peek into any of those files and start bidding on cases," Margo suggested.

"You know I can't do that," Bonnie said. "And when was the last time you bought a case?"

"I just hope I proved myself with this welfare thing and that Earl will give me another good one."

"You did," Shipman said. "Earl was impressed. I think he has a lost cat caper in store for you." Margo grabbed Bonnie's paper and swatted him.

"Gimme that," Bonnie said. "I usually don't allow myself out into the light of day without reading my *Tribune.*" As she turned to her favorite section, the light of day disappeared and it began to drizzle. We headed toward a small pavilion a few yards from our picnic table.

I was helping lug our stuff and found myself behind Bonnie, who had made an instant tent of the paper and hid her head beneath it. As she spread it out to dry in the pavilion I picked up the soggy first section.

TEEN SUICIDE SHOCKS SKOKIE;
YOUTH LEAVES PUZZLING NOTE
SKOKIE — Police in this north Chicago suburb are questioning friends and relatives of a popular Skokie South High School senior, 18-year-old Brian Lawrence Dahlberg, Jr., who apparently committed suicide at the fashionable family residence here last night.

The youth was found in the garage, behind the wheel of his father's late model car, police say. The engine had been running with the garage door shut, and indications are that the boy's own sports car had been idling in the garage as well.

Ironically, it was the young Dahlberg's father, owner of Dahlberg Industries, Inc., Chicago, who found a six-page letter from his son on the kitchen table, then ran to the garage where he attempted to revive the boy. He has been unavailable for comment.

Speculation among police is that the boy was despondent over the accidental death of a close friend nearly three months ago. They say his letter was "mostly incoherent," and while it has not been released to the press, a police spokesman read the last paragraph, which he said followed three solid pages of "I'm sorry. I'm sorry. I'm sorry."

The final paragraph read: "Sorry doesn't work. I feel no better. I can't forgive myself. It's better I'm gone. Sorry, Dad."

There was more, but I could read no further. I sensed Margo and Larry reading over my shoulder and talking to me, but I didn't respond. My heart raced, and I felt as if I were about to explode. I whirled and looked to where I had parked the car. "Margo," I said, not even looking at her, "can you get a ride home with Larry or Earl?"

"Sure, but Philip — "

I ran to the car and felt the cold October rain flatten my hair and stream down my face. A car pulled in next to mine. I didn't know where I was going, but I had to go. As I started the car Earl shouted at me, and I saw a water-distorted view of him sharing an umbrella with a woman who had just gotten out of his car.

Paige. Earl would understand.

With rain dripping from my hair onto my neck and down my collar, and with tears welling in my eyes, I could hardly see to drive. I went three blocks without turning on my wipers, and I never did think to turn on my lights. I failed to obey a yield sign and heard an angry horn.

Not knowing exactly where I was, and suddenly exhausted, I pulled to the side of a residential street and rested my head against the steering wheel.

"God," I prayed aloud, alarming myself with the tightness of my own voice, "why do I always wait?" I sensed no reply. It was a question without an answer. I could think of nothing else to say. The phrase echoed in my mind, and I sobbed. There is always a reason to wait, always a reason to put it off, always a better time, a better situation, a better place, a better way to bring a person to a higher level of receptivity.

Receptivity. My conversation with Margo the night before haunted me. I had all the answers. While I had been telling her of Brian's "real needs" as opposed to his symptoms, and while I had it all figured out that what he really needed was an anchor in the universe, he was writing his suicide letter.

Margo had asked me why I didn't think he was ready.

The business about how you never know when a person may be hit by a car or die in his sleep had always been a churchy cliché to me. Not only did I now have a friend who was a victim, but I had also had the chance to offer hope. And I had blown it. I had waited.

No one could console me. I didn't need counseling. I was disgusted with myself, and I had a right to be. I hit-and-missed my way back to the Edens Expressway and headed south. I would wait no longer.

All the way to the Keith home, I tried to think of what to say and how to say it. I prayed for the right words. I knew I was being impulsive and that I might make a fool of myself, but I was also hit again with my question, "Why do I always wait?"

I had heard so many times that if there's anything worth becoming a fool for, it's the salvation of men. If I was about to become a fool for Christ, so be it. I would simply talk to the Keiths about Brian, try to insist that they not take any of the blame — though I knew Mr. Keith would after having hedged on his forgiveness and leaving the boy in despair.

And then I would tell them that I just had to say to them what I had wanted to say to Brian. I would tell them that their wonderful family and their airtight morals and their church attendance were not enough, that if something should happen to them or their daughters as quickly as it had happened to their own son and to Brian Dahlberg, they would need to have received Christ, His love, His pardon, His salvation.

It wouldn't be smooth. They might not understand. The time might not be right. Their receptivity might not be at the best level. But I would not wait. I would not have another experience like the one I had just endured. I didn't want another person I knew to have the chance of being lost simply because I had waited for a better time.

That included Earl, and the Dahlbergs, and Larry, and Bonnie. Margo and I had our priority list, and Earl was right at the top, but I couldn't wait on the others until we got through to Earl. I didn't want to alienate people, and I prayed that I would not do more harm than good or go off half-cocked. I wanted to be sensitive, loving, genuinely concerned. And now when I felt it so deeply, I had an entrée and I would use it.

The Keiths had not seen the paper and were speechless. The man hung his head, and I told him I thought I knew how he felt.

"Do you know that I nearly called him last night to tell him that my wife was right about my reaction?"

I shook my head.

He continued, "And do you know that I wanted to talk with him then? He said we would talk. I said we would talk. I had been horrible to him. I wanted to forgive him, but like you, I waited. You say you had this important message for him, and while I don't understand it and am not sure I even agree with it, I can identify with you. I had a message for him, too. But I waited. I figured I could call him in a few days. I knew my wife would invite him on an outing. I'd get my chance. Only I didn't get it, did I?"

His wife put her arm around his shoulders and patted him. She looked up at me. "We're not really religious like you are, Mr. Spence, but we go to church and try to live right. We'll pray for Brian as we pray for Justin."

I wanted to argue theology with her. I wanted to tell them that all their attempts to do what only God could do would get them nowhere. But I had already said it. They had heard it. They may not have understood it, and they may never. But someday someone will say it again, or they'll read it somewhere, or their pastor will start taking his sermons from Scripture instead of human literature, and the seed I planted will be watered.

"If you have any doubt that you are in right relationship to God, I urge you to seek Him where He can be found, through Christ."

They nodded tolerantly and said they hoped I felt better for telling them, as if I had gotten something off my chest.

Something told me I would no longer be satisfied to just be a sort of Christian hit man, blitzing people with the message and moving on to the next prospect. There was much more to this than just spilling the story and hoping for the best.

On the way to the Dahlberg home I almost found myself debating the timing. If there ever *was* a valid reason for waiting, this might be it. But I couldn't wait. I told Mr. and Mrs. Dahlberg that I was a friend of their son. Then I began with: "There was something I really should have told him last night, and I would give anything to be able to tell him now." They were anxious to hear what it was, and while they responded no more encouragingly than the Keiths, I know they were glad to hear from any friend of Brian's.

NINE

"How are you, sweetheart?" she asked.

I sighed deeply and leaned up on one elbow without turning on the lights. "I don't know," I said, thickly. "Just tired."

"Want to talk?"

"I guess."

"Want to meet me somewhere? Are you hungry or anything?"

"No."

"I just want you to know I'm with you," she said.

I couldn't speak. She heard me fighting not to cry again.

"Talk to me, Philip. Then you can go back to sleep."

"Why do we always wait?" I said.

"I don't know."

"Why do we *always* wait? We've always got some reason, some priority, some idea. Can you believe the baloney I was feeding you about this time last night? I sure had all that wisdom confirmed, didn't I?"

"Philip, you can't feel responsible. That boy — "

"Brian."

"Brian had a lot of deep, deep problems."

"I'm not saying I could have prevented his death, Margo. But I had an answer for him. He may not have understood or cared, but he would have had an option."

She didn't say anything. I love that about her. When she speaks, she says the right thing. And when she doesn't speak, it's because that's the best course.

"I learned the same lesson from this, you know," she said finally. "Even though I never knew Brian and couldn't care for him the way you do."

"I hardly knew him myself, Margo. But, yes, I do care for him. Did, anyway."

"Do you want to talk about where you went today?"

I told her about the meetings with both sets of parents. "I'm sorry I left you stranded," I said.

"You didn't. It was sweet that you made sure I could get home before you left. I don't think I would have done that."

"How was the assignment meeting?"

"Earl postponed it. You know he doesn't like to have those without everyone there to put in his two cents' worth. It's scheduled for Monday morning."

"I wonder if Earl will let me talk to the staff for a few minutes."

"Probably. He knows you're upset, and he understands. He wishes you could have met Paige, but he knows you had to leave."

"When will I get to meet her?"

"Sunday afternoon. The rain ruined our picnic, so we're trying again. Same time, same place. We'll have time to change after church and get up there."

"So, tell me about her."

"Wouldn't you rather be sleeping?"

"I *am* sleeping. Tell me about Paige."

"She's really special, Philip. Everything Earl said she was. A selfless, loving person, just the type you'd love to have for a mother or a sister or a nurse or whatever."

"I didn't get a good look at her. What does she look like?"

"She's cute. I know that's a strange description of a forty-year-old woman, but she's cute. Fresh, wholesome, bright. We all just loved her."

"Well, it'll be good to meet her. I'm happy for Earl. So, what are you doing tomorrow?"

"Don't you remember? That's why I called you tonight, because I'm leaving early in the morning to spend the day in Milwaukee with Bonnie. One of her kids lives there, and we were going to just blow the whole day. I'll cancel if you want and stay with you. Bonnie will understand."

"No way, hon. You've been looking forward to this."

"Well, why don't you go with us? It'll get your mind off Brian a little."

"Nah. That's not my idea of a diversion. You guys enjoy yourselves. I need a good day with nothing to do. If I get bored I may talk Earl and Ship into going downtown or something."

"You won't be talking Earl into anything. You can bet he'll be with Paige every waking moment."

"Right. Anyway, have a good time, don't worry about me, and I'll pick you up Sunday morning at nine."

"I love you, Philip."

"Of course you do. You can't help yourself."

"Oh, shut up. At least you still have your sense of humor."

"Yeah, and isn't that wonderful?" I said, wryly. "Sometimes we Christians bounce back so quickly it's disgusting."

"Don't be too hard on yourself."

"I won't. I'm just tired. I'll see ya."

I slept until nearly noon on Saturday, then went out for lunch, deciding to walk about a mile-and-a-half to a greasy spoon. My trench coat felt baggy, though warm against a shivery breeze, and I spent a couple of blocks trying to decide why. The answer was at the edge of consciousness, and I worked at trying to keep it there. It was an idle, stupid exercise, something I have often done. As the obvious answer took shape, I tried to think of other things, scolding myself for playing grade-school games as the truth forced its way into my head: *Your trenchcoat is baggier than usual because you're not wearing a suit coat like you usually do.*

Silliness. I used to like being alone. Now I was weird alone. I needed a wife. I needed Margo.

I hadn't completely dried my hair after my shower, and the wind made me shudder. *Grief,* I thought, *I need more than a wife; I need a mother!*

I pulled my collar up around my neck and thrust my hands deep into the pockets of my coat. *Why am I walking so fast?* I asked myself. *Nothing to do today, no obligations.* I slowed and then deliberately veered off the sidewalk to walk through some leaves.

But they weren't dry and crackly. They'd been rained on and were merely mushy and muddy. I still liked the odor. Sweet. Not yet moldy with death, but dead just the same. And from death, life. The greatest truth of my faith.

My leather heels clicked on the pavement as I crossed a street and entered the Hole-in-the-Wall, a most appropriately named hash house. I ordered a Polish sausage and a Coke.

I ate slowly, trying to push everything from my mind. But as the food and drink worked their magic on my system, I began to eat faster. It suddenly became important to get finished, to head back, to call Larry, to do something, anything. I wasn't going to vegetate. I couldn't just sit around. I had to do something, even if it wasn't productive — a mutation of the Protestant Work Ethic, married to the Now and the Me generations. Do something, have fun, experience, whatever.

I walked briskly back to my apartment, ignoring the sights and sounds and smells I had enjoyed on the way. I played no more silly mind games. Earl's car was gone. He would be with Paige. What was Larry's home number? I looked it up in the office and called him from there.

"Hey, Philip, glad you called! Margo's gone with Bonnie, huh? I just had a guy stiff me who was gonna drive into Indiana with me today, so I'm looking for something to do. Whatcha got in mind?"

"Oh, I don't care. Anything. I'd be happy to drive to your place if there's anything going on around there. Hold on a second, Ship, there's a call coming in."

"We don't answer on Saturdays," Shipman said.

"No, I'd better take it. Hang on." I never have been good at ignoring ringing phones or doorbells. It was Earl.

"I've been trying to reach you at home," he said. "Glad I caught you. You OK?"

"Sure, thanks. I want to talk to you about it sometime, Earl, but for now, yeah, I'm all right. I've got Larry on the other line. What can I do for you?"

"Oh, good. I wanted him too. Listen, is there any chance you two could come to the rehab center today? I don't want to tell you what it's all about yet, but I need your help. Anyway, it'll give you a chance to meet Paige."

"No problem for me, Earl. I'm free. Let me ask Larry. Hold on."

"The rehab center is about midway between us," Larry told me. "If we each leave within the next fifteen minutes, we can meet there in forty-five. See you there."

At least there'd be something interesting happening today, even if it was simply getting to meet Paige.

When I pulled into the parking lot at the institution, Larry and Paige were waiting with Earl in his car. I slid into the backseat with Larry, directly behind Paige. She turned around and smiled. What a doll. She reached back and took my hand as Earl introduced us. "I've heard so much about you," she said. "And your fiancée is a lovely girl. You must be very proud."

I told her I had heard a lot about her too, was glad to meet her, and all that, but I was nearly speechless otherwise. Had it been the middle of the night, Earl wouldn't have needed his headlights. She glowed, just as everyone had said. I wanted to ask Earl what he wanted, but he and Larry were already involved in conversation. Paige turned completely around in her seat and leaned over the back to whisper to me.

"Philip," she said, "I was horrified to hear about your young friend, and I want you to know that if there's anything I can do, or if you want to talk about it — or even if you *don't* want to talk about it, just let me know."

"I appreciate that, Mrs. Holiday. And I think I don't want to talk about it for a while."

"I understand," she said. "These things can be traumatic. Well, then, tell me about yourself and where you're from. Margo already told me about your unusual meeting and courtship, but I know very little about your background."

I told her about my home in Dayton, Ohio, and that I had always wanted to be a free-lance artist until I got involved with Earl. "He's quite a guy," I said. She smiled and crinkled her nose.

I tried to get her to talk about herself, but she just told me what Earl had said, that she was a widow and had lost her only child at birth. "And you're from — ?"

"Saint Paul," she said. "Been there?"

"Nope."

"You'd love it. Did Earl tell you that there's been some encouragement with Earl, Jr.?"

"No! Earl," I interrupted, "what's this?"

"Paige says he seems to be responding to her, mostly when no other children or adults are around. He might have smiled and once even tried to talk."

Paige nodded.

"Incredible!" I said. "That's unusual after this long, isn't it? I mean, he's how old now?"

"Thirteen," Earl said.

"Has he responded to you, Earl?"

"Not yet. I can't really see any difference, but it's all I can think about right now."

"That's a switch," Larry said, winking at Paige. She tried to suppress a smile and stole a glance at Earl.

"We'll talk later," she said, looking deep into my eyes and turning back to the front seat. "OK?"

"Sure," I said. Neat lady.

Earl pulled into a posh restaurant. "Oh, no," I said.

"Have no fear, gentlemen," he said. "This one's on me."

"I'd love to help you celebrate this progress with Little Earl," I said, "but I just ate."

"That's all right, Philip," Paige said. "You can watch us eat."

"Anyway," Earl said, holding the door for everyone, "we're not here to celebrate, although that's not a bad idea. I just may have a new case."

"A new case?"

"Let's order, and then I'll tell you about it."

As we looked at the menus, Paige asked Larry about his career as a stringer for the local papers and broadcast media, obviously picking up where they had left off at the aborted picnic the day before. She really had a way of bringing out the best in people. She could talk to men in front of Earl without flirting or ignoring him. In fact, she had a way of including him, even when he wasn't really part of the conversation.

I didn't know how far their relationship had progressed, whether he had even told her of his affection for her, but it was obvious that she cared for him. She cared for everybody, but I sensed that she even knew what he was thinking. Her inner beauty, which manifested itself in her expressive face, was even more amazing to me when I learned a few minutes later that our next case would revolve around her.

I never would have guessed anything was out of kilter in her life, the way she had given herself to conversation and to the group. I could tell why Earl was so taken with her, and why he would ask us to join him to start the investigation — or whatever was necessary — with all the heads available.

"I'm going to tape this so Bonnie and Margo can know what you boys know," Earl explained. "I want all the help I can get."

TEN

"Do you want to tell the story, Paige?" Earl asked.

"No, you go ahead. You know at least as much of it as I do."

"When I took Paige back to the rehab center after the picnic yesterday, there was a note from her supervisor that she was to report immediately. I waited around, since she was not really on duty anyway and we were planning to go out.

"When Paige returned from her meeting, I could tell she was troubled. I had never seen her show even a trace of fatigue or frustration or depression before."

I knew what he meant. I couldn't imagine Paige looking troubled. Even now, she was simply listening to him the way she listens to everyone.

"It took a long time for me to drag it out of her, but it seems a young girl, sixteen or seventeen, showed up at the center Friday and demanded to see Paige Datilo. The supervisor told her the only Paige on the staff was Paige Holiday.

" 'That's her,' the girl supposedly said. 'Holiday was her maiden name. Unless she's remarried, her name is Datilo, just like mine. Tell Paige Datilo her daughter was here.' "

Shipman and I looked at each other, and then at Paige and Earl. "So, what's the truth?" Shipman asked, as if it were the most obvious and logical question he could think of. "What *is* your maiden name, Mrs. Holiday?"

"Nothing ethnic, that's for sure," she said. "Just Greene with an *e,* that's all."

"Can you prove that?" Larry said.

Paige did a double take, and Earl scowled. "Sorry," Larry said. "Just askin'."

"Somehow the interviewing techniques I admire so much in you don't seem to be called for here," Earl said coldly.

"Are you sure you can be objective about this one, Earl?" Ship asked.

"Absolutely."

The way he said it proved him wrong, but he was too close to see it. "And if you want to try interrogating someone, why don't you start by tracking down this little opportunist and finding out who she is?"

"Where do we start?" Larry asked.

"Three guesses," Earl said. "Really, Larry, you want me to tell you where to start looking for someone?"

"I suppose I should start with the only woman we know of who has seen her."

"I suppose," Earl said, condescendingly. Paige touched Earl's arm and spoke his name quietly. It seemed to transform him. "I'm sorry, Ship," he said. "But you're one of the best in the business. You don't need to ask, 'Where do I start?' do you?"

"Of course not, Earl, and forgive me, Mrs. Holiday. I shouldn't have sounded accusatory."

She flashed that warming smile and assured him it was OK. "My supervisor's name is Marilyn Fleagle. She works Tuesdays through Saturdays until six."

"Then she's still there," I said, looking at my watch.

"Oh, both you guys are up for gold stars," Earl said, still frustrated with Larry but pretending to be kidding.

"I'm not eating," I said. "Why don't I just head over there?"

"Because we have only one car here, dummy," Earl said, smiling. I smacked myself on the forehead with an open palm. Larry laughed. Paige looked sympathetic. I wanted to hug her. An hour later, we all sat in Mrs. Fleagle's office.

"Mr. Haymeyer, I already answered your questions. Must we take more time?"

"If you don't mind," Earl said, "I would appreciate it if you would fill in my colleagues. Mr. Shipman here will be handling the case."

"The case? What case? Mrs. Holiday's or Datilo's daughter comes in here to see her and you call it a case?"

"We'll be investigating it."

"Investigating it? Now it's more than a case. It's an investigation. What *is* all this?"

Shipman answered. "You don't think this girl was lying?"

"No. Why should she lie? She looked a little like Mrs. Holiday."

"In what way?"

"As I told Mr. Haymeyer," she said, shifting her mass in the high-backed chair and scowling under a full head of white hair, "she had those even teeth that Mrs. Holiday has. Her coloring was much darker, and her hair was jet black. But she was built small, and there was a resemblance."

Paige had said nothing. "Doesn't it bother you, Paige, that your boss thinks this girl could have been telling the truth when you say there's nothing to it?" I asked.

Paige smiled knowingly at Mrs. Fleagle. "Not really," she said. "Our disagreements go back about six weeks when I first joined the staff. I didn't have the experience she wanted, but I was good with the children and she needed someone."

"That's not quite all of it, is it, Mrs. *Holiday?*" the old woman said, putting sarcasm into the name as if certain Paige was hiding behind it.

"I don't know what you mean," Paige said, still unruffled and looking the woman right in the eye.

"I mean that this is not the first time I have caught you in a lie."

Earl reddened. "Surely you don't mean you have caught Paige in a lie," he said. "You may have disagreed about something, but why wouldn't you fire a person you think has lied to you?"

"As Mrs. *Holiday* herself just said, I needed someone. People who deal with this type of handicapped children are not easy to find." The woman immediately softened as she remembered that Earl was more than a detective; he was also a father. "I'm sure you know what I mean," she said carefully.

"Yes, I do," Earl said. "And I've never seen anyone deal with autistic children the way Paige does."

"There's more to dealing with them than smiling at them," Mrs. Fleagle said.

"Good grief, what are you saying?" Earl said. "Is there something wrong with a woman trying to draw out an autistic child with a beautiful smile?"

"Of course not. It's just that she doesn't draw them out. She just says she does."

"Could we rephrase that?" Paige suggested. "I'd rather think that if I am wrong, I am simply mistaken. I don't just say that I've drawn a response. I truly believe that I have. Only you or someone else more qualified would know for sure. But you haven't been present when the children have smiled at me or tried to communicate."

"Indeed I have not. And in fact no one else has been around, have they?"

Paige seemed to smile forgivingly at the old woman. It was as if she had thought of just the right sarcastic remark to put Mrs. Fleagle in her place, but Paige held her tongue. I was proud of her. And nearly as defensive of her as Earl was.

"Earl," Shipman said, "I wonder if Mr. Spence and I could talk with Mrs. Fleagle alone for a few minutes. It's obvious there is tension between these women, and you have two reasons to have a vested interest in this. What do you say?"

Earl started to argue, but Paige nodded to him.

"I did say you would be handling it," Earl said. "We'll be outside."

When just the three of us were left in the room, Shipman turned on his boyish charm. "Please forgive Mr. Haymeyer," he said. "He's a professional like you are, but I'm afraid with his son having been here since he was a toddler, and with his obvious affection for Mrs. Holiday, whom he barely knows, he is a little defensive."

"Oh, that's quite all right," Mrs. Fleagle said. "I understand."

"May I call you Marilyn?" Shipman asked.

She was ready to say no, I'm sure, but when she raised her eyes to glare at him, she had to return his huge grin. "I suppose," she said hesitantly, "as long as you don't insist that I call you Larry or Shippy or whatever it is they call you."

She hadn't meant it to be funny, but Larry threw his head back and laughed loudly. "Well, they call me a lot of things, Marilyn, but Shippy isn't one of them. You can call me anything you like, as long as it's clean, know what I mean?"

A smile invaded her face. "I prefer to call you Mr. Shipman, if you don't mind."

"Not at all. Now, Marilyn, the first thing I want to know is if we have already overstayed our welcome" — she looked as if she had been waiting for a chance to graciously get rid of us — "because if we have, I want you to feel perfectly free to just tell us and name the date and time so we can reschedule. It's no problem for us to cancel other appointments and coordinate our calendars and make the trip down here. You just tell us."

"Well, how much more time did you want?"

"Just a few minutes, ma'am."

"Then I'd just as soon finish this tonight. I can stay a little later to finish my work if I have to. Clarence is working late tonight himself."

"Your husband? I'd love to meet him some day."

"No, you wouldn't," she said, laughing. "I've been waiting years to say that!"

Shipman realized she considered that funny, and he roared a little too late and a little flatly, but she didn't notice. He had her now.

"Why do you think Mrs. Holiday is using her maiden name and doesn't want to see her daughter, Marilyn?"

"Oh, I didn't say that."

"But you think it, don't you? I mean, you really tend to believe the girl more than your employee for some reason."

"Yes, I suppose I do."

"Why? Is it because Paige is naive? Because she comes in here with no training and thinks she's reaching the unreachable?"

"That's not totally it, Larry, uh, Mr. Shipman. But I suppose it's part of it. At first I liked it. Anybody would. She's a beautiful woman, that smile of hers and all. And she does seem to care for the children. But she's not reaching them any more than I reached them when I had her job for more than twenty years. You love those children until it hurts; you give them everything you have to give. You try every new technique and therapy that comes along, and only a handful out of the hundreds ever seems to make any progress."

"I understand, Marilyn. So it bothers you when she is optimistic."

"I would never begrudge anyone optimism. The point is that she lies."

"But she admits she could be wrong, and she says you would know."

"It's not a matter of being wrong. She lies."

"Those are pretty strong words," I interrupted, feeling Shipman's stare because I had stepped on his choreographed system of drawing her out. Now I had offended her.

"Perhaps they are," she said. "But I have caught her in lies."

"Actual lies?" Larry said, raising a hand to keep me out of the conversation.

"Actual lies."

"She admits them, when she's caught?"

"No, and that's what bothers me. I've had any number of employees who tell little white lies to stay out of hot water. If they lose something, they say they never saw it. If they break something when no one's around, they deny it. But when they are caught red-handed, they just apologize. It's human nature. But this woman never admits her wrong doing. I'm telling you that if I were to believe this woman, I would have to think she was nearly perfect. And now I'm supposed to believe that she's getting through to some of the toughest cases we have? No, sir."

"Marilyn," Larry said softly. "I think you know people, and I'm not trying to patronize you." He hesitated, and they smiled at each other as if both knew he was full of hot air. "But I want you to tell me everything you can about this young girl. I want to find her and talk to her, and you have my assurance that if she *is* Mrs. Holiday's daughter, we will report back to you and see that this situation is rectified."

"I might as well tell you, and you can tell Mrs. Holiday," she said, "that any major shenanigan like this will not be tolerated. If she's lying about this, she's gone, short of staff or not."

"I understand, Marilyn," Shipman said, "and thank you very much."

ELEVEN

Somehow, Larry talked Mrs. Fleagle into letting me make copies of everything in Paige's personnel file. I made two so Larry could take a set home.

He filled in Earl and said he was confident we could clear the thing up. When Earl took Paige home, Larry and I lingered in the parking lot to chat.

"The supervisor bothers me as much as she does everyone else," he admitted. "But I don't think we're going to get anything out of her by putting her on the defensive. Anyway, now that she's given us Paige's files, she really doesn't figure into the case anymore. Unless the girl shows up here again."

"I disagree," I said. "I think this woman has it in for Paige somehow. She could be making up this whole story. Even so, it would be nice if in the course of the investigation, we could make things smoother for Paige to work here. It can't be any fun when your supervisor doesn't trust you."

"True enough, but Paige seems like she can hold her own and make the best of any situation. I think she derives her pleasure and fulfillment from working with the kids."

"I'm anxious to get into her file and see her background," I said. "There's something special about her."

"How many do you know?"

"Who are like she is, you mean?"

"Yeah."

"Not many."

"That's what I thought. See you at the picnic tomorrow, and don't bring any business."

"I won't if you won't," I said.

Paige's file reflected everything she had told us. "Maiden name: Greene. Last previous residence: 314 Main St., St. Paul, MN. Marital status: widow. Children: None — lost unnamed male in childbirth, 1969."

Her forms showed six years of nurses' aide experience, followed by eight years of public school teaching in the largest elementary school district in St. Paul. She had moved to the Chicago area when her forte, special education, was phased out of the public school system and put under another state department. She wrote on the application that she could have taken a job with the state in a similar capacity, but since her husband had died the previous summer, she decided to simply start over in another city.

I admired her. She was self-confident, sure, but even the most aggressive people are hesitant to pull up stakes at age forty and start over. I wanted to take the file with me to the picnic Sunday and talk to Larry about it, but I had promised. I would, however, have it in the car so Margo could see it and so I could tell her all about what had happened.

She called at about eleven to tell me she and Bonnie had returned safely. "I'm almost too exhausted to think about church tomorrow," she said. I think she was waiting for me to tell her not to worry about it, so I didn't say anything. "But, I guess I'll try to make it, at least for the worship service at eleven," she said.

"Well, I was going to tell you about a big new case we're all going to get involved in, but I suppose it can wait until later."

"See you at nine sharp," she said.

I fell asleep with Paige's file all over the bed.

There was hardly time to tell Margo everything during the short ride to church the next morning, so she insisted on taking the file inside with her and peeking at it while we waited for the service to begin. I kept making faces at her, but she was fascinated.

"What do you suppose this Fleagle woman's problem is?" she asked.

I shrugged.

On the way back to Margo's apartment, where I would wait in the car for her to change and get a picnic basket ready, she told me to read the miscellaneous memos attached to Paige's file. I thought I had seen everything of any relevance, but I agreed.

"I'll be right back," she said, bounding up the stairs. I opened the folder again and dug out the notes that had passed between Mrs. Fleagle and her boss, who was known in the file only as J.T. She gave J.T. a glowing recommendation on Paige and suggested that she be hired, even though it was proving difficult for the personnel department to track down the references Paige listed. "All have changed jobs, moved, or died within the last eight months," she noted.

"References are not as crucial at this level as they might be at another," J.T. had replied. "If you are confident of her potential, proceed."

"You think that's relevant?" I asked as Margo returned.

"I don't know, but it is a loose end. The kind Earl always catches."

"He wouldn't have caught this loose end. It's a chink in Paige's armor."

"Oh, it is not. It's not her fault her references are hard to locate. And Earl would too have found it. He's sharper than that."

"Not when it comes to Paige, believe me."

"I'm going to ask him at the picnic."

"C'mon, let's not talk business there. I promised Larry I wouldn't even bring the file."

Now it was Margo's turn to wait in the car while I changed. On the way north to the forest preserve, she read the entire file again. "Sure doesn't appear that she could have had any connection with anyone named Datilo, or that she has a daughter anywhere. Even the child she lost was a boy."

"Where does it say she went to college?" I asked.

"University of Minnesota. Why?"

"Just curious. Should be easy enough to corroborate all her information."

"Why do you suppose she took such a low-paying job here, compared to what she had before?" Margo said.

"Ever try to get a teaching job without local tenure? She probably took this job so she could eat, and then liked it so much she wanted to stay."

"I don't imagine she's had any time to look for other work, now that she's been seeing Earl," Margo said. "It's too bad this supervisor has it in for her. It would be a tragedy for the kids if they lost a friend like Paige."

When we arrived at the picnic it was obvious before we got out of the car that I needn't feel guilty about bringing the file. Larry had his out and was reading it to Bonnie. Earl and Paige were peering over their shoulders.

"You turkey," I shouted, "I thought you weren't going to bring work!"

Everyone looked up and smiled, except Shipman. "This is all I needed to see," Earl said. "You guys did the job. I'm just curious about the young girl now, and I want to know what her scheme is. What do you think? Does she want money? A free ride? What?"

"Does she sound like anyone you have ever known, Paige?" Margo said. "A relative, an old acquaintance?"

Paige thought and shook her head.

"Hold it!" Bonnie said. "That's enough business. Earl, if you don't put a stop to this and get on with the picnic, I'm leaving. I love this work just as much as the rest of you, but we've got to put it behind us for one day and relax."

"This isn't business," Earl said, a little too curtly. "It's Paige."

Bonnie flushed. "I'm sorry, Earl. I know you're worried about it."

"Worried? Naw. Why should I be worried? It's probably just some local high school kids pulling a prank. Let's have a picnic!"

When we started breaking out the goodies, I overheard Earl tell Paige and Bonnie, "I'm not going to even let it enter my mind any more today. Why waste time on trivia?"

Later, while we were tossing a football around, he told Ship, "You guys'll have this thing wrapped up quick, and we won't even have to bother with it any more. It's silly. Not worth even talking about."

As we were leaving, Earl put his arm around me. "Hey, don't worry about this thing with Paige. I've put it out of my mind. No sense letting it get in the way of business. You guys give it another day or so and get a bead on this kid and meanwhile, I won't even think about it."

I just looked at him. He was spending so much time not thinking about it that it was running his life. Even Paige looked a little tense, but as usual, she put everyone else's needs before her own. She was the one who pitched in first for serving and cleaning up and running errands. Earl was a lucky guy. Now if she could just get him to *really* forget about her phantom high school tormentor and the boss who had fooled on her so quickly.

"Have you thought about the possibility that Mrs. Fleagle might have fabricated this whole thing?" Margo ventured. I saw Larry give her the quiet sign from behind Earl's back and shake his head. But it was too late.

"I have," Earl said, putting his foot up on our bumper and warming to the subject. "Has she given you reason to think she might do something like that, Paige?" he asked.

"I hadn't thought of it," she said. "I doubt it. Behind that crusty exterior is a woman who is really a professional. Even though I fear she has me misjudged, I don't think I could accuse her of making up stories to hurt me."

"Well, that's just the way you are, Paige," Earl said. "I think you may be right, Margo. Let's talk about it at our meeting in the morning. Meanwhile, I'm putting the whole thing out of my mind." This time no one reacted. And no one smiled. Earl was becoming obsessed.

Just before Earl and Paige pulled out of the parking lot, I jogged up to his door. "Earl, would it be all right if I spoke to the staff for a few minutes tomorrow morning?"

"What about?"

"Well, it's just that everyone knew about the case I was working on with the Keith boy, and that his friend Brian killed himself. I just want to bring everyone up to date, you know."

"Yeah. You're not going to get religious on us now, are you?"

"No guarantees, Earl. I promise not to take more than ten or fifteen minutes if you will agree not to put any restrictions on what I can talk about."

"Now Philip," Earl said, "we've been through this before, and many of us even know what you're trying to pitch. I just think — "

"Earl, you have no idea how important this is to me. I want to tell you guys what I wish I'd been able to tell Brian Dahlberg."

Earl pursed his lips. "If I let you do this, will you agree not to pressure anyone or keep after them if they don't want to talk any more about it?"

"Sure, but what if they do?"

"They won't, but that's up to them. All right. Ten minutes. You can have the first ten in the assignment meeting, then it's all business. Fair enough?"

"Fair enough. And thanks, Earl."

"Yeah, yeah," he said, driving off.

I skipped back to my car, jumped in, and embraced Margo, planting a huge kiss.

"What's this?" she managed. "You get a raise or something?"

"He said yes!"

"Yes what?"

"Yes I can talk to the staff tomorrow for ten minutes."

"That's not enough time, Philip," she said, suddenly serious.

"It is for me," I said.

"Slow down, Billy Sunday. You're gonna have to really plan and pray."

"Mostly pray, I think."

"That's more like it. You want any help?"

"You bet. Anything you've got."

"All I have is encouragement, but I have a lot of that. Let's drive down to the beach, and you can start planning how you're gonna use your ten minutes."

"It really doesn't sound like much, does it?"

"No. But it is. It's ten minutes more than you ever had before," she said.

"I think maybe we'd better go to church tonight and go to the beach after that." Margo smiled.

TWELVE

On our way out to the car from church that night, Larry Shipman met us in the parking lot. "I'm glad I caught you," he said. "I had no idea how long these rallies lasted."

"You mean church services?" Margo asked.

"Whatever. Anyway, what are the possibilities you two could spend some time with me right now?"

"Well, we did have a date at the lakefront," I said. "What's up?"

"It's this thing with Paige. I think we've all got our heads in the sand over it, and I want Margo to hear the original tape of our dinner conversation and look again at Paige's personnel folder."

"I'd like to hear it," Margo said, "if you think it's necessary. There'll still be time to go to the lakefront, Philip."

"What I want to do," Larry said, "if you don't mind, is to have us listen to the tape at your apartment, Philip, since it's so close. I'd rather not be listening to the tape in the office when Earl gets back from Paige's place."

"Why not?" I said. "He wanted Margo to hear it, didn't he?"

"Yes, but frankly I think we're going to come to different conclusions than Earl, and we won't know what to say when he walks in if we've just been discussing how to properly investigate this thing without his interference."

"Without his *interference?*" Margo said. "Yes, Larry, I think we'd better talk."

We tossed our coats across the bed and stretched out on the floor to hear the tape. "I don't want to prejudice you any more than I already have," he said, "but listen carefully. You were there, Philip, but maybe hearing it again will give you something new. Margo, tell me what you hear."

Nothing hit me. It was just Earl telling the story of the young girl who had claimed to be Paige's daughter. I shrugged as the tape ended.

"So, what did you hear, Margo?" Shipman asked.

"You mean beyond what you guys had already told me?"

"I mean what did you hear with your heart?"

"Ship," I said with a snicker, "you sound like a B-movie."

"Just listen," he said, rewinding the tape and starting it again. I went to the kitchen and made some popcorn. I didn't care how many times I heard it, I didn't know what Larry was driving at. He was going to have to tell me.

I brought in a big bowl and then started pouring Cokes. Margo said, "When I listen emotionally — that's what you're getting at, isn't it, Larry? —" he nodded "— I hear nothing but Earl."

"Right!"

"Of course she hears Earl," I said, frustrated. "Earl told the story!"

"But I hear more than the story, Philip," she said. "I hear Earl's love of Paige getting in the way of his reason."

"He's been that way since he first met her," I countered. "So what else is new?"

"It hasn't affected his work that much," Larry said. "He's been dreamy about her, but you said yourself that when he talked business he was right on the money. He's nowhere near precise on this one. And he doesn't really want us to check it out. He wants us to bury it."

"Do you know something we don't know?"

"No, and I wouldn't accuse Earl of that, either. It's just that he can't fathom Paige with any dark corners in her past."

"I can't either," I admitted.

"Nor I," Margo said.

"Well, none of us can, don't you see?" Larry said. "That's why we're all breathing collective sighs of relief when we read her personnel file."

"It *does* document what she says," Margo offered.

"No, it doesn't. We want her to be telling the truth so badly that we use her records to corroborate her testimony, a cardinal sin of evidence gathering. Who do you think filled out the lousy personnel forms?"

Margo and I looked at each other. "Paige, of course."

"Of course. Now here, look at the file again."

We ignored our snacks and bent over Ship as he spread the documents on the floor. "Her maiden name was Greene. There are probably a ton of those in the Twin Cities. And, if we're going to be picky, catch this address: Main Street. How many of those do you suppose might be in Saint Paul?"

"Excuse me, Larry," Margo said, "but why do we want to suspect Paige's personnel file? This stuff should be easy enough to check."

"You're right, but Earl may not want us digging into her past, not because he suspects anything, but because he *doesn't* suspect anything."

"I don't follow," I said.

"He's so sure that she's the tormented victim here that he doesn't want to insult her by checking up on her. In fact, he doesn't want *us* insulting *him* by checking up on her."

"So you're saying," Margo decided, "that we should routinely check her background, just as we would any new client, because so often the client doesn't tell us the whole story."

"Exactly."

"And you're convinced that Earl won't see the logic in this?"

"Want to hear the tape again, girl?" Larry asked.

"No."

"Or do you just want to think back to the picnic today and the number of times Earl put the whole thing completely out of his mind?"

Margo and I looked at each other and smiled. "So, how we gonna pull this off, Ship?" I said.

"I want you to check it out," he said. "You may have to go to Minnesota."

"I'm going to Minnesota without Earl knowing? No way. He's not blind."

"I can handle it," Shipman said. "Maybe I can arrange to trace the girl to Minnesota, and you would go there to track her."

"You mean deceive Earl? I couldn't."

"Then let me. Philip, you have to realize how important this is. We'll find a logical reason for you to go north, and while you're there, confirm the information Paige put in her personnel file. That's all."

"OK, Ship," I said. "If you can find me a legitimate reason to go. Otherwise, no."

Margo and I spent an hour-and-a-half in the car at the Lake Michigan waterfront around midnight, praying and planning what I would say the next morning. We needn't have bothered. Earl met me as I came in the office door at 8:00 A.M.

"Philip," he said, "I'm not the type to back out on a promise — you know that. But I'm going to have to ask you to postpone your little talk. More has come up in this case with Paige, and we need the time to hash it out. I guarantee you I'll reschedule it, and you'll get up to a half hour, no restrictions, OK?"

I was really disappointed, but I had no choice. I couldn't hold my boss to his promise, and he *had* made a major concession. Just before the assignment meeting I spoke quietly with Margo.

"I feel like I'm waiting again," I said. "And I determined never to wait again."

"You can't control this situation, babe," she said. "Be glad he gave you more time.

You'll be able to explain it all clearly, without fear of slipping into cliches and sounding religious — "

"Which seems to be Earl's biggest fear."

"Right. Let's take this as if it was meant to be and make the most of it."

When we were all assembled, Earl began. "I'm asking Bonnie to contact all our clients whose cases are in the pending file to tell them we'll be getting to them as soon as possible. There are several interesting ones there, and I'm sure you will each be pleased at your assignments. But for now, I want this business with Paige cleared away."

"But you said yesterday that Philip and I should just give it a few more days and be done with it."

"I know that, Ship," Earl said. "If you'll just let me continue. Paige called early this morning and said one of the neighbors in her apartment complex told her a young girl had been nosing around, asking questions and claiming to be Paige's daughter. It's really starting to get to her, and I'd like us to concentrate on finding this girl fast. I want to know what her angle is so we can put Paige's mind at ease."

"Do we have a lead on the neighbor?" Larry asked. "It would be good to have someone talk to her."

"You can check that out with Paige. I also want someone to talk with Mrs. Fleagle again. She doesn't work Mondays, but you should be able to locate her. I want to know if she noticed whether the girl appeared to have been traveling, or was local, or what."

"You still want me to handle this?" Shipman asked.

"Yes, I do."

"Then may I make a suggestion? I think you should simply observe and make recommendations. I really feel you're too close to this to be making judgments and decisions. I probably should have told you that in private, but I feel it's important."

"Forgive me for speaking up," Bonnie said. "I'm not supposed to speak in these meetings, I know, but I think Larry is right. Earl, you owe it to yourself and to Paige to stay out of this investigation."

Earl was hot. There's no way around it. I thought he was going to blow and tell us that he could handle the pressure and remain objective. But he didn't. "I suppose you're right," he said, not sounding totally convinced. "I want to spend a lot of time with Paige until this is over anyway, so I don't suppose I'd be too valuable. What's your first move?"

"Is Paige working today?"

"Yup."

"I want Margo to go with you to see her on her break. Get the whole picture of what her neighbor told her. Meanwhile, Philip can talk to Paige briefly and then track down the neighbor to get her complete statement. I'll go to the administrative office and see if I can get Marilyn's address or phone number."

"Marilyn?" Earl said. "Who's Marilyn?"

"Mrs. Fleagle."

"Somehow she doesn't hit me as a Marilyn," Earl said, shaking his head.

"Let's get going," Larry said. "We'll meet in my car in the parking lot at ten thirty this morning to report."

I started my search at the rehab center, calling Paige away from her job for a minute to get the name and address of her neighbor. "I don't even know her name," she said.

"She lives a floor above me and she works. Lives alone, I think. I'm sorry I can't be more help. She came by to tell me this morning on her way to work."

"But you don't know where she works or anything?"

"No."

"What does she look like?"

"Oh, average build. Middle-aged. Brown hair. Plain."

"Great."

"I know I haven't been of much help, Philip. And I'm sorry."

"That's OK. If that girl was nosing around, I'm sure someone else saw her too. Wish me luck."

She flashed me an appreciative smile and gave me a thumbs-up sign. "Oh, I almost forgot," she said. "Will you tell Earl something for me?"

"You can tell him yourself in a few minutes. He and Margo are coming to see you."

"Oh, good, because Mrs. Fleagle came by today and threatened to make trouble for me if I didn't shape up."

"Make trouble for you? How?"

"She didn't say."

"And how are you supposed to shape up?"

"I don't know, Philip. I wish I did. I guess if I'd admit to some rules infraction or something, she'd like me more."

On my way out I saw Ship and Earl and Margo in the waiting room. "She help you much?" Earl asked.

"Not really. Good thing I'm good at this."

Everyone smiled.

At Paige's apartment building I talked to everyone at home on six floors, and none of them had seen a teenage girl they hadn't recognized. Most knew Paige, the new tenant with the lovely smile, but no one on Paige's floor or on the ones immediately above and below hers fit the description of the plain, average, brown-haired, middleaged, single working woman, and no one knew of her, either.

It was nearly ten thirty, and I had little to report but my puzzlement.

THIRTEEN

"What've you got?" Shipman asked me as I got into the car. Earl and I were in the backseat, Margo on the passenger's side in the front next to Larry.

"Not a thing," I said. "Whoever that woman was, she's disappeared or never existed."

"What do you mean by that?" Earl demanded. "Are you saying Paige dreamed this up?"

"I'm saying, Earl," I said coldly, "that no one else saw the girl, no one recognizes the woman by Paige's description, and no one there looked like her. Paige doesn't know her name, describes her as plain and average and alone and a working woman. No, I'm not saying she dreamed her up. I'm just saying I had a frustrating morning and this thing is starting to appear pretty strange."

"Well, just be careful about ascribing to Paige any — "

Larry interrupted. "I'm sorry, boss, but this *is* starting to stink. I gotta tell ya, Paige may not be coming clean with us."

"What are you talking about?" Earl said.

"C'mon, Earl!" Larry said, exasperated. "I think we're all just a little tired of your defensiveness. Paige is a wonderful gal, and we're all impressed with her — though admittedly not in love with her — but we're checking this thing out just the way we check everything, and we're turning up some disconcerting information. Are we not allowed to double-check any of it, or should we just sweep the whole thing under the rug?"

"There's nothing to hide. But you'd better tell me what you mean by the fact that Paige may not be coming clean with you."

"You don't want to know what I've got."

"Of course I do."

"Look at this."

Larry held out a handwritten note penned in a heavy back-slanted style that read, "Dear Peggy: You have until exactly noon on Tuesday to get out of my life. Otherwise, I make no guarantees."

It was signed, "Your former mother."

"So what?" Earl said. "What is it, where'd it come from? Who wrote it?"

"Mrs. Fleagle said Paige brought it by her house this morning and demanded that she give it to the woman at the reception desk inside and instruct her to give it to the teen girl if she showed up again. Here's the envelope."

It read: "Peggy Datilo."

Haymeyer swore. "That's ridiculous," he said, "And Margo will tell you why."

"It does look like Mrs. Fleagle is doing just what Paige claimed she would do," Margo said. "She told us this morning that Mrs. Fleagle threatened to pull something like this."

"She said something to me like that this morning too," I said, "but I thought she said yesterday that she didn't think Mrs. Fleagle would stoop that low."

"Well, she has, hasn't she?" Earl said.

"I don't suppose this is Paige's handwriting, then?" Larry said.

"Not even close," Earl said. "Hers is very neat and slants forward."

Earl flopped back against the seat in the back. I leaned against the door. Margo turned around in the front seat to face Larry who sat with his head resting on his fist. We were all stumped.

"Is Marilyn Fleagle our woman?" Margo asked, as if it came as a great surprise.

"I don't think so," Larry said.

"What're you talking about?" Earl said. "If she's not, Paige is, and you have absolutely nothing to base that on."

"Think of this, though, Earl. If it was all fabricated — Mrs. Fleagle made up the whole thing, in other words — why the story about someone telling Paige that the girl had been at her apartment building? It's a story we can't substantiate, and it serves only one person: Paige. It makes it appear that the girl really has come around."

"I could see this Fleagle woman's purpose," Earl said. "She could have sent the 'neighbor' to talk to Paige this morning. Perhaps she just said she lived on the next floor. No one would have noticed a woman of such average description."

"It's a long shot," Larry said.

"It is not a long shot," Earl said. "It's the most likely possibility we have."

"All right, Earl, if you want to run with it this way," Larry said, "where do we go from here? How do we determine that it's Marilyn Fleagle who dreamed up this whole thing? What's her point? What's she trying to accomplish?"

"I don't know. That's what we need to find out. What would you suggest?"

"I would suggest that we not put all our eggs in Mrs. Fleagle's basket, and if you argue with me, Earl, you're going to regret it."

"How do you mean?"

"Simply that you are not functioning at full capacity, because you are in love with a woman who could be doing a number on us. I'm not saying she is, mind you. I'm just saying that if it were any other situation and any other case, you would not think twice about simply checking out the stories of *both* women."

"What's there to check out, Larry? Mrs. Fleagle says Paige gave her a note for the young girl, which raises more questions than it answers. It's not Paige's handwriting, she wouldn't be dumb enough to try it anyway, and besides, she has no teen daughter."

"Philip should go to Saint Paul and check her out," Larry said. "And soon. Who knows what this noon tomorrow threat is all about?"

Earl pressed his lips tight and shook his head in resignation. "I said you could handle this thing, Ship, so do whatever you feel is necessary. I suppose you know this is coming out of my pocket. I mean, just exactly who are we representing here?"

"Is money the problem, boss?"

"Of course not. I just think you're barking up the wrong tree."

"Don't worry, Earl," Larry said. "While Philip is in Minnesota, I'll be Marilyn Fleagle's beagle."

"Cute."

"For now," Larry said, "I've got to get Philip to the airport."

"Then I'm heading back to the office," Earl said. "Tell Paige I'll call her tonight and see her in the morning, OK?"

I arrived in St. Paul early that afternoon and started with the phone book. Sure enough, there was a P. Holiday listed at 314 Main Street. I headed to the University. Student records showed that Paige Greene had married a Holiday while a junior, but their records were incomplete after her first job as a nurses' aide in a suburban hospital.

My cab bills mounted as I traveled to the medical center. "Yes," I was told, "Paige Greene was an employee here, and a good one, until she went into teaching special education in the early nineteen seventies." I left for the school board office.

A gentleman in records there said he did not know any of the employees personally, but he did note that a district supervisor had, added a comment on Paige Greene Holiday's record. "Would you care to read it yourself?" he asked.

I turned the file folder to face me. "Mrs. Holiday has been an exemplary employee. Our loss is Maplewood's gain. Highest references."

"Maplewood?" I said.

The man reorganized the folder and stepped to the file cabinet. "It's a facility for severely retarded young people. We've lost more than a few teachers to Maplewood."

"But I thought the special education in the public schools had been phased out and reorganized under another state department."

"Pardon me?"

"Not so?"

"No, sir. There have been cutbacks in some areas, but special ed was not one. Of course, teachers can make more money and can often rise faster to higher levels of responsibility when they choose to move to private centers, but no, there has been no phasing out of special ed in our school district."

"I'm sorry. Tell me again when Mrs. Holiday left the employ of the district."

The man didn't even have to check the file again. "At the end of the last term," he said. "Five months ago."

"Maplewood Center for the Mentally Retarded," I told the cabbie, and I began digging through Paige's personnel file once more.

There was no record of Maplewood. She had simply left it out. Either it was a short-term job, or she never really took it. Her records showed that she put her affairs in order, rented her apartment, and packed to move. By the time we pulled into the grounds, the administrator, Mr. Richards, was short of time. "We're closing," he said.

"Just a moment, please," I said. "It's important. I'm a friend of Paige Holiday's, and I just wanted to double-check on her work record here."

The man was taken aback. "How do I know you're a friend of hers?" he said.

"Um, well, what do you want to know? I'll tell you to prove it."

"Where did she work before she came here?" he said, sounding as I had sounded all afternoon.

"School District number seven-oh-nine in special ed," I said.

"And what is her husband's name?"

"I, uh, don't know that, sir, except I know that he died some time back."

"I'm sorry?" Mr. Richards said.

"You didn't know that?"

"Who's asking whom the question here, young man?" he said. "This is highly unusual."

"I know it is, but someone is trying to set up Mrs. Holiday or scare her or something, and I'm a private investigator from Chicago trying to help her."

"Do you have any identification?"

"Sure." I showed him my card.

"You're not a very good special agent for the EH Detective Agency, are you, Mr. Spence?" he said, reading carefully.

"Sir?"

"I say you are not a very good one, are you?"

"That may be, sir, but I don't follow."

"I mean you know very little about the woman you claim to represent. You did say you are representing her, did you not?"

"I'm not sure I said it, but yes, in this instance I am representing her, yes, sir."

"And you say her husband passed away some time ago."

"Not real long ago, as I understand it." I felt stupid. He had somehow put me on the defensive, and I couldn't stay with him.

"Tell me more about Mrs. Holiday," he said. "Convince me that you know her personally."

"I thought you were short of time, sir."

"I've got plenty of time for this. Go on."

"Well, she lives in Chicago and works in a rehabilitation center for autistic children. She worked as a nurses' aide before she taught special ed in the schools here. She went to the University of Minnesota."

"Very interesting."

"But not true?" I said, sheepish for some reason.

"Mostly true. Tell me, Spence, what does she look like?"

I didn't know what in the world Richards was driving at. It wouldn't have surprised me if he had said the woman was his own wife and then produced her from under his desk. He really seemed to enjoy sporting with me.

"Well, ah, she's about forty, and — "

"You know she's forty from her records. What does she look like?"

"Right. She's average height. Built sort of cuddly — " I knew when I said it that he would raise his eyebrows. He did. "Um, she's got pretty dark hair and bright eyes, a beautiful smile."

"Was that pretty hair that's dark or hair that is pretty dark?"

"Honestly, Mr. Richards, must we play this game? Do I have the wrong place or the wrong woman, or are you not really the director here, or what?"

The hint of a smile left his face. "I thought you had been putting *me* on," he said. "Now you say *I've* been playing games. I'll tell you this, I don't consider terribly funny your coming in here and asking a lot of questions about a short-term employee."

"I hadn't intended them to be funny."

"I don't consider it even appropriate."

"I'm sorry. I'm puzzled again."

"The woman's husband is not dead, Mr. Spence. And I guarantee you she is not living in Chicago or working anywhere. She's buried less than a mile from here."

FOURTEEN

I must have turned white. I couldn't speak. "Obviously someone is playing a very dirty trick on you, Mr. Spence. How can I help you?"

I was nearly choked up. All I could think of were the ramifications. Was it possible that everything Paige had said was a lie? Why would she want to pose as someone else, and a dead woman at that?

"I think I'd like to talk to her husband," I said. "Would that be possible?"

"I don't know. I'll call him. Would you care to wait in the outer office?"

"Sure. Is there a phone I can use to call my office collect?"

Bonnie answered. She could tell I was shaken. "What's the matter, Philip?"

"I need to talk to Earl right away."

"He just left and took his infrared camera with him."

"Is anyone else around?"

"No, they're all at the rehab center, I think. I was about to leave for home myself. What can I do for you, Philip?"

"Just have someone meet me at O'Hare just after midnight. If I can't make the late flight out of here, I'll get a message to you somehow. Otherwise, be sure someone is there."

Mr. Paul Holiday, located at 314 Main Street, was not excited about my visit, but he was cordial. I asked him to tell me about his wife.

"There's not much to tell. We never had any children, except one that died at birth many years ago. Paige loved children and liked helping people, so she always worked at jobs that served others. I make a good living as a construction engineer, but we really thought our ship had come in when she was offered the job at Maplewood. It was close to home and meant a tremendous increase in salary. I think she always would rather have had children, but short of that, she was fulfilled by helping people and being successful in her career."

"Do you mind my asking how she passed away?"

"She was killed in a car accident."

"I'm sorry."

"I am, too. It really hasn't been that long, you know."

"Mr. Holiday, do you know any *other* Paige Holidays?"

"Nope, not any more."

"Any more?"

"My younger sister's name was Paige. For the first couple of years of our marriage that really caused a lot of confusion. My wife had been Paige Greene and married me to become Paige Holiday, giving us two in the family. Strange, huh?"

I heard myself saying, "Yeah, I'd say that's strange," but I don't know how I got it out. "Your, uh, sister, she didn't, ah, happen to marry a guy by the name of Datilo, did she?"

I caught Mr. Holiday in the middle of lighting his cigarette. He stopped and the match burned close to his finger before he shook it out, squinting at me all the while. "Nicholas Datilo," he said. "You got it. Nicky. A bum. He changed her."

"Sir?"

"I don't want to talk about it."

"Where is your sister now?"

"I don't know, and I don't want to know."

"Is she in trouble?"

"It sounds like you know, Mr. Spence. Why don't *you* tell *me?*"

"I just want to be sure I've got the right woman. I embarrassed myself earlier by thinking I was talking about your sister when I was talking about your wife."

"That *would* be embarrassing," Mr. Holiday said. "There's no comparison."

I hoped that by getting him to talk more about his wife, he'd tell me enough about his sister so I would know if we were locking horns with her or with someone using her name and his wife's history.

"No comparison, huh? They don't look at all alike?"

"Not really. I'd have to say my sister is the more striking. Paige, my wife, was never a raving beauty or anything. Pleasant enough looking, but she didn't have my sister's smile. Ah, I don't want to talk about it."

"Your sister's husband changed her?"

"She used to be a great girl. A long time ago, admittedly. But by the time she had her second child, he had changed her."

"Two kids?"

"A girl and a boy. Peggy's about sixteen by now, I'd say. Nobody knows where she is, either. She left about three years ago when little Ronnie died."

"The brother?"

"Yeah. There was a big investigation because my sister and her husband accused each other of having beaten him before he died."

I was in over my head. I could hardly comprehend all this. "So, when did her husband die?"

"Nicky? He didn't die. The kid, the three-year-old, Ronnie, he died."

"Your sister isn't a widow?"

"No. Divorced."

"Could I ask you something, Mr. Holiday? Do you think your sister beat your nephew to death?"

"Yes."

"Sure?"

"Yes."

"Why?"

"Because Peggy told me she saw it happen, and Peggy never lied."

"Were you close to Peggy?"

"Not close enough, I guess."

"Ever hear from her?"

"Now and then. We never know where from, really. The postmarks follow her around the country. She called me one night and asked if her mother had left town. I told her I would try to find out. When the phone had been disconnected and the mail returned unforwardable, I knew her mother was gone."

"You don't know where she is?"

"No. And like I say, I don't care to know, except that Peggy wants to find her."

"Do you know why?"

"I'm afraid to think why."

"Sir?"

"She once said she wanted to kill her, but she was waiting for her to get out of the Twin Cities so it wouldn't be so obvious."

"I need to get back to Chicago," I said. "I sure appreciate the time you've taken and how forthright you've been with me."

"Quite all right. Depressing, isn't it? You never did tell me why you wanted all this information."

"We may have found your sister in the Chicago area."

"Well, you can have her. I just hope you don't find my niece there, too."

FIFTEEN

Mr. Holiday rummaged around and came up with old photographs of both his sister, Paige Holiday Datilo, and his niece, Peggy. I assured him I would mail them back as soon as possible. It was eerie to stare into the beautiful smile of Earl's love and to know that she was not at all what he thought she was.

With the way this case had been going, I knew I should double-check her brother's story. Who knew what reason this man might have for discrediting his own sister?

The cab had been waiting, the meter clicking, and the cabbie reading the *Twin Cities Telegraph*. He looked up and smiled when I opened the door. "Any more stops, pal?"

"I've got a problem," I said. "I need to get to the office of the paper you're reading, and then I need to get to the airport for an eleven o'clock flight."

"Start the countdown, commander," he said, grinning in the rearview mirror and racing off.

We arrived at the newspaper office with only a few minutes to spare before their public information center closed. "Please let me check something on microfilm real quick," I begged the girl.

"Do you know exactly what you're looking for, or are you going to have to check through a bunch of films?"

"Just give me June, three years ago, and I'll be outa here in fifteen minutes."

She popped open a box and threaded the machine in seconds. Deftly whipping the crank, she rolled to the front page, June 1. "There you go," she said. "I want to leave here at ten after."

"You got it," I said, and I started cranking. When the June 9 pages rolled into view, the headline appeared in the lower left-hand corner of the third page:

MOTHER ACCUSED OF CHILD
MURDER STANDS TRIAL TODAY

The article told the story of the tragic death of three-year-old Ronnie Datilo and the finger-pointing by both parents. One paragraph reported the police opinion that the thirteen-year-old daughter might have been a witness, but that she had been scared out of testifying and was in seclusion.

I cranked through the folowing days' coverage of the trial and came upon a photo of an unsmiling Paige with a bandana covering her hair, her collar turned up, and her eyes hidden by sunglasses. She was acquitted because she had successfully turned enough attention onto her estranged husband. The opinion of many jurors was that he had committed the crime, but that "even if she did it, he should share the blame."

There was great public outcry, and Mrs. Datilo left for parts unknown. Her husband never stood trial, though the papers reported that the daughter was believed to be staying with him. According to Paul Holiday, Paige Datilo's brother, she didn't stay there long. She had been chasing her mother all over the country.

And now she had found her. I ran for the cab.

"You've got plenty of time now," the cabbie said. "You could get out of the Twin Cities by nine."

"That's what I want to do," I said.

I landed at O'Hare Field at a few minutes after ten and ran through the terminal to the rental car desk. I was huffing and puffing as I asked for whatever car was available and slapped my credit card on the counter. "O.J. Simpson you're not," the girl joked. I couldn't even smile.

On my way out to the car, I phoned Bonnie's home. "Tell whoever was going to pick me up that they don't have to now."

"I was going to pick you up," she said, "so this *is* good news. Did you turn up anything there?"

"I really don't have time to go into it, Bon. I'm sorry. I gotta go."

"I understand, Philip. Are you aware that the girl showed up again?"

I had nearly hung up the phone. "What?"

"Peggy Datilo showed up at the rehab center asking for Paige after hours. Mrs. Fleagle was not in, but the receptionist phoned her at home and let Peggy talk to her. Peggy told Mrs. Fleagle where Paige was to meet her tonight."

"Tonight? Peggy's meeting Paige tonight?"

"That's what she wants."

"Do you know where they're supposed to meet?"

"No, but Larry and Earl and Margo do. They're on their way to Paige's apartment now."

"If you hear from anyone, Bonnie, tell 'em I'm on my way there too. And tell 'em not to do anything until I get there, including allowing Paige to meet with Peggy."

I was lucky to avoid a speeding ticket on my way to Paige's apartment building near the rehab center. I pulled into the parking lot where Margo, Larry, and Earl were just getting into Larry's car. I flashed my lights and wheeled close to them before realizing that they would not recognize the car. I saw Earl reach inside his coat just in case.

"It's me," I said, rolling down the window.

"Let's talk in my car," Shipman said, and we all climbed in.

"Bonnie told me that Peggy is demanding a meeting," I said.

"That's not all," Larry said, "Mrs. Fleagle claims she told Paige that Peggy wanted to meet her in the unlit northwest corner of the municipal park in Mount Prospect about an hour from now, and warned her not to bring anyone with her. Earl called Paige to see what she was going to do, and she claimed that Mrs. Fleagle had never told her any such thing and that she wouldn't sit still for any meeting anyway, especially with some crazy girl claiming to be her long lost daughter."

"I think we've got Mrs. Fleagle dead to rights," Earl said. "But I still don't know what she's trying to pull."

"But the girl exists," Larry said. "The receptionist told us she saw Peggy."

"She could have been saying what her boss told her to say," Earl said.

"No, she wasn't," Margo said. "That woman was not lying."

"You can't know that," Earl said.

"We can find out," I said, producing the old photograph of the girl. "Let's show this to the receptionist. I think I've found Peggy Datilo."

"What's *this* all about?" Earl said.

"I'm not sure yet," I said. "Let's check and see if the woman at the receptionist desk identifies her. Meanwhile, you can tell me what you're doing here."

Larry started the car. "Paige told Earl she wanted to be alone tonight and asked him not to come over," he said. "Margo got suspicious and wondered if maybe Mrs. Fleagle was telling the truth and really *had* told Paige about Peggy's demands. When Earl called Paige to double-check, there was no answer. We got no response at her door, and her car is gone."

"Do you think she'll try to meet Peggy?"

"If there *is* a Peggy," Earl said, still dubious.

Larry stopped near the front door of the rehab center, and we all trotted in. "That's her," the receptionist said, studying the picture. "She's older, but this is the girl."

"All right," Earl said. "The girl is for real. And maybe Mrs. Fleagle has been telling the truth all along. Philip, I've gotta know what you found out."

I told the story fast as Larry sped back to Paige's building. Earl stayed in the car with his head in his hands while the other three of us ran to the elevator.

"We really need to know where she is," Larry explained as he whacked loudly on the door. No answer. "Help me, Philip," he said, and we lowered our shoulders into the door.

It creaked and cracked, but it was heavy and wouldn't give. Larry motioned me out of the way and drove his foot into the right side, just under the knob. The door blew open, ripping the inside frame molding with it. We flipped the lights on. The apartment was empty. No clothes in the closets, no pictures on the walls, nothing but furniture and a little trash.

"Now," Margo said, "is she going to see Peggy, or has she simply left?"

"I don't know," Larry said, "but we can't take any chances after what Philip says she told her uncle."

We waited as long as we could for the elevator, then bounded down the stairs. Earl was not in Larry's car, and Earl's car was gone. "This is all we need," Margo said.

"It's time to go to Mount Prospect," Shipman said.

Larry turned off his lights as we neared the park and rolled to the curb about a block and a half away. "Is that Paige's car down there?" Margo asked.

"It's hard to tell," Larry said, "but if that other one is Earl's — and I think it is — he can see it more clearly. I don't know what he thinks he's going to do."

"Maybe shoot pictures with his infrared camera?" I guessed.

"No way," Margo said. "He left it right here on the floor." She pulled it up to show us.

"Let me see that," Larry said. "A few well-placed shots will at least prove Paige was here, in case she tries to deny it later."

"Why would she do that?"

"Who knows why she does anything?" Larry said. "I can't figure the woman. How does she maintain this incredible facade?"

"That's me too," Margo agreed. "It's hard to believe."

"I just thought of something, Larry," I said. "Are you carrying a gun?"

"You know I'm not licensed yet."

"I know. But are you carrying one anyway?"

"No, Earl finally made me give him all of mine so he wouldn't get in trouble if I got caught with one."

"Great."

"Why?"

"Because the only one of the four of us with a gun is Earl. And Peggy did — at one time at least — intend to kill her mother."

"Earl knows that, and I don't think he'll let Paige get out of her car if Peggy shows."

"But Earl is more concerned with his relationship with her than with this meeting," Margo said. "Isn't he going to want to know how she could have lied to him so much? Won't that be the first thing on his mind?"

"You may be right," Shipman said, tinkering with the camera and thinking. "Paige doesn't want to see him again, I think."

"How do you know?" I said.

"Because she's packed for the road. She probably figures a short meeting with Peggy will be easier than a confrontation with Earl. I think she's getting ready to totally stiff him. He'll never hear from her again."

"But Larry," Margo said, "there are a few things working against Paige right now, and Earl is the least of them. She doesn't know her daughter wants to kill her — "

"Don't be too sure about that," Larry interrupted. "She's not stupid. The girl has had a horrible life and was surely traumatized by what she saw. In fact, she was probably an abused child herself."

"OK, but still, I doubt Paige knows that Peggy has actually said she wanted to kill her mother. Anyway, regardless of what Paige feels or doesn't feel for Peggy, she *is* her daughter, and Paige has to be curious. I'm betting that Paige wants to get a look at her, even if she's afraid to actually talk to her."

"You don't think Paige is concerned with Earl now?" I asked.

"Not really," Margo said. "She has to know that what she's done to him can never be justified or reconciled. She's gonna just leave him in the dust. She may communicate shame or sorrow to him someday, somehow, but for now, she's leaving him behind."

Shipman appeared to have the camera figured out. "What do you think, Philip?" he said. "Is there anything to what Margo's saying?"

"She knows the female mind," I said. "In fact, she often knows the male mind, too. I wouldn't bet against her."

"So what's Earl going to do, Margo?" Larry asked.

"I already told you. He knows the story, knows Peggy is more than a figment of someone's imagination, and knows that Paige has been phony. He just wants to know how she could have done it. I say he'll be ignoring Peggy and concentrating on Paige."

"So why doesn't he approach Paige's car?"

"I don't know. Are we even sure those cars belong to who we think they do? And if they do, and we've got the right place, where's Peggy?"

"Right there," Larry said in a whisper, pointing down the street at a slim, young girl walking resolutely into the park. She passed under a street light and into the shadows where she stopped and leaned back against a huge tree.

And waited.

SIXTEEN

"Keep your eyes on Paige's car, Margo," Larry said. "She probably doesn't know how to get out without letting the inside light come on. If you see that light, let me know. Philip, you watch Earl's car, though you probably won't see anything, even if he gets out.

"I'm counting on your amateur psychology, Margo," Larry continued. "When Paige realizes she can't get a good look at her daughter from where she is, I say she'll venture out."

"And that's when Earl will make his move?" I said.

"Earl is going to be hard to figure tonight, Philip. If I were Earl, I would want to get to Paige before she gets to her daughter, knowing what we know. Maybe he's just here to see if she lied to him about coming, and once he's sure it's her, he'll leave."

"You think he'll leave when he sees Paige get out of her car?" Margo asked, incredulous.

"Right."

"Wrong," she said. "No way he's gonna drive off and leave her to her daughter, no matter what she's done to him."

"But he knows we're here to protect Paige," Ship countered.

"He also knows you're not carrying a gun," Margo said. "What're you gonna do, shoot it out with a camera?"

Larry shrugged.

"Here we sit," Margo said. "C'mon, we've got to do something."

"Let me think," Larry said. "But keep watching those cars. Do either of you have a long comb?"

"I do," Margo said, digging it out of her purse without taking her eyes off Paige's car. "What do you need it for?"

"You'll see." Larry opened his door a crack and pressed the comb against the button that keeps the light off when the door is closed. "If I can jam it in here right," he said, "we can all get out without worrying about the light coming on and giving us away."

"All of us?" Margo said. "What am I supposed to do?"

"I want us to beat everyone to the punch," Larry said. "Earl may be already out and in the park, but we just don't know. I think I can walk around the block and come in the park from behind where Peggy is. If I can pull it off, I'll be behind that big stone hearth over there about twenty feet to her left and behind her about ten feet. See it?"

Margo and I stole a peek from our car vigils. "Yeah," we said.

"Philip," Larry said slowly, "I have a real chore for you."

"You do, huh?"

"Are you up to it?"

"Depends."

"No, it doesn't depend. In many ways we have to be like the military. Either you're ready to do exactly as you're told, or your job is in jeopardy. You realize I'm in charge of this."

"Of course, Larry. I was only kidding."

"This isn't the time to kid. I want you to get to the other side of the tree Peggy is leaning against. You'll have to be quieter than you've ever been in your life, and you'd better take some kind of a weapon in case she's armed. Which she very well could be."

"How do I get there without her noticing?"

"You go the major part of the way with me, then veer off to the right behind the trees. It's important you get to her tree because you may have to keep her from harming Paige."

"I have no weapon."

"I have two substitutes in my glove compartment. Take your pick while I watch Earl's car."

I dug around in the glove box and came up with a folded wire hanger Shipman used when he locked himself out of his car, and a huge flashlight. "I'll take this," I said.

"Just make sure it doesn't go on," Shipman said. "It'll light up the whole place. Margo, I want you to walk down the other side of the street. There are no lights between here and Earl's car, so you won't be seen. If you happen to get there before he gets out, I want you to do whatever you have to do to keep him right where he is. He's going to be good for nothing here tonight, so if there's a way to keep him in that car or at least out of the park, do it. OK?"

"OK."

"What'll you be doing, Ship?"

"Taking pictures. Say, 'Cheese.' Let's go."

The three of us made it out of the car without incident, though Margo had to climb over the back of the front seat to get out Larry's jimmied door. "I would take your assignment, Philip," he explained before Margo left, "but I'm a lot bigger than you are, and I don't think I could get close to her without her hearing me."

I knew it was true, because I knew Ship was fearless and usually demanded the most dangerous assignment. He'd be close enough if there was trouble.

We could see Margo moving slowly up the far side of the street, a long block from Earl's car. "Don't walk on either heel or toe once we get into the park," Larry whispered. "You want your foot to hit flat, distributing the weight and deadening noise." He demonstrated in the gravel at the side of the road as we crossed the street to enter the far side of the park. It was as if he were walking in stocking feet on carpet.

"What if Paige drives off?" I asked.

"We watch to see what Earl does. If he goes after her, we go after him. Let Peggy fend for herself; she seems to have done all right up to now. I just want to be around for Earl's confrontation with Paige. I don't think he'd do anything rash, but I want to protect his pride, too. It would be sad if he made a fool of himself."

"He probably thinks he already has," I said.

We were about 150 feet from Larry's station. He put out a hand to stop me. "No more talk," he whispered. "I'll just signal you."

We crept up behind the hearth, running our fingers along the huge rocks and cement that made up its back side. Larry was just ahead of me and motioned that I should follow him. When he got to the edge of the far side he stopped and bent low, peeking around the corner. He grabbed my shirt and pulled my ear close to his mouth. "I have a perfect view of her," he whispered. "You go back around the other way and take your time getting to the tree. Silence is the priority, not speed. If anything happens before you get there, I'll handle it."

By the time I had sneaked around the other side of the stone hearth I could see Peggy's silhouette between me and a distant streetlight. I wasn't thirty feet from her, yet I was convinced she could hear my heart crashing against my ribs. I took a step, cracked a twig, and stopped dead. She hadn't heard. She didn't move. Neither did I.

I waited. When my breath came a little more evenly, I ventured forward again. I was trying to walk so quietly I could hardly keep my balance. I could barely see the metal of the flashlight in my left hand. *What in the world am I gonna do with this?* I wondered. I looked past Peggy to the street. I couldn't see either car, though I knew if either Earl or Paige got out without fixing the light button, I'd see.

By now, Margo had to be at Earl's car, and for that I was grateful. I was convinced she could keep him away long enough for us to find out if Peggy was really going to try anything.

When I was twenty feet behind Peggy, any possible view of me was hidden by the tree she leaned against. I stopped to catch my breath and relax a little. The stretch where she could have spotted me had seemed like a hundred miles, though it wasn't really more than forty feet. Now I had to get up behind her. She wouldn't see me unless she heard me and came around the tree to look, so I had to be slower and quieter than ever.

There were big trees between us, so if she did come, I could hide momentarily. Maybe it would give me time to either blind her with the flashlight or yell so Ship could help me, but we'd really have to get the drop on her to elude a weapon of any force. I couldn't imagine a sixteen- or seventeen-year-old girl carrying a gun, but this was no ordinary girl. Who knew where she had been living, or with whom, for the past three years? And what must it have taken for her to track down her mother, who was using her maiden name and her sister-in-law's history?

I was ten feet from the big tree. It was so immense that I couldn't see her. I knew she was still there because otherwise I would have heard her leave. My eyes had long since adjusted to the darkness, and I was amazed at what I could see in what had at first appeared pitch black. I would have to avoid a small branch on the ground, and I was glad the leaves in the area were still moist. There was no way I could have moved undetected through crisp dry leaves. As it was I felt like an elephant in baseball cleats trying to tiptoe through peanut brittle.

I had to open my mouth to keep from making too much noise breathing. It seemed as if I were gasping, my chest heaving. Surely she could hear me. But she didn't. Or at least there was no indication that she did.

Now there was nothing between me and the big tree. Nowhere to hide, nowhere to run. I had to make it and press myself up against it. By now I should have been in Larry's line of sight, and for some strange reason I wanted to appear brave and self-confident, should he be watching. I took a slow and, I hoped, quiet, deep breath, straightened up, and began moving, one torturous step at a time. The last three steps were excruciatingly slow and painful because the tension had caused cramps in my legs and even in my back.

I couldn't imagine that she didn't hear me, because I could hear her. Every time her weight shifted or she sighed, it was as if she were standing right next to me. Which, of course, except for several tons of tree trunk, she was. I laid my cheek up against the cool bark and smelled deep of the wood. I could see the shadowy outline of Larry's form crouching twenty feet back and ten feet over at the end of the hearth.

Somehow, his being there lent very little comfort. I was not five feet from a girl who might be intent on killing someone tonight, and if I got in her way I could be the victim. What could he do? I wondered if he was already taking pictures and what in the name of Sherlock Holmes he thought he was going to do with them.

I couldn't relax or slow my heart rate or breathing. Any sound or sensed movement from the other side made me flinch, and I was certain she knew I was there. I didn't dare peek around to see if anyone was coming because it would have brought me too close to her line of sight.

I watched Larry for several minutes, trying to take my mind off my predicament, anything to make the time move faster. Where was this going to lead? At one point I thought I saw him raise a fist and then duck back behind the hearth wall, as if to encourage me to hang in there.

Finally, I heard footsteps from in front of the tree. I wanted to look, but I knew I would be seen. I stayed still. The steps stopped about ten feet in front of Peggy. I heard Peggy move forward a foot or so, but neither person said anything for several seconds. Peggy spoke first.

"I'm glad you came, Mother. I wasn't sure you would."

"I've been here quite a while, actually," Paige said, still sounding sweet, though a little subdued. "I just wanted to watch you for a while from the street."

"I don't hate you anymore, you know," Peggy said.

"No, I didn't know."

"I might have killed you if I had found you six months ago. But I started living with a guy who slapped me around a lot, the way Daddy used to do to you. It made me crazy. It made me want to kill my guy and my dad, but it changed how I felt about you a little."

Paige did not respond. The girl sounded so calm, as if she had carefully planned what she was going to say. She waited and then spoke again. "I still hate what you do, passing yourself off as someone else, refusing to try to get in touch with me. I know you don't love me, but you can quit worrying that I'll come forward and tell what you used to do to me and what you did to Ronnie."

"I may never quit worrying about that, Peggy," Paige said. "You were always a rebel, always a conniver, always saying whatever you had to to get your own way. Why should

I trust you now? You know where I am; you know my alias. I don't remember loving you since you were a baby, so what do you want from me?"

I could hardly believe what I was hearing. There must have been a lot about this strange relationship that I didn't know. The daughter tries to make up with the murdering, abusing, and abused mother, yet the mother suspects her.

"I want nothing from you. I just wanted you to know that my search is over. I'm not forgiving you for anything, and I'm not even sure that keeping silent is the right thing to do, since you did kill Ronnie. Regardless of the pressures you were under, you didn't have to beat him. But you *were* under pressure, and now I know that. That's all I wanted you to know, and I'm satisfied to be through with you. You've been through with me for longer than I can remember."

"Why don't I trust you even now?" Paige whined, as if she really wanted to.

"I don't trust you either, Mother, so don't worry about it."

"I *am* worried about it. And I *don't* trust you. And that's why I must make sure you don't tell what you saw."

"I just told you not to worry about it."

"And I told you I didn't trust you."

Paige fumbled in her purse, and it dropped to the ground. Peggy spun around to my side of the tree, bumped into me, and screamed.

Seventeen

I flipped on the flashlight and twisted around to the other side just as Paige flew forward, a gun in her hand. I dropped in front of her and heard the shot as she tumbled over me, flashlight and gun flying in different directions.

I grabbed her around the waist and pinned her to the ground as Larry gathered up the gun and flashlight. Earl ran past at full tilt after Peggy, with Margo not far behind.

"I can't stop him!" Margo cried. "He thinks Peggy shot her mother!"

Larry took off after them, shouting and waving the flashlight. "When I arrived," he said later, "Peggy was on the ground, staring into Earl's revolver and pleading for her life."

Peggy was not held after she was questioned at the police station. Paige was booked on attempted murder but refused to talk to Earl or let him try to bail her out. He was exhausted.

The day had begun to get to me, too. I had been up early, thinking I was going to get to tell my friends and co-workers about my faith, and since then I had been in another state, had run around in a park, and nearly got my head blown off.

Margo sat close and put her arm around me. "Earl needs us," she said quietly. We sat in a spare interrogation room and asked Earl if he wanted to talk.

"I don't know," he said, his voice thick. "You know if she hadn't pulled this tonight, she could have been home free. Now she may never be free again."

There was nothing to say. On all of our minds was her performance over the past several days, living someone else's life with someone else's name, and winning our hearts. Especially Earl's.

"I don't know what I would have thought of her if she hadn't done this tonight," he said.

Shipman stared him full in the face.

"I think maybe I would have been able to forgive her, to see her side of it, to understand why she had to hide from herself and her past. But now. She had no compassion, no honesty. Hardly anything that came from her mouth has been truth ever since I've known her. I just wonder what she thought of me."

"Do you really want to know?" Ship asked.

"Probably not. Maybe she's trying to tell me right now. I did love her, there's no getting around it. She was, or seemed, a wonderful, loving person."

He was fighting tears. "We all need sleep," Margo said.

"I won't be sleeping tonight," he said, sounding old. "What do you make of this, Margo?"

"Pardon?"

"What do you make of the fact that I seem to get one break, one chance at love after all these years, and it not only goes up in smoke, but it nearly consumes me in the process."

"I don't know, Earl," she said. "I just know that we all love you and care about you, and we're feeling terrible for you."

He nodded without looking at her. Shipman stood and clapped Earl on the shoulder, letting his hand linger.

"What'd you get in the way of pictures tonight, Lar?" Earl said.

"Aw, nothing really."

"C'mon! I know you were shooting. What'd you get?"

"Well, I got several shots of Peggy waiting at the tree, and a few of Philip behind her. And, frankly, I think I got a shot of Paige and Philip just before she fell over him."

"In other words," Earl said sadly, "you have a picture of Paige trying to shoot her own daughter."

Shipman dropped his head and nodded. "You asked," he said.

"That's my camera, right?" Earl said.

"Yeah."

"And that was my film, too, right?"

"Yeah."

"May I have it, please?"

Larry handed it to him. Earl carefully took the camera from its case and popped the back off. He pulled the film from its cannister and dropped it into the waste basket. He rose wearily and pulled his coat on.

"Take a day off tomorrow, kids," he said. "I'm going to."

We trudged out to Larry's car and rode in silence to the street next to the park where Earl had left his car. "You gonna be all right, chief?" Larry asked as Earl got out.

"Yeah. I'll see you Wednesday. Philip, walk me to my car."

I got out quickly, puzzled. Earl didn't say anything.

"I want you to know that what Margo said goes for all of us, Earl. No matter how hot we might have gotten at you during the course of all this — "

"I know," he said. "Philip, I just don't know how to explain all this, and I don't want you to even pretend to try. But I do want you to talk to the staff Wednesday morning like you were going to today. Grief, it seems like a week ago.

"Anyway, take all the time you need. No restrictions. And I'm not telling you I'm about to buy any of it; in fact, I probably never will. But I think I know a little of how you felt when this Dahlberg boy died. If you've got something you want to say, I want you to say it."

He stuck out his hand. I couldn't remember when I had last shaken hands with Earl. I gripped it hard. "See you Wednesday morning," I said.

"Bright and early," he said.

"Bright and early."

ALLYSON

Philip is assigned the biggest investigation of his career. The beautiful Allyson is in search of her father's history, a history that seems to have vanished. The case takes Philip to Israel and jeopardizes his love for Margo.

ONE

I WAS SURPRISED WHEN ALLYSON SCHEEL ENTERED OUR SIDE OF THE BUILD-
ING, but I confess it wasn't the first time I had watched her return from lunch. And I
wasn't the only one. Even the two women in our office — my fiancée, Margo, and
Bonnie, our receptionist — had caught themselves staring more than once.

It wasn't anything strange. Allyson, whom we guessed to be about twenty-five, was
just one of those people who knew how to dress, how to carry herself, how to walk
purposefully yet without conceit. She looked like somebody. She *was* somebody. And
her long red hair and appropriately pink complexion didn't hurt, either.

Allyson and her mother, Mrs. Beatrice Scheel, owned the boutique on the first floor
of the building, so we were on enough of a nod and smile basis that I knew when and
where she usually lunched, and I just happened to be gazing out our second-floor window frequently at 12:30 P.M.

Margo wasn't jealous. I had tagged along once when she visited the Beatrice Boutique, and she had commented on Allyson's striking appearance. "I wouldn't even call it
sexy, would you, Philip? More dynamic, classy."

"Yeah," I had said, watching Allyson move from behind the counter to the little office
where her mother sat behind a desk. I got the impression that neither Allyson nor her
mother personally waited on new customers.

That little visit had taught Margo and me a few things about Beatrice Boutique, too.
Margo tried on a couple of dresses and then asked the salesgirl, "How much is this one?"

"Excuse me?" the girl had said.

"How much?"

The girl betrayed a flash of condescension and tried to hide her surprise. "You mean
you'd like to know the price?"

Undaunted, Margo said, "Yes, I'd like to know the price."

"One moment. I'll check."

By the time the girl returned with the news that the dress was about a hundred
dollars more than Margo had in mind, we had figured that a boutique without price
tags, where customers were expected to sign for what they wanted and pay whatever
total arose, was slightly out of our class.

Still, the young co-owner was fun to look at. And now here she came, entering our
side of the building.

I was peering down from close to the window — to see if maybe I was mistaken and
she was just heading to the drugstore or somewhere — when I heard her trotting up
the stairs. I wheeled around so it wouldn't be too obvious that I had been ogling her

every step. Our huge outer office and double glass doors were between her and me, and with Bonnie at lunch, I was supposed to be watching the phone and the door. I hurried out of my office just as she stopped at the top of the stairs to read our sign: "EH Detective Agency/Private Investigations."

It would have been classier, I know, to have let her decide if she was at the right place, but I had momentum, after all. I pushed the door open to ask if I could help her and almost knocked her back down the stairs.

As I gushed apologies, somehow blurting her name in the process, she smiled forgivingly. "How do you know my name?" she asked.

"Oh, well, you know, we're detectives and all, ha, ha."

She raised one eyebrow to indicate that her question still needed an answer.

"No, seriously, we, uh, I, uh, well, you know Earl, Earl Haymeyer, my boss, owns this building, and even though he has a firm that maintains it and collects the rent and everything, he's still the landlord, and he knows you, I mean, he knows, ya know, that your mother and you own the boutique here."

I sat in Bonnie's chair at the switchboard and gestured to a visitor's chair for Allyson.

"So Earl, your boss and my landlord, talks about me?" She appeared slightly amused.

"Oh, no, no, it's just that we see you around, ya know. We figure Earl knows the regulars, so we asked, or at least Ship asked. Larry Shipman — he's one of our men. Well, he's our only man 'sides Earl and me. We're a small shop here. Private investigations."

"So your sign says."

"Right."

"Right," she said.

Allyson looked expectantly at me, and I didn't know if she expected me to whip out a menu of what we charged for various kinds of cases or what. The phone bought me time. It was Margo calling from the deli down the street. "Yeah, Babe," I said, "mustard and mayo. The usual, the way we like 'em. Got somebody in the office. See ya soon. Bye."

Allyson had been glancing around the office while I talked to Margo, and I was able to compose myself somewhat. I don't know why I felt so guilty. There wasn't anything wrong with watching someone walk down the street, was there?

"So, Allyson," I said, "is there something I can do for you, or were you just checking out the rest of the building?"

"No, I did that a long time ago," she said. "Mother and I have been in this building for many years more than even your boss, as you probably know. We like what his ownership has meant to the place, and while I haven't been up here on the second floor for a couple of years, I'm not surprised to see that he runs a handsome office. But no, I'm here on business, I think."

"Well, he lives right here in the building, you know," I said. "Just down the hall. So he can kind of keep an eye on the agency that's supposed to be keeping an eye on it for him. I live here, too, just down from Earl."

Allyson nodded politely, and I wondered why I had said that. She couldn't have cared less. "I'm sorry," I said. "You're here on business?"

"I think."

"Right. How can I help you decide if you are or not?"

She smiled a huge smile that started slowly but was worth the wait. Her perfect teeth, full lips, and long, thin nose set off her wide-set green eyes and made her look as if she had been put together from a kit. She pressed her lips together to resume a serious demeanor. "Well, I have a problem, and I've debated for months whether I should seek help with it, pursue it myself, or just forget it. I've seen your sign downstairs but never worked up the nerve to come up here. This was hardly the day for it, being our biggest shopping day of the year, but I'm sort of impulsive and knew today was the day I would look you up."

I liked her already. She didn't appear the type who had to work up the courage to do anything, yet she admitted not only that but also that she was impulsive. I've never been the type who makes myself vulnerable with strangers, and the self-confidence that evidenced in her made her all the more attractive. I wanted to tell her that, but all that came out was, "The day after Thanksgiving is your biggest day of the year, huh?"

"Yeah. That's true with most places." She looked tolerant again.

"I'm sorry," I said. "I keep getting off your subject. Who'd you murder?"

Her bemused look returned, and I was suddenly apologizing again. "I know I shouldn't do that," I said. "Someday I'm going to say that to the wrong person and get an answer."

"I could get to like you, Mr. — ?"

"Spence," I said. "Call me Philip."

"My problem is nothing like murder," she said, smiling. "And nothing like yours."

"I do have a problem, don't I?" I said.

"If that's your opening line with every prospective client, you do for sure."

We laughed.

"Are you really a prospective client?" I asked, trying to get serious.

"I think so."

"There you go again. Thinking. Let *us* do the thinking. Are you, or not?"

"There are a lot of things I'll want to know first," she said. "And there are a few things I'll want to tell you about me and my problem to see if you're interested. But your lunch is on its way, and I don't know if you're, I mean, are you the one who — "

"It's all right, Allyson. And no, I'm not the one who would screen you. Earl does that. I would probably sit in on it since you talked to me first, but Earl's the one you'll need to officially start with. You'll like him, and he'll be able to tell you if we can help you or not. I gotta admit I'm curious, but I won't ask. You can save it for him."

"I wouldn't mind telling you, Philip," she said, "but why don't you just tell Mr. Haymeyer that I would like you to sit in on our meeting."

"OK."

"And when will that be?"

I rummaged around Bonnie's desk, trying to find a note with Earl's schedule on it, and Allyson jumped up to open the door for Margo, who was balancing a cardboard tray of food.

"Thank you," Margo said, breezing in, delivering the food, and taking off her hat and coat seemingly in one move. "You're Allyson from the boutique, right?"

"Right," Allyson said, looking directly into Margo's eyes, the way she had mine. "And you must be Babe."

"Babe?" Margo and I repeated in unison.

"Isn't that what you called her on the phone?"

"Oh, yeah — no, this is Margo, an investigator on our staff. That's just what I call her. Babe."

"Don't let me interrupt," Margo said. "I have work I can do if you're talking, and there's nothing hot here that will suffer from getting cold."

"No, no," Allyson said. "I have to run, but I will be back to see Mr. Haymeyer — when, Philip?"

I turned back to my rummaging at Bonnie's desk, but Margo saved me the trouble. "Two-thirty," she said, "Give him half an hour and drop in at three. If we find he can't see you then, Bonnie will call you at the boutique."

"I appreciate it, Margo. And Philip." And she was gone.

I can't say I wasn't disappointed that Margo had shown up before Allyson and I had really finished talking. And that made me feel guilty.

"So you finally get to meet your dream girl," Margo teased.

"You're my dream girl, you know that," I said, leaning to kiss her. She offered only her cheek and grunted her disbelief.

"And was there some reason you didn't tell her why you call me 'Babe'?"

"I guess I assumed it was obvious. Sorry."

"Uh-huh. And how long was she here?"

"I don't know. Why?"

"Long enough that you should have asked to take her coat?"

I smacked an open palm on my forehead and turned toward the food. "Yeah." I shook my head.

"What's her problem?" Margo asked.

"Problem?"

"Well, she wasn't up here just to see you, was she?"

I laughed. "No, unfortunately." Margo was not amused. "I don't know. She's gonna tell Earl this afternoon. Where is he, anyway?"

"He and Larry are on a domestic case in Chicago, not far from Larry's apartment."

"I thought Earl didn't take domestic squabbles."

"It's more than a squabble, and it's a relative of Larry's. Bonnie knows more about it than I do. Ask her. You gonna pray before you're finished with that sandwich?"

" 'Spose I should."

"If you don't want God to give you a tummyache," she said.

I tossed a pickle at her.

"Anyway, you're gonna be finished with your lunch before I take a bite."

"Sorry." I reached for her hand, and we prayed.

I was tossing my garbage, and Margo was still munching when Bonnie returned. Late fifties, motherly, and superefficient, she was the office glue. But right now, she was crying.

TWO

Margo hurried to Bonnie, helping with her coat and steadying her as she took off her boots. "What is it, Bon?" Margo said.

I turned my back to them and tried to look busy, but there was nowhere to escape except to the darkroom or Earl's office, and that would have looked phony.

"I lied to you, and I feel terrible," Bonnie blurted. "I'm not a lying person, you know that. It's not like me."

"Bonnie, sit down," Margo said. "Philip, will you catch the phone if it rings?" I sat at Bonnie's desk again, and Margo and Bonnie sat at mine.

"Now, what did you lie about? Whatever it was, I'm sure you had a good reason."

"I told you that domestic case Earl and Larry are working on concerned a relative of Larry's."

"Yes. And it doesn't?"

"No, it's my daughter!"

"Bonnie, it's all right. You don't have to be ashamed. We're with you. Do you want to talk about it?"

"I guess. It's hard living alone and seeing your daughter's marriage failing and not having anyone to talk to about it."

"You know you can talk to us."

"Thanks, Margo. Well, it's Linda."

"Linda? The one we visited in Milwaukee last year?"

"Right."

"I would have thought — I mean — "

"I know — it's all right. I would have thought if one of my daughters was going to have trouble at home, it would be Tracy. She always was a pistol. But you know, she and Lew are happy as larks. 'Course, there are no little ones yet."

"Yeah. And Linda has the daughter, um — "

"Erin. She's thirteen now."

"Right. So, are things bad? Linda and Greg seemed so happy when we saw them."

"Well, you know Greg was never really thrilled with his job in Milwaukee, but Linda only reluctantly went along with the move back to Chicago. They were coming to a higher cost of living area for a sales job with lots of potential but less salary and commission to start."

"It was a risk."

"Yes, and one Greg was willing to take for the sake of his family. At least that's what I counseled Linda. No doubt I was being selfish. I had always dreamed of having Erin close enough to visit whenever I wanted. I don't even mind her staying with me when they're gone, but they aren't gone much — together anyway."

Bonnie turned away from Margo and stared out the window. She pressed a tissue to her face and broke down again.

"Job pressures are always tough on a marriage, aren't they?" Margo tried.

"That's just it," Bonnie said. "It has nothing to do with the job itself. Linda was suspicious from the beginning about Greg's big sacrifice for the sake of her and Erin, and I guess she was right all along. I don't mind being wrong; I have no illusions about my judgment, but I kept telling Linda that Greg was doing it for her."

"And he wasn't?" Margo was trying to lead Bonnie without prying. I felt for her. It was a delicate spot. Bonnie obviously wanted to talk about it, but Margo didn't want to appear too eager.

"No, he sure wasn't," Bonnie said with a heavy sigh. "Maybe I should wait and see what Larry and Earl find before I start jumping to conclusions the way Linda has."

"What are Linda's conclusions?"

"Oh, she thinks Greg moved back to Chicago for an old girl friend."

"Oh, no."

"I'm afraid so. Her name is Carla. Greg was engaged to her when he was in college. Linda had met her once but had never worried about her until now."

"What makes her think Greg's seeing the girl now, after all these years?"

"She's only the boss's secretary in Greg's office."

"You're kidding. And Greg didn't know that when he took the job?"

"That's what he claims, but how could he not have known? He came to Chicago three different times about this job, and he was in the office every time. He had lunches and dinners with the sales staff and the big boss. You can't tell me he didn't know."

"But that's what he claims?"

"That's right. Linda says he hit her with it a few days after they had moved. He comes home from work and says, 'Guess who works in our office?' Some surprise, huh?

"Linda was steamed about it for a few days but kept telling me that even though she figured Greg knew Carla worked there, he had kept it from her just to protect her."

"But she's not giving him the benefit of the doubt anymore?"

"Hardly. Now she's convinced not only that Greg moved back to Chicago because Carla works here, but also that Carla recommended him and greased the wheels."

"Carla's not married?"

"She was once. No more — no kids — " She sighed. "A real number."

"Even if Greg did come because Carla was here, does that necessarily mean he has to be seeing her?"

"Not necessarily, but Linda is convinced he is. He's withdrawn, moody, irritable. He's gone a lot, blaming it on the work schedule. He's caught on that he should never mention Carla's name at home, so he doesn't. Not ever. That makes Linda even more suspicious. She tried to challenge him on it, accusing him of moving his family to Chicago for another woman, and he wouldn't deny it. He just blew up, told her she was crazy and if that's what she thought she ought to act on it."

"What did he mean by that?"

"That she should leave him, file for divorce, or something. I don't know. I've said enough."

"I can see why you're upset, Bonnie," Margo said. "Far be it from me to advise you, but I agree that you should be careful about judging Greg until you hear from Earl. You never really know what's going on."

"I know. And I will. It's just that I'm tired of trying to explain away his actions to Linda when she knows him so much better than I do. They've been married nearly fifteen years. They've had their problems, but this is a new one for me."

"How long has this been going on?"

"About six months."

"I'm amazed. You've known about it all this time?"

"Just about."

"You haven't let it affect your work."

Bonnie sat up straight, then rose. She dabbed her eyes and moved toward her desk. I smiled at her as I left her chair. "I would never let it affect my work, Margo," she said, sounding almost offended. "I take almost as much pride in my work as in anything else in my life."

"We know," Margo said, and I nodded. "And it shows."

Bonnie smiled gratefully and began to arrange her papers. I raised my eyebrows at Margo as I passed her on the way to my desk. I had just sat down when Earl arrived, reached for his messages, and nodded to everyone as he hustled back to his office. Usually there's a tendency for everyone in the office to line up at his door, waiting for an audience, but Margo and I figured Bonnie had the most pressing need for him. We were both a little surprised when she didn't follow him.

"I wish he wouldn't do that," she said. "Walk right past me with hardly any acknowledgment, especially when he knows I'm living and dying for some word."

Earl poked his head out.

"These two know what's going on?" he asked. He has a nose for knowing what people have been talking about. Of course, with Bonnie's red eyes, it didn't tax his investigative powers.

"Yeah," Bonnie said.

"Just as well," he said. "Hard to keep secrets around here. No need anyway, I guess."

"Right," Bonnie said.

"Well, there's not much to tell, Bon. Larry's gonna stay on it tonight as late as he has to. He and I saw very little today. Greg went out to lunch with the boss and Carla and a couple of other people. There were five of them, two women. Nothing inappropriate that we could see. I'll say this, though, if I were Greg's wife, I wouldn't want him going out to lunch with Carla in a group of a hundred."

That didn't comfort Bonnie much, but still she thanked Earl. He and Larry were donating valuable agency time to a domestic problem, the very type of a case Earl never accepts. "Can't pay me enough to follow unfaithful spouses around to bars and hotels," he had said more than once. But as a freebie, and for the best secretary and receptionist he'd ever had: anything.

"Whose lousy handwriting is this, Philip?" Earl called from his office a few minutes later.

Bonnie and Margo enjoyed that, and I grimaced. Earl appeared in his doorway again with my Allyson Scheel note in his hand. "You just got licensed to carry a handgun, didn't you, Philip?"

"Yeah."

"We're gonna have to go out and get you a piece this afternoon, but if you shoot the way you scribble, I'm in as much trouble as you are. Now, who is this, and why does he or she want to see me at three P.M.?"

"Allyson Scheel. She's the — "

"The good-looker from the boutique, yeah?" Earl said, suddenly studying the note carefully. "What does she want?"

"I don't know. I didn't talk to her long. She just dropped in and said she had a problem and was thinking about talking to us about it."

"C'mon, Philip, you usually do better than that. I appreciate your letting her know that I handle the initial interviews — you did tell her that, didn't you? — but you usually give me a little to go on, something to look for, something to expect."

Margo cut in. "Excuse me, chief, but I think it's safe to say that your junior colleague was just a little intimidated by Miss Scheel and didn't handle the conversation in his usual professional style."

"Is that right, Philip?" Earl said with a grin. "I can't say I blame you." As he turned back to his desk he called over his shoulder, "Bonnie, please call Miss Scheel at the Beatrice Boutique downstairs and tell her I can't see her until four this afternoon. Philip, give me a few minutes, and then let's go shopping."

It was always sort of fun to watch, or at least hear, Earl at work. He could get more done in fifteen minutes with a dictating machine and the telephone than most people could accomplish in half a day. He sped through correspondence and details so he would have time to think, to ponder, to pore over files and notes on cases. "Thinking is the life's blood of our profession," he would remind us. "Don't get bogged down in clerical work."

Earl was a mover, always on the run. I listened closely for the end of his last phone call because when I heard the familiar squeak of the chair celebrating his leaving it, I reached for my coat. If I didn't he would wing past me and would be out the door, down the stairs, and in the car by the time I got started. And here he came.

I fell in behind him, pulling my coat on. I blew a kiss to Margo and waved to Bonnie. Earl backed out of his parking space as I was shutting the passenger side door. "So, how do you feel about this, kid?" he wanted to know.

"About getting a gun? I don't like it. You know that."

"You've always said that, Philip, and you've been with me nearly two years without any pressure to get one, but now that you've had your training and your orientation to shooting and everything, there's nothing standing in your way. Is there?"

"I've never needed a weapon. You've always told me this isn't like on TV where the guys are shooting out someone's tires between commercials."

"You're right, and you know I haven't fired my gun in the line of duty in twenty years."

"I know your rule of never drawing your gun unless you're prepared to shoot, and never shooting unless you're shooting to kill."

"It's a good basic rule, Philip, and I live by it. Whenever you can avoid shooting someone, whenever you can subdue him by any other means, that's what you want to do."

"So why am I buying a gun?"

"You're not. I'm buying it. But you're going to carry it, and it's going to be valuable to you, even if you never use it."

"It still makes me uncomfortable."

"It did me too, at first. Now I wouldn't feel comfortable in church without one."

"You don't go to church anyway."

"You know what I mean."

Earl parked in front of a sporting goods store, but suddenly wasn't in such a hurry. "Tell me," he said, "how are things between you and Margo?"

"OK, I guess."

"Really?"

"Yeah."

"Only OK?"

"Yeah."

"But OK?"

"Yes!"

"Then why hasn't she been wearing her engagement ring for the last three days?"

THREE

I was speechless.

"Are you tellin' me *you* haven't noticed?"

I shook my head.

"I don't mind telling you, Philip, I care about you two."

"I know," I managed.

"But you can't, you must not, let your love problems interfere with your work."

"They won't, Earl. You can depend on that, but I don't know what this is all about. I hope I'll find out she's got dishpan hands or isn't used to wearing it in cold weather or something. It's not like her to stop wearing it and just hope I'll notice."

"No, it doesn't sound like her. That's why I figured you knew."

"I hate to admit I hadn't noticed. I guess I just took it for granted."

"Well, hey, if you're not aware of any problems, it's probably nothing. Sorry I brought it up." Earl started to get out of the car but hesitated when he noticed I wasn't moving.

"I'm not saying I'm not aware that she's had second thoughts," I said. "We've done a lot of serious talking lately. She's not interested in anyone else, and she says it isn't that she doesn't still love me or anything like that. But she did want a cooling-off period."

"Well, that's it then," Earl said, uncomfortable in a counselor's role, especially on this topic.

"No, that's not it, Earl," I said. "I thought we had agreed not to have a cooling-off period yet. We've both been working on important cases, and we didn't want any emotional strain right now. I agreed to quit pressuring her for a wedding date, and she agreed to hold off on any moratorium on the relationship."

"Well, you'd better find out what's going on then, Philip. I don't need to know. I just want what's best for both of you, and I don't want to lose either of you, regardless what happens. Have you thought about how awkward it might be to work in the same office if your relationship changed?"

"Earl, Margo and I go back a long, long way, maybe not in terms of years, but we've been through a ton of trauma."

"I know that. Maybe that's why she needs a break. But have you thought about what I said?"

"No. It never crossed my mind. Sure I've thought about what it would be like in the office if we were in limbo for a while, but I never even considered the possibility that she would sever the relationship."

"And *you* would never sever it?"

"Of course not."

"Don't you think she opens the possibility of its ending when she proposes a moratorium?"

"I hope not."

"You're being naive. And I'm out of my field. Just know that I'm concerned, more for the two of you than just keeping our super team together, but that *is* important."

"I know. And thanks, Earl."

"Sure. Let's buy a gun."

It was hard to concentrate on the sales pitch from the clerk, but I was brought back to the present when he whispered that he could "work it out" if we didn't have licenses.

"We have licenses," Earl said, "because we are private investigators who care about the law, particularly handgun laws."

"Oh, certainly, yessir. I do too. I just meant that — "

"I know what you meant, partner," Earl said. "And if you want a quick sale, forget the rest of the pieces and show us a Colt snubnosed thirty-eight."

The clerk became quietly efficient then and pulled a handsome box out from under the counter. Even a passive type like me had to admit that it was a beautiful handgun, as handguns go. It was heavy in my hand as I had remembered from the practice range. "It's a powerful mass of metal, Philip," Earl said. "I've always been able to sense its potential violence just by holding it."

"I know what you mean," I said. It was cold, blueblack, threatening. "What do you want to hear, Earl? If this is what you want me to carry, I'll carry it."

"Do you want a belt, pocket, or shoulder holster?" the clerk asked. I looked to Earl.

"Carrying it on your belt or in your pocket, especially the way you feel about it, will make you constantly aware of it. It can get in the way when you sit and stand and get in and out of the car. With a shoulder holster, once you get the hang of slipping it on and off each day and get used to the feel of the straps, you'll wear the gun without thinking about it. It'll fit between your ribs and your stomach and will be out of sight."

"That's what I want," I said.

Earl pulled out his credit card and the papers showing that I was licensed to carry a concealed weapon, that it would be registered in the name of the EH Detective Agency, but that I would be the sole user. I was amazed that the total price, including ammunition, was more than two hundred dollars.

"It's the confidence," Earl said, carefully loading the pistol. "It evens the score. You have a last ditch form of extremely efficient protection should you ever need it. It makes alleys less dark, strange places less strange. It slows your pulse a few thumps during tense situations. You'll get used to having it, Philip."

"I hope so."

It was nearly three-thirty by the time we returned to the office. Bonnie told Earl that Miss Scheel would see him at four. "I forgot to tell you she wanted me in on that, Earl," I said, "if it's OK."

"Sure."

I found it difficult to look at Margo. She looked up from her work and smiled a greeting as I approached, but I didn't hide my emotions well. I leaned over her desk. "Would you tell me why you're not wearing your ring?" I whispered urgently.

"Yes, but not here, not now, Philip. Later, OK?"

"I don't know if it's OK or not," I said. "I know what we've been discussing, but no one here knows, I hope." I knew that sounded like an accusation, but I couldn't help it. She shook her head to assure me that she had discussed our business with no one.

"But they sure know when you don't wear your ring for a few days," I said.

"Did *you* notice?"

"No, frankly, I didn't. Earl asked me about it. Can you imagine how it made me feel? Margo, you have the right to do anything you want and make any decisions you want, but don't you feel you owe it to me to tip me off when you decide to quit wearing your ring? It looks like we've broken our engagement. Is that what you want?"

"I don't know."

"Well, it's obviously what you want it to look like."

"I'm *sorry*, Philip," she said, sounding more defensive than sorry. "I didn't intend it to look like anything. I've been going through some real doubts about myself and us, and I just didn't feel like wearing the ring the last few days. I was relieved when you didn't notice. I didn't want to hurt you, and I thought if the feeling passed or I came up with some answers, I would start wearing it again. Do you understand?"

"No, I don't. Not everyone in this office is as unobservant a detective as I am. Earl probably noticed the first day. He said this is the third day you haven't worn it."

"He's right," she said.

"I'm hurt."

"I'm *sorry*."

"I wonder."

"Now *I'm* hurt, Philip. Whatever other problems we have, I don't need you accusing me of lying."

"You're right," I said, stealing a glance to see if Bonnie could hear us. "It's just that you don't sound sorry, and not wearing your diamond without even discussing it with me is insensitive."

"We discussed my doubts, Philip."

"But you never mentioned not wearing the ring."

"I suggested a cooling-off period."

"But I thought we had decided to put that off!"

"A cooling-off period on the cooling-off period? Yes, I guess we did, but I just can't put my feelings in the deep freeze until our work schedule gets lighter. Who knows when that'll be? Philip, I think we need to take the time to discuss this and get it settled."

"A moratorium on our engagement doesn't sound like a settlement to me."

"That's because you don't want it."

"And you do?"

"Of course I do."

"Then you're right we'd better talk about it," I said. "How about tonight at dinner? Earl is concerned that we don't let our problems get in the way of our work."

"So you don't want me to say anything to anyone here about our problems, yet you discuss them with Earl?"

"He brought it up, Margo! He noticed you weren't wearing your ring."

"And he's more concerned with the work than with us?"

"You know better than that."

"Do I? You know, Philip, talking about splitting with you, even temporarily, is a scary thing. I'm nearly an orphan without you. If I have to worry that Earl is going to throw me — or us — out unless we get married — "

"I'll set you straight about how Earl feels about it tonight, OK? Where do you want to go?"

"Anywhere quiet. Don't spend a lot of money, especially when I'm feeling this way. You deserve better than that."

"I'm worried about you, Margo."

"So am I."

"Mostly I'm curious about why you were so offended that I didn't tell Allyson we were engaged when it's apparent you wish we weren't anyway."

"I don't know, Philip. I don't even understand myself. That's one of the reasons I want a break, not an end. It would be unfair to both of us for me to dump you when I'm not sure of my own feelings. That's the point."

"I'll pick you up at seven tonight," I said.

I made some final notes on a case I had finished investigating the day before and delivered the documents to Bonnie to be typed for Earl. Then I told him I thought I was free for another assignment, and we were chatting in his office when Bonnie buzzed him and announced Allyson Scheel.

"Maybe this will be your next case, Philip," he said. "Are you going to be up to it, regardless what happens with Margo over the next few days?"

"Sure," I said. But I wasn't sure.

Allyson looked exquisite as ever. I adjusted my chair so I could watch her when she talked. I had to remind myself not to keep staring when Earl was talking. She had to be used to people's watching her, though. I wondered if she had ever been through an ugly duckling stage. Someday I would ask her.

"You've met Mr. Spence," Earl said as he directed her to a chair.

"Philip," I reminded her.

"And I'm Earl Haymeyer. You can call me Earl, or Mr. Haymeyer, whatever you're most comfortable with. Anyway, what can we do for you? We're eager to help in whatever way we can, short of investigating domestic quarrels."

"Well, no, it's nothing like that," Allyson said, crossing her legs and interlocking her fingers. "Do you mind if I ask some questions about you and your agency first?"

"Not at all. Please."

"Since it's a small firm, could you tell me about the backgrounds of your people?"

"It's pretty simple," Earl began. "I've been in detective work for about twenty years, first as a local police officer, then as a special investigator for the US attorney's office. I started this agency a couple of years ago with Philip, who was a commercial free-lance artist before that and whom I trained from scratch. He has also had a professional training course since joining us, as has Margo Franklin, who also started without experience. She is studying criminology in night school.

"Larry Shipman was a free-lance communications expert in radio, television, and print journalism, and had worked often with our office as an undercover agent when I was with the US attorney. Despite the limited backgrounds of these three, each has distinguished himself over the past two years, and I'm proud of how each has progressed. I would trust any one of them with just about any case."

"Even mine?"

"I haven't even heard it yet, but yes, even yours."

FOUR

"I start every investigation with the proper paperwork," Earl explained, pulling from his desk drawer a manila folder and a pad of forms entitled EH Detective Agency Client Registration. From another drawer he produced a black felt marker and printed A. SCHEEL in neat block letters on the folder.

"I'm going to ask you a few questions," he said. "You may refuse to answer any that you wish, but I want to make clear that every answer is helpful to us and that we pledge one hundred percent confidentiality. I also want you to know that if in the course of our investigation we find that anything you tell us here has been intentionally misleading, we drop the case."

Allyson nodded but appeared uneasy. "I have no reason to lie to you, Mr. Haymeyer," she said.

"I'm sure you don't. I just want you to know how important this preliminary questioning is. We base much of our work on the mundane facts we get from the client, and if those facts are wrong, it will cost us time and you money. And if they were intentionally wrong, we simply don't have time to mess with it. It's difficult enough to investigate a problem without having to investigate the client as well."

"I understand," Allyson said.

Earl placed his pad of forms over the manila folder and pulled a black, ball-point pen from his shirt pocket. "Full name please," he said.

Allyson glanced my way with a slight smile, almost as if she was beginning to enjoy this. I knew the feeling. "Allyson Abigail Scheel," she said.

"Date and place of birth?"

"August 31, 1954, Chicago."

"Home address?"

"Old Depot Towers, One Green Bay Court, Wilmette, Illinois."

"Occupation?"

"Co-owner, with my mother, of the Beatrice Boutique, Glencoe Road, Glencoe."

"Nature of the business and your role?"

"We sell designer fashions, mostly imported. I'm the buyer."

"Annual income?"

Allyson flinched.

"Let me tell you why I ask," Earl said. "There are people who can't afford us, and we either help them find assistance, or we are able to charge reduced rates in special instances."

"I understand. That won't be necessary. I assumed when I came up here that this would be expensive."

"Not terribly," Earl said. "We charge two hundred ninety per day for up to twenty-four hours when necessary."

"Do you still need to know my income?" Allyson said.

Earl nodded. "It would be helpful."

"It depends on the year," Allyson said. "For the last two years Mother and I have drawn sixty-five thousand dollars each from the business. This year we're planning to draw closer to seventy-five thousand each. I do appreciate your pledge of confidence about that." I was still shaking my head.

"The nature of your problem?" Earl continued.

"It's hard to explain, Mr. Haymeyer," Allyson said, settling more comfortably in her chair. "I suppose it won't be the type of investigation you're used to. There's no crime, no villain. At least I hope there's not. It's just that for as wonderful as my life is and has been, there are gaps in my history — centering on my father — and I want to put the pieces together."

"I'm not sure I follow," Earl said. "Is your father living?"

"Oh, yes."

"Are your parents still married?"

"No, they divorced when I was a baby."

"I want you to tell me this story, Allyson. Tell me anything you want and don't make me fish for information. If I need to know something, I'll ask. Otherwise, I want you to tell me just what your problem is and exactly how you feel we can help you."

"OK."

"Do you mind if I tape this, for our purposes only?"

"I guess not."

Earl leaned back in his chair and opened a cabinet behind him, revealing a huge reel-to-reel tape recorder. He flipped it on and shut the cabinet. "The microphone will pick you up. Just go ahead," he said.

"Well, my first memories of my father were of meeting him at the train station in

Wilmette. He was, and still is, a garment cutter in Chicago, and he still lives in the four-room flat on the West Side where he and my mother lived after they were married in 1952. Following their divorce in 1955, Mother and I moved to a small apartment in Wilmette and she worked as a dress design trainee in a small store in Kenilworth.

"She didn't talk much about my father, and I didn't ask much at first. All I know is that from as far back as I can remember, she and I would walk ten blocks to the train station the last Sunday of every other month and would meet Curtis Scheel as he stepped off the train. He always dressed the same. He still does. He wears black oxford shoes with thick rubber soles that must last eight or ten years. His suits are drab and dark, and he probably has never owned more than three at one time. They are hard to tell apart. The pants have cuffs, the coats are singlebreasted and always buttoned, and he always wears sweater vests over white shirts and a plain dark tie.

"As a child I thought him strange. He spoke with a thick accent that I learned was German. He always wore a hat, even in the summer, and he always carried himself formally, but not necessarily with dignity. There were no airs about him. In fact, he would not be noticed in any crowd. He was always neat and clean and closely shaved, and his hands were always immaculate. They still are. I tell you, Mr. Haymeyer, it's hard to separate what he was then from what he is now, because other than the loss of some of his hair and the graying of what's left, he appears the same."

Earl interrupted. "Do you mind if I stand as I listen?" he said. "I won't if it bothers you."

"Not at all," she said. "Am I getting anywhere?"

"I don't know. I'm not sure yet. But please continue."

"Well, anyway, I began to look forward to those visits. When I was tiny, two months between visits seemed so long that I couldn't put it into perspective. After he visited, I would badger my mother for days to tell me when he was coming again, but I didn't understand answers like 'in fifty days,' and things like that. By the time he returned, I would have almost given up hope of seeing him again."

"But you wanted to see him? These visits were enjoyable for you?"

"Oh, yes! I had not yet put together the idea that other kids had live-in fathers and I didn't. I'm not sure I even knew that a father was the male equivalent of a mother. A mother was the only person you knew from forever, and a father was a small, shy, formal man who hugged you tight and cried when he met you at the train station every other month.

"He would kiss me all over my face and hold me like he never wanted to let go, and then we would walk back to our apartment where my mother fixed dinner and I played on the floor with my father until it was time for my nap. When I woke up, we had a light meal, and then Mother and I walked him back to the train. There he would hug me and kiss me and cry again. Once I said, 'Bye-bye, Daddy,' and he firmly but kindly told me, 'I'm not your daddy. I'm your father. Call me Father.' I said, 'OK. Father. Come and see me again soon.' "

Earl had been standing with his arms crossed, staring intently down at Allyson. Now he walked slowly over to the window and thrust his hands deep into his pockets. He appeared depressed, but Allyson wouldn't have been able to tell. She stopped speaking when he moved to the window, but he gestured that she should continue. She turned in her chair to face him, but it must have been disconcerting to address his back. He was staring at the sunset, yet hardly seemed to notice it. I found Allyson's story a little sad too, but I wasn't hearing it through Earl's ears. He was a widower whose only son was autistic. Even a strained, on-again off-again relationship between parent and child was more than he had enjoyed with a son who had never recognized him.

"As I got older," Allyson said, "I was able to understand what my father and mother talked about during those every-other-month Sunday dinners. He asked once in a while to take me back to his place, but she refused. Their divorce had been amicable. They were not at all hostile to each other. She was cordial to him, but she made it clear that she would not let me visit him at his apartment until I was older, and that she didn't care to go there with me. 'Let's just keep it going this way,' she suggested. He was not a fighter. He never argued with her. Sometimes he would just beg to have me to himself. I wished for that, too, but my mother was protective and didn't want things to change.

"Which they didn't until I was in sixth grade. Every time my father had visited for the previous year or so, I had peppered him with questions about his past. I was developing a curiosity about this man, and I never got the answers I wanted and needed. My mother finally told me that the marriage had simply not worked out. Neither had been mean to the other. There had been no fights. It just didn't work out. I couldn't understand that. If you got along, you could stay married — that was my idea.

"And my schoolmates mostly had two parents at home. I was embarrassed that my parents were divorced, but I bragged about my father and made up stories about him to make him appear even more romantic to my friends. I told them that he brought me expensive gifts every month, when in truth he brought me trinkets. At Christmas I would get something nice, but I couldn't understand why my father was never at our family gatherings. My mother's family is Irish-American and have loud, happy celebrations. They don't like my father and don't invite him, but she told me — and he later confirmed this — that he doesn't care to come anyway. That was when I asked him why I had so many aunts and uncles and cousins and even two grandparents on my mother's side, and none on his side."

"They were all in Germany still?" Earl said, his back still to Allyson.

"No" she said. "He said he was an orphan and never knew his parents. He had virtually no relatives. It was so sad I could hardly take it in. Then I wanted to know everything about the orphanage where he grew up, but he said it was too painful and that he had shut out all the memories. I wanted to know how he had come to the United States, and he said he had just saved his money until he could get a ticket to sail here. He said he found New York too big and Chicago not much better, but he had no more money to keep moving, so he settled and found a job with the trade he had been taught in technical high school.

"I'll never forget the night when I was in junior high and I asked my mother to tell me everything she knew about my father. I couldn't stand those sketchy ending-the-discussion stories I had heard all my life. I loved my father, but I resented that he had no roots. I felt life had been unfair to him and thus to me. He had no family, and so I had no family on his side."

"And so did your mother tell you anything you hadn't picked up before?" Earl said, finally turning to face Allyson.

"Did she ever."

FIVE

It was dark outside. Bonnie knocked softly and opened Earl's door. "I'm heading home unless there's anything else, boss," she said, smiling and winking at Allyson.

"Thanks, Bonnie," Earl said. "I think we're all right. See you tomorrow."

"Margo's going home with me, Philip," Bonnie said. "She told me to tell you that if she didn't hear from you by five-thirty she'd take a rain check and not to worry about it."

"OK," I said quickly, hoping that Allyson wouldn't assume that Margo and I were going together. That made me feel despicable, but I was feeling sorry for myself because of Margo's attitude, and I found myself hoping I could keep my options open. I nearly shook my head, disgusted with myself.

Bonnie pulled the door shut behind her, and Earl asked if either of us was hungry. "I'm good until about eight o'clock," Allyson said.

"Me too," I said, wanting to have something in common with her.

"Feel up to continuing?" Earl said.

"Sure. Mother told me she had met my father while she was touring a garment factory as part of a class she was taking. The students weren't supposed to talk to the cutters and the others on the line, but she said Father looked so sad and shy and withdrawn that he was a challenge. She had been the spark plug of the class, the witty, funny, loud one, so when she had a question for the tour guide, she asked it and then insisted that Father answer it. He blushed and demurred, but before the tour guide could rescue him, Mother went right over to his table and said, 'C'mon now, we both know you're gonna be running this place someday. Tell me what happens when you feel a cloth shipment price is too high. Do you bargain, do you go elsewhere, or do you just refuse to buy until the price comes down?'

"The class was tittering and clapping, enjoying the show, and Father brought the house down when he said, just above a whisper, 'I don't have not'ing to do wit' cutting da prices. I cut only da cloth.' There was an uproar as Mother threw her arms around him and kissed him on the cheek. 'You're a good sport, man,' she said, and as she walked back to the group she said, loudly enough that he could hear, 'I wouldn't mind seeing him again sometime.' When the laughter died down, Father was heard to say, 'You know vere to reach me. Dis is vere I am everyday.'

"Mother told me that, to the astonishment of her friends, she went back to the factory two days later and waited for Father at the gate. He almost turned white before he turned crimson, but she was so drawn to him that she just took over, insisting upon showing him the town. She got more money from her father, who was putting her through school, than he earned as a garment cutter, so she even financed their first night out on the town. They went up to the top of the Prudential Building, they visited the lakefront, they walked up and down State Street, and they went to the movies.

"Mother says he was very quiet even that night, but it was obvious that he loved the attention. I don't know if you've seen my mother — " we both nodded " — then you know she's a very attractive woman. Here was a small, shy, immigrant laborer being dragged around the city by a beautiful Irish-American. She could have had any guy she wanted, and was asked out all the time, but she began to turn down everyone else. If she didn't hear from Curt often enough, she'd call him. He never became very conversant, but she had won his heart, and he had won hers. Her family couldn't believe the match and refused to consent to the marriage. They predicted divorce, which had not tainted the family name for generations, but my parents were married anyway, alone, before a justice of the peace."

"Is that why your mother never remarried?" Earl asked. "Family pressure?"

"Partly, I suppose. But she is a woman of such high moral standards, I think she feels she doesn't have the right to remarry as long as my father is alive. I know that sounds old-fashioned, but I think that's how she feels. Her family is Catholic, and she has never even dated, to my knowledge, since the divorce more than twenty-five years ago."

"Can I ask a question, Earl?" I said.

"Sure."

"What caused the divorce — the lack of things in common, the different cultural backgrounds, the big difference in personalities, what?"

"This is the strange part, Philip," Allyson said. "My mother finally told me that the reason she divorced my father was that she was as frustrated by being shut out of his former life as I was. She told me she couldn't penetrate that memory, she couldn't get past the obscure orphanage in Berlin, a city big enough to have dozens of orphanages. She heard no names of friends, relatives, or even acquaintances."

"But that's not enough to cause a divorce," Earl said. "Frustrating, yes. Something that would lead a spirited woman to despair, sure. But divorce?"

"There was more than that, Mr. Haymeyer," Allyson said. "It was not simply that my father had no family and no history. It was that he maintained this posture despite recurring nightmares that scared my mother to death. He would scream out in the darkness, clutching his pillow, pleading for his life, calling out in German she could hardly understand. He would not even wake himself up. He might rise and calm down, and go to the other room and sit for long periods, but he never admitted to remembering the bad dreams the next day.

"My mother says she badgered him, 'You mean to tell me you don't know that you woke the neighbors with your screams in the night?'

"And he would say, 'Nonsense.'

"She would ask him what certain German words meant, and he would cloud over and become sullen. She had a way of getting the definitions out of him, but she always regretted it. What he was saying in terror were things like, 'Wait! Don't! Please! Mama! Father! I'm sorry! Your blood is on my hands!'

"She begged him to tell her what it all meant. The closest he ever came to convincing her was when he said that if her accounts were true of his terror in the night, perhaps it was something common to orphans who never knew their parents.

"She didn't want to hurt him or falsely accuse him, but she suggested to him once the possibility that he had harmed his parents or even killed them and had been sent to an orphanage after that. He refused to discuss it, except to say that he had been told all his life that his parents had died when he was an infant. By murder, accident, illness, he didn't know.

"My mother finally got to the point, when she was pregnant with me and had been married for two-and-a-half years, that she couldn't take it anymore. There was too much hidden in the man, too many dark secrets, too much pain and sorrow and despair. She was depressed. She loved him, yet she couldn't bring him out. Then she wondered if she really wanted to. She was afraid of what she might find beneath the surface of his personality. She begged him to see a psychiatrist, but he would have nothing to do with it. Sometimes he would sit for an hour, staring into space and crying softly, hardly aware he was doing it. Occasionally my mother would joke with him, tousle his hair, treat him the way she had when they were courting. Then he would smile faintly and tell her that he loved her and couldn't live without her and would do anything for her. He told her she was the only flower in his life, yet he refused to seek help or to even tell her what was wrong.

" 'Do you deny that you are a man with deep pain?' she would demand.

" 'I cannot deny that,' he would say.

" 'Do you not want to be healed of this hurt?'

" 'Nothing can heal the pain of the soul,' he would say, 'especially when I don't know where the pain comes from. Perhaps it is common to orphans.'

"She had heard enough. She told him she wanted to hear no more of his past unless he told her the truth. She accused him of having his name changed when he came to the United States. No one in Germany spells Kurt with a 'C,' she would remind him. He said it was common for immigrants to Americanize their names.

"Finally my mother told him that she could not go on. She extended an unending offer to come back to him, to help him, to do anything he wanted her to do, and even to love him again if he would but be truthful with himself and seek help. She began sleeping in the other room, and after I was born, she never slept with him again. When one of his nightmares woke me one night, she asked him one last time to let her help him. When he refused, we moved out. Six months later her divorce was granted. She and my father worked out the visitation program, no alimony was involved, and that was that.

"I was raised by my mother, my father visited when she allowed, and he begged to have me visit him rather than his always visiting us. When I was a freshman in high school, she finally relented. He had visited like clockwork for years, and now she was going to let me take the train to the Chicago and North Western Station downtown, where he would meet me. It was no small sacrifice on her part. She worried herself sick over me. It was the fall of 1968, and there had been race riots in Chicago. She would not let me stay overnight at his place, and I didn't want to, anyway, fearing I would hear him cry out in the night."

"What kinds of visits were those?" Earl asked. "What did he have in common with you, and what did you talk about?"

"They were formal and uncomfortable. I loved him, and I knew he loved me deeply, but since my mother had told me the stories, I was wary of him, almost afraid of him. He would ask me about school and my plans for the future. By then my mother was assistant manager of a store and was making decent money. She talked of buying her own store someday and training me to be her partner and buyer. There was nothing I wanted more. 'That's good, that's good,' Father would say, every time I told him about the plans.

"That's when I told him that Mother thought it would be good if I spent my last two years of high school overseas to learn fashion design and the whole business. My father fell silent and then gravely asked me if he could tell me a secret. I began to tremble. Was he going to tell me something he had not even told my mother when she had been his wife for nearly three years?

" 'Yes,' I whispered, frightened. 'I will keep your secret.' And I have kept it, Mr. Haymeyer. I have not even told my mother, who probably deserves to hear it. I have told no one in the world. Until now."

SIX

Earl had been leaning against his bookcase for a long time, and he moved back to his desk and sat on its edge, dangling one leg over the side. He was a couple of feet from Allyson, whose face was taut. Her body appeared relaxed, except for her fingers, which were interlocked again, knuckles white. I felt an urge to put my arm around her, to comfort her, to encourage her to keep talking. She seemed so vulnerable.

I knew what was going through Earl's mind, because I'd heard him say it before after hearing someone's story: "It was impressive, but I don't see how we can help." I hoped he wouldn't say that this time, because I wanted to help. I didn't even know what Allyson wanted, but whatever it was, I wanted to be in on it.

"My father pointed into his bedroom, and I stood in the doorway as he shuffled in and knelt by his bed, pulling a shoebox from beneath it. He brought it out and we sat on his heavy old couch. He opened the box and then quickly closed it again, rose, and went back to his bedroom. He returned with another shoebox, opened it, and showed me various amounts of cash in small bills, a brochure from a travel agency, and a savings account book.

" 'I'm going to take a leave of absence one of these days and return to my homeland for several weeks,' he announced, his accent still thick after all those years in the States. He had less than a hundred and fifty dollars in his savings account, and the cash still left him short of two hundred dollars. 'It will take me another few years,' he said, more excited than I had seen him in ages, 'but I will get there.'

" 'What will you do there, Father?' I asked him. 'If you have no family, what is there for you?'

" 'You don't understand,' he said. 'We are talking about my homeland. My homeland. When you have no family and no wife, your homeland is your family.' He began to cry, and I embraced him, which had the opposite effect than I intended. He held me close and cried out in great wrenching sobs, 'Allyson Abigail, you are the only flesh and blood I have left who loves me. There is no one else! Don't leave this country for schooling overseas unless you go when I go.'

" 'But, Father,' I said, 'Mother is sending me in just a couple of years. Will you be ready to go by then?'

"He shook his head sadly, turned away from me, and said, 'No.' I spent my two years overseas, and he never really forgave me for it. Oh, he was thrilled when I returned, but there was a sad distance between us that had never existed before."

"And did he ever get back to Germany?" Earl asked.

"No, but he hasn't given up. That's the reason I'm here. He told me recently that after all the years he's served his company, he has been able to combine three weeks of vacation and a brief leave of absence with no fear of losing seniority, and he will be leaving in two weeks for his homeland."

Allyson acted as if she had finished her story, catching Earl and me by surprise. "Why did he want this kept from your mother?" Earl said.

"I'm not sure. I think he feared that she would see hope in his visit, perhaps want to go with him and trace his family history, see the orphanage, or whatever."

"Why does he fear that?"

"I don't know. I honestly believe that after all these years, my mother still loves him and would be happy to be his wife again if he would get these haunting threads from his past tied together."

"Are you serious?" Earl asked, incredulous. "That's a long time."

"Absolutely," Allyson said. "She's never said anything like that, and she's never acted affectionately toward him in my presence, but by the same token, she has never once run him down. I think she merely pities him and remains frustrated by his refusal to seek help. She feels she did all she could before she gave up. There's certainly no one else in her life."

Earl pushed in his desk chair and offered Allyson her coat. "Let's all go get something to eat, and then you tell us how we can help. If one of us trails your father overseas, our daily price is increased by fifty percent. I'm sorry to talk business after that story of yours, but I wanted you to be aware of it."

On the way down to Earl's car, he continued, "One thing I'm puzzled about is why you need someone other than yourself to follow him. He'd probably be thrilled to have you go along."

"That's just it," Allyson said. "There's more to the story. He's not going to Germany."

"Where *is* he going?" I said.

I opened the front passenger door for Allyson and then got in the back on the same side. I slid all the way over behind Earl so I had a better angle from which to talk to — OK, to see — Allyson, and I noticed Earl's amused look in the rearview mirror. He knew exactly what I was up to.

"I'm not sure where Father is going," Allyson said. "But it's not Germany. He's not booked on any flights out of O'Hare to Germany. He's booked on one to Kennedy Airport in New York, but nothing to Germany from there."

"So, you're a little detective yourself, huh?" I said with admiration.

"Oh, it didn't take much to track that down. I just want to know where he's going."

"Really?" I said. "Is that all? You don't want us to follow him?"

"Depends on where he's going," she said.

Earl pulled into the restaurant parking lot and turned off the engine. He turned sideways in his seat and faced Allyson. "Something's still sticking in my craw," he said. "A person who is inquisitive by nature, like you are, and a person who cares so much about her father and his history, like you do, is not going to let that first shoebox go. Didn't you wonder about it? Didn't you think maybe there was something in there he didn't want you to see? I don't get it, Allyson. Why didn't you go after that box one day when the situation was right?"

"I did," she said, opening her door. "Aren't I a good girl? I'll tell you all about it."

Earl and I waited in the lobby for a table while Allyson excused herself for a few minutes. "What do you think?" I said.

"I dunno," he said, as if he wished he really did know. "She's got a real mystery here, and I need to take the time to think it through, listen to the tape again, see what it's all about."

"But are you interested in following her father to Germany or wherever just to find out why she doesn't have any relatives?"

"No, there's got to be more to it than that. I mean the undying curiosity of the orphan or the daughter of the orphan is just not enough to spur Allyson into investing in our services. She could find out that stuff herself, and I'm a little surprised she hasn't been to Germany already to do just that. I'm guessing that she or her mother, or both, already have a hypothesis she wants to try out on us. If she thinks her father is someone or has done something bad and she wants us to check that out, then, yes, I'd be interested in following him wherever he goes. In the US, that is."

"What do you mean, 'in the US?' Are you saying you wouldn't fulfill the wishes of a client willing to pay for international work?"

"Of course not. I'm just saying that *I* would follow him in the States. If he leaves this country he's yours."

"You're kidding."

"Would I kid you?"

"Yeah."

"But not this time. You want a good case, a little travel, an important assignment? This could be it, but don't start banking on it. If all she has is what she's told us already, I'll be declining the case. I can't afford to be chasing ambiguous puzzles where the clients give you nothing to go on and you're not even sure what they want you to find."

The hostess approached. "A table for three is ready for you, Mr. Haymeyer."

Earl looked quickly for Allyson. "I'll watch for her," I said. "I need to call Margo at Bonnie's anyway. We'll find you."

Bonnie answered just as Allyson came out of the women's washroom. I pointed her toward Earl. She winked her thanks, my heart skipped, and I said, "Hello, Allyson?"

"Uh, no, Philip," Bonnie said. "Who did you call?"

"Sorry. I just wanted to tell you, I mean Margo, that I was sorry I couldn't make dinner and that I appreciated her willingness to take a rain check."

"You can tell her. Just a minute."

I repeated the message to Margo. She was cool, but not unkind. "I know you want some straight answers from me, Philip. And I think I'm ready to give them. You may not like them, but you need to know."

"Great," I said, sarcastically.

"I'm sorry, Philip, but the way we both feel right now, we probably should get together on this as soon as possible."

"OK. Tomorrow for dinner for sure. I'll clear the decks and check with Earl."

"Good."

"Margo?"

"Hm?"

"Are we through?"

"You mean through talking?"

"No, I mean finished through."

"I don't know. Maybe."

That wasn't what I wanted, or expected, to hear. I knew she was having problems with our relationship, but I had been hoping she would say it had just been a phase, a stage, a mood. I didn't understand how she could so casually say that maybe we were through.

I hung up uneasily and with a sense of dread. Not much earlier I had almost wished I were free of the engagement with Margo that had begun so beautifully and now seemed to be ending in frustration. I had thought I wanted to be available to pursue Allyson, but as I headed toward the table I realized the folly of that. I didn't even know her. Besides a little of her sad history, I knew nothing about the girl except that she had a seemingly precious personality, looked people in the eye when she talked to them, and was a beautiful, beautiful lady who had the ability to hide the fact that she knew it — if indeed she did.

"Sorry," I said as I sat down.

"Did you break your date with Margo smoothly?" Allyson asked.

"Oh, no, it wasn't really a date," I said, not quite lying. "We were just going to talk about something."

"A case?"

"Something like that."

Earl stiffened. My evasiveness surprised him. He couldn't imagine that I would be hiding my engagement to Margo from anyone, even if it *was* on the skids. I couldn't imagine it either, but that didn't stop me. I knew it was foolish, but when Allyson innocently forced the issue, I rationalized a half truth I would live to regret.

"I got the impression that you and Margo might have something going together," she tried.

"No, uh-uh," I said. "Not really. No."

Earl's face was buried in his menu, but his eyes burned accusingly at me from over the top.

SEVEN

Earl decidedly froze me out during the small talk before ordering, ignoring every attempt by Allyson to bring me into the conversation. I couldn't blame him. He could have just called my bluff, told Allyson that Margo and I had been engaged for months and in love for a lot longer than that, but he was going to let me stew in my own juices.

When our salads were delivered, Allyson bowed her head slightly, closed her eyes, and appeared to be praying for a few seconds. I couldn't believe it. I don't think Earl even noticed. I had to ask her.

"Do you mind if I ask why you did that?"

"Did what?"

"Appeared to be praying there?"

"I was. I always pray before I eat."

"Why?"

"Well, Philip, it would take a while to explain. Maybe we can talk about it sometime."

"No, I know why you did it. It's because you know that God is the source of our provisions, and so you thank Him for them before you eat. Right?"

"Right."

Earl saw his opportunity to nail me without blowing my cover on the relationship I was hiding. "You believe that too, don't you, Philip?"

"Yes, I do, and so that's why I was wondering, Allyson, if you were — "

"Then why," Earl interrupted, "don't *you* pray before you eat?"

"I usually do," I said.

"Not around me you don't," he said.

"Well, I don't want to offend you. I know that you don't share my view about God, and — "

"I certainly share your view that God is our provider. Most sane people know that. I just don't buy your gungho, prosyletizing, drag everybody and his brother into the kingdom ideas."

I was hurt. "Those aren't my ideas. I just believe that followers of Christ are called to share their faith and — "

"And you believe Christ is the only way to God."

"Right."

"Well, I don't," Earl said.

"I do," Allyson said kindly.

Earl nodded that that was all right with him, but I couldn't leave it alone.

"You do?" I said, a little too loudly. "I mean, you're a Christian, not just religious?"

"Yes," she said. "My mother had hardly ever taken me to her Catholic church, but when I was overseas from nineteen seventy until nineteen seventy-two when I graduated from high school, I got in with a group of kids who introduced me to Christ."

"Grief," Earl said, smiling for Allyson, but dead serious for me. "I'm surrounded by 'em."

"My mother didn't like it too much when I wrote her about it. For a while she even hinted that she was going to bring me home, but I think she eventually sensed a change in me, even through my letters."

"How does she feel about it now?" I said.

"She's become a Christian. She started going to church with me in the mid-seventies and now we're in this thing together, as they say."

"Margo's a Christian too," Earl said, staring at me. "Christians stick together, right?" He was really twisting the knife.

"I sense you aren't too open to the idea yourself, Mr. Haymeyer," Allyson said. "Am I right?"

"I wouldn't say I was closed to it," Earl said. "But I do like to separate business and religion, and I have had the whole pitch from Philip here, sometimes even on company time."

"I wouldn't mind trying to change your mind about aggressive Christians someday," Allyson said. "I think people can be told about Christ without being forced into the church. I might even pay two ninety a day for the privilege of telling you on work time."

"For two ninety a day I'll listen to anything," Earl said, and we all laughed. But when he caught my eye, his smile died. Misrepresenting my feelings for Margo was bad enough for me, not to mention Margo. But for what it was doing to my example before Earl, I was ashamed. What could I say? What could I do to make it right?

"Anyway, Philip," Allyson was saying, "it's great to know I have a brother working for me."

"Yeah," I said, less than enthusiastically. I was cringing under the heat of Earl's eyes. When we had finished eating, Earl asked if we could get back to business.

"Sure," Allyson said, reaching for her fashionably large leather purse. She pulled out a half-inch-thick manila folder as Earl produced a mini tape recorder and placed it near her.

"I waited three years for the chance to see what had been in that first shoe box," she said. "It wasn't until after I returned from high school and was allowed to stay overnight at his apartment that I got it. I was taking a huge risk, I know, but when he was in the bathroom in the morning, I hurried into his bedroom, dropped to all fours, and dug around under the bed for the shoeboxes. The first one had the cash and stuff in it. I shoved it back underneath. I pulled a big rubber band off the other and dumped its contents into my overnight bag, being careful not to let the stuff fall out of order. I was nervous the rest of the time that weekend, worrying that Father would discover that everything was missing from the box. Saturday evening I told him I had an errand to run, and I went to the public library and spent a lot of money photocopying everything from the box. I copied fronts and backs of pictures and every document. The next morning I replaced the contents in the same order I had taken them, but I broke the rubber band on the box. I tied it together and put the knot on the bottom, then dove back out into the other room when I heard Father leaving the bathroom. I don't know to this day if he ever noticed."

"And what you have in this folder are the photocopies of what you found in the box?" Earl said.

"That's right, but I have a few questions first."

"That's fine," Earl said, "and I want you to know that we are not interested in the photocopies."

Both Allyson and I snapped our heads up. "Why not?"

"They could be extremely valuable to us in investigating whatever it is you want investigated, Allyson, but until I know what that is, I wouldn't touch them. And if you should ever want to see your father prosecuted because of anything you found in the box, you'd have a tough time because of how the material was obtained."

"Why would I want to have him prosecuted?"

"I don't know. *Do* you?"

"No, but that's the whole point. If you find something in the course of your investigation — let's say you're just helping me discover his parents, even if it means in some German cemetery somewhere — and you run across a crime he committed. Are you bound to expose him for that?"

"Not necessarily, Allyson," Earl said. "It depends on the crime committed, where, and how long ago.

"Can I ask you a little more specifically without incriminating him?"

"Sure. I won't pursue any line of questioning unless you tell me more than you want to."

"Let me ask this way, and you tell me if I'm treading on dangerous ground. Hypothetically, referring to any such crime or any such criminal, is there a time limit as to how soon a murderer has to be caught before he can be prosecuted?"

"You mean is there a statute of limitations on murder?"

"Yeah."

"No."

"Just curious. And is there a statute of — what did you call it?"

"Limitations."

"Yes, is there a statue of limitations on war crimes?"

"That depends on the war and the crime. Most of the war crimes committed in this century are beyond prosecution, but of course the war crimes of the Nazis in World War II are still open cases. Nazis have been found in this country and elsewhere ever since the Nuremburg trials, and the perpetrators are still tried, often convicted, and sentenced." Earl was abruptly quiet.

A pall had fallen over the evening. I stared at Allyson, unable to speak. The waitress came by and asked if anyone wanted dessert. We all shook our heads. Allyson put the folder back in her purse. Earl put the recorder in his suitcoat pocket and flapped his credit card down onto the check. We sat in uneasy silence until the waitress picked it up and Earl was able to direct his energy toward small talk with her.

I helped Allyson with her coat on the way out, she thanked me and then Earl for opening the door for her, and that was the extent of our conversation until we arrived back at the office.

"That's my car right there," she told Earl.

He pulled next to it and shifted into Park. "Allyson," he said, "the preliminary interview is always free, no matter how long it lasts. The way it stands now, you had a nice chat with a couple of friends. If you want to contract for our services, you know the terms. I would need to know only precisely what it is you would like to have us find out, and we would do everything we could to find it out. Let me just add this: if you have any reason to believe about your father what you intimated tonight, I would not hire private investigators — at least law-abiding ones — to check out any part of his background. The study of a childhood in an orphanage or the tracing of long-since-dead parents could lead to areas you want left undetected. The atrocities of World War Two are history. The man you know as your father seems gentle and harmless, though tormented by something in his past. If you don't want to be responsible for what could happen to him after more than thirty years of hard work in this country, I would leave the whole thing alone. Do you understand what I'm saying to you?"

"Yes, I'm afraid I do," Allyson said, her voice trembling as I had not heard it all day. "But if my curiosity gets the better of me, and I just have to know?"

"My offer stands," Earl said. "My only fear is that if we find something you don't want to know, you may wind up having hired us and being our enemy all at the same time."

She reached a hand across to Earl and shook his. "Thank you, Mr. Haymeyer. I appreciate your counsel." She reached back to me. I took her hand warmly. "And thank you, Philip. I imagine I'll see you both around." She left the car and trotted to hers.

Earl removed the mini tape recorder from his suitcoat and turned it off.

We sat in his car until she drove away, then went up into the office. "It never even crossed my mind that her father might have been a Nazi," Earl said. "I hate to admit it, but I never thought of it until she mentioned it. I suppose I should have, figuring her age and the age her father would be. He would have been in Nazi Germany as a young man, military age or so, at the time of Hitler."

"Is it true that if those facts came out about him in the course of a routine investigation, you would have to turn him in?"

"That or face charges of protecting a war criminal, which could be regarded as treasonous."

"And how about your advising her that she should leave it alone if she suspects that? Would that not be regarded the same?"

"I don't think so," Earl said. "I have it on tape just in case. I was — in my opinion — advising a family member, who would not be required to testify against her father anyway. If she was the only one who knew or suspected, he would never face charges."

"Do you feel you should go to the authorities with what you heard tonight?"

"I didn't hear anything tonight, Philip. And neither did you."

EIGHT

"You know how my conscience is, Earl," I said. "Please tell me that I shouldn't feel guilty about keeping her suspicions quiet."

"Philip, think about it. She gave us nothing. A German immigrant has nightmares, and she wonders if war crimes have a statute of limitations. There is nothing there to share with anyone. If you have a conscience, my boy, it oughta be working overtime right now anyway, wouldn't you say?"

"I suppose. You were pretty hard on me, ya know."

"You deserved it."

"I know." And that was true. I knew I had to pray about it, but, frankly, I was afraid of how God might lead.

"What's going on, Philip? Can't you and Margo have a few serious discussions about your relationship, maybe even a few quarrels, without you turning on her and then jumping ship?"

"That's not it, Earl. I just don't see why I should get in the way of any potential I might have with Allyson by telling her I'm engaged, especially if my fiancée wants to end the engagement. You never heard me deny my love for Margo before."

"True enough, but you sure seem eager to get it over with now. I thought Margo's breaking it off would be harder on you."

"Allyson could make it easier."

"Get off it. First, it takes an incredible ego to think you could get to first base with a girl like that. Face it, pal, if Margo hadn't had big troubles and been attracted to your chivalry, you probably wouldn't have gotten anything going with her, either."

I couldn't believe I was hearing this from Earl. What was he saying? I never claimed to be much to look at or listen to, but why should I feel like a second-class citizen? Earl could tell he had as good as punched me in the stomach.

"Don't take it so hard, Philip. All I'm trying to say is that you'd better not get your hopes up on Allyson Scheel. She's a classy young lady, an international traveler, smart as a whip. She's got money, she's got security."

"But she needs me."

"Whatdya mean? All you two have in common is that you pray before meals, and *you* don't even do that half the time. It'll take more than religion to start anything smoldering with her."

"How many times do I hafta tell you it's not religion?" I said.

"And how many times do I have to tell you that it's only you and your religious friends who say it's not religion? Everyone else says you're religious and that you've got religion, so no matter what you say about it being a person or a relationship or a way of life or whatever else you call it, to most people that's religion. You act as if there's something wrong with religion so you'd like to pretend that faith in God or Christ or the church is something other than religion."

"It's better than religion. Religion is a trap, confining. Christ is freedom."

"So you're better than everyone else."

"I didn't say — "

"You're even better than other religious people, because they call their religion religion, but to you it's a trap. Don't you see that that's what stands in the way of people buying your package, Philip? You are one of the nicest kids I know. Except for a few occasional incidents of inconsistency, which heaven knows I can't criticize people for, I think the world of you. But your religion — excuse me — your faith would be less offensive if it was more live-and-let-live."

"But one of the major tenets of Christianity is that it is evangelical," I said. "I don't want to badger you, to drag you to Christ. I just want the right to tell you about Him, to share with you what He has to offer. That's all. No obligation. I can't make you buy it. You can reject it. But don't deny me the right to tell you about it."

"I never have, Philip. I've even given you time to tell the whole staff. All I'm saying is that you had better have your own life in order, and you'd better be careful about your better-than-everyone-else attitude before you start the pitch."

He had me, and I knew it. You don't sell even the best product on the market with a we-don't-need-you-you-need-us attitude. I pursed my lips and nodded. Message received, loud and clear.

"And like I say, Philip. Don't take it too hard. I want to see you mellow out a little, but don't think I'd want you without your relig — your, uh, faith. I want you pretty much just the way you are. If there is any truth to all this, I'm gonna need you around."

I forced a smile. He *was* well-intentioned. And worst of all, he acted like more of a Christian than I did in many ways. He was honest, forthright, compassionate. Right then I felt the opposite.

Earl was tidying up the office, and I was switching off lights. "Whatdya think, Philip?" he asked. "Is Allyson going to be back asking for our help?"

"I don't know. I guess if she just can't stand the tension she will. I'm intrigued by this idea that he's going somewhere, but not to Germany. Where could he be going? If she's even close with her fear about his past, he'd be pretty brave to travel far internationally, wouldn't he?"

"Good thinking. If you really are going to try to see her again, let me know if she finds out where he's going. I'd like to help her, if we can. Hey, here's a note from Shipman. He was here! What time is it?"

"Quarter to eleven. Why?"

"It says to call him if I'm back before ten thirty. I think I'm gonna try him. I want to know what he found out for Bonnie today. Get me his home number from her file and then listen in on the extension."

I did better than that. I peeled off my coat and tossed it over Bonnie's chair, found Larry's number, and dialed it from her switchboard. When it was ringing, I buzzed Earl.

Shipman answered groggily. "Hello?"

"Boy, when you say ten thirty, you mean ten thirty, don't you?"

"Oh, hi, Earl. Yeah, I guess. I was sleepin'."

"You wanna talk, Ship, or you wanna go back to sleep and call me in the morning?"

"Naw, I'm awright. Let's talk. I spent some time at the son-in-law's office today, nosing around. It's weird, but the scuttlebutt in the office is that this Carla can hardly stand to be around Greg. Everybody knows they were engaged years ago, and the way they play it at work is that they aren't even on speaking terms. If they're faking it, they're good at it. She tries to nail him at every turn. She forgets to give him important phone messages, leaves his name off the routing slips on memos from the boss, embarrasses him, and is openly hostile. He tries to be nice, but it appears she's out to get him."

"I wasn't expecting *that*, Ship. How long has it been going on? Wasn't she partly responsible for getting him hired?"

"No, if you can believe the flunkies in the office. The word is that she opposed it from the beginning and had to be sweet-talked into it by the boss. He made her promise to make the best of it, pledged to keep them apart, and all that. She really resents having to go along on luncheons when he's involved."

"Hey, Lar," Earl said slowly. "How'd you get all this dope?"

"Oh, uh, I was sorta the, uh, copy machine repairman today. Amazing what a charming supplier can get out of the secretaries if he's friendly and speaks generically about the strange office he just visited. I told a girl there that one of my clients has all kinds of scandal in the office. 'I don't suppose you have any of that kind of excitement around here,' I suggested. Before you knew it, it all came out: the best potential for scandal. A single woman works with her former fiancée, who is now married. But it's *not* a scandal. She seems to hate him. Hard to know if it's true or just a sham, but if it's a game, he's being hurt by it."

"You know I don't like us to misrepresent ourselves, Ship," Earl said.

"I know, chief, but what did you want me to do, announce that I'm a private investigator looking for facts about the Greg and Carla affair for Greg's mother-in-law?"

I laughed.

"Is that you, Philip?" Shipman said.

"Yeah. How ya doin'?"

"Fine, but, Earl, you gotta tell me when Holy Joe is listenin' in so I don't make some wisecrack about God or whatever."

"He can take it," Earl said. "Thanks for the information, and get back to bed."

"I am in bed — I'm just not asleep. Or maybe I am. Anyway, that's not all I've got."

"It isn't?"

"No, and I'm not sure Bonnie's gonna want to know what else there is."

"What're you saying?"

"First tell me Bonnie's not listening in, too."

"It's just the two of us, Ship. Now what'd you get?"

"Well, after I got what I wanted from Greg's office, I drove over to his and Linda's apartment. I don't know what I expected to find, but my timing was perfect. Remember the guy, good-looking, about forty, who went to lunch with Greg and the boss and Carla and the other woman?"

"Yeah."

"I saw his sports car parked at the apartment building."

"What time was this?"

"About one-thirty in the afternoon."

"OK — "

"So I put on my painter's hat and coveralls and grabbed a can and hung around the hallway near Greg and Linda's apartment, always within view of their door. I don't know how long he had been there before I got there, but he came out of their apartment at three twenty, exactly ten minutes before Erin, the thirteen-year-old, arrived home from school."

"Who is this guy?"

"Name's Johnny Bizell. A friend of mine in the sixteenth precinct ran a ten twenty-eight on the license number for me."

"That's the worst news I've heard all day, Ship. Thanks a lot."

"You know Bizell?"

"No, but the thought that Linda is covering her own garbage with stories about her husband is going to kill Bonnie. I wish I was working for *his* mother instead."

"I'm going to stay on it, Earl. I want to be sure before you tell Bonnie anything. Good night, boys."

Earl and I gathered up our stuff and trudged down the hall to our respective apartments. There was nothing to say, but Earl said it anyway as he stopped to unlock his door. "I didn't need this tonight," he said.

"I know what you mean. Hey, Earl, I need to have dinner with Margo tomorrow night. Can I avoid overtime?"

"I think so, unless we get another Allyson-style walk-in. I want to see things work out for you and Margo, you know."

"I know. I appreciate it."

"You don't sound too optimistic about it, Philip."

"I'm not."

NINE

I didn't sleep well. I knew I should be planning what to say to Margo the next evening, but after all, it was her party, not mine. As far as I was concerned, as long as she wanted to continue our engagement and build toward marriage, I certainly did, too. It was only lately, when she quit wearing her diamond and hinted that she wanted out, that I became resentful.

I'm sure I would not have considered any potential with Allyson Scheel had Margo not been in her present state of mind. I had always enjoyed watching Allyson, sure, but so had everyone else in the office. I had never had roving eyes for anyone. But now, when I should have been planning strategy or trying to figure what was making Margo tick or what it would take to convince her that we were right for each other, all I could think of was Allyson.

I felt guilty about it, and disloyal. Even fickle. I lay on my back with my hands behind my head, staring at a ceiling I could hardly see in the darkness, reliving the past few hours. Most of the conversation had been between Allyson and Earl, but I had caught her eyes a few times. We were communicating. We shared moments. When Earl said something funny, she threw her head back and laughed and looked at me.

God was nudging my conscience. I ran from the feeling and continued to dwell on Allyson. She wasn't afraid to be a kindred spirit. And when she was talking or listening to me, she looked me full in the face. That's flattering, no matter who does it. But when it is someone who is simply so exciting just to look at —

I knew there was nothing to it yet, and that she would have no idea what I was thinking. I was not so immature that I would think she was excited by me the way I was about her. And I also knew that if she *was* made aware of my interest, she would have been surprised. She was obviously an old-fashioned girl, practical to the point where she wouldn't put much stock in the heartthrobs of someone who had seen her around and had spent a few hours with her.

Anyway, I knew Earl had a point, though a painful one. Here was a girl out of my class. Of course, that had never stopped me before. Margo had been full of pain and problems, yet compared to me, she had been raised as a rich girl, cultured, exposed to the finer things of life. That was not intimidating to me. In fact, I had learned a lot from her. She always said I was better for her than she was for me, but even my social graces, graceless as they were, had been revolutionized by observing her in public.

Allyson had that same air about her, and I was glad that I had learned from Margo to be calm and collected and matter-of-fact in social settings. Good grief, I was using things I had learned from my fiancée to try to make a good impression — or at least to avoid making a bad impression — on a new woman.

A new woman. Wouldn't that be nice? Not that I had grown tired of Margo. But if she wanted out, what was I supposed to do? This was no old movie where the star pines away, remains true to his rejecting love, and wins her back in the end because of his persistence. Margo wasn't the type who would consciously want me to work at keeping her. If she wanted a break, I would give it to her, and I wouldn't penalize myself by waiting for her and pretending that I still was a one-girl guy.

I was rationalizing, and I knew it. But the guilt wasn't as strong as the desire.

I rolled onto my side and pulled the ends of the pillow up around my ears. I stared at the red digits on my clock radio and watched them change to 2:17. I shut my eyes hard and commanded myself to sleep. The next morning the staff would meet for its weekly session. Several cases were in the works, and Shipman would report on the Greg and Linda affair, uh, matter. Bonnie would not likely be allowed to attend.

I always looked forward to those meetings because the new assignments were made, and Earl was at his best, making suggestions, offering tips and reminders. Since the A. SCHEEL case was obviously not going to take me overseas, I wondered what else he would have in store for me. The fact that he would even consider me for such a plum and the bonus it involved (Earl always shares the additional income on unusual cases with the investigator) encouraged me. I knew he was happy with my work, and I wanted to show him that I could be trusted with anything he thought I was ready for.

I needed to sleep to be at my best. The next time I looked at the clock, an hour had passed. I turned to a classical music FM station, thought a little about Margo and a lot about Allyson, and finally fell asleep.

It seemed I hadn't seen Larry Shipman for days. In fact, I hadn't. Our cases, seldom calling for us to work together, had scrambled our schedules to the point where he was in the office when I was out, and vice versa. That was another advantage of the weekly staff meetings.

"Mornin' good-lookin'," he said, giving Margo a brotherly squeeze when she arrived.

"Hi, Lar," she said. "Who's on the desk over lunch today?"

"Believe you are, kid," he told her.

"Wonderful."

"I know you love it. Where's the chief?"

Bonnie could hear us from the switchboard. "He'll be here any minute," she said. "I'm not joining you this morning. Hope that means good news."

"Hope so," Margo echoed.

Larry and I already knew differently.

"Want Philip and I to bring you something back from lunch today, Margo?" Larry asked.

"Yeah, thanks. Where you going?"

"I dunno," he said. "Where do you wanna go, Philip? Or maybe I should ask Margo where she wants us to go. I'm not particular."

"I might not be able to go with you," I said. "I'll let you know mid-morning."

"Something going with the boss, huh? Ambitious?" Larry said, jabbing me on the shoulder.

"Naw."

"Then he's cheatin' on you, Margo! I just knew it!"

When neither of us laughed or looked at each other or even at him, Larry stage-whispered, "Whoops! Not the day for that line, huh? Sorry, kids! Anyway, Margo, I'll check with you before lunch to see what you want."

Earl, looking grim, drew the door shut behind him, greeted everyone a bit more formally than usual, and quickly turned on the tape recorder. "We've all got a lot of work to do, so let's get rolling. How is everybody?"

We all responded with some form of signal. Margo shrugged. I stuck out one hand, palm down, and tipped it back and forth. Larry signaled thumbs up, but added, "Except for what I found yesterday."

"Oh, no," Margo said. "Was Bonnie right? Was Linda right?"

"Worse than that," Larry said, waiting for Earl's cue and then telling her the whole story.

"That's terrible," she decided. "What next, Earl? How do you deal with that, finding the opposite of what you were looking for?"

"You just keep looking," he said, "until you know all you want or need to know. Then you tell the client as gently and as forthrightly as you can, and let her do what she wants."

"But Earl," Larry said, "what do I say to the client this morning when she asks what I saw yesterday?"

"Use your imagination. I'm telling you that you can't talk yet about what you saw, because nothing's been confirmed yet. And you know that's true."

Yeah, but you know as well as I do that it looks pretty bad for Linda to have a man in her apartment all afternoon, leaving just before the daughter gets home."

"Still, Ship," Earl said, "what *are* you going to tell Bonnie, based on what I just told you?"

"You don't want me to tell her anything now, yet you don't want me to appear evasive?"

"You got it."

"I'll think about it."

"Margo," Earl said, "tell us where things stand on your case."

Margo sounded tired, but her thoughts were clear and she represented herself well, as usual. "I've traced a major part of the drug supply at Glencoe High School to a history teacher, a Mrs. Millicent."

"A married lady?" Shipman said.

"No longer married, and hardly a lady, I'm afraid," Margo said. "She puts on a good front, doesn't appear to be any less than the model mid-thirties, with-it teacher. But too much points her way."

"Should we inform the drug prevention boys at the Metropolitan Enforcement

Group?" Earl asked. "The school board liaison just wanted a good lead before going to the police, and my guess is that we've used up their budget for this. How long have you been on it now?"

Margo checked her file. "Today will be thirteen days."

"They allotted five thousand dollars," Earl said, studying his client registration sheet. "That gives you four more days if you have a plan. What will you do, or should we just give 'em what we've got?"

"I want to go in there," Margo said. "I want to be a transfer student from anywhere, and I want to get next to Mrs. M."

"Not a bad idea, but can you pass for an eighteen-year-old, and can you look hungry for drugs within four days of meeting her without scaring her off?"

"I could pass for *sixteen,* unfortunately," Margo said. "As for the four days, probably not. But if they want this woman nailed in the act of selling, they're gonna need me."

"But a police undercover agent would be cheaper. In fact, free," Earl countered.

"Yeah," Larry interrupted, "but those kids know every stinkin' one of 'em."

"That's right," Margo said. "I'd say it would be worth asking the board for a little extension, say another ten days. Could we maybe give them a price break?"

"For what?" Earl said. "Volume?" We laughed. "I'll just tell them we need ten more days. If they want a break on the price, let 'em ask for it. I'm sure not going to hand it out unless they ask."

"They'll ask," Larry said.

"And I'll probably relent," Earl said. "This is one case I'd like to see through to the end. Get her, Margo. It's bad enough kids are getting drugs from the sleaze on the streets without having to see this kind of an example at school. I'll grease the wheels for your transfer. Where do you want to be from?"

"Better make it Atlanta," she said. "It's the only place I can talk about intelligently other than Winnetka, and there would be too many people with friends in Winnetka who haven't seen me in high school lately."

Earl coached Margo on how to keep a low profile while getting next to the teacher and casually getting on the subject of liberal views of freedom, and so on. It made me wish I was in on it, and I knew Margo would do a good job.

"Now, Dr. Spence," Earl said expansively. "Even though you've been in my doghouse a bit lately on peripheral matters" — Larry looked puzzled; Margo didn't — "I must congratulate you in the presence of your peers for your outstanding work on the Ussry missing person report. As the rest of you probably remember, the police didn't want to touch the case of Mr. Ussry's missing son because there had been some contact made through friends, indicating that the boy — what was his name, Philip? Right, Frank — was happy and healthy but that he had no interest in reestablishing any relationship with the family. As he was eighteen, there was really nothing the police could do, and Mr. Ussry, being a man of some means, contacted us. According to Philip's report" — he dug out the copy Bonnie had typed the day before — "within eight days Philip was able to locate the boy in Cleveland, visit him, negotiate a meeting between father and son, and completely satisfy the client. Excellent work."

"I can't say the boy will be coming home," I said. "In fact, he won't be. But he was able to explain to his father his reasons for feeling he had to leave. He refused any financial support and insists on making it on his own. He prefers that his father not try to contact him anymore, but Frank promised to keep him posted on his well-being. I think it will be all right in the end."

"Well, it was a fine piece of work, Philip. You're progressing well, and I hope you can tell how pleased I am. We don't have time this meeting, but on your own, Margo and Larry, I want you to read this report and see how Philip found the boy and what he said to both parties to start the healing process. Sometimes our work involves more than just sleuthing. There's compassion and psychology involved."

"Thanks, Earl," I said, feeling less high than I thought I should after such a compliment.

"Now," he said, "I want to bounce Allyson Scheel's story off the two of you who haven't heard it yet."

"The Allyson Scheel from downstairs?" Shipman said, leaning forward in his chair.
Earl nodded.

"I'm all ears. And eyes."

TEN

Earl played selected portions of the tapes he had made the night before. "What do you hear that I'm not hearing?" he asked after an hour.

"Well, my guess is that she won't be back, chief," Larry said. "Are you sure you want to spend the time on it?"

Before Earl could answer, Margo cut in. "You're wrong. She'll be back. She loves her father, and she wants to know, she *has* to know about his past. It's not just curiosity. She cares. She wants to help. Earl, you should have told her that she can't testify against her own father, even if he *was* a Nazi. And you can't use any of the solid stuff she gives you if it came from a shoebox she obtained illegally. I don't know how she's going to help him if he was a Nazi, but maybe she can find a way to help him deal with his guilt."

"Well, as long as we're going to talk about it," Shipman said, "I did hear something. According to what she said, her father never told her he was going to Germany."

"Whatdya mean?" I said. "He told her several times he was going to his homeland, and he said he was raised in Germany in an orphanage. He also showed her the box of savings toward the trip."

"She saw a brochure from a travel agency, but she didn't say for what country," Larry said. "And he never *said* Germany."

"I think it was just the way she repeated the story, Larry," Earl said. "But let's keep it in mind. The man has a German accent, but he has never talked much about his past."

"I say he was born somewhere else before being sent to the orphanage in Germany by officials, church people, distant relatives, or someone," Larry continued. "He probably knows of that country and wants to go there either to trace his family or to claim it as his homeland, as he says."

The rest of us looked dubious, but I was intrigued. It always amazes me what others hear in conversations that I don't.

"I've got a few potential cases I want to go over with you, Philip," Earl said. "Meanwhile, Margo will stay on the school board assignment; Ship, you hang in with Greg and Linda; and I'll try to stay available if Allyson Scheel returns. That's all for now."

It was nearly lunchtime, and as we headed back to our desks, I heard one of Shipman's all time great lines. Bonnie asked him what he had learned about her son-in-law the day before. "Nothing to speak of yet, Bon," he said. "Nothing to speak of."

Bonnie, Earl, and Larry quickly organized to go out for lunch together and took Margo's order as she got situated at the switchboard. "I'll see you tonight," I said softly. She nodded.

As I left I heard Larry asking her, "Where's the rock today?"

"Home," she said, as noncommitally as possible.

I bounded down the stairs and out the door, strode up the sidewalk to the other end of the building, and ducked into the Beatrice Boutique, not realizing that I was out of breath. "May I help you, sir?" a salesgirl asked.

"No, uh, yeah, I'd like to see Allyson."

"May I tell her who's calling?"

"Sure."

"Your name?"

"Oh, yeah, Philip. Philip from upstairs. No, don't tell her from upstairs. She'll know."

I didn't want her mother to know she was seeing anyone from the detective agency in case Allyson hadn't told her anything about her plans.

The girl returned. "Allyson asked if I would tell you that she is still thinking about it and will call you." She started to walk away.

"Thanks," I said, "but that isn't what I wanted to see her about. Could you ask her if I could talk to her for just a second?" She hesitated, then went back to the office again. I smiled when Allyson appeared, but she didn't flash her usual response.

"Hi, Philip. Listen, my mother doesn't know I've talked to you and Mr. Haymeyer, and I'd just as soon keep it that way until I decide what I'm going to do. I appreciate your interest, but I got the impression from your boss last night that he thought maybe I shouldn't pursue this. Does he know you're checking with me again right away?"

I held up both hands to try to get her attention, and she finally gave me an opening. "I'm not here on business," I said. "We never try to talk people into retaining us, anyway. It's unprofessional, and it doesn't work. You would prove that all over again. Anyway, we have plenty of work. I'm here to see you."

She smiled but said nothing.

"I was wondering if you were free for lunch."

"Well, I usually just run down the street here for a sandwich. I don't take much time to eat because I like to get back and help Mother with the books and all. One of our clients is coming in today who orders her spring wardrobe about now each year, and she will not talk with anyone except Mother and me."

"I would enjoy taking you to lunch, Allyson," I said, finally having caught my breath. "We can go to your usual spot, or you can go with me to one of my usual places, and I promise to have you back here whenever you say."

She cocked her head and gave me a pretty, closed-mouth smile. "Fair enough," she said. "If we leave now, which is a little earlier than usual for me, I can take an hour."

"Great, that'll give me time to take you to a neat Italian place I think you'll like. You do like Italian food?"

"Love it. Let me get my coat."

As we walked to my car, I purposely slowed her down to make sure that my three co-workers would be gone by the time we rounded the corner. They were, but I realized as I opened the door for her and then went around to my side that Margo would have a perfect view of us from one of the office windows if she chose to look, as I did nearly everyday. I didn't dare look up to see.

Allyson smiled a lot and talked a little. While we waited for our food, I asked if I could talk business just for a minute. "It's not really business, because I really do care after hearing your story last night. Whether we take the case or not."

"It's OK, Philip," she said.

"It's just that one of our guys, Larry Shipman, noticed that your father never told you he was going to Germany, so maybe you shouldn't be so surpised that he isn't booked on a flight to there."

She thought for a moment. "He's right. Father never did say Germany. I just assumed — "

"So did I," I said. "So did Earl."

"So my next step is to find out where he's going, even if I don't retain your firm."

"Yeah, and I'd be curious to know when you find out. Just curious for my own sake, I mean."

"I appreciate that, Philip. Sure. I'll tell you if I find out."

"Thanks. Enough business for today?"

"Yeah. Hey, you know a lot about me because of last night. How 'bout telling me about you?"

"There's not much to tell," I said, but I told her anyway.

"Do you miss illustration work, now that you're out of it full time?" she said in the car on the way back.

"Not really. I still draw on my own time now and then, but I regret not having gotten into detective work earlier. Of course, then I probably wouldn't have had the chance to learn the trade under Earl. He's the best, you know."

"I sensed that. Are you talking business again, selling me on him?" She was smiling.

"No. I say that even to people who aren't prospective clients."

"I believe you do," she said.

I dropped her off in front of the boutique. "Thank you very much for lunch, Philip," she said, her eyes locked on mine. "It was a good idea, a good place, and I enjoyed the company."

"My pleasure," I said, as if I had just delivered her paper.

"Thank you," she said, almost shyly. " 'Bye."

I was high at work that afternoon, but something was eating at me, too. I had told her about how I met Margo and that bringing her to Chicago and helping expose her mother as a murderer had led us both into detective work. But I never even hinted that Margo and I had fallen in love and were engaged. Of course, maybe after tonight we wouldn't be engaged, but I could have just told Allyson that. She wouldn't have thought it improper for me to be taking her to lunch when my fiancée had quit wearing her engagement ring. I think.

But I didn't want her to think for a moment that I was showing interest in her because I was on the rebound from a disappointment. Because of Allyson, the disappointment I probably would have felt over Margo was dispelled somewhat. I knew that was rotten, but it was the truth. Maybe Margo was right. Maybe we were taking each other for granted and were tired of each other. That wasn't exactly what she had been saying, but with an exciting newcomer in my world, maybe Margo *was* beginning to seem routine.

I didn't think I would have felt that way if Margo had still been excited about me, about us, about our future, but I couldn't be sure. Something had pulled the plug on her feelings for me, and it was hard to take. I didn't want to force anything, so maybe I should just let it happen. We could still be friends. In fact, we'd always be more than friends. We had been through so much, and she had received Christ. We were family. We didn't have to be in love.

I told Earl about my conversation with Allyson without telling him I had taken her to lunch. I knew I wouldn't be able to hide it long if I continued to see her, not with all of us together in one big, happy building.

"Unless her father is going somewhere really unusual, I doubt we'll ever hear from Allyson again," Earl predicted.

Well, we might not, I thought, *but I will.*

"Take a look at these two folders this afternoon, and let's talk tomorrow morning about them," Earl said. "We've got to get you back into circulation soon, don't we?"

"Yeah. Listen, Earl, do you mind if I take the afternoon off and get some sleep? I didn't sleep well last night, and you know I've got that important dinner with Allyson, I mean Margo, tonight. I'll read the case files late tonight and be ready for tomorrow morning, OK?"

"Sure."

ELEVEN

I told Margo what I was doing and asked if she would mind calling me when she left work so I could get up and get ready. For some reason, because of the strain between us, I felt uneasy asking such a favor, and I sensed she felt the same, though it was the type of thing we had done for each other without question before.

When my phone rang at 5:30, I assumed it was Margo, but it wasn't.

"Can I talk with you tonight, Philip?" Allyson said.

"Sure, what about?"

"Business," she said. "I'm still not sure I want to retain EH, but I just have to show someone what I found in the shoebox. Can I do it off the record just to see what you think? I found out where Father is going by asking a friend in a travel agency in Evanston to check my father's name through all the airline companies."

"Where's he going?"

"I'd rather tell you in person, Philip, if you don't mind. And I want to show you the photocopies of the contents of the box first anyway. Is that OK?"

"Sure. When?"

"Soon?"

"Oh, I can't, Allyson. Ya know I was supposed to have a meeting with Margo last night, and I canceled. I just can't cancel tonight."

"How about later? Will your meeting last long?"

"No, I hope not. I mean, I don't think so. Why don't I call you when I'm free, and we can meet somewhere?"

"Fine, and thanks, Philip."

I called Margo to be sure she hadn't been trying to reach me.

"No," she said. "But I was just about to. When should I be ready?"

"Why don't we just go from here?" I said, realizing I sounded a little eager to get on with it.

"OK, but I'm not gonna look like much."

"I thought you said I shouldn't treat this like a date, that I shouldn't spend much money because of your state of mind or something like that?"

"Yeah, you're right. But I do like to look nice when I go out."

"No need. You look fine. We won't go fancy. Where do you want to go?"

"You decide," she said.

"No, it's your deal, really. I mean, it is, isn't it? You know what I mean. Just anywhere you want will be fine."

"Well, I don't want to spend all evening trying to decide where to go. Let's just go somewhere quiet where we can talk and get a decent meal."

"Fine, Margo. You name it."

"Oh, all right. The Italian place."

I gulped. "Well, I, uh — yeah, that's good. Give me a half hour here to get a shower, and I'll come get you."

"Don't dress up, Philip."

"I won't."

I called Earl to tell him of the development with Allyson, but he was still wary. "I don't want to hear anything incriminating about the man unless she's going to hire us, Philip. Remember that."

We talked about the various possibilities until I realized that I had just ten minutes to get ready. I figured I had treated Margo badly enough lately without showing up late, so I showed up with damp hair instead.

She had retained a bit of her humor in spite of her emotional turmoil. "I said not to dress up," she said, "but you didn't have to go overboard."

I hurried through my meal, hoping we could get on with whatever it was Margo wanted to say. She sensed it. "Got another date tonight?"

"Naw. Just something I'm going to check out for Earl if I have time. No rush."

When we finished dessert and the dishes had been cleared, she was finally ready to talk. "Philip, I know I've been unfair to you with the ring business. You were right, I was wrong. There was no excuse for it, and I want you to forgive me."

"No, it's all right," I said. "If you didn't feel right about wearing it, I understand. I just wish you would have said something so I would have known before other people started to notice."

"That's what I mean. That's what I'm sorry about. I can't say I'm sorry that I'm not wearing it. I do miss what we had, but I don't think we have it anymore, and I need time to sort it out."

"I'll buy that we don't have what we had," I said, "but I confess I don't know why. My feelings for you never changed. I was still in love with you, excited about you, eager to marry you. What happened?"

"I don't know, Philip. Now that you see me in one of my confused states where I am down and moody and troubled and uncertain, what does it do to you?"

"It makes me feel rejected, like I deserve better. I know that's selfish and probably unreasonable, but that's the truth. You asked."

"Yes, I asked. Does it make you love me less?"

"No."

She sensed my hesitation."No?"

"Well, I don't know. I feel I have lost a lot of what I felt for you."

"You see?"

"Well, does that bother you? I mean you're the one who wants to break the engagement, to have a cooling off period, to think things over."

"Yes, it bothers me. It proves to me that I need more than a husband has to give. I need someone who will love me and stay with me and see me through times like this. You know I had a weird childhood and that I carry scars that even my faith doesn't seem to erase. I need you to stay with me when I'm upset and confused."

"Stay with you, but not be engaged to you? That's what you call staying with you? I loved you. Supporting you, in my eyes, meant loving you and being your fiancée. You're asking a lot for me to stay by you and be your strength while your emotional trauma evidences itself by shutting me out."

"I know. It's too much to ask. I'm being unfair. Just forget it."

"Margo, if I had known at the beginning of this that this was what you wanted, maybe I could have been ready for it. But I felt pitched out like so much cold dishwater, and I was just adjusting to the fact that you wanted no more of me."

"Well, it didn't take you long to mourn my loss, did it? You sound quite over it by now."

"That's not fair. You should be glad I'm not an emotional cripple over it. You might feel responsible."

"An emotional cripple like me, is that what you're getting at?" she said.

"I didn't mean that at all."

We were silent for several minutes. I found it difficult to look at her. Finally, I spoke. "I thought that maybe I could handle it. That we could be friends, better than that, best friends. We have been through so much together. We could be buddies for life. I could watch you find someone new and get married and always be welcome at your home and with your children. You would be interested in my life, too. We'd be examples of a loving brother and sister in Christ."

"That's nice, Philip, but that isn't what we were building. If it can't work out between us, that would be wonderful. But I don't want second best. I want you as my lover and husband and the father of my children."

I was completely thrown. "What am I supposed to make of all this, Margo? You wring me out and hang me up to dry, I deal with it the only way I know how, and now you change your mind on me."

"I haven't changed my mind. I just don't know where I am. I feel we've lost something, and until we get it back, my dreams won't work. Maybe I'm too romantic. Maybe it's unrealistic to think that the warm fuzzy feelings will last over a long engagement."

"Which I agreed to for your sake," I reminded her. "I knew we had fallen in love under very unusual circumstances, and I agreed that we should really be sure. But I was sure. And I thought you were, too, until now. What do you want, Margo? I'll be or think or do anything you want."

"Well, that attitude, for one thing, I do not want. I would much rather be saying that to you and have you advise me on exactly what I should do. Prescribe the medicine, send me to bed, tell me it'll all be all right in the morning."

"But you really don't want that, do you, Margo?"

"I guess not. I want to give you your ring back, take a break for a while, see what happens to me spiritually and emotionally, and then come running back to you when I'm ready and sure."

"And if you do that, how will I know that we won't go through this again?"

"You'll just have to take my word for it. And I'll make you one pledge right now. If I come back to you, ready to take up again where we left off, I'll want to marry you as soon as we can get organized."

I was dumbfounded. "And what should I do in the meantime."

"Wait for me."

"Wait for you?"

"Yes. Be patient. It may not take as long as you think, but I don't want to make any promises."

"You also don't want to keep any," I said unkindly, accepting the ring from her outstretched hand. "Are you telling me that I should live under the restrictions of an engaged man while enjoying none of the privileges?"

"What are you saying, Philip?"

"That I'm not sure it's fair that I should deprive myself of a normal life — as I might have if I weren't engaged — when for a while, and perhaps permanently, I am not engaged."

"I missed something," she said.

"No, I think *I* missed something."

"Wait, Philip. You're telling me that if you're not engaged, you'd like to play the field a bit, is that it?"

"Maybe."

"*I* won't be doing that."

"That's your prerogative."

"Philip, I thought it would be torturous to break our engagement, and I expected you to tell me you would wait forever for me to come to my senses, which I probably will do. But you're taking it remarkably well and are even eager to get back into the free life."

I felt foolish, as if I had already confessed that I had taken Allyson out. "And what if I did wait forever for you, and you didn't come back? Then what?"

"Well, I would have let you know at some point that it was completely over."

"So, this is just a trial period, a time for thinking, a cooling-off period, but you'll let me know when it's for real?"

"You make it sound pretty shallow."

"There's a good reason it sounds shallow, Margo."

We were silent again. I paid the check and returned to the table. I looked at my watch.

"Can you leave it this way, Philip?" Margo asked, incredulous. "Could you go and handle your errands for Earl without our resolving anything here tonight?"

"I'm afraid we *have* resolved something," I said. "I get the impression that you're going to play me for the fool, expect me to wait until you're ready for me, and then pull me out of the mothballs and put me on again."

"Philip, I'm shocked. What do you want, full freedom? Surely I couldn't ask for any commitment from you. But it's not going to help my decision-making if you ran right out and start dating while I'm trying to sort things out."

"Margo, you're asking too much. I pledged my life and my tomorrows to you, and the ring you just gave back to me was my symbol. If you want to hang it up, even temporarily, that's *your* choice, not mine."

"You're telling me that if I want you to wait for me, I have to keep the ring and keep wearing it? That would make a difference to you, knowing how I feel right now?"

"No, I would not *offer* the ring to you, knowing how you feel."

"And I wouldn't accept it from you, knowing how *you* feel."

"Fine, then. We're through. You know where to find me."

"Terrific, Philip. I can see working at the office is going to be just peachy under the circumstances."

"We owe it to Earl to not let this get in the way of our work."

"Oh, certainly." She was on the edge of tears.

I could hardly believe what I had heard myself saying. Was I doing this just to justify Allyson in my life? *Was* she in my life? Would she be for long?

"Will you at least take me to my car at the office?" she asked.

"Of course."

On the way she broke down and sobbed. I reached to touch her shoulder, but she shrugged my hand away. When we stopped, I said, "I hate to leave you this way."

"Oh, never mind," she managed, opening the door.

I reached in my shirt pocket for Allyson's home number.

TWELVE

"Philip, can you come to my apartment?" Allyson wanted to know.

I hesitated. "I suppose," I said.

"We can meet somewhere else if you wish," she said. "But my mother is already here and — "

"Oh, well, if you're mother is there."

"Philip," she scolded. "I wouldn't invite you to my apartment alone — "

"I know."

"You did *not* know."

"You're right," I said. "You threw me. Listen, where is your mother on all this?"

"I told her almost everything so far."

"And I don't like it much," Mrs. Scheel said a few minutes later, after I had found my way past the doorman and the glassy, carpeted labyrinth that led to Allyson's place. "I have made it a practice — in fact, since Allie returned from high school overseas — to let her make her own decisions. I didn't force her to work with me or for me. I live in this building, but on a different floor. She doesn't answer to me."

"But you *do* tell me what you think," Allyson said.

"And would you have it any other way, dear?"

"Of course not. I need your counsel now more than ever. I don't want to do anything that would hurt either you or Father."

The women were a study in family beauty. Beatrice Scheel appeared a spirited, handsome woman with an open, honest face and hair dyed jet black. Allyson's soft smile and the flowing red hair around her face were invitations to stare. The women looked good together, like they belonged to each other. And they conversed openly, maturely. The mother stood.

"Philip," she said, "Allyson trusts you. She's a good judge of character, and I have implicit confidence in her. I want to tell you exactly how I feel about this whole thing, and then I want you to advise me. Regardless how I feel about it, then it will be up to Allyson whether she decides to follow up on it. We'll all have to live with the consequences."

She moved to a wing chair near the end of the couch where I sat, leaving Allyson in a love seat directly across from me. Mrs. Scheel tucked her legs beneath her, letting her floor-length lounging coat cover her feet. When she was situated, she reached out without looking, and Allyson handed her her saucer and cup of tea as if it had been choreographed. She set it carefully on the arm of the chair and didn't touch it again until she was finished talking.

"I can understand Allie's need to know. I lived with that need for years. I should say I *have* lived with that need. I never outgrew it or got over it. I loved that man. That has dissipated somewhat because I have all but given up on finding the key that unlocks him. I have prayed for him for the last several years, but I have not asked him about his past for more than a decade. He is a closed book.

"I was not aware of his wish to return to Germany, or his original homeland, or wherever it is he wants to go. I confess that intrigues me. Allie is right when she assumes that I wouldn't mind going along. You see, I still am curious. I would have bet my life that I could have changed that man a little by marrying him. But that sweet, shy disposition that so drew me to him from the beginning turned to a fierce protectiveness, a privacy, a wall around his, his — the — his being itself, if you will. I'm telling you, the man is locked up tighter than a drum.

"I know what Mr. Hampshire, is it — ?"

"Haymeyer," Allyson corrected.

"Haymeyer is driving at, warning Allie to be careful. I know none of us wants to admit our fear, but we have to. If we're going to let Allyson pursue this, or you for that matter, Philip, you are going to have to know who and what you are dealing with. We all fear that he might have been a Nazi. And the terrifying nights I lived through with him — though I thank the Lord he never laid a hand on me — nearly convince me that he could have been in Hitler's army.

"There's a slight hitch to that, though. Is it possible that a man with a history like that could never slip up once and say something that would give himself away? There is no doubt in my mind that his American name is not the same as the one he brought with him when he emigrated from Germany. He would not even admit that. But I know it's true."

"You *know* this?" I said. "It's more than a logical guess?"

"Yes."

"Forgive me, but how do you know?"

"Well, it started with the black eyes."

"The black eyes?"

"When I first saw Curtis, the time Allie told you about, at the factory, he still had traces of black and blue rings under his eyes. I could hardly see them in the dim light on the cutting line, but when I hugged him, I got a better look. The first time we went out was at night, and I didn't get to confirm it. But about a week later on a picnic, I noticed that it was almost gone. But there is no doubt both eyes had been blackened."

"Mother, you never told me this."

"It didn't seem significant, honey."

"I don't see how it ties in," I said. "I'm sorry."

"Well, I couldn't even get Curtis to admit that he had been injured. He denied that the traces of bluish and yellow marks around his eyes were even there. He told me it was my imagination, but when I tried to touch them lightly to show him where I meant, he pulled away. I let it drop, but I went behind his back to others in the factory to see what they knew."

"You asked his *friends* about him?" Allyson said. "People you didn't even know?"

"Well, he didn't have any real friends," Mrs. Scheel said. "And hardly any of them would talk to me. They thought I had come on too strong with him and that I was brassy to be talking to them about him behind his back.

"The personnel manager said no one had ever seen Curtis mad, ever raise his voice, or even seem upset, and he'd been on the job maybe four or five months by now. He took everything in stride, almost too much so. Some of the guys thought they could never count on him if they wanted to file a grievance or something."

"How did he explain it?" I asked, looking at Allyson, who appeared completely nonplussed.

"Just like every other puzzle in his life," her mother said. "He didn't. He ignored the questions, brushed them off, or just made up an obvious tale to let you know you had asked him something he would never answer. I never met a more stubborn, self-contained person in my life. I might have been able to live with it if he hadn't been so full of pain and remorse, but when you combine that kind of guilt with a closed personality, you have one sick person. I couldn't handle it. I wish to this day I could have had more strength, but I exhausted every trick I knew."

"They weren't tricks, Mother. You used your personality, and you were loving him."

"You're right about that," Mrs. Scheel said, looking away and growing quiet. "He just frustrated me so," she whispered. "Maybe that irks me more than anything. He was such a challenge. I loved to make him laugh, even just to smile. He never got any attention from anyone else. There wasn't a person alive I couldn't draw out, and sometimes I think I finally left just because he defeated me, but then I realize that he didn't do it intentionally. There is something stopping the man from opening himself to anyone, even a woman who loved him with everything she had in her — "

Mrs. Scheel's voice broke, and she hid her face in her hands. She was not crying, really, but she had to compose herself before she could speak again. Allyson knelt by her and put an arm around her.

"Why do you assume he changed his name?" I asked. "You knew his first name was Americanized in its spelling, but what about the last name?"

"Well, the only other thing the personnel man told me about Curtis was that it took a long time to get his application cleared through social security and the immigration service because of his name change. Of course, he could not — and would not — divulge Curtis's original name. Once Curtis got his papers and his social security card and was naturalized, that too was a closed book. He seemed more relieved than proud, and if he had been evasive about his German name before, now he was stony. The most I ever got out of him was that his German name had probably either been made up or assigned to him at the orphanage. I don't believe he even really thinks that, otherwise, how does he think he's going to trace his heritage?"

"Do we know that's what he wants to do?" I said.

Neither woman said anything.

Allyson moved back to the love seat. "Philip," she said, "I have withheld from Mother two things."

"What?" Mrs. Scheel demanded.

"Please, Mother, you promised. I want to know if Philip thinks I should tell you."

"Oh, hey," I said, "that's out of my league. I don't know what you've kept from her, and I'm not sure I want to know, but I would guess she has withheld an item or two from you as well."

The women looked at each other. Beatrice lowered her eyes. Then she smiled slightly. "Are we about to work a deal?" she asked.

"I think we'd better," Allyson said. "Just from the new things I've heard tonight I feel more determined to get to the bottom of this."

"How do you feel about the possibility that we all might suffer from what we find?" Mrs. Scheel said.

"I agree that's paramount," I said.

"We couldn't suffer more, could we?" Allyson said. "Mother, you have pain and emptiness from a one-sided relationship. Father is going to explode before he dies if he doesn't drag his poisonous memories into the light of day. And I'm loving and pitying a man I never got to know. He's a father who wasn't a father, a man with no history, no future, no goals. A man who left me without half a family. Maybe it's selfish, Mother, but I have to know. If we can find out without hurting him, and I know there's no guarantee, I think I want to pursue it."

Mrs. Scheel stared at me and then at Allyson. She sipped her cold tea and touched cup back to saucer with a cultured tick. She took it back to the kitchen and returned. My eyes met Allyson's, and it was obvious we were both hoping for the same thing — her mother's agreement that something had to give.

"I'll go this far," her mother said, one knee resting on the arm of the love seat. "I'll tell you the only other significant memory I have of your father if you tell me what you haven't told me yet."

THIRTEEN

Allyson told her mother the story of the shoeboxes. Mrs. Scheel nodded sadly throughout. "I know that shoebox," she said finally. "I saw it a few times myself. Once I even caught him clipping items from the paper to put into it. So we shared the same secret, Allie."

They clasped hands, comforting each other.

"I don't mind telling you I'm still in the dark," I said, "but I don't want to press."

"I'm sure Allyson came to the same conclusion I did when she saw the material. It was the only part about Curtis that didn't fit. He was so secretive about everything else, yet that shoebox full of newspaper clippings and old photographs from Germany was so loosely hidden under the bed that it was as if he were begging for it to be found.

"I asked him once if he wanted to talk about it, and it sent him into one of his silent, softly crying hours. 'No,' he said eventually, 'I just feel drawn to my homeland. I keep articles about it here. The pictures are of people they tell me were my family. But there is no resemblance. I do not believe them. But they are pictures of Germans, and so I keep them.'

"But he did more than keep them. Every few months I would see him with the box, studying the photographs. Once when he was gone I dug out the box and studied the pictures. I disagreed with him. I saw a family resemblance, and I think I even saw Curt as a young boy. The face was different, but I was convinced it was him. The names of the people in the pictures had been scratched over and marked out, and there had even been some erasing. I couldn't make out any names, only dates. Mostly the pictures were taken in the early nineteen thirties. The unmarked ones could have been later."

"What kinds of clippings did he save?" I asked.

Allyson and her mother looked at each other and then at me. They started to speak together, but the older woman deferred. "I have photocopies in my folder," Allyson said. She went to get it.

I didn't know what to say to her mother while Allyson was gone. It didn't seem right to talk about Mr. Scheel, so I talked about the only other thing that had been on my mind the last two days. "You have a very beautiful daughter."

Mrs. Scheel smiled. "I know," she said, not immodestly. "And let me tell you something from an admittedly biased point of view, Mr. Spence. I raised that girl, I trained her in the business, I have been her boss, and now we are partners. We have lived together, we have lived apart, and I have given her her freedom. Still no one knows her like I do. That beauty is deep inside her, too. It goes right to the soul."

I wanted to tell her that I sensed it, that I didn't doubt her in the least, but Allyson returned. She could tell by the quick silence that we had been talking about her, but she was so intent on the file folder that she ignored it.

Though only a half-inch thick, the folder had that heavy feel of a sheaf of photocopies. She and her mother sat together and waited as I leafed through it. The photos had been ganged about five to a page. They showed working-class Germans in typical group-shot family poses, very slight smiles when smiling at all. The progression seemed to show a small family of perhaps five, the children growing larger and the parents a little older in each of about a dozen shots. The photocopy of what had been written on the backs of the pictures was nearly useless. Tiny year listings from the 1930s were all I could make out.

The newspaper clippings were the shockers. They weren't the scrapbook style clips an immigrant would save, fun little features and picture-story travelogues of his homeland. No, these were follow-up stories on World War II in Germany. They chronicled the rise and fall of the Third Reich. They were clippings of not just big, front page articles about Hitler and the SS, but also little three-inch items from the back pages of the old *Chicago Sun* and the *American,* the *Daily Tribune* and the *Daily News.* Many were dated before Curtis Scheel had claimed to even have arrived in the United States, so he had obviously obtained back copies. But the clips were also as recent as the late sixties when Allyson had found the box.

"I'd love to see what's in there today," Mrs. Scheel said. "If Allyson retained your firm, could we find out?"

"Probably not," I admitted, not looking up from the photocopies. I shuddered at the abundance of short pieces about the discovery of Nazis in the U.S. and Canada and other countries, their trials, their convictions and acquittals. Mr. Scheel had a file of clips on the Adolf Eichmann trial that would have rivaled that of any library, yet the clips had been neatly folded in a shoebox under a bed for more than a decade when Allyson had found them.

I spent a depressing half hour trying to speed read the file. "I don't think I'm going to be able to show this to Earl," I said, "even if you let me take it. He will not use evidence gained illegally, and under the circumstances, this could be very damaging. I don't know what other conclusion to draw from this, and I frankly don't know, Allyson, what good you'll be doing yourself or your mother or your father to have us confirm this. The man seems to have a very valid reason for living in fear. Maybe the orphanage story is a sham, if these photos of what look like his family are any indication. But if he has been able to maintain silence all these years, even from the woman he was married to, I don't think we'll do him any service by trying to purge his tormented mind with a confession. He has had every opportunity to come forward."

"Do you have to expose him based on what you know?" Allyson asked.

"Earl doesn't think so," I said. "And I feel no compulsion to, though there would be many who would disagree and would want to see him brought to trial. I suppose if there were evidence that he wasn't remorseful and was just gleefully living off the fat of the land and flaunting his freedom, I would feel differently. Frankly, I think the man is in his own prison and is suffering as much as any jury could impose upon him."

"But I want him out of that prison," Allyson said.

"You'll just be putting him in a literal one," Mrs. Scheel countered.

"Maybe not," Allyson said. "If we can arrange it that Philip and Mr. Haymeyer can find out who Father really is and can confront him with it, perhaps he can experience some kind of emotional release. We can't testify against him, and I'd much rather have it be we who expose him than someone else."

"What makes you think someone else is onto him?" Mrs. Scheel said.

"Because he lives in such fear and torment."

"Because he may be guilty of heinous crimes. We may be interpreting the guilt as fear. Maybe he is less fearful after having eluded prosecution for more than thirty years."

"Well, if he travels internationally on his phony name, he may run into trouble he hasn't expected," Allyson said.

"In Germany?" her mother asked. "And he's had that phony name longer than he had his original. It's official in the US. He's been naturalized with it, he has papers, official ones, with that name all over them. It *is* his name now."

"You forget, I found he's not going to Germany. It's the one other thing I haven't told you. And it's going to convince you that Father needs protection."

"What *are* you talking about, Allie?" Mrs. Scheel said.

"I'm talking about the fact that I wouldn't worry so much if Father were flying nonstop to Germany, but he's not. It's not even on his itinerary."

"I'll bite," her mother said. "Where's he going that's going to put him in danger of being exposed?"

"Israel," Allyson said. "More specifically, Jerusalem."

Her mother drew a hand to her mouth.

"He is booked on a Zion Air nonstop from New York to Tel Aviv, and he has arranged for a car and a driver to take him immediately to Jerusalem. He's reserved a room for four nights at the King David Hotel, and his return flight has been left open. That's all I know. I don't know what or whom he is going to see, but I know I want him either confronted before he leaves or guarded while he's there. I have no idea how a German could be discovered and exposed after thirty years in the United States, but I have a feeling deep inside me that this is an unwise trip for him. Mother, do you agree that we should put Mr. Haymeyer's agency on this to either talk Father out of it or follow him to Israel?"

Mrs. Scheel couldn't talk. I didn't know what to say.

"Mother, I know what you're thinking," Allyson said. "When it finally hit home what all this was about, and I started considering the possibility that my worst fears were true, my first thought was of all the Jewish women we have dealt with over the years on the North Shore. From customers who are the backbone of our business, to associates, to suppliers, to service women, to seamstresses, can you imagine the impact if they knew the history of our own flesh and blood? And you know I'm not thinking in the least about the business impact."

"Of course I know that, Allie," the older woman said. "I know exactly what you're saying. Sweetheart, this whole thing has been on your initiative from the start. I think you have to do what you have to do. I'll support you either way. All I ask is that you keep me informed and don't ask me for any more information."

"You've given Philip all you have anyway, haven't you?"

"Almost."

"Let me have it all," I said. "Please. Don't make this any more difficult for us than it already will be."

Mrs. Scheel studied her hands. "It may be nothing," she began slowly, "but, Allie, do you recall that your father never wore short-sleeved shirts?"

"I guess so, yes. I never thought much about it because he was almost always dressed up when I saw him."

"If you think about it, you'll know that you *never* saw his bare arms."

"OK — "

"Well, I did, and sometimes I think I am the only person who ever did. Philip, did Hitler's troops have any sort of swastika or other insignias tatooed on their forearms?"

"I really don't know. I'd have to check that. Why? Did he have anything like that?"

"No, but he had one of the nastiest burn scars on his forearm that I have ever seen. It was so clean, in a perfect rectangle, that it almost looked as if it had been done intentionally to cover something. I asked him about it only once. He said he had no memory of it whatever. He assumed it was a birthmark, but if it was, it was unlike any I've ever seen."

FOURTEEN

"So, I hope you don't mind that I didn't get to those case files you asked me to read," I concluded the next morning.

"Nah," Earl said. "It looks like you're going to be busy enough for a while. Is Allyson coming up to sign the papers?"

"I assume. You want me to pay her a visit?"

"Maybe. But first let me see that folder with the photocopies of the stuff from the shoebox."

"You're kidding. I told Allyson and her mother that you probably wouldn't want to see it, knowing your feeling about using evidence that was gained illegally."

"What are you talking about, Philip? This is a whole different ballgame from when Allyson first talked to us. We're not trying to find out who or what her father is or has done. That's not our problem. Our assignment is protect the man. Any and all information Allyson or Mrs. Scheel can give us that will help us protect him, we want."

"And if it shows that he is a Nazi?"

"We'll deal with that at that time. Frankly, I don't think — from what you've said about the contents of the box — that anything in there will give him away. It may show that he's a German, and maybe even that he was not really an orphan, but lots of people collect news stories about Germany. I have a little nephew who knows more about Hitler than anyone I know."

Earl studied the file carefully, spending most of his time on the photographs. "I'd really like to know if these were taken in Germany," he said. "It would be helpful to know if the little boy in this picture and the older boy in this one are both Mr. Scheel as a child. If they are, and these were taken in his original homeland — and it's not Germany — maybe he really was an orphan, deserted by his parents or left alone when they died or something."

"How will that help us, Earl?"

"It might help us track him."

"But Mrs. Scheel is sure he changed his name."

"And she's probably right, but why did he change it? Who in his hometown, maybe the oldtimers, would recognize the people in these pictures? If you could find that out first, you might be able to save yourself a trip to Israel."

"But what if I go to Austria or Germany or someplace, and then still have to go to Israel? That could get pretty expensive for Allyson."

"Let's let her be the judge of that. Go see her."

I couldn't think of anything I'd rather do, and was grinning to myself — which isn't easy if you think about it — as I moved quickly out of Earl's office and over to my desk to throw on my suit coat. I walked right past Margo, hardly noticing her. "Good morning," she said, formally.

I realized immediately that I should be acting a little more deliberately and mournfully too, the day after breaking my engagement. I let my shoulders sag. "Hi," I said softly. "How are you?"

"Fine."

"Good. That's good. I want you to be fine."

"I am."

"Good."

"Thank you."

"Right."

"I'm really OK, Philip. Don't worry about me."

"Oh, I wasn't. I mean, well, I *was,* but OK, I won't."

"Fine."

"Good." I felt like a jerk. I *was* a jerk. She raised her eyebrows as if she was finished with this ridiculous conversation if I was. So I put on my suit coat and hurried downstairs, realizing only when I caught a glimpse of my reflection in the plate glass window of the boutique that my coat collar was sticking straight up in the back. I tried to straighten it with one hand and open the door with the other.

Allyson was on her way out. "I was just on my way up to see you," she said, reaching for my collar and helping smooth it down. I had never been so close to her. I smelled her delicate perfume and was inches from her eyes. If it hadn't been for the concern evident on her face, I could have savored the moment. "I just got a call from my friend in Evanston — the travel agent — and I have to talk with you and Mr. Haymeyer. Is it all right?"

"Sure," I said, spinning on one heel and leading her back out the door. I could hardly keep up with her and wound up following her into Earl's office. If Margo looked up, it wasn't until we had passed her.

"Good morning," Earl said.

"Hi," she said quickly, sitting down without taking off her coat. "I need to retain your firm immediately and have my father followed to Israel. I'm afraid for his life."

"Whoa," Earl said. "Easy. Let's take it from the top."

"I got a call from my travel agency friend in Evanston this morning. She said she thought I might want to know that while my father was booked on a flight to Tel Aviv from New York on December fifteen, he was also wait-listed on one this evening. A seat opened, and he's going. She checked with the agency in Chicago that booked him and found that he had already changed all his arrangements, hotel, driver, everything, so he could fly tonight and arrive there tomorrow."

"Allyson," Earl said slowly, trying to change the pace, "none of us is dead certain about your father. We don't know if he's German, though it's obvious he grew up there from his accent alone; we don't know he was an orphan, though we have no solid reason to doubt him; we don't know he was a Nazi, though he could have been in Germany during Hitler's reign of terror, and he would have been the right age for military service."

"And he is a tormented man with a haunting past," Allyson said.

"All right," Earl said, "but are you certain his life will be in danger if he visits Israel? My point is, are you sure you want to invest in air fare, meals, lodging, and miscellaneous expenses, plus, let me see, two hundred and ninety plus half of that again, carry the one, four hundred and thirty-five dollars a day to have him tailed?"

Allyson dug a pocket calculator out of her handbag. "If it took three weeks, that would be a little over nine thousand dollars, plus expenses. I think I can afford to have one of you go there and stay as long as he can afford to stay."

"And that's what you want to do? Send one of us to protect him?"

"Without his knowing it," Allyson added.

"That may not be easy after a while," Earl said. "Especially if we need to keep a close watch on him. And you know, we guarantee nothing, especially with only one of us going. There's no way one man can watch another twenty-four hours a day unless they're handcuffed together and sleep at the same time."

"I understand, but I'll expect you to do your best."

"I'm not going to be able to go," Earl said. "I'll be sending Philip."

Allyson turned and looked me full in the face, unsmiling. "That makes me feel very secure," she said.

I couldn't pull my eyes away. I wanted to tell her without saying a word that I would do everything in my power to protect her father, as if I were protecting her.

"You can't take your gun, Philip," Earl was saying. I reluctantly turned to look at him. "There's no way they'll let you on a plane to Israel with a firearm, and they'll check your bags too, so forget it. You're going to be on your own over there."

"How am I going to get there if seats are so tight on the airlines?"

"I asked my friend to put you as high on the wait list as she could without getting in trouble," Allyson said. "She's gonna call me later this morning. In fact, maybe I'll call her now." She stood.

"Would you sign this, please?" Earl said, turning a clipboard toward her. She leaned over the desk and wrote her name in a small, neat script.

"How much do you need in advance?" she asked.

"Figure fifteen hundred for air fare, including Chicago to New York, and another six or seven hundred for hotel and meals and transportation for a few days. My hope is that if Philip learns anything in Israel about your father, perhaps he can talk him into coming back soon. That will be cheaper."

Allyson looked dubious about that as she quickly wrote out a check to the EH Detective Agency for thirty-two hundred dollars. "I'll let you know as soon as I hear about the Air Zion flight," she said. "It leaves New York at eight tonight, so you'd better get an early afternoon flight out of O'Hare."

Bonnie booked me on a New York flight for one o'clock while I was packing. "Take enough for four days so you can travel light," Earl had said, "then get to know the valet in the hotel. You'd better stay at the King David and plan to spend a lot of time in the lobby so you'll know when Scheel's leaving."

I was ready to go by ten o'clock and sat fidgeting at my desk. "Have a nice trip, and be careful," Margo said.

"Thanks," I said. "Hey, I hardly noticed how young you look. You startin' high school today?"

"Yeah. I'm nervous. Scared is a better word for it."

"Me too. We've finally hit the big time, huh?"

"Well, I wouldn't put working undercover as a high school girl in the same league with globetrotting after war criminals, but, yeah, I'd say we're at least fullfledged junior deputies by now."

We smiled at each other, and I wondered if mine looked as pained as hers. I hoped it was just a result of anxiety over her assignment, but I knew better.

We both spun toward the door as Larry Shipman bounded up the stairs and blasted through in his characteristic style. "Bonnie, my love, how are ya?" he shouted, winging past her without looking, trenchcoat tails trailing him. "Philip, Margo," he said in greeting as he blew past and into Earl's office. He shut the door.

"He didn't look at me," Bonnie said. "He always looks at me when he comes in. That must mean bad news."

"Oh, don't be ridiculous," Margo said, stealing a knowing glance at me. "It could just as easily be good news, or, knowing Ship, no news." Bonnie turned back to her typing, obviously unconvinced.

Earl stuck his head out. "Bon," he called, "did the morning paper ever come?"

I started to remind him that he had picked it up on the way in when we both arrived at about seven, but he stared me to silence.

"I don't see it anywhere," she said. "Anyone else seen it?"

Margo shook her head.

I didn't know what Earl was up to, so I stalled. "Today's paper, you mean?" I said.

"Bonnie, would you run and get me one?" he said. "And while you're out, could you run my car over to the Standard station? Tell him I want that lube job special they're advertising. They'll bring you back."

"Sure," Bonnie said, "and then will you tell me what Larry has found?"

"You'll be among the first to know," Earl said.

As soon as Bonnie was out the door, Earl motioned Margo and me into his office with a nod. "Tell 'em, Ship," he said as we sat down.

"Bad news," Larry said. "It was as I suspected. Greg had been gone not ten minutes — and the daughter, Erin, about five — when loverboy Bizell shows up in the 'Vette. He was in there for an hour or so, and I was getting impatient. I put a ring of keys on my belt and put on an old cap. I was already wearing grubbies. I picked the lock with Earl's famous steel piece that's quicker and quieter than a key, and as I swung the door open, I hollered, "Maintenance! Anybody home?"

FIFTEEN

Margo and I sat there with our mouths open. Was there no end to Shipman's imagination, let alone his gall?

"So they'd been sitting on the couch. She jumps up off his lap, and he stands up, too. 'What *is* it?' she demands, 'and what do you mean, barging in here without knocking?' Bizell looks like he's seen a ghost.

" 'I'm so sorry, ma'am,' I said. 'Just checkin' to see if you got any water from the leak upstairs.'

" 'No,' she says, 'I didn't even know about it.'

" 'That's all I needed to know,' I said, and there was a lot of truth to that. 'Sorry to bother you, Mr. and Mrs. — uh — ah — ' and I'm checking a slip of paper. Bizell says, 'Gibbons,' so I repeat it, backing out into the hall. Then I came here."

Margo was angry. "That woman," she said. "Casting aspersions on her husband's reputation when it's been her all along!"

"We can't be certain Greg is totally innocent," Earl said. "But I'm afraid you're right. How would you like to have to tell Bonnie this?"

"You wouldn't do that to me, would you, Earl?"

"Of course not. I run the place. I authorized the free service. I relay the bad news. The thing that never ceases to amaze me is the number of times you turn up things in a case that are the opposite of what you thought you were after."

We sat in silence. The phone rang at the switchboard outside. Margo, nearest the door, jumped up to get it.

"Philip, it's for you. Allyson from downstairs."

I shouldn't have appeared so eager to talk to her, grabbing the phone from Margo with hardly an acknowledgment. Allyson had bad news, too. This had not been our day. "My friend has us, I mean you, at the top of the wait list," she reported, "but Air Zion is not expecting any no-shows. I guess these are booked so far in advance that people hang onto their reservations."

"Let me punch Earl onto this line," I said. I told him the story.

"Those are seven forty-sevens, aren't they?" he asked. "Surely someone will be sick or late or something. We're talking about a lot of people. More than three or four hundred, right?"

"Yeah," Allyson said, "but we can't bank on that. What if Philip gets to New York and then can't get on? He just has to be on the same plane with Father." She sounded frantic.

"Can you come up here, Allyson?" Earl asked.

"Sure."

We met in his office again.

"There's one more option," Earl said.

"You're not talking about a charter flight, are you?" Allyson said.

"Hardly. Even you couldn't afford that. This plan will cost you, though."

"I'm listening."

"You can buy someone's spot on the plane."

"How do I do that? What if Philip tries to talk someone out of his reservation for some money and no one takes him up on it?"

"He couldn't do it that way, anyway," Earl said, "from what I know about Israeli security. He would have to have a ticket in his own name and then prove it with his identification documents. By the way, Philip, you're going over there as a tourist, you know."

"What do you mean?"

"I mean that when they ask you the purpose for your trip, if you say you're playing clandestine bodyguard to a Nazi war criminal, you're not going to get far."

I nodded. "I've never been there," I said. "So, I *will* be a tourist."

Allyson was getting impatient. "I'm sorry, gentlemen, but how are we going to get Philip on that plane?"

"It'll have to come through the travel agency," Earl said. "Your friend is going to have to get on the blower and start calling booked passengers, informing them that a party is willing to pay a certain amount for their reservation. If she can find anyone, the ticket will be rebooked in Philip's name, and he's set."

"She's going to have to get moving on it," Allyson said. "What would be a good offer? I'm willing to pay for it."

"Oh, I would think a hundred dollars or so, plus a hotel room for the night in New

York. Whoever you talk into it is going to need a seat on the next available flight to Israel, no doubt. I would advise your friend to call people who appear to be traveling alone. Families will not likely want to split up, even for money, and the individual passenger who is not on a tight schedule might opt for the money and a free night in New York."

"Can I call from here?" Allyson asked.

Earl turned his desk phone around to face her.

Her hands shook as she dialed. She hung up before anyone answered. "It's all right," she said. "I'll call from downstairs. I need to tell Mother what's happening anyway." Still unsmiling, she winked at me on her way out. I was going to miss her. She trotted back and leaned to whisper in my ear. "If I get you on the flight, can I also drive you to the airport?"

"Sure," I said. "O'Hare or JFK?" It almost drew a smile.

I was getting antsy. Within half an hour I would need to be leaving for the airport. There was no sense going to New York unless I was booked to Tel Aviv. I tried reading a file and making some notes, but I was anxious to hear from Allyson. Bonnie was in Earl's office for a long time.

When she came out, she was in tears, red-faced, seemingly in shock. "I can hardly believe it," she said as Margo embraced her. "I'm so ashamed."

"It's not your fault," Margo said, leading her to the coat rack and helping her on with her coat. "She's a grown woman, married fifteen years."

"But she's not going to make sixteen, is she?" Bonnie said, covering her face with her hands.

"Stranger things have happened," Margo said. "Sometimes people are able to forgive and to rebuild." I had always been impressed with Margo's gentleness and spirit of encouragement.

"Earl said I could take the rest of the day off," Bonnie said. "I'm going home."

"Do you need any company?"

"No, thanks. Larry's not going to like sitting at the switchboard with you off at your high school assignment and Philip flying to New York."

"Don't worry about him," Margo said. "It'll be good for him. Let me walk you to your car. I'm going to the school now, anyway. Are you sure you'll be all right?"

Bonnie nodded.

For a few minutes I enjoyed watching Larry try to familiarize himself with the switchboard. He had manned it during the lunch hour before, but it had been programmed to ring on just one line. Now he would have to answer the appropriate phone, transfer calls to Earl, and everything.

I realized I hadn't said good-bye to either woman. I could be gone by the time either returned to work. And when I saw Allyson's slight smile as she appeared at the top of the stairs, I knew I *would be*. I stood as she entered.

"It worked," she said. "My friend found a man who didn't really need to be in Israel until early next week. It's going to cost about two hundred dollars, but it's worth it. I feel a lot better."

"You look a lot better," I said.

"Thanks."

"If that's possible." It was my first even close to bold statement to her.

"Thanks again," she said, smiling. "Ready?"

Earl had been listening from his doorway. "Keep in touch, Philip," he said. "Don't be afraid to call with questions. Our client will pay for it, and she's loaded. Just remember the time change."

I assured Allyson that she could just drop me off in front of the American departure terminal, but she insisted on parking in the garage and walking me to the gate. She was nervous, talking more than usual and continually checking her watch.

"We're OK," I told her. "We're a little ahead of schedule." I suddenly felt very close to her. Probably it was just that our energy and concentration was centered on her father. "I hope I can protect him and that whatever he wants from Israel, he'll get," I said.

She said nothing.

"I'm going to miss you," I said.

She had been staring out at the planes lined up on the runway. "Ah, no, you won't," she said.

"I will," I said, growing bolder. "I'll miss you very much. I'll be eager to get back to see you."

She looked flattered, but only smiled. I had planned to be among the last on the plane, since I had a seat and a reason to linger, but when the boarding call was announced, Allyson looked at her watch, thanked me for "being so sweet," reminded me that my Air Zion ticket would be at the will call desk in New York, shook my hand, and hurried off more quickly than she had moved all day. I hoped maybe she was hiding an emotion she didn't want to admit, but I wouldn't have bet on it.

I tried to sleep on the way to New York, knowing that the long flight to Tel Aviv would take its toll, but it was impossible. By the time I had had my Coke and a snack and an early dinner, we were "beginning our descent," as they say.

I got to the international terminal a couple of hours early, and the sights there were an experience in themselves. It appeared that 90 percent of the passengers were carrying more bags than would be allowed, most were from Israel, and many were religious Jews, dressed in full garb. The place was jammed, as if the plane was about to take off.

Hardly anyone but the desk clerks spoke English, and tired children wailed the whole time. I pulled two photographs of Curtis Scheel from my wallet and began surreptitiously scouting him out.

Forty minutes later, when I finally reached the head of my line, I had still not spotted him. As the girl checked my reservation, I asked if Mr. Scheel had checked in yet.

"I'll check." She entered his name on her video screen. "Two Scheels have checked in and another has a reservation. First initial?"

"C," I said.

"There are two. Is he from Cleveland?"

"Chicago."

"Yes, Mr. C. Scheel of Chicago has checked in. Would you like to be seated near him?"

"Not necessarily. I was just curious if — "

"I'm sorry," she said. "I couldn't get you near him anyway. That section is filled, and so is the one behind it. I'm afraid you will be forty or so rows behind him."

"That's all right," I said. "That's fine."

I just hoped I would get a look at him before we hit the ground. "What seat is he in?" I asked.

"Seventeen G. Just ahead of the forecabin lavatories."

At security, I was asked the purpose of my trip, whether I had been to Israel before, who had had access to my bags, had anyone given me any gifts, packages, or messages for anyone in Israel, how long was I staying, and on and on. When I was finally cleared and my bag had been checked, I felt relieved. I sat and waited more than an hour and a half to board, and by the time the announcement came, I was already exhausted. I had not seen Curtis Scheel. And it had already been a long day.

He would enter the plane from the front entrance, I from the rear. I knew I would have to mosey up the aisle at some point during the flight and get a look at him. And from that point on, I couldn't let him out of my sight except when he was in his hotel room. He would be vulnerable even there, but I was only one man. I would have to take some chances.

People all around me were reading prayer books and praying quietly. I dug my Bible from my carry-on bag and read, wishing that I was in Israel for pleasure rather than business. So many friends had told me how the Bible had come alive when they had visited Jerusalem and all the other historic Christian sights. Maybe one day Margo and I would come back to see it as pilgrims.

Margo. Was she still that entrenched in my mind? What was I saying? It's hard to shake the thoughts of a future life with someone, even when that possibility has ended.

The flight was grueling. It was nonstop to Tel Aviv, and there were several meals and various other boredom-interrupters, but not enough. I slept for a while, but a feeling of claustrophobia crept up on me, and even after walking around a little, squeezing past other bored passengers in the aisles, I was unable to sleep anymore. Jet lag was hitting me already, and the only thing I had to look forward to over the next several hours was more of the same. I was just getting ready to make my way up to the front section when the lights were turned off, the window shades pulled, and the movie begun.

I thought I would try again when the movie was over, but the plane was kept dark for those who wanted to sleep. Had I blown it already? What if I couldn't get a look at Scheel before going through customs at Ben Gurion Airport? What if the plane was emptied from front to back? He might have twenty minutes on me and get to the King David Hotel first. If anyone knew he was coming and meant him any harm, I could lose him before I ever saw him. I didn't even know whether he was on the plane.

Sixteen

My muscles ached and my mind was numb as the plane droned on, if a jet can drone at 600 miles per hour. It seemed as if we would never arrive. When the window shades were finally opened and the Middle Eastern sun invaded the cabin, I jumped up to head for the lavatories and to see if I could catch a glimpse of Curtis Scheel. At least, I had to know what he was wearing in case I lost him temporarily in the crowd.

Everyone else had been waiting for daybreak to go to the bathrooms too, so I stood in long lines for more than a half hour. Finally I made it up to the forward cabin. He was not in his seat, but a vinyl flight bag was tucked beneath it. As I snaked back to my seat, a man squeezed past who could have been Scheel, but I didn't want to look too closely for fear he would remember me if he saw me again in Israel.

When we finally touched down, a common expression clouded the faces of the hundreds of passengers. The women's makeup was no longer doing its job. Most of the men needed shaves and wore blank expressions of fatigue that would be remedied only by an afternoon and all-night sleep. I wanted to get to where I would be able to see Scheel as he got off the plane, but sure enough, they let us off from front to back, and he had a big lead on me. Several buses carried us from the runway to the terminal, and he was at least two buses ahead of me.

I hoped the bottleneck at the passport check-in stations might give me a chance to catch him, but I received such hateful stares from the other tired passengers when I tried to get ahead of them that I waited until I got to the baggage claim area to make my play. Though I was among the last to crowd around the two conveyor belts of baggage, no luggage had appeared yet. Even when they did start their mechanized parade, I ignored the bags and scanned the faces. Several times I thought I saw the little man, hidden behind taller people, but I lost him. I moved away from the claim area to the final check-through to ground transportation. If he had been on the plane, he would have to come through here.

And then I saw him, a short, middle-aged man. He wore a dark brown suit with cuffs on the pants, plain black oxford shoes, and a hat. His tie, unlike those of most of the rest of the passengers, was still snug at the neck. He wore an olive sweater vest under his suit coat. The vinyl bag I had seen on the plane was slung over one shoulder, and a modest suitcase was the only other item he carried. It was bound by thin string, almost like a Christmas present. When he passed I turned to watch him from behind. He walked slowly, hesitatingly following others who had found their bags. While he was in line to have his luggage checked at security, I dove into the crowd to find my suitcase, looking over my shoulder every few moments to check on his progress. For a long time he was stalled in the line, but then he seemed to be moving up farther every time I looked.

Finally, he was gone. I had found my bag, but I didn't have time for anyone to pick through it for contraband. I set it and my carry-on piece off to one side and dashed to the inspection area. "Bags?" the guard said.

"No."

He checked my passport quickly, and I ran out into the waiting area for ground transportation. My man was approaching a cab driver. I walked to within earshot when he said, "Can you take me to the King David Hotel in Jerusalem?"

"Many shekels," the driver explained.

"OK," Curtis Scheel said.

I ran back inside and got my luggage, sweated through a careful inspection, and hurried back out. The cabs were filling. A limousine with draped windows idled at the curb. "Is this car for hire?" I asked.

"More than cabs," the driver said. "Happy to take you."

"How much?" I asked.

"How much you want to pay, Mister?"

I didn't have time to bargain. I got in and told him I would pay him extra if he could get close enough to follow a certain cab, even though I hadn't yet figured out the money system. We didn't catch the cab, and I probably got rooked on the fare, but I had no choice.

I asked the registration clerk at the King David if John Scheel had checked in yet.

"No, sir. The only Scheel we have checked in today was a Curtis, who was just put in three eighteen. Would you like to call him or leave a message?"

"No, thank you."

I waited until the head clerk was busy so he wouldn't think I knew Curtis Scheel and make the mistake of saying something to him about my looking for him. I stepped to the counter and was waited on by a young assistant. "Any chance of getting a room on the third floor?" I asked.

"Certainly. Several rooms are available on three. Any preference?"

"What do you have?"

"I'll check. All of the odd teens are open, also the evens except for three sixteen and three eighteen."

"Oh, I don't care. Put me in three seventeen."

"That's a double room, sir. Are there two of you?"

"No. But that's OK. I'll take it."

"Room three eleven is a single for much less money, sir."

"No, that's OK. I'll take three seventeen."

Once settled, I put my ear to the service door connecting my room with Scheel's. He was just climbing into bed, if I could trust my ears. I listened for more than five minutes until he was snoring softly.

I dialed the phone.

"Front desk."

"Double-checking on Mr. Scheel's wakeup call in three eighteen," I said.

"We have no wake-up call recorded for you, sir. When would you like to be called?"

"Oh, no. I'll call you later."

"Very well, sir."

I dragged one half of one of the sectioned double beds over to the service door, then unpacked my suitcase. I hardly had the strength to undress, but when I finally stretched out on the cool sheets, I was asleep within minutes. I hoped my head was close enough to the door that I would be awakened by any noise coming from Scheel's room.

At about 11:00 P.M., I awoke with a start. The room was pitch black, and I had not heard anything. At least I thought I hadn't. Then why had I awakened? I wasn't sure. I sat up and leaned over so my ear was flush with the door to Scheel's room. Sure enough, the bed squeaked as he moved. Was he going somewhere, or was he simply moving in his sleep? I listened without breathing. He dialed the phone.

"Hello," he said. "Can I get food in my room? . . . Call vat? . . . Room service? . . . Vat's de number? . . . T'ank you."

He dialed again. "Vant food in my room," he said. "T'ree hundred and eighteen . . .

Vatchu got? . . . Menu? No, I see no menu . . . Just tell me vat you got . . . OK, just tell me sandwiches. I can get sandwich and coffee? . . . OK, OK. T'ank you."

He left the bed, and I heard water running in his bathroom. I took my phone into the closet and dialed room service. "Did you just take an order for room three eighteen? . . . Well, listen, when he delivers, could you have the boy explain the wakeup call system here?"

"I could tell you, sir," the man said.

"No, just have the boy tell when he delivers, OK?" And I hung up.

A few minutes later, ear pressed against the service door again, I heard the puzzled bellman ask Scheel if he had asked about the wakeup call system.

"No. Vat that is?"

"Well, if you want to be awakened at a certain time, you just call the desk downstairs and ask them to call you at that time in the morning."

"I could call them even now?"

"Sure."

"No charge?"

"No charge."

"I to tip you for bringing food?"

"That would be fine, sir."

"How much?"

Scheel obviously held out his hand with change and bills in it. "One of these and one of these will be just right, sir," the bellman said. "You ask around and see if I took too much, OK?"

I wanted to get back to sleep, but I waited until Scheel finished eating to see if he would phone for a wakeup call. "Car and driver to pick me up here at nine in morning," he told the desk. "Can you vake me up vit' phone at eight? . . . T'ank you."

I pulled my bed back to its normal position, called in a 7:30 wakeup call for myself, and slept soundly. When the phone rang, I assumed it was my wakeup call, but my watch said it was only 6:00.

"Hello? Seven-thirty already?"

"No, but I couldn't sleep anymore. I've been sleeping since we got here, and now I'm ready for the day to begin."

I sat up and swung my feet off the side of the bed to the floor. "Allyson? Is this you!?"

"Of course."

"Where are you? You sound close!"

"At the Diplomat Hotel."

"In New York? Where?"

"Right here, silly. I'm about five minutes south of you, according to the cab driver."

I was finally awake. "Allyson, you'd better be kidding."

"I'm not."

"What're you doing here?"

"I came to help you. You can't keep an eye on my father yourself."

"But you can't help! If he sees you, it's ruined."

"Philip, I was on your flight to Tel Aviv. I caught a United flight out of O'Hare about fifteen minutes after you took off, and I had my friend pay *two* people to stay off the Air

Zion seven forty-seven. If you didn't recognize me, why should my father?"

"I don't believe you."

"I was only a few rows behind you, Philip. I was the little old lady in the burgundy shawl."

"If you were disguised as a little old lady, how did you get past the passport people?"

"I just straightened up and took the scarf away from my face. They probably thought I was one weird young lady to be dressed so frumpy."

"Allyson, I'm having a hard time taking this all in. How come I didn't even see a little old lady in a burgundy shawl?"

"I'll bet you can't describe ten of the people you saw on that plane. You were tired, and nervous, and you were looking for a little man in his late fifties, not a little old lady. And you were concentrating on the front of the plane, not the back."

"I still don't get it, Allyson. If you planned to come with me, why didn't you just tell me?"

"I had to hide from Father anyway, and I was sure you and Earl would not let me."

"We couldn't have stopped you."

"No, but you would have tried awfully hard to talk me out of it."

"True, and I'm going to have to try hard to talk you out of getting too close to your father, too. I don't know if anyone else is following him, or what they might do to him if they are. That's what I'm here for, remember?"

"Philip, I want to see you."

"I want to see you too, Allyson, but I can't have distractions."

"I'm a distraction?"

"You bet your life."

"You wouldn't make me hole up in the Diplomat Hotel when we're this close together and thousands of miles from home, would you?"

"I hope you don't think we're going to get to sightsee or shop or go out for dinner."

"Of course I know we can't do that. I just want to help you, and I want to be kept up to the minute on what's going on with my father. Is that too much to ask?"

"I still can't believe this isn't a dream."

"Did you get enough sleep, Philip?"

"Yeah. Woke up hungry, though."

"Me too. Would you be able to come down here for breakfast, or are you expecting Father to be up and moving soon?"

I told her he was meeting his car and driver at nine and that I would have to be back for that. "I'll be there at seven for breakfast," I said.

I called the desk and double-checked on the wakeup call for 318. It was still for 8:00. I told the clerk to cancel the call for 317.

In the huge lobby of the sprawling Diplomat Hotel, Allyson reached up and grabbed me by the shoulders with both hands. The sun was already fairly high in the sky, and through the lobby windows we could see a man and his camel parked near a tour bus.

"I just saw you off yesterday in Chicago, I know," Allyson said, "but being this far from home calls for a long-lost style greeting, don't you think?"

I wished I had the fortitude to tell her what kind of greeting I really preferred. She looked radiant, though she couldn't hide the concern in her eyes.

SEVENTEEN

I couldn't get over how pleased I was to see Allyson, even under those circumstances. We enjoyed the typical Israeli breakfast of eggs, cheeses, fruit, and even vegetables.

"How will you keep track of Father today?" she asked.

"One of two ways," I said. "The hard way is to get a cab and tell the driver to 'follow that car.' But with the unrest and tension here, limo drivers are wary of being followed. They don't always know who their passengers are or who might be out to get them, so I might not get far that way. I'm sure a cab driver would try it for the right money, but the limo driver would likely catch on, even if your father didn't notice."

"What are your options?"

"Well, Earl has been training me how to get information about people without lying to get it. I was really having a moral problem with it as a Christian. Earl is one who believes the end justifies the means where the life of someone may depend on what we know and what we do. So he often just tells outright lies. Like last night, he might have tried to duplicate your father's voice on the phone to get information out of the desk clerk. Or he might have told the clerk that your father was his uncle and that he needed to keep an eye on him or that he wanted to surprise him or something."

"Crafty."

"Very. Earl's the best. And in many ways in this business, the end *does* indeed justify the means. But I was raised to tell the truth. So even when I tell a lie for what some may feel is a good cause, I'm not good at it. Of course, I could be trained to get better at it, but it's hard for me to live with."

"So what do you do?"

"I asked Earl to think of an alternative, because I couldn't. It took him a few days, but he came up with one. He tells me to be bold, to ask questions, and let the listener draw whatever conclusions he wants. Like I told the desk clerk I was double-checking on Mr. Scheel's wakeup call. That was entirely true. I had heard your father call it in for eight o'clock, and then I was double-checking it. I didn't say I was Mr. Scheel, and if the clerk wants to think I was, it doesn't bother me. When I asked the room service manager to have the bellman explain the wakeup service, I didn't say Mr. Scheel had requested it. I just told him to do it."

"So, how will that help you this morning? Can you avoid the risk of the 'follow that car' routine?"

"I'm thinking about it."

"Good luck."

"Thanks."

Allyson and I were finished eating, and apparently finished talking, too. I looked at my watch, and she looked at hers. "I would appreciate your staying close to the hotel here today," I said. "I don't know where your father is going, but it would be very dangerous, or at best unfortunate, for you to run into him if you're out and about."

"Could you call me and tell me where he's gonna be when you know? Then maybe I can get out to a museum or something. I'll go crazy just sitting here waiting."

"I'll see what I can do."

We were silent again. I had about twenty minutes before I had to start heading back to the King David. I looked into Allyson's eyes. There was nothing to say, but the shyness was gone from both of us. I had no idea if she was feeling for me what I was feeling for her, but I was past the point where I was uncomfortable looking at her for longer than a moment. Usually I looked away after a few seconds, and more often, she looked away. Now we simply stared at each other from across the table. I put my hand over hers. She didn't pull away, but she didn't respond, either. I smiled at her, wondering if I had surprised her. When the waiter came, the moment was lost.

We strolled through the lobby again, and Allyson took a picture of the camel through the glass. I wanted to hold her hand, but I didn't want to push her or scare her. I was dying to know what she was thinking, feeling. "I gotta go," I said.

"I'm sorry," she said, softly.

"About what?"

"That you have to go."

"That makes me feel good," I said.

"It was meant to."

"You're very forthright, aren't you?"

"So are you," she said.

"I think you're special," I said.

"I am," she said, burying her head in my arm and giggling. People turned to look. I laughed.

"How long has it been since I've been free to act like a child?" she said.

She was suddenly serious.

"What is it?" I asked.

"You have to go, and I'm battling two emotions. I'm scared and upset and troubled about Father. I keep having second thoughts about your being involved, but as Earl says, your assignment is to protect him, not to expose him. And then here I am acting like a schoolgirl because I like being around you. That's hard to keep straight in my head, one feeling so dark and threatening, and the other so pleasant."

"I'm facing exactly the same problem," I said. "I need to be razor sharp to handle this case, and yet I think about you all the time."

"You do?"

"I wouldn't have, maybe, if you hadn't come to Israel."

"I'm sorry. I had to."

"I'm glad you did."

"Me too," she said. "And like I predicted in your office just a few days ago, I'm getting to like you, Mr. — " she teased.

"Spence," I reminded her.

"Right. Mr. Spence. Now get going. And if you can call me and tell me where I can go without running into Father, that'll help."

"I will. 'Bye." She gripped my hand and made me pull away to get in the cab. I wished I didn't have to work.

"You here to pick up Mr. Schwartz?" I asked the first limo driver in line at the King David.

"No, Mr. and Mrs. Young," the driver said.

I asked the second the same question.

"No, sir," he said. "Mr. Scheel."

"You're not with Feinstein Livery?"

"No, sir. I'm with Carmel Touring."

"Thank you."

I jogged into the lobby and called Carmel Touring. While I waited for them to answer, Scheel walked out past me, hesitating and half-stepping and looking around as usual. He asked at the desk if the limo driver would come in or wait for him outside. "He may come in if you're late," the man said. "Otherwise, he'll be outside."

As he went out the door and the limo drivers called to see if he was their man, a woman answered my call. "Carmel Touring."

"Double-checking on Mr. Scheel's itinerary today," I said.

"Is that Mr. and Mrs. S. Scheel, or C. Scheel?" she said.

"C."

"Starting the day at the Yad Vashem Memorial. The rest of the day is open, the car available until four-thirty this afternoon."

I took a cab to Yad Vashem, not realizing until I arrived that it consisted of various beautiful memorials to the martyrs of the Holocaust. Inscriptions, sculptures, even planted trees had been placed in this setting to commemorate the six million who had been massacred by the Nazis in World War II for their "crime" of existing as Jews. I confess I was shaken to the core to realize that Curtis Scheel would come here. I had hardly been aware of the museum and the various remembrances, and now I was face to face with them, realizing the limits of my own knowledge of the tragedy. We had studied it in school, sure, but there was something sacred and eerie and soul-twistingly somber about this place. And it hadn't even opened to the public for the day yet. Curtis Scheel joined the crowd of a couple of hundred or so who milled about the Warsaw Ghetto Memorial Square. There were school children, tourists of several nationalities, religious Jews in varying styles of dress, and perhaps some survivors or children of survivors. No doubt, there were also in the crowd some relatives of the martyrs.

Scheel stood away from the rest, gazing somewhat confused — I thought — at a modernistic sculpture on the Wall of Remembrance. I studied it for several minutes, trying to put together what little I knew about Jewish symbolism and art, and the best I could make of it was that it honored the Jews who rebelled against the Nazis in Poland rather than submitting to their barbarism.

When the doors finally opened, many filed slowly into a huge dark room where nonreligious Jews and Gentiles whose heads were uncovered were given cardboard caps. I had trouble keeping mine on, but I soon forgot about it as I stared at the flame and the markers that plotted the concentration and death camps that had dotted all of Europe during the domination of the Third Reich. An English-speaking guide quietly told his group about the various places and the atrocities committed there. It was moving, but I had to keep watching Scheel. He stood rigidly, directly across from the marker for Chelmno. After several minutes he moved down to stand before the marker for

Treblinka. I remembered these names, not as famous as Auschwitz or Buchenwald, but names from history lessons nonetheless. I wondered what memories they conjured for Mr. Scheel.

As the crowd moved slowly and silently out, many of us dropping our cardboard caps back into a box, Scheel lagged behind. As his driver and car waited in the parking lot with many others, he sat on a bench outside the museum itself and stared at the ground. Oh, to know what was going on inside that head. Was this his final purging? Did he want to see what the Jews had put together in their museum to force themselves and the world to remember? Would he be moved to any sort of confession in his soul, not the subconscious type that had violated his dreams for years, but the kind that might wring out his being and bring him to his knees before his victims?

A tour group with a German-speaking guide moved into position before the artwork that graces the wall that separates the two wings of the museum. When Scheel heard the explanation of the symbols in the art and the story it told of Jewish persecution through the years, he rose heavily and edged close enough to get the whole presentation. He appeared puzzled, as I must have, even when I heard the English tour guide talk about it. There was something strangely beautiful about the stark sculpture on the wall, and I remembered how meaningless it had appeared before I heard someone point out the elements.

There was something strange, too, about the crowds that moved through the museum. They went in from our right, knowing full well that they were going to get an eye-opening educational experience, but having no idea of the emotional impact it might have on them. They chatted quietly with each other, smiling, though basically reverent. No one was acting inappropriately, but there were incidental conversations. As they came out into the open again from the first leg of the tour and headed into the final portion, those of us waiting to get in saw them afresh. They walked more slowly. They spoke not at all. Some looked on the verge of tears, most appeared stunned. It made me more curious than ever to see what awaited us, and I wondered anew what effect it would have on a Nazi. How many had slipped in unnoticed to see it?

EIGHTEEN

Just more than a dozen people entered the museum with Curtis Scheel. I stayed behind him and out of his line of vision no matter where he turned. I realized quickly that I should have tried to go through the facility alone first so I wouldn't be tempted to stop and look at the stark, high contrast blowups of black and white photographs and read the captions. This, I realized, made up the bulk of the museum, and I was fascinated.

But I had to keep Scheel in view. I stole glances at some of the first photographs, documenting Nazi oppression of the Jews in Europe before the camps had opened. Signs calling for the blood of the Jews and banners with derogatory slogans against the

Jewish race gave evidence that the Nazis quickly quit trying to hide their reasons for wanting to do away with the Jew. They didn't trump up charges against him. They didn't frame him or entrap him. They didn't push him into wrongdoing. They needed no other excuse than that he was a Jew. That was enough. That was punishable by death.

I put myself in a position where I could watch the movement of Scheel out of the corner of my eye as I read and studied the photographs. He was not twenty-five feet into the gallery when his already slow pace simply stopped, and he stood staring at the photographs, laboring to read the English captions. He had no trouble with the German phrases and words in the pictures themselves.

He stood granitelike as other patrons filed past, reading more quickly, taking in the flow and progression of the story. It was education, it was history. It was moving and dramatic, and it assaulted their eyes, taught them lessons, opened their minds. But it did nothing to them compared with what it did to Curtis Scheel.

It became obvious that he could barely take it in. I moved closer to the wall and pretended to be trying to get a better view of a small photograph, but I really wanted a look at his face, at least from the side.

He was simply staring at a picture of a young Jew and his German girl friend who had been caught together in the man's apartment. They had been forced to wear signs in public, admitting their "disgraceful" relationship. Scheel stared at the picture, and his face grew taut. He squinted, his eyes darting around the background of the shot, perhaps remembering landmarks of his youth. Finally he moved slowly along and stopped at the next picture.

He spent several minutes at each one, seemingly unable to move away until something inside him had assimilated what his eyes had taken in. His entire body was more rigid. He seemed unable to bend his legs at the knee, walking slowly like a robot, sometimes seeming to hardly move. All it did was make me want to study the photographs even more and read the captions more carefully, but I didn't dare linger lest he suddenly regain his composure and slip out with the dozens who had passed him in the last several minutes.

I almost forgot I was there to protect him. From what or whom, I didn't know. I doubted that anyone recognizing him, regardless who Scheel really was or had been, would try to harm him there, but stranger things had happened. I moved closer to him. We had been in that section of the photo gallery, a blackened room with small lights illuminating the photographs, about three times longer than the usual spectator. Scheel arrived at the photos of families who had been forced to dig their own graves, then strip and stand together in line while they were machine-gunned into the holes. I stood transfixed, looking over his shoulder at the pathos evident on the faces of the young mother and father as they tried to comfort terrified children. There could be no explanation, no pacifying. And there was no escape. The parents were stoic, comforting their babies in their arms before the bullets drove them to their deaths.

My throat was tight. I didn't know what I felt toward the Nazis. That emotion that most sane people in the free world nurture deep in their bosom, that outrage and incomprehension of the atrocity, is something that doesn't need explanation. It was simply wrong, dead wrong, unconscionable what the Nazis did to the Jews. And worst of all, there was not even an attempt to justify it. What was I feeling toward Scheel? How could I pity him?

Yet in a sense I did. He had lived with this all of his adult life, and now it was staring him in the face in more vivid and horrible detail than he endured in his worst nightmares. And he wasn't running from it. He couldn't. It had him in its grip, and he was forced to face it. I didn't know if it would be therapeutic or not. All I knew was that it had stopped him in his tracks. Was this the reason he had come to Jerusalem? Had he read about this place, and had he known that it was the link to his past, the only link — painful as it had to be — that would do a number on the demons that tormented him?

As he moved slowly to an even more horrifying picture of hundreds upon hundreds of emaciated bodies in a tangle of arms and legs and torsos, buried stiff in a huge pit, Curtis Scheel drew his right hand slowly to his mouth and completely covered it so his breath was forced through his nostrils. It was as if the hand on his mouth was the only thing keeping his head erect. He nodded in protest, trying to look down or turn away, yet he held his head in place with the fingers that kept his mouth shut. His breath began to come in great draws and blows through his nose, causing some passersby to wonder at him, but he was oblivious to all around him. I stood directly behind him and shielded much of the view others might have had of him. I fought conflicting emotions again of outrage against the Nazis, yet pity for this man who faced the evil in photographs that may have been shot just for him.

His chest heaved, and his loud breath came in broken gusts. When people stared, I stared back, and they moved along. Finally he tore himself from the picture and turned to look at the other side of the room. It was as if he simply couldn't take another closeup view without a break. He had been lingering at horrible depictions for nearly an hour, and his spirit had been stretched to its limits. His eyes were red, the pupils large in the darkness, and he looked me full in the face for the first time, his hand still covering his mouth. I looked away quickly and focused on another photograph.

More people moved past, and finally Scheel turned back to face the display of pictures. When he arrived at a shot of a conveyor belt delivering the cadaver of a naked Jewish man to the door of a crematorium, it was more than he could take. He covered his mouth with both hands now and forced himself to look at the photograph. The man operating the oven held the door open and was shoving the body in with a steel bar. Scheel began to moan, only the hands over his mouth keeping him from being heard throughout the room. The painful cries of mourning came through his nose, and he pushed his hands higher so the noises were pinched off and sounded like the cries of an animal trying to get out of a sealed box.

The more he moaned, the more he tried to stop, but the harder it became. He shut his eyes hard, and his arms tightened to stifle the cries, but it was futile. His head dropped to his chest and great tears gushed from his eyes and cascaded over his knuckles, still pressed against his nose. His whole body shook, his knees bent. People stared and turned away quickly, unable to deal with the anguished cries. The pictures and captions were enough for them. They didn't need this.

I didn't know what to do. I was drawn to embrace him, but I was not ready to give myself away, and I had no idea why I felt such compassion. If he had been responsible for this in any way, he needed this reckoning. It was all he could do to continue breathing while sobbing and trying to stifle his terrible moaning at the same time. He moved back into a tiny alcove where no one would pass him, and I saw him fall to his knees and move his hands up over his eyes. His cries could be heard now by anyone near, so I stepped up to block everyone's view, as if I were his son, protecting his privacy. His fingers trembled and he let the tears fall in giant drops on the floor.

When his sobbing stopped, his tears continued. He worked hard at regaining his composure. He stood, his face still to the wall, and tried to straighten his suit. There would be no hiding the fact that it had been he who had broken down at the sight of this, but when he shuffled back out of the alcove to resume his tour, he sought me out, though I tried to elude him. He leaned close. "Speak English?" he asked.

I nodded.

"I am grateful for your kindness," he said.

I didn't know what to say. How he could be aware during his grief that I had helped in a small way to protect his privacy, I couldn't understand. I touched his shoulder lightly to indicate that he was welcome, and I walked ahead of him. He caught me, ignoring the rest of the photographs in the first half of the museum. "Are you a Jew?" he asked.

I shook my head. If he was looking for someone to talk to, a Jew to apologize to perhaps, I knew he would have little trouble finding one. "This place is run by the Jews," I said, realizing immediately that only an imbecile would not know that. As we moved across the open area to the other side, I pointed to workers and helpers.

He nodded and followed me to another huge room of pictures. "Would you like me to walk with you?" I asked.

"I vould, yes, very much," he said, shyly. I assumed the worst of his emotional trauma was over.

I was wrong.

NINETEEN

Scheel ignored many of the subsequent photographs, but he spent a lot of time laboriously reading the English translations of the captions, particularly under the shots of Nazi leaders. His lips moved slowly as he worked on the quotes of the men trying to defend their murdering of the Jews.

I sensed his body reacting anew, and I wondered if I could shield him again from the stares of others if he broke down. It happened when we encountered first a pathetic shot of a few teenage girls in just their slips, nearly finished disrobing before their executions. Their faces evidenced more confusion than anything, but the fear in their dark eyes reached out to Curtis Scheel's throat and caused him to gasp loudly and turn away.

But he found himself face to face with one of the more grotesque pictures in the collection, a difficult choice in this place where the Jews have chosen to force upon the world in the form of photographs the horror that was forced upon them at the hands of the Nazis while the rest of the planet stood by.

He crossed his arms and hugged his shoulders while he gazed at the image of a woman who had been used by Nazi physicians as a guinea pig to test procedures and drugs. She was crippled and dying, due only to their callousness. In fact, she was healthier looking than most of the imprisoned women because she had been fed and taken care of to be a better specimen. It was a stark, horrifying thing, and it caused Scheel to run. He pushed past people and charged up the stairs, blindly looking for the exit.

Younger and faster, I zigzagged behind him, staying close. I was the only thing close to a friend he had in this place. He looked wildly from right to left, and when he reached the bottleneck at the exit where people picked up literature and left their contributions, he suddenly slid to a stop and dug deep in his pockets. He still had not changed his American currency into shekels, and he withdrew several large bills, probably totaling more than a hundred dollars. He shoved them into the box, his lips quivering, fighting to keep from sobbing aloud again. He reached for more money.

I gently took hold of his wrist. "This is not the answer," I said. "You will never be able to pay enough."

"I vant to support this shrine," he whined. "The vorld must see this."

"Shalom and thank you very much," a young man at the desk said, reaching across the counter for Scheel's hand.

"Shalom," Scheel said, his voice breaking. "Are you a Jew? Of course you are."

The young man smiled. "Yes, and you?"

I flinched at the irony of that, until I heard Scheel reply.

"Yes, I am a Jew. I am a survivor. I am an escapee." He put both arms on the counter and dropped his head, bursting into tears again.

I was numb.

"Bring him back here," the young man said. His nameplate read Yaacov K. "Call me Jacob," he said. "Are you a relative?"

I was still reeling, lightheaded from this thunderous revelation.

"Yes," Scheel answered for me, and the three of us ducked into an office.

"What camp were you in, sir?"

"You may call me Kurt, vit' a *K*," Scheel said. "The last name is Burghoff, and I vas sent vit' my father and mother and brother and sister to Chelmno, December 8, 1941."

Jacob trotted to a shelf on the other side of the room and pulled down a huge three-ring binder. "Bring the Treblinka book, too," the older man said. "Ve vere transferred there October 4, 1942." Jacob turned back and brought it.

He carefully leafed through the pages of Burghoffs, asking Kurt for the first and middle names of his father and mother and brother. As he reached each name, he paused. "Are you aware of their dispositions, Mr. Burghoff?"

Kurt nodded sadly. "I escaped in the August second revolt vit' a couple of hundret others in 1943, but none of my family reached our meeting point. They vere killed."

My mind raced, frantically striving to put together all that had led all of us to believe the opposite of the truth about this troubled man.

"Here is your confirmation, sir. I'm sorry." Jacob turned the book so Burghoff could read for himself. His father's name and birthplace and date and his death camp number were listed, followed by the notation, "Caught in escape attempt, August 2, 1943, sentenced to death for conspiracy to escape. Executed August 5, 1943."

For his mother, the same, except the execution took place a day later. For his older brother, it read, "Wounded by shooting during escape attempt, August 2, 1943. Executed same day."

"And vere is my name?" Kurt said.

"Right here, sir. It says Kurt Burghoff, born November 12, 1923, Leipzig, Germany, #116075. Reported escaped August 2, 1943. Assumed dead."

Burghoff stood with a swagger, removed his suit coat, and rolled up his sleeve to expose the ugly burn scar his wife had told me about. Jacob looked at it for only an instant and then into the man's watery eyes. Jacob doubled a fist and raised it in the air, a celebration of Kurt Burghoff's defiance.

With the same aplomb, Burghoff rolled the sleeve back down, buttoned it, and replaced his coat.

"I have lived for nearly thirty years vit' the guilt of having escaped vile my family suffered," Kurt said. "How I vish I had been captured again or killed in the escape."

"That's not what your family would have wanted," Jacob said earnestly, his hand on the man's arm. "Let me find your sister's name here, just so your mind will be clear on all of these. Yes, here it is." He turned it and read it as we did.

"Rachael Burghoff, born May 15, 1926, Leipzig, Germany, #116076."

"Ven did she die?" Kurt asked.

Jacob spun the book back around and peered at the listing. "When there is no death date we must check the release book," he said. "I don't want to get your hopes up, Mr. Burghoff, but let me check to make sure. If she is not in the release file, you can assume she was executed or died, and the date was simply not available."

But Burghoff could hardly contain himself. He had lived in guilt and torment for years, and the very idea of a flicker of hope had not entered his mind. Now it crashed down on him with its full force, and he was pulled from his chair once more. He followed Jacob to the release book and hung on his elbow as the young man looked up Rachael's name. As he began to read, Kurt whooped and spun in the air. "She's alive, she's alive!" he shouted.

"Now, take it easy," Jacob said, trying to get more light on the page and read the listing aloud. "Very often we find that people who survived until the Allied victory have since died." Kurt fell silent, and Jacob read: "Rachael V. Burghoff, among the survivors at Buchenwald, where she was transferred after the destruction of Treblinka in late 1943. Married Jonathan Haase, Berlin, September 23, 1949. Divorced, October 10, 1951. Married Frederich Speigel, Frankfurt, January 16, 1953. Widowed May 24, 1960. Married Michael Nissim, Haifa, Israel, December 20, 1964. Last reported address, 53 Victoria, Haifa, Israel."

Kurt was beside himself. "I must go to see her!" he said. "I must go now!"

"Let us call her," Jacob suggested.

"No! She vill never believe a crazy man on the phone. I must go see her! How far is Haifa? Can I make it today by car?"

"Certainly. But please, Mr. Burghoff, remember that Mrs. Nissim could have moved or even passed away since she last updated her listing. She may be difficult to find."

"No," Burghoff said. "It vould be cruel of God to do that to me now."

He pumped Jacob's hand vigorously and promised to see him again, then he hurried out to the car as I trailed him. "Please let me talk to you before you go to Haifa," I begged.

"Come vit' me," he called over his shoulder.

I debated whether to tell him that his daughter could go too, but I decided against it. As thrilled as she would be to see this reunion, or as much help as she could be if Kurt *was* disappointed, I thought he needed to do this alone. The healing of his immediate family would begin soon enough.

He told the driver to get him to Haifa as fast as possible, then turned to me. "Are you sure you vant to go along?" he said. "I can's guarantee a ride back. I don't know how long I might stay vit' my sister."

I resisted the urge to warn him against wishful thinking and simply told him yes, that I really needed to talk with him. I wasn't sure he could take it with all the emotional upheaval he had already endured and the potentially traumatic meeting with his long lost sister, but I told him straight out that I had been sent to follow him, just for his own safety, by his daughter and with his former wife's approval. I said nothing about their suspicions. He was shocked. And moved.

"Mr. Burghoff," I said, "if you don't mind, I'd like to make a suggestion. I would like to help you locate your sister and then make the first contact with her. It could be very difficult for both you and her if you meet all of a sudden. Just let me prepare her and then bring you in. What do you think about that?"

"I t'ink it will be hard to vait in the car," he said, "but I see the visdom in it, and somehow I trust you, Mr. Spence."

Late that afternoon in Haifa, the driver asked directions to Victoria Street while I dialed the number listed for the Nissims at that address. I prayed the phone book was new and that they still lived there. A young woman, maybe a teenager, answered in Hebrew.

"I'm calling for Mrs. Nissim," I said, slowly, wondering if she could understand English. She did, and called her mother to the phone.

"Hello?"

"Mrs. Nissim, my name is Philip Spence, and I'm here in Haifa from the United States. I have some news for you about an old acquaintance of yours from the States, and I was wondering if I could see you for a few minutes to bring a greeting."

"I have several friends who are now in the States," Mrs. Nissim said. "Can you tell me who the message is from?"

"I'd rather wait until I see you, if you don't mind."

"I guess not," she said, hesitating. "My husband will be here," she added, perhaps as a warning.

"Very well. We'll see you shortly."

My youth and nonthreatening appearance helped put Mrs. Nissim at ease. Her daughter flitted in and out of the room as we talked, and her husband sat reading in the corner. "Mrs. Nissim, I have very good news for you," I began, "probably the best news you've ever had in your life."

She raised her eyebrows. "I have had a very difficult life, Mr. Spence," she said. "It doesn't take extremely good news to be the best I've ever had." On her arm, where her brother had a self-inflicted wound, Mrs. Nissim bore her death camp number in a faint blue tattoo.

"This is extremely good news," I said. "Someone you thought was long since dead is alive."

She stood quickly, squinting at me. "Tell me it's Kurt," she said. "Please tell me it's Kurt!"

Her husband let his newspaper drop into his lap, and her daughter returned from the kitchen.

"It's Kurt," I said.

"Where is he?"

"I can arrange for you to see him soon, but I'm concerned that you are calm and can take the shock of seeing him after all these years."

"This is too good to be true! I've felt it in my heart for as long as I can remember; even when I saw in the listings at Yad Vashem that he was assumed dead, I didn't think so. I knew from people in Leipzig that he had come back to our place for some personal effects before fleeing underground. I just couldn't imagine that he would have let himself be caught again after escaping." She sat back down and looked troubled. "You know, Kurt saw more than any of the rest of us. He saw many, many people die. He was tortured. Is he all right? Has he come through this all right? Oh, I have so many questions. You said he lives in the States. When can I see him?"

"If you will compose yourself, I'll bring him in," I said. But she would have none of that. She followed me out the door and her portly middle-aged body passed me when Kurt emerged from the car. She hesitated at the sight of a face altered by years and surgery, but then he said her name in dialect as he must have as a child. Their tearful embrace moved me like nothing I had ever seen. Her husband and daughter came slowly across the street. The driver got out, and the four of us stood by the car, surrounded the curious-looking couple, and silently wept.

EPILOGUE

I left Kurt Burghoff in Haifa with his sister and returned to Jerusalem, where I arranged for his belongings to be sent to him. Allyson wanted to see him, but I had not even told him she was in the country. "I don't think he could take it right now. Why don't you and your mother prepare to welcome him back to Chicago when he comes," I suggested. "I think some things may change in your lives, even after all these years."

A cable waiting for me at the airport in Tel Aviv the next morning informed me that even Margo's case had turned out the opposite of what we had expected. The teacher she had suspected of being a pusher was herself an undercover police officer!

On the flight back to New York, I boldly put my arm around Allyson and held her as we talked excitedly about her plans to rebuild relationships between her father and mother and herself. "I've become very fond of you," I said.

"And I of you." She let her head drop to my shoulder. "But I'm scared."

"Of me?"

"Sort of."

"Why?"

"Because I'm falling in love with you. And the last time I did that I got hurt."

"Bad?"

"Um-hm."

"Wanna tell me about it?"

"No, but I owe it to you, because it could get in our way. I was engaged."

I stiffened.

"I loved the guy and wanted to marry him. He felt the same. There was no problem. In fact, that *was* the problem. It was too perfect. It worried me. I had never been really serious about anyone before, and now I was ready to commit myself to someone for life."

"Yeah? So what happened?"

"I asked for some time. That's all. Just some time."

"Did you get it?" I asked, barely able to get the words out.

"I'm still serving it. When I needed time, he didn't have it to give. He was married to someone else within six months."

I was speechless.

"Are you all right, Philip? Does it bother you that I was engaged?"

I shook my head.

"There was nothing about me he didn't like, he told me. He just couldn't handle it when I asked for a little time. She came along at just the right moment, and that was that. She got him."

"Are you sorry?" I managed.

"Not really. That said so much about his character that I would have hated to learn the hard way, after we were married. What if I had asked for some consideration then? It wasn't in him to allow that."

I pulled my arm back and sat staring out the window into the morning sun.

When I didn't speak for several minutes, Allyson touched my arm. "What is it, Philip?"

"I need to talk to you about something very important," I said. "Will you bear with me?"

"Of course."

"You said you were *falling* in love with me."

"Yes."

"But you haven't fallen, have you?"

"I hardly know you, Philip."

"Right. Good. Because what I'm about to tell you will help you get to know me. And then I'm afraid our relationship will have to change."

Telling her about Margo made for a painful trip home. I realized what I had done to both women. Allyson forgave me, but her tears hurt me deeply. It was my own fault. With her phrase "There was nothing about me he didn't like" ringing in my ears, I knew I had no reason to dump Margo. It wasn't just that there wasn't anything about her I didn't like. I loved her. I had loved her from early in our friendship. And I would always love her.

"She needs to know that," Allyson said. "You and she will grow from this, you know."

"I wish you and I could always be close," I said. "You'd like Margo, too."

"You know that would never work," she said, still fighting tears, as I was.

"Yeah, I do. But do me a favor, will you? Never forget that I admire you and appreciate you. You are a beautiful person."

"Thank you, Philip," she said. And she laid her head back on the tiny pillow and closed her eyes.

ERIN

Linda Gibbons's boyfriend, Johnny Bizell, is found murdered. Among the suspects are Greg Gibbons, Linda, Bonnie, thirteen-year-old Erin, and an unidentified mainte- nance man who once barged in on Linda and Johnny but who does not fit the descrip- tion of anyone working in the apartment building.

ONE

WHEN YOUR BOSS CALLS AT FOUR O'CLOCK IN THE MORNING, you respond the way you would if he called at four in the afternoon. At least you should.

"Hello?" I said groggily.

"This is me," came the familiar voice of Earl Haymeyer, calling from just a few doors down the hall. We lived on the second floor of his two-story building, the floor that also housed his EH Detective Agency.

Earl sounded serious — appropriate, I thought, for waking someone.

"I need you to go with me to Proviso West High School in Hillside," he said.

"Right now?"

"Of course right now. You think I'm calling now to set a date for later? Johnny Bizell was found murdered in his car."

Johnny Bizell. I'd heard that name enough during the past several months. How many times had Earl's secretary, Bonnie, said Bizell was the one man she could kill without losing sleep over it?

"Shipman will meet us there, Philip," Earl was saying, "but we've gotta move. We'll be lucky if they haven't moved the body already."

"Margo going?" I asked, switching a light on and squinting.

"No. I'm enough of a chauvinist yet to think a woman might be better off not seeing this. Now Philip, let's go! I'll be waiting in the car."

I splashed water on my face and dragged a comb through my hair as I heard Earl's door shut and him trotting down the stairs. I didn't think it was fair for him to dress before calling me and then make me look slow. Two minutes later, wearing only blue jeans, a T-shirt, moccasins (no socks), and my trench coat, I slid into Earl's car.

"Bring your gun?" he asked.

"No. Should I?"

"No time. Forget it."

The night watchman who guarded the drug store, boutique, and professional offices in Earl's building tipped his cap as Earl swung out onto Glencoe Road to the Tri-State Tollway south.

"I got the call from an old nemesis of mine," Earl explained. "Chicago Homicide Detective Sergeant Walvoord F. Festschrift."

"What in the world kind of a name is that?"

"Who knows? Wally says his mother was Jewish, married a German, and always wanted to live in Holland."

"Do I wanna know what the *F* stands for?"

"Feinberg."

"Mercy. So what's the deal on Bizell, and why is Chicago in on it if it happened at a suburban high school?"

"I'm not sure yet. Festschrift was really gloating over the fact that he and I would be locking heads over this one. He was my first boss when I went plainclothes in Chicago. He's got a lot of ability but no ambition. He never wanted to be anything more than a homicide detective, and he's turned down promotion after promotion. Problem is, when the guys he's trained and brought along are then promoted over him because he won't take the promotions, he resents them."

"And that's what happened to you?"

"Yup. It was awkward to become his boss, but I always felt I treated him fairly. He was tough to supervise, though. Sarcastic. Condescending. Always accused me of being a glory-seeker."

"Were you?"

"Probably, but I hid it well."

"From everyone but Fet — "

"Festschrift."

"Right."

Earl drove on in silence, neither of us willing to mention the possibility that anyone we knew could have had anything to do with the murder of Johnny Bizell. When Earl exited to the Eisenhower east and we were just a few minutes from Hillside, I asked, "How did this Festschrift guy know to call you at all?"

"That's what I'd like to know."

We passed the Hillside Shopping Center and the front of the huge Proviso West Campus, a prime example of a sprawling educational plant that gives suburban kids advantages that few others enjoy. The events sign at the edge of the front lawn was still lit, and I shot a double take as I realized the implications: INTERNATIONAL GYMNASTICS EXHIBITION TONITE ONLY.

"Erin?" I asked.

Earl pursed his lips and nodded.

"Bizell was here for that?"

"Apparently so."

"But still, how would Festschrift know of our connection, and why would Chicago Homicide — ?"

"I don't know, Philip. I told you, I don't know."

Even at this early hour, a small group of onlookers had gathered, attracted by the police car and ambulance lights. "You can bet Wally doesn't have his dashlight on," Earl said. "Hates that kind of thing."

Earl was right. As we walked to the edge of a roped-off area near the field house, I spotted the unmarked Chicago police car. The blue light on the dash was dark. The suburban cars all had flashers going and an ambulance was backing into place, also lit up like a Christmas tree. The man I guessed to be Sgt. Festschrift was swearing.

"Get these lights off," he railed. "You wanna draw the whole town? Mi's well blow yer sirens too!"

Earl and I stood at the edge of the rope and watched the fat man. He wore giant rubber-soled black shoes and white socks, which you could see when they peeked from under his too-long and low-riding suit pants — pants that were baggy at the knees but too tight-waisted to cover his ample belly. One shirttail hung out, his tie was loose, and his hands were on his hips, pushing his overcoat and suit coat back. Beyond him about fifteen feet was the silver Corvette of Johnny Bizell, the driver's side door open. I knew Bizell had to still be inside or close by, but I couldn't see from where we stood.

Finally, Festschrift noticed Earl and waddled over. "Let this man in," he told the uniformed officer at the rope.

"He's with me," Earl said, pointing at me. "Philip Spence."

"Yeah, yeah, good to know ya, Spence," Festschrift said, offering a meaty paw. He led us around the ambulance to the door of the 'Vette where the body of Johnny Bizell sat behind the wheel. The inside light was getting dimmer, indicating that he had sat there for hours. "It ain't pretty, Earl, but then these never are."

Earl was suddenly more polite than I'd ever seen him, asking Festschrift's permission before doing anything. Later he would tell me that this was merely the etiquette of the jungle and that if he had been in charge of the investigation, he would have expected the same treatment from Festschrift.

"Can I take a peek inside, Wally?"

"Yeah, but don't touch anything, and leave that murder weapon, such as it is, right where it lies."

I knew Earl would be offended that he was being told by a detective sergeant to not touch anything at a murder scene. As if Earl hadn't investigated dozens of murders in his career as a policeman, special investigator for the U.S. attorney, and now a private detective. But he didn't let it show and motioned that I should follow him to the other side of the car.

We peered into the passenger side window, but the light from one of the parking lot lights reflected off it and distorted the view. We could see that Bizell's head lay back on the headrest and that his eyes were open. His right leg was over the hump on the floor and his right hand, covered with blood, rested outstretched in the seat.

From the edge of the roped-off area, Larry Shipman called to Earl. "Wally," Earl said, "that's another of my men. Can he join us?"

The sergeant appeared annoyed but let Shipman in. Larry, who's been around such things a lot more than I have, started taking notes and looking at every angle. After he was introduced to Festschrift, he plunged right in. "Hey, Sarge," he said, "how 'bout opening that passenger door? You can do it with a wire or something without affecting fingerprints."

"I know, kid," Festschrift said. "I ain't 'xactly a rookie myself, ya know. I got a team of forensic types comin' out here at dawn, and I don't want you rummies messin' up the crime scene for 'em."

"Then why did you call us?" Earl asked.

Festschrift looked as if he wanted to tell him right then and there but decided against it.

"Just let us have one closer look before you move the body," Earl said, dripping with deference, which his old companion ate up.

"Awright, but don't touch a thing."

Festschrift fished a hooked wire from his pocket and moved quickly to the passenger door. He fastened it to the handle without touching anything with his hands, and gave a sharp yank. The door popped open and Earl leaned in, reaching out behind him without looking, as if he expected Festschrift to hand him something. Festschrift produced a flashlight.

"Philip," Earl called. I could hardly hear him with his head deep into the car and his back to me. I leaned in. Shipman was staring in from the other side of the car.

Violently deceased bodies are something I don't think I'll ever get used to. I once asked Earl how he got used to them. "I didn't," he said simply. But now he was bent over the passenger seat, his head a few inches from the wide-eyed face of a dead man whose blood had flooded the front left bucket seat, the console, and much of the floor. Earl backed out, nearly bumping me. He handed me the light. "Look on the floor between the seats," he said.

"Do I want to?"

He stared at me. I leaned in. Despite the great amount of blood, it was mostly dry, another clue to timing. The smell nauseated me. On the floor, right on the edge of a tiny pool of blood, was what appeared to be a small plastic toy, purple colored. I pointed the light directly at it and noticed a reflection, as if it had metal imbedded in it.

The death wound was a gash at the right side of Bizell's neck, and the blood had poured from him on that side. But his left hand, dangling at his side, also had a small laceration. Earl had noticed it too. As the paramedics moved into position to move the body and Festschrift supervised the shooting of several photographs, Earl and I hurried around to the other side of the car where we joined Larry. "See that?" he whispered, pointing to the small tear in the victim's left hand. We nodded. "I have a theory," he said.

Festschrift approached. "Save it," Earl told Larry, handing the flashlight to the sergeant.

"You boys got time for some coffee?" the old cop asked.

"I s'pose," Earl said, "though I hate to be seen in public looking like this. But it's probably the only chance I'll get to find out what you're doing here, and why you called me."

"You got it," Festschrift said with a grin.

I felt greasy and grundy as we slid into a booth at a combination bakery and coffee shop at the nearby shopping center. We were the first customers of the morning. It didn't help much that I was jammed into a booth next to Sergeant Festschrift and sitting across from Haymeyer and Shipman, who were not successful in hiding their glee at my plight.

"So, this is your crew, huh, Earl?" Festschrift said, stuffing half a sweet roll into one side of his mouth and dousing it with coffee so hot that none of the rest of us had even dared get close enough to blow on it yet.

"Basically, Wally," Earl said. "I've also got a young woman, Margo Franklin, and we have a secretary/receptionist."

"I know," Wally said. "Mrs. Bonnie Murray, widowed several years, a couple of married daughters, one living in Chicago named Linda Gibbons. Separated from her husband Greg. Has an only child, Erin, who is fast becoming the talk of international gymnastics."

"Uh-huh," Earl said slowly, an unbitten Danish melting in his fingers. "What else do you know, and more importantly, why?"

"I know that Johnny Bizell is the reason the Gibbonses are separated, and I know that the daughter Erin and the grandmother Bonnie have been none too thrilled that he has injured the marriage."

"So, what are you saying?"

"I'm saying I don't know what that little hunk of plastic and metal in that 'Vette is yet, but something tells me that when I do, it's gonna lead to someone who had a reason to kill Johnny Bizell."

Shipman and I caught each other's eyes. Earl didn't flinch, but the topping on that Danish was dripping onto the table. "All right, Wally, for whatever problems you and I may have had in the past, we've always been straight with each other, and we're both after the same thing, so why don't you tell me exactly what you're up to."

"You gonna eat that Danish, Earl?" Wally said, stalling. Earl handed it to him and watched it disappear in another wash of coffee. Festschrift leaned forward and across me to grab an ashtray, pushing the table into Earl and Larry's ribs. He lit a cigarette, took a deep drag, squinted as he pushed his chin in the air, and blew a blue cloud over our heads. He placed the cigarette carefully on the edge of the tray and wriggled out of his overcoat, exposing a dark green suit, frayed at the cuffs and worn at the elbows, that looked as if it had been on the job as long as he had.

"You're wonderin' why Chicago is in on a suburban murder, is that it?"

Earl nodded, apparently annoyed at Festschrift's dramatics. The fat man wanted Earl to have to drag it out of him, but Earl wouldn't bite.

"OK, Earl," Wally said, finally. "We know as much about the Gibbons situation as you do. You know because you want to keep your secretary informed. We know because Bizell is a Chicagoan with mob ties."

"We guessed that," Earl said. "But why the inordinate interest?"

"The Vice Control Division has had Bizell under surveillance for some time and they just kept a portfolio on his contacts. When they noticed that you and your people were tailing him too, they wanted to know why. It wasn't hard to find out. When Bizell turns up dead, I inherit the case. And my first suspects may be friends of yours, maybe even co-workers." Festschrift looked at each of us with a slight smile. Haymeyer continued to stare.

"You want me as an ally in this investigation, or an adversary?" Earl asked, eager to switch to the offensive.

"Do I have a choice? Do *you* have a choice? You might want to be my ally, Earl, but when I start poking around your office, suspecting your secretary and your secretary's son-in-law, and asking everyone in your shop what Bonnie Murray has said about the now dead home wrecker, we'll be adversaries whether you want to be or not."

"Are you seriously suspecting my secretary?"

"You see, Earl? Your secretary is the best suspect I've had on a homicide in three years, and you can't see it because she's an employee and, I imagine, a friend. But think about it. The woman surely has a motive. She's not a small person, so with the right means she could conceivably have done the job. The lab will tell us if that 'weapon' on the floor was the means. You want me to tell you about her opportunity? Can't have a murder unless you've got a motive, means, and opportunity."

"Let me guess," Larry interrupted. "You're gonna tell us that Bonnie was at Proviso West last night for the gymnastics meet. Well, so were thousands of others, and few with as good a reason as the grandmother of the women's all-around champion."

"Anyway," I said, wishing later I hadn't, "Margo was there with her." Larry and Earl looked at me as if I had lost my mind, volunteering information like that. Chicago Homicide Detective Sergeant Walvoord F. Festschrift merely smiled.

"And when can I meet this Margo?" he asked.

Two

It was due only to my own foolishness that Margo and I were not still engaged. Sure, she had been childish, insecure, fickle, but then what did I expect? I knew her background. She had never had a normal adolescence, if there is such a thing.

She had seen her parents' marriage break up, had for years carried the dark secret that her mother was a murderer, finally exposed her, and then saw her die in prison. In many ways, Margo Franklin was an emotional cripple, yet I spent so much time trying to convince her that I didn't feel sorry for her or pity her and that my love for her was genuine and simply inspired by the person she was, that I actually began to believe it.

It was largely true, but Margo was *due* some pity. I should have seen that. I should have been able to let her be what she was, a deep girl, rich in character and inner beauty (not to mention outer), but who needed time, even at this stage of her life, to grow up, to find herself in the truest sense.

But I had not been patient. She had wanted time to think. The small, dark, fine-boned and delicately featured beauty had virtually disappeared from my life. I saw her every day in the office, and we were more than cordial. The difficult, uncomfortable time was past. We were now fairly good friends, but I'd rather it had remained uncomfortable. Because I knew now, more than ever, that I loved her deeply.

It hurt me to see her grow emotionally and especially spiritually and to know, first, that I had nothing to do with it, and second, that I wasn't even seeing it firsthand. And yeah, OK, I wondered if she had a new mentor, someone who had swept her off her feet, some super-spiritual type who could be all and more to her than she needed.

But she didn't. She never dated, as far as I could tell. She was very active in a small church, and although I considered switching from the large church we used to attend together, I knew she would feel threatened. I wanted her to feel loved, not threatened.

Around the office, everyone could sense a selflessness in her that was attractive, not obnoxious. She was not putting on just for attention: she really did think of others first. Even in talking to me, she would ask and ask and ask and rarely tell. You could talk to her for twenty minutes and go away feeling good about yourself, only to realize later that you had learned nothing about her, except that she was something special.

So now I was ready with my pity, and she was no longer in need of it. I was more understanding of what she had been going through, and she was no longer going through it. She had even become accurately introspective. I'll never forget the night she called and asked if I could meet her somewhere to chat. I thought she was ready for us to get back together.

But she didn't even know that that's what I wanted. Maybe if she knew, she could start thinking about it too — But that wasn't even on her mind. In fact, when I suggested a few meeting places that she had to associate with our betrothal days, she politely declined and we settled on neutral ground. We met in the lobby of her apartment building.

For the first several minutes she asked me about myself. Of course she knew the day-to-day stuff, but she asked about my parents, my new car, my feelings about Earl's having talked me into carrying a gun (he had talked her into the same thing, but dumb me didn't think to ask how *she* felt about it), and about my plans for the future.

My plans, I told her, included simply doing the best job I could for Earl, learning as much as I could from him, and just growing where I was planted. She asked about church and even my spiritual life. I was taken aback, yet there was no gall, no guile. It made me uncomfortable, probably because I knew she was surging ahead of me by leaps and bounds.

I told her I was still hangin' in there, and I could tell by the look on her face that she knew I was being purposefully vague. Then she finally began to talk about herself. She went on for about five minutes about how God had apparently used our "crisis" to put her where He wanted her. Well, He hadn't put her where *I* wanted her, but on the other hand, I knew that was selfish and that I certainly couldn't argue with how she had grown as a whole person.

"My point in telling you all this," she had concluded, "is just to let you know that I wanted time, and I got it, and I'm glad. God has used it. I've learned that Christianity is not a part of life that can be compartmentalized. It's not a filter through which we view everything else. It is life. It's everything *and* everything else."

I was tempted to unkindly ask who she had been reading lately but something told me that this was the mind I had always appreciated in her — loved, in fact. This was the analytical bearing of a person who had endured dark times in her life and had been forced to evaluate them and make sense of them.

"So, I want you to know how special you are and will always be to me, Philip. I will never forget you and your struggling faith, and your caring and your love. And of course I can never thank you enough for introducing me to God. I know what a pill I was, and for sure, I can't say that's entirely behind me now, but you deserve more than an apology. I have no more to give, so you have at least that, and I want you to forgive me."

I was speechless. Forgive her? Somehow in light of that request I couldn't remember what a rascal she had indeed been at times. Her impulsiveness, her lack of logic, her verbal cruelty all came into perspective somehow. I'm not saying she was right or had excuses, but she did have reasons. And I had harbored bitterness in spite of them.

I had wanted to take her in my arms that night, tell her I loved her and that she never had to ask my forgiveness for anything, but I was frozen. She had not called me to make up with me, to become attached to me again, to melt me back into a relationship. She was serious, she was sincere. She had seen herself for what she was and had simply asked forgiveness.

She repeated her request and all I could do was nod. She thanked me for coming, carried the rest of the conversational pleasantries so I could leave without making a fool of myself, and that was that.

For the next several days I had tried to get next to her, to be her special friend, at least, in the office. But she treated everyone the same. I tried catching her eye and smiling at her, and without being unkind she simply smiled right back, just as she did for everyone else. I couldn't hold her gaze the way I had been able to when we were in love. That hurt, but she hadn't intended it to. If she had intended to freeze me out, she easily could have, and it would have made it simpler for me.

Earl was concerned that we not let our love problems surface at the office. We were aware that few establishments even allow engaged couples to work together. But she was so oblivious to my feelings for her that any formality or coolness in front of others was eliminated. She treated me the way she treated everyone else, and *everyone* loved her.

I would ask her out, she would ask if it would be all right if three or four of us went together, and I didn't want to be a sourpuss by saying no. I had made my feelings clear to her when we broke up, and she had believed me. I didn't know how to express to her that I had been wrong and was sorry. Perhaps if I hadn't seen such a change in her, I wouldn't have changed my mind. Did that mean my love for her was conditional? I didn't know. Conditional or not, it was there now and stronger than ever, and I needed a way to prove it to her.

She had begun spending a lot of time with Bonnie. Bonnie lived alone on another floor in Margo's building. She had asked Earl and Larry to check on her daughter Linda's husband, because Linda had told Bonnie that Greg was being unfaithful. She had been terribly hurt by the knowledge that it was Linda who had been seeing another man.

The investigation proved that rather than Greg Gibbons's seeing one of the secretaries from his office, Linda was seeing Johnny Bizell, the leading salesman in Greg's office. Needless to say, Bonnie was horrified, and Margo spent much of her time trying to convince Bonnie that she could not blame herself.

Mostly, Bonnie was worried about Greg and Linda's daughter, Erin, who had recently turned fourteen. Not long after Earl and Larry had told Bonnie what they found, Linda and this Johnny Bizell — one of those great-looking forty-year-old bronze types from the covers of fashion catalogs — quit being so careful to cover their tracks.

Erin had seen him at the apartment a couple of times and recognized him from her father's office. When she raised the question in front of both parents, things deteriorated rapidly. Linda finally admitted the relationship but insisted that it was over. For about a month, it appeared she was telling the truth. Greg had moved out, and divorce proceedings had begun, but things stalled when it appeared that Linda was no longer seeing Bizell.

How Greg was able to work in the same office with Johnny, I'll never know, but I guess except for their common "appreciation" of the same woman and their selling of the same office equipment products, they ran in entirely different circles. At least, that's what I gathered from what Sgt. Festschrift had said early Saturday morning.

What had really complicated matters was that the press had become aware of the marriage problems. None of the details (like Bizell's name or even that Linda was seeing someone else) were printed, but the fact of the separation was public. Why? Because of Erin.

She had been interested in gymnastics since she was a tiny child after having seen first Olga Korbut and then Nadia Comaneci in the Olympics on television. In spite of the fact that Greg was never into big money and Linda even had to work part time to help make ends meet, they scraped up enough to send Erin to gymnastics camp a couple of years in a row, let her join the school team, and finally signed her up on a local AAU team.

That team had a traveling squad of the best eight girls who competed throughout the Midwest, but it also carried three or four dozen other girls and gave them a place to learn and work out and train. When Erin was eight, nine, and ten years old and had been in the program for several years, she talked her parents into taking her to the meets so she could watch the traveling squad and cheer for them. Greg was never much interested in it because he couldn't envision his gangly little daughter ever reaching that level, but Linda had taken her to the nearby meets.

Something happened in Erin's mind when she saw her older friends begin to really, truly improve and become competitive under the tutelage of their coach, Nik Adamski. At first her friends were embarrassing, but through the years as they grew in strength and grace, and as their parents allowed them more time for workouts, their scores started edging upward. The dozens of girls under the traveling squad who made up the rest of the team began to see themselves as teammates, and they exulted as much as the participants with each victory.

As an older girl moved up or out or off to college, someone from the lower levels would be chosen to replace her. Not even Erin remembers when she started to foresee that possibility for herself. She had always performed in the lower half of the fifty or so girls in the practice meets that were held for parents' eyes only. But then she asked permission to train the year around.

Most of the parents of the other girls were well-to-do and fully supported their daughters, sending them for expensive specialized training over the summer. Greg and Linda could not afford that, but they were able to sponsor Erin's staying on the team all year every year. And she began to improve.

By the time she was twelve, she had moved into the top fifteen, and then, her grandmother says because her father finally took an interest, she blossomed. She grew a couple of inches, gained a little strength and a lot of self-confidence. And finally — her coach attributes this to his brainwashing — she developed a singlemindedness for excellence in her sport that transcended everything else in her life.

She ate, drank, and slept gymnastics. There were only four Olympic events, she reminded her mother often, and she would perfect them all. She became a marvelous free exerciser and vaulter, and Coach Adamski began to push harder for her to reach her potential on the uneven bars and the beam.

He worked with her all one summer, and when competition began in the fall, she was the first alternate. She worked out all week just like the rest of the first team, but week after week she failed to compete in any meets. No one was injured or sick and she was unable to sneak in past the last girl on the squad during pre-meet tryouts. What was worse (or better, depending on your perspective), the entire team was getting better.

Nik Adamski had worked his magic over the years and had built one of the most respected gymnastics programs in the country. For two years running they were national AAU champions and sent four young women on to the national team to compete overseas and host meets in the U.S. The girls below Erin were getting better, and the girls on the first team were internationally ranked. She came to the slow realization that at the tender age of twelve she was ninth woman on the best team in the United States and among the best fifty or sixty women gymnasts in the world, yet she had never competed in an actual meet.

One of the girls Erin idolized was the best gymnast Nik Adamski had ever coached. Larisa Cumiskey, sixteen the summer Erin turned twelve, had strength and grace and precision that won her the all-around competition in every national meet she entered. Internationally, she was always a threat, winning at least one event and finishing high in the overall standings each time.

The other girls would sit wide-eyed listening to Larisa tell about competing in Poland and the USSR and Czechoslovakia and Germany. Everyone wanted to be Larisa's friend, and most were, at least those on the first team. Somehow she had been able to avoid the haughtiness that so often accompanies brilliance. Erin decided that if she could ever get next to Larisa, she could help make her a great gymnast too. But Larisa had been on the same team for years and had seemed to hardly notice little Erin.

Then came the week that Erin showed such class and flair in vaulting that, in front of everybody, Nik Adamski told the last vaulter on the first team that if he were selecting only the best competitors in each event and not the best all-around performances, she would have lost her place on the team.

That girl didn't burst into tears and run from the room. Instead she agreed and shook her head in admiration of the tiny twelve-year-old who had drawn applause from the whole team. Larisa and the others gathered around Erin and patted her on the head and the back, encouraging her to keep working hard.

When the excitement died down, Nik said in his broken English, "I vant volunteer or two to vork vit' dis girl. She been close to first team for too long and is now ready for big move."

Erin could have died when Larisa Cumiskey stepped forward and said, "I'll work with Erin." It was the start of an unusual friendship.

THREE

According to Margo, who had grown close to Bonnie and thus to Erin and even her friend Larisa, the older girl really took Erin under her wing.

After practice every afternoon — and sometimes, with permission, even during practice — Larisa would personally coach Erin on the uneven bars. Where Coach Nik was a shouter, a demanding, team-oriented, Dutch uncle type, Larisa had her own brand of praise and encouragement.

Nik enforced unity on the team, insisting that there be no jealousy, no territorial protection even in this highly individualized sport. It was probably the reason Larisa had volunteered to help the young upstart. She had learned her lesson well and truly believed that it was the togetherness Nik had fostered that had made their team the best in the country. And if this little girl could improve that last 10 percent that could make her superb, the team would be that much better.

During the Christmas vacation, there was no meet competition and Nik held only a few practice sessions. But Larisa and Erin were at the gym for several hours each day, getting to know each other, but more importantly, pushing Erin to heights she had never imagined possible. The age difference was just right, because she held such a reverence for her mentor that any praise she could elicit was that much more meaningful.

When Erin flew through a stratospheric routine on the uneven bars, Larisa was exultant. "Erin, that was a nine-point-oh if I ever saw one. I am not kidding, Erin, you've arrived."

Erin was red-faced, hardly believing it. The years she had invested in dreaming and working hard at the fundamentals Nik drilled into the team every day had given her a base upon which to add creativity and courage. "Now all you need is abandon on both the beam and the bars," Larisa said.

"Abandon?"

"Right. Let yourself go. Lose your tentativeness, your last shred of fear. You're good, now believe it. You've been trained well by a great coach, and you're not going to hurt yourself. Start adding daring and speed to every move until you're confident and can nail a dangerous routine as easily as you do a normal one."

Erin was eager to try it, and within ten days she was flying through routines that thrilled her. When the coach and the rest of the team returned for an all-team tryout before the next meet, Erin seemed to have grown up overnight. The advice that had moved her from being good to excellent on the bars and the beam had made her among the best three on the team in floor ex and vault.

All of a sudden, Erin was a first-team member of the defending national championship women's gymnastics team, and she could hardly wait for her first meet. Yet when it came it was an exhibition against some of the best gymnasts in the world. She wasn't expected to place in any of her events. Indeed, it would be a chore for even Larisa to win anything but the uneven bars.

When it was over, the best performance by a U.S. team member was a 9.7 on the bars, good for third place, by Larisa. Erin choked and was unable to produce the same daring she had exhibited during workouts. In her best event, the floor ex, her 8.6 didn't even put her in the top ten. She missed her dismount off the beam and landed on her seat. She stubbed her toes at the start and in the middle of her uneven bars routine. Her vaulting was uninspired. She was humiliated.

In the locker room after the meet, Larisa and a couple of other girls tried to console her. "You don't wanna know what my first meet scores were, Erin," one said. "I didn't even crack an eight until my third meet, I was so scared."

"I didn't feel scared," Erin insisted through her tears. "I just couldn't do what I wanted to do!"

"That's what scared feels like," another said. "There are a lot of girls who would love to have had your all-around score tonight."

Within four more meets, Erin Gibbons was the second best gymnast on her team in every event. By the end of the year, she was within five hundredths of a point of Larisa in the vault and floor ex and within two tenths on the bars and beam. And they were closer than ever as friends.

When Larisa returned from off-season international competition, she found a thirteen-year-old who had not only drawn to within an eyelash of her in every event, but who also had begun to shave her legs and wear makeup, emulating her idol, her teammate, and her rival in every respect. "My mom won't let me wear the makeup except during meets," she said, and Larisa and her friends laughed. "She thinks I need to look older to the judges or they won't believe they're seeing a good routine."

Erin confided to Margo once that she and Larisa had had a good heart-to-heart talk during the wee hours at a slumber party in the mansion home of Ernest and Jean Cumiskey. Larisa told Erin that she should never let their friendship come in the way of their competition, that they could continue to like and respect each other while striving their hardest to beat each other. "Our team will only benefit from it," Larisa said. "I was raised to be number one, and that means someday I'd like to be the best in the world, but if you wind up better than I am, then we'll be one and two. I don't mind telling you I'd rather be first, but we may be the only real competition each other has this year. We can keep our team winning by trying to outdo each other."

The girls also shared family secrets. Erin was already suspecting the future of her parents marriage because of continued fights and threats. Then she was convinced her mother was seeing a man from her father's office. She even learned his name — Johnny Bizell — and knew his car, a late model silver Corvette.

Larisa's problems seemed to pale in comparison. While the greatest embarrassment to Erin, outside her mother's deceit, was that she could hardly bring a bunch of friends to a small apartment for a party, slumber or otherwise, Larisa's was that she had a stage father.

Her mother wasn't too bad at the meets. She was proud of her daughter and often had to restrain herself from charging onto the floor and hugging her when she won an event or a meet, but it was Larisa's father, Ernest, who was the talk of the circuit.

"He wants me to be number one worse than I do," Larisa once told Erin. "He believes in being number one so deeply that it drives him crazy that my little brothers are twins.

I think he actually favors Bobby over Billy because he appeared eight minutes sooner nine years ago. When he watches them play junior hockey or soccer or baseball or football, he's thrilled if one of them is the best, but he's obsessed with the fact that the other is not."

Sometimes Larisa laughed about it; other times she did not. Finally the day came when Erin had to ask, "Has your father's attitude toward me changed since I started to give you more competition?"

"I don't think he ever had an attitude about you," Larisa said. "I know his attitude toward me has sure changed since you've been coming on. He's forever badgering me about my diet, my sleeping habits, everything. He wants to know if I'm working out as much as I used to. He wants to know if my age has affected my weight or muscle tone. I'm only seventeen years old and he fears I'll be over the hill by the time the next Olympics rolls around. He doesn't realize that once you get into the high nines, it's hard to improve without getting tens. He says my goal should be to break Nadia's record of seven perfect scores in one Olympic game. I've yet to score one ten in competition. It's not good enough for me to be the best in the US or even in the world. I have to be the best in history, and now it looks like you'll keep me from that."

Larisa put her arm around Erin's shoulder to show that she didn't really mind the competition. "Anyway, why did you ask? Has Daddy acted differently around you lately?"

"Oh, yeah, if it's not just my imagination. He used to greet me, talk to me a little — mostly about you, of course — but now he acts like I'm not here."

Margo talked the rest of the staff into going to a six-team invitational meet in Chicago one night, and it happened to be the night that Erin edged Larisa in an event for the first time. Larisa still won the all-around, but Erin was a close second after topping her by a tenth of a point in, of all things, the uneven bars — Larisa's best event.

I don't know gymnastics except what I remember from high school and a little of the Olympics on television, but from what I could see, Larisa made no mistakes on her routine. She scored in the high nines, but Erin really flew. It was worth the extra tenth of a point, I guess. In fact, I thought Erin did better on the floor exercise than Larisa too, but the judges didn't agree.

It wasn't long after that that Erin and Larisa visited Erin's grandmother Bonnie at our office. They were going to go shopping late in the afternoon on a non-practice day. I was intrigued by the lithe little things, so close and yet such competitors. Their figures were so youthful, yet their calves were taut and their hands calloused and bony. They were just about to leave when Larisa's mother called to tell her that her father was insisting that she work out that night at the gym, even if it had to be alone.

She was in tears when she left, assuring Erin that it was all right and that she didn't mind not going shopping. Erin offered to work out with her, but Larisa wouldn't hear of it. "Maybe this way, Daddy will think I'm getting the jump on you," she said, trying to smile.

"You probably will be," Erin said. "Maybe I'd *better* come along." But she didn't.

What impressed me through it all was that both girls seemed to excel in spite of their parental problems.

I kind of got hooked on gymnastics, especially when Bonnie's granddaughter was competing, and Larry Shipman and I took in several meets whenever we could. We were there when Erin first tied Larisa for an overall first place. Larisa had won the uneven bars competition by two tenths and Erin had won the floor ex by the same margin. They had tied on the other two events, and you should have seen them beaming on the victory stand, arm in arm, waving.

Larisa's father was furious and drove home by himself, leaving his wife and two sons to fend for themselves. Was Jean Cumiskey embarrassed! She got a ride with Bonnie. I never heard what she said to her husband later, but I can imagine.

A real battle was shaping up for the national AAU finals, which were to be held at the University of Illinois Chicago Circle Campus. Wide World of Sports was there to tape the competition, and the place was a madhouse. I was really becoming an aficionado. Getting to know Erin better was a joy, and yet you can't get to know Erin without getting to know Larisa. They are inseparable, and I decided Larisa was one classy young lady — a truly beautiful person, a lot more like her mother than her father.

He was president of a national sales organization, and he looked the part. Everything he did and said (and wore) exuded class and the looking-out-for-number-one mentality. He found it impossible to talk to anyone about anything without categorizing, prioritizing, sizing up, and finding out where you fit in, whether you were number one or had the potential to be number one, and how you planned on getting there. He also found it impossible to talk for more than three minutes without bragging on Larisa, which I thought was OK, except that he seemed to take the credit for her excellence when I was convinced it was in spite of him.

Anyway, Larisa won the national all-around title, even though she finished third in one event and second in two others. A girl from Dubuque surprised everyone by winning the balance beam competition. Erin was second, a fraction ahead of Larisa. Erin finished first in floor ex and the vault, giving her more gold medals than anyone, but Larisa again was just a fraction behind in each event, and when she finally hit a perfect score on the uneven bars, it gave her enough margin to overcome Erin for the aggregate.

Strangely, however, the talk of the meet — mostly because of the national TV coverage — was of the thirteen-year-old teammate of the great Larisa Cumiskey who had come within a point and a half of winning four gold medals. A great deal of time was spent explaining not how Larisa had salvaged the all-around gold with a rare 10, but how close Erin had come to a dramatic sweep of the meet.

Larisa's experience in international competition aided her when she and Erin both made the United States team and competed around the world. In two meets, Larisa and Erin finished first and second to give the US women's team its first international victories ever. In other meets they finished second and third, usually with Larisa on top, but everyone knew, because of age, that Erin was fast becoming the top female gymnast in the United States, and that world recognition would not be far off.

Erin finally pushed her way past Larisa for the first time the Friday night before Johnny Bizell was found murdered. I had been with Earl and Larry at a White Sox game, and we hadn't returned to our apartments until nearly midnight.

Now, having been awakened by Earl at four and having met the reknowned Sgt. Festschrift, I wanted to read the paper and go back to bed. "We've got to find Bonnie," Earl said as he parked back at his building.

"I'll try to call her," I promised. "What else can we do? If she's not at home, she may be out with Margo or with Erin and Larisa."

"That's all we need," Earl said, yawning. "I want to get to all of them before Wally Festschrift does."

"If *we* can't find 'em, *he* sure can't," I said.

"Don't kid yourself," Earl said. "They could be being fingerprinted right now."

I laughed. He didn't.

"I'm going to be in the office this morning waiting for the lab report," he said, "so I'll try to reach the gals by phone. Get some sleep. We may be in for a lot of overtime the next few days. I told Larry he could go back to bed, so fair's fair."

"When you gonna get some sleep, Earl?"

"I never sleep. You know that."

I jogged down to the corner for a newspaper, then flopped onto my bed to read myself back to sleep. It wasn't easy. The front page carried the story of Johnny Bizell's death and Festschrift's intimation that it may have been a gangland hit. I knew as well as he did that he didn't believe that for a minute. Nothing about the murder looked clean enough for a mob job, but talking like that was his way of taking the heat off his real suspects, and off Earl too, though Earl was too smart for that. Festschrift thought Bonnie had the best motive — I couldn't argue with that — and he didn't want the media or anyone else in his way while he made his case. Everyone else, he hoped, would be looking the other way when he closed in on the real murderer.

The sports page mercifully buried the story of the White Sox late inning loss to the Yankees under a splash for Erin Gibbons, the new sensation, who "thrilled the home-town Chicago crowd at Proviso West High School last night with a quartet of 9.85s on the balance beam, the uneven parallel bars, floor exercise, and the vault to win all four events and the all-around gold, carrying the U.S. women to victory" over four visiting European teams. Larisa Cumiskey, now regarded as a "veteran," finished no lower than fourth in any event and won a silver in the all-around competition.

I wondered if Erin would get to enjoy her victory before hearing of the news of Johnny Bizell. Would it add to her euphoria? Or would she not be surprised in the least?

FOUR

I found it difficult to sleep, wondering why — even on the sports page — the newsmen felt it necessary to point out that Erin's performance was even more impressive, given the fact that she was from a broken home and had been raised in an apartment, no less. What would they do if they found out that the home wrecker had been murdered?

Earl called at about noon and asked me to join him and Larry at the office. He had heard nothing from Wally Festschrift about the lab report yet, but he wanted to prepare some charts to determine everyone's whereabouts the night before, starting with the time work ended.

"I haven't been able to reach Margo or Bonnie," Earl said. "For all I know, Wally has already gotten to Linda and Erin Gibbons."

"Did you try calling *them?*" Larry asked.

"Naw, I hardly know 'em. Anyway, I don't want to irritate Wally just now. He'd really be hot if I started questioning people before he did. I *would* like to see their reactions to the news, though. Anyway, let's get to work."

Earl used a felt-tipped marker and wrote several names on a big sheet of white cardboard.

He started with himself, Larry, and me. He wrote, "work, Peppercorn's for dinner, White Sox Park, home."

Then he wrote "Bonnie, work, home, Margo's for dinner, Proviso West, home."

"I know they went together. Do you guys know who drove?"

"Margo," I offered.

"You sure?"

I nodded. "That was the plan. And Erin was supposed to come back with them and stay with her grandmother."

"Are you serious?" Earl asked. "What about Larisa? They're usually inseparable."

"I don't know. I didn't hear anything about her coming back with them."

"Where would they be now?"

"Who knows?"

"Something bothers me about their relationship," Shipman said. "Doesn't it seem a little too good to be true? Larisa's eighteen goin' on nineteen, will graduate from high school this June; Erin just turned fourteen and won't start high school until this fall. Yet they seem to get along. The only thing they have in common is gymnastics."

I tried to explain it to him the way Margo had tried to explain it to me. Gymnastics can't be described as an "only thing." It's too much more than that. It's such a huge part of life to these girls, especially at this level, that everything else seems insignificant. "The biggest thing is that I think Erin has won Larisa's respect and even admiration, more than just for what she can do on the apparatus, but by her courage and determination and all that. Plus, remember they have traveled the world together in competition."

"Yeah," Larry said, "but maybe I'm more realistic. Does it make sense that Larisa's not jealous or even contemptuous of a little girl who's stealing her thunder?"

"That's not as much realism as cynicism," I said.

Earl interrupted. "We're getting nowhere. We have to take Erin and Larisa's relationship at face value until we see or learn otherwise. While you're in the mood for talking, Ship, why don't you tell us your theory about the wound to Johnny Bizell's hand you were so hot about last night?"

"I wasn't so hot about it. It just made me visualize the murder, that's all."

"Now you're psychic," I teased.

Larry explained. "My guess is that the assailant inflicted the neck wound from the driver's side of the car, probably leaning in through the window."

"The door was open," Earl countered.

"And the wound was on the right side," I said.

Larry held up a hand to silence us. "But there was a wound in the victim's left hand. My guess is that the lab guys will find tissue on the inside door handle where Johnny tried desperately to get out."

"But why would he get out of the car on the side where his assailant is standing?"

"For one thing, the assailant wouldn't have still been standing there. The weapon, or most of it, is still in the car. The death wound was inflicted in one move, and there was nothing more the perpetrator could have done to have wounded Bizell any worse. He probably sensed that and ran off as Bizell reached up to his neck with his right hand — thus the bloodiness of it — and tried to jump out of the car, either for help or to get a better angle on stopping the bleeding."

"I still don't see why he wouldn't have tried to avoid the assailant by heading out the other door," I said.

"Well, the car has bucket seats and a stick shift on the console. Even with all that adrenalin flowing, Bizell must have known he didn't have time to navigate *that* obstacle course."

"Why couldn't the murderer have come in from the passenger's side and murdered him that way?" Earl asked, not challenging, just trying to draw a bead on Larry's logic.

"He could have, but it appears to me that the murder was a surprise. Bizell probably wasn't sure what was happening until it happened. And opening that door so frantically that he injured himself doing it proves that he probably did it after he was mortally wounded. If he had seen someone coming after him from the other side, he probably could have gotten out and escaped injury."

"It's a long shot," Earl said. "But interesting, and you're thinking."

"Thank you, teacher." Larry mocked. Earl ignored him.

"We don't really know what happened, then, to anyone else, including Bonnie and Margo, after we saw them leave work," Earl said.

Larry and I shook our heads, and Earl drew big question marks after their names. We heard heavy footsteps coming up the stairs and wheeled around to see Wally Festschrift burst through the door in the same tacky outfit he'd worn that morning. "My sentiments exactly," he said, huffing and puffing from the climb and motioning to Earl's chart with an unlit cigarette.

"Just tryin' to do our jobs," Earl said

"Yeah, well, me too," Wally said. "May I?" he asked, dragging a chair between his legs and engulfing it with his body. Earl didn't respond. "So, where is everybody?"

"Everybody who?" Earl said.

"C'mon, Haymeyer, " Festschrift said, "what're ya doing, harboring every suspect I got? I ain't found anybody but Greg Gibbons, and that poor sucker is disappointed that he *wasn't* responsible for Bizell's death."

"Are you sure he wasn't?"

"Positive. He's got an airtight alibi. He went to that tumbling meet or whatever you call it at the high school last night, but right afterward he had a meeting — guess where — with Larisa Cumiskey's old man." Wally put the still unlit cigarette between his lips and dug around in several pockets to produce a bent up notepad. "Ernest, Ernest Cumiskey is after Gibbons for a job with his company. Likes the young guy a lot, I guess."

"That doesn't compute," I blurted. Earl put his finger to his lip, but Festschrift caught it.

"Don't shush him, Lieutenant," Wally said, referring to Earl's rank when he was Festschrift's boss years before. "I thought we were all in this thing together and you got nothin' to hide and all that. Why doesn't it compute, kid?"

I looked to Earl for permission. He was giving me one of those you-got-yourself-into-this-get-yourself-out-of-it looks. "I just can't imagine Ernest Cumiskey in the mood to talk business after his daughter had humiliated him in the gymnastics meet."

"I read in the paper that she finished second in the all-around," Shipman said.

"You don't understand," I said. "In her father's eyes, that's worse than breaking a leg. I've seen him so angry after meets where she's lost just one event that he will leave his family behind to find their own way home."

"Gibbons said Cumiskey seemed a little nervous," Wally said, "but that was all. He didn't represent it as anger, just preoccupation. I'll tell you frankly, I think Gibbons is just happy with the way his job interview went — and since you're not gonna bite and ask where they were, I'll tell ya. At our little breakfast spot."

"Charming," Earl said, intimating that he had heard nothing constructive so far. "You were going to call me with the lab findings."

"Well, hey, ain't an in-person performance better than a call? You should be flattered."

"I couldn't be more," Earl said dryly.

Festschrift flipped a few more pages in his grimy notepad and tossed it onto Bonnie's desk where he could read from it while he finally lit up. Earl moved to open a window and let a cool breeze in. "I was gonna take my coat off," Festschrift whined. "Now I gotta leave it on."

"Suit yourself," Earl said.

"So, anyway, the autopsy shows that there was an initial wound at the front of the right side of the neck that left almost an inch-deep gash. In what they think was a simultaneous action, a slicing wound extended from that initial puncture back about an inch and a quarter, deep enough and long enough to sever both the carotid artery and the jugular vein."

"I've heard of going for the jugular," Shipman said. "What does the carotid artery do?"

"I'm glad you asked that, kid," Festschrift said, gesturing with both hands. "I've been wanting to show off my medical knowledge ever since I learned this. The veins carry blood back to the heart. The arteries take it away from the heart. Whoever pulled this job knew what he — or she — was doing. Those two workhorses, the jugular and the carotid, do the job on blood to and from the heart and brain. If only one or the other had been affected, Johnny's reflex action to stop the bleeding might have helped. But with the blood flow to *and* from the brain crippled, he lost the facility to do anything for himself."

"What did the coroner think about the wound to the left hand?" Shipman asked.

Festschrift slowed him down. "I'll get to that. Don't you want to know more about the death wound? The coroner says it was caused by a combination of something as sharp as a razor and as blunt as something fibrous. When we showed him the hunk from between the seats, it was like the last piece of a puzzle. Exhibit A. The lab guys would like to find a duplicate so they don't have to wash it apart. They can't get a fingerprint off the plastic part, and although they have taken a couple of chips of the blood from it, they want to leave it as is. There is, they are sure, a razor blade imbedded in it."

"A homemade weapon?" Earl asked.

"They don't know for sure. We'll know soon, though. These guys are unbelievable."

"Yeah, they can trace almost anything," Larry said, "like the cause of a wound on a dead man's left hand?"

"Awright, awright, the coroner says that was caused by a blunt instrument, likely metal. Guys on the scene found tissue on the door handle and the coroner is satisfied that that's the solution."

Larry beamed and looked at Earl and me. It was a nice piece of deduction on his part, but I wasn't sure it told us anything substantial.

"Have they determined when Bizell died?" I asked.

"They're not entirely sure, but given the location of his car, it could have been during or after that gymnastics thing. He was really in a spot back there where none of the spectators getting in their cars could have seen him or the assailant. The coroner put the time of death at before midnight but he's only guessing how much before."

"How was he discovered?"

"A local squad car cruises through the parking lot every few hours, and the cop on that beat said he thought he saw a light glowing between the air-conditioning units and the garbage bins the first time around, but he didn't really check it out until his second time through at about three forty-five A.M. Speakin' of that, I'm tired."

"You oughta be," Earl said, a modicum of respect in his voice for the first time since at the crime scene.

"But I gotta get a line on some of these other people before I hit the rack. We gumshoes like to take weekends off, ya know, so I can suffer through today if I can line up some interviews for Monday. How 'bout lettin' me in on the whereabouts of your people and givin' me a break, Earl?"

"I'm telling you the truth, Wally. I don't mind saying that I would rather talk to Bonnie and Margo and even Erin before you do, but if I knew where they were right now, I'd tell you."

Festschrift squinted at his old friend as if to size him up, then nodded. "One thing you never did was lie to me," he said. "Will you let me know when you find 'em?"

"Yeah, I will," Earl said, standing, as if to signal that the party was over. Festschrift didn't move.

"And will you let me talk to them first?"

"I can't promise that," Earl said.

"You don't want to obstruct justice, do ya, Earl?"

"That's another thing I've never done, Sergeant," Earl said evenly.

Wally cocked his head and raised his eyebrows, nodding agreement as if to silently apologize. "But you're not conducting an investigation, are you?" he said.

"Of course I am. Two of these people work for me and the other is very close."

"But you're not representing any of them, and you can't protect them the way their lawyers can."

"I wouldn't want to protect anyone I thought had murdered someone, but yes, I am representing Bonnie Murray. You wanna see her file? She engaged me to put her son-in-law under surveillance on a domestic matter."

"No you don't, Earl," Festschrift said, exasperated. "This ain't no domestic case now. Anyway, everybody knows you don't take domestic cases. And besides, if you were watchin' Mr. Gibbons, you had the wrong party."

"We learned that," Earl said. "And I took this domestic case because Bonnie's a friend."

"She's also my prime suspect."

"And if I can prove that she came straight home from the gymnastics meet with Margo Franklin, will you let her off the hook?"

"Of course, depending on the trustworthiness of this Margo Franklin, who I would also like to meet soon."

Festschrift was startled when the three of us burst into laughter. "Sorry, Wally," Earl said, "but documenting the character of Margo Franklin will be the easiest job you've ever had."

"I could use an easy job."

The phone rang. "Yes," Earl said, "he is."

"Yeah, this is Festschrift. Uh-huh, yeah, give it to me." He motioned frantically for his notepad and pen. I scooped them up and delivered them to him, noticing the inscription on the barrel of the ballpoint: *Stolen from Harry's Union 76.*

Earl paced with his hands in his pocket while Festschrift scribbled. "A razor, huh? Yeah. Interesting. Yeah? I don't know. Let me know when you find out."

Wally hung up and folded his notepad, stuffing it into his shirt pocket. "Craziest thing," he said, wanting us to beg for information. None of us would. "All these hotshot scientists workin' on the dumb thing, and a secretary winds up recognizing the murder weapon." He paused again, but we just waited. "It's a broken off piece of a lady's shaver, the cutting end of one of those disposable jobs."

"How do you know it's a lady's?" I asked, accusingly.

" 'Cuz it's purple, boy," he said, smiling. "Would you shave wit' a purple razor?" Earl and Larry laughed. "They're checking on the brand now to find out where it might have been bought. That could help us a lot."

I wasn't sure I wanted to know all that that might tell us. I didn't want the murder weapon to be so femininely identified. And I suddenly felt the need to get the sleep I never really caught up on from the pre-dawn trip south. It wasn't to be, though. Margo was trotting up the stairs.

"Margo, where have you been?" Earl said.

"Oh, you're Margo," Wally said before she could answer. He extended his hand.

"Yes, Margo Franklin. And you're — ?"

"Wally Festschrift. Chicago Homicide."

"Margo," Earl jumped in, "did you and Bonnie bring Erin home with you last night after the meet like you planned, and did Larisa come with you?"

Margo looked at Festschrift and back at Earl. "Well, no, Larisa wasn't coming with us, anyway, but as it turned out, I drove home alone."

"How did Mrs. Murray get home?" Wally asked.

"I'm not sure she went home. She said something about attending to some business and then going with Erin and Linda to Linda's apartment. The three of them had planned to spend the night at Bonnie's, but I called there early this morning and got no answer. So, what's going on?"

FIVE

"I'm sure your boss will be more than happy to fill you in on what's happened, Miss Franklin," Festschrift said, "but I have jurisdiction in this case and I have a few questions for you, if you don't mind."

"I mind," Earl said.

"I asked her if she minded, Earl, not you."

"You're in my office, Sergeant, and I'd rather you not conduct your business here."

"Earl, please," Margo said, "has something happened to Bonnie?"

"No. Johnny Bizell was murdered, and Sergeant Festschrift here — "

"I can speak for myself, if you don't mind." Wally briefed Margo on the case. "Tell me, Margo — may I call you Margo? — tell me, did Mrs. Murray ever say anything that would lead you to believe that she had an interest in harming Mr. Bizell?"

Margo was stunned. She stared past Festschrift and out the window, her hand drawn up to her mouth. "Oh, no — " she said quietly.

"I didn't get that, ma'am," Festschrift said politely. "Are you saying, no she didn't, or are you saying, oh no, because you recall that she did?"

"Of course she had a motive," Margo said absently.

"Of course she did. But did she ever say anything about acting on it?"

Margo looked desperately to Earl and then to me. We both shook our heads.

"Don't make it difficult for both of us, Miss Franklin. I know you spend a lot of time with Mrs. Murray, and I'm sympathetic to her distaste for a man she believes broke up her daughter's marriage. It's not illogical that she might have said something threatening, and it's not necessarily incriminating, either." I was amazed at how articulate Wally could be when he wasn't playing his illiterate cop routine.

Margo slumped into a chair, and Festschrift leaned back against a desk, directly in front of her. "Well, Earl," she said, "you may hate me for telling this, but Bonnie has been saying daily for weeks that she would kill Bizell if Greg and Linda's divorce ever became final. But it never did. In fact, Linda has not been seeing Johnny for a month. Bonnie, *and* Linda for that matter, have been optimistic about a reconciliation."

"But she said she would kill him?" Wally pressed.

"She didn't mean it! It's something you say when someone messes up your world or harms your children, and that's what happened."

"She may not have meant it," Festschrift said, scribbling madly again, "but somebody did it for her."

"You're saying she paid someone to do it?"

"I'm not saying anything except that her wish came true. Anybody here got anything more for me?" He buttoned up his coat. We said nothing. "Where can I find Mrs. Murray, if not at home?"

"I have no idea," Margo said. "I thought they'd be at either her place or Linda's."

"Why don't you try 'em on the phone one more time," Festschrift suggested. Margo looked like it was the last thing she wanted to do.

"Why don't *you?*" Earl said, but when Wally reached for a phone, Earl added, "on your own phone."

Festschrift straightened up, stuffed his notepad and pencil in his coat pockets, and left his hands there too. "So, the lines are drawn, huh, Earl? We're not gonna help each other on this?"

"Apparently not," Earl said "It's not like you to be so eager to pin a murder on the first suspect you come up with, but that's where you're heading and I won't be part of it."

Festschrift turned his back and walked to the door. Without turning around, he said, "Just be sure of two things, Earl. Don't be guilty of the opposite, protecting extremely viable suspects. And don't obstruct justice by harboring criminals, witnesses, *or* suspects."

Earl stepped to the window and watched the detective pull away, heading the opposite direction from Bonnie's apartment. "Try Bonnie on the phone," he told Margo. "Fast."

As she dialed, Earl dictated the priorities to Larry and me. "Either of you on cases that can't be shelved for a few days?" We shook our heads. "Our top priority is to locate Bonnie and Linda and Erin. Festschrift hasn't even thought about Larisa yet, but she's so far removed from the situation that he may not even want to question her. Let's do whatever we have to do."

"Bonnie!" Margo said. "I've been trying to reach you! Have you heard what's happened. Yes, yes. Where are — "

Earl grabbed the phone. "Bonnie, listen," he said, "don't answer the phone. Just pack a few things and come over here as soon as you can. We'll talk then. Yes, I know. They aren't? You can't? Well, where could they — ? Never mind for now, just hurry."

He hung up and spun around. "Larry, I want you to get over to Linda Gibbons's place and watch for her. Bonnie doesn't know where she and Erin are. You'll have an advantage over the cops who will also be staking out the place because you know what Linda and Erin look like. You have to get to them before Festschrift does."

As Larry bounded down the steps, Earl told me to arrange for a double room at the Holiday Inn in Northbrook just off the Edens "close enough to us, but just that much farther from downtown. Make it in Larry's name; I think his was the only one Wally didn't hear."

I was still on the phone when Bonnie drove up. "That was quick, Bonnie," Earl told her. "Good work. We're on our way to Northbrook. You can leave your car here."

Margo and Earl and Bonnie and I piled into Margo's car, Earl dragging his big white chart with him. As Margo blasted up the Edens, Earl questioned Bonnie. "I gotta know where you were and what happened last night," he said.

"Well, after the meet I had arranged to chat for a minute with Erin's coach, the guy with the funny name."

"Nik Adamski."

"Right, Nik. I told him that I was prepared to finance Erin's training this summer if he could give her individualized coaching when she returned from the European tour. That's been the dream of her life. He told me that it wouldn't be necessary because he had already been promised a grant by the U.S. Olympic Committee and that both she and Larisa had qualified to train under the grant. Then I told him that things were looking better for Linda since Johnny had dropped her."

"You told him *that?*" Earl said, incredulous.

"Of course. Nik and all the girls know that story from way back," Bonnie said. "It's no news. He said it was important that they all encourage Erin during this difficult time."

"So what is the story with Linda and Greg? Are they getting back together? Did this Bizell really dump her?"

"Yes, he dumped her, and much as I hate to admit it, she loved him and it hurt her. She hated him for it, because she said she had been willing to break up her family for him. She's still kicking herself over that and says she couldn't blame Greg if he never forgave her, but she wants him back and will do anything to see that it happens."

"Meaning what?"

"Take all the blame, admit she was wrong, beg his forgiveness, whatever. She told me that while their relationship, hers and Greg's, had deteriorated over the years, he really did nothing that justified her affair. But the fact remains that she did fall for Bizell and she virtually gave up her husband for him, and then he dumped her."

"How did she take it?"

"Not well at first. She tried to get back at Johnny."

"Did she ever threaten him?"

"Oh, I'm sure she did."

Earl hung his head. "Did you ever hear her threaten him on the phone or anything?"

"No, only to me."

"She told you she had plans for him?"

"She only told me that, wrong as she was to have made the decision, there was no way she could let him get away with leaving her when she left her husband for him."

"C'mon, Bonnie, was she ever specific? Did she hate him enough to kill him for it?"

Bonnie bit her lip and looked away from Earl, watching the Saturday morning traffic on the expressway. "Where're we going?" she asked.

"To jail if you can't tell me more, Bon," Earl said gently.

"I don't want Linda to go to jail," she said, fighting tears. "I'd go first."

"You might." Earl told her about the involvement of Chicago Homicide and the fact that Margo had no choice but to repeat some of the things Bonnie had said about Bizell.

"Margo, how could you?" Bonnie said. "You know I was just raving as any mother would do! You would have said the same things. Yes, I hated Johnny Bizell enough to kill him, but you didn't hear me say that stuff for long after Linda admitted that she was as much to blame and that she'd made a conscious decision to break up her family for the creep. I nearly cheered for him when he dumped her."

"Bonnie, what could I do?" Margo said. "I was asked point blank if you had ever said you wanted to kill Johnny Bizell. You can't deny you said it many times, and I couldn't deny you said it, either."

"Don't blame Margo, Bonnie," Earl said. "What I want to know is whether Linda ever said the same things."

"Of course she did," Bonnie admitted.

Earl took Bonnie's hand. She was twenty years his senior, but he talked to her as if she was his daughter. "You know I love you, don't you, Bonnie?" She nodded. "You also know I have to ask you some hard questions, don't you?" She nodded again. "I'm going to ask them now, and when we have you and Margo settled in your hotel room, I'm going to want your answers. You must tell me the truth, Bonnie. I won't be the only person who asks, so be straight with me and we'll put everything we've got behind protecting you."

Margo exited at Lake-Cook Road and headed west to the light at Old Skokie Road/Route 41.

"Did you murder Johnny Bizell last night? Did you see him last night? Did Linda murder him? Did she see him?"

Margo turned left twice and then right into the parking lot of the Inn. Once in the room, the four of us sat on the edges of the beds. Bonnie was crying. "It's time to talk to me, Bon," Earl said gently.

"I know," she said, holding a tissue to her face. Margo put her arm around the woman. "I didn't murder Johnny Bizell, much as I would have liked to have the courage. Yes, I saw him last night. When Linda joined Margo and me in the stands, she pointed him out to me."

"I didn't know that," Margo said, dropping her arm.

"I know, honey," Bonnie said. "We didn't want you upset about it."

"Upset?"

"Anyway, that's when we decided to change our plans. Erin and I were going to stay at my place, but I wanted to talk to Linda and be with her in case Johnny wanted to cause trouble. We couldn't imagine what he would be doing there after having not seen Linda for a month. What was worse, Greg had phoned Linda just before she left for the meet and told her that he might be there near the end himself and that he would try to greet her if he could. It was as encouraging as he'd been since Linda and Johnny broke up. She was excited about it like a first date, but she didn't see Greg and when Erin won the all-around, there was too much pandemonium and we didn't even look for him."

"Bonnie," Earl said, "were you with Linda every minute then until you picked up Erin and went home?"

"No."

"Where did she go, and for how long?"

"She told me to wait for Erin and bring her to the car. She didn't know I was going to talk to Nik anyway, but she wanted to look for Greg at the exits and in the parking lot, so she said she would wait in the car."

"So how long were you apart?"

"Maybe twenty-five minutes," Bonnie said.

"Ouch."

Bonnie hid her face in her hands. "I know," she said. "It crossed my mind, too."

"When did it first cross your mind?"

"This morning when Erin came running in with the news. She had gotten up early to watch the news on TV to see if she would be on."

"How did Erin react?"

"She was just shocked. Not remorseful, just stunned."

"And Linda?"

"She burst into tears. She had, after all, loved the man, if only for a short time. I came home to get some things so I could stay with them a while longer, but when I called there before leaving my place again, there was no answer. I took Linda's car, so I have no idea where they are."

Earl shook his head. "Are you ready for one more tough one?" he asked.

"No, but go ahead."

"Are you fairly certain that Erin was in the locker room the whole time you talked to Nik and the rest of the time you waited for her?"

Bonnie stood as quickly as a matronly woman in her late fifties could stand. "No, you don't, Earl," she said, pacing and pointing at him, unable to restrain her tears. "Don't you dare cast aspersions on that child."

"I'm sorry, Bonnie, but I have to ask you if Erin ever said anything threatening about Johnny Bizell."

"No, you don't have to ask. Earl, you are talking about a thirteen-year-old child!"

"Fourteen," Margo corrected.

"Whatever! How dare you ask such a question?"

"Bonnie, why does it upset you so? Don't you know that my whole point is to establish alibis for all of you? I can't manufacture them, and I wouldn't."

"And I wouldn't expect you to! Don't you believe me, Earl?"

"Of course I do, but I have to know where Erin was between the time the meet ended, the interviews were over, and you picked her up outside the locker room door."

Bonnie went into the bathroom and shut the door, sobbing loudly.

"What are you after, Earl?" Margo asked.

"I'm not sure. I just don't like the way she exploded when I asked about Erin. I wasn't after anything when I brought it up. I was just trying to cover all the bases. But now I wonder if she's being straight with me."

"Do you believe her about not leaving the field house until she went to the car?"

"Oh, yes. I don't think Bonnie could have murdered Bizell. I don't even think she would have confronted him, though she might surprise me on that."

Bonnie returned. "So are we done, Earl? Is Margo going to stay with me until this thing is over, and are you going to protect me from having to answer questions from the press and the police?"

"I don't know, Bonnie. I can protect you from the press but not the police forever. And anyway, I don't think you're being fair with me."

"You're accusing me of lying?"

"I didn't say that. I have to know that you and Erin went directly to Linda's car when Erin came out of the locker room."

Bonnie fidgeted. "I lied to you, Earl, and I'm sorry, but you must believe me, it was only on one minor detail. I know you're trying to help, so I want you to believe me when I say that I am going to straighten out that lie and that I won't lie to you again."

"Of course."

"I waited longer than twenty-five minutes for Erin. It must have been closer to twice that. I spent the first fifteen or twenty minutes with the coach. Then I waited about half an hour until Larisa came out of the locker room. Other girls had been filing out and meeting their families, but Larisa recognized me and said that Erin had left earlier. She said she had skipped her shower and had ducked out to avoid the press. I ran out to Linda's car, and Erin was already there. I was going to scold her, but Linda said she had thought it would be better if she didn't leave Erin alone in the car, and she didn't want Erin running into more newsmen by going back in after me."

"How long had Linda waited in the car before Erin showed up?"

"It was the other way around. Erin waited outside the locked car for awhile with her parka hood up so no one would recognize her. Linda had looked around quite a while for Greg before giving up. I hope Larisa found her mother."

Earl looked depressed, deep in thought. "Huh? What? Found her mother?"

"Yes, she asked if I had seen her mother. She said her mother was going to meet her but that she hadn't appeared yet. I told her I didn't think I would know her mother if I saw her, and she said she would be the one with two bratty nine-year-olds fighting with her."

Earl took me into a corner to talk quietly. "I want you to go out and find a pay phone," he said. "Call Festschrift and tell him that I will personally apologize about my actions today and am willing to help all I can, but that I want the report on any fingerprints they may have found on Bizell's car."

"So, what do you think, Earl?" Bonnie was saying as I pulled on my coat.

"Well, I don't like it much," he said.

"What don't you like?"

"I don't like the fact that of all the people I've ever even heard of who were at that meet last night, I can't think of one, except maybe the coach, who has an alibi. I suppose the other girls on the team can vouch for Larisa up until the time she left the locker room, and maybe the ones who came out while you were waiting can vouch for you, but unless they knew you, you might have blended into the crowd. I don't even have an alibi for the Cumiskey twins, let alone their mother. Where was the father? Where was Linda? Where was Erin?"

"I just told you where *they* were," Bonnie reminded him.

"But an alibi, Bonnie, means someone can substantiate your whereabouts. Not even Margo is clean on that score."

Six

"Where's yer boss?" Festschrift wanted to know.

"Tied up at the moment," I said. "He just wanted me to ask for the information."

"What was your name again, kid?"

"Spence. Philip Spence."

"Yeah, right, Spence. Listen, why don't you come on down to the sixteenth precinct and learn a few things about the business?"

"I know a *few* things about the business," I said. "I've been in it a while myself."

"Yeah? You ever sit outside a lab waiting on some important piece of information, a hot bit of evidence?"

"Not exactly, but — "

"Well, then come on down. You know how to find us?"

"I think so."

"Good." *Click.*

A quick call to Earl brought permission and the insulting reminder to not proffer any of the information I had heard from Bonnie.

"I *know,* Earl," I said while driving him back to his Glencoe office in Margo's car.

"I suppose you do, Philip," he said. "Meet me back at the office later. I'll be trying to track down the missing gymnast and her mother. If you find out that Festschrift and Company have gotten to them already, call me immediately."

Festschrift was sitting on a wood bench in a grimy hallway outside the forensics lab when I approached. It was the only place he had looked at home since I had first seen him running the show in the parking lot of Proviso West High School. I didn't realize until I was upon him that he was dozing.

He sat with his ankles crossed — I guessed he hadn't crossed his legs at the knees for many moons. His top coat was buttoned, though champing at the gaps, and his hands were folded in front of his belly. His chin rested as close to his chest as possible. He made no noise, but his breathing was even and deep. I couldn't bring myself to wake him. He had been up as long as I had, but he hadn't had the luxury of trying to nap between dawn and noon as I had.

His face had grown dark with stubble, and he looked pitiable. I quietly sat at the other end of the bench and studied the man. He was good, Haymeyer had said. What drove him? Who was he, really? Why did he so love the work of tracking homicidal personalities even above getting ahead, making more money, gaining power? There was something pure about that.

And what about his bluster, his sarcasm, his earthiness? Was it just a show? Why the contempt for his former protégé and then boss? Was he just filling a role, or did he really resent Earl?

I determined to ask him. I also prayed that he would give me the right opening to talk about what I thought was important. I had regretted waiting for perfect opportunities before, and it wasn't going to happen again.

A door swung open from the lab and a white-coated and bespectacled woman emerged carrying a clipboard with a stack of forms on it. She leaned close to Festschrift's face and stooped to look into his eyes. She glanced at me. I held a finger to my lips and shook my head.

"You with him?" she mouthed. I nodded. She beckoned with a finger and I jumped up, almost too quickly. We walked down the hall and stood under a dim light over a washroom door. "You're on the Bizell case, right?" she asked. I couldn't lie.

"Yes," I said.

She began flipping pages. "You got all this weapon and wound stuff this morning, right?"

I nodded again as she kept turning pages and mumbling to herself, "Wound on left hand, blood type, carotid, jugular, uh-huh, yeah, yeah, yeah. You ever talk, uh — ?"

"Name's Spence, Philip Spence. I'm sorry."

"You ever do more than nod and say your name and that you're sorry, Spence?"

"Uh, sure, sorry."

She looked at me, bemused. I was embarrassed and not unimpressed. She looked deep into my eyes and then back at her clipboard. "So you just want the new stuff, right?"

I nodded.

"There you go again," she said, smiling.

"I'm sorry," I said, knowing immediately that I had set myself up again. It isn't easy letting someone think you're something you're not.

"OK," I said, "uh, forgive me, but yes, I just want the new stuff, thank you."

She flashed the smile again and turned back to her papers. "OK, Mr. Spence, we have fingerprints from the driver's side, Bizell's only. On the passenger's side door and window we have what we think are prints from three different hands, two big ones and a small one. Our bets are on two men and a woman, but we don't want to rule out a young boy or a very small man, maybe a girl."

"Thank you."

"Sure. Will you give this stuff to Rip?"

"Rip?"

"Van Winkle?"

"Oh, yeah, sorry."

"How come you're so sorry, Spence? You like workin' Saturdays as much as I do?"

"Yeah, plus I feel guilty."

"Hm, I haven't heard this line before. Let's have it."

"It's not a line, ma'am, it's just that I let you think I was with Festschrift."

"Uh-oh," she said musically, raising her brows and taking back the clipboard.

"Oh, no, I don't mean I lied to you. I mean I am with Festschrift, but not in the way you think."

"Well, you're not dating him, are you? Who are you?"

"I gave you the right name. I'm with a private detective agency, and I *was* invited here by Sergeant Festschrift."

"But you're not supposed to have direct access to this file, are you?"

"No, ma'am, I'm afraid not."

"Forget the politeness, Spence. You just swindled me out of classified information."

"I'm sorry."

She swore. "I've already heard that one, remember?"

She stomped back down the hall to Festschrift and swatted him on the hands with her papers. "Here ya go, Sleepy. Can I go home now?"

"Huh? Oh, sure, Marilyn. Sorry you hadda come in. Take the rest of the day off."

"Everybody's sorry," she said. Festschrift looked puzzled, but I was grateful she hadn't told him what I'd done. She probably would later.

Festschrift shifted his weight and leaned toward the light, holding the papers close to his face and scrounging up a pair of half glasses with his free hand. He read each page carefully, all the fine print, then announced that there wasn't much of anything new but that he might have to begin fingerprinting everyone who had been at the gymnastics meet the night before. He looked so serious that it threw me. Then he let his head fall back and cut loose a belly laugh that echoed throughout the precinct headquarters. I smiled.

"So what's yer philosophy of life, Spence?" Festschrift said.

I was floored. "Pardon me?"

"I study death to make sense of life," he said. "You made sense of it yet?"

"I think maybe I have."

"Oh, yeah? One of the myths of youth. Seems we all know more about life the younger we get. Have you found that?"

"I guess I know what you mean," I said. "I mean, I do realize every day how little I know about everything there is to know."

"Yeah, me too," he said, staring off into space as if he was about to fall back to sleep. I didn't want to let it drop, but I had never heard of a way to segue from a question like he had just popped to a cogent argument for faith in God.

"Do you really wanna know my philosophy of life?" I asked.

"Not really, no," he said, smiling apologetically. "I ask that of a lot of people, just to see what they'll say. But, OK, go ahead, what would you have said if you had known what was coming?"

"Well, I'm a Christian," I said.

"Yeah, well, hey, we've got a few of those on the department. More than a few I should say. They've got some kinda lodge or club called Cops for Christ or somethin'. They come on a little strong, and I'm not in the mood right now, so I'll make a deal with ya. You save your sermon, and I'll buy you the best steak in town."

It was apparent he *wasn't* in the mood, and the offer sounded too good to pass up.

Festschrift's unmarked squad car looked and rode like the hand-me-down it was. With its blackwalled tires, whip antenna, spotlight, and city license plate, it screamed cop car louder than any Chicago blue and white with lights.

The ride was rough, the squeaks loud, the brakes metal on metal. It rolled on the curves and rocked at stoplights. Inside it looked like a cab with a couple of hundred thousand miles on it. Festschrift admitted to only 160 thousand plus.

He drove like an old lady on her way to church, which didn't seem to fit. I knew he was tired. We dined at a stuffy little place he called cozy. In reality, it reminded me of the inside of his car, decorated in Early Akron. He appeared a connoisseur of good food, however, and in that I was not disappointed.

We sat in vinyl covered kitchen-type chairs at a square formica table on linoleum floors and were waited on by men who understood so little English that we had to point out our entrees on the menu. "Plenty of it and plenty good," the sergeant said. And he was right.

He was greeted by a half dozen or so patrons as the night wore on. "I eat here often," he said simply. He'd identify the acquaintances by precincts "The old lady left me goin' on four years ago," he said, always with his mouth full. "We'd been together, if you can call it that, sixteen years and had four boys, every one of 'em a bum. I even got one behind bars right now."

I didn't know what to say. "I never had time for her or them," he said. "It's my own fault and I know it, but then my old man never had time for me and I turned out awright, didn't I?"

I wasn't sure exactly how he'd turned out, with four no account sons and a divorce.

"I still see her around. She's OK. I don't blame her. I'm no prize. I love the job more than anything or anybody, and I can't change that. But I don't hate her, and she takes a big chunk of my check every two weeks, so we might's well be on speakin' terms."

"Why do you love the job so much?" I had to ask. He didn't seem like such a sensitive, loving, humanity-oriented person.

"I'm a justice nut. I like the puzzles, the mystery. Every homicide is different, ya know. Like this one. I got me an idea on this one that's kinda bizarre, and I'll trade you secrets if you want. I know you know something 'cuz my guess is ol' Earl has found one of the women I'm looking for. Wanna trade?"

"I don't know. I don't think so."

"You just tol' me something, you know that?"

"No. What'd I tell you?"

"You tol' me I was right. You told me that Earl found one of 'em at least. You're deciding not to tell me what you learned, but you did learn something just like I said."

I cocked my head. He had me. "But I really can't say anything," I said.

"No, 'course you can't, and I can't bully Earl with my obstruction-of-justice routine either. He knows that. These women aren't wanted yet, so he's not harboring anything."

Wally ordered a carafe of wine, offered me some, then drank the whole thing over the next forty-five minutes with no apparent effect on his mind or speech. This was a man used to eating and drinking heartily, and then, in a succession I wouldn't have guessed, he decided he was ready for dessert. "I never drink on duty," he said. "And I'm takin' tomorrow off. That oughta give Hayseed a real jump on me, but I'll get to all the people eventually whether he sees 'em first or not."

He busied himself with his deep dish apple pie and what appeared to be a pint of ice cream.

"Tell me something," I said. "Have you ruled out any mob connection in this murder?"

He gestured and tried to talk, even with his mouth jammed as never before, as if I had come up with an idea so ludicrous, so obviously in left field that he couldn't let rebuttal wait until he had swallowed. "Oh, no, small time, small time. In fact, if Bizell had been snuffed two days from now, I wouldn't have had the honor of handling it. The vice control division thought he was tighter with some south suburban mobsters, but all he was into was some porn and some dope. He had no real connections. They just trailed him a little and found that he was nothing but a super salesman type, number one in his company, who liked to run in some fast circles. But he was all show. Some of our informants told us he was too loud for their tastes. They like to play it close to the vest, you understand, and you don't do that with his golden mane and that hot silver 'Vette o' his. He found himself uninvited to the kinds of gatherings we like to keep an eye on."

"But they were still watching him at the time he was murdered?"

"Just barely. They knew he was home much of the evening and then went to that gymnastics meet. They didn't expect much there, so they left him. It might have been the last tail of him anyway, so when the call hit ISPERN, one of our guys recognized the name and called VCD. Then it fell to me."

"ISPERN and VCD?"

"Illinois State Police Emergency Radio Network and Vice Control Division. Anyways, Bizell was strictly a small time womanizer with a few bucks, fewer friends, and hardly any family to speak of. This sucker gon' be buried without much fanfare."

"Sad."

"Think so, huh? Wait 'til you been in the business as long as I have. Like I tol' ya, I'm a justice freak. People have to pay for what they do. I was a lousy husband and father, and I don't like the price, but I'm payin' it. I'm a good cop, and I earn the rewards for that. It's fair. Sad because a creep like Bizell buys it? Not me. But whoever did it has to pay, regardless of the reason."

"And you've got a bizarre idea about this one?"

"Yeah, but you're not in the market for a trade, am I right?"

"You're right."

"Ah, who cares? I got nothin' to lose. If I'm right, Earl can't protect her anyway."

"I know you think Bonnie did it, but that's not so bizarre. I don't think she did, but she sure had a motive."

"Nah, I'm past that. I haven't totally ruled her out, you understand. One of the things I like about this work is that I often come back to someone I've eliminated early. It's all part of the game. Anyway, I'm thinking gymnast."

"Gymnast? Erin?"

"Gymnast, yes, Erin, I don't know. She might be a little small. I'm guessing whoever did it leaned in the window on the driver's side, reached around behind Bizell's head with the right hand, and did the damage quickly. But it had to be someone that Bizell didn't fear. He had to think of the gesture as affectionate or a greeting or not know what it was to let someone do that. He probably never saw the murder weapon; it would have been tucked into the hand. A little girl might have arms long enough to pull that off, but I don't know."

"But why a gymnast, and if a gymnast, why not Erin, who has a motive just like her grandmother does?"

"A gymnast because I studied up a little at the library early this afternoon and I learned that those little beauties develop incredible muscles in their hands. They can grip and squeeze and take punishment. They have hand strength like grown men, and that's what it would take to have inflicted this wound so successfully. Grown women anyway."

"But you're not thinking of Erin?"

"Oh, I s'pose if I knew more, I might think Erin. But I say I'm not thinking of her only because I really have nothing to go on. I need to chart the comings and goings of everyone at the meet who might have had a motive. The way Earl was doing in your office today."

"You learn that from him?" I asked.

"You kiddin'? He learned it from me. Ask him."

"You like Earl?"

"Love him." He said it without a moment's hesitation.

"You mean it?"

"You bet I do. He's one of the best I've ever seen, straight as an arrow. My kind of a guy."

"You don't act like that around him."

"You think I want him to know? A guy's gotta keep some advantage. Don't you?"

"I don't know. Nah."

"That's *your* advantage."

"Pardon?"

"That self-effacing bit of yours. You gotta be good or Earl wouldn't waste his time with you, but you pull that Columbo, poor-dumb-me act and I'm guessing you're dumb like a fox. Am I right?"

I was embarrassed. Flattered. I shrugged.

"See?" he said. "I was right."

A beeper went off in his pocket and he nearly had to stand to get his bulk out of the way so he could reach it. He clicked it off and headed for the phone. On the way he passed the waiter who had our check. "Jes' put it on the cuff, Georgio," Wally said, "and t'row in a fifteen percenter for yourself, huh?"

"Earl put your cohort on the Gibbons residence today, huh?" Wally said when he returned.

It was apparent he already knew, so I didn't feel I was breaking any confidence by nodding.

"Well, he blew it. We got to Linda Gibbons before he did, and when he appeared, she identified him as someone she had seen before. She said he was a maintenance man she had seen once in the building. He once walked in on her and Johnny Bizell. You wanna go see him?"

"Where is he?"

"We busted him. Had to. He's in the slam at the nineteenth precinct station. Not far from here. You can bail him out if he's got an alibi."

SEVEN

I called Earl on the way out of the restaurant, and he was none too thrilled that I had let so much time elapse before contacting him. I didn't want to tell him that I actually found his old nemesis fascinating.

"Well, you told me to call you if I found that Chicago had found Linda and Erin before Larry had. And they have."

"You're not doing your homework, Philip."

"What do you mean?"

"You're giving me second-hand information."

"Well, sure I am, but it's what Wally Festschrift said based on a phone call he just took."

"Did he actually tell you that *both* Linda and Erin were picked up?"

"I guess I just assumed — "

"Assumed is not homework. Call me from the nineteenth and I'll tell you where *we* have Erin."

In the car I asked Festschrift how they happened to find Linda without finding Erin.

"We just staked out the apartment, saw a little too much of your buddy there, what's his name?"

"Larry Shipman."

"Yeah, and when we saw him approach a young woman, we moved in. The woman was Linda Gibbons, she was on foot, and she still hasn't told us where she dumped Erin."

Linda had agreed to questioning at the precinct house, but no charges had been filed and she was free to go. She had not contacted a lawyer, and from what she told the police, it was apparent she didn't need one. Not that she had an alibi; she didn't. She just told them very little.

She said she had left the gymnastics meet alone to look for her estranged husband at the exits and in the parking lot. When she was unsuccessful she headed for her car because it was locked, and she didn't want her mother and her daughter to get out there first and have to wait for her. As it was, her daughter was already waiting for her and her mother came along some time later. The story was so much like Bonnie's version that it was eerie. It could have been the truth, or it could have been tailor-made.

Festschrift asked her where she had been when he had looked for her that morning.

"My mother went home in my car to get some things so she could stay with us longer, but a few minutes after she left I had this fear that the press would somehow put it all together and try to badger Erin about it. We just threw some things together and jumped on a bus, but I'd rather not say where we went. Anyway, she's there now."

"It shouldn't be hard to guess," Wally said. "I'd say she's either with her coach or with her friend Larisa."

Linda stiffened, but Festschrift didn't pursue it. "The time will come when we need to talk to her, Mrs. Gibbons."

She nodded. "I know. But not yet."

A desk clerk approached. "There's a Mr. Hayworth on the phone for you, Sergeant."

"Haymeyer?"

"Oh, yessir, that was it."

"I don't remember your name, but I know you work in Mother's office," Linda said. "You've been at some of the meets."

"Yeah, quite a few of them actually. I'm Philip."

"Oh, yes, Philip Spence. You used to go with Margo."

"Yeah."

"You must think I'm a terrible person, Philip."

"Oh, no, well I, uh — "

"You do, and you're right. I am. But I hope you don't think I'm so low that you can't give me a ride home — " and she leaned close to whisper " — or to see Erin when I leave here. I'd rather not have to ride back the way I came, with the cops."

"Sure. I don't blame you, but you'll have to ride with Sergeant Festschrift as far as the sixteenth precinct where my car is."

She nodded as Festschrift returned. "Well, I'm gonna let your comrade go," he announced.

"Larry? Why?"

"That was Earl. He said you guys were at the Sox-Yankees game last night."

"I could have told you that," I said.

"Well, good, I've got two unimpeachable sources."

Linda was puzzled. "So I *had* seen that guy before? I remembered him from the time he walked in on Johnny and me, but he's with Earl too, huh? What was the maintenance man bit all about?"

"That was back when your mother thought *you* were the innocent party, and she was trying to get Greg in trouble."

She fell silent.

"We'll likely want to be talking to you again soon," Festschrift told Linda as Larry entered. "Stay accessible."

She didn't respond.

"I haven't seen so many lowlifes in a cell since high school biology," Larry said, eager to get going. "Philip, can you take me to my car up there in Linda's neighborhood?"

"Sure! I mean, that is, if it's all right with you, Linda, that Larry goes along. Is it?"

She shrugged. "Make it a party," she said.

Festschrift dropped us off at my car and said he was going home for some sleep. I was the last to slide out of his car and he grabbed my wrist. "Lemme tell ya something, kid," he said. "I like you, so I'm gonna let you in on one more thing we found at the scene. I'll only tell ya if you assure me we're after the same thing here: justice."

I nodded.

"Perfume," he said.

"Perfume?"

"Perfume. It has different ingredients than men's cologne and the like. On the back of the collar of the dead man and a little on the back of his neck, there were traces of the elements in perfume. When the lab beefed it up by adding to each element and mixing, they matched the smell of a brand name fragrance. Experts — that is, the women in forensics and a few secretaries, not to mention the girls behind the cosmetics counter at Carson's down the street — agree unanimously. It's something they call Chantilly. Ever heard of it?"

"No."

"Well, you've probably smelled it. I recognized it. Not real common, but something you remember." He pulled a heat-sealed plastic packet from his pocket. "Take this," he said. "Take a whiff when you get a chance. And if you smell it on any of our suspects, let me know. You owe me one."

I knew at least *that* was true. "Get some sleep," I said.

"Don't worry, I'll probably be asleep before I get out of the car."

"And thanks for dinner."

"Don't mention it, and hey, keep your advantage."

I knew what he meant, but I pretended I didn't.

Speaking of pretending, Larry put his head against the window and pretended to sleep as the three of us rode to the north side and Linda's apartment. But with Linda in the mood for talking to someone who couldn't put her away for murder, I was sure Larry didn't miss a syllable.

"Since we're all adults here and there's no hiding it from you guys, you wanna know what the toughest thing is for a woman who's had an affair she regrets?"

"I admit it wasn't the first thing on my mind this morning," I said, "but, sure, I'll listen."

"It's that you get put in a bag. Compartmentalized. I'm an average woman. I had always been a faithful wife. I worked. I was a good housekeeper and a good mother. But I met a guy from my husband's office, and something happened. I was bored with my life and here was a gorgeous guy who paid attention to me. I fell in love with him.

"It was wrong. He was wrong; I know that now more clearly than ever. And I regret it, but do you think I'll be able to erase it from my life? Never. Even if Johnny hadn't been killed, I never would have really been forgiven. I can even see it in *your* eyes. An edge has been taken off. I'm seen as worse than just someone who has made one mistake. By people who know, I will never be considered worthy of normal status again. Am I right?"

I didn't know what to say. Of course she was right. She was even right about how I viewed her. "I'm in no position to condemn you," I said.

"Well, that's nice. Maybe you've made a mistake or two in your life too, huh?"

I didn't exactly want to put myself in her category, and there I went, doing just what she predicted, categorizing her. I couldn't stop the next line from coming out of my mouth. "Well, not that kind of a mistake, no. But, yes, I have made some serious mistakes. Why do you think I'm no longer engaged to Margo?"

"I couldn't tell you. I don't know her well, but from what I can tell, you should have hung on to that one. But anyway, did you just hear yourself? You've made some mistakes but nothing as horrible as mine."

"I didn't — "

"I know you didn't say that or mean to imply it, but it's what you think, and I can't blame you. I used to react the same way. I thought the only people who could cheat on their husbands or wives had to be disgusting wanton types. I'm telling you, it happened to me, a normal person, but I'll never be normal again. The worst part is, my husband looks at me and talks to me and treats me the same as everyone else does. Something has been damaged, and no matter what I do, I won't be able to fix it."

I was more than bewildered by this woman unburdening herself to me when I was just this side of being a total stranger. She must have been implying by that openness that she couldn't even say these things to her mother because her mother was as guilty as the rest of us. And why do I say guilty? Are *we* guilty? Is there something wrong with seeing someone in a different light who has nearly ruined the lives of everyone around them by their behavior? Or *were* we unfair, especially now that she was admitting it and not blaming her husband or her lover?

"Greg and Erin and I will probably have to move away to escape this reputation," she said quietly, defeatedly. "That is if he'll ever have me again."

I wanted to tell her that of course, he'd take her back, but I didn't even know the man. I wanted to change the subject, to ask her about perfume, anything. But talking about something else would merely tell her that I didn't care about her problem. And, strangely, I did. I don't know why; I guess she just reached me with her argument.

I knew the right thing to tell her was that there was Someone who could forgive her, Someone who understood, Someone who had experience with people who had sinned and wanted forgiveness, in fact, even with women who had committed adultery. But with Larry in the backseat, pretending to sleep so as to avoid commenting on her treatise, I wasn't ready to hit her with it.

"How did you feel about Johnny's death?" I asked.

"I cried."

"I know, but how did you feel? Sad? Angry? Guilty?"

I knew I shouldn't have said that.

"Guilty? Hardly. You think I killed him, don't you?"

"No, I — "

"You *do!*"

"No, I don't. I meant that it's very likely that whoever killed him thought they were doing you a favor. Therefore if you didn't kill him, you still might feel responsible for the fact that someone did."

"The only person responsible for Johnny's death was Johnny. The way he chewed me up and spit me out qualified him for getting what he deserved. No, I didn't do it. And I wasn't angry or sad. Shocked is the better word. I had been in love with him, or at least I thought I had. I've never lost anyone close to me except my own father, and that's been a long time ago, and he had been sick quite a while. I could accept that. This was horrible. The thought of someone I had known intimately being murdered — " She shuddered.

I parked at the curb, not far from where I had seen Johnny Bizell's car several times. As soon as I shut off the engine, Larry came to and headed out the back door. Before shutting it he leaned back in, touched Linda on the shoulder, and said, "A piece of advice to take or leave: Forget what people think. Only you know what's inside, and that's all that matters. See ya," and he slammed the door and trotted to his own car.

"Oh," she said softly, as if she had been wounded by the perfection of his words. I sat there wishing I had said them. "That was sweet," she added.

I decided that if she had been any woman other than one who had been willing to let her family fly apart, I would have treated her like a lady. "Hang on a second, and let me get the door for you," I said.

I ran around to her side and then walked her up to her apartment. She handed me the key, and I unlocked the door. "Can you come in for a minute?" she asked.

"No, I really shouldn't. I've got to call my boss."

"You can call him from here."

I hesitated.

"You're afraid of me, aren't you? You see? I'll never be able to be a normal person again."

"Let me tell you the truth, Mrs. Gibbons — Linda — I'd be afraid of Snow White if I were alone with her."

She laughed sympathetically. "I'll tell you what I'll do, Philip," she said. "I'll leave the door open, and I'll sit in the living room, and you can use the phone. But hurry, because I have to talk to Earl too. I need to see if he got a call from Coach Adamski — who is also afraid of me, I might add — and was able to pick up Erin from his home. I didn't know where else to take her; I didn't want to burden the Cumiskeys."

"I'll find out for you."

Earl asked that Linda get on the extension phone. He told us that Coach Adamski had reached him at the office shortly after I had dropped Earl off. "I picked her up at his place, and she's with Bonnie now."

"I want to see her," Linda said.

"You can, but we'll have to be careful. It's likely you're being watched, and you could lead the police right to Bonnie *and* Erin. Philip can bring you to the office where we can talk. When we are sure no one is tailing you, we can scoot you over to see them."

"Where are they?"

"I'd rather not say on the phone. How did things go downtown?"

"Not bad. I just told them my story, nothing that should clear me, I wouldn't think, but they fingerprinted me and let me go quickly."

"They fingerprinted you?"

"Yeah."

"Did they charge you with anything?"

"No."

"Were you informed of your rights?"

"Yes, but I thought it would be better if I didn't appear to be hiding anything."

"If they fingerprinted you it means they may have found prints on the car."

"They did, Earl," I said.

"Let's talk about it when you get here," Earl said.

On the way to the office, I asked Linda if she knew anyone who used Chantilly perfume. "Of course," she said, "Larisa has everyone on the team using it. Erin uses it when she gets some from Larisa or I can afford it."

"But Larisa started it?"

"I think so. Her mother swims in it. I can tell when she's coming or even when she's been somewhere. Why?"

"Just curious."

At the office, Earl told Linda that Bonnie and Margo and Erin were at the Northbrook Holiday Inn and that everyone was fine. "I know you've been asked a ton of questions, and Philip has filled me in on your version of what happened last night, but I need to get some more information from you if I can. Do you fear that someone you know and love might have killed Johnny Bizell?"

Linda lifted her chin and looked at the ceiling, catching a short breath and then exhaling. She closed her eyes and dropped her chin to her chest in a pose that reminded me how Festschrift had looked not so many hours earlier.

"Yes," she said, barely above a whisper. "I do."

"Who?"

"I don't know. Erin knew all about him but would never talk to me about it. I can't see her having done it, and I probably couldn't accept it even if she told me she had.

"My mother had the desire but not the drive. I don't think she could have done it, though she wanted to and threatened to many times. When she got the whole story, I think she would have rather murdered me.

"It's my husband I worry about. He said he was going to be there, but I never saw him. I didn't expect to see Johnny, but I did. I don't know. I wish I knew where Erin and my mother were after the meet, and I'm sure they're wishing the same about me."

She was still staring at the floor. "The first several times Greg accused me of seeing Johnny, he blamed it all on Johnny. He couldn't see that I was as much at fault, because that threatened him too much. I don't know if he ever got past that blinded view of it. He probably still wants to blame it on Johnny, and I know he hated him enough to kill him. Whether he did or not, I couldn't say."

"Well, he's been virtually cleared by Sergeant Festschrift, " Earl said.

"Oh?" Linda didn't appear fully relieved about that.

"Yeah. Seems he was with Ernest Cumiskey for a couple of hours immediately following the meet."

"Larisa's dad? What for?"

"Talking to him about a job with Cumiskey's company, I guess."

"No kidding? Greg has always admired Ernest. He's such a go-getter. Goes after only the best people. That says a lot about Greg. Had he been selling well lately in spite of all this, do you know? It doesn't seem likely. Even when we were happy and life was relatively normal, Greg was always just a little above average in the company as far as sales went. Maybe something else about Greg impressed Mr. Cumiskey. Was he offered a job? Did he take it?"

"I have no idea," Earl said. "Excuse me."

He answered the phone and his face clouded. "I see, yes. Thanks, Wally. Yes, I will."

He replaced the receiver and walked deliberately to where Linda sat. She looked up at him expectantly. "I'm afraid I won't be able to take you to see Erin just now," he said. "I've been instructed by the police to hold you here for a few minutes until they arrive."

"What is it, Mr. Haymeyer?"

"Sergeant Festschrift left instructions that he was only to be awakened if anything important turned up. When your fingerprints matched those on the passenger door of Johnny Bizell's car, they thought it was important enough. And so do I."

EIGHT

Sure enough, we had been tailed to the office, and in just a few minutes, homicide detectives had entered, read Linda Gibbons her rights for the second time that day, and took her downtown to await arraignment on charges that she had murdered Johnny Bizell.

"I'm not ready to bring Bonnie out into the open yet," Earl said. "Maybe tomorrow or Monday." I could tell he was seething. "I don't know if Linda is guilty or not, but if she isn't, she has only herself to blame for our not being able to protect her. How could she have seen Bizell recently without telling even her mother?"

"Are you sure she didn't tell her mother?"

Earl got on the phone. "Yes, I know it's nearly midnight, Margo," he said, "and I'm sorry, but I must talk with Bonnie."

He told her that Linda would be charged with the murder because of the fingerprints, her motive, and her lack of an alibi, and he said he wanted Bonnie to hear it from him first. "It'll make the Sunday papers," he said.

Erin was sleeping, and Bonnie and Margo agreed not to tell her. "I'll come over there tomorrow morning and spend some time with you," Earl said.

"Tell Margo to be ready to bring your car back here and go to church with me," I said.

He told her. "She says she'll meet you at her church at nine-thirty." Oh well, it was worth a try.

I was exhausted, but I couldn't keep the wheels from turning as I undressed for bed. There was no way this investigation could be this cut and dried. No one had an alibi for Linda, and she had lied about not having seen Johnny except from across the field house. Apparently, she had been in or near his car.

But if she had murdered him, wouldn't she have been more concerned with convincing people — like Larry and me — of that rather than holding forth about the injustices, meted out to fallen wives? In my mind, she had been truly concerned about how to overcome the consequences of her actions against her husband and her marriage, not actions against her former lover.

One thing I hadn't asked her and wished I had. I wanted to know if she had ever used her daughter's perfume. She said she only bought it when she could afford it or when Erin borrowed some, but did women use each other's perfume? I didn't know. I would ask Margo in the morning. That is, if I could get up early enough to meet her at her church at nine-thirty.

If I had known what I would be getting into, I probably wouldn't have made the effort.

I slept without moving for seven hours, rose, showered, dressed for church, went out for a paper and a roll and coffee, brought them back to my apartment, and sat eating and reading for an hour. It was hard to get past the front page when the banner head-line screamed the news: MOTHER OF GYM STAR CHARGED.

If Erin could keep her equilibrium in the face of all this — I wondered if she would continue to compete. How could she? The most important meets of the year were approaching, but how could she be at her best? How could she even have her mind on her training? She was a fine-tuned machine. A lack of concentration at the level she performed would not only affect her score, but it would also be terribly dangerous. You don't just throw yourself at a balance beam four inches wide and four feet off the ground or fling your body around uneven parallel bars at breakneck speed without having 100 percent concentration.

Margo's church may have been small, a white clapboard structure that looked out of place in the sprawling North Shore, but it was crowded. I arrived early to watch for her but still had to park a block and a half away. I was strolling toward the front of the church when she arrived with a car full of kids who were still a few years shy of ten. She was shouting instructions to them, straightening their hair, making sure each had his or her Bible, tucking in shirts and blouses, and shouting, "I'll see you right here at noon, and no running!" They were all running.

"Hi, Philip," she said, still moving. "Good to see you. Listen, I have to make an announcement in each department and then lead a discussion group in our Sunday school class, so if you wait for me there I'll be a little late." She pointed the way down the stairs and past the washrooms, through the primary department and near the piano at the end of the fellowship hall, behind the partition. "That's where we meet."

"I'll find it," I said, but I had not looked when she had pointed. I just kept staring at her. She was radiant in dark blue with just the right accessories as usual. Energetic. Eager. Enthusiastic. She saw that I wasn't paying attention to her directions and stopped. "Philip," she scolded, blushing. She physically turned me around and pointed over my shoulder. "Down there," she said, "and left past all that stuff I just listed."

I turned and watched her hurry away. She stopped and ran back. "I forgot to tell you, our class breaks up early because the choir uses that piano to practice just before the service. And I'm in the choir, so save me a seat near the front, OK?"

I nodded. No wonder she liked this church better than the one we used to go to. She owned it, or at least she ran it. So many people greeted her that it was obvious she knew everyone and was a favorite.

I was the first to arrive at the partitioned off young adults class area near the piano, so I just sat and waited. The first few people didn't greet me, but after a bunch had arrived, I was asked to introduce myself. I just said my name and that I was with Margo Fr — and I could hardly get any more out amid the cacophony of *ohs* and *ahs* and *oh reallys* from the women and men alike.

"Are you going with her?" someone asked.

The others interrupted. "You shouldn't ask *that!*" some said, but they all waited for my answer.

I wanted to say that we used to be engaged and that we were sort of going together again, but we weren't, and she might not want people to know of her broken engagement, so I just said, "No, we work together."

When Margo arrived, she was again greeted by seemingly everyone, made her announcement, took a very active role in the discussion, and when we broke up into smaller groups, she led ours. I was ill with admiration for how she had blossomed, and painfully aware that it had been without my input. In fact, there was no way she could have emerged like this had we stayed together. No wonder she didn't appear to need me anymore. She had everyone else.

I would have gotten a kick out of it during the worship service if she had eyed me from the choir for a quick smile or even a wink, but I didn't get so much as a glance. She was into her work, concentrating, doing it right. I hadn't even been aware that she had an interest in singing, let alone ability.

After the service, I stood in the background while she chatted with dozens of different people, touching them, smiling, asking, working her magic, making them feel great.

Men, women, the elderly, children, peers. She should have been running for office. I can't even say she neglected me. She introduced me often, pulling me next to her to meet people, telling them that I was a bright young investigator with an unlimited future, all that stuff. I wanted to believe it in the worst way.

I followed her to her car where she piled the kids in, turned on the radio, and then stood outside to talk with me. "I'm sorry I was so busy," she said. "But that's what I like about this place. I think the problem I had for so long was that my faith was inactive, inward, stagnant. I enjoy exercising it, but I hope I didn't make you feel like a tagalong."

"Well, I felt that way, but it wasn't your fault, and I wouldn't have wanted it any other way. I just hope I wasn't in the way."

"Of course you weren't."

"Anyway, you'll have lunch with me, won't you?"

"Sure, why not? After I drop the kids off. I'll take the car back to my apartment. You can pick me up there in a half hour. Dutch?"

"No, I'm buying, and I want you to know that it bothers me when I ask you out and you adjust it so it's a double date or a group or Dutch like we're merely co-workers."

She was embarrassed, and I was sorry I had gotten into it right then and there. She looked back toward the kids in the car who were climbing back and forth over the seat and eager to get home for dinner. "You're right, Philip, and I'm sorry. I accept your invitation for lunch, and I'll be ready when you arrive." And I finally got my wink. Now what was I going to do with a half hour when it only took ten minutes to drive to her apartment?

I went to the office, straightened my desk, walked down the hall to my apartment, searched for a section of the paper I hadn't read but couldn't find one, straightened my tie, ran a damp towel over my shoes, brushed my teeth, and headed out, still with time to kill.

I pulled into the parking lot at Margo's building at the same time she did. She jumped from the car, waved as she ran to the building, and was back in less than ten minutes. She had changed from her blue dress gathered at the waist to a sweater and slacks outfit in beige and tan, highlighted by tiny gold chains around her neck. "You look great," I said.

"Thanks. So do you. I suppose you know that Linda called Erin last night."

"You're kidding."

"Nope. She was given one phone call, and she called Erin. She was pretty crafty too, because the room was in Larry's name and she had to remember the name of everyone on our staff and ask if they were booked. She finally hit on Shipman and then rang the room. She told Erin that she wanted her not to worry or to feel too badly and that she had wanted her to hear it from her mother, not from anywhere else. She also told Erin that she was innocent and that she would be cleared, even though it looks bad now. Erin said her mother told her, 'If you know for sure, because I'm telling you, that I didn't do it, you can concentrate on your gymnastics and not let it affect your scores. I'll be rooting for you.' "

"Wow."

"I know."

"What do you think, Margo? Who killed Bizell?"

"You really want to know what I think? I think it's strange that of these three women, Bonnie, Linda, and Erin, each thinks either of the other two could have done it."

"That's true. Does that make it likely that one of them did?"

"Oh I don't think so, Philip. I mean I'm not sure that it wasn't one of them; in fact, I'd lean more toward Linda right now with the fingerprints and all, but just because they fear the guilt of each other doesn't prove anything."

"I'm frankly a little wary of Greg Gibbons in this whole thing," I said.

"And don't leave out Larisa."

"Larisa?"

"Yes, Philip, I think Larry might have been onto something there when he first questioned that relationship. It may be because I never enjoyed one like it, but it is a little too good to be true. And either way, Larisa could have had a motive."

"Either way?"

"Whether she loves Erin or hates her for stealing her glory. If she really cares about Erin and wants her to be happy, she might have taken it upon herself to eliminate the problem in Erin's life. And if she has been phony all this time and really resents Erin, perhaps she murdered Bizell, hoping either that it would appear that Erin or her mother did it and would ruin her career."

"Bizarre."

"Not when women are involved. It could happen, Philip."

"That doesn't make it any less bizarre."

"Oh, this place is supposed to be neat," she said as I parked in front of a small French restaurant. "I hope we're done talking shop."

"Almost," I said, hoping the same thing. "I just need to know who in that gymnastics bunch of girls and their families uses Chantilly perfume."

"Chantilly? Um, you gotta start with Larisa's mother, then Larisa, then Erin, then Linda and then the rest of the girls."

"Linda uses it?"

"Occasionally, why?"

"I'll tell you later. Does Linda buy it?"

"I don't know. You asked me who uses it, I told you who I've noticed, starting with the heaviest user on down."

"Mrs. Cumiskey uses a lot?"

"Well, I shouldn't have said heaviest user. It's just that real perfume causes different reactions on different people. The same amount I use might smell like twice as much on her. Let's just say it's her trademark. Larisa got the rest of the girls using it. You know I'm not gonna leave you alone until you tell me why you're asking."

"Trust me, please. I will tell you, but later."

I was preoccupied at lunch, dying to think of a way to broach the subject I had been thinking about constantly, even during the murder investigation Margo was cheery and fun to talk to, but everything was peripheral. She wasn't playing dumb or hard to get. I knew she knew I was interested in her again, but she didn't know how to react either. She had to protect herself from getting hurt again. I had to show her that because of the changes in both of us — not just in her (which were more obvious) — we would not run into the same kinds of problems again, that she would not need time to sort it all out, but that if she did, I would be willing to allow that without dumping on her.

"I thought we'd come here to symbolize an attempt at a new start," I tried.

"That was a good idea, Philip," she said, earnestly. "I would have felt uncomfortable at one of our old haunts."

"But you feel more comfortable here?"

"A little."

"You're not comfortable with me?"

"Not totally. We've been through a lot, Philip, and I don't know what I feel for you. I feel it very deeply, whatever it is, but even with all the time I've had, I don't know if it's just gratitude, appreciation, friendliness, or what."

"I know what I feel for you, Margo."

"Do you? Really? Or are you just guessing too?"

"I know for sure, but I'm hesitant to burden you with it just now when you're doing so well."

"Your feelings for me will be a burden?"

"Sometimes I think so. They were in the past."

"It wasn't your feelings then; it was your reaction to my feelings."

"What I'm getting at, Margo, is that I am surer about how I feel about you now than I've ever been, but if you're not ready, I don't want to push you. You're blossoming into such beauty, inner beauty to match your looks. Looks. What a weak word. You know what I think is physically beautiful about you?"

"Are you going to embarrass me, Philip?"

"I imagine. But let me tell you anyway. It's how you move, your hands, your fingers. Your face and hair, of course. That's obvious to everyone. But I appreciate the whole picture."

She studied her menu, and I hoped I hadn't sounded corny.

We ordered and were both grateful, I think, for the lull in the conversation. But as we waited to be served, I wanted to make her feel more at ease. "If you're not ready for me, I understand. I really don't have any more patience than I used to, but you are worth the wait. I can hardly believe I almost lost you for good."

"If I wasn't ready for you, would I have come to lunch with you?"

"I don't know, would you have?"

"No, I would not."

NINE

By Monday morning, Earl wanted Bonnie and Erin checked out of their hotel room and moved back into Bonnie's place. He asked her if she was ready to come back to work, knowing full well that Sgt. Festschrift, at least, would want to question her.

Larry Shipman came in early, none the worse for wear after his brief stay in the cooler at the 19th precinct.

And while we hadn't even told each other yet, Margo and I were in love again. She wasn't ready to make any commitments about the future, but I felt she was mine, and I *knew* I was hers.

Erin, who would be bored staying at her grandmother's place, asked if she could go to Cumiskeys' and stay with Larisa. Earl said he thought it would be all right if it was OK with the Cumiskeys and Bonnie. It was.

But when the morning paper was delivered and the murder weapon was described, things began to happen. Included in the story was the news that although Linda Gibbons's fingerprints were found on the car, so were two other sets of prints, as yet unidentified. The police were seeking to fingerprint anyone associated with the case, and many were balking at the prospect. But one was not.

Greg Gibbons not only came forward, willing to be fingerprinted, but he also told police that they would likely find his prints on the car. "There is a reason they're there, but that will be your problem to figure out." He was printed, the prints were matched, and he was booked, demanding that his wife be freed. She was not.

Festschrift would not comment for the press; he told Earl, however, that he couldn't decide which suspect had the best motive. "I know he was in the vicinity of that parking lot that night though, don't I?"

"Do you?" Earl asked.

"He met with Mr. Cumiskey at the donut shop later."

"So why don't you bust Mr. Cumiskey then? And Coach Adamski, Bonnie, Erin, everybody?"

"If I find their prints on that car, you can bet I will, Earl. You can bet I will."

About midday, Earl took another call from Festschrift, who wanted to question Erin. Earl told him she was not home or at Bonnie's and that he preferred not to tell him where she was.

"Her parents are both in jail, and the man who split them up has been murdered, Earl," Festschrift said. "You think I can traumatize her any more?"

"She'll be at the Cumiskey home," Earl finally conceded. "I'll call out there and tell them you should be allowed to talk with her privately this evening."

"I'd appreciate that very much, Earl," Festschrift said, as if maybe he really didn't and expected nothing less.

"Would you mind, however, if I sent someone out there to be with her?"

"Like a lawyer maybe?"

"Maybe. No, seriously, Wally, we're talking about a child away from home here. Let me have Margo and Philip go out there with you. In fact, come by here and they'll drive out with you."

"Fair enough. Will you be there?"

"Probably not; I've got my own leads to follow up."

"You sharing all your leads with me?"

"Ask yourself the same question, Wally. 'Bye now."

Earl and Larry spent the afternoon at Linda's apartment with a key provided by Bonnie. They had convinced her that Linda's and Erin's best interests were at heart and that they should search the place thoroughly before the police did so there would be no surprises. "The only rub, Bon," Earl said, "is that if I find anything incriminating, I'm going to have to share it with Sergeant Festschrift." She nodded and gave him the keys.

Earl and Larry called from Linda's apartment a couple of hours later. "Would Erin have taken her mother's overnight bag and left her own?" they asked Bonnie.

"Oh sure, she does that frequently. Switches off."

"Does Linda ever use Erin's overnight bag?"

"I don't think so, no."

"Put Philip on the phone, please."

"Yes, Earl, Philip here."

"Philip, I want you to call Festschrift and ask him to meet me at Linda Gibbons's apartment. And I want you to beat him here, hear?"

"Yeah."

I raced over to Linda's, but I arrived only a few minutes before Festschrift and one of his men. "Can't you see the signs on the door, Earl!" Wally demanded "It says it's off limits until we've been through it."

"So what're you going to do, book me for violating a police barrier? You know I wouldn't keep anything important from you. Besides, you don't need to go through it any more, Wally," Earl said. "Larry here found what we've all been looking for. He grasped it with a tweezers and plastic bagged it for you, so all you have to do is match it, fingerprint it, and pick up another suspect."

Larry produced a Baggie containing the broken off handle of a lady's purple razor.

"Where'd you find it?" Festschrift asked.

"In this overnight bag. Erin's name is on it."

"How come she didn't take it with her to her girlfriend's house?" Wally's partner asked.

"Who knows?" Shipman said. "Maybe she took her mother's just to feel closer to her right now."

"What do you make of this, Earl?" Wally asked. "I don't mind tellin' ya, I'm stumped. What have we got here, a family murder?"

"Unlikely. But they *were* all there. Each had a motive. Two have fingerprints on the car, and the daughter has the hand strength to do it. I hate to say it, but I have to concede that among the three of them, you probably have your man."

"Or woman," Festschrift said. "Or child. You wanna come with me when I pick her up?"

"This is a very unusual situation, honey," Festschrift told Erin an hour later in the car. "We have a warrant for your arrest, but because you are a minor, we must secure a lawyer for you before we ask you anything. Mr. Haymeyer here will serve as your guardian while you're downtown, in the, uh, absence of your parents."

"I don't care if I have a lawyer or not, Mr. Haymeyer," Erin said. "I won't be answering any questions or offering any information."

She sounded so grownup it was disarming. But for the rest of the trip downtown, she said nothing. At the precinct station, she was assigned a lawyer and a custodian, and Festschrift and Earl and I headed back out to the Cumiskeys'. Larisa was still at school when Ernest and Jean sent the twins out to play and took us into their fashionable family room.

Ernest sat with his arm around his wife, seeming very subdued compared to the shows I had seen him put on at gymnastics meets. Before the competition he would greet all his friends and other fathers of gymnasts with very physical handshakes, hugs, pats on the head, the whole bit. A real outgoing, boisterous type. Then, during the meet, depending upon how Larisa was doing, he could be seen going through any number of gyrations, shouting, turning red, fuming, pacing, stomping. If she lost, he'd storm off to the car. If she won, he was more gregarious than ever, again greeting everyone with a cupped-hand smack on the cheek or a slap on the shoulder. When he wanted to, he could make you feel like a million bucks.

This evening, he was merely subdued. "You wanna do the talking, honey?" he said.

His wife, smelling heavily of Chantilly, leaned forward on the edge of a couch facing us. Her husband's hand still rested on her back.

"Yes, well, gentlemen, this is not an easy thing to say. We love Erin like our own daughter. They get along so well together and enjoy each other so. You know, even with the difference in ages, there is no problem. However, you might think that Larisa, being older, would be a good influence on young Erin and make her want to act older. In many ways, this is true and it works out that way."

Mrs. Cumiskey was a handsome, deeply tanned woman with short hair and stylish sports clothes. She appeared to be the country club type that she was.

"However, in some other ways, I have to admit that Erin has also been an influence upon Larisa. Sometimes when several of the girls are over for a slumber party, which we let Larisa have at least once a month, usually more often because we are more fortunate than some" — and here both made unsuccessful attempts to appear humbly grateful for their opulence — "well, occasionally the girls get tired and silly and giddy."

"Yes," Festschrift said, pushing her, "and they do things they might not otherwise do? Things that girls only Erin's age might do, even though she's the only one under sixteen in the bunch?"

"Yes, that's right," she said, almost smiling. "But frankly, we've run into things that are embarrassing. Things we wish they hadn't done, regardless how playful or seemingly innocent."

"And you've discovered something more?" Festschrift tried again. "Something that concerns you, especially in light of what's happened."

"Yes," she said, "especially in light of what's happened."

"That's right," Ernest said, as only he could, as if he had so liked the way Festschrift and his wife had put it, "very much so in light of what's happened." He ran his palm up to the back of his wife's head and let it linger in her hair.

She stood and hurried quietly to a desk in the corner and dug a sheaf of papers from a bottom drawer. "My husband was not very pleased to find these, I must say," she said, returning and sitting closer to him. He leaned forward with his arm around her back to look at them with her. We all edged forward too, but she wasn't quite ready to let us study them.

"You should say I was disappointed," he said. "Very, very disappointed. I didn't find them funny at all."

"No, he, well, neither of us found them funny in the least. He was very disappointed. And I would say upset."

"Yes, I was upset, that's right. Upset."

The stack consisted of white notebook paper with blue lines and three holes in one side. The writing, from my perspective, was girlish with back-slanted and heavily rounded letters with stars or flowers rather than dots over each *i*, and lots of underlining.

"I might as well tell you. From the outset that these *are* in my daughter's handwriting," Mrs. Camiskey said.

"Yes," her husband agreed. "There'll be no hiding that. You could have found that out very easily, and I should say that we could have burned these papers very easily as well. However, we didn't and I felt, we felt, that you should see them and be aware of them. Go ahead, honey."

Festschrift shifted impatiently. "Why not give them to us one at a time, starting with me," he suggested, "and we'll read them in sequence. That way you won't have to read them aloud."

The officious husband took them from her and began peeling them off one by one to Wally, who read each stonily and passed them on to Earl and then to me. Wally shook his head occasionally, and Earl grunted now and then. Finally, the first of several sheets came to me. It may have been in Larisa's handwriting, but it was likely dictated by several girls in the wee hours of some slumber party morning when they were in some kind of a mood. Here's what Larisa wrote:

> My name is Erin Gibbons and I'm thirteen years old. My friend Larisa Cumiskey and I will one day rule the gymnastics world as the best in every event. We don't care who's first or who's second, as long as each is one of us.
>
> My mother has forced my father to leave us because she is seeing another man, a man named John Bizell. He drives a silver Corvette, and some might say he is good looking, but he is not a good man.
>
> I have been watching them for some time now, and my friends and I, all the girls on Nik Adamski's AAU Gymnastics team, are getting ready to ambush him. That's right, literally ambush him.
>
> We know where he works, because he works where my dad works. And we know his hours, because we know when he most often comes to see my mother. Since my father moved out, he doesn't even try to be gone by the time I get home.
>
> We will ask Larisa's father to get us some guns because he can get a good price on anything. Maybe we'll rent them, because we won't have any more need for them after we shoot Mr. Bizell and any police who try to get in our way. The only person we will try to protect will be my father and my mother if she says she is sorry it happened.
>
> We'll wait for him to arrive at our apartment, then I'll make an excuse to go out. I'll call all my teammates, and they will meet me at the corner. Larisa will bring the guns in a grocery bag. We'll hide behind the other parked cars and when he comes out to get in his car, we'll all shoot at him from different directions to make sure somebody gets him.
>
> We'll make sure he's dead by cutting his heart out. Larisa's father can also get a good price on a big knife.

Then, with nothing for me to worry about any more, nothing to bother me when I practice, Larisa and I will just have to keep getting better so we can be the best in the world, the best ever. And Mr. Cumiskey will be glad he provided the guns and the knife, but he will never know the reason.

"Did the girls ever mention anything like this to either of you?" Festschrift asked. Mrs. Cumiskey shook her head. Her husband spoke.

"Of course not. It's just a little girl's fantasy and I'm embarrassed that my daughter let herself be dragged into it. She hates violence and would be scared to death of a gun or a knife."

"If you're convinced it's just a little girl's fantasy, Mr. Cumiskey, why did you feel it necessary to show it to us?"

"Because the little girl's fantasy came true, didn't it? I just thought you should be aware of it. Plus, if any of the other girls who were here that night feel guilty about it, they might mention it and it could look bad for both Erin and Larisa."

"And you want it to look bad only for Erin, is that it?"

"Why, no! But, but — well, Larisa had no reason, I mean. Oh, come now, you're not seriously suggesting that Larisa — "

"No," Festschrift said. "I just want to know what you think about Erin. Could she have murdered this man?"

"I don't think so," Mrs. Cumiskey said.

"I wouldn't be too sure," Ernest said. "I've heard her talk about him. She hated him. She blamed him for everything. She even blamed the fact that she was troubled about him for her scores being lower than she thought they could have been, and at that time she was number one in two events. I think she's capable of getting rid of or stepping over anything that gets in the way of her winning."

Mrs. Cumiskey appeared a bit startled by such a harsh statement and flashed a doubtful look at her husband. "Oh, Ern, I think she's a little too sweet for all that, isn't she?"

And he finally got excited. "Are you kidding me? Have you seen that look of hers when she walks up to the beam or onto the mat? I'm telling you, the girl has a winning determination about her. She ought to, she learned it from the best. You fellas wanna see the gallery of fame I've built for Larisa?"

"Ernie, please, I don't think that would be appropriate under the circumstances — "

"Nonsense. You guys would have time for a little peek, wouldn't ya? It'll only take a second."

There was nothing we could say. "I've not got a lot of time," Festschrift growled, "but sure, let's have a look."

Mrs. Cumiskey excused herself, and we were ushered upstairs to Ernest's paneled den, which was as large as most people's rec rooms. On the walls he had awards from every company he had ever worked for, plus a couple of certificates naming him first in his class at some sales or management course.

"Got all your awards here, huh?" Earl said cordially.

"Nope. Just the first places, the number ones. I've got a raft of seconds in my time, but I don't keep those. Anything less than first is last, I always say. The philosophy hasn't hurt my career, I'll tell you that."

A couple of dozen pictures of Larisa, all of her waving from the top step of the awards platform, graced the walls. "I used to put up a picture every time she won an event," he said, "but now, at her level of skill and accomplishment, the only things that count are winning the all-around competition. I've got this nice big one here of her first perfect ten score, but I'm leaving room for the world's championship in Helsinki next month and of course the Olympics. That will be the ultimate. Her first Olympic gold. I can hardly wait."

"I'll bet you'd put up a picture of her from the Olympics, win, lose, or draw," Earl said. "Am I right?"

Cumiskey appeared annoyed by the question, but he broke into a grin and threw his arm around Haymeyer's neck, forcing Earl's head into the crook of his elbow and pretending to batter him with his other hand. "Don't even mention such a thing, you son-of-a-gun!" he said, laughing. Earl tried to smile.

And we left.

TEN

"I'm gonna do somethin' crazy," Festschrift said in the car. "I've had it with this case!"

"This is a little early for you to be giving it up, isn't it, Wal'?" Haymeyer said. "We've only been on the chase less than forty-eight hours."

"Yeah, but I've got too many suspects, and I don't like any one of 'em. If this was a crime of passion, any one of 'em coulda done it, but none rings true with me."

"Me either," Earl conceded. "But we're gonna have a tough time getting around that razor handle."

"Yeah, especially if it's got Erin's fingerprints on it. Let's call and find out, because if it doesn't, I'm gonna see if I can't get all three of 'em released."

I couldn't believe my ears. Neither, apparently, could Earl.

"You've got to be kidding," he said.

"No, I'm not. Even if one of them is the murderer, letting them off on their own recognizance won't threaten the case. It's not like they're gonna try to kill anybody else except those of us trying to find the truth, and we're not worried about that, are we?"

Earl shook his head, still wondering what Festschrift was up to and whether he'd really go ahead with this weird scheme. Yet when I thought about it, I wasn't worried about either Linda or Erin actually harming me. Greg I hardly knew.

"If I let 'em out, I think each of us should take one of 'em, and I'd like the little girl."

"What do you mean, 'take' one of them?" Earl said.

"Question them, stay with them, try to learn where they're coming from. See if we can trip them up. You know what else I'm concerned about, and what your Margo can help with?"

"What's that?"

"I'm a little uncomfortable with Mrs. Murray's actions Saturday morning. Could she have planted that razor handle and then hit the road?"

Earl scratched his head. "Where do you come up with these, Wally? What would she be up to?"

"I'm talkin' about whether she could have done it."

"Nah, I'm not accepting that yet."

"But you're open to it?"

"No, not really, no."

"Earl," I asked, "what would you and Sergeant Festschrift think of my going back to the Cumiskey's tonight, sort of unannounced, to ask if I can chat with Larisa as a friend?"

"*Are* you a friend?" Festschrift asked.

"Yes, he is," Earl said. "He's been following Erin and Larisa for some time. It might not be a bad idea."

"It's awright with me," Wally said, " 'cause it'll take me time to get these three released anyway. I'm gonna have to talk to each of 'em first. Ooh, the press is not gonna believe this! They'll put their front pages together with the news that an entire family is in custody for murder, and by the time the papers hit the street they'll be wrong!"

"You're really gonna go through with this?"

"I am. Maybe I'm ready for the nut house, but let's you and me and Philip and my partner and the crime lab keep that razor to ourselves and see who's the first suspect — or nonsuspect — to say something about it, something they shouldn't know."

"That sounds like a lot of people to keep a secret," I said.

"It is. But are you gonna be the one who blows it?"

"No."

"Is Earl?"

"No," I said again.

"Well, I know my partner, who is off the next three days, and he never breaks a confidence. And do you know that the crime lab people can't talk outside the room or they automatically lose their jobs?"

"Is that right? Well, maybe you *can* pull it off."

Wally and Earl dropped me off at the office, where I learned that Bonnie would be spending the night with Margo. Shipman was busy with Earl's other cases, trying to keep the business going while the rest of us found ourselves up to our necks in the Bizell case. Margo was becoming antsy and wanted to get in on the action.

"I'll be all right at your place if I know you'll be back later," Bonnie said. "You go with Philip."

"But is that all right with Earl and Sergeant Festschrift?" Margo wanted to know.

I was wondering the same thing, but I wanted so badly to talk with Margo alone and to have her along that I assured her it was fine. "I'll take the heat for it if it's not," I said.

"I'm not concerned with who takes the heat, Philip," Margo said. "I just don't want to go if it wouldn't be right."

"It's all right," I said. "Come on."

We were only a few miles up the Edens when Margo admitted, "I'm glad I came."

"I am too."

"I love Bonnie, but I get tired of her crying and moaning all day long. I don't know what else to say or do for her. You know she's convinced that either Linda or Erin killed Bizell, and I think she's leaning toward Linda."

"Is that right? I think Greg thinks it was Linda too; that's why he's turned himself in. There's probably a logical reason for his fingerprints on Bizell's car. They work out of the same office, don't they? They probably park in the same lot. He could have leaned on the door while chatting with Bizell or something."

"But would they chat? It seems like they'd be having a cold war these days, wouldn't they, Philip?"

"Maybe, but remember, Johnny hasn't seen Linda for a month."

"So Linda says, but we know her prints were on the car too, so she must have seen him not long before he died. Are you ruling out Greg as a suspect, Philip?"

"I think so. If it was Greg, how could he have planted the other part of the razor in Linda's apartment?"

"Planted what?"

I winced. "Oh, no! I promised Festschrift and Earl I would say nothing to anyone! I can't believe I did that! Margo, you hafta promise not to repeat that, especially to Bonnie, no, not to anyone. They're trying to flush out the murderer with information only he or she would know about."

"Well, I'm not the murderer, Philip, and I'll promise to keep it quiet if you tell me what you're talking about. You found the other half of the razor at Linda's?"

"Shipman did. It was in a soft, zipper-style overnight kit of Erin's."

Margo was silent, thinking.

"You think that incriminates anyone other than Erin?" I asked.

"Well, Philip, we can't be naive about Greg's access to the apartment. He must have a key."

"I never thought of that. I also forgot that the one name Festschrift didn't mention when he rattled off the list of people who had to keep our discovery a secret was that of the guy who found it."

"Larry? He'd never leak a secret."

"I know. But he doesn't know it's a secret. I'd better try to reach him."

I pulled off to a gas station and found a pay phone. I couldn't reach him at the office or at home, and I couldn't exactly call Bonnie at Margo's place and leave a message. Margo and I didn't know what else to do except pray that he would somehow not talk about it to anyone.

"I missed you today, Margo," I said.

"I missed you too, and I'm not just saying that, Philip. I know it's the natural response, but that hasn't been a natural feeling for me until today."

"Ouch. You mean you haven't missed me for so long you were getting used to being without me?"

"Oh, you know I missed you when we first broke up. That was a miserable time. But it did start to get better, the more I got active and the more I relied on God. That's one thing I must not do this time, Philip. I must not switch my reliance from God to you."

"You can count on me for some things, can't you? I need to feel needed."

"Of course. I learned that when I started missing you today. I think I missed hearing that someone loves everything about me, not just my face or even just my character, but even the way I move — was that what you said yesterday?"

"Yeah," I said, embarrassed. "You didn't think it was corny, then?"

"Of course I did, but I love corn. I eat it up."

We both laughed. "You eat it with butter and salt, don't you?" I said.

"Canned, popped, or on the cob," she said and leaned close. "You can be as corny as you want with me, Philip Spence."

"You're a crazy girl," I said.

"And you love it."

"You."

"Hm?"

"I love *you*."

"Thank you," she said, not flippantly. "It's good to have you knowing that I love you again."

"You love me again?" I asked.

"No, I never quit. It's just good to have you aware of it again."

"You're right that I wasn't aware of it. You hid it well."

"I thought I should. I didn't know if it would be returned or not."

"I probably never quit loving you either, Margo, but I didn't know it."

"I know."

"You do?"

"I think I do. I could see it when you got back from Israel. I didn't know if it was pity or remorse or love, but then I never knew that for sure about your love for me from the beginning."

"Do you now?"

"I'm just gonna take your word for it."

"You do that."

"Is Larisa home?" I asked Mrs. Cumiskey at the front door.

"Well, yes, as a matter of fact she came home early from practice, and I don't believe she's feeling well." She lowered her voice. "Her father is not real excited about her missing practice so close to the big meets, especially when she's undisputed leader right now. Ernest and she are not speaking right now, if you know what I mean."

"Well, is she ill?" Margo asked. "Because if she is, we could come back another time. We just thought we'd see how she was doing during this difficult time for everybody."

"Let me see if she feels up to talking. Come in."

Mrs. Cumiskey trotted upstairs and we could hear her husband railing before she shushed him. ". . . chance to be the best in the world and she spends her evenings moping around the — "

Apparently Larisa thought we were worth seeing. She bounded past her mother and down the stairs and right into Margo's arms. "Margo, Philip, thanks for coming. Come on into the family room." She had been crying.

We sat on either side of her on a huge couch. Her brothers were outside shooting a basketball. We hadn't even said anything when she hid her face in her hands and began crying again. She leaned over onto Margo who stroked her hair. "It's all right, 'Risa,"

Margo said quietly. "It's all right; we're with you and we love you."

She sat up and tried to stop crying. "It's all my fault!" she said. "If I had just thrown away those silly papers. All we were doing was humoring Erin. We never intended to do anything to that Bizell guy. You saw the papers, Philip, do you think they looked serious? We were just being crazy, writing out a fantasy. It made Erin feel better and that's all we cared about."

If this was an act, she was one great actress. "It's not like I left them out for Daddy to find. He had to ransack my room to come up with them. They were just tucked in a drawer somewhere. Margo, they were at the bottom, *beneath* the bottom. My mother lines my drawers with paper, and this stuff was *under* that paper!"

"Why would he do that?" Margo asked.

"I don't know. Doesn't trust me, I guess. More likely, he's just looking for an edge for me over Erin. Well, I've got it now and I can't concentrate enough to take advantage of it. I hope he's satisfied."

"Why did you keep those papers, Larisa?" I asked.

"That's just it. If they had been serious, we'd have gotten rid of them, burned them. That's what Daddy should have done, especially after getting my side of the story. But we added to them each time the girls got together. That wasn't written all at one time. It was just silliness. I'll tell you, it sure freaked out the other girls when we heard about the murder, though. Not that any of us suspected Erin or anything. It was just eerie. I wonder what Daddy thought then."

I looked at Margo. "You mean he found those papers before Bizell was murdered?"

"Oh, yes, probably a month ago. That's why I think he just wanted to use them to scare Erin. She knew, just like all the other girls, that he had found them, and they were all scared their parents would find out. Not as scared as they were when they heard the news, though."

"I imagine not," I said.

"Larisa, what's the matter today? Is it just too much for you to think about Erin under suspicion?"

The high schooler nodded, fighting tears again. "I can't believe Erin had anything to do with it at all!"

"Well, if she didn't, she'll be cleared. You know that, don't you?"

"I guess. But that razor business makes me wonder, and I feel horribly guilty for even letting it enter my mind."

I stiffened. How could she know about the razor? Or was she even thinking of the same thing I was?

"What razor?" Margo asked.

"The newspaper said they had determined that the murder weapon was a lady's razor with half the blade exposed. Oh, Margo, I don't know what to think!" And we were back to tears and tissues and stroking her hair again.

My heart was pounding. Why was this girl associating the murder weapon so strongly with Erin if she didn't know the other half of it had been found in Erin's bag?

"You think because Erin uses that kind of a razor that she could have used one on Johnny Bizell?" Margo asked as gently as she could.

"I don't wanna think that, especially since she got started on that kind of razor at another slumber party here."

"Honey, lots of girls use that brand. It's very popular."

"I know." She didn't want to talk anymore. I gave Margo the eye that we had to get to the bottom of this. "I don't believe Erin murdered Johnny," Larisa said slowly. "I just want the doubts out of my head so I can concentrate on my gymnastics. So I can concentrate on *anything.*"

Margo was silent. I took up the conversation. "Why do you have doubts?"

"I don't wanna talk about it anymore."

"I don't blame you, Larisa," I said. "But maybe I can allay your suspicions. Isn't it significant that hundreds of thousands of razors just like that one that killed Johnny Bizell are sold in the Chicago area every year?"

She nodded, but I could tell she was unconvinced. For some reason, she was putting that razor together with Erin when there was no solid connection she should know about.

"Thanks for coming," she said, standing. "You really did help a lot, and I appreciate it."

"You want some good news?" I asked, trying a different tack.

"Sure."

"I think the whole Gibbons family will be released before tomorrow."

"You're serious? Oh, that's great! How did they get around Erin's broken razor? Or didn't she even tell them? I guess she wouldn't have had to tell them, would she? Unless they asked."

I was stunned. "What are you talking about, Larisa?"

"You mean *you* don't know about it?"

"I didn't say that. I want to know what you know about it."

"Oh, Philip, I can't say anything about it if *she* didn't, but I hope she's being cleared in spite of it because it was the only reason I couldn't shake my doubts."

Margo said, "Larisa, do you trust us?" She nodded, but I tried to signal Margo not to say any more. As it turned out, she wasn't giving anything away anyway. "I need you to tell me what you know about Erin's broken razor. It's very important."

Margo said it with such sincerity and urgency that Larisa sat back down, cleared her face vigorously with a tissue, and told us an ominous story.

"I broke that razor myself," she said. "We were going to have a slumber party, and I had agreed to pick up Erin after school and drive her first to practice and then to my house. I drove over to the junior high and parked in a no parking zone. I ran in, laughing and yelling at her to hurry up because I was going to get a ticket. So, she hauled everything out of her locker and started throwing it at me. I caught most of it, but I was falling backward when she tossed her little overnight kit and it slid under my foot. I skipped to keep my balance and stepped right on it and heard something snap. We peeked in the bag in the car to see what I broke and I saw that razor, split right at the top, exposing the blade. I told her to be careful when she threw it away, and we remarked how lucky I had been that it hadn't sliced through the bag and my foot. I remember Erin said something like, 'Yeah, it could've cost you your ranking as the number two girl on our team.' We always kid each other like that.

"Anyway, that's the last I saw that broken razor and the last I thought about it until I read the paper this morning. Whatever you do, don't breathe a word of this to my dad. He'll have her strung up without thinking twice. But I don't care what that broken razor means, I won't believe Erin murdered anyone unless she tells me herself."

ELEVEN

Margo and I stopped to grab a sandwich on the way back to Glencoe, then I dropped her off at her car near the office and ran up to talk to Earl in his apartment, just down from mine.

"How'd it go downtown?" I asked.

"Everything's still up in the air, Philip," he said. "If this weren't so serious it would have made for a great comedy today. Every time Wally tried to release one of the Gibbonses, the suspect would confess to the murder and try to tell how he or she did it. Each thought one of the other two was guilty and tried to take the credit. What makes it more confusing is that now Wally is convinced that *none* of them had anything to do with it."

"Why? And isn't it going to be difficult to release them when they have made confessions?"

"That's just it; their confessions gave them away. All three of them described killing Bizell by surprising him, coming through the passenger door and slashing away at him. But the only wound other than to his neck was that minor gash on his left hand from trying to open his own door. Wouldn't you think he would have fended off the attacker with his hands if he had been approached from the other side?"

"Yeah, but that doesn't prove one of them wasn't telling the truth."

"There's more, Philip. Festschrift told me tonight that before we got to the scene and Shipman badgered him to open the passenger door, he had already had to nearly lie across the victim to reach the door lock with his wire. Then he could open the door when Shipman asked, but it had been locked."

"Yeah?"

"Yes, and how many murderers do you know who surprise a driver by coming through the passenger door, sinking a razor deep into his neck — which the coroner insists could not have been done without considerable pressure and not by a swiping motion — and then backing out and locking the door before shutting it? It's absurd."

"But not impossible."

"Granted, but here's the kicker. Wally gave them each one last chance to prove their claims. He asked them where they got the murder weapon, where the other piece of it was, whether their fingerprints should still be on it, and where was the location of Bizell's car at the time of the murder."

"How'd they do on those?"

"Laughable again. Greg said he bought the razor and hoped to make the murder look as if it were committed by a woman, but not by his wife because he didn't think she used that brand razor. He also said he broke the razor on Bizell's neck and threw the handle away as he ran and that we'd probably find it in the parking lot of the school with his fingerprints on it."

"You're sure this is all full of holes?"

"As sure as I'm sittin' here. You wanna know where he said the murder occurred? In the northeast corner of the parking lot."

"Not even close," I admitted. "Could he have been mixed up in his directions?"

"Nah, Philip. Think. Even if he had the wrong corner, all the corners are exposed. There's no way to commit a murder in any corner of that lot and have it go undiscovered for hours. Impossible."

"Is there any chance he could have changed his mind about protecting his wife and daughter and misled Festschrift on purpose?"

"No."

"So what was Linda's story?"

"She said the razor was one of her own, that she broke it and threw the other part away and stashed the blade end in her purse until the time was right. I loved that. She wants us to believe that she carried that thing around until she happened to run into Bizell at a gymnastics meet. She said the broken part would have been tossed with the garbage weeks ago, and she placed Bizell's car with all the other cars in the lot, not secluded between the garbage bins and the air-conditioning units. Festschrift asked her if she hadn't read in the paper about how the car wasn't discovered until some time after all the other cars were gone. If she had murdered him between the end of the meet and when she met her daughter at the car, surely someone would have seen the car sooner. She said it was parked at one end away from the parking lot lights."

I was tired. I stretched out on Earl's floor and asked about Erin's account.

He said Festschrift was pleasantly surprised to get anything out of her and assumed that when he said he was letting her go, she figured her mother had been exposed. "So, she concocted her own story, which Festschrift could have believed except that he had already learned that the razor handle had no prints on it."

"*No* prints?"

"None."

"What do you make of that, Earl?"

"What do you make of it, junior deputy?"

"That it was a plant. If Erin had just left it in her overnight kit, it would have her prints on it. It was wiped clean?"

"Clean. Very good, Philip. You're gonna make it after all. But there's another reason we know it wasn't Erin. She could have told us that we'd find the razor handle in her overnight bag in the apartment."

"And she didn't?"

"How could she? She didn't know it was there."

"How can you be sure, Earl?"

"Because she *wanted* credit for this murder. That's the best way she could have gotten it, to point us right to the other piece of the murder weapon. But she couldn't do it. She was closer than anyone to guessing the location of Bizell's car, but that's all it was, a guess She says she sat in the car with Bizell and talked to him, then surprised him with the blade. Wally was beautiful on this one. He asked if she was right-handed. She said of course. He said she was lying. The only way to inflict that wound on Bizell by sitting next to him would be by a left-hander getting his elbow up and back behind the head-rest, then plunging the blade in. Wally can visualize the murder now. It was someone reaching in from the driver's side window and getting his hand around behind Johnny's neck and up near the front on the right side."

"Then he couldn't have seen it coming."

"Or if he did, he didn't see it as menacing. That makes me wonder if it was a woman leaning in and embracing him or taking his head in her hand."

"But if not Linda or Erin, who, Earl?"

The phone rang. It was Margo. She told Earl that Bonnie was no longer at her place, nor at her own. "Don't worry yet, Mar," Earl said "We'll find her."

"Bonnie?" I asked.

"Yeah, shoot. This is all we need. Let's check the office." As we hurried down the hall, Earl assured me that he didn't think Bonnie could have murdered Bizell. "He wouldn't exactly let her get her arms around him while he sits in his car either, you think?"

I had to chuckle at the thought.

"Hey, here's a note from Larry." Earl tried to decipher it as Margo entered.

"What do you think?" she said. "Where could she be?"

"She's with Larry," Earl said. "Did you try to call there?"

"No, I didn't think of it," she said, dialing.

Earl motioned me over. I looked at the note over his shoulder. It read:

> See you soon.
> Under the circumstances,
> I thought it would be all right to
> counsel Mrs. Murray over dinner.
> I will call before bringing her back.
> Don't worry about her.
> All is fine. Be back soon.
> Larry

"There's no answer, Earl, but I guess we needn't worry if Larry is with her. Earl?"

He was still studying the note. I had read it and turned away. I turned back. "What is it, Earl?"

"Larry's handwriting. It's never been this neat. And why the big explanation? Why not his usual 'Bonnie and I have gone to dinner'? He's trying to tell us something."

Margo joined us and read it carefully. "It's as plain as day," she said, dread in her voice. "Just read the first letter of each line."

Earl swore. "She thinks her daughter killed Bizell, I'll bet anything," he said. "We need to tell her otherwise. It wasn't Erin either, not even Greg."

"Our possibilities are narrowing," Margo said.

"My money is on the Cumiskey twins," I said, trying to be funny. Neither Margo nor Earl appreciated it.

"All we can do is wait for them," Earl said. "Who knows where he might have taken her? I've never known him to go to the same place twice without being dragged. Anyway, I'm glad you're both here. I wanted to talk to you."

Margo and I looked at each other and followed Earl back to his office. He dragged his chair out from behind the desk and rolled it up next to the two side chairs. He offered his chair to Margo, and we all sat down. "I don't know how to tell you this," he said, "but I have been talking to Wally Festschrift about God."

Nonplussed is too weak a word for our reaction. "I, you, wha — ?"

"I know it sounds crazy. And mostly, I've felt inadequate."

"But, but — "

"I know, Philip. I'm not even qualified. It's not like I'm trying to even give him something I've got because as you both well know, and as Festschrift himself would say it, 'I ain't got it myself.' But if there was ever a person who needed and could use what you two have, it's Wally Festschrift."

"And so you're, I mean — "

"Yes I'm telling him. What do *you* call it? Witnessing?"

"You're witnessing to Festschrift?" I finally managed. "But, witnessing is — "

"I know, Philip. It's telling about something you have personal knowledge of. Legally it means giving an eyewitness account."

Earl sat there waiting for further reaction. I had none.

"Are you trying to tell us something, Earl?" Margo tried.

"No, as I said, 'I ain't got it myself,' but I'm telling it anyway."

"Uh, just what are you telling him?" I asked.

"All the stuff you've tried to tell me over the years. I'm sure I'm getting some of it wrong, and that's why I want you to help me. He needs it, kids, and if he's not getting it from you, he's gonna hafta get it from me."

"You've been telling him what?" Margo said. "That he needs God, or religion, or what?"

"Oh, give me credit for more than that! If there's one thing I have gotten out of all your preaching around here — of which there hasn't been much lately, by the way — it's that what you've got and what you've talked about is not religion. It's a *Person*. How'm I doin'?"

"Great. What else did you tell him?"

"I told him that you admit you have done wrong, admit it to God, I mean. And you pray that Christ will forgive you and save you and give you peace. How's that?"

We just sat staring. "That's unbelievable," Margo said.

"That's what I've been saying for two years, Margo," Earl said "But somehow it makes sense to Festschrift. He's a little embarrassed to ask you any more about it, Philip, but he was impressed with you, I'll say that. We got to reminiscing and reconciling and recreating the old days, and he started telling me how remorseful he was about much of his past. Then it sort of popped out."

"It popped out? What popped out?"

"All that stuff you two have been telling me over the years. Wally was lamenting the fact that you can't turn the clock back, that you have to pay the price for your mistakes, that you can't undo wrongs, and all of a sudden I heard myself telling him that, by God, you *can* let someone else pay the price, and I wasn't swearing."

"How'd he react?"

"Well, if you think you guys were stunned by what I just said, that was the *last* thing Wally Festschrift thought he'd ever hear out of me. But he listened. He always did listen to me, even when I was a brash rookie and he was already the weather-beaten veteran. He told me he was sorry for the way he had treated me over the years, that he didn't know why he'd been that way, and that he had a lot of people to apologize to, including his wife and kids. You know what I told him? You're not gonna believe this."

"Try us," Margo said. "I'll believe anything now."

"I told him, 'See, Wally, we've only been talking about it a few minutes, and it's working already!' He thought that was pretty funny at first, but you know he laughed until he cried. That's when I knew I would have to come back to you and tell you that something struck a chord with him that was never struck with me. At least not until he started crying. That hit me, I don't mind telling you.

"But anyway, I knew I needed more ammunition. What do I tell him now?"

"Would you like us to talk to him, Earl?" I said. "Should I tell him how to receive Christ into his life?"

"I don't think so, Philip. I think he'll take it from me but not from you at this point. There's a lot of complexity in that guy. I thought of your saying that all you have to do is to realize that God loves you and wants to forgive you and become part of you, but all I could think of to tell him was that you just do that by praying and meaning it. But I knew that was too simple, so I didn't say it. I'm here for another crash course."

"You've learned well, Earl," Margo said, her voice unsteady. "You tell him that and get him into a good church, and you'll have your first convert."

"That's all there is to it? I should have known. That's what you've been trying to tell me. I haven't always liked the way you went about it, but I never did find any superiority complex in either of you, and I've been watching for it. I *have* been disappointed in some inconsistencies, especially in you, Philip, but I also know that you've told me a million times to not judge God by His children. I think I know what that means now."

"So where are *you* in all this?" Margo asked.

"How do you mean?"

"I mean what is Earl Haymeyer thinking about what he told Sergeant Festschrift?"

"You mean am I ready?"

"Yeah."

"Let me say it this way. I don't need any more encouragement. If both what I told Festschrift and what I almost told him is on track, then I know all I need to know to make my own choice and take my own action, don't I?"

We nodded.

"Then I will or won't on my own — is that fair enough? That's the way I've always been and the way I always will be. Philip, you told me once that God would take me just as I was, right?"

"Right."

"I resented that then. I thought you were saying I was some no account skid row type. I know what you mean now. If I do want God to take me, He's going to have to take my independence and all the rest."

I wanted to assure him that He would, but silence seemed appropriate. Margo couldn't take her eyes off Earl. He grew restless, embarrassed. "So," he said, slapping his knees with both hands and rising, "if I'm on the right track with Wally, I'll keep at it."

We followed him back out to the main office, our eyes meeting in wonder.

"Let's talk a little business," he said. "Tomorrow morning I'm going to want Larry to meet with the Gibbons family. Believe it or not, our work can sometimes be conciliatory, and I think we have a classic case here of people trying to cover for each other. There's a base of love there, and if nothing else comes out of this crazy case, maybe we can see that family reunited. Do we all agree that this would be a valid goal?"

I was thinking that Earl was right: "It" had started working already.

"Now then," he continued, "if we eliminate Greg and Linda and Erin as suspects, who's left?"

"Don't be so quick to eliminate all of them," Margo cautioned. "Two of them are women, and they might be smart enough to have misled you. You can't tell me that Erin didn't know that razor handle was still in her overnight bag."

Earl glared at me. "I'm sorry, Earl, it just slipped out, and Margo has told no one, I swear."

"You swear! Honestly, Philip. If that had gone any further it could have affected the interrogations Wally conducted today. What if those suspects had known we had already found that razor piece? They all could have been misleading us!"

"Well, Shipman was never reminded not to say anything."

"He wouldn't — he wasn't? You're right, he wasn't!"

Margo heard a car and stepped to the window. "You can have your fears confirmed or denied in a minute, Earl," she said. "It's them."

Twelve

"No," Larry said. "Of course I knew better than that. Really, Earl, you insult me."

Earl told Bonnie the good news, and she broke down. Margo appeared troubled because she hadn't shaken her fear that Erin knew more than she was saying, but she was also grateful that Bonnie could stop worrying — even if only temporarily — about the guilt of her daughter and granddaughter.

"You know, I was so afraid that Linda or Erin might have had something to do with Bizell's death that I could have killed myself. I couldn't stand the turmoil in my mind. I didn't want to know the truth if that was it."

"Really?" Earl said, playing dumb but nodding to Larry behind her back to indicate that we had gotten his cryptic message.

Earl gave Larry his assignment for the next morning and suggested he call the parties and arrange for them to get together early. "What I'm going to want to do, besides attempting the reconciliation, is to find out how Greg and Linda really explain their fingerprints on Bizell's car, in light of the fact that it's been shown they didn't murder him."

"I'm curious about that, too," Margo said. "Among other things."

I followed Margo and Bonnie to Margo's place so I could say good-night to Margo in the hall while Bonnie went to bed. I told her about my conversation with Linda Gibbons and how I had sensed the comparison between her story and that of the woman taken in adultery whom Jesus had forgiven in the New Testament.

"And when you hear that Earl is doing our job for us, it makes you want to get back in the game, doesn't it?" she asked.

"You got it."

"I'll be praying for you, Philip. When are you going to try to talk to her?"

"I don't know. Sometime this week. I wish I knew Greg better and whether his plans are to take her back or what, because I think this could be good for him, too."

"You gonna wait until after the big meet tomorrow, or will Erin even be competing?"

"There's a gymnastics meet tomorrow?"

"Only the national regional. One of those do-or-die jobs on the way to the national championships. That's all."

"Where's this being held?"

"At the Rosemont Horizon."

"The Horizon? That's huge."

"Well, there'll be teams from all over the Midwest, even down to Texas. The place is sold out, and the meet will be televised nationally."

The next morning Larry met with Greg and Linda Gibbons and Erin at Linda Gibbons's apartment while I was tracking down AAU gymnastics coach Nik Adamski. Earl had asked that each of us verify at least one remaining principal's movements from the previous Friday night. Believe it or not, Margo had drawn the Cumiskey family, twins included.

I found Nik Adamski at the Y in Mount Prospect. He was a recreational director there, but he was doing nothing but doodling, experimenting with various lineups, some including Larisa, some not, some including Erin, some not, and some including neither.

"I haf no idea whedder dese girls be wit' me tonight or vat," he explained. "Larisa, she has been down since she lost ze all-around to Erin at Hillside. She say she iss upset about Erin, bot everybody know she can no kill a man, so I think Larisa, she just upset wit' herself."

"Uh, Mr. Adamski, it's part of my job to determine your movements after the meet Friday night."

"Oh?" he said. "Vy is dat? I am suspect?"

"Well, everybody is. I even had to account for where I was."

Unexpectedly, Nik Adamski stood. "I grew up in Poland during de Hitler regime," he said, standing rigidly. "I come here to stop accounting for self. I need tell no one vere I go, vat I do, not'ing."

"You can tell *me*, Mr Adamski. I can't hurt you. I can help you. If the police ask and you don't tell them, you could be in trouble."

"How can I be in trouble when I have done not'ing?"

"You can't, but you don't want the police bothering you now, especially when you have so much to do before tonight's meet. It might interest you to know, by the way, that Erin has been released. And I can't imagine Larisa's father allowing Larisa not to compete for any reason."

He sat back down. "Erin released? Dat good news. She be out of shape though. Can't count on first places."

"She competed brilliantly just Friday night," I said. "That's just a few days ago."

"She scored four 9.85s, Mr. Spence. Highest all-around I ever coach. You don't do dat again four days later vit' no work. You don't understand mind. It's not just body. It's mind, and her mind been troubled plenty lately and probably still is. She released, but her mama released too?"

"Yes, and her father."

"But do dey know who kill Bizell?"

"No, do you?"

He glared at me. "Of course not. I never saw de man. Just hear about him everyday for months make me vant to kill him if I did. But if dey not know who kill him, how peaceful can Erin be? She need peace to do well."

"That I don't know. That will bother Larisa too, won't it?"

"Only t'ing bother Larisa is Larisa," he said.

"Still, Coach, could you tell me what you did after Friday's meet, after you talked to Mrs. Murray?"

"Mrs. Murray. I no talk to a Mrs. Murray."

My heart nearly stopped. "You didn't talk to Erin's grandmother about personalized coaching for her this summer?"

"Oh, Erin grandmother. Yah, yah, I did."

I breathed again.

"Then what did you do?"

"Was interviewed for local television. Den meet wife at back door and drive home."

I knew it would be easy enough to check. And it was. Nik Adamski was clean, which was no suprise to me, though he threw me with that "I no talk" to Bonnie line.

Margo learned that Mr. Cumiskey "kicked a few chairs — I'm like that when I'm frustrated" and left even before the awards ceremony, "not because I was so upset, though I admit I was, but because I had an appointment with Erin's father about a job interview."

Ernest Cumiskey admitted that it was difficult to work up much enthusiasm for the father of the girl who had swept his daughter in four events, but he had done the best he could. Margo asked him, "Isn't it true that normally you go after only the number one top sellers from other companies?"

He had been flustered. "Why of course, that's my trademark."

She just stared at him, leaving unasked the question of why, then, Greg Gibbons when everyone knew that he wasn't even close to the top salesman in his firm.

"Why Gibbons then, you're wondering?" he said, reddening. "I don't know. Always liked the kid, I guess. I'd seen him around socially, ya know, at meets and stuff. Maybe I wanted to do him a favor for the sake of his daughter. She's a good friend of my daughter, ya know."

"Still, if you don't mind my saying so, you're not known for hiring people to do them favors."

He was getting angry. "Yeah, well, listen, uh — "

"Margo Franklin."

"Yeah, Miss Franklin, truth is I was only humoring Gibbons. He came to me, see, and I have a few openings. I knew from the onset that I wouldn't be hiring him, but I thought, hey, what the heck, it'll make him feel good to be interviewed by the president of a top firm, right? Maybe make him look good to his wife. Maybe they can get back together and I can have a little to do with that, huh? You follow?"

"Yes. Very generous of you."

"Yeah."

"And very sacrificial."

"How's that?"

"That you'd set up a strictly cosmetic meeting like that for right after a big international meet. You couldn't have known that your daughter was not going to win. In fact, you probably expected her to win plenty."

"You bet. I always do. I have to get *her* thinking the same way. She'll win everything tonight on national TV. You gonna be there?"

"Wouldn't miss it. But if you don't mind my pressing this point, why would you set up this meaningless meeting that would force you to leave a gymnastics meet so quickly?"

Margo told Earl and me that it was apparent Cumiskey *did* mind her pressing the point, and he told her so. "What are you trying to say, sweetie? I mean I don't mind answerin' a few questions, and you can check with the clerk at the all-night donut shop in the mall over there to see when I met Gibbons and when I left. Now if there's nothing more — "

"No, nothing more." And here Margo tried to change his mood. "You're real optimistic about Larisa's chances tonight?"

"Oh, yeah. There'll be more competition, just in numbers, than there was with the Europeans Friday night, and there are some super American girls too. That gal from Dubuque will be back. But I think without Erin in the lineup, Larisa will rise to the occasion. Could win everything. No flukes tonight."

"Erin's performance Friday was a fluke?"

"Oh, I wouldn't say that, but four 9.85s? Come on. Luck? Coincidence? Not even Larisa has had an all-around score of 39.4. Had 39.3 once. Erin's good. Ought to be; Larisa made her what she is. But they're not really in the same league. Not really. See you tonight?"

After her visit to Cumiskey's office, Margo visited once more with Mrs. Cumiskey.

"We had a report from Mrs. Murray, Erin's grandmother, that she saw Larisa waiting for you after the meet. We'll have to check on what Larisa did and where she was after that, but would you mind telling me where you were?"

"Not at all," she told Margo patiently. "I don't know if you're aware that my twins are hyperactive?"

Margo shook her head.

"Well, let me tell you, that's bad enough when they're toddlers and preschoolers, but when they hit eight and nine and get some size and can fight each other and everyone else, it's all I can do to keep them reined in."

"I can imagine. So, you were with the boys?"

"Well, yes. I watched the awards ceremony because I wanted to see how Larisa took her disappointment. I thought she did remarkably well. She looked on the edge of tears, and yet I know she was very happy for Erin."

"No jealousy there?"

"Oh, some, I'm sure. No one likes to have someone else pass him up. Ernest could hardly take it. He was swearing and carrying on so, I was just glad he had that appointment so he could get out of there. Pity the poor prospect, though. I'll bet it wasn't a good meeting for Mr. Gibbons. I was unaware, by the way, that he had become top salesman in his company."

Margo stared. "I was too," she said matter-of-factly.

"Well, anyway, the boys had left me about midway through the meet, and I had to track them down by looking in all the auxiliary gyms. I found them, with the help of a janitor. They had scrounged up a volleyball or a soccer ball or something and were using it as a basketball, running with a bunch of other kids and sweating to beat the band. It was all I could do to drag them to the car, and by then Larisa had been waiting quite a while."

Margo had found the janitor on duty that night who had led Mrs. Cumiskey to the impromptu basketball game.

"Good work, Margo," Earl said in the office. "Larry, how'd you do?"

"Well, Greg and Linda embraced when it was all over, if that's what you're after."

We all clapped.

"And I got a few straight answers for once, though Erin was pretty stony. She didn't want to talk there but she asked me in private if she could come and talk to you, Earl. She said she'd heard good things about you from her grandmother."

"Fine. When does she want to meet?"

"After the competition tonight. Possible?"

"Sure. Where?"

"Bonnie's apartment. She's going to spend the night."

"So what kind of straight answers did you get from Greg and Linda?"

"Well, they were so impressed with the fact that each had tried to confess to protect the other that it was hard to get them to do anything but make eyes at each other."

Bonnie was listening intently, obviously pleased.

"But Greg finally admitted that he and Johnny had attended the same sales meeting Friday, and in his haste to avoid Johnny he left without picking up all his material. Johnny had brought it back to the office and when he saw Greg in the parking lot, he just called him over to the car and handed it to him. They were formal, short of cordial, according to Greg, but he did thank him, and Greg had, indeed, leaned on the car door when he picked up the stuff."

"Simple enough," Earl said.

"Yeah. Johnny's visit to Linda wasn't so simple though. It seems she had something of his that he wanted back. She gave him what for on the phone, saying that if he so much as showed up, she would make a scene he would regret. He said he was coming anyway. And he did."

"He was at Linda Gibbons's the day he died?"

"That's right."

"I'm gonna have to ask Wally how VCD missed that," Earl said.

"It was a short visit. She saw him arrive from the window and was out and down before he had even parked. She opened the passenger door and threatened him."

"She threatened him? She didn't just give back whatever the gift was?"

"No, she threatened him. She said that's why she burst into tears upon hearing of his death. To her it was as if her threat had been a prayer and she felt responsible. She still has the gift."

"What was it?"

"Just a bottle of perfume. I don't understand that. Why would a guy like Bizell want a bottle of perfume back? How much could it have cost?"

"That's the kind of man he was," Bonnie said. "That's why he was so despicable."

"What kind of perfume was it?" I asked.

"What's the difference?" Earl said.

"I just wanna know."

Margo shot me a doubletake when Larry said, "Chantilly. According to Linda, it's not even her brand. It's Erin's."

"Weird," Earl said.

"Philip," Margo said, "is that why you asked me — "

I shushed her, but Earl wouldn't let it drop. "What's going on, Philip? Do you know something we all should know?"

"Oh, it's just a little secret that Festschrift confided in me. I don't know how important it is since so many people use that kind of perfume."

"Philip, I have never known Wally Festschrift to do anything but *trade* secrets. He never just gives them away. What'd *you* tell *him?*"

"I didn't know we had any secrets *he* didn't have," I said. Earl squinted at me, just short of contemptuously. "I think he gives secrets to people he likes and trusts. I didn't have to trade anything." Earl was cool to me for the rest of the day.

Everyone from our shop was planning to go to the meet that night. Tickets were not easy to come by. Larry was to ask Erin if she would talk to all of us, including Sergeant Festschrift. "If she knows anything more than what we've got, we have to jump on it," Earl said. "Everything's closing up on us."

I took binoculars to the Horizon that night and watched less of the gymnasts than I did the spectators. I sat with Earl and Larry while Margo and Bonnie sat with Greg and Linda Gibbons in a different section.

"I'm sorry about that secret business today, Earl," I said. "This is all it was." I took the packet out of my pocket, told him what the lab had found on Bizell's body, and pierced the plastic with my finger. "They call it Chantilly," I said.

"It makes me think of Mrs. Cumiskey," Earl said as other spectators turned around to see where the scent was coming from.

"Yeah, I know," I said, "but don't jump to conclusions, because Larisa also uses it, and most of the girls on the team use it too because they admire her so. Erin uses it as much as anyone, and Linda has been known to borrow hers. "

"I can see why you didn't think there was much to it," Earl said. "It hardly narrows our field, does it?"

"Nope."

"I still don't like the idea of your withholding something from your co-workers."

"I know, Earl, and I'm sorry. If it had turned out to be more important, I would have remembered to tell you. It won't happen again."

THIRTEEN

I don't believe Ernest Cumiskey knew Erin would be in uniform until the AAU team ran out from the locker room. Larisa led the way with Erin prancing right behind her, looking bright and fresh in spite of it all. I turned the glasses on the Cumiskeys, who rose with everyone else to applaud the country's best team, but when Cumiskey saw Erin his hands stopped in midair and he ranted to his wife.

She stopped clapping too and followed his pointing finger. I got the impression she attempted to soothe him.

As the girls sat next to each other in metal folding chairs on the perimeter of the floor, I focused in to see the interaction between Larisa and Erin, assuming they would be thrilled to have been reunited. But they weren't even looking at each other. And when their teammates did exceptionally well or exceptionally poorly, they might congratulate or console them, but they never exulted together, and they seemed to never even speak to each other, though they sat right next to each other.

I had seen them in meets before, talking so much and so animatedly and encouraging each other, sharing secrets, cheering the scores of everyone. This was strange. I couldn't figure it. I turned back to the Cumiskeys, who were carefully studying the competition as the lesser ranked girls performed their routines.

Mr. Cumiskey started by recording scores on his program as he did at every meet, but by the end — regardless how well or how poorly his daughter did, that program would be unrecognizable, having been used for a megaphone, a whipping post, or whatever.

When Larisa's teammates performed, he grew pensive, waiting for Larisa. When Erin was up, he was dark and moody, not ranting, not cheering, regardless. Always, until Larisa performed and he felt uncomfortable unless he stood and moved, he sat close to his wife, his arm alternately around her back, her shoulder, the back of her head.

I asked Earl to watch him while Erin performed. "He sure looks possessive, doesn't he?" Earl said. "It would seem she'd get tired of that, but he was doing the same thing when we were at their place, wasn't he?"

I nodded and took the binos back. Erin had scored under 9 on the uneven bars, and she sat quietly weeping next to Larisa, who ignored her. When Larisa was up, Erin looked the other way. The older girl scored only slightly higher than Erin, and they stood ninth and tenth at the end of the first event. Coach Adamski sat with his head in his hands. The fourth best uneven bars performer on his team had surprised him with her best score ever, but even she was only in sixth place.

To the uninitiated, it may have seemed too early to be giving up on a repeat national title, but with such a huge field and your stars off their games, it was already virtually over.

Neither Erin nor Larisa scored as high as a 9 all evening. There were four different winners of the four events. The girl from Dubuque won the all-around with a 39.14 with neither of the favorites even in the running. Ernest Cumiskey was beside himself. We discovered later that he left his keys with his wife and let her take the family home. He showed up near midnight in a cab, not entirely sober. It was a first for him.

Wally Festschrift was waiting at Bonnie's apartment when our whole gang trouped in, much more subdued than we expected. After having talked with Erin's coach earlier in the day, I was less optimistic than the others about how she might fare, but not even Adamski could have predicted that dismal showing. And what had been wrong with Larisa?

Erin was teary and sullen, quite obviously humiliated, but determined to go through with talking to Earl. They sat with Wally and Bonnie at Bonnie's dining room table with the rest of us — Larry, Margo, and me — sitting in a row on the couch. We didn't want to appear too eager to hear everything, but we were, and there was no sound but Erin's tiny voice. I couldn't get over how grownup she looked with the makeup she wore only for meets. The eyeshade and the bright lipstick didn't fit the little person and voice, but she was something to listen to.

"I wanted to talk to you, Mr. Haymeyer, because my grandma told me you might understand. I'm not as comfortable as I thought I might be with all these people here, but I guess it's all right."

"They've all been working on this case, Erin," Earl said "Mostly because we love you and your grandmother and they'd like to see that nobody, especially you and your family, gets in trouble for something you didn't do."

"I know. And that's why I'm here. See, I know who killed Johnny. I admitted it until Sergeant Fest — "

"Festschrift."

"Uh-huh, until he tripped me up on some questions, but everybody thought I did that to protect my mother or father. I know them better than that. Neither of them could have done it. Well, maybe they could have, but they didn't, and I knew it."

"How did you know, Erin?"

"Because that thing that was used to cut Johnny's neck used to be part of my razor. But I never had it at home, so where would they get it?"

Erin looked at Bonnie and started crying. "I know why she did it. She did it because she loved me and because she didn't want to see me hurt. She didn't want to see my parents split up for good."

Earl was startled. "Honey, your grandmother has witnesses who can account for her whereabouts at the time of the murder."

"She's not accusing me," Bonnie said. "She has someone else in mind."

"Larisa," Erin said painfully. "She and I broke that razor when we were messing around. She told me to be careful when I threw it away. And I was. I threw it away at her house in the waste basket in the master bedroom where we had our slumber party."

No one spoke. Earl leaned forward and put his hand on Erin's arm, but it was Festschrift who asked the next question. "Do you remember throwing away both pieces?"

"Huh?"

"Both pieces. It broke in two, didn't it?"

"Yeah. Of course I threw away both pieces. What would anyone want with a worthless piece of plastic?"

"What, indeed," Festschrift said, standing. "Earl, there's only one more piece to this puzzle, and we can make an arrest."

"What will happen to her?" Erin asked, sobbing.

"I don't know, Erin," Earl said. "Let's just say that your friend is going to be one very sad and disappointed young woman." She was crying softly on her grandmother's shoulder when we left.

Festschrift spent most of the ride home moaning to Earl about "just two more small items, well, one not so small."

"I'll bite," Earl said.

"I wanna confirm my suspicions about the perfume, and I wanna come up with a motive."

"The motive is simple," Margo said. "Jealousy."

"But the murderer is usually jealous of the victim. If that were true in this case, Erin would be dead."

"It's more convoluted than that," Margo said.

"First tell me what *convoluted* means, and then tell me what you're talking about."

"I just mean it's more involved than simple one-on-one jealousy. The whole family is jealous of Erin's athletic superiority, whether they all admit it or not. Erin chooses the wrong place to throw away both the weapon and the evidence that will be put back into her bag to implicate her. The girls have talked about murdering the man, and even put it in writing. Ironically, the night the murder is planned, Erin provides more reason than ever by destroying Larisa in every event. After that, it was as good as done. Erin would be suspected, and Larisa would be left at the top of the heap."

"I like it," Festschrift said. "I mean, I don't like it, but I mean, you know what I mean."

The next morning at nine o'clock, Festschrift and Earl and I visited Mrs. Cumiskey, who was home alone. "It's very important that we talk to your husband," Wally said. "Would he be at work?"

She panicked. "Why, what is it? Has something happened to Larisa or the boys?"

"No, ma'am," he said. "I really prefer to talk to him alone first, if you don't mind."

She appeared troubled. "Well, he would be at the health club this morning and then he would arrive at work, always at ten sharp. Can't you tell me what this is about?"

"I wish I could, Mrs. Cumiskey," Festschrift said. "You won't be in the dark long. I assure you."

As she showed us to the door, Wally uncharacteristically put his hand carefully on her shoulder and up to the back of her collar, which he gently straightened. He expressed his thanks.

In the car he held out his hand to Earl and me so we could smell the heavy scent of Chantilly. "Enough to transfer to a man's skin if I touched him," he said.

We arrived at Cumiskey's office and pulled into his parking space at 9:45. It seemed a long wait, but a few seconds before ten his sleek black Oldsmobile 98 swept into the far end of the parking lot and down toward us.

From a few car lengths away, Cumiskey could see that we were in his space. He tooted twice and then laid on the horn, but when Festschrift emerged from the car, Cumiskey stopped and slowly broke into a wide grin.

"Sergeant, what're you doing here, old pal?" he said, waving and rolling down his window, as Bizell must have done the Friday night before at his rendezvous in another parking lot.

Festschrift walked briskly to the window as if to greet him warmly, the way Cumiskey always greeted everyone, but Ernest's smile froze as the sergeant's hand came out of his overcoat pocket, not with fingers extended, but as if holding something in his palm.

He reached in behind Cumiskey's neck as if to hug him, as the murderer must have done to Bizell, but Cumiskey was a wary victim and screamed, ducking as Festschrift playfully dragged a fingernail across his neck, at the same spot Bizell was mortally wounded.

"Gotcha!" the sergeant said, showing the trembling Cumiskey his empty hand.

Ernest sat up slowly and let his head rest on the steering wheel. He sobbed.

Earl and Wally joined Margo and me for dinner late that night after a full day. I could tell that Earl, at least, was eager to get back to the discussion they had carried on during the few uninterrupted minutes they were able to carve out of the past few days.

I dropped them off at the corner near Earl's building before taking Margo home, and as we pulled away, we saw them walking toward the office, Earl with his arm around the old cop and gesturing earnestly with his free hand.

SHANNON

Can a woman be acquainted with every victim in a series of murders without being involved in the crimes? Shannon is linked with six slayings that paralyze Chicago, yet she maintains her innocence. Is she protecting someone? Is she herself a target?

ONE

I HAD DRIVEN MARGO TO HER APARTMENT and had even ridden the elevator to her floor. I walked her to her door, and we joked about whether I should also check every room in her apartment before feeling confident about leaving her.

"And even if I do," I said, "who'll see *me* home?"

We were more than thirty miles from the scene of the last unsolved slaying in a series of six, yet the fear we covered with nervous humor reached from the heart of Chicago to every suburb.

Though the murders had been linked because of bizarre clues, there was little other pattern. All had occurred within ten miles of the Loop, the last two right downtown.

But four of the six victims had been men. A four-month gap separated the first and second murders, two days separated the second and third. The last three were three to four weeks apart, the most recent just two nights before.

Not that it was easy to know if the murders were actually taking place at night. Night-time seems to fit our fears of mass murderers, but in reality the times of death were difficult to pinpoint. All anyone knew — and because of the media coverage, everyone knew — was that six people of different ages, backgrounds, occupations, and economic means had been shot through the back of the head apparently by someone they trusted enough to allow into their homes or apartments.

There had been no evidence of struggle, and while the perpetrator had not seemed to move the bodies an inch from where they had fallen, he or she had tidied up each scene with the victim's own dish towels and water. The spent slug of a .357 magnum high-velocity shell, which in one case had been fired from such close range that it destroyed the victim's brain before passing through both sides of a wall and imbedding itself in a door jamb, was always removed from the scene. Authorities knew the size of the slug because of careful studies of trajectory and damage to both the victim and the room. And because of one other puzzling fact.

Although the murderer took great pains to dig the slug out of the wall or the door, and in one case even the ceiling, he or she also was careful to leave the one empty shell in the victim's hand. Etched onto each shell, apparently with a vibrating tool used to identify appliances, was a squiggly but unmistakably carefully marked message in tiny block letters: "THANK YOU, S.D."

Even on the placid streets of the affluent North Shore there had been the usual run on dead bolt locks and peep holes. Few people went out alone after dark.

Margo and I had discussed the case for hours, fearing that despite our titles as private investigators for the EH Detective Agency, we had little more insight into it than anyone else reading the papers every day.

She leaned back against the wall in the hall outside her door, and I stood with my face close to hers. "So, when are we gonna get married again?" I said, changing the subject.

"Oh, ho! Again?"

"You know what I mean. When are we going to get engaged again?"

"When you're ready."

"I'm ready," I said.

"And when you ask."

"I'm asking."

"You're not ready."

I rolled my eyes. I could have been irritated with her stalling, but I wasn't. I deserved it. The last time we'd been engaged she had asked for some time to think things over and get her mind settled. Hurt, I had immediately begun seeing someone else.

By the time I realized what I had done to us and quit trying to blame it on her, she had learned a thing or two about dealing with me. We'd been seeing each other again for several months, and there was little doubt in anyone's mind that we would be married, but she was not pushing anything. I was, but I wasn't seriously worried about the outcome.

She smiled up at me. "Good things come to those — "

"Oh, now you've classified yourself as a good thing," I said.

"You got it, pal." She is so beautiful when she's mischievous, so much sweeter than in the past when her tone was edged with sarcasm.

I asked if she wanted me to check out her apartment. "No," she said. "I carry more weapons than you do."

She was right. We both carried handguns, of course, but she also had a whistle and a pretty little decorator tear gas dispenser. "Someday you're gonna mistake that for cologne and set yourself free with it," I said.

"Are you still planning to see Earl at the office tonight?" she asked.

I looked at my watch. "Yeah. Gotta go. You sure you'll be all right?"

"Of course," she said, cupping my face in her hands. "I love you, Philip Spence."

Earl Haymeyer and I live in the same two-story building that houses his detective agency. His apartment is just down the hall from mine, but we're not exactly just another pair of tenants. He owns the building, and all the shop owners on the first floor pay their rents to him.

Not yet forty, Earl has a wealth of law enforcement experience that makes him a great guy to work for and learn from. He can make me feel younger than the ten years that separate us, but he's never condescending. He's all cop, and he's brilliant.

I was surprised to find him with Larry Shipman, who — besides our matronly receptionist, Bonnie — is Earl's only other employee, an investigator like Margo and me. "I thought you had to be up early tomorrow morning, Lar," I said, pushing open the double glass doors to our outer office and shedding my trench coat.

Neither responded. "I'm sorry," I said. "Am I interrupting?"

"Nah," Larry said. "Change of plans. I'm not going back down to my apartment tonight anyway. I'm staying with Earl."

"Afraid of the 'Thank-You Shooter,' huh?" I teased, drawing only a cold look from Earl. Shipman hadn't even looked at me since I walked in the door. "Whoa, I'm sorry, guys," I said, quickly slipping my coat back on. "Gimme a call if you need me."

"Oh, sit down, Spence," Shipman said. "You're gonna hafta know about all this eventually anyway."

Earl stood and motioned us to follow him past the four desks in the outer office and past the darkroom into his private office. Shipman, as usual, wore his off-duty jeans, flannel shirt, armless insulated vest, and construction boots. The most casual I had ever seen Earl was when he took off the jacket of his three-piece suit and rolled up his shirt sleeves. Tonight the jacket was off, but the sleeves were down.

It was unlike either of these two to keep secrets. The agency had always worked as a team, almost a family. Though Larry lived in Chicago and the rest of us lived in or around Glencoe, we were tight.

Earl had reminded us time and again that we were not working on the mass murder case, but newspaper photos of the victims and details of each crime were tacked on his wall. Just two days before, during our staff meeting, he had added the latest victim, listed personal characteristics, and allowed us to brainstorm for a while, "just for practice."

We couldn't be officially involved in the investigation because it was Chicago Police Department business and was, of course, being handled by the Homicide Division. Anyway, we had our own caseload to worry about, and although none of our current projects was anywhere near as provocative as the one on everybody's lips, we were busy enough.

I think Earl knew we'd be trying out our own hypotheses on each other all day long if he didn't give us a chance to gas about it as a group once in a while.

"Your news or mine?" Shipman asked Earl as I tried to appear patient.

"Mine," Earl said. "Philip, you know how much heat has been on the Chicago P.D. since the second murder?"

"Yeah, even since the first."

"OK, but it's been building, and the department is really feeling it. It's not just the public, but also the media, the mayor's office, everybody. And with good reason. I mean, it's not that Homicide isn't doing the job, but this is a tough one, and if they don't get some results soon, heads are going to roll."

"Is your old friend Festschrift getting any heat?"

"They all are. He's not heading up the investigation, you know, but he's in the thick of it."

Sergeant Walvoord F. Festschrift had been Earl's commanding officer when Earl was a young cop, several years before Earl left the department to join the state's attorney's office as an investigator. In fact, when I met Earl he was special investigator for the US Attorney for Northern Illinois, James A. Hanlon. When Hanlon announced what turned out to be a successful run for governor, Haymeyer went into private practice and opened our agency.

"I spoke with Wally Festschrift a few days ago, Philip," Earl continued. "I offered to help, but we both knew that was impossible. The Homicide boys are embarrassed enough that they don't have any solid leads without having to admit they're seeking the advice of private detectives."

"So he doesn't want your help?"

"It's not that. He'd love all the help he can get, but there probably isn't another man down there who'd stand still for it. The problem is, and Wally doesn't even know this yet, Jim Hanlon called me today and he wants us involved."

I shook my head. "The governor can involve us in a city police matter?"

"The governor can do just about what he pleases in this state, within reason. He offered state assistance early on in the investigation, but the mayor coldly accused him of political maneuvering and said that when the city needed help, it would ask for it. The fact that the murders have all taken place within the city would make it difficult for Hanlon to push state detectives into the picture. He tried to assure the mayor he wasn't trying to embarrass anyone, and, to hear him tell it, all he really cares about is the safety of the public."

"You know him, Earl," I said. "Is he genuine?"

"Oh, yeah, I have no doubt about that. That's why he's asking us to become involved. The state will pay for it, but anything we get has to be carefully fed to Chicago, and no one can know."

"It sounds impossible," I said. "What can we do that Chicago can't do? And how can we do anything without their permission? We need information. We need access. You can't get that without arousing suspicion.

"Not without Festschrift we can't," Earl said.

"But you just said he agreed that our involvement would be impossible."

"Only if the brass know we're involved. I'm going to ask him if he'll consider me a consultant. He's at a level where he doesn't have to clear the use of every expert or contact he might employ. He won't pay us. We'll be invisible — for the most part." Haymeyer and Shipman traded glances. "No one will be embarrassed, yet we'll have the access we need."

"Even to the murder scenes?"

"Probably."

"And what happens to Festschrift if anyone finds out he's cooperating with the state? I can just see the headlines."

"Festschrift can't know. That's one of Hanlon's conditions."

"You're not going to tell your old friend that you're using him to make money off the state?"

"I'm hardly doing it to make money, Philip. You know better than that. Hanlon couldn't pay me enough for the cases we'll have to postpone, let alone the ones we'll have to reject."

"You're going to put everybody on this?"

"Of course."

"I can't believe Festschrift won't get suspicious of all the time and effort he sees on our part," I said.

"I know," Earl said. "He's good enough to sniff anything out, but it's as important to us as it is to everyone else involved that no one knows the basis of our interest. He must see little effort on our part and must view me as just an interested observer."

"Earl, you know I think you can do anything, but I just don't see how you're going to be able to pull this off. Hardly a cop in Chicago even takes his day off anymore. They've got everybody on the case. The biggest job they've got is just coordinating all the activity. How can we help without being in the way, and what in the world can we do without anyone knowing?"

"That's where you come in," Shipman said without emotion and still without looking at me.

I stared at him, then back at Earl.

"That's right," Earl said. "Festschrift likes you, right?"

"Well, yeah, but — "

"He likes you, right?"

"Well, we only worked on the one case together, and — "

"And he has you just a little underrated, doesn't he?"

Earl pressed.

This was something I could warm up to. Festschrift *had* always called me Kid and seemed surprised whenever I came up with anything of value.

"Yeah," I said tentatively, more as permission to continue than in agreement.

"I'm asking Wally to take you under his wing for a few months in a special internship program I'm initiating for my junior guy."

"C'mon, Earl. I've lived with that junior business for so long it's getting old. I know Larry's been around longer and all that, but haven't I earned a spot yet?"

Shipman broke in, finally looking at me. "Philip, listen, this has nothing to do with the way we feel about you. Your place is secure here. We're thrilled with your progress."

I looked pained.

"OK," Larry said, "not just your progress. We feel you've arrived." He looked to Earl for confirmation, and Earl nodded. Larry continued. "Earl's idea is to play on Festschrift's view of you. He'll buy the internship thing, let you spend time with him and all that, and won't suspect anything. In fact, he'll *want* you to share things with Earl and will likely pump you for Earl's reactions. Sort of a nonthreatening way to get help."

"Sure, OK, but will you have to deceive him, lie to him to get him to agree to this?"

"Me?" Earl said, feigning a wound. Even Larry almost grinned. "No, in fact, not even *your* lily-white principles will be violated by this. I really am initiating such a program. It'll be good for you; it'll go on your record and into your resume if you're smart. It'll make you a better investigator. You'll have to give me oral and written reports on what you learn."

I was catching on. "And in the process, you'll get enough information so everyone on our team will be able to get their heads together on the Thank-You Shooter case."

"You got it, pal," I heard for the second time that night.

I sat back, thinking. "So you're going to suggest to Wally that I tag along with him for the next couple of months, or until the case breaks." Earl nodded. I continued. "Meanwhile, I'll be coming back to you with every tidbit we turn up, and you'll be trying to feed back to Wally, through me, anything that might help him — and thus Homicide Division, Chicago P.D., and the mayor — solve the case by himself but really with the help of the governor, who doesn't want any credit."

"It does sound preposterous, I guess," Earl said. "But that's basically it."

"Do I have a choice?" I asked.

"Not really. You don't want to do it?"

"It's not that. It just has to sink in."

"Fair enough. We can settle on the details tomorrow. I want to meet with everyone here to go over the case one more time anyway. Margo knows nothing of this yet."

I nodded. "Now," I said, "Larry has news too, right? Something that's got him so troubled that it's affected his sense of humor and even his ability to look me in the face. I hope it's not a problem with me."

"Of course not," Larry said, irritated. "It's just the kind of news I wish I didn't have. Even before you start running around with Festschrift, provided Earl can talk him into that, we already have some information you can feed him."

"You've already got something on the murder case for Festschrift?"

"Do I ever."

TWO

I had met Larry Shipman long before the EH Detective Agency had even been formed. I was a free-lance artist in Atlanta and was awkwardly trying to help my new friend Margo Franklin unravel some of the most complicated personal problems I had ever encountered.

Her mother was a circuit court judge in Chicago mixed up with the mob and even a murder. Anyway, Earl Haymeyer, then of the US Attorney's office, was assigned to the case, and in the process of the investigation he used a free-lance media junkie, journalist, informant: Larry Shipman.

What a character Shipman was. He liked to be near the action, regardless what the action was. He was convinced that more happened with the police and the news media than anywhere, so he taught himself to write, became a stringer for one of the big Chicago dailies, and hung around radio and television stations long enough to pick up the technical know-how to handle writing and reporting for them too.

But his area of expertise for Earl's purpose back then was as an informant. With his ability to look any part, he posed as a convict and Earl got him put in the same cell as a mob hit man. Later he helped expose embezzlers at a downtown bank by working for several weeks as a teller. Larry helped me with the first "case" I ever had as a private detective. I'll never forget climbing down from a second-floor apartment patio into his waiting arms and both of us tumbling down an embankment, laughing our heads off while trying to remain undetected.

Larry wasn't the moody type. He was usually up. He wasn't a Christian by any means, yet he wasn't hostile either. He carefully stayed out of the discussions about God that Margo and I frequently had with Earl. We figured when he wanted to talk about it, he would. He was basically an honest guy and had a real sense of justice, a prerequisite for working for Earl. He didn't even have any obvious vices or bad habits, though we knew he dated several different women and never seemed to develop a relationship.

He seemed to genuinely like everyone he worked with. He was particularly good to Bonnie, our receptionist, a widow who has had a rough life. Basically, we all like Ship; and because he's so steady, his mood shifts are very noticeable. And right now, I was noticing.

"I have a friend," Larry began, "well, not a friend actually. More just an acquaintance. Her name is Shannon Perry and she's a newswriter for WMTR-FM, Metro Radio in the city. I never dated her or anything, but I worked on a few stories with her a couple of years ago when I was stringing for Metro. She's a good kid, kinda straight, real ambitious. Cute."

Larry stood and went around Earl's desk, stopping directly behind Earl — which Earl doesn't like, but he didn't complain this time. Larry studied each face of the victims pinned to the corkboard. I wanted to ask if he thought this girl knew anything or was involved or what, but Earl is usually the one who pushes Larry to get to the point, and I figured if he could be patient, I could too.

"The only one I had ever even seen before was number five here," Larry said quietly. It wasn't like him to let his work get to him. I didn't know why he mentioned it again. We all knew that he had a nodding acquaintance with Frances Downs, the murdered twenty-six-year-old producer of local TV shows for Channel 8.

"Did your friend, uh, Shannon, know Frances Downs too?" I tried, but Earl shushed me with a look and a gesture.

"Yeah, uh-huh," Larry said finally. "They knew each other somewhat, about as well as Shannon and I knew each other."

I was in an interrogating mood, but Earl was still staring me down, so I waited.

"Shannon swore me to secrecy, Earl," Larry said, suddenly louder and turning to face the boss.

Earl leaned back in his chair and blankly returned the stare. "You said yourself you would break a confidence only for a good reason. I think this is good enough. You told me, it was your idea to tell Philip, and tomorrow you're going to tell Margo."

Larry sat on a corner of Earl's desk, another pet peeve Earl now chose to ignore. Shipman's shoulders sagged. "Shannon lives on the far north side, almost into Evanston," he said.

He said that simply, as if it had significance in itself. I had to think about it for a minute. The first Thank-You murder had taken place up there somewhere. "How far from where this Ng guy was killed?" I asked.

Larry looked at me squarely and recited the facts the way Earl often did. "Lawson Ng, Filipino male, age thirty-three, slight build, athletic, bachelor, Park District recreational director six years, found murdered in his second-floor apartment Wednesday, June second, by a bullet wound through the brain from the back of his head, a wound the coroner says was inflicted most likely during the day on Tuesday, the first."

I knew all that. "So," I said, "how far from — "

"Same block," Larry said coldly.

"Wow."

"Yeah, wow. Some coincidence, huh?"

"Could be," I said. "Surely it's not unusual to have a crime committed in one's neighborhood, and it's not really that bizarre to have slightly known someone who became a victim. Are you trying to make something of the fact that this Shannon has had some kind of connection with two of the victims?"

Larry and Earl glanced at each other. "I wouldn't," Larry admitted, "if that was all there was to it. The thing is, Shannon herself is obsessed by it. I've never seen her this way. I mean, like I say, I don't know her that well, but she's usually just a nut, a fun-loving type who's a good little writer and has a real future."

"Well, *you're* apparently convinced there's nothing to the coincidence, so can't you just talk her out of worrying about it? Or *are* you worried about it?"

"Let him finish, Philip," Earl said. "There's much more to this, or Larry wouldn't be giving it a second thought."

Larry seemed detached again, standing and looking at the board again. He faced the wall as he spoke. "Victim number two, Annamarie Matacena, Italian female, age fifty-one, heavy build, divorced, nurses' aide in the pediatric ward, Mid-City Hospital on the near north side, found murdered in her tiny Uptown apartment, same method of operation, apparently on her day off, Thursday, September second."

We'd been over these so many times; I wanted to say something, but Earl was indulging Larry still. I let him talk.

"Shannon knew this woman, too," he said. "She had almost forgotten about it and probably wouldn't have put it together except that the picture in the paper brought it back to her."

"Where did she know her from?" I asked.

"Shannon was researching an in-depth piece on Mid-City's care of handicapped children, and while Mrs. Matacena was not interviewed, she was assigned to help Shannon find her way around for an hour or so."

It was a wild coincidence, but I was still having trouble worrying too much about it. What was Larry saying? What was Shannon saying? Did she feel she ought to be under suspicion? Was she worried that some strange second nature overtook her and that she herself was murdering these acquaintances?

Then Larry recited the details of the third murder.

"The Reverend Donald Pritkin, male, age thirty-eight, father of three, pastor of the Ashland Congregational Church, murdered by same modus operandi, found in the modest parsonage by his wife when she returned from shopping, Monday, September sixth. He was still wearing his golfing clothes."

I looked questioningly for the connection between this pastor and Shannon Perry. "She attended a friend's wedding at that church a few months ago," Larry said. "Reverend Pritkin officiated."

I made a face and shrugged, looking at Earl. He cocked his head as if he agreed that this one was a long shot. That piqued Larry. "I didn't say some of these weren't a little farfetched, did I?" he said, almost shouting. "But you can imagine how this girl feels!"

Earl raised a calming hand again, and I wished I hadn't made the face. Larry looked disgusted with both of us, but after a minute he turned back to the wall. "Dale Jerome," he began, and I could hardly believe it. "Male, forty-one, LaSalle Street lawyer, divorced, living alone on Lake Shore Drive, discovered murdered, Wednesday, September twenty-second, same MO, by landlord when his office called, concerned because he had missed an appointment with a client's corporation counsel."

Larry paused as if in thought. "Several years ago, when Shannon first started working in Chicago, the editor of the paper she wrote for recommended Dale Jerome to her to defend her against a suit filed by the other driver in a minor auto accident. He handled the whole thing with the insurance companies, it never went to court, she only met with him once, and that was it. But she remembered his name and like any of us when we hear news about someone we've had any contact with before, she said, 'I know that guy!'"

"A lot of people knew *that* guy," I said, trying not to sound too disparaging. "Even back when he represented her on that little case he was handling big publishing firms and other corporations. It's not unusual that he would have many, many acquaintances."

"I know that, Philip," Larry said, more patiently than before. "But putting it into this context, I mean in light of the fact that she had some contact with each victim, makes it even more significant, wouldn't you say?"

"I suppose," I said, not entirely convinced. Yet.

Wearily, Larry turned back to the board. "Victim number five," he said. "Frances Downs, female, twenty-six, local TV producer, discovered by a friend in her Sandburg Village high-rise, Saturday, October sixteenth."

"This is one that puzzles me," Earl interrupted. "This girl was living above her means."

"TV producers make good money, don't they?" I said. "And she was single. No family expenses."

"Yeah, but she wasn't making nearly enough to afford a penthouse in that building. We're talking big bucks here."

"OK," Larry said, "so she may have been a kept woman. We can investigate the rest of her past after Philip gets rolling with Festschrift, but for now, I'm interested in the fact that this is another acquaintance of Shannon's."

It was getting very late, and I was tired. But the newspaper clippings of the sixth murder hadn't even yellowed on Earl's wall yet. Two days before, on Wednesday, November 10, Thomas McDough, a forty-eight-year-old dentist, was discovered murdered, apparently by the Thank-You Shooter, in his Marina City Tower condominium. Dr. McDough, a married man whose children were grown and gone, was found by his wife when she returned from an overnight trip. He was Shannon Perry's dentist.

I had to admit it was eerie. Individually, the fact that Shannon Perry knew each victim wasn't much more of a coincidence than that Larry knew number five, Frances Downs. They had been in similar occupations. Earl admitted that he had known the lawyer, Dale Jerome. "At least I knew who he was. His name was familiar to me."

I knew none of them, had not even heard of one of them. But then I had not been a Chicagoan for long. Margo had not mentioned having been familiar with any of the victims either. To know or to at least have had some contact with all six? It was a boggler. I wondered how Larry learned about it.

"She told me," he explained. "I see her every now and then when I visit the old haunts. She's always cheerful and has often asked me to join her at her desk for lunch. But the last few times I've seen her, she's been different. Preoccupied."

"Like you tonight," I suggested.

"Yeah," he admitted, smiling. "I guess. Anyway, I asked her if anything was wrong, and she said maybe she'd tell me about it sometime. I never put it together with the fact that each time I saw her, another murder or two had been committed and that each one cut her deeply because of the name recognition thing every time it came over the newswire. You know, because of her position, she was learning of these murders before anyone else. It got to the point, she told me yesterday, where she dreaded hearing about another murder, wondering what acquaintance or friend would be dead this time."

"How did she finally decide to tell you?"

"Well, I was in to see Chuck Childers, the morning man over there?"

"Yeah."

"And when I went past Shannon's office she didn't even look up. Well, she never misses a thing, so on the way back, I went slowly past her window and made a face, and even though I know she saw me, she didn't respond. So I just walked right in and asked her what was up. She was really distraught. Her boss had told her that her work was suffering for some reason. She was an award winner for years, but now she couldn't meet deadlines, missed facts, and all the rest. He wanted her to take a couple of weeks off, with pay. She was humiliated — at least that's what I thought."

"She wasn't?"

"I suppose that was part of it, but that wasn't what was bothering her. She said she had not been able to tell anyone what was bothering her, and that she had been hoping I might come around because she felt somehow she could trust me and she knew I was a private detective now. That got my interest and I assured her she *could* tell me. She closed the door and burst into tears. I'm tellin' ya, it took forever to drag it out of her, and I had to promise the moon, not to mention protecting her confidence. When it was all over she asked if I would tell her boss, another old friend of mine, that she was taking him up on the offer of a couple of weeks off, that she was grateful, and that she would be back. And I took her home."

"What do you make of it, Larry?" I said. "It's too much of a long shot to be coincidence, I admit. Is this a dangerous or sick person?"

"Dangerous, no. Sick, possibly. I'd be sick too if it happened to me, wouldn't you?"

I nodded.

"The thing is," he continued, "Shannon has airtight alibis for several of the murders, at least for the ones during which she can remember where she was, like the most recent ones. I got those out of her by asking the most roundabout questions you've ever heard. The last thing I wanted to do was to make her think that I thought there was any possibility she could have been involved. When I had the alibis all sorted out in my mind, I recounted them to her to assure her that no second personality or darker side of her could have committed murders she didn't know about. She demanded to know then who would be murdering people to get at her, as if I would know."

"But she was right, of course," Earl said. "If she didn't commit the murders, we're agreed that there are too many coincidences here for this to be other than deliberate on someone's part. Someone is either trying to frame her or is leading up to threatening her life."

"Of course," Larry said, "but I couldn't tell her that, could I?"

THREE

Margo's first question at our hastily called Saturday staff meeting the next morning was directed at Larry. "Do we know the floor plans of the murder scenes — I mean of the entire apartment, condo, or house in each instance?"

"We can get them from Festschrift, I assume," Larry said, "but if you don't mind my saying so, that wasn't the first thing I expected to hear from you."

Margo looked puzzled.

"Me either," Earl said.

"OK," she said, "I'll bite. What was I supposed to say?"

"I thought you'd challenge our plan to break her confidence," Larry said.

"Oh, no, I don't think so," Margo said. "You're doing exactly the right thing, and I'm sure that down deep it's what Shannon wants, too. She has sworn you to secrecy, Ship, but you've shown her that her worst fear is unfounded: the fear that she has been involved in the murders without knowing it."

"But she doesn't want anyone to know that she's had knowledge — limited though it may be — of every victim," Larry said.

"No, she doesn't want the public to know. But why do you think she told *you?* It's not just because you're a trusted friend, because, let's face it, you really haven't been that close. She wants protection. She has to know, whether she admits it or not, that you're going to feel responsibility for her safety. And don't you?"

"Yeah, I should say I do."

"Then don't feel guilty about your plan to at least tell Festschrift. Even if she insists that no one else knows, at least it will give *him* a place to start. You know her name is going to come up in this thing eventually anyway. I assume Chicago Homicide is checking into every member of the Congregational church and will try to round up guest books from all the weddings there in the last year. You know she'll be on at least some ancient list of that lawyer's, even though he won her case for her and she may not be thought worth questioning unless everything else fizzles. The dentist's patient list is being scrutinized now, and she'll be more recent and prominent on that one than on any of the others. I don't know how they'll connect her with the Filipino or the Italian woman, but when her name turns up in the orbit of even two of the others, she'll be under a magnifying glass."

Somehow Margo had summarized what we'd all been toying with since Larry gave the rundown. "You're becoming quite a detective," Earl said. "It makes me wonder why you want to know about the layouts of the murder scenes."

"It's the dish towel part of the MO," she said. "We're pretty confident, because of the absence of unfamiliar fingerprints at each scene, that the murderer was wearing gloves. And based on the careful digging and scraping to remove the slug, the tidy cleanup work, and the placing of the shell in the victim's hand, we can guess that the murderer was wearing small, thin gloves, maybe even rubber or surgical ones. Those would frighten someone, however. No one would let someone in wearing surgical gloves. So we can guess that the murderer was wearing regular gloves over rubber gloves upon entering the house or apartment."

"I'm with you so far," Earl said, "but I confess I don't know where you're going."

"Who wears gloves at this time of year? Certainly not men for the most part."

"Handymen might," Larry said. "Maybe repairmen, maintenance men, garbage men."

"Well, that's true," Margo said, appearing to resign from whatever hypothesis she had been building.

"But what does that have to do with the layout of the scenes?" Earl asked again.

"Well, I was thinking I was on a track that might make us lean toward a female perpetrator," Margo said. "I don't guess the gloves angle is exclusive to women after all. But I was hoping to put that together with the fact that the murderer always soiled a dish towel in sopping up the blood."

"Keep going," Larry said.

"Never a bathroom towel," Margo said, "never a rag from under the sink or anything else lying around? What does that say to you? Anything?"

"So what you want to know," Earl said, "is whether any of the murders occurred closer to the bathroom than to the kitchen, and if so, why did the murderer use a dish towel rather than something handier."

"Exactly."

"Good question. I'm not sure it's necessarily a feminine thing to choose, but it could be. It could also just be part of the sick pattern here."

"If so, it would have no significance," Margo said.

"Right, but let's check it out if I can hook Philip up with Wally."

We were all eager to know what our various assignments would be on this most important case — assigned from a higher level than ever, too. Earl started by having us call every client on our active cases list and inform them that their investigation was being either canceled, postponed, or reassigned to another company. It was our job to pacify them without giving them any reasons. In some cases we would refund a major portion if not all of their fee, even if the case was being reassigned.

When Larry and Earl were finished with their calling they split up for separate trips to Chicago, Larry to tell Shannon what he wanted to do about her problem, and Earl to sell Wally Festschrift on his idea for me. I called Bonnie.

"Earl asked if you could contact the agency that runs the building for him and see how long that vacant apartment will be open," I told her. "He'd like to have it available for agency use for the next month or so, at least until December 15."

After lunch Margo and I drove up to Highland Park to a mostly deserted playground. A few kids played softball with their coats on, and we smelled charcoaled burgers and hotdogs as we strolled. "Earl has been so close," Margo said. "I hope working with Sergeant Festschrift again will be a good thing for him."

She was talking about Earl's interest in God. Ever since we had known him, Margo and I had struggled with just how to tell him what Christ meant to us and that we had found Him to be a personal God. Earl had gone from amusement with us to hostility to reluctant listening, and then to a roller coaster of reactions that seemed to depend on his moods or what was happening in his life at the moment.

We had decided on a moratorium on overt selling and just prayed that somehow God would use us to show Earl what we had been unable to tell him. Just to think of the people — even other non-Christians — whose advice we sought for how to share the most important thing in your life with someone you care about. Someone I asked told me, "The very phrase 'share with someone' has a religious ring to it that'll turn him off."

For a while we were uncertain about the effectiveness of our new resolve to do more living of the faith than preaching it in front of Earl. He seemed to enjoy the truce. It's not that we had ever put him on the spot or challenged him, but I confess I had frequently spiritualized things and had unintentionally come off holier than thou. For a while it seemed all I did was ask for chances to tell the staff all about Christ. When he finally relented, I didn't feel I had done well, though no one seemed offended.

We wanted so badly to see those people we loved come to Christ. But again, there was that terminology so foreign to them. The strangest break came, however, when Earl's old friend, Wally Festschrift, reappeared out of the past.

Oh, he had been there all the time, but the men had basically lost touch over the years. It wasn't just that Earl had worked for Wally when he first became a cop, but as Earl rose quickly through the ranks, he passed Wally up and the latter wound up working for him for a time. And did he give Earl fits then.

Maybe it was jealousy. Wally denies it. Maybe he really was — as he claims now — trying to make Earl a better cop. Maybe he hated to see the department lose Earl; Wally says he saw it coming two years before it happened. "He was too smooth, too good; you just knew somebody in politics was gonna snap him up. I just didn't want him to get too big for his britches before he left us. Yeah, I gave 'im a hard time. So what?"

A hard time was understating it, to hear Earl tell it. He says Wally was the toughest guy to supervise in all of Homicide. "I mean, there's something going on when a guy is in the same position, sergeant in Homicide, for fifteen years, and that's after several years as a homicide detective."

Wally explained that it simply was and always will be his first love. The mystery, the people, and most of all, as he once told me, the sense of justice when the heat finally comes down on the guilty.

I liked Festschrift, though he took some getting used to. First impressions are always worst, especially when it comes to Wally. But regardless of how interesting he was — and how excited I was at the prospect of working closely with him again on this new scheme of Earl's — the most important thing was that Wally and Earl had not just made up for their past squabbles. They had developed a new relationship.

Wally is divorced, and his kids have turned out bad. He is a lonely old cop. Earl is a young widower whose only child is an institutionalized autistic who has never recognized his father. Neither would admit his loneliness, though Festschrift once confessed to me his failure as a husband and father.

But you should have seen it when they were reunited on a case that happened to overlap Chicago Homicide with the EH Detective Agency. At first there was formality, cautious sparring, maneuvering, diplomacy, politics, a few flare-ups, and territorial scuffles. But then they realized they needed each other, and the old professionalism and camaraderie of the fraternity of cops took over and they were old war buddies again. It was exciting, not to mention educational, just to hear them reminisce about some of the old cases.

That was when Festschrift finally tried to explain away his despicable performance as a subordinate; not as a cop, mind you, Earl used to always concede, but in a boss/employee relationship, he was near impossible to deal with. Wally had been a good boss, Earl said, but he made a lousy subordinate.

"It wasn't jealousy, no matter what you say or what you think," Wally said a dozen times during the Johnny Bizell murder case, which brought the two back together. "I was just the stone that polished you into what you are today." Whereupon Earl would swear, and then excuse himself.

Somewhere during that renewed relationship, Earl started telling Wally Festschrift about Christ. I know what you're thinking. You're thinking you missed something, that I forgot to tell you when Earl's mind and heart got changed and he became receptive and prayed to become a Christian. But he didn't. I'm saying the man started telling his friend that Christ could forgive his past and could give him a new and abundant life, and Earl hadn't even dipped into the gift for himself yet.

"And he still hasn't," Margo said, as we chatted in the park.

"No, but remember when he said he'd noticed that we'd been strangely silent about these kinds of things for a while, and that made us ashamed of our strategy?"

"Yeah," she said, "but in reality I think the strategy had a lot to do with it. He started asking more questions on his own, and we were able to answer without feeling as if we were shoving anything down his throat. For as classy a guy as Earl is, he's also proud and he's not about to be sold a bill of goods or be badgered into anything."

"That's for sure," I said. "I've seen him with more than one can't-miss salesman who missed. Remember when he told the one that he wasn't motivated by great amounts of money?"

Margo nodded and laughed. "Where was the poor guy supposed to go from there? He told Earl he could donate the profits to his favorite charity and Earl said, 'You're looking at it.' "

We watched the kids play ball for a while, and Margo grew serious. "I also remember when Earl came to us after he had started talking to Wally and told us that all he could remember about how to receive Christ was that you just pray, confess your sins, and believe. He knew there had to be more to it than that, so he wanted a little counsel before he headed back out to his little mission field."

It had been a shocking revelation to us. Here was Earl, "sharing" a faith he didn't have, doing the work we should have been doing, and yet not afraid to ask us for input. He also made clear that night that he had all the information he needed to make his own decision about it, and so he expected to be left alone to make it. We got the point, but that didn't make it any easier over the ensuing months.

The Bizell case was solved, Earl continued to talk with Wally occasionally, but they eventually drifted apart — that's what the thirty miles between the Loop and the North Shore will do to you — and as far as we knew, neither of them made any commitment. We tested the waters with Earl a few times, but he just reminded us that we had done our part and that the rest was up to him.

That didn't stop us from praying, of course, and we found ourselves doing that more than ever. "It's what we should have been doing all along," Margo said. "Instead of talking so much."

She's always been hard to argue with, especially when she's right.

We leaned against a huge tree and pulled our coat collars up higher around our necks. Her full, brown hair waved in the wind, and she hunched her shoulders to keep warm. I had been stricken by her beauty long before I fell in love with her. I had been so involved in her personal problems that I assumed anything I felt for her was merely pity. And when I realized otherwise, it was hard to convince *her* it wasn't pity.

But over the few years, through all the rough times we'd seen, even through our brief breakup not long before, I had loved her. And I had seen her grow. Better than that, she had seen *me* grow.

If she hadn't, we wouldn't have been standing there in the park, looking deep into each other's eyes. Her smile always reached me. I loved her. I loved her before I knew it. I loved her when I thought I didn't. I loved her before she loved me. I loved her when I was certain she didn't love me anymore, and when she had reason not to. We loved each other now, and regardless what would happen to her love in the future, mine would never waver again.

"I never quit loving you," she said softly. "Even if I acted like it. Even if I thought you didn't deserve it — "

"I didn't — " I said, but she put a finger to my lips.

"I was hopelessly in love with you even when I thought I had lost you to someone else, just because I had asked for some time. I was willing to give you up if that's what was meant to be, but I can't imagine what my life would have been without you."

I loved to hear her talk like that, but saying so would have only spoiled it. I reached up to her face and slipped my fingers between her hair and her neck and pulled her face to mine. As we kissed, two little boys giggled and pointed. Margo turned and winked at them and embraced me.

FOUR

By the time I entered our office Monday morning, more things had been set in motion than I had even known were planned. I got in late Sunday night and was unaware that Earl and Larry had moved Shannon Perry into the vacant apartment at the end of the hall.

Earl had also arranged for me to meet with Sergeant Wally Festschrift at the precinct house downtown, and had somehow talked Wally into tutoring me for the duration of the Thank-You Shooter investigation.

Bonnie was filling me in at our front desk. "Does this mean I'm not going to get to meet Shannon before I hook up with Wally?"

Before she could answer, Earl poked his head out and asked Margo and me to join him and Larry in his office. "There's someone I'd like you to meet," he said.

Margo straightened her desk and caught up with me. When we entered Earl's office, a young woman of about twenty-five stood and extended her hand. Medium height and slender, Shannon Perry was a pretty girl with dark brown, short-cropped hair, bright blue eyes, and a gleaming though tentative smile. She wore a pale pink blouse with a contrasting burgundy ribbon bowed at the neck and a cream-colored crocheted vest with a leather belt over a pleated, light gray skirt. Signs of her trauma became evident as we talked.

Earl had a couple of extra chairs dragged in, then filled us in on the arrangements he and Larry had made with Shannon.

"You were right, Margo," he began, "about Shannon's real desire for protection. As far as we can tell, no one knows she's here. She'll stay with us for the entire two weeks she has off, unless she comes under suspicion by the Chicago P.D.; then we'd have to inform them of her whereabouts. Meanwhile, while Philip is working with Wally downtown, we'll be grilling Shannon about everyone in her life to see what the story is."

"I don't look forward to that," Shannon said quietly, "but I know I've had enough of this torture. That's why I didn't really mind when Larry told me he had confided in you as friends. I think if he had not prefaced it by assuring me that you could help and that you were all convinced I was innocent, I wouldn't have felt good about it at all. I'm still not sure what to make of this contact you're making with the Chicago police sergeant."

Overarticulate is the only way to describe Shannon's precise, cultured speech. She had a way of saying exactly what she meant.

"We feel it's a real break," Earl said. "We'll have access to information, and Sergeant Festschrift will have our input in a nonthreatening way, and maybe we can get a good bead on the murderer."

Shannon nodded but didn't speak.

"You know," Larry said, "we can be pretty certain that the murderer is someone you know well, Shannon."

"That's scary," she said. "What does it mean? Is someone trying to frame me?"

"I don't think so," Earl said. "The advertising on the shells has nothing to do with you, does it? Is overpoliteness one of your things, or do you know anyone with the initials *S.D.?*"

"No. In fact, when I heard of the first murder, of that young man in my neighborhood, I assumed the murderer was someone who wanted to be caught. This fastidiousness at the crime scene and the message and initials on the bullet just seemed like the work of someone who was crying out for help or at least for capture."

"That could still be," Margo said. "Yet with five more murders and no more clues, I'm beginning to wonder."

"There's something I'm feeling guilty about," Shannon said. "We all know there are literally hundreds of Chicago policemen combing the city right now, looking for clues, interviewing door to door in the neighborhoods where the murders took place. I was even questioned after the Ng murder because I lived so close. If you're so sure the murderer is someone who knows me, shouldn't we help them focus their search a little better?"

Earl stood. "That's what I've been wanting to hear," he said. "We were worried about your request for secrecy. You know if we tell Chicago, they'll probably take the case out of our hands, and it will be difficult to keep your name out of the news. My fear is that when this leaks out, and you know it will if that many people know about it, it'll scare the murderer out of the city and we'll never be able to track him."

"Or her," Margo said, and Shannon flinched.

"Her?"

"Very possibly," Margo said. "I would start this investigation with your girl friends, your co-workers, even your relatives. Someone knows you very, very well to be killing people who are such a relatively small part of your life. It's almost as if it were someone with access to your records, your datebook, your wallet, or something."

"We've got a problem," Larry said ominously. "If Shannon was interviewed after the Ng murder in June, she's on file. And when that dentist's client list is cross-referenced by computer with all the other names associated with the other murders, it's going to spit her name right into their hands."

Earl grimaced. "You're right, of course. Let's see, is there any way that she could be associated with any of the other victims, officially I mean? I can't see how they could associate her with the Matacena woman. And it would be ages before she would be placed at a wedding officiated by Pritkin. Did you go alone to that wedding, Shannon?"

"No, in fact I had a date, and a bunch of us went from work."

"Who was your date?"

"Jake," she said.

"Jake Raven?" Larry said. "Your boss?"

"Right. You know Jake well."

"I don't know him like I know Chuck — "

"Childers?"

"Uh-huh, but we all used to hang around together in the old days."

"It wasn't that long ago, Larry," she said.

"Yeah, I know. Just seems like it."

"We're getting off my point, Lar," Earl said. "The fact that several people from W — "

" — MTR-FM," Shannon offered.

"Yeah — went with you to this wedding must mean that several people from work also remembered it when the murder was announced."

"Yes, we talked about it."

"Well, let's take this slowly then," Margo said. "I see what Earl is driving at. The odds are that since the Ng murder was the first and it did just seem interesting at that point for it to have happened in your neighborhood, Shannon, there was no reason to hide that from your friends. It must have been normal to talk about how spooky it was to have something like that happen on your street, in your block. You must've talked about staying with someone for a while and having new locks put in and all that."

"Exactly," Shannon said. Looking first at Larry, then at Earl, she added, "Sometimes this girl knows me better than I do," and she leaned over and squeezed Margo's hand to assure her it was a compliment. "As a matter of fact I did stay with Jeanie for a couple of nights, but I never did go through with my plan to get better locks. I realized I had the best you can buy anyway, and the strange thing is that there had been no forced entry into Mr. Ng's place. All the reports said it had to have been someone he trusted. I didn't know anyone that he knew, and I had only spoken with him a time or two, so I cautiously moved back home."

"But Margo's point is that everyone at work was aware of your apartment's proximity to the victim's, right?" Earl said.

Shannon nodded.

"And it's likely you expressed some reaction when the Matacena woman was murdered," Margo tried.

"Oh, yes. I reminded some of the people who were with me on that assignment. We're a small staff; that meant almost everyone in our office."

Margo began scribbling notes and stood to study the clips on the wall. "Everyone at work knew Frances Downs too, so that's when the panic started to set in. That brought it right downtown and applied it to someone who was more than just a neighbor. Am I right to assume you all had seen her at various news events and social functions, maybe had lunch with her a time or two?"

"Yes, that's right."

"So, the big question is whether everyone in your office knows that you were also acquainted with the lawyer, Jerome, or the dentist, McDough. If they did, then you aren't the only one with the terrible secret. Of course, whoever's murdering these people knows of your acquaintances with them, however limited. But who else would? Somebody else where you work, I mean."

"I think no one," Shannon said after a moment. "By the time Mr. Jerome was found murdered, I knew enough not to tell anyone. I may have mentioned him in passing before that, you know, like when his name hit the news for some other reason. I could have told someone at that time that he had helped me out once. But I kept my mouth shut when he was murdered. I was sick of the coincidences by then."

"And nobody mentioned it, nobody asked you? Not even whoever it might have been that you had mentioned his name to before?"

"No."

"I'm still stuck on your date at the wedding, Shannon," Larry said.

"I told you it was Jake."

"But I don't remember your seeing Jake socially."

"Oh, I never did, really. I mean, we didn't actually date at all like Chuck and I used to. In fact, I was kind of coming down off of breaking up with Chuck around that time, and Jake was just doing me a favor. We sat together, that's all. I think we went to dinner once or twice, but you know his divorce hadn't come through yet and it made me feel uncomfortable."

"His divorce has been final for some time now, but you still don't date him, do you?"

"No, I was never really interested in him, and he knew that. Still, when he was officially married I didn't want to be seen socially with him in any formal situations that could look compromising."

"I don't think the guest register from that wedding will be checked for quite some time," Earl said. "But I think we're narrowing the possibilities anyway. We're going to want to get into your relationships with the men at your office some more, but let's cover your reaction to this most recent murder. Who at work knew that McDough was your dentist?"

"I'm not sure, but I know I didn't mention it when it happened. I figured that anyone who happened to know could ask me about it. I wasn't volunteering any information at that point."

"And no one brought it up?"

"Chuck might have. Or Jake, I don't remember. Yes, it was Jake because he asked if that was what was bothering me when he suggested a few weeks off. It was just after that that I saw Larry."

"Let me ask this, and then I've gotta go," I said. "Did you feel that anyone at work grew suspicious of you or acted wary of you when they put together the Ng, Matacena, Pritkin, and Downs murders?"

Shannon thought a moment. "No, I don't think so. There may have been some talk about the coincidences, but then you see, almost everybody there had had as much contact with Matacena, Pritkin, and Downs as I did."

"The question I have," Earl said, sitting again, "is why everyone there isn't a little paranoid. Are news people so egotistical that they think they routinely come into contact with three people who wind up murdered by the same perpetrator? You started getting a sickening feeling pretty quickly, Shannon, and admittedly, you have some connection with *every* victim. But it seems to me everybody in that office ought to be wondering the same things you are. Is it me? Am I the murderer? Or am I the next victim? Or is it one of my co-workers?"

Shannon appeared almost relieved. "I see what you mean," she said. "I don't know if any of them knew all six, like I did, but even knowing half of them is too much of a coincidence, isn't it?"

"You bet it is," Earl said. "Philip, let me see you before you go."

Earl walked me down to the car where we chatted in the cold wind. "By the time you see Wally he could be onto this girl," he said.

"How do you mean *onto* her, Earl? Do you think she's — ?"

"I don't know. Larry is confident of her alibis. We'll check them out more closely later. What I'm saying is that while the three victims everyone else in her office had some contact with will be hard to connect with Shannon or any of the rest of them — except this Downs girl, and they'll all be talked to about that one eventually — Shannon will certainly be linked with Ng and McDough, and when they check to see if she was at the Downs funeral, that will make a pretty stark list. It won't take long for them to find her on Jerome's old client list; that had to be only five or six years ago. And when they ask questions of her co-workers, as you know they will at that point, she's going to be quickly matched with every victim."

"But won't her alibis protect her?"

"From conviction, if they're solid. From publicity? This will ruin her life. We're confident the murderer is someone with something against Shannon and this is either a way to try to frame her — which I doubt — or to scare her to death, or to lead up to her murder. Frankly, I fear the latter, but our first concern is that if Chicago gets onto this soon — and you know they will — we have to continue to protect Shannon."

"Are you saying we won't tell Chicago we've got her out here?"

"You can tell Festschrift, but we're buying his confidence."

"I don't follow."

"Don't tell him anything until her name comes up. You know it will, Philip. It won't take long. He'll check with her boss and learn that she's off for a couple of weeks, and all of a sudden there's an all-points bulletin — "

"And all of a sudden we're harboring a suspect."

"Yeah, unless you tell Wally quickly enough that he can take some heat off. If he can protect her privacy, we'll let him come out here and talk to her. We'll give him everything we've got because we're convinced she can lead to the killer if all the noise doesn't scare him or her off."

"And if Wally doesn't mention her name today or tonight?"

"Then you keep your mouth shut. I'll see you later."

I was supposed to meet Wally Festschrift for lunch at 11:30, and I was running late. I didn't know whether to just head straight for his favorite sit-down burger joint or try to catch him at the precinct house. He often ran late for everything except lunch, but I knew he had the smell of blood in his nostrils on this one and might lose himself in the chase.

Here was his chance to show well again. It had been a couple of years since he broke a big murder case. Every few months he tracked down a tough one, but even he couldn't deny that there was a certain amount of satisfaction — even if he was immune to pride — in seeing your name in the paper as the one whose hunch or unusual insight led to the capture of some particularly horrifying perpetrator of a heinous crime.

He was the best in the business, according to Earl. And Earl should know, because many consider *him* the best. Earl's opinion of Wally is shared by many, including Wally. He admitted it to me once, but I didn't detect an ounce of braggadocio.

"I just flat care," he said. "Just like the card company on TV that says they care enough to do the very best or something like that."

Apparently Wally doesn't watch enough TV to get the commercials down precisely, but it was close enough and I knew what he meant. He was careful. He was tireless. He wanted justice. And his car was in the lot at the station.

It was hard to miss. It looked like a renovated taxicab. It was the shade of green painted only on cars bought in fleets. Blackwalled tires, a city license plate, two whip antennae, a spotlight, a bash here and a ding there. This was the most marked unmarked squad car in the city. It had more than a hundred thousand miles on it, rocked when it stopped, and lurched in the turns. You wore seatbelts, when you could dig them out, more for safety within the car in the normal trips around the city than for any other more ominous possibility. This wasn't a car that would ever be junked. It would be shot.

Of course, Festschrift fit the car. It was his responsibility, so it wasn't as if he were inheriting all those ills. There were things on it that he could have had taken care of and then be reimbursed by the city, but cars weren't his thing. Murders, and more specifically murderers, were his thing.

When I jogged up the steps of the station house, Wally was coming out of a seminar room with a couple of dozen other plainclothes detectives who were pocketing their notepads. Someone was trying to tell him a joke, it appeared, and he was pretending to guffaw — too early, of course — while continuing to scribble notes on the backs of several of his business cards with a stubby pencil.

The jokester turned away, shaking his head as Wally absently slowed to a stop in the middle of the lobby, unknowingly forcing everyone in the area to detour around his massive frame.

His greasy hair, which was either cut very short or was in need of it depending on when you caught him — right now he needed it cut, probably because he'd been putting in fourteen-hour days — hung in strands over his ears. His bald spot was visible as he bowed to make his final note. I stood by the door, waiting for him to notice me on his way out.

He was a sight. His meaty hands stuffed the business cards into his breast pocket wallet, which was then jammed not in his breast pocket — "Can't stand those big things makin' yer jacket hang sideways" — but in his hip pocket. With his big trench coat in a ball under one arm he unbuttoned his green suit jacket, hiked up his pants, and went through contortions to tuck in his white shirt, which was suffering from a bad case of gapsiosis. His tie had to be all of six inches from the loosened knot to the crown of his girth.

Pulling his pants up over his belly exposed his sensible shoes, the type with the huge rubber soles. And of course, white socks, trademarks of the detectives who have been detectives through several decades and never bothered to notice a change in the fashions.

Dragging the trench coat on but making no attempt to button it, the big man finally started moving toward the door. As if he had known I was standing there all along, he threw his arm around me without seeming to even look at me and said, "Philip, my boy, welcome to Chicago Homicide, where we do it right. Wait till I tell you what we just learned from the fancy-schmantzy psychologist."

FIVE

"The regular but make it two," Wally said as we sat at a table in his kind of restaurant.
"One for each?" said the man behind the counter.
"Ah, no," Wally said. "Philip, you want what I'm havin'?"
"Sure, why not?"
"OK, Julio, make that three regulars."
Wally peeled off both his topcoat and his suitjacket and piled them on one of the empty chairs. "Very interesting," he said. "Really. Here, let me show you. I love this psychology stuff, I really do. I think if that poor Dr. Shrink woman ever saw a murder scene she'd be packin' for Podunk, but she does seem to know her stuff, and some of my own research bears her out."

Wally waited to see if I thought that sounded funny. It did, but I wasn't going to laugh at him. When I didn't, he did. "I'm dead serious," he said with a twinkle, and I knew he was.

He dug into his hip pocket for the wallet, almost having to stand to get to it, and produced the batch of cards on which he had recorded an hour's lecture on the potential characteristics of the Thank-You Shooter based on the computerized evidence Homicide had presented to the psychologists.

"Look at this," he began, leaning forward and showing me the back of one of the cards. I wouldn't have been able to read one word of it if my life depended on it, but I nodded as if I was following his finger. "She says they're pretty sure this murderer is actually committing mass suicide, killing his or her own personality or alter ego."

I cocked my head, not knowing what I thought of that and certainly not knowing what Wally thought of it.

"Either way, it's interesting, isn't it?" he said.

"Yeah, I'll grant you that. But how did they come up with that?"

"Well, you know we've been interviewing everyone connected with all the victims, except this dentist, of course, 'cause that just happened and we're still tryin' to get a bead on everyone in his sphere. I like that word *sphere,* don't you?"

I nodded. It wasn't one of my favorites, but I was willing to like whatever Wally liked.

"It makes me sound like a shrink, doesn't it?"

I nodded again.

"But what I'm gettin' at," he continued, "or what she was gettin' at anyway, and I tend to agree with her, is that there is indeed a pattern with these victims." I nearly jumped, but it wasn't what I had thought. "I mean, we still don't know if the murderer is male or female. Lots of us have different views on that."

"What's yours?"

"It's irrelevant at this point, Philip," he said. "Which is a nice way of saying that I don't have the foggiest and I'm not sure it would help me if I did. Yet, that is. Knowing the sex of the murderer will become very important as we start closing the net, of course, because you'll cut off half your prospects — which is a nice trim if you can get it, know what I mean?"

I wasn't sure, but I nodded anyway. And our food was delivered. Mercy. His regular was a half-pound burger and a mountain of cottage fries with a Coke in a milk shake tin. He had two of everything. One of each was going to be more than enough for me, yet he would finish first, even while carrying the bulk of the conversation (no pun intended).

"The point is this," he said, depositing a quarter of the burger into one cheek as if storing it for the winter — amazingly, it didn't affect his coherence in the least; it was as if his mouth was still empty — "a pattern of types among the victims is important in getting a bead on the murderer, right?"

"Sure." I wasn't, but it sounded good.

"OK, I don't mind tellin' ya, this case has had me buffaloed for a long time. It drives me nuts that this guy, or girl, or whatever, is still out there when there are such loud clues being left at each scene. I know the guy — and let me call him or her that for the sake of briefery or whatever they call it — is going to make a mistake one of these times and give himself away, but see my goal is to nail him *before* the next one, not after. We just can't let another murder happen. I was hurt bad by this dentist buyin' it because even though we didn't have much of a lead on the killer, I thought we were making enough racket that we could scare him off for a while. Apparently I was wrong, and it's gonna take more than what we had to either flush him out or keep him down for a while. If we can just keep him quiet for a while, we can get him without his killing anyone else. I got some associates who want him to kill a few more people just so we'll maybe get more clues. That's sick. Don't you agree that's sick?"

That was not hard to agree with at all. I was getting a little impatient. "So, what's the pattern among the victims? Whatever it is, it hasn't come out in what we read in the papers, because we can't seem to put anything together." I wasn't lying. We hadn't put Shannon together with the victims. Shannon had. From our studying, we had drawn a blank.

"Oh, and I just know ol' Earl is a-studyin' those clippings, even though he knows better. We're not giving the papers everything we've got, though I must admit we don't have much more than you read. But I never knew of anyone solving a murder by reading the papers."

Wally had downed one of the Cokes and a burger and was polishing off the last of the first mess of fries. He didn't appear to be slowing down. "There *is* a common denominator among these victims," he said. I knew that, but I hadn't thought he did. Luckily, his was different from mine.

"Let me give you some basics of what we've found and see if you don't come to the same conclusions," he said. "I'll take them in order: Ng, Matacena, Pritkin, Jerome, Downs, and McDough." He did that without notes. The details of this case had long since been burned into this brain. He noticed my awe of that recital. "I haven't been on another case since the second murder," he said.

"Now, with Ng, he's one of these quiet types. Doesn't have trouble with the language, but is still shy, almost as if he does. He's detail-oriented, an organizer, a super athlete type. Likes to get the kids of the neighborhood involved in the Park District programs. But here's the thing that sets him apart, aside from being kind of a shy loner. Nobody really knows him well. He keeps to himself basically, at least in relation to adults. Never dates. Was never married. But spends lots of time with kids.

"Never brings them home. His landlady said she never saw any kids at his place, but said he seemed to work long hours. His boss attested to that. He was salaried, no overtime pay, but worked long days. Maybe because he had nothing and no one else. But anyway, his boss also said that in spite of his modest salary, he had kids in programs who couldn't pay the fees and somehow the fees got paid. The boss knew Lawson was paying. Now what does that tell you?"

Wally took me by surprise. I wasn't sure it told me anything. I was enjoying hearing him wrap up the information he had gathered. "I didn't know there was gonna be a test," I said, smiling weakly.

"Well, there is. What does that tell you? What do you know about Ng based on what I told you? We've gotta know the victims if we're ever gonna know the culprit."

He took a long drink of his remaining Coke, somehow never taking his eyes off me. I felt as if I were on the hotseat. I would hate to be a suspect he's interrogating. "He's a nice guy," I tried, "a loner. Organized?"

"C'mon," he said. "You can do better'n that. Anybody can figure that out. His friends and neighbors knew that before he got snuffed. What do you know about him that's not so much on the surface, something we might put together with another victim that would make a pattern?"

"He's apparently sympathetic to the down-and-outers," I said.

"That's it!" he said, using his burger bun to sop up the catsup from his fries. "It ain't big, I'll admit, but keep that in your head as you hear about the rest of the victims." He stood heavily and peeled a ten from his wallet and began the process of putting those coats back on. He pressed the receipt into his shirt pocket as we left and loudly bid farewell to every non-customer in the place. They all smiled their blank, uncomprehending smiles in wonder at the man who ate big, tipped big, and always ordered the same. They didn't understand much of his English, but they liked him and he liked them and that was what feeding Americans, or anyone, was all about.

"Good place, huh?" he said, squeezing behind the wheel of the Festschriftmobile.

I was stuffed, almost sore. "Yeah," I managed. "Good place. Thanks."

"Thank the City of Chicago, brother. I'm on duty and you're, what does Earl call it, an intern?"

"Yeah."

"Yeah, an intern. Sounds good. Anyway, you wanna hear about victim number two?"

"Sure."

" 'Course ya do. Annamarie Matacena," he announced in an Italian dialect. "Another quiet foreigner. At work she keeps to herself. She's quiet. To her, language *is* a barrier. She's a sad woman with a tough life. She's never gotten over her divorce, and money is always tight. She makes so little that her food and rent is subsidized. She's a hard worker, not lazy. Not quick or ambitious, but a selfstarter, never in the way but always there when you need her. What would you guess she's like at home?"

"Same way, just like Ng," I said, wondering why Wally always spoke of the victims in the present tense, as if they were still alive.

"Not a bad guess. It was my guess too. If you get any comfort out of being just as wrong as the best homicide cop in the city, welcome. Even though this woman is fifty-one years old, she's got a daughter and two grandkids living with her, plus a couple of more grandkids from a no-good son who ran out on his wife. Are you ready for this? She also takes care of a couple of Mexican kids in the neighborhood.

"Now, Philip, it's one thing for a woman with an ethnic background that is big in family relationships to take care of her own and be embarrassed by divorce and a son gone bad, but to take in other kids, not her own and not even her own nationality. What have we got here?"

"Another Ng?"

"You got it. The woman cares about the down-and-outer. She's got nothing to live on, but she's got plenty of company helping her live on it. But the quiet, out-of-the-way, keep-to-herself type at home? Nope. We were both wrong on that. She was loud, an intruder in neighborhood politics. She screamed at her family, all of 'em, her own and the borrowed ones. They fought long and hard and at the top of their lungs, but they were fiercely loyal to each other and watched out for each other."

"So, Ng and Matacena are sympathetic to the underprivileged," I said. "And Matacena is underprivileged herself. What does that tell you?"

"I'm the teacher here, kid. And it doesn't tell us anything yet. Let's talk about the third victim, the preacher. Beautiful family. Beloved guy by the congregation. Not all preachers can say that, ya know. Anyway, if he had a fault, it was that he went above and beyond the call of duty. I know these guys are supposed to have a higher calling anyway, and you might think that because he was golfing on his day off — that Monday — that he was a typical suburban pastor, kinda affluent, a country club type. Fact is, he was a duffer. Had only taken up golf in the past few months. Used second-hand shoes, borrowed clubs. His wife said he rarely took his whole day off. He might shoot a round of golf or go fishing, but he liked to be home when the kids got home from school so he could play with them in the yard or go bike riding or something. But Monday nights he was downtown doing volunteer work with the Salvation Army. Can you beat that?"

"That *is* hard to believe. Puts him in the sympathetic category again, doesn't it?"

"So why is someone killing off nice guys, especially in light of what the shrink told us today? Is the murderer a nice guy who doesn't want to be? Maybe he'd rather speak his mind, stick up for himself, do something for himself once, but he's weak. He hates the nice guy in him because the nice guy isn't nice at all. He just gets walked on. He does what people ask."

"Interesting."

"Uh-huh." Wally fell silent, carefully picking his way through Loop traffic on his way to South LaSalle Street. Cabs and small trucks that attempted to cut him off didn't get far, and when they got a good look at the car they backed off. At a city-owned parking garage that would have charged the price of our lunch to park for more than an hour, he wiggled from behind the wheel, deftly flashed his badge, and we headed down the street to a tall office building.

He mashed a button on the elevator and said, "I live with these victims every day, Philip. I mean I know them better now than I would've if I'd been their friend. It's because I know everyone who knew them. I know who liked 'em, who didn't, who they liked and who they didn't, who they worked for and who worked for them. Friends don't have that kinda perspective, but I do. I know when they got up in the morning and when they went to bed at night. I think about 'em, eat with 'em, dream about 'em."

"Don't you ever get tired of it?"

"Tired of them, maybe, but not tired of *it*, because *it* is all there is. *It* is what I am, kid. *It* is the search, the trail, the puzzle, the game. My boss doesn't like to hear me call it a game, and somehow, now that I'm older and more mature than when I was givin' your boss fits, I know what he means. When it's the murderer of some scum bag or socialite who never gave a care for anyone else anyway, only the justice and the mystery keep me going, because regardless of the quality of the life that was taken, it shouldn't have been taken, and it's my job to deliver the guilty party to the people. But when it's a mass murder of decent people and when the poor sucker pulling these jobs is leaving us clues and begging us to catch him, then I gotta agree, it's more than a game. And, no, I never get tired of it."

We exited left off the elevator and padded down a dimly-lit, carpeted hallway past a security guard who hardly looked at Festschrift's badge. We entered a huge mahogany door with a half dozen names painted in gold on it and found ourselves in a waiting room with three couches and several large wing chairs. The receptionist sat behind a great dark desk that would have been appropriate in a corporation president's office.

"Chicago Homicide," Festschrift said softly. "We'd like to talk with the secretary to the late Mr. Jerome."

"Hello, Sergeant," the receptionist said. "You're aware, I assume, that you're not the first to see Miss Severinsen this week — in fact you're the fifth or sixth, and I know you've been here a couple of times before."

"Oh, yeah?" Festschrift said, unimpressed. "Is she complaining about that, or are you the only one around here who doesn't care if we find out who did it?"

It was cold, but it was beautiful, and the receptionist pushed a button. "Miss Severinsen?"

"Yes?"

"A policeman is here to see you."

As she escorted us back to the inner office, the receptionist said, "I know you've got your job to do, but I can't imagine there's any more the poor woman can tell you. You just caught her, you know. Within the hour she'll be cleared out. She's leaving."

"Oh?"

"Yes, the gentleman who's replacing Mr. Jerome brought his own secretary and, rather than take another position with us, Miss Severinsen is moving to another firm."

The slender, graying, middle-aged secretary was teary-eyed as we entered. Festschrift introduced me as his associate. She was taping the top of a box, but she offered us chairs and then sat down herself. "Is there anything I can tell you today that I didn't tell you last time, Sergeant?" she said, not unkindly.

"Probably not," Wally said, more compassionately than I had ever heard him. In spite of his appearance, he could be gracious when he wanted to. All as a means to an end, admittedly, but then again, perhaps there was more real sympathy in there than I thought. "I know this is terribly difficult for you and that you were very close to Mr. Jerome. Basically I just wanted to come by and wish you the best in your new job and to tell you that I would be thinking of you and hoping that it will in some small way help take your mind off this difficult memory."

Miss Severinsen dabbed at her eyes. "Well, thank you so much. I'm looking forward to it, under the circumstances."

There was an awkward silence as she apparently wondered if that were really all Festschrift had come for. "You could do me one little favor," he said finally, and I detected a slight stiffening in her. "It might be the easiest question I've ever asked you about Mr. Jerome." She appeared willing to hear the question at least, but she said nothing. "You've told me that he was basically a wonderful guy and that he was excellent at his profession. But could you tell me anything else that would help me get a picture of his personality, something in the area of selflessness or helping the little guy. Everybody knows these high-powered lawyers have lots of money and influence, so it's kind of easy for them to appear gracious and humanitarian. But I get the impression from you that he was genuine in his concern for the down-and-outer."

"Well, maybe not the real down-and-outer, because, as you may know, there isn't too much that a lawyer of Mr. Jerome's stature can do for a truly disadvantaged person, but yes, there were people he helped who couldn't afford to pay him at the level he had become accustomed to. It wasn't unusual for one of his big clients to ask him to represent one of their employees, for instance, someone involved in a small civil suit or even a real estate deal. He handled those for just a few hundred dollars. Of course, a very good lawyer like Mr. Jerome rarely had any trouble winning such cases for the clients, and he was always glad to do it on his own time."

Festschrift looked over at me knowingly. His point had been proved. Another champion of the people. But he didn't know what I knew, and that gave me a delicious, albeit guilty, feeling.

Six

Back in the car, Festschrift radioed in that we were back on the street:

"Oh-nine-six-H to central."

"Central, go ahead six-H."

"I'm ten-eight in the Loop."

And received word that he was to call his office:

"Ten-four, six-H. Oh, six-H?"

"Yeah."

"I've got a ten-twenty-one from your office here for you."

As soon as he was out of the worst of the traffic, Wally shot down a side street and headed for a pay phone. "Might be something good if they don't wanna tell me over the box."

While he was on the phone the dispatcher called for him again. "Oh-nine-six-H." I didn't know whether to answer for him or not. I waited.

"Central to oh-nine-six-H," came the call again.

I grabbed the mike. "Oh-nine-six-H is, uh, he's uh, he's on the phone."

"Ah, ten-four. Advise six-H to change that previous message to a ten-twenty-two."

"OK. I mean, ten-four."

He was mad when he returned to the car. "I told you to come in, not call in, Sergeant," he mimicked his lieutenant. "How am I supposed to know? The dispatcher says call, I call. It wasn't my fault the dispatcher got it wrong."

"The dispatcher called while you were on the phone and changed the message from a twenty-one to a twenty-two."

"Beautiful," he said, screeching away from the curb. "Now it's so hot the junior deputy in blue has to tell me in person and not even on the telephone. It better be good."

In the five minutes it took us to wend our way through the midafternoon rush to the Homicide Detail headquarters, Wally cooled down enough to resume his rundown of the victims and how he felt they tied together. "Victim number five is this TV producer gal, Frances Downs. And you know what she's known for?"

"You mean other than television?"

"No, I mean television."

"Yeah, I know she's in TV and known for that. Does good work and all that, has won a few awards, local and national."

"C'mon, specifics, Philip. What's her bag in television, and if you tell me producing or some other such obvious baloney I'm gonna take a hard left and open your door."

I got the feeling I was taking the heat he'd like to have given his lieutenant, a man more than ten years his junior. "Ah, you mean what kinda programs."

"You got it. What kinda programs is she known for?"

"I dunno."

Festschrift rolled his eyes and shrugged. "I bet you can guess."

"Programs spotlighting the down-and-outers?"

"Praise be. A shiny star for you. Frances Downs likes to produce shows that emphasize the plight and the accomplishments of the poor, ethnic, underprivileged in Chicago. She's — "

"Central to oh-nine-six-H, did you get that ten-twenty-two?" the radio interrupted. Wally angrily grabbed the mike and depressed the button.

"Yes, sir, Mister Dispatcher. Mister zee-ro-ninety-six Homicide is just now ten-sixin' at Homicide HQ, ten-four?"

"Ten-four, six-H," the dispatcher said timidly. "Sorry, Wally."

"You'd better wait here," Wally said. "I shouldn't be long."

I trotted to a pay phone at the corner. "Hi, Bonnie, let me talk to Earl.... Hi, Earl, it's Philip.... Good, listen, all Wally seems to have at this point are some interesting characteristics about each of the victims that might tie them together somewhat, things like the fact that all appear to have had a soft spot for the underprivileged. They were selfless types, and Wally is trying to make that fit with something he heard from a police-appointed psychologist who believes that the murderer is someone who is, in effect, killing himself over and over. Maybe someone who's nice but wishes he weren't."

"Is Wally convinced the perpetrator is male?"

"No, he doesn't know yet."

"And he's not onto Shannon yet?"

"Could be. He just got called into his headquarters. What do you want me to do if that's the news?"

"Hold off telling him for a while. If they think she's a prime suspect, they'll probably not want to scare her off. Let him discover that she's not working and not at home and then see what he wants to do. If he recommends an all-points bulletin, that will blow the secrecy and all the cops will know, and you know what that means."

"That the media will know too, and then the whole town."

"Right. And the more we talk to her here, the more convinced I am that she's not involved in the murders. She's a little weak on her memory of some of the murder dates, but I'm still banking on my judgment of character. I've been fooled before, but if this girl is a mass murderer, I'm the Easter Bunny."

"Here comes Wally. So, what do you want me to do if he says anything about an all-points bulletin? Quick."

"Tell him we've got her, but swear him to secrecy first. Don't mess it up. It won't be easy, but don't mess it up."

"Gotta go."

I tried to read Wally's walk as he headed for the car, tucking a document into his coat. When we were both in the car he put the key in the ignition but didn't start it up. "Bingo," he said softly, giving me a tight-lipped smile. "Persistence and modern technology pay off."

"Oh?" I said, trying not to betray nervousness.

"We've got a woman who's linked to three of the victims."

"Really? Who?"

"She lives on the same block as Ng, and if I'da been on the case that early, I'd have questioned her myself. I didn't talk to neighbors when we started the double-checking after the second murder. I just questioned his landlady and his boss."

I tried to steady my breathing.

"Anyway, her name came up on the client list of the dentist, McDough, which they just ran through the computer this morning. It was quite a list, and get this, you know *why* it was quite a list?"

I wasn't listening. "Huh? No, why?"

"Because the guy has two offices. One within walking distance of his Marina City Tower condo, and the other on the south side. Philip, it's a free clinic."

"Uh-huh."

"Uh-huh is all you can say? We've got a downtown dentist here who can afford a condo at Marina City, and he runs a charity clinic on the side. Does it fit? Has Wally put a team together?"

"Yeah, I guess."

"The problem is, Philip, that the lists don't often help. Here I've got a warrant for the arrest of a girl who lives in the neighborhood of the first victim and is a client of the last, and the mother of the second to last recognized the name when my boss called her. Mrs. Downs said, yes, this woman was an acquaintance, that she remembered the name and believes she was at the funeral. So what does my list mean? What do all these interesting characteristics mean? We don't know. Because we don't know anything about, um — " he dug the warrant out of his pocket "Shannon Perry."

I said nothing.

He looked at his watch. "Still time to catch her at work," he said. "She's at some two-bit FM station in the Loop." And he started the car.

While he was busy driving, I mustered the breath to speak casually. "It sounds like a real break," I said. "But could it be coincidence?"

"Oh, highly unlikely. Three outa six ain't bad. I gotta admit I'd like something a little more solid on her relationship with each of these, but my boss has people on that right now. Living in the same block as a dead guy is no crime, and neither is happening to know someone in your profession. Goin' to the dentist seems like a crime, but in and of itself, it's not incriminating. Point is, a judge thinks three times is the charm, and I hafta agree. Don't you?"

My mind was racing.

"Philip?"

"Yeah, I guess. Sure."

"You thought it would be more exciting than this, did you? Sometimes this is all there is. You search and search and then a few things cross-match and all of a sudden you've got prime suspect number one. I wish I could say it was something I did, but if this is right and we get a killer off the streets, hey, what more can we ask for, huh?"

He grabbed the mike as an afterthought and informed central that 096 Homicide was ten-eight in the Loop. "You know how wet behind the ears my boss is?" he said gleefully, as if he could hardly contain himself now that he had a good suspect.

"No."

"My badge number is oh-nine-six, right? His has four digits!" And he roared.

I expected him to leap from the car when we cruised up to a small cubbyhole of an entrance that read *WMTR-FM, Metro Radio, Chicago* on its glass door. But he parked a few doors down and turned off the engine. "I wanna do this without scarin' anybody off or giving myself away as a cop. If she's not here, there's no sense everybody in there knowing that we're after her."

"You want me to ask for her? I can do it innocently enough."

"But can you get her to come with you?"

"Yeah, I'll tell her her car lights are on."

"How do you know her car is here? Where do they park?"

"I dunno."

"Forget it. What if she doesn't drive? Then she'll be suspicious and we'll lose her."

He turned the ignition switch far enough to keep the radio on. "Oh-nine-six-H is ten-six in the Loop."

"Ten-four."

"Sit tight, Philip."

A few minutes later Wally was back with the news that Miss Perry had taken a couple of weeks off. "That's not good news," he said, "but I didn't press for details because I didn't even want them to know why I was asking. The receptionist asked if I wanted to talk to her boss, but I said no. We've got her home address here."

He spread the warrant out in front of him. "It's way up on the north side, almost into Evanston. I think I'm gonna make one more stop before we go," he said. "Wanna try the radio?"

"Sure," I said, feeling more deceitful by the minute. I hoped Earl and Larry and Margo were taking advantage of every precious minute I was stalling for and were getting enough information to help clear Shannon.

"Tell the dispatcher that I'm back in the car and enroute to South LaSalle Street where I'll be out of the car for a few minutes again. And do it all by the book."

"Where we going, Wally?"

"Where do you think? As long as we've got a minute, I want to see if we can find a link between this Perry woman and Dale Jerome."

My heart sank. "Oh-nine-six-H to central," I said.

"Central, go ahead."

"We're ten-eight and enroute to South LaSalle where we'll be ten-six."

"Ten-four, six-H."

Wally clapped me on the shoulder in mock congratulations for a job well done on the radio, but I couldn't get enthusiastic. Lying by omission made me uncomfortable. Here I had hoped there'd be a lull in the investigation so I could raise some of the issues he and I had discussed during our last case. I wanted to know what Earl and he had talked about and what he thought of what Earl had to say. But Wally had been strangely silent about anything spiritual this time. It would have been natural for it to come up. The previous time, he had raised the question. And he had to know that Earl told us of their talks.

But then Wally was so immersed in this case, and now that it seemed to be breaking for him, it appeared there would be no time to talk of anything but leads and suspects. I knew that even when he discovered that Shannon wasn't the prime suspect he thought she was, he would still consider it the biggest break of the case, because if she wasn't guilty, she had to be the reason someone was murdering these people.

As we parked near the law offices, Wally got a message to phone his office again. "Good grief, soldier blue is impatient today," he whined. "He wants to know what's happening every step of the way. He's gonna want to know if I picked up the Perry girl and if so, why am I going somewhere else before I bring her in. Dumb."

In the lobby of the office building, Wally made his call. I could hear his condescending tone from a few feet away. "If I had picked up the girl, I'd be delivering her right now — sir. She's not at work, and she lives all the way up almost to Wisconsin. . . . No, I'm exaggerating. She's on the far north side, just south of Howard Street. But I wanna see if I can link her with Jerome before I make the trip. . . . Yes, I'll be making the trip anyway, but don't you think a fourth link would nail the lid on this coffin? . . . Yes, sir. Yes, sir. I will."

He slammed the phone down. "He told me to get going up north immediately." He stood thinking for a moment. "I can't. I just can't. Let's go."

He quickly shuffled to the elevator, and when we emerged he actually got ahead of me in the hall. "Miss Severinsen is gone," the receptionist said. "Home, I presume."

"Where is that?"

"Park Ridge."

"I haven't got time to go to Park Ridge. Can I see Jerome's files?"

"Well, I don't know, I — "

"I can get a warrant. Make this easy, huh?"

"Let me talk to Mr. Norris."

"No, let *me* talk to him. Get 'im out here."

When an irate-looking Mr. Norris emerged, Festschrift showed his badge and led him to a quiet corner. "I hate to cause you any trouble, sir, but I need access to Mr. Jerome's files right now. I'm sure you want the murderer caught as much as any of us do, and we have reason to believe it could have been one of his clients."

Without a word, Mr. Norris led Wally and me back to Jerome's empty office and unlocked six file cabinets. "Have at it," he said. "Need any help?"

"No, and thanks. We'll let you know when we leave."

"Philip, look up Perry, and I'll check under the call letters of the radio station."

I raced quickly through and found nothing, then stepped quickly over to the file for Field Enterprises, owners of the *Sun-Times* and the now defunct *Daily News*. Wally was just slamming his file drawer shut when I found the name, "Perry, S., auto, civil suit, see auxiliary file." He was walking over.

I straightened up and shut the drawer. "Nothing," I said, feeling rotten.

"Shoot," he said in a hiss, jamming his hands into his pockets. He paced the room for a few seconds, then headed toward Mr. Norris's door. He knocked and entered and I followed. It was obvious we had interrupted a client consultation. "I'm sorry," Wally said.

"No problem," Norris said. "Excuse me just a moment." He stepped outside. "Find what you need?"

"No. Would Jerome have had any other files, like on cases he did on his own time and not for your firm?"

"His secretary would have taken those. She's the executor of his will."

"I need to see those. Would you be able to release her phone number?"

"Certainly."

He led Wally and me back out to the receptionist, where he instructed her to find Miss Severinsen's number. She pursed her lips and hesitated, whereupon Mr. Norris quietly said, "Right now."

"And may I use your phone?" Wally asked her. Her anger was obvious.

"Yes, you may," Norris said firmly. "Why don't you take a little break, Margaret." She stomped off. "Just dial nine, Sergeant," Norris said.

Festschrift explained his urgent need to Miss Severinsen and asked her to check the files for Shannon Perry and to call his dispatcher with a message of simply either positive or negative and it would be relayed to him. "Thanks a million. I'll let you know how this turns out, and please don't mention anything about this to anyone."

Sergeant Walvoord F. Festschrift was psyched. I could have enjoyed it, and him, if I didn't feel so lousy about leading him on this wild goose chase. He was gathering information he would eventually need, but I could have saved him all the effort. We weren't far north of the Loop when the dispatcher radioed that Wally's lieutenant had been trying to get hold of him and that he was to call in as soon as possible. Wally jumped on the mike. "Tell Lieutenant Merrill oh-nine-six is enroute to the north side and that if he needs to talk to me about anything else, I'm here."

Apparently that was all the pesky lieutenant had wanted. We were near the Hollywood exit off Lake Shore Drive when another message came over the radio. "Central to oh-nine-six-H."

"Go ahead, central."

"You were expecting a message from a Miss Severinsen?"

"Ten-four."

"Message follows: positive."

Wally looked over at me and extended his fat hand for slap. I gave him five and wished I could die.

S E V E N

When Wally made his first pass of Shannon's two-story apartment building — hers was the upstairs flat — he asked me to jot down the license number of the car parked at the curb. Then he pulled around the corner out of sight of her building and shifted into park.

"Oh-nine-six-H to central," he said.

"Central, go."

"I need a ten-twenty-eight on Illinois plate JE nine nine two eight."

"Stand by, six-H."

I was in no mood to talk as we waited. Wally didn't want conversation either, but he did talk to himself. "Four out of six, whew! Wonder how she hooks up with Matacena and Pritkin. She wouldn't have wasted her own pastor, though she *did* blow away her dentist. Hmph. You wouldn't put a woman together with this MO, would you?"

He wasn't asking me, so I didn't answer.

"Maybe she's a big girl," he said. He looked at his watch and then around the neighborhood. "Nobody at the windows as far as I can tell." He sniffed. The man was a terrible waiter. So was I. I jumped when the radio crackled.

"Central to six-H."

"Yeah, gimme it."

"Your ten-twenty-eight on JE nine nine two eight. Registered to a blue/grey 'eighty-one Ford Granada two-door hardtop. Owner Perry, Shannon, no middle name, born nine-nine-'fifty-six, female, white, seventy-five fifty-five North Hoyne Street, Chicago six-oh-six-four-five. Five-foot-five, one hundred fifteen pounds, brown hair, blue eyes, no restrictions, no violations, not reported stolen."

Wally thanked the dispatcher and told me to be ready to run around to the back entrance, "in case she meets us as we come up the walk and decides to make a run." I nodded, knowing we were opening an empty package.

As we left the car, he pointed down an alley that led to the rear. We buzzed her from the first floor. When he got no response, he said, "You'd better scoot around back," but before I could, the landlord poked his head out of his first-floor flat. "Can you let me upstairs fast?" Wally said, producing his badge.

"She ain't up there," the man said. "Hasn't been around since Sunday night when she stopped in to get her things and then left with a scruffy lookin' young guy in a little yellow car."

"You know him?"

"Nope. Never saw him before. Looked like a construction worker or somethin'. Dressed that way anyway. None too big. You don't got trouble with her, do ya, Captain? My guess is yer after the guy. He's a drifter, ain't he?"

"Yeah, something like that. Listen, you hear from her or see either one of 'em, you call me at this number, huh?"

"Right, Captain."

Wally looked dejected trudging back to the car. He swore. "Somethin's goin' down," he said. "At least my boss can't tell me I would have had her if I hadn't taken the time to visit Jerome's office. I'm not looking forward to this call."

"This call?"

"I gotta tell Merrill that she's blown."

He went around to his side of the car, and I asked him over the top, "What happens then?"

"He puts out an APB and she becomes an instant fugitive. She'll be much harder to find this way, I can tell you that."

"I can't let you do that," I said as he opened his door.

He had started to climb in the car, but now he straightened up, his hand on the open door. "You can't let me do what?"

"Have them put out an APB on Shannon Perry."

His face screwed itself into the most puzzled expression he could muster and he cocked his head. With half a laugh he managed, "Wha — ?"

"I know where she is," I said, wondering if he was going to go for his gun and drop me where I stood.

He was speechless. He squinted at me. "I've never thought much of your sense of humor, Spence," he said. "But you had better not be serious."

"I'm serious, Wally. I know where Shannon Perry is."

His wheels were turning. "Does Earl have her?"

"Yes, sir."

Wally took one step back and slammed his door so hard that it bounced back open and hit him. He kicked it shut on the rebound and something metallic broke loose. He spun in a circle and brought both fists crashing down on top of the car. I stood there, letting his eyes burn through me, hoping his wrath would somehow vindicate me.

"I'm sorry I deceived you, Wally."

He couldn't talk. He just shook his head and stalked off down the sidewalk, once turning back as if to say something but deciding not to. He cursed in a loud, raspy whisper, and as he stomped along, his trench coat flailed in the breeze behind him. I moved to follow him.

"Get away from me!" he yelled over his shoulder.

"Hadn't you better call in?" I said.

"Get away!"

"Wally, they're going to send help up here if they don't hear from you, aren't they?"

"And what am I supposed to call in?" he demanded, stopping and turning around, hands on his hips.

I looked down.

He came back, closing the gap between us and shoving his red, sweating face next to mine. The veins in his forehead and neck were bulging. He whispered, "Huh? What am I supposed to call in?" He swore again. "Am I supposed to tell them that my partner, my unofficial in-, uh, in-, intern or whatever you call yourself and my old friend from the division have been harboring the prime suspect in a mass murder case?"

He was about to explode. I didn't know what to say. Telling him I thought we could prove she was as innocent a victim as the deceased would have only set him off more. He had my lapel in his fist.

"Let me explain," I said.

"Oh, you'll explain all right," he snarled. "But let me tell you something first. I don't much care how this shakes down, but I wanna impress on your brain what it means to give your life for something. We're talking about total devotion here, Spence. Oh, yeah, I've told you about the fun of this job, but you've also seen some of the drudgery. And you've only seen the tip of the iceberg. Do you have any idea how many personal, one-on-one interviews I've conducted since Friday, September third, when Annamarie Matacena was found with her brains blown out? Of course you don't. Nobody does.

"And can you imagine how I felt September sixth and September twenty-second and

October sixteenth and then last Thursday? I'm out here from the time I get up in the morning until the time I crash into the rack around midnight every night, seven days a week, and I don't sleep too good because with all the work I been doin', I'm not gettin' any closer to the murderer. I can feel it when I get closer, and I haven't been. Until now, all I had was a list of nice-guy victims and a psychologist tellin' me it's really a mass suicide. Well, lead me to the suicidal murderer so I can help her finish the job.

"I don't know how this Perry woman fell into your laps, but you can bet it wasn't because you been poundin' the streets for two months!" Festschrift released his grip, took two long strides to my side of the car, and kicked a huge dent in the door. "Today was a typical day, Spence," he said, still shaking his head. "Interviews in the morning, then a seminar with the psychologist, a fast lunch, then downtown, back to see the boss, over to the radio station, back to the lawyer's office, then up here. This is what it's like. You see why I dream about breaks like these? Do you?"

I nodded, but it didn't slow him down. "You let me go to that radio station and all the way up here? You probably knew there was a connection with Jerome, too." I nodded dejectedly, almost feeling as if I should admit that I saw her name in Jerome's files at the downtown office. I resisted the urge.

Festschrift was puffing and sweating and I feared for his health. He went around to the driver's side and opened the back door. He shed both coats and flung them in the backseat, slammed the door, wrenched the front open, and slid behind the wheel. He had started the car and shifted into drive before I realized I was still standing outside the car. I jumped in as he pulled away, but I found it difficult to even look at him.

"Central to oh-nine-six-H, come in, please," came the urgent sound of the dispatcher.

"Yeah, I'm here."

"You need assistance, six-H?"

"Negative."

"Your office requests immediate status report."

"I'll ten-twenty-one 'im, ten-four?"

"Negative, six-H. Lieutenant Merrill is right here."

A new voice came on. "Yeah, Festschrift, what do you think you're doing up there? Have you got the subject or not? You need help? What's the story?"

"Negative. Suspect has been located. Can you meet me in Glencoe?"

"Glencoe?"

I put my hand on Festschrift's arm. "You can't bring your boss to see her," I said.

"Stand by, sir," Festschrift said. "I'll be right back to you."

He slammed on the brakes, sending us both into the dash. Throwing the mike on the floor, making the spring cord bounce and dangle, he pushed his meaty index finger near my nose. "Listen, Philip, that's enough. I'm gonna do anything I please and if you or your boss or anybody up there interferes with the apprehension of this suspect, I'll bust every one of you for harboring a class-X felony suspect and obstructing justice. You got that?"

He was trembling. So was I. I nodded. "Can you at least ask him to come alone?"

"I don't care if he brings the national guard."

"Festschrift, get back on the blower!" Merrill was shouting.

"I'm back," Wally said. "Let me give you an address where you can meet me and have access to the subject."

"You're sure the subject will be there?"

Wally looked to me. I nodded.

"Affirmative. One more thing, sir. Come alone."

"Come again?"

"Come alone."

There was a pause, then a resigned voice. "Ten-four, Wally. This had better be good."

We were about twenty minutes from Earl's office, and Wally knew it would take Lieutenant Merrill another forty-five minutes from the Loop, at this time of day, so he pulled off the road. "I don't want to get there before Merrill does. I'm not sure what I'd say to Earl."

"You know Earl's got an explanation."

"Oh, sure, and I can't wait to hear it."

"Can I call him?"

"Oh, I'm sure! Not on your life."

It was still hard to face Wally. He looked out his window and I looked out mine. Darkness was falling fast as we sat and listened to the static traffic on the Motorola. With nothing to say I was able to concentrate for the first time on the stench in that car. *Years and years worth of drunks and cigarette butts,* I thought. *Not to mention your basic grime.* Then it hit me. "Hey, Wally, you've quit smoking!"

He turned slowly to get a full look at the idiot who would think of something like that at a time like this. "Yes," he said patronizingly, "I did."

"Well, that's good. I think that's good. Don't you think that's good?"

"Yes, it's good."

"I mean, you feel better, don't you?"

"Yes, I feel better. Thank you."

"Well, good. You're welcome. I mean, good." I slapped my knees and looked out the window into the night.

"Hey, Wally?"

After a pause, "Yes?"

"You're not mad, are you?"

His laugh started deep in his belly and shook him from head to toe. It came out first as a low wheeze and grew to a great roar, culminating in a series of shrill, falsetto hoots I thought would wake the dead. He buried his face in his hands and continued to bounce long after the sound had died away. As my remark continued to work on him he would laugh anew, muffling it in his palms. He laughed until he cried and the tears poured through his fingers, and I wasn't sure he was crying from laughing or crying because of the emotional investment he had spent on me, getting off his chest the frustration of this most taxing task.

For the next several minutes, as he wiped the tears away, little bursts of laughter would squeak out against his will, and he would shake his head and look at me and laugh some more.

"You're gonna drain me of all the wrath I was saving for Earl," he managed.

"You *saved* some?" I said, and he burst into laughter again.

After a while he looked at his watch and slowly pulled away. "We'll have the residents calling the cops on us soon," he said.

"Can I tell you what we're doing with your prime suspect at our place?" I said.

"Yeah. Give me a head start. Why should I have any more surprises today?"

I told him that Shannon had approached Larry before she had become a suspect and that Earl and Larry had invited her to stay in our custody during her two weeks off. "Larry is convinced she's got alibis. Earl is getting more confident."

"Larry's the owner of that canary yellow car, isn't he?"

"Uh-huh."

"So he was the construction worker type who pirated Shannon Perry away Sunday night. How is Larry?"

"He was OK until now. He's pretty worried about Shannon."

"He oughta be, Philip. She's in big, bad trouble."

"But she turned herself in."

"To the wrong people. And you can't really call looking for help turning yourself in. She's scared to death, and she's looking for any port as they say."

"The point is, Wally, if she does have alibis, there's no way around the fact that whoever's committing the murders is doing it for its effect on her."

"For sure. But forgive me if it takes me a while to move too quickly away from her as a suspect and to her as a victim. I mean, I've got a girl here who's linked with four of six murder victims, remember."

"Six."

"Six?"

"She's connected with all six."

"How is she connected with Matacena?"

"She ran into her at the hospital when she was doing a story on pediatrics."

"And Pritkin?"

"She only attended a wedding he officiated."

"That would have taken awhile to put together. All six, huh?" Festschrift let out a long whistle through his teeth. "You know we're going to have to take this girl into custody until we can verify her alibis, don't you?"

"I suppose."

"We won't be able to verify them on a Monday night, you know. At least I don't see how we can."

"But if she's a target, rather than the murderer, can't you use her to catch him?"

"It's possible."

"But if there's any publicity about your taking a suspect into custody, won't that blow that angle?"

"There doesn't have to be any noise. My boss is a reasonable man. Grief, I can't believe I just said that. Seriously, for whatever faults he has, he knows the difference between a victim and a perpetrator, and the sooner we can determine which Shannon Perry is, the better shot we'll have at the murderer."

"How were you able to get a warrant for someone's arrest for murder who was not seen with the victims on the days they were murdered?"

"For one thing, we don't know she wasn't seen with them. The lieutenant will be able to tell us more on that. But in a case like this, it's not at all hard to get a warrant to pick someone up on suspicion of murder when their name is linked to two, let alone three of the deceased. It grew to four by midday and now you tell me she's at least remotely connected to all six. Put yourself in a judge's position, even ignoring the public and media hysterics after going this long without a lead. Would you issue a warrant for Shannon Perry's arrest?"

I pretended to think for a moment. There was only one answer, of course. "Sure."

Wally waited at the corner near our building for the sight of a blue-and-white carrying Lieutenant Merrill. When it appeared, two men were in the front seat. It followed us into the parking lot of the EH office, and Wally rolled down his window facing the other car's passenger side. "You couldn't come alone?" he asked.

"Be cool. He's leaving. You're going to drive me and the suspect back downtown. Now tell me what's going on, and who's that?"

When Wally had finished briefing him, Merrill stepped out. He was a youngish forty, prematurely gray, trim and in uniform. He looked none too pleased that all the lights were off on the second floor. And neither did Wally.

EIGHT

The office was closed and locked. No one was in Earl's or my rooms, and I wasn't sure I wanted to tell Lieutenant Merrill or Sergeant Festschrift that they could all be in the apartment at the end of the hall.

"I don't guess they'd venture out in public for dinner," I said.

Merrill gave me a look I thought had been patented by Wally.

"They must be at Bonnie's," I said. "Should I call over there?"

"Sure, and scare 'em off?" Wally said. "Forget it. Just take us there."

On the way, Lieutenant Merrill sat stonily in the backseat. "So, what do you think, Sergeant?" he said finally. "Is the woman armed and dangerous and should we approach it that way, or do we step in nice and cordial-like and depend on the level-headedness of the former head of Chicago Homicide. That is the Earl Haymeyer we're talking about, isn't it?"

"One and the same."

"He's an impressive fellow."

"You know him?" Wally and I said in unison.

"Only by reputation. Remember he was a few bosses before me, but he's the one who left the longest-lasting mark on the operation. His systems and procedures and standards are pretty much still intact, and anybody who was around back then has nothing but praise for him."

"Except me," Festschrift said.

"Right, except you, except I don't believe a word you say. Did you give Haymeyer as bad a time as you give me?"

"Worse."

"I'd have to see that to believe it. I can tell down deep you liked Haymeyer. You'd have had to unless you were a real bozo, and much as I'd like to, I can't lay that rap on you."

"I guess that was a compliment," Festschrift said.

"Yeah, and the way you treat me must be your form of compliment, especially if you treated Haymeyer the same way."

"I didn't. I said it was worse."

"Then you must have liked him more."

"Of course."

I couldn't believe the good mood. Apparently these men had enough confidence in Earl that they felt there was little danger either that Shannon Perry was the murderer or that they'd lose her if she was.

"We doin' this by the book or not, boss?" Wally said as we pulled into the parking lot at Bonnie's apartment.

"How do you mean?"

"Code says we have guns drawn on a felony arrest, and we go in loud, badges out."

"Forget it. We're just making a social call on Mr. Haymeyer and his friends. If one of his friends happens to be Shannon Perry, we have a little piece of mail for her."

"You're the boss."

"Thanks for reminding me. Remind yourself occasionally."

I rang the bell at Bonnie's door and heard the conversation cease inside. Someone stepped to the door and, I assume, was peering out the peep hole. I waved self-consciously. "It's Philip and Sergeant Festschrift and someone else!" Bonnie said, opening the door, and we heard Earl call out, "Wait!" but it was too late. Festschrift stepped past me and through the door before Bonnie could even think to shut it again.

The three of us moved past Bonnie, who was wearing a large apron to cover her clothes, and we were met by a dinner table full of people who had just started eating. Margo and Larry and Earl and Shannon Perry stared at us over steaming plates. "Ah, real good work, Philip," Earl said, and I tried to laugh but nothing came out.

"Well, let me get some more chairs and you men can join us. How'll that be?" Bonnie said.

"I don't think — " Wally started to say.

"Oh, nonsense, Sergeant," Merrill said. "I haven't eaten dinner. Have you?"

"Well, no."

"Then we'd be delighted, thank you, ma'am."

Bonnie and Larry searched for more chairs while Margo dug around for more plates. Everybody scooted around, and soon eight of us were shoulder to shoulder around Bonnie's dining room table.

There was an awkward silence, everyone ignoring the obvious, until Merrill spoke. "You must be Earl Haymeyer," he said, shaking hands.

"And you must be the current head of Homicide."

"You say current as if you consider the job transitory."

"It has been. I'm sure you'll spring from it to bigger and better things."

"As you did?"

"Well, I wouldn't say that. I — "

"Oh, of course you did. And did this rascal give you as much trouble then as he does me now?"

"Well, I used to work for him, you know. I guess I gave him a little trouble myself before the tables were turned. I imagine I deserved whatever he dished out."

"Well, I don't deserve it!"

And there we all sat, most of us laughing, some of us staring, and one young, dark-haired girl focusing wide-eyed on the head of Chicago Homicide and unable to bring her fork to her mouth.

"Dessert now or later?" Bonnie asked as she began to clear the table.

"This isn't my party," Lieutenant Merrill said, "but it's about to be. Ma'am, you invited me in here and you can throw me out, but Sergeant Festschrift and I would like permission to talk to Mr. Haymeyer and Mr. Spence and Miss Perry in another room, if we may."

"Certainly," Bonnie said, and she ushered us into her living room, where Earl and Shannon sat on the couch and Merrill and I sat on the coffee table. Wally sat on the arm of the couch.

"Miss Perry," the lieutenant began, "you and I have some serious talking to do."

"I understand," she said softly.

"I'm afraid I have to tell you that you are under arrest on suspicion of murder in the first degree. You have the right to remain silent. Anything you say can and will be held against you in a court of law. You have the right to have an attorney present while you are being questioned. If you cannot afford one, an attorney will be appointed for you. Do you understand these rights as I have read them to you?"

"Yes," she said, barely audibly.

"And do you wish to have an attorney present?"

"No."

"Do I understand you correctly that you are waiving your right to an attorney for the purpose of this questioning?"

"Yes."

"And will you also waive the right to silence?"

"Yes."

"Good. Is there anyone here you would rather not have present?"

"No."

"And is there anyone you would like present who is not here?"

"Yes, could Larry be with me?"

"Certainly."

Larry joined us and squeezed onto the couch between Earl and Shannon.

"Are you armed?" Merrill asked Shannon.

"No."

"Do you own a weapon?"

"You mean of any kind?"

"Yes."

"I have one of those Mace cannisters, and I carry a sharp instrument on my key ring."

"Do you own a gun?"

"No."

"Have you ever owned a gun of any type?"

"No."

"Do you know of anyone who owns a handgun?"

"I think Larry does."

Larry nodded.

"Have you ever handled Mr. Shipman's handgun?"

"No, I've never seen it."

"Did you know Lawson Ng of Hoyne Avenue in Chicago?"

"I didn't really know him. I knew who he was, spoke to him occasionally. I don't think he knew my name."

"Did he ever help you change a tire on your car?"

Shannon looked surprised. "Why, yes, I had forgotten about that."

"Do you remember when that was?"

"No, well, I know it was hot out."

"So it was during the summer?"

"I think so. It was very hot."

"Could it have been June first?"

"Yes, it could have been. I remember it was his day off. He was jogging or something and noticed I had a flat."

"Are you aware that he was murdered that day?"

"No, I thought it was the next day."

"His body was discovered the next day, but the coroner puts the time of death as late afternoon, June first, a Wednesday."

"I was at work at that time."

"Can that be proved?"

"Oh, yes, there are careful records."

"But you don't punch a clock, do you, Miss Perry?"

"No, but our office coordinator keeps a careful record of how much time we spend on our various projects for purposes of cost control. I'm certain she would have a record that shows I was in the office from late morning — I was late because of the tire — until early evening."

"Did you mention the help Mr. Ng gave you to anyone in the office?"

Shannon thought a moment. "Yes, I think I told Chuck Childers, our morning man. I was going with him at the time, or we had just broken up, I don't remember. Anyway, we have always been on good terms and I'm sure I mentioned it to him."

"And was it an item in your office when the Ng murder was announced?"

"Sure. Everyone wanted to know if I knew him and how close I lived to him and all that. In all the excitement I must have forgotten about the tire changing thing until now."

"Tell me about your relationship with Frances Downs."

"I didn't know her well. I always respected her and felt that she did good work. Mostly I was impressed with how she concentrated much of her work on the underprivileged."

I stole a glance at Wally, who was scribbling notes. He broke in with a question. "Did you mention that to anyone?"

"You mean about respecting her for that?"

"Right."

"Oh, yes, I suppose that's all I ever said about Frances. I'm sure people got tired of hearing me say that."

"Somebody apparently did," Wally said.

Merrill took over again. "Were you aware that Miss Downs was what some would call a 'kept woman'?"

"You mean that someone was paying for that big apartment at Sandburg?"

"You're aware of that then?"

"Of the apartment, yes. Everyone knew about it."

"Did anyone wonder how she could afford it?"

"I guess we all figured she had a guy. No one knew who, though. It could have been any one of a number of men. I tried not to talk about her in those terms. I'm not a goody-goody or anything like that, but I usually talked only about the positive things about Frances, because there were many. I didn't figure it was any of my business if she was whatever you say she was."

"Who's your dentist?"

"Dr. McDough."

"Dr. Thomas McDough in the Loop?"

"Yes."

"When did you see him last?"

"In October, I believe."

"October twenty-ninth, a Friday?"

"That's possible. Yes, it could have been. I don't remember exactly."

"You didn't see him after that, socially, on the street, anywhere for any reason?"

"Not that I recall."

"He wasn't in your offices during the first week of this month?"

"Yes! I'm sorry. He was. I don't know what he came in for, but he was in to see somebody and he ducked in and waved at me. I didn't even speak to him."

Merrill looked concerned, as if he didn't like these sudden recalls of memory. "And did you say anything about him to anyone?"

"I may have said something to either Chuck or Jake Raven, our boss. I don't think I said he was my dentist, but I said we ought to do a story on his free clinic on the south side sometime."

"And when he was murdered did you mention that he was your dentist?"

"No, by that time I was getting paranoid because I had been acquainted with so many of these victims. I didn't say anything about it at all."

"You didn't mention to the girls in the office that the dead man was the one who had come through the week before?"

"No."

"And you didn't say anything about it to the one you suggested the special program to?"

"No."

"And whoever that was said nothing to you about McDough?"

"No."

"Are you aware how implausible that sounds?"

"I guess. But it's the truth."

Merrill stood to stretch, leaned down and whispered to Festschrift. "Did you say she's linked to the others as well?"

"There's evidence of that, yeah."

"You wanna ask a few questions?"

"Sure."

Merrill sat back down. "Miss Perry, do you mind answering some more questions?"

"Not at all, especially if it'll keep me from having to go downtown and being booked or whatever."

"I can't guarantee that it will," the lieutenant said. "We cannot, of course, take only your word for these alibis, you know."

"But they should be easy enough to check," Larry said.

"By whom? Would you like to start verifying them tonight?"

"I would."

"Well, you probably would, but I can't let you do that. Let's continue here, and I'll have to decide what we're going to do with Miss Perry in light of this warrant. Sergeant Festschrift?"

"Yeah, Shannon, you don't mind if I call you by your first name, do you?"

"No."

"Isn't it also true that you are at least somewhat acquainted with the second, third, and fourth victims in this murder spree?"

"Yes, I'm afraid so. That's why I sought out Larry. It was starting to get to me."

"I can see how it would. Now, as I understand it, you had only one contact with Annamarie Matacena?"

"Yes, she was sort of my guide when I was researching a story at the hospital where she works."

"Did you know where she lived or anything else about her?"

"No. Nothing. In fact, I only remembered her name from her nameplate and then from the name of the hospital when her murder was announced."

"And of course you made mention of it at the office."

"Sure, several of us had been at the hospital."

"Who, specifically?"

"Well, Jeanie, another writer; Steve Lacey, our part-time sound guy; and Jake."

"Your boss was there?"

"Yes. He's teaching Steve how to do sound engineering, so he went along on that trip to show him what to do when the actual interviewing crew went back."

"And who would have been on that crew?"

"An announcer. I'm not sure which one, maybe Chuck. Then a sound man, probably Steve. And one assistant, either me or Jeanie."

"Well, did you go back or not?"

"I don't think we ever did. That job may still be in the hopper."

"Why hasn't it been done yet?"

"I really don't know. I thought Chuck was going to be the announcer on it and so I told him what to look for, but I never heard if the show was done, and I probably would have heard if it had. Maybe the murder of the woman who worked there made it seem inappropriate for now."

"Is there anything you want to tell me about the Reverend Mr. Pritkin, other than that you attended a wedding at his church and he officiated?"

"No, that's about it. I think everyone was there from work."

"By everybody you mean — ?"

"Our office coordinator, Jeanie, Jake took me, Steve wasn't there, and I guess neither was Chuck. Somebody from night crew came."

"Whose wedding was it?"

"A girl who used to do the traffic for us on afternoon drivetime."

"Did Reverend Pritkin make any impression on you?"

"No, not really."

"Did you know he was an unusual guy at all?"

"Unusual in what way?"

"I'm asking you."

"Well, yes, now that you mention it, the girl, wow, I don't even remember her name now, but the bride told us that when the pastor heard they were both putting themselves through college, he refused to accept a fee and wouldn't even accept any money for the use of the church."

"So that made an impression on you?"

"Yes."

"Would you have told anyone about that?"

"I might have."

"Would you have discussed it with anyone?"

"Probably the people I went to the wedding with. We went out afterward, even though I was sort of with Jake. We all went to dinner as I recall."

"And that was a topic of conversation? The fact that the pastor was really nice to the wedding couple?"

"Probably so."

"Would anyone at work have known that you were once represented by Dale Jerome in a civil suit?"

"Oh, probably, though they might not have put the name with it."

"Why not?"

"I'm not sure I always used his name when I remembered his kindness."

"But you might have talked to someone at work about it?"

"Sure."

"That's a big thing with you, isn't it?"

"What's that?"

"Talking about people who do things for you or for others?"

"Yes, I guess it kind of is. I don't know enough people who go out of their way for others. I don't do it much myself."

"So, you talk about it?"

"I guess I do."

"You told people about Mr. Ng helping you with your tire. And you told them how nice Mrs. Matacena was. And it impressed you what a kind gesture Reverend Pritkin made to the young couple, even though you can't remember the bride's name. You remember a kindness from a high-paid lawyer from six years ago. You are so impressed with the soft spot in Frances Downs's heart for the underprivileged that you forgive her for her loose morals."

"I never thought of it that way."

"And your dentist, a part of life most people would rather not think or talk about, gets your vote of confidence because he runs a free clinic. You're almost too good to be true."

"I am? I don't think so. I don't think it's unique to be impressed by selfless people."

"Are you a selfless person?"

"No. I wish I was. Sometimes I am, but never enough. I'd really like to be."

"Why? Because they get nice things said about them or even their faults covered because of it?"

"No, it is just the way I was raised and I'd like to be that way."

"But you're not?"

"Not as much as I'd like to be."

"You were raised to be selfless?"

"Not exactly. But to be nice, do things for people. And if you can't say something nice about someone, don't say anything at all."

"How does that fit in with your profession? Newswriting is hardly ever good news."

"Maybe that's why I talk about people who do good things, I don't know. When I get a chance to do an in-depth piece, I usually go for something like that. There's enough bad news."

"How much does it bother you that you're not as good and selfless as you want to be?"

"I don't think I dwell on it. I hope it just spurs me to do better, to do more. I don't let it get to me."

"It doesn't get to you to the point where sometimes you feel you'd like to kill someone who's better than you are? Do you sometimes feel you'd like to murder them? Shoot them? In the head? In the brain? To get rid of that part of them that thinks such good thoughts that it allows them to be the nice, selfless person you just can't match?"

We were all stunned at this performance by Festschrift. Even Earl was taken back. Merrill stared intently at Shannon. Margo and Bonnie had entered the room without our even noticing.

Shannon stared right back at Wally, but she didn't respond.

NINE

Finally, Earl stood. "Is that the end of your questioning, Wally?" he said.

"Now just a minute," Lieutenant Merrill said, raising a hand. "I'm a guest here, but I *am* in charge of the questioning, and Miss Perry has not answered the question."

Shannon was trembling. "May I ask a question before I answer that one?" she said.

"Certainly," Festschrift said.

"I want to know if that's what you think."

"If what's what I think, honey?"

"If you think I murdered all those people because they were nice and I'm not."

"That's not for me to decide."

"You can sit there and accuse me of that and then tell me it's not for you to decide?"

"I didn't accuse you of anything, dear. I merely asked you a question."

"Please stop with your endearing names, and please don't call that diatribe you just finished a mere question. Did you ask me that because you think it's the case?"

"I asked you that for two reasons. I wanted to see if you would deny it, which you did not — "

"Well, I'll deny it — "

" — Excuse me, Miss Perry. Which you *did not*. And I also asked it to see what kind of reaction I would get if you did *not* deny it."

"I'm denying it. No, I didn't kill anyone. I never even thought of it. And just because I admit I'm not always as selfless as I'd like to be is no reason to think I would kill anyone who is. I admire them. I talk about them. I don't go around murdering them. Can't a person admit a shortcoming without your thinking they're a murderer? Saying that I'm not always as selfless as I want to be is a bit of a selfless statement in itself."

Larry put his hand on Shannon's shoulder and shushed her.

"Let her talk," Wally insisted. "I want her to tell me that she's not all bad. That she does do some good things."

"Of course I do!" She was crying now. "I wasn't admitting to anything terrible. I told my boyfriend, or my former boyfriend, to look up Mrs. Matacena because she was so nice. I was complimenting her and making his job easier. Is there something wrong with that? What did you want me to say? That I'm perfect? That I always do things for others at my own expense? That I'm as nice as Mr. Jerome or Dr. McDough?"

She dropped her head and cried. "How did I get into this mess?" she sobbed. "I was just trying to answer truthfully, and he turned it all around."

Even Festschrift appeared a bit self-conscious, as if he felt he should defend what he had done to everyone glaring at him now. "She'll get tougher questions than that in court," he said.

Earl stood again. "Are we through now?"

Merrill looked to Festschrift, who nodded. "I'm afraid we are going to have to take you downtown until we can check on your whereabouts at the time of each of these murders," Merrill said.

"Are you telling me that I'm going to be spending the night in jail?"

"It won't be that bad. We can keep you at the precinct lockup by yourself."

"And you don't think that'll be bad? Oh, Larry, do something!"

"Earl," Larry said, "can they take her downtown without a female officer in the car?"

"No, you can't," Earl said.

"That's right," Merrill said, "and that's why I was going to ask for the loan of either your secretary or Margo Franklin here."

"I'll go," Margo said.

"No, wait a minute," Earl said. "You're still working for me, right, Margo?"

"Of course."

"Then I'm telling you I don't want you to go. Lieutenant, you'll just have to have a matron come out here tonight. Otherwise you can leave her in my custody."

"Oh, come on, Haymeyer, be reasonable. You know how difficult it'll be to get a policewoman driven out here at this time of the night."

"You bet I do."

"What's the point of leaving her in your custody?"

"Several points. First, I believe every word she's said. Every one. Even the sudden memories. If she was lying she wouldn't try something that stupid. Second, I think her alibis are going to hold up, and there's no sense detaining an innocent young woman in a jail cell. Third, I want to hear more about everyone in her office, because if I'm right and she's innocent, she's more than innocent, she's a catalyst. Someone is murdering these people because of her, and we'd better find out why. You take her downtown and it leaks out that you've got her, whoever it is at that station who's committing these crimes will wrap himself into a cocoon you'll never penetrate."

Merrill appeared to be softening. "Earl, you realize the risk I'd be taking. This is the biggest murder case in Chicago since John Wayne Gacy. I'd be hung out to dry if something happened to my only suspect."

"I'll sign anything you want. You put her in my custody and I'll see that she stays put. She'll be here when you need her. Frankly, I think we're going to need her for bait eventually. It's up to you, Lieutenant. Either you trust me and leave her with me, or you can call downtown for a matron."

Merrill and Festschrift huddled alone for a moment. "All right, Earl," Merrill said finally. "I'm gonna trust you."

Shannon hugged Larry in relief.

"I hate to be so ornery about this, gentlemen," Earl said, seeing the men to the door. "But you were pretty tough on her, Wally."

"Forget it."

"Hey," I said, "can you take me downtown to my car?"

Festschrift motioned that I should follow him, and I almost forgot to kiss Margo good-bye. "I've missed you today," she said.

"Me too," I said. "I can't wait to tell you about it. You gonna be up when I get back?"

"Depends. Are you going to be talking with Festschrift until all hours like you did last time?"

"Hm. Probably so. Don't wait up for me. I'll talk to you when this thing's over."

"Who knows when that's going to be?"

Wally's car was idling by the time I raced into the parking lot and jumped in. The ride back to Chicago was pretty quiet. I got the impression that the two men had already discussed whether they had done the right things, Wally in pushing as hard as he had and Merrill in leaving the suspect in Earl Haymeyer's custody.

Wally dropped his boss off at Homicide and then tooled over to the precinct house and pulled in beside my car. He turned his engine off and rolled his window half way down. I was glad he appeared in a talking mood. "So, what'd ya learn your first day as an intern, huh?"

"Not to get you riled."

Wally appeared to laugh, but no sound came out. "Yeah, well, I'm not takin' back a word of it. Even now that I see the whole picture, I don't think Earl should have put you up to stalling me like that. Aside from all the grief it put me through, it's an insult to me. Look how it turned out; the girl is still with Earl and his people. We're not goons. Earl doesn't have to worry about us. We're reasonable people."

"I'm impressed."

"Don't be smart."

"I'm not. I'm serious."

Wally turned sideways toward me and rested his knee on the seat between us, wedging his foot into the Motorola. "Good to have that thing off for a while," he said.

"Oh, I still kinda think the radios are neat, listening to all that stuff."

"Aah, you get to the point where you tune out everything except your own numbers unless you hear certain codes, like B & E or something."

"Breaking and entering?"

"Right."

The fat man let out a long breath. "Whew, big day," he said. "Big, big day. I'm gonna sleep tonight, I'll tell you that."

"What time'll you get up tomorrow?"

"I always get up the same time, no matter when I get to bed. 'Bout five-thirty, quarter to six. Gotta get rollin', get the juices flowin', see what we've learned so we can lower the net on somebody."

"You about to lower the net on somebody?"

"Oh, yeah, I think we're closer than we've ever been in this case."

"You think Shannon did it, really?"

"What? Are you kidding? What do you think?"

"I don't think she did, Wally. I really don't."

"Well, neither do I."

"You don't?"

" 'Course not. But don't tell her that. I need her on edge, in case I'm wrong. I've been wrong before."

"You're not wrong this time."

"Well, I don't think I am either, kid, but let's not get overconfident."

"Who do you think did it?"

"Well, we all know it's gotta be somebody at that radio station. But you know what really threw me about this case at first?"

"Hm."

"The days of death."

"The *days* of death?"

"Yeah."

"I don't follow."

"Well, Ng was found on Wednesday and had been murdered on Tuesday. Matacena was found on Friday and had been murdered on Thursday. Of course, at that point I wasn't thinking about the days; I was thinking the way the reporters were thinking, that this killer had a thing about foreigners. Then Pritkin, a red-blooded American, is murdered on a Monday and I start wondering if this nut is going to try to rack up one for every day of the week. Not even three weeks later we find Jerome's body and the death day is set as Wednesday, OK? We've got Monday through Thursday so far, but not in that order. Now I'm betting that if another murder is committed, it's gonna be on a Friday. Four Fridays come and go, and nothing. Then on Saturday, October 16, Frances Downs is found. The lab says she died on Friday.

"Now I live and die for Saturdays and Sundays, because while I've got no other leads except my nice-guy theory, I'm convinced we've got a calendar freak on our hands. Three weekends go by with nothing, and the creep surprises me with a Wednesday hit on Dr. McDough with a Thursday discovery. Shoots my theory sky high. I don't know what I was gonna do with that information anyway. I didn't stop any murders."

I yawned.

"You wanna get back home to bed, right?"

"No, no, Wally. I want to hear whatever you've got to say. I think this thing is going to be nudged around in your head until it all falls into place."

"Well, I had another theory that got blasted. After the first three, Ng, Matacena, and Pritkin, I was thinking we've got a murderer who can't stand poor people, right? I mean, when the preacher is the one with the most means of the three, you've got some poor people here, am I right?"

"Yeah."

"Yeah, but look at the next three. A lawyer, a kept woman who makes almost enough to keep herself, and a dentist. Three poor ones and three rich ones. What am I s'posed to do with that?"

"It must be nice to finally have a pattern that seems to make sense."

"Well, you're right, it does, but you know what I was saying to Shannon a little while ago made some sense too."

"That was scary. You sure convinced me you believed it."

"I convinced her too, didn't I? I wonder if she was starting to doubt herself and her own alibis there for a while. I'm tellin' ya, our psychologist woulda been proud of me."

"Were you proud of you?"

"You mean do I enjoy that, playin' district attorney? No. I'm good at it, and Merrill counts on me for it. You noticed how he played the soft and smooth role and I got to play the heavy? We do that a lot. I don't particularly enjoy it, but it has its place. I've surprised myself a few times with what I've dragged out of people."

"Were you surprised tonight?"

"Not really. She reacted the way an innocent woman would react. Only a murderer guilty as sin would have looked me in the eye the first time around and said, 'No, sir, you're wrong.' "

Wally asked if I wanted to go somewhere for some dessert or something. I couldn't think of a worse suggestion, and I told him so.

"Well, then do you mind if I get something?"

"No, go ahead. I want to talk to you about something anyway."

"Uh-oh, here it comes."

"Here what comes? You don't know what I want to talk to you about."

"Don't I? You want me to write it on a piece of paper and see if I'm right?"

"Sure, go ahead."

And he did. He scribbled on one of his business cards and tucked it in his pocket.

Then he drove down to the corner to an all-night diner where he ordered a big piece of pie with ice cream. I had ice water. "So, what did you wanna talk to me about?" he said.

"About having played a part in deceiving you today," I said.

"Oh, hey, forget it. I gave you a piece of my mind. I meant it. It was a lousy thing to do to a guy, but I can forget it. Why don't you?"

"I don't want to. I felt horrible about it all day, and I feel worse the more I think about it."

"Then don't think about it."

"How can I not think about it? You were so right, even in your anger. I don't know when I've seen someone as mad, but you know you made sense. Every word made sense. You were beside yourself, yet your logic would have won any debate. You shot our reasons out of the water, and you convinced me that I had been part of a dirty deal."

"Good. That's all I wanted to do. I didn't want to put you so far under that you can't resurface. Come up for air, boy. It's over."

"Well, I want you to forgive me."

"I said I was forgetting it. What more do you want?"

"I want forgiveness. Sometimes forgetting glosses over forgiveness and there's still bitterness there deep down. Well, I can't blame you for the bitterness because of all the reasons you gave me when you were screaming at me. But I want you to forgive me, and if it's too early and the stench is too fresh in your mind, I can wait. I just want you to know I want to be forgiven and that I've learned a lesson.

For once, Wally Festschrift was at a loss for words. He looked straight at me while shoveling down a couple of mammoth bites, then spoke. "That's real nice, Philip. You know, that really is. I think you mean what you're saying. You're not just trying to make yourself feel better. OK, then, I forgive you. On your terms. Forgetting *and* forgiving, no glossing over. No trying to say it wasn't as bad as it was or that there was some reason for it. Just plain old unconditional forgiveness. Good enough?"

"Good enough." And we shook hands.

"Well, you got me," he said as we went back to his car.

"I got you?"

"Yup. Here's what I wrote on the card."

It read: *Preaching. Just like Earl.*

I laughed. "I'm glad you brought that up," I said.

"Oh, no."

"C'mon, you *want* to talk about it, I can tell."

"You can, huh? How can you tell?"

"You brought it up, didn't you?"

"Yeah, I guess I did."

"You know, you brought it up last time too."

"I did?"

"Yeah. You came right out and asked me what my philosophy of life was or something like that."

"I remember that."

"So, what did Earl talk to you about?"

"You know."

"Well, I know what he told us, but I don't know what you thought of it."

"I thought it was strange. You know, it was the last thing I expected to hear from Earl. 'Course it would be even more surprising to hear something like that from an old coot like me, but Earl is so self-sufficient and smooth."

"Don't I know it."

"I s'pose. But he was givin' it to me with both barrels. And he wasn't trying to say he was better than me, either. That's what I thought was so weird. He was telling me that I needed God in my life and that God can be personal and all that through Jesus Christ. Well, it sounded pretty good. He was giving me all the unconditional love business about forgiving my past and making something out of what was left of my life, even with all my failures. He made it sound pretty attractive and simple. I told him I didn't see myself as a church-goin' type, and he said the same went for him. But you know what he said? He said he thought one day he probably was going to take the step, be a Christian, start going to church and the whole thing."

"He said that?"

"Sure as you're sittin' there."

"How did you react?"

"I told him if he did, I would."

"But he didn't?"

"Not yet. I was going to talk to him about it, but there hasn't been time, and we lost contact up until today."

"You know, Wally, what he decides really has nothing to do with what you decide."

"I know that. You know, a funny thing happened though, when it was all over and we had gone our separate ways. I quit smoking."

"Well, I noticed that, but what did that have to do with what Earl was talking about?"

"I'm not sure. I said something about my smoking while he was preaching at me, and he insisted that smoking had nothing to do with it. He kept harpin' on the fact that it had nothing to do with my doing good things or not doing bad things, it was all what God could do for me if I'd let Him. I got the point, I mean I really did. The fact that I can remember it now tells me that I got the point real good. But for some reason, I decided I wanted to quit smoking after all these years, and I did. It wasn't easy, but I did it. Something about just having talked with Earl about all that stuff made me feel better about myself or something, and I just found the strength I never had to quit."

"What made you feel so good about what he had said?"

"I guess it was just the idea that God might really love ol' Wally Festschrift after all. That I was worth something to somebody, even Earl, after everything. And if there's anything to it, and if I do someday take the step Earl might take, well, at the time I felt good about that."

"And how do you feel about it now?"

TEN

"Right now I feel tired about it," Festschrift said.

"So do I, and I don't want to push you, Wally," I said, "but if you don't want to talk about it, you can just tell me. You don't have to blame it on fatigue."

"I'm not, kid. Really, I'm not. In fact, I *want* to talk about it some more, maybe with you *and* Earl. I wouldn't even mind showin' up at your church there with you and your fiancée. 'S long as Earl will come too."

"Margo and I would love that, but she's not my fiancée."

"She's not?"

"Well, we're not officially engaged."

"Well, what're you waitin' for? She's a terrific girl. Smart, too."

"Oh, I know. I'm waiting for her to finish waiting for me."

"You'll have to explain that one."

"Well, she asked for time the last time we were engaged and I got huffy and almost dumped her. Now she's all grown up and mature — I mean she really is; it's amazing how she's changed since then. Anyway, I think it's given her unusual insight into me. Whether I think it or not, *she* does."

"Does what? Have insight or think she does?"

"Both. And I think she feels she has a better idea than I do of when I'm really going to be ready for a lifetime commitment. I disagree with her on the surface. I love her and feel I'm ready. But I have a nagging fear. More like respect, really. I'm so afraid that she might be right that I'm not pushing her. It's not like she's acting like we're *not* going to be engaged again."

"And you're not gonna push me either — on this church thing, I mean?"

" 'Course not, Wally. That's the last thing I'd want to do. But, you know, I had a young friend I was careful not to push and he committed suicide before I ever really got to the point with him. And when you really believe what you're talking about is a life or death matter, that hurts."

"Ouch. I'll bet it did. But I'll tell you what, I'm not even considering suicide."

"I know, but who knows what could happen? An accident, a heart attack."

"Hey, don't start with me. The only worry I have about heart attacks is when my friends double deal me."

"Guilty. I thought you'd forgotten and forgiven."

"You're right. I have. Tell you what, let's make a deal. The Sunday after we solve this murder case, I'll talk ol' Earl into goin' to church. We'll make it a foursome."

"It's a deal, but you're in trouble now. When I tell Margo, she'll start praying that it'll happen this week, and when she starts praying, things start happening."

"I'm all for that. I'll be prayin' the same way. This case has got to break soon, kid."

I opened the door and walked around to my car. Wally started his and rolled his window all the way down. "Listen, Philip. I don't want to lead you on or anything. What I mean is, I don't want you to get your hopes up about me, or even Earl for that matter.

I don't mind talkin' to you about this stuff, and that's more'n I can say for the way I was when we first met. But just don't read too much into it. There's a lot of water over my dam, and some things just never change. OK?"

I wanted to argue with him, but he wasn't in the mood. I knew of worse characters than Wally Festschrift who'd been changed by God. But I just nodded, he touched his fingers to his forehead in a little salute, and we drove off.

I was telling Margo all about it in the office early the next afternoon when Earl called everybody into his office and asked Larry to see if Shannon could join us. As is Earl's custom, he didn't say a word until everyone was in and seated.

He interlocked his fingers, tucked them under his chin, and rested his elbows on the desk in front of him. "Chicago Homicide has been busy this morning," he began. "They have a plan, and I like it. They have done some undercover checking on your alibis, Shannon, and they feel fairly confident that you can be used to lure the murderer out into the open."

"Does that mean they believe me now?"

"If they still had doubts, I don't think they'd let you out of their — or our — sight."

"Well, I'm relieved, but are you sure they aren't just trying to set *me* up? Are you sure they don't still believe I'm guilty and are just trying to put me in a position to prove it?"

"I know how you could feel that way after last night," Earl said, "but they've done their homework today and now they agree with us that though it's unlikely that you are involved with the murders, no doubt you are either a target or the catalyst."

"It's *unlikely* I'm involved? Is that all you can say?"

Larry broke in. "Shannon, surely you know by now that we all know you're innocent. Earl is trying to emphasize that you are also in the middle of this thing. Have you let that sink in? All these grisly murders that have been in the news every day for months have revolved around you."

"I thought of that first, remember? And I'm sorry. I know you all believe me or you wouldn't have taken care of me so well. I'm not sure I want to be involved in luring any killer out, though."

"Think about this," Margo said. "We're all pretty sure the murderer is not only someone you know, but also someone you work with who must have some sort of a morbid fascination with you. It's time to start thinking who that might be. It may seem unfair to lay that responsibility on you, and you can shirk it if you want to, but why not seize the moment? How much better to grit your teeth for a few more days for the sake of saving more people."

No one said anything for a moment until Earl spoke. "Well, Margo, you took the words right out of Lieutenant Merrill's mouth. In effect, that's what he told me on the phone this morning. He wasn't quite so eloquent, but you've read him well on their view of Shannon's role. They'd like us to meet with their psychologist, a woman named Dr. Mary Stone from International University. They've been feeding her all the information they have, virtually everything that pertains. And now they want you to tell her what you can about your office, the people you work with, your relationships, everything. Are you willing?"

"Sure."

The five of us met with Dr. Stone, Merrill, and Festschrift in a hotel room in the south suburbs. A stack of computer readouts lay before her, and Dr. Stone had taken copious notes. As we arrived, several plainclothesmen were leaving.

"You're last on the docket today," Wally said as his eyes met Shannon's. "We've never had this many men on one case. Dr. Stone has all the information except yours."

Shannon appeared not to be listening. Wally put his hand in front of her and she slowed. "Miss Perry, please. I know you're upset with me. Let me explain."

"There's no need," she said, her tone cold. "I know you were doing your job." She tried to walk past him but he put his hand gently on her shoulder. She looked impatient but she didn't pull away.

"Hey, I sometimes hate that part of my job," he said. "You've gotta understand that."

"You didn't appear to hate it last night."

"That's all part of doing it right. I'm sorry if I hurt you. Will you believe that?"

"I'll try."

We were all introduced to Dr. Stone, a handsome woman in a tweed suit who appeared slightly detached, as if she had just crammed for a test and didn't want to run into anything for fear she would lose half of what she had stored in her mind. Indeed, that was the case, she admitted. "I need to tie the loose ends of all this information together so I can make some sense of it," she said. "And perhaps I can offer something useful. If you're ready, Miss Perry, I'd like to just ask you several questions."

"I'm ready, and please call me Shannon."

"OK, Shannon. I want you to tell me about the office where you work. It's a radio station, and you're a newswriter, I know that. Tell me about the physical layout and the people, and please sketch the floor plan on this board as you talk."

"I'm not much of an artist," Shannon said, taking the two-foot by three-foot chalkboard and chalk and beginning to etch a large square. "The office is here in the back, and we're basically in one big room with little offices around the perimeter. The office coordinator and an assistant newswriter and a part-time secretary have their desks together in the middle of the open area, and then my office is here, then here's the entrance to the control room and then the booth beyond it. Then on the other side of the entrance here is my boss's office and the workshop."

"Thank you, that's good," the doctor said. "Put names with these people please, just first names if you wish."

"Could I ask a question first?" Earl said. "How far is it here between your office and your boss's office?"

"The doorways would be about ten feet apart."

"And it appears you can see each other if you want to, while each of you is in his own office, I mean."

"Right."

"Do I see three doors on your boss's office?"

"Yes, Jake can come into the large office area, go into the control room, or into the workshop."

"I'm sorry," Earl said, "can I ask just one more? What happens in the workshop?"

"Oh, all the equipment repair, storing extra mikes, remote equipment, that kind of thing. Our part-time sound man, Steve — he's about nineteen — spends most of his time in there when he's not in the control room. Jake does a lot of maintenance work on the equipment, too."

"The boss does?" Earl pressed.

"Oh, yes. We're a small station. Everybody does double duty. I even have to take my turn as receptionist, and I'm making union scale as a newswriter."

"I'm sorry, Doctor," Earl said.

"It's quite all right, sir," Dr. Stone said. "If there's one thing I'm fairly confident about in this case, it's that we're dealing with a volatile individual who is increasing the rapidity with which he or she commits violent acts. Anything you notice or need that will help us locate this individual, please feel free to mention.

"Now, Shannon, the office coordinator is?"

"Betty."

"And your relationship with her?"

"Strictly business. Never social. We get along very well. She likes me, I think."

"Any doubts?"

"No, in fact, people have told me that she says nice things about me, which is the best kind of compliment."

"And the assistant writer — "

"Is Jeanie. We're friends. Not close, because she works for me, but we will see each other socially. I don't confide in her or anything, though I think she'd rather I did. Sometimes she tells me personal things, but she hasn't lately because I've never traded secrets."

"Do you think that bothers Jeanie?"

"Oh, not really."

"Do you think she has any grudges against you, any jealousies? Could she hate you or have any reason to get back at you for anything?"

"I'd be surprised. We've had our minor arguments and hurts over the past two years. She had a little trouble adjusting to me as her supervisor because she came out of college thinking she was ready to take over for Dan Rather. But I think I've taught her some things along the way."

"Does she think so?"

"She wouldn't admit it in so many words, but yes, I think she knows I've been good to her and fair with her. The only problem she has with me is that she can't get me to gossip. She loves to talk about people, and I love to listen. But I won't do it myself."

"Does this bother her?"

"You mean enough to make her do something terrible? No."

"Since she works for you, you are responsible for her hours, and so forth?"

"Yes."

"Has she had any unusual absences, or is she basically there during the normal business day?"

"Well, we all are. Yes, she's always there. The only people with irregular hours are the secretary, Debbie, and then the on-air people who work a couple of hours before and a couple of hours after their shifts on the air. Like Chuck works four A.M. to noon but is on the air only from six to ten. Steve is going to school, so he works mornings. And Jake works eight to noon and four to eight."

"Why those hours for Jake? You said he was the boss?"

"Right, it puts him in the office for the sake of the office staff and he also catches, let's see, half of four different DJs' shows."

"Is he ever there in the afternoons?"

"Oh, yes. Sometimes he'll save some of his shop work for his off time. I think he does some work on his own stereo equipment there, too."

"Does that bother anyone?"

"Oh, no. Nothing Jake does could bother anyone."

"How do you mean? And while you're answering that, explain as carefully as you can, your relationship with him."

"I was in awe of him at first. Everyone is. He's been around. He was a big rock DJ in a couple of big markets in the sixties."

"Do you know where?" Lieutenant Merrill asked.

"Both coasts, I think. L.A. or San Diego and then Baltimore, I believe. And he's an impressive guy. He's a good looker, tall, wide-open face, thinning blond hair that's naturally curly. Wears those big glasses. A really nice guy, too."

"Excuse me," Margo said. "Earl, I've been listening for some connection with this S.D. inscription on the shell casings. Shannon, do you know what this Steve's middle name is? You said his last name was Lacey, I believe."

"Yes, and I do know his middle name because we kid him about his initials spelling S-O-L, *sun* in Spanish. His middle name is Owen."

"OK, and then you mentioned that Jake was a DJ in San Diego. Los Angeles is called L.A.; is San Diego ever called S.D.?"

"I'll check on it right now," Wally said, rising. "My guys have been investigating Childers anyway, and I want their input too. It shouldn't be too hard to trace Jake Raven to San Diego if he ever worked there."

"Ask his agency," Shannon said. "Farrar on Michigan Avenue."

"He's got an agency?"

"He still does emceeing and grand openings and stuff like that. He's a real pro. We've all learned a lot from him."

"I'm also gonna check on this Lacey kid's attendance at his afternoon classes on the days of the murders. The coroner has pretty much concluded that they were all afternoon jobs, committed by someone who studied their patterns and knew when they would be home."

Dr. Stone stood and paced, questioning Shannon for almost another hour. "Please go back to your relationship with Jake. Is everyone so enamored of him?"

"Yes. He's really quite special. He has high standards and he gets the best out of everyone, but I don't think he has ever hurt anyone. He can correct you, even criticize you, and make you feel good about it. He never puts anyone down, seems to be fairly close to everyone at work, but he's divorced and lives alone."

"I understand you dated him a few times."

"Well, not really. We thought up reasons to sort of go out together, but they weren't official dates. One was to the wedding, and once was a dinner to celebrate my anniversary with the station. Stuff like that. I don't think I would have gone out with him if he officially asked me. For one thing he was only divorced recently, and come to think of it, he did ask me out after his divorce was final. That was a sort of a celebration of that. See? Always reasons, not real dates. I just wouldn't feel comfortable dating my boss. Not just because he's my boss, but because I really do kind of have him on a pedestal. He's in his early forties, and, no, I wouldn't actually date him for real."

"How does he feel about that?"

"He kidded me about it a few times, saying I was rejecting him or something. He's a cut-up. He did that in front of people. Of course, he never really asked me out for a date-type date. But he knows I wouldn't accept anyway. I really wouldn't. It would scare me to death."

Wally returned. "Have you talked about Childers yet?"

"No, we were just getting to him," the doctor said.

"Has anything hit you yet with the others?"

"This Jeanie could have some latent hostility for Shannon, and I'm a little fuzzy on the student, but I don't think there's anything else here so far."

"Well, the student, Steve, has perfect attendance in his afternoon classes except one week when he was at his parents' home, and that checks out."

Dr. Stone, who had added first names to the office positions on the board, leaned over and X'd his name off.

"But we've gotta talk about Childers," Wally said. "Chuck Childers. When I asked the agency if Jake Raven had ever worked out of San Diego, they said no. L.A., Pittsburgh, and Baltimore before Chicago. Never San Diego. But you know what they said? They said, 'You must be thinking about the guy who works for Raven, the morning man.'

"I said, 'Yeah?'

"And they said, 'Yeah, he was the biggest thing to hit San Diego in years before he went to Oklahoma City.' "

We all looked at each other.

"I knew he was in Oklahoma City, but you know he never told me he worked in California," Shannon said.

"You dated him for how long?" Dr. Stone said.

"For about a year up until May or so."

"And he never told you he had lived in California?"

Shannon shook her head, her eyes tearing.

"There's something else he didn't tell you, Shannon," Wally said. "My boys have reason to believe he's the guy who'd been paying Frances Downs's rent for the last two years."

ELEVEN

Shannon pressed her hands to her temples and closed her eyes. Dr. Stone put a hand on Shannon's knee. "We're going to have to talk about this."

Shannon nodded, grimacing, her eyes still shut. "Not Chuck, no, please not Chuck. Even after we broke up, I confided in Chuck. He knew everything about me."

"Even who your dentist was?" Festschrift asked.

"Of course. We went together. We were nearly engaged."

"Were you intimate with him?"

Shannon nodded. "I never lived with him or anything like that, but yes."

"Did he tell you he was divorced?"

"Yes."

"It's not true," Wally said. "He's separated, but he is not divorced. He has two children in Oklahoma City."

Shannon covered her eyes with her hand. "He said he never had children."

Dr. Stone brushed off her skirt and crossed her arms. "What would you gentlemen like to do? You can, of course, pick him up in connection with the Downs murder, I imagine. Do we need carry this any further?"

"We still don't have a motive," Merrill said.

"Of course you do. She broke up with him, right? Rejection. Humiliation. Revenge."

"But why all the little people in her life? It still doesn't add up," Wally said.

"Anyway," Lieutenant Merrill broke in, "I don't want this guy on one suspicion of murder if I can get him on six. He sounds like first class low-life, but lying about your marital status is no crime unless you're guilty of bigamy. You didn't marry the guy, did you?"

Shannon shook her head.

"And there's no law says you can't pay a woman's rent, either. He was likely guilty of adultery — well, we know that — but we're not on vice detail. If this is the guy and he's as volatile as you say, Doctor, let's find out what sets him off and then let's set him off. Tell Shannon what it is she's doin' that makes him do what he does, and then we'll catch him in the act."

Shannon was shaking her head. Margo spoke to her. "Honey, listen, I know you're still finding it hard to believe this guy would lie to you and cheat on you and then act this way just because you wanted out of the relationship, but think about what he's done to you and to other innocent people. Can't you consider doing whatever you need to, to stop him?"

Shannon ran to the bathroom, and we could hear her sobbing for several minutes. Dr. Stone conferred with Merrill while the rest of us fidgeted. Margo walked over to me, and oblivious to the others in the room, wearily put her head on my chest and wrapped her arms around me. "Bizarre," she said quietly.

We all fell silent when Shannon reappeared. "I'm ready to do whatever I have to do," she said. "But can it wait until tomorrow?"

Dr. Stone looked to the lieutenant.

"The actual work can wait, but we'll need to set it all in motion today. I want Dr. Stone to determine what it is you say or do that pushes this guy over the brink. Then I want you to call your boss and thank him for the time off but tell him you're better and you want to come back to work. Then you work on Childers and we'll keep him in sight every minute."

"I think I can help you even more," Dr. Stone said. "I believe this man can be programmed to go after someone specific. Would that help?"

"Would that help? You bet it would. If we can use some bait and stake out the place where we think he's heading, we'll have him red-handed."

"Well, no matter who we try to set him up for, you'd better protect Shannon too, because I think he's leading up to her. I'm guessing that her propensity for talking up these minor characters in her life whom she sees as so wonderful drives him crazy. In his mind, if he can do away with all these selfless people, he will have no competition left. Yet this man knows himself. Imagine how many people he will have to destroy before he's the best one left."

"If that's true, then isn't Jake vulnerable, too?" Merrill asked.

"Do you talk about Jake at work the way you did here today?" Dr. Stone asked.

"Well, no, not really. Everyone pretty much feels the same about Jake. Even Chuck. It's sort of a given. No one says much. I've said it to Jake, of course, but Chuck and I haven't talked about Jake that much."

"But you have, as you think back on it now, talked about these people, all six of them, in a good light to Chuck?"

"Yes. All of them. The thing is, he must be a great con man. Besides all this stuff I'm finding out, he always agrees with me when I say good things about people. I can't believe it's all an act. I just can't believe it."

"I'd still like to know how he gets into people's homes and makes them trust him to the point where he can murder them with no signs of a struggle," Merrill said.

"He's a charmer," Shannon said. "He could talk you into anything."

"I want to be the bait," Larry said suddenly. "I want this creep."

"Oh, hey, I don't know — " Earl said.

"Me either," Merrill said. "We've got plenty of undercover cops who can play a role."

"No, he's maybe onto something here," Wally said. "He's a natural because it's for real. Shannon can truthfully say that this guy has been very nice to her lately. When she was distraught over personal matters, he helped her. It's perfect."

"I agree," Dr Stone said. "I mean, it's not my place to even suggest such specific detail, but I do know it will help Shannon if she can be telling the truth even when she knows she's playacting for a purpose. It will make it easier."

Shannon stared at Larry. "Larry, you've become very special to me these last few days. I can't think of risking your life in this."

"You can't talk me out of it, Shannon. You deserve more than this. I want to do it and I'm going to."

Dr. Stone raised a brow at Merrill. "I believe the ball is in your court, sir."

Merrill looked to Earl. "Wally is apparently for it. How'bout you?"

"Aah, I don't know. I don't like it much, but we're going to make it airtight, aren't we? Heavy stakeouts? People hidden within a few feet of Larry all the time?"

"Of course," Merrill said. "Larry, if you're willing to sign a few releases and your boss frees you to do it, I can pay you one day's patrolman's wages."

Larry looked to Earl, who shrugged. "Why not? You've done crazier things."

Shannon and Dr. Stone spent another hour carefully going over the way Shannon would act in the office. "It's important that you try to return to normal, at least to the level of normalcy you were at last week. The key is to continue to say good things about people, especially Mr. Shipman."

"That's right," Lieutenant Merrill said. "Make it natural. Tell whoever you would normally tell that Larry has been so kind to you."

"See, I know Chuck," Larry said. "It would be the most natural thing in the world for Shannon to talk about me in the office. I'm sort of a regular around the place anyway; I get in there every few weeks or so."

"Did Chuck tell *you* he's worked in San Diego?" Shannon asked.

"No, I thought he'd gotten his start in a small station in Oklahoma and then moved to the big one in Oklahoma City before coming here. I gotta tell ya, though, it doesn't terribly surprise me about his relationship with Frances. I thought about warning you a few times how he talked about women, but about the time I really thought I should, you broke up with him anyway."

"Was that a traumatic break?" the doctor wanted to know.

"Well, it was for me, but Chuck was so good about it. I can see why, now. Jake was wonderful too. He was upset with Chuck for a while, assuming Chuck must have hurt me in some way, but that wasn't it. I was just feeling crowded, and I was uncomfortable carrying on a relationship with someone I worked with."

"Was there any one thing that brought about the break?"

"Not really. He did want me to move in with him, but I just couldn't. As I told you, I'm no prude, but I haven't gone quite that far astray from the way I was raised."

"Was he upset?"

"Disappointed. He acted hurt for a while, but he agreed we could still be friends and that he wouldn't hold a grudge. It was an item of conversation around the station for a week or so, but it's been since May now and I thought we had overcome it. I really did."

"You still talk with Chuck a lot, like you used to?"

"That's just it. More than ever. I didn't talk to him about what's been troubling me lately because I was embarrassed. I thought I was going crazy and that everyone was seeing all the coincidences like I was. But we talked every day."

"What did you do about Jake's being upset at Chuck?"

"I told him I really thought Chuck was being nice about it and to please let it blow over. They've always had a good relationship. Jake hired Chuck, you know, and he's proud of him. We all are. Were anyway."

"Do Chuck and Jake socialize together?"

"No, not much. Jake tells his people that he'll go with them in a group, but that his policy is that he can't favor any over the others away from the office."

"But he appeared to want to favor you."

"Oh, that was just to cheer me up after I split from Chuck. It was hard on me for a while, but Jake was so nice. They both were."

"And even though they don't socialize away from work, they're on good terms?"

"They must be."

"Why's that?"

"Because Jake often talks to me about things I discuss with Chuck. He'll bring them up and I'll just know it's something I talked to Chuck about but not to Jake. I talk to them both, like I say, but there are differences in the things we talk about. I'm a little more personal with Chuck, naturally."

"Does it bother you that Chuck shares these things with Jake?"

"Chuck denies it. He says I must have told Jake and didn't remember, but I'm not that dumb. I told Jake once that I wasn't so sure I liked Chuck telling him what I talk about, and he tried to make me believe that I had told him, too."

"Where does all this talking go on, at a lunchroom or something?"

"No, Chuck doesn't go anywhere but straight into the studio and then either to Jake's office or the workshop or home. I talk to him during the music when he's on the air. Unless Jake can read lips — his office is in the line of sight through the studio window, but of course, the studio is soundproof — I can't see how he can tell what we talk about if Chuck isn't telling him."

"Why would Chuck tell him?"

"I don't know. It's nothing big. I don't badmouth anybody. I guess it isn't even worth worrying about, but you can imagine how it makes me feel. It isn't often, you know, but once in a while Jake just happens to mention something I know I haven't talked to him about and I somehow feel as if Chuck has betrayed me. It's like my privacy has been invaded. Oh, it's no big thing."

"Yes, it is," Dr. Stone said. "It's a very natural reaction. I frankly don't know how it fits into the picture I'm getting of Chuck Childers, but in a way it says something interesting about Jake, doesn't it? Sometimes we're tempted to tell someone that we know something about them that they don't think we know. However he's getting the information — apparently from Chuck for some reason, who may be subtly showing off to Jake that he's still close enough to you to hear personal information — Jake is possibly trying to say, by repeating it, that he is concerned with your personal life too. He may want to convince you that you were the one who told him, in the hope that you will bring him into that kind of a relationship."

"But I'm just talking about things like when I get my car fixed or when my mother is coming to town or when a check bounces. Those aren't the kinds of things you tell Jake, or any boss, I imagine."

"That doesn't negate my point," Dr. Stone said, smiling. "In fact, it's the very type of thing Jake would want you to tell him about if he's more interested in you than you think."

"Oh, I doubt it."

"Could it be he's getting this type of information from one of the girls in the office?"

Shannon thought for a moment. "Well, I tell more of it to Chuck than to anyone, but I suppose it's possible. I doubt it, though. That's just not the kind of things they talk to Jake about, and sometimes the period between when I've mentioned something to Chuck and when I hear it from Jake is so short that I just know Chuck is the big mouth."

Festschrift stood and looked at his watch. "I don't want to rush you, but it's after four and Jake should be back at the office. Shannon should call and tell him she wants to come back to work tomorrow."

"I think we're through," Dr. Stone said. "Anything else you want to tell me, Shannon?"

"Just a question. How am I suppposed to feel about this? I feel guilty already, playacting and pretending. Plus bitterness toward Chuck."

"That's understandable. Calm yourself as much as possible and remind yourself of the terror this city is going through. You have a chance to do something about that. This man has lied to you. It's not unfair for you to avenge that by stopping him from what he's doing."

"Sergeant Festschrift, what should I say to Jake?"

"Tell him you're sorry about your work lately and that you have just been overtired. Promise to do your best work and all that."

While Shannon was waiting for an answer at the station, Festschrift began gathering information from Larry about the location and floor plan of his apartment. "I'm gonna want to see that tonight and spend the night there. We'll decide who'll be stationed where and I think four of us should be able to handle it, inside and out."

"Hello, Debbie," Shannon said, and we were all silent, "this is Shannon. . . . Hi, fine. . . . No, in fact I think I'll probably be in tomorrow. . . . No, just tired, you know. Is Jake around? . . . Thanks."

Shannon's hands shook, but resolve was written in her face. "Hi, Jake, listen, I think I want to come in tomorrow. . . . No, I'm OK, really. I was just overtired and I feel a lot better since resting over the weekend and today." She held up her crossed fingers and we smiled. "No, I appreciate it, but I'd just as soon come back to work. I'm going crazy here." There was truth to that. She made a face as if he was insisting that she stay away a few more days. "Really, Jake, a friend, well, you know Larry Shipman? Yeah. He's kind of taken me under his wing and I feel better now, so unless you're going to lock me out, I'll plan on being there tomorrow at eight. . . . No, I wouldn't if I wasn't sure I was ready. I'll be back in my old form, and if it doesn't show right away, you can send me home, I promise. OK, Jake? . . . Thanks. I'll see you tomorrow."

She hung up and flopped into a chair. "I thought I wasn't going to be able to talk him into it!" she said. "I must have really been doing lousy work last week! He's so sweet. He kept saying that they missed me but that he didn't want me to come back until I was sure I was ready and not to feel pressure or feel obligated or anything. It was almost like he didn't want me to come back!" But the look on her face made it clear that he had convinced her of the opposite and that he was just watching out for her. She was still obviously nervous about the next day, but she was pleased, too.

TWELVE

Dr. Stone shook hands all around and tucked her briefcase under her arm. At the door she turned. "Shannon, I'll be thinking of you tomorrow. If you talk to Chuck Childers as easily and naturally as you just talked to your boss — and if you even use pretty much the same words — we'll know soon enough if he's our man."

Lieutenant Merrill said she should even act embarrassed and noncommital if anyone asked — as they surely would — whether there was anything going on between her and Larry. He insisted that the most important part, and they rehearsed it several times, was that she should mention that she wished she would have taken one more day off because Larry was off all day Tuesday. "You might even ask if you can get off a half hour early, even though you hate to ask Jake because you talked him into letting you come back before you needed to."

They ran through a few role plays, interrupted only when Shannon wondered aloud if she was up to it. But a pep talk from Margo and Wally helped her begin to warm to the idea that she could kill two birds with the same stone. She could protect society while repaying Childers for his deceitfulness.

Shannon provided Lieutenant Merrill with photos of the people in her office. Chicago Homicide arranged for a stakeout of her apartment, where she would spend the night and then report to work as usual. Margo was asked to be in on that surveillance while Earl would work with Lieutenant Merrill outside Larry's apartment building, and would alert Wally and me inside when anyone was coming. "I wouldn't have chosen you first necessarily," Wally told me, "but the way Larry describes that utility closet in his kitchen, it sounds like you'll be the only one who can fit between the water heater and the washer/dryer."

Just to be safe, all the squad cars were exchanged with personal cars and the stakeouts were set early that evening. It was unlikely anyone was onto us, but even if they were, they wouldn't have looked for us to start getting into place the night before when we didn't expect any action until the following afternoon.

Those of us on the Shipman detail grabbed some fast food and ate at Larry's little kitchen table. "Wally, this is up to you," Merrill said, "but since the kitchen is right off the entrance here and the dining room is out of sight off the kitchen, I would think you'd want to be in the dining room and Philip in this closet, as you say. With that closet light off, Philip will be able to see out through the crack between the louvered doors without Childers seeing in. We want him in the process of doing whatever it is he does, and then you should take him. If he's just talking or going through some ritual, that's one thing. When he gets to the point of putting a gun in his hand, don't wait."

"Please," Larry said. "Don't wait."

Lieutenant Merrill continued. "Wally will be just around the passageway from the dining room to the kitchen; that's why it's important for you to steer him into the kitchen, because if he gets into the living room, he'll be able to see Wally in the dining room."

Earl wedged himself in the closet where I would be the next afternoon. "I could almost do it, but if I sneezed I'd blow the water heater."

Everyone laughed except me. "I'll be within three feet of Larry and Childers standing there," I said. "Won't he be able to hear me breathe?"

"You won't be breathing," Earl said, and again everyone but me was laughing. Earl turned serious. "You know, Philip, if anything goes wrong, you'll know first. If he should grab that gun and start waving it around or trying to force Larry to stand somewhere, you haven't time to call for help. Maybe Wally will hear enough to make him come in immediately; maybe he won't. You'll be able to see everything, and if you have a doubt in your mind, you've got to drop the man."

"You mean — ?"

"You know what I mean." He shut the closet door and turned the light off. I heard him empty the bullets from his snub-nosed revolver and drop them into his pants pockets. "That's the one thing I'm doing that you won't do," he said. "Now I'm standing here with my gun in my right hand, my arm is bent at the elbow, and the gun is pressed to my chest, just under my chin. Keep your eyes on me."

There was nothing to see. The closet was dark. Even though we knew he was in there, it almost seemed as if he weren't. We waited several seconds, no one moving, all eyes on the door. We jumped when it burst open and Earl stood there, arm extended as if it had all happened in one motion, his gun to my head.

I let out a huge sigh.

"But you don't come out of there unless you mean to drop the man," he said. "That means you're kicking the door and firing at his head in the same motion, probably two shots as fast as you can because you're not making this move unless he has the three fifty-seven in his hand. Until he does, you stay put. Ideally, Wally should enter and you should come out slowly at about the same time, just before the man actually raises the weapon. That's much cleaner, and you'll avoid having to kill a man."

I stood quickly and walked into the living room, suddenly overheated and short of breath. Pulling back the curtains, I pressed my forehead against the cool glass of Larry's eighth-floor picture window and pretended to study the Chicago traffic below. I half expected Earl to come and give me one of his famous welcome-to-the-big-leagues pep talks, but he didn't. In fact, no one at the table said a word as Earl sat back down.

I wasn't sure I was ready to kill a man, justified or not. It wasn't a moral issue. A man who has killed six people in cold blood should be shot on the spot if he was standing with his gun pointed at victim number seven. I just didn't know if I was cut out to do it. I had thought that if someone came into the apartment with a gun in his pocket, we could just grab him and take him in and hope we had the right gun, the etched shell, and enough of the rest of the pieces of the MO to make it stick. And we probably could have. But with the crazy legal loopholes and the restrictions put on law enforcement people these days, it's always better to catch your criminals in the act.

I sat on the couch and folded my hands in my lap, letting my head fall back. I stared at the ceiling. "You wanna get in on a game of cards, Philip?" Larry called out.

"Nah," I said, my voice sounding strange because of the position of my neck. "You guys feel free." I wouldn't have known how anyway, but that wasn't the whole problem, and Larry knew it. I heard some quiet talk. Then Larry came in and sat next to me.

"Wanna talk?" he said.

"Not really."

"Wanna listen?"

"OK."

"I just want to give you my perspective on this," he said. "I appreciate you and your straight life and your beliefs and all that, I really do. I think you and Margo are special people. But let me be a little selfish here for a minute. Let me think of me and my neck. I volunteered for this assignment. I mean, I made 'em let me do it. I don't mind tellin' you, it scares me. I'm not backing out, but I want you to if you don't think you can protect me. If something, anything, makes you hesitate when you should be acting, I'm a dead man. Don't let anyone shame you into this, Philip. You gotta go into it with the full confidence that you'll do whatever you have to do. You don't have to like it, but you've got to do it. Otherwise, tell us now so we can get some other skinny little guy to stand in the closet."

He slapped me on the knee and went back to the kitchen. I started to pray about it, then I realized the unique nature of the prayer. I had never asked God for the kind of courage this would take, and it took me a while to settle it in my head. Was I asking for the strength, the courage, the ability to be an agent of death? Or of justice? I confess I was not exactly awash in any peace borne of a commitment to justifiable homicide, but after a few minutes I did rise and shakily retake my seat in the kitchen. "I'll do it and I'll be ready," I said, looking at the floor.

No one responded. I watched them play a slow, somber, unspirited game of cards until almost two o'clock in the morning. Before Merrill and Earl left, the lieutenant gave his last bit of instruction. "Shannon will call us when Childers leaves the office tomorrow, and it will be radioed to me. I'll radio it to Wally up here. I don't want her or anyone else calling here because a busy phone could scare off our man. And remember, nine out of ten stakeouts are just long waits for nothing. Shannon's going to do everything she can to let Chuck know that Larry is home today, but who can know the mind of a madman? He might not be ready to move for another week or two."

"On the other hand," a weary Sergeant Festschrift said, "he just might be ready tomorrow."

"That's why we're here," Merrill said.

The sergeant and I stretched out in the living room, but I can't say I slept much. Wally snored some, but every few hours he would sigh and move about. I got the impression Larry wasn't having an easy night either.

In the morning we freshened up a bit without shaving and sat around small talking and letting our beards grow. At about ten Lieutenant Merrill called on a special frequency on Wally's walkie-talkie. It sounded strange that they didn't have to use code numbers. "Hey Wally, come in."

"Yeah boss."

"We just got a call from Shannon. She feels pretty good about how it's going. She told Chuck she might ask Jake if she could get off a little early because Larry was off today, but she had hardly been back at her desk for two minutes when Jake buzzed her and asked if she could work late because he's expecting some wire service guys to come in at four thirty. What do you make of that?"

"Sounds legit. She'll keep us informed when Childers leaves work at midday?"

"Yeah. This Steve kid isn't working today. Exams or something."

"Thanks, boss."

"Something else, Wally. Childers asked Shannon a few questions about Larry. Like did he enjoy his work and what did he really do with the agency, stuff like that."

Wally didn't answer.

"You get that, Wally?"

"Yeah. I don't know what to think."

"We don't talk about it much, now that I think about it," Larry told Wally. "He knows I work at EH but that's all. He never asked for details."

Wally nodded. "Lieutenant?"

"Yeah."

"We don't know if that means anything. We're out."

"Merrill over and out."

"I'll bet the sound from that studio is piped into Jake Raven's office," Larry said, almost to himself.

Festschrift was antsy now. I was just quiet.

"You guys wanna watch some TV or something?" Larry said. "This is like waitin' for Christmas."

"Not exactly," I said.

"Well, not exactly, no, but the time is draggin'."

"Sure," Wally said. "I'm up for a little TV."

We must have been a sight, lounging in Larry's living room watching inane game shows that marked the half hours with panels and prizes and celebrity guests and commercials. At eleven-thirty the phone rang. Wally jumped up and turned the TV off. "Take it in the kitchen. We'll listen in out here."

We were in direct sight of the kitchen phone, so Wally put his hand on the receiver and signaled Larry when to answer. Wally and I pressed our faces together so we could both hear.

"Hello, this is Shipman."

"Hi, Larry. You recognize my voice, don't you?"

"Yeah — "

"Don't say my name. There are some things I'd like to talk to you about in light of your line of work, and I'd rather not discuss them by phone."

"OK." Larry nodded vigorously to indicate that it was Childers. "What do you want to do?"

"Well, listen, you know the girl I was going with for a while? The one you're seeing now?"

"Well, I'm not actually seeing her — "

"You know what I mean. I just want to know if you know who I'm talking about without mentioning her name."

"Yeah, OK, I know who you're talking about."

"Well, I think you also had a pretty good idea that I was seeing someone else at the same time, right?"

"Yeah, I think so."

"You know who I'm talking about?"

"Yes."

"And you remember what happened to her?"

"Yes."

"What I'm wondering is, do you think that will be discovered?"

"Well, it was already discovered," Larry said. "I mean, what happened to her and everything."

"I'm asking you because of the line of work you're in if you think my, um, involvement with her might be discovered. Do you think if someone saw me with her or saw me at her apartment or something, is it possible I would be questioned or anything?"

"It's possible. But you know, that's not the kind of, uh, project my company is into, you know. That's handled by the city."

"I know. I just thought, as a friend, you might be able to shed some light on that. You know, it would be not too good for me, I mean my career and everything, my reputation, for it to be in the paper that I was even involved with her, let alone if I was under suspicion or something."

"I know what you mean," Larry said.

"What would you think about my turning myself in and just telling someone straight out that I was seeing this girl but that I had nothing to do with what happened to her? Do you think if I did that they could do whatever checking they need to do without it getting in the paper?"

"I don't know. It sounds like a pretty good idea, and you can be sure that if they discover this involvement before you tell *them*, it could be real noisy and make you look worse."

"Listen, Larry, I gotta get back to work here, but I could use some advice on who to talk to and how to go about it, but I don't want to do it by phone. Could I maybe come and see you today?"

Festschrift nodded to Larry.

"Uh, sure. I'll be home all day. You know where I am, don't you?"

"I'll find it. I gotta go. I have to stop by my place first, but I'll try to see you before three."

Larry hung up, folded his arms, leaned back against the kitchen wall, and focused a puzzled stare at Wally.

But Festschrift was already on the radio to Merrill, recounting the entire conversation, almost verbatim. "Well, I think he went for the bait," Merrill said. "But I'll bet he never used that line before to gain entry for one of these jobs."

"Tell him I was almost convinced he was sincere," Larry said.

Wally radioed the message to Merrill.

The answer came back: "Tell superbait not to bet his life on it."

It wasn't funny.

Time: 1:07 P.M.

Merrill: Wally, you there? Over.

Festschrift: Yeah, boss.

Merrill: Shannon called HQ about two minutes ago. Childers has left the office. Let's not buy his story about going home first. You might want to get into position. We're where we can see him if he enters either side of the building. We'll follow him up there, but we'll have to be at least a minute behind him to be safe. By the time he's been in there a minute, we'll likely be right outside the door. But after I tell you he's on his way up, you gotta kill the radio so he doesn't hear any static.

Festschrift: Gotcha. Thanks. Over.

Time: 2:35 P.M.

Merrill: Wally, we're comin' up there.

Festschrift: What? What have you got?

Merrill: The jig's up, Wally. It's over.

Festschrift: What're you talkin' about? What's goin' down?!

Merrill: We've got another murder, Wally. Same MO.

Festschrift: Who?

Merrill: Chuck Childers is dead, Wally. We're comin' up there.

THIRTEEN

Wally snapped off his radio and tossed it on the couch in the living room. Larry flopped down in a kitchen chair as if he'd been bowled over. I emerged from the closet, cramped and sweaty.

We were speechless. Wally took off his shoulder strap holster and placed it carefully next to his radio, then sat down, his mass lifting his feet off the floor as he settled in. I leaned over the kitchen table and rested on my hands.

"What now, Wally?" Larry said finally. But Wally just shook his head sadly.

Larry went into the living room and I straightened up and stretched. The phone rang. "Can you get that, Philip?" Larry said.

I picked up the phone. "It's Earl!" I said, and Wally grabbed the extension.

Earl was panting. "You got your radio off up there?"

"Yeah," Wally said.

"I had to run two blocks to this phone! We just spotted Raven. He should be there any second. We're on our way."

Wally hunched himself up off that couch, grabbed his stuff, and lumbered into the dining room. I hung up the phone and jumped back into the closet, pulling the door shut and trying to control my breathing. Larry headed for the kitchen. "Stay in the living room," Wally whispered. "And don't be too quick to answer the door."

Less than a minute later the doorbell rang. Larry waited. It rang again. He approached the door and looked out the peephole. "Who is it?" he called out.

"Congratulations, Mr. Shipman," came Jake Raven's deep, resonant voice from the hall. "You've won WMTR-FM's Lucky Bucks Game!"

"Jake, is that you, you old sonofagun?"

"Yeah," Raven said, laughing. "Let me in, turkey!"

Larry opened the door. Raven was not yet in my line of sight. "Hey, for a minute there I thought I'd really won something!" Larry said, a little too loudly. "I s'pose it'd look a little suspicious if your friends won the money though, huh?"

"Yeah, I suppose. Listen, you got a minute?"

Raven's voice sounded farther away, as if he was inviting himself to the living room.

"Yeah, I got some time. C'mon out here and I'll take your coat and find you a beer."

As they entered the kitchen, Larry pointed to the chair in front of my closet and Raven sat down and put a leather briefcase down on the floor beside him. Larry draped Raven's coat on another chair. "What brings you around here, Jake?" he said, opening the refrigerator but careful not to turn his back on his guest.

"Well, believe it or not, I really am giving away one of our prizes today."

"Yeah? In this building?"

"No, down the street, but I remembered you lived around here, so I thought I'd stop in and see if you were home. Didn't really expect to see you. You're not workin' today?"

"Nope. Day off," Larry said, popping the top and setting the can before Raven. "I didn't know you got to give the money away."

"Yeah. It's fun. Sometimes it's a thousand or two, you know."

"Yeah, I know."

"Anyway, DJs don't wanna do that kind of work. But I enjoy it. People are thrilled."

Larry slowly sat down across from Raven, stared into his eyes, and said nothing. Raven took a long swallow and set the can down again. Rising, he moved to his left and put his briefcase flat on the counter. Larry started to stand.

"Don't get up," Raven said evenly, his friendly tone gone. "I want to talk to you for a minute."

Larry sat back down, his face taut, one finger tapping silently on the table.

"May I use a towel?" Raven asked. Larry nodded and Raven carefully removed a dishtowel from a rod on the wall. Folding it neatly in half, he held it under a stream of water until it was drenched. He pressed the excess water out of it in the sink and set the towel down next to his briefcase. By now I knew he was in Wally's line of vision and that Wally had to have moved a few feet to his right to remain undetected. My breathing was short and shallow.

I strained to get a better view when Raven tripped the spring latches on the briefcase and delicately set the top open. I held my breath, knowing that if he pulled a pistol out of that case, I would have to make my move.

He pulled out two tiny, white gloves, the type film editors use when they're splicing film. Larry watched unblinking as Raven almost daintily tugged the gloves on, and it was then that I noticed the perfection of his clothes.

He wore light brown patent leather shoes, expensive tan slacks that stopped at the top of the heel just so, and a rust colored knit shirt. He looked as if he could have just had a shave, and his razor-cut hair was in perfect shape.

"Is that how you get in, Jake?" Larry asked. "You tell people they've won the radio money prize in that great voice of yours?"

Raven stiffened. "Silence," he said.

"Forget it," Larry said. "You can stand there and blow me away like you have all the others, but you're not gonna tell me I can't ask a few questions."

Raven ignored him and leaned over the table to grab the beer can. He poured the remainder down the sink, ran the water again, wiped his fingerprints off the can and the faucet with his gloved hands, and tossed the can in the trash. Then he wiped his chair and the table and the counter. I wondered how much more we'd need before taking him. Earl and Lieutenant Merrill had to be pressed up against the door by now.

My .38 snub-nose was heavy in my hand, and I wondered if I'd be able to move if I had to. I was ready, but my job was to stay put unless I saw that gun in his hand. And so far, I hadn't even seen the gun.

"Talk to me," Larry said. "Sit down and talk to me."

Raven snorted. "Oh, sure," he said. "I have nothing to say to you."

"C'mon, give me a break for old time's sake."

"You think I'm going to come this far and then give you a break?"

"Hey, I'm curious, Jake. At least tell me what the initials mean."

Raven looked genuinely puzzled, as if he really didn't understand what Larry was asking.

"Ohhhh," he said, finally. "You mean these." He reached into his case and produced a bullet with the high velocity slug. "This one's just for you. I had to make two of these today."

My eyes darted to Larry's face, and I saw him press his lips together as if to keep himself from saying, "I know." If he had, even the deranged mind of a Jake Raven would have computed that Larry had inside knowledge and was setting him up.

He played with the bullet in his fingers as he stood towering over Larry, just far enough away that he could thwart a move if Shipman tried anything. "Yes, Larry. The prize trick has worked every time, except I didn't need it for Frances or Chuck."

"Chuck?"

"Chuck."

"Or me."

"Or you."

Raven suddenly clasped the bullet in his fist as if he were through chatting.

Larry spoke. "You've told me this much; at least tell me about the initials."

"If you'd been in L.A. in the sixties you would know."

"I wasn't. I'm sorry."

"I'm sorry too. You missed a great show. I was the morning man. And I was big."

"I'll bet you were."

"Don't patronize me. I *was* big. And my trademark was a cute little closing at the end of my gig every day. At ten o'clock, Pacific Time, I would say, 'Thank you, everyone. Thank you for turning me on.' "

Larry wanted to stall him some more, looking as if he too wondered what Wally was waiting for. Unless I saw the gun, I wasn't going to do anything. Wally was to handle every other eventuality.

"Are you gonna make me beg you to tell me what the initials mean?" Larry said.

Raven laughed a sad laugh and leaned his hips against the counter. "Don't you remember those crazy names we DJs had back then?"

Larry sat silent.

"Well, don't you?'"

"Yeah, sure."

"I had a beautiful name. I went by Stacks DeVincent. Stacks DeVincent! Don't you love it?"

And with that, Raven turned his back to me so that he could still watch Larry out of the corner of his eye. He brought the bullet up to the thumb and forefinger of his right hand and reached into his briefcase, which was now blocked from my view, with his left.

Two bounding steps from the dining room entrance shook the whole kitchen and with a loud grunting shout Wally Festschrift smothered Raven with a crashing bear hug, driving him across the kitchen into the far corner where I heard flesh and bone give way against the lip of the formica counter top.

Upon the initial impact I blasted out of the closet as Larry went under the table, and Merrill and Earl came through the front door in low crouches, guns up. With my gun barrel pressed against Raven's forehead on the floor, I searched frantically for his weapon. It had clanged into the sink, the lone bullet spinning into the drain basket. He never got the bullet into the chamber.

Still astride the writhing Raven, whose face mirrored the pain of that blow against the counter, Wally fished handcuffs out of his belt. When Earl saw Raven's right forearm, however, he told Wally, "Just cuff his left to your right. He's goin' nowhere."

Raven's right wrist and hand jutted out at a cockeyed angle and his forearm appeared crushed. As Wally helped him up, ignoring the yelps of pain, he thrust his hand into the crying man's rib cage. "He's got some severe damage here, too," he said.

Before Earl and Larry and I left the precinct house downtown that night, Wally came out to say good-bye. I was still shaken, as was Larry. I'm sure he was as eager to see Shannon as I was to see Margo.

Wally shook hands with Larry first. Neither spoke. Then Wally grabbed my hand and smacked me on the shoulder with his free hand, almost knocking me off balance. "Be glad you're not in the kitchen," he said with a big smile.

As he took Earl's hand and threw his arm around his neck, Haymeyer said, "Wally, you're something, you know that?"

"Yeah, I know that," the big man said. "You're really gonna think I'm somethin' when you find out what I got us roped into." He winked at me.

"What's this?" Earl said, trying to break free of Wally's grasp. Wally wasn't budging.

"I made a deal with the kid over here," he said, "but you're part of the bargain."

"You can't make a deal for me," Earl said, still buried in Wally's embrace.

"Well, maybe I can't, but I did, and a Festschrift deal is a deal. Right, Philip?"

I nodded.

"Tell your sweetie that your boss and me will see you Sunday, huh?"

I nodded again.

CHRISTIAN HERALD ASSOCIATION AND ITS MINISTRIES

CHRISTIAN HERALD ASSOCIATION, founded in 1878, publishes The Christian Herald Magazine, one of the leading interdenominational religious monthlies in America. Through its wide circulation, it brings inspiring articles and the latest news of religious developments to many families. From the magazine's pages came the initiative for CHRISTIAN HERALD CHILDREN and THE BOWERY MISSION, two individually supported not-for-profit corporations.

CHRISTIAN HERALD CHILDREN, established in 1894, is the name for a unique and dynamic ministry to disadvantaged children, offering hope and opportunities which would not otherwise be available for reasons of poverty and neglect. The goal is to develop each child's potential and to demonstrate Christian compassion and understanding to children in need.

Mont Lawn is a permanent camp located in Bushkill, Pennsylvania. It is the focal point of a ministry which provides a healthful "vacation with a purpose" to children who without it would be confined to the streets of the city. Up to 1000 children between the age of 7 and 11 come to Mont Lawn each year.

Christian Herald Children maintains year-round contact with children by means of a *City Youth Ministry.* Central to its philosophy is the belief that only through sustained relationships and demonstrated concern can individual lives be truly enriched. Special emphasis is on individual guidance, spiritual and family counseling and tutoring. This follow-up ministry to inner-city children culminates for many in financial assistance toward higher education and career counseling.

THE BOWERY MISSION, located at 227 Bowery, New York City, has since 1879 been reaching out to the lost men on the Bowery, offering them what could be their last chance to rebuild their lives. Every man is fed, clothed and ministered to. Countless numbers have entered the 90-day residential rehabilitation program at the Bowery Mission. A concentrated ministry of counseling, medical care, nutrition therapy, Bible study and Gospel services awakens a man to spiritual renewal within himself.

These ministries are supported solely by the voluntary contributions of individuals and by legacies and bequests. Contributions are tax deductible. Checks should be made out either to CHRISTIAN HERALD CHILDREN or to THE BOWERY MISSION.

Administrative Office: 40 Overlook Drive, Chappaqua, New York 10514
Telephone: (914) 769-9000